Praise for *The Godless Boys*

'Dystopian novels of faith, power and resistance crop up regularly. So the form can feel stale. Yet this assured, involving debut finds a new vehicle – although one that knows its own tradition – to explore this ground . . . Wood sketches the back-story with crafty discretion, while a richly imagined setting allows the fable to flourish with the minimum of preaching.'   *Independent*

'Wood conjures a time-warped world in which xenophobia, resignation and defiance fight for expression, and where unpleasant truths about human nature are conveyed in convincingly archaic slang. At its best, the result recalls the less fantastical parts of Philip Pullman's *Northern Lights* trilogy.'
Financial Times

'This tale of faith and power from a young British writer is bound to get tables talking . . . An exploration of gang terror with whispers of *A Clockwork Orange* and a nod to *Lord of the Flies*, the novel also has shades of 2006's film *This is England*. But it's the surprising tenderness and cliché-free sentimentality that sets this story apart. Vibrant and evocative language give a tangible bitterness to this sharp story about lives saved, and doomed, by religious faith.'   ***Stylist*, Book of the Week**

'Wood's use of language is deft and ambitious . . . Wood is only twenty-seven yet her writing already has distinction'
'terary Review

The Godless Boys

NAOMI WOOD was born in 1983 and lives in
London. She studied at Cambridge and at UEA for
her MA in Creative Writing. Originally from York, she has
gone on to live in Hong Kong, Paris and Washington DC.
She is the Eccles Centre Writer in Residence at the
British Library. This is her first novel.

Naomi Wood

The Godless Boys

PICADOR

First published 2011 in paperback by Picador

This edition published 2012 by Picador
an imprint of Pan Macmillan, a division of Macmillan Publishers Limited
Pan Macmillan, 20 New Wharf Road, London N1 9RR
Basingstoke and Oxford
Associated companies throughout the world
www.panmacmillan.com

ISBN 978-0-330-51336-4

Printed and bound by CPI Group (UK) Ltd, Croydon, CR0 4YY

For Mary Wylie: 1914–2007

And for my parents

England

It was the summer they burned the churches again.

Sunrise broke over Berwick: the shadows clipped close to the walls; the sky broken only by Saint Gregory's spire. Laura checked the rear-view mirror. There was no one around.

It had been a quiet journey here. Someone higher up in the Movement had told them where to meet and what time; no more. They had travelled for an hour or so, no one saying much, the glass bottles, full of petrol, clinking against each other in the boot. The two men had both taken the back seat, one in army green, the other in black.

As the car had pulled in to the church lane, there'd been a moment, sitting there altogether, as if someone were considering saying something, perhaps *good luck*, or *goodbye*, but nothing was said. Instead the two men took the cases from the boot, and, as casually as worshippers, they walked toward the church, a case held tight in either hand. And Laura had stayed at the wheel, waiting.

She watched the first smoke start to drift upward from Saint Gregory's, drawn away on the wind, then building into a column, the smoke getting darker, richer. So here it was: the Secular Movement, alive again. Not since 1950, since the Church had taken power, had England seen such violence. And in the intervening years? God had come down on England like a cage, and all those involved in the violence of 1950 had been expelled to the Island. But the Secular Movement had retrenched and grown stronger, and, though they had been quiet until now, in the summer of 1976, the churches burned again.

Glass broke, somewhere close. Still there was no one on the Berwick streets. There followed a louder explosion and she thought – surely someone would wake and come to look, but no one emerged.

Last week, Laura had helped cut the petrol with tar so that it would better stick to what it caught. As she took Sarah to school she wondered if the other mothers might smell it on her. Soon, it would cover the pews, and then the curtains and the paintings, and anything else that was in its path. The two men would be launching the last of the glass-bottle bombs, now, lighting the soaked wicks and throwing them hard into the church windows. Laura thought she could smell fuel, probably from the boot – its metal stink flattening the air.

Blue light suddenly filled the car, strobing the mirror. Laura scrabbled for the handle but the door didn't release. She couldn't find the lock. Where was the lock? This was not her own car. The plastic snapped when she pulled at it. When she was outside the sounds of the siren filled her ears like water, and then she began to run.

Her teeth smashed against each other as she ran past terrace houses. Sleepy faces emerged from net curtains. From some way off a car screeched. She should have stayed in the car. She should have driven away. Somewhere in her mouth she tasted tin and blood. She should have driven away home. *They will persecute me for their names and I cannot give them up!* She thought of her husband and Sarah, her daughter's hair the colour of rust. What was she doing here, saving these strangers?

The big grey sky made the two men seem smaller than they were in the church yard. One had a flaming bottle but he dropped it when he saw her. The other scaled the far hedge and dropped out of sight before she had even said the words. 'Police! Police!' The heat was starting to come off the church now. Then the other man began to run.

'Police, police!' That's all she had managed and she knew that she too should run but she didn't: she had stopped running altogether. Why this impulse to save these two and not herself? She had no care for them; felt no sense of decency, and yet here she was. Steps ran toward her; there was nowhere to go, she wouldn't be able to make it to the hedge in time. A hand clamped her neck, another jerked her arm up, and then she was level to the ground.

In the cell, in Newcastle, she would remember the taste of gravel on her tongue, and the blood, from before, when she'd bitten down on her lip.

Laura saw the boots of the other policeman run on. A window of some stained and colourful Biblical scene smashed to the ground. 'Godless bitch,' the policeman spat in her ear.

Laura lay unmoving. Sirens circled as the fire grew stronger.

The Island

Ten Years Later

1. The Island

England, across the way, though it could not be seen tonight. The Sound was long and still. The boy crouched by the hedge, moonlight white on his skull. Underneath him was Lynemouth Town, slipping down the hill slope toward the sea. A few lights were on here and there but mostly it was dark. You could think, up here, that the Island might be alone in this, this sea; a great glob of earth, with nothing else for miles but water.

Looking at the Sound like that, looking so deceptively calm, always made Nathaniel think of his da, and how the sea had gobbled him up in its brackish waters. His da's boat would be out there, its keel dragging along the seabed, his body wet and strewn.

His da was one of the first men of the Secular Movement to be expelled to the Island, in 1951, a fact which made Nathaniel very proud. Jack Malraux had been a plumber in Hartlepool before being found responsible for one of the church-burnings in the summer of 1950 and deported here.

On the Island, Jack's trade was fishing and he'd done well from it. Nathaniel remembered the excitement of greeting his dad in Warkworth Bay when he came home for the weekend, and the rolling sound of the chains fixing the boat to the pier. When he left again, on the Monday morning, Nathaniel would accompany him down to the jetty, in the plum-blue mornings, in the winter months when the Island was all diamonded frost and sheeted ice, his hand in his father's hand, as they walked down toward the water's edge. Nathaniel would watch the boat leave, his da waving from the deck, knowing himself to be a softly shrinking dot in the distance, as his father sailed away to fish.

It was an English boat Jack had sailed out on. An English boat Jack had gone down with. No rocks or storms; most likely the caulk had given and the boat had sunk. Nathaniel imagined the English laughing when they had given the Islanders that boat, they must have known it could not be seaworthy for long.

A very English murder, this: unseen, bloodless, far away in time.

The moon was a dab of light now, not much more, what with the clouds tonight. Nathaniel wondered if there might be a twin of him, in England, a bald boy too, looking out across this sea, thinking about him. He wondered if his English twin also imagined descending on his scalp a cudgel to watch the blood ream. He'd like that; he'd always imagined English blood thick, like a pool of liquorice he'd seen melting one day last summer. The boy ranked his da's death as one of the Island's finest humiliations at the hands of the English. Worse than the Newcastle riots, worse than the Secular Deportations of '51 or '77; his da's death in that English boat rankled most.

*

Nathaniel set off up Marley Hill. He was a bald boy with a long throat, dressed in tight trousers and a military jacket, with gold braid on the epaulettes. The sleeves were a touch short and the studs of his wrists were frozen in the night. The trousers too were short of his ankles so that they showed the slope of his boots, which had been his da's, and which he'd given a rollicky-polish this evening to prepare for the scrap tonight. The boy wore handkerchiefs in the boots to stop his feet slipping. Red braces swaddled him neatly like a baby.

That afternoon, in his ma's bathroom, he'd smeared something on his lips called Pomade Divine. He knew it was meant for hair but he smeared it richly on his lips. On the front of the tin was a man with slick hair and a leer; Pomade Divine tasted of apples.

The hill was steep and the grass nearly bald with the Island's shearing winds. It was freezing, but he wouldn't shiver: because what was November on the Island but a cold to knock the breath from you? And leafless trees, and freezing nights, and the wind from off the Sound enough to make your balls into clams?

In the dark peat, further from the path, mushrooms grew, a whole moony lot of them. Something about their soft bright bonnets made him feel sick, or maybe it was not that, but the gills underneath, that made him pure want to heave. Nathaniel looked out for the Island's flowers his da had told him of: bog cotton, sandwort and rock-cress, but it was too dark to see anything but the mushroom domes. Just before the hilltop he ambled over to one of the swelling white patches and mashed the mushrooms into the grass.

Warkworth Bay was visible now and you could see where the skerries were from the waves' white froth. The pier, which would welcome the English boat tonight, had disappeared in the dark.

Nathaniel placed his boots down hard, since a misplaced foot could send a boy tumbling off the cliffs to the Sound. Where up at the summit Warkworth Town had been a shimmer of white, the houses now reared above him, their walls thick and coated in sea spray, the slated roofs dark. Handkerchiefs slipped gently in his boots. He wondered when he would fill them.

Shop awnings were going mad in the sea's fetch, and the Islanders were scurrying about beneath them, thronging the grocer's, and the fishmonger's, their coats billowing out from them, big as sails. Nothing much had changed in Maiden's Square since the emergency powers had brought the first men and women of the Movement here in 1951. In an elegant hand, the signs that hung from the shop fronts read: *Stansky & Sons* (above the fishmonger's), *Buttons* (above Mrs Bingley's clothes shop), *Caro's Launderette*, *Forrester's Funerary Services*, and a grocer's, doctor's, and hardware shop, for 'tools, cutlery and hardware', and 'oils, paints and varnishes'. And in rippled black glass, the walls unpainted, unlike the rest, the museum stood at the northeastern corner of the square. Walled in photographs, it told the Island's short history, and held the books and pamphlets the Church sent over to educate their godless kin. Mostly, they ended up graffiti'd – often by Nathaniel and his boys.

The boat, which was called the *Saviour* and came

weekly from England with supplies – potatoes, generators, rope, fish-tackle, medicine, newspapers and religious propaganda, amongst other things – did not deliver cigarettes. In fact, there had been no cigarettes on the Island in the past thirty-six years. The Islanders had always seen it as yet another form of punishment from England, though the men could have lived a lot longer with their untarred lungs, had it not been for the Sound filling them up so frequently, and fatally, with its lusty waters.

Nathaniel, however, had cigarettes. Tonight, he lit one, not caring who saw him. The shoppers gave him a funny look. He grinned: a smile which broke his face in two like a split egg. He stretched out on the bench, waiting, and watching. Mr Forrester, in the funeral home, was working at his desk. Two girls from school were walking arm in arm from the launderette; one had a dress draped over her arm. Nathaniel winked at her and told her he'd take her somewhere nice in that; she flushed and looked away. Fish-skins glistened in the monger's. Arthur Stansky went about his work, pausing here and there to drag scale and innards down his pinny. Arthur was a bloody mess but he seemed not to mind.

And there Jake came, lumbering along, a little late, something about his get-up – which was the same as Nathaniel's – a little askew, the jacket too tight about the middle, the boots a little dull. Aye, his boots could do with a polish. He didn't look like a Malade; not like him; not as sharp by halves. Jake was an enormous boy, a head taller than Nathaniel, with his arms hanging down to those hands the width of a spade apiece. His soft bulk always surprised Nathaniel, as if a separate, leaner Jake existed in

Nathaniel's imagination. Aye, there was something whale-like about the boy, something gentle but irritating about the boy's great tonnage.

'I told you not to let your hair grow so long,' said Nathaniel, when the boy was close enough. Bristles spun from the boy's crown.

'Aye,' Jake said, scratching his head.

'Well?'

'Mam's asked me to grow it a bit. She says I look like a victim of summat, when I'm all shaven, like.'

'On yer bike, Jakob. Your mam's got nowt to do with it.'

'*I* can't help what she says.'

'Did you say you were a Malade? That this is what our gang is for, now? That all us boys are like this?'

'No.' And then: 'Aye.'

'And what does "No. Aye," mean now?' Jake shrugged and eyed Nathaniel's cigarette hungrily. 'How is your mam?'

'Well,' said Jake, 'and Mammy Malraux?'

'Fine,' and then, to goad him, 'When is your mam to invite me to fish supper?'

'You know you're not allowed back to mine,' Jake said, and Nathaniel knew this but still liked to crab him about it. Just to get Jake upset was pleasure enough for him.

They watched people come in and out of the shops, carting their plaid trolleys or shopping bags, their faces flat in the lamplight. Nathaniel and Jake were waiting for the rest of the gang, the Malades, waiting for their skulls to come bobbing down Marley Hill toward Maiden's Square.

Tonight, Nicholas Tucker was to be initiated into the gang.

They didn't speak for a bit, and Nathaniel was reminded of Jake's habit of wetting his lips, over and over again, furtively, with his tongue. Nath was about to reprimand him, but something about his eyes, their baleful stare, hooded by the wide flat lids, stopped him. Jake's hands, on the spread thighs, looked babyish. Who knew where the bones were in those things?

'Can I have a cig, Nath?'

'No. I don't have many left.'

'Are you getting no more from the Boatie tonight?'

'No. Not tonight. Got nothing to exchange them for.'

'Your ma's pills?'

'There's not enough left. I have to leave some for her, aye.'

'Have you been taking them?'

'Stop crabbing me, Jake! You're an old woman at times. My ma forgot to order more. So no pills, no cigarettes. We'll get more next week.' Nathaniel squashed the cigarette onto the bench. He had smoked it too quickly and a yellowy sort of nausea passed from his gut to his throat. An explorative belch made him feel better. Arthur held a fish by its tail in the monger's waxed light. Without taking his eyes off it – *It might be skate! And how long was it since he'd eaten fish!* – Nathaniel said: 'When are the boys coming?'

'At six. As we arranged.'

And though he knew the answer already he asked, 'And who is it? Who's to be the Freshcut?'

'Nicholas Tucker.'

'Lumme.' Nathaniel's hand over his scalp produced a lovely rasp; he wondered if only he was party to the sound. 'What a good idea. Did he suggest it himself?'

'Aye. Said he wanted to be in the gang. So I said I'd ask you.' Nathaniel nodded his assent, then slipped off the bench, and tilted his head for Jake to follow him.

Buttons was a big long shop with all the original fittings and fancy ironwork. A bell rang as they came into the shop, which was warm, much warmer than outside. Mrs Bingley emerged, took one look at them and her face turned stern. An elderly lady with white hair and thick calves, she wore a paisley dress with brown tights the colour of the peat on Marley Hill. Mrs Bingley folded her big soft arms across her big soft chest. 'What do you want, now? I'm not wanting any trouble. It's too late in the day for that.'

'Hallo, Mrs Bingley. Nice to see you, too. We're not causing trouble. Promise.'

Mrs Bingley touched her hair, pushing up the curls; they had a lavender tinge. 'How's your mam?'

'Well, well.'

'You shouldn't be causing her any more ache than she's already got, you know.'

'Aye, I promise you, Mrs Bingley. I want to buy Ma a present, that's all.'

'Like what?' Old-fashioned dresses hung from the walls as well as corduroy trousers and tweed skirts. There was a sharp smell, as if the clothes had brought with them the scent of the boat's bilge. 'This is all I have.'

'Mrs Bingley. Now, now, now. Is there nothing new here?'

'Oh no, dear. We haven't had any clothes from England since six months now. I have a mind of having a word with the Boatman.'

'And why don't you?'

'On your way, he'd scare me half to death. Not on your life am I talking to an Englishman. No. It wouldn't be proper.' She looked both prim and thrilled by the thought of converse with an Englishman. 'Imagine his churchy hands on me!' For a moment, her gaze was far away. 'On with your business, now. What did you have in mind?'

Nathaniel shrugged. 'Something for my ma.' Mammy Malraux needed something new, something to lift her spirits. He didn't know what to do; he worried after her. If only he could be as good to his ma as he intended to be . . . but the wall of smoke that hung in the living room, the intolerable warmth, the long blab of the television set . . . That living room sent him mad for the scrap, so that as he sat for hours in front of the gas-fire, all he could think of was the boys, the Malades, his gang! He knew he disappointed her, but he couldn't seem to help it. 'I don't know. I'd like to buy her something. So that she might think about stepping out here and there. She doesn't leave the house, aye.'

Mrs Bingley suggested one or two dresses much the same as her own, but they were all drab. Nathaniel held up the dresses to himself in the changing-room mirror. 'Nothing slimmer? Or slimming?'

'This is all I have,' she said, gesturing around her.

A clapping sound came from the outside, of boots against the flagstones. It must be six. The boys passed the length of the glass, their scalps passing in whitish blur, settling near the stage, talking excitedly.

'Let's off, now, Nathaniel,' said Jake. The boy stared through the cold glass, his gigantic hand now banging the pane and waving to the boys outside.

'Oi! You leave well alone of that window, you hear!' Mrs

Bingley's eyes shuttled from the gang outside to the boys in her shop. Her whole face had gone a shade of crimson. '*I told you*, Nathaniel, I said I don't want any trouble. You sharking about outside my shop does not help business, d'you hear me, son?'

'Bye, Mrs Bingley!' Jake said as he pulled open the door and ran out. Cold air burst in. Nathaniel put the dress back to its rail. He did his best syrupy voice for her, as if he were talking to his own mam, and took her plump old hand in his. 'Don't you worry, Mrs Bingley. We'll be right as rain. Don't you worry about us. We're Island boys, we shan't be any trouble!' And he gave her hand a squeeze, before dashing into the square.

The Malades were a beautiful bunch, in the way that scraping the scalp of all the fuzz brought out their bonny eyes, their full boys' lips. What slick little outfits they had managed! They were all dressed like Nathaniel and did not wear much, for November. Their mams pure despaired of them, urging an extra scarf on them, or a more sensible jacket, which they always – in fear of Nathaniel – refused, because who might know what kind of mood he was in, whether the humiliation might be a whole-scale attack, or something worse; total exclusion from the gang. They were all so pale; no one darker than a candlestick. But there was something very pretty about them, too, quite a nursery of daft infants.

The boys gossiped about the Islanders, who might be showing signs of churchliness and who might be their next target. They talked about their mams and what they were up to. For those fortunate enough, they talked about their da's on the fishing boats, and what they had done with them on the rare weekend that they were back on Island soil.

One boy stood apart. He looked nervous, and was moving a finger up and down his collar. He was a good-looking boy, soft-featured, younger than the rest, his eyes darting from Nathaniel to Jake, not knowing which one to settle on. He stood in front of Forrester's funeral parlour. 'All right, boy,' Nathaniel said to him across the way, 'you're right at the dead centre over there, aye. Why don't you come and have a chat with us?'

'Aye,' he said, but he didn't move. In the latening evening, the night had become cooler still.

'I hear you want to be in our gang.'

The boy took cautious steps toward them. 'Aye,' he said.

'Have you been to the museum, of late?'

'I went last year.'

Nathaniel's laugh was high and easy. 'Not good enough. You have to go often – many times – once a month, maybe, or every week, so you can ken your past. You've got to see the church-burnings, you've got to see how the Movement were kicked out of England in '51, and then again in '77. You've got to see how easy it is for faith to hijack your head! Oh, aye, you've heard what your mammy has said, and your da, as he dandled you on his knee before the fire. But unless you go to the museum, and often at that, you won't understand the English mentality. You won't under-stand how God has grown up around the English like cobwebs, while they weren't paying attention, and how it could, any minute, here, if our boys aren't alertful of the signs. You've got to go so you can understand who you are.

A child not just of Mammy and Pappy, aye, but of the Movement. So it's baneful shocking, you see, to hear it was a
year ago you went.' The boy's lips trembled. There was
nowhere to hide his shame and it rose as a pink wave from
his throat to his brow. 'Och, now, Nicholas, not to worry.
Next time, aye?' And Nathaniel chucked him on the back
of his pate, lightly, and smiled at him, so that Nicholas lost
the watchful look and he smiled back, hesitantly. 'I like
your hair, Nicholas, did you do that yourself?'

'Aye,' he said.

'Did your mam blub when she saw you?'

'She gave me a right bollocking, yeah.'

The boys were a ring around him now, their baldheads
half in shadow, half in light. Some of them laughed,
remembering how their mams had been when they too had
shaved their scalps. 'Well, you're all done now. And your
scalp shines like a lovely penny. Now we're just going to ask
you a few questions, get you to commit to some things.
We've all taken the oaths. Don't worry. No fish heads or
guts or any of that daft shite you might have heard of. No,
boy. Just some firm moral matters of principle, which you
might find in any tough boys' gang. We're a good lot, us,
but we don't like casuals. Understand?' Nicholas nodded
his head. Nathaniel leaned in and said very tenderly, like a
father might, 'Then you'll be a Malade, like me, like Jake,
like all of the boys, and you can help us with the cause.'

Nathaniel looked around the group. 'There is a ring of
spies on this Island, working for England. Trying to get us
back into God's acre. Soon the Island will be as faithful as
London! Aye, aye: the walls of the church are not built in
the freezing air but in the ramparts of the heart! Here, an

aunt may be praying at night. There, a brother may be caught reading the English rag – or worse, fingering pages of scripture. One moment they'll merely be faithful, the next moment they will be at Warkworth beach welcoming English warships. So,' he turned to Nicholas. 'This is what I'm going to ask you. Have you ever been a Got?'

'No,' the boy said.

'Are you sure, now?'

'Aye.'

'No one in your family, either? A Got? A believer?'

'No.'

'Tell me, boy, have you ever believed? Have you ever felt the blood of God in your veins? Or heard his words in your mind?'

'No.'

'Are you sure of that, boy? We'll understand if you have. It can be nice. The soft babble of God in your ears.' Sweat had pricked high on Nicholas's forehead. Where his skin had been white it was now greenish about the chops, froggy and damp. 'He's a great comforter to those lost at sea.'

'No.'

'Not a prayer, sweetheart? Not a moan for a molly-coddle when Pappy popped his boots? The sea is cruel to us, you couldn't say we're not in baneful need.'

Nicholas's voice was barely a whisper. 'No. Nothing. I promise.'

The boys were tense and ready. Their boots kept edging them closer. He felt a great ministry within him, a great stillness, holding back until they were really at the damp-ish verge. Though Nathaniel's sight was fixed on Nicholas, the other boys hung, weightless, in the corner of his vision. 'And if your ma had gone all syrupy with faith? And decided to spy for England? Or your da? Would you tell us? Would you let your boys in kin know of the failings of your family?'

'Aye, aye.'

'What about your sister? Lovely Charlotte? If she were spying for England, trying to get the Island back to the Ministry, would you tell us, so that we could treat her how she deserved?'

'Aye, aye, I'd tell you.'

'One last thing; then you'll be just like us: a Malade, through and through.' Nathaniel reared his fist and caught his knuckles on the boy's lips. Blood issued from his mouth, as red as jam.

The boys' laughter was a distant sound as if they were a great way from him, beyond the Sound, even. Nathaniel slipped his index finger into the wet hollow of the boy's mouth. 'Now a Malade,' he said again, 'through, and through.'

For a moment, Nicholas was aghast. Something hallucinatory about the blood coming from – where was it? His tongue? Or had it been his nose that had burst? It was a brown taste in his mouth. Seconds passed, and he cupped his face in his hands: he had expected this, this predicted violence. And it had not been so bad. And so he smiled, the blood like a tonic on his tongue.

Nathaniel cooed, 'Aye, Nicholas,' and ruffled the baby spikes of his hair, declaring the boy one of the gang.

Oiled on all of this sudden affection, Nicholas smiled with the blood still coming from his lips and gums. He spoke quickly, lightly, laughing, 'See I knew you'd do that. Knew it. Knew I was in for some questions, and then a bit of the scrap. But I was ready. Ha! Yes. Now I'm a Malade, a marauding Malade, just like you!' Nicholas mopped his chin with a hankie.

Jake called: 'Down to the Sound now!'

'Off with you,' Nathaniel said, because the whim took him, 'I'm not going down to the Sound tonight.'

'But the dunking, like with Sammy, and me '

'No. That's not part of the game any more. We don't go down to the bay any more.'

'I'm only saying that when I was a Freshcut, there was a dunking in the Sound after the Square and now—'

'Not any more. *Listen*, Jake. Listen to what I say.'

Nathaniel lit a cigarette and passed it between the boys so that the earthy smell of tobacco filled the square. The boys smoked, concentrating hard. They looked with some degree of fascination at the smoke now clouding the air, and the ashy, not unpleasant tastes in their mouths. Jake refused the smoke, his mouth pouting and cross.

'All I envy them for. Those cigs.' After the boys had had their smokes, Nathaniel had the last of it then flicked it out across the square. It went burning in a pleasing arc. 'If the Gots had their way, faith'd spread through the Island like the flu. If someone sneezed you'd catch God in your nose. No, no, no, there's more to life than sacrificing everything for Old Man upstairs.' His face cracked into a philosophical smile. 'But they make a fine cigarette. I must say that. And it hurries them up to Kingdom Come, so at least the cigmaker is possessed of all his senses.'

A wave of tiredness passed over him, as it always did,

and Nathaniel felt that familiar restive feeling – not dis-satisfaction, quite, but something close to it. This always happened after the scrap, as if the violence were not big enough to dispossess him of some sad and unknown memory. 'Who's on for Wednesday night, then?'

'Eliza Michalka?' said Sammy.

'Nah,' said Nathaniel, 'I'd rather stare at that pudding all day than throw rocks at it. Another time. Once I've crabbed her, perhaps.'

'As if you could crab her without paying for it.'

'That I could, Jakob Lawrence, I'd be down to the Grand and have her pudding before I could even ask for the spoon.'

Jake looked away, as if embarrassed.

'Mrs Richards, then,' said Sammy.

'The maths teacher! Lumme,' said Nathaniel. 'Why? The evidence?'

'I hear she talks to the girls after school. Teaching them Bible and scripture. It's thought she's in contact with the English. She's a spy, all right. Through and through.'

'Grand,' said Nathaniel. 'We'll check her out. We're all on dispatch tonight and tomorrow night. See who comes in and out of that house from seven o'clock onwards. We don't want to crab her while the big man is there. All right, boys?'

And the boys ran from the square, following Nathaniel, this gang who would come and clap faith from any beating heart. The night was now a dark black lump, but they knew the Island instinctively, like worms in soil, and they were happy, the whole sleek lot of them. Six Malades now, aye.

Oh, life was a laugh, a lark, a love, on this Island of his!

2. Miss Eliza Michalka

Tonight was no especial occasion: Eliza had stood any number of hours in that doorway, come seven o'clock, under the sweep of the museum's shadow. Arthur Stansky had not yet seen her; not tonight, nor the other nights she had come to watch him, with all the rapture of a child at a television set.

Eliza had arrived at Maiden's Square just as Caro was closing the launderette. She had made some show about getting a dress that she knew would not yet be ready, all the while keeping her eye fixed on Arthur in the fish shop opposite. The launderette smelled of carbolic and made her nose itch. Caro had shrugged her shoulders and told her it was not yet ready, and that she was closing, mumbling something about having it up to here with this Island and these boys at their tricks. Eliza did not know what to say, offered some platitude or other, and stepped from the launderette to the museum's doorstep, jamming herself down into its shadow. Arthur would not see her here.

The monger's let out a square of yellow light. Under the window frame, deep maroon tiles; above it, an awning, with gold lettering. Eliza thought the fish shop the nicest place on the whole Island; the most perfect place. Beatrice Spenser was now Arthur's last customer: she was not really dressed for the cold, and looked rather wan. Beatrice was a deportee from the second wave – one from the 1977 boat – and she had never really mixed in with the other Islanders, save finding someone to father a child with her. Who he was, was a mystery to everybody. Eliza knew – just as everyone else did – that Beatrice Spenser would tomorrow slip into the museum and steal the English newspaper that was brought on the weekly boat. Beatrice missed home, Eliza thought, more than the others.

Arthur, however, was always kind to Beatrice. Eliza wondered what pleasantries they might exchange: the intemperance of the weather, perhaps, or details of the latest catch, or what the English boat might bring the Islanders tonight. Eliza had had only the most minimal of conversations with Arthur these past couple of months. What would she give, to hear him talk of cod or the cold?

Arthur pulled a long slender fish from the ice. Tenderly, as if it were a newborn, he held it from its tail, the fish flashed in the light, Mrs Spenser nodded her head, and he slit it down its belly with a long grey knife. He pulled out bladder and intestine and who knew what else from the hole. Mud-coloured and stringy, he washed the mess from his fingers. He grated the fish and sheared off its scales, which flew into the air like sparks. Oh, to be that knife; to be that fish! Wrapped in paper now, the fish was bundled under Mrs Spenser's arm, and she said her goodbyes.

Moments passed when no one was in the shop. The monger moved to the doorway, looking to the square from the gridded glass: tall, good Arthur. He seemed to be searching for something. Eliza shrank into the museum's shadows, wondering, if their eyes met, if he would see her. She doubted that.

The memory came back to her, painfully, as it always did, of the night they had spent together at the Grand this summer. It had been very warm: her room had seemed to creak with the heat, the air wriggling as it became stickier. She remembered, outside, the press of grey clouds above a strangely still Sound. A storm was approaching. She remembered Arthur's ropey, sweaty hair, his waistband too tight, as if he too were expanding in the softening heat, as if he were only kept narrow by the Island's winters. She remembered his parting words: 'Forgive me, Eliza.' Then months had passed, the cold had come, and nearly nothing had been said between them.

And now, very late November, and nightly she came to Maiden's Square, to stand and watch him, in the shadows, constant as a ghost.

In bloodied apron, Arthur proceeded to clean the shop. He moved a cloth against the glass and marble, pushing the scale and bone and blood into the claw of his other waiting hand, as if he were returning his countertop to a state of grace. Eliza wished dearly that she could lay herself naked down on the tablet, near the skate, and the sole, and the salmon, and find herself a thing of Arthur's worshipped hygiene.

He let go the handful into the bin.

Into a bag he gathered the old fish, put on a coat, unlocked the door. He switched off the light so that the square was dark. Arthur was invisible, now, just like her. The lock clicked again. Now he would set off toward Warkworth Bay – but he stopped at the door as if he had detected something. Cries of gulls scratched the air. Why had he not begun the walk? Had he seen her? Was he coming closer? Would he shout at her, or dismiss her as a lunatic? Eliza stayed very still and did not breathe, wondering what on earth she would say to him if she were discovered here.

He fiddled with some keys, and then set off. His shoes rang against the flagstones until he reached the peaty ground, and then the sound and sight of him was lost. She was disappointed; she had half-hoped for discovery. The herring gulls moaned. Eliza stepped out of the dark, straight into the soft bosomy front of Mrs Bingley.

'Oh,' she said, with Mrs Bingley looking equally frightened. Buttons had been dark; Eliza had had no idea anyone was still in the square.

Mrs Bingley held her hand at her breast and breathed heavily. 'Eliza Michalka, for pity's sake, stop haunting this doorway! Do you not think I have enough trouble with these boys? If it isn't them, it's a full-grown woman sharking about my shop and causing me trouble.'

'I—'

'I don't want to hear it. Not a moment's peace! This Island will be the death of me yet. Keep away from my doorway, miss, I've had enough hassle for one evening.'

'I'm sorry, Mrs Bingley, I didn't mean to scare you.'

Mrs Bingley flicked her eyes from Eliza's head to her boots. Her mouth clenched a little. 'What are you doing here, anyway?'

'I,' she paused, 'I came to see if you had a delivery from the Boatman.'

'The English boat is here tonight. We collect the goods

tomorrow. You know that. Why doesn't anyone know that? This Island's all gone soft.'

'Aye. Aye. Silly of me. I'm sorry. I'll come tomorrow, then.'

'Shan't you be on your way, then?'

'I'm waiting for a friend . . .' Arthur would be coming back soon. She willed Mrs Bingley to leave the square. 'Janey.'

'Bet you are. Don't get cold, then. You'll turn to ice at this rate.'

'Aye. Goodnight, Mrs Bingley. Safe on.'

'Aye.' Mrs Bingley muttered into her scarf and set off. Eliza saw Arthur returning and she slipped back under the museum's gable. His empty bag now blew open in the wind as he stopped to chat to Mrs Bingley. Then he returned to his apartment above the monger's.

The rooms above Stansky & Sons gave out a watery glow. She saw a shadow move against the north wall before she saw him. No doubt he would create for himself a handsome meal of fish and potatoes, though perhaps he tired of it during his labours. Perhaps he hankered for meat, though there was none to be had on the Island. The Islanders had never had meat: it couldn't come on the benefaction boat, and they couldn't rear livestock on the hill here. Beef, pork, lamb; Eliza wondered what they tasted of. Perhaps, like an expensive piece of furniture.

Arthur sat. At one point she thought he put his head in his hands and wept. But when he stood, he took a newspaper from the table and he moved to what she knew was the living room, and Eliza left.

*

She walked away from the square very quietly, heading for Warkworth Bay. She knew she should not torment herself with the sight of all that good fish only just on the turn, but she thought of it as a kind of offering, one that Arthur made to the world, and why should she exclude herself from the bounty just because she loved him, and he no longer loved her back?

Down at the bay, the birds circled the bluff, diving and picking from the fish flesh; all beak and wing and claw. How like ghosts they were, so white in the dark, but infinitely more solid, quick, and sure of their purpose. What a hash she'd made of tonight. Eliza had sworn she would talk to Arthur, but she hadn't even got close to the shop front.

On her brow that evening, Eliza had penned the word *Courage*, close to her hairline, underneath her fringe, to encourage her to talk to him. She had made a habit of this since starting at the Grand (that June, and so unwillingly!), pulling up her fringe and penning little messages of hope – or self-pity – on her brow. One word, or two, like *Courage*, or maybe *Resilience*, or maybe *Take Heart!*, and she'd go around the Island with her blonde lock of hair covering the words, murmuring the message in her head, hoping for inspiration.

But tonight! What a coward she was. *Courage!* Pathetic. She had no courage. She felt like that fish Arthur had shorn of all its scales: dull, and missing its brilliance.

The sound of a boat came up from the harbour. The tide, too, was quickening. It must be the boat from England. Eliza left the gulls and took the steps down the cliff face, toward the beach.

When she reached the sand, the boat was already docked, with its pale orange top, life rings on its railings, and the black belly of it bringing up the sea spray. Eliza crouched behind the rocks, so that for the second time that night she would be hidden.

The engine stopped. A big bow wave travelled to the beach, then the sea was almost flat and waveless again. Nothing could be seen through the cabin's windows. The name of the boat was written in large yellow letters on its side: the *Saviour*. The Boatman, bald and fat, shut the door of the cabin and unlatched the cargo door. Eliza had heard of him – many of the Islanders were frightened of him – but had never seen him; not in the flesh. He walked down a series of steps and came back up with a box of supplies.

Here, then, was the English benefaction. Ever since the emergency powers, and when the weather permitted it, England had weekly delivered the Islanders their goods. It was done at no cost whatsoever, so that those lost in the night-time of the Lord could eat, and think from what hand they ate; use light, and think from where this light had come; fish, and know who it was that provided them with twine and hooks. Most of the time it was accepted with a sneer, since there was no way of showing the English their rebuke, and since there was no possibility of rejecting the charity.

The Islanders received the *Saviour* with a heavy heart, though without it they would have died, or gone mad. They did not like to think of themselves as beholden. Not to the English. There'd be another boat next week, but then it would not come again until the new year. Aye, the Islanders were left to cope alone for the winter, when the winter fogs would come, thick as mud, and make passing the Sound an impossible task.

Tomorrow morning, the men would come down to the jetty and distribute the things as they saw fit; to the fishermen, the plumber, Caro, the doctor, the grocer and Mrs Bingley, if there was anything in there for her. You wouldn't steal; people didn't steal English things, which were English at least until they turned up in the shops and had to be paid for. Theft would be what the English expected and so the Islanders did not do it. The Boatman shifted the first box to the end of the pier. It looked a heavy thing and he stopped for a cigarette at the end. He looked rather peaceful, sitting there, despite the threat of foreign turf; he could almost be waiting for someone.

Eliza made to leave, when something on the boat caught her eye: there, on the deck, a girl stood. Just as the birds had solidified the air, here stood a presence of breath and blood and bone, rendered from the dark. The girl stood still, quite white, looking into the Island. She turned around to the massive Sound, that breadth of water before the North Sea began in earnest back to England, and then she turned again to the Boatman. He had nearly finished the cigarette.

Eliza felt her heart club as the girl climbed over the rigging and onto the pier. A stowaway? An *English* stowaway? On the *Saviour*? She started to edge down the pier, and Eliza's eyes darted from the girl to the Boatman, urging the cigarette to slow itself of its burning. The girl walked quickly down the pier, her eyes trained on the cigarette's orange light. No sound issued from her step. Just as the Boatman took his last smoke, and flicked the end to the beach, the girl reached the shore and dropped to the beach, crawling between the pier's legs, where she was lost again in darkness.

Over the next twenty minutes the Boatman brought the rest of the boxed provisions to the Island. He was still oblivious of the girl. Eliza concentrated on the dark tent under the pier. She could see nothing of her, which could only be a good thing, for now.

The Boatman stayed a few minutes longer, after his labours, idling by the boat. He had a small box in his hands. He lit another cigarette. When he finished that one he gave up and without further fuss stepped back into the boat and shut the cabin door. Moments later, the engine gunned and the waves began foaming again at the beach. The engine smoked as the boat turned. Eliza watched the mast until it disappeared into the sky and sea.

As soon as the *Saviour* had gone, the stowaway lunged toward the cliff. As she came toward the rocks, Eliza saw her water-blue eyes and freckles, dense as a bruise against her skin. The girl's hair, the colour of rust, flew in the wind. Eliza let the girl climb the steps and go over the top, before she too gained the rutted boards, intending to catch up with her at Maiden's Square, and, if her courage served her well (she pressed her fingers to her forehead – *Courage! Courage!*), she would talk to the girl and tell her she could spend the night with her at the Grand. They might be friends – the English girl, after all, would be sore pressed to find another on the Island. She wondered what on earth the girl was doing here.

Eliza arrived breathlessly at the top. The girl was gone. She was not even on the path toward the square. The fish, too, all gone, and the gulls with them. Eliza's stride broke into a run. Halfway to the square she stopped suddenly, looking back toward the Sound, terrified that minutes into being on the Island the girl might have jumped. Then it would be Eliza's fault for not acting quickly enough. Another score in the post for her inaction! No, no, she thought, hurrying along to Maiden's Square, a good English girl, one with faith and God and all manner of things she could not imagine were the privilege of that country's children, would not give up so easily.

Up here, the houses shone with the salt from the Sound, brought to the innermost part of the Island in rough storms. Arthur had probably finished his dinner, now, and might be doing his dishes; good man. Eliza just saw the girl between the museum and the hill: what a quick-ferreted thing she was to move at such a pace, and for someone who could not know the Island. Now, now, she might catch up with her, and ask her about London, and Walkmans, and churches, and motorways, and England! Eliza hurried along, no longer caring if Arthur saw her, when she caught the sound of other footsteps, apart from this time, they were following her.

The boys surrounded her quickly, like a leaking organ suddenly circled in blood. All her breath left her in an instant. Eliza turned around to see if there was anyone else left in the square but knew there would be no one, and then she craned her head to see if she could still see the girl. The rucksack, and the orange hair, slipped agonizingly from view. She might take any path from there; any road or pass, any which way. *Damn them*, Eliza thought, *damn them*.

She took a step away from the scalped boys but they were already a ring around her. 'Hello, dear.' This was Nathaniel; she did not know the names of the others.

'Evening, Nathaniel.'

'A fine night, Miss Eliza. We don't often find you in the square at this time.'

'No.' She looked around her. 'I was running an errand. For Musa.'

'At this time? That's awful late.'

'I might say the same to you. What are you doing here? The lot of you. You should be at home with your mams.'

'As you should be with yours.'

'My mam's dead; you know that.' He showed nothing. 'What are you doing? You've been told to stop it now. This sharking about.'

'Aye. And we haven't put a person to their displeasure. Not tonight. Isn't that right, Jake?' A tall boy nodded, touching his finger to the jacket's braiding. There was another boy with a bruise that looked just fresh. The ring of them seemed closer though she knew they had not moved. Eliza told herself these boys were nuisances, merely. Nathaniel lit a cigarette; where did he get them from? 'And your ma, what does she think about this? Her only son, skulking about the Island smoking English *cigarettes*. Shame on you.'

'She doesn't care.' Nathaniel touched his hand on her hip. 'Do you care, do you care for me, Eliza?' His lips were close to hers. He was sixteen – somewhere around that age – but he had the height over her.

'Get off me.'

'Oh. Firm with me now, are you?'

'Aye. I'll be firm with you yet.'

'Why? Do you not like us? Are you a woman of faith? A Got, lady?' This was Jake, now, stepping forward. Something about him made Eliza's courage shrink.

'A Got? On your way.' She tried to square herself up to them; she only just now counted how many there were. 'I was born on this Island, just like you.'

'Have you been up at church?' Nathaniel now. 'The old ruined one at Lynemouth?'

'Even if I have, it's none of your business.'

'Every bit of our business,' said Jake. 'If you're an English spy.'

Nathaniel walked the length of the stage, wagging his finger into the air, as if he were a mathematician vexed by a problem of logic. 'What I can't square is how you might carry on, dear Miss Michalka, in your line of work, with your heart pumping your devotions and with your other hand pumping—'

'Stop your mouth.'

He swivelled around, fingering his lip. 'Stop it for me.' There was a moment's silence before the gang cracked up. Loudly now, Nathaniel shouted: 'Stop my mouth, Eliza, our lady of the Grand!' He jumped from the stage and joined the ranks around her. He leaned in as if he was about to kiss her.

A window flew open above the monger's. Arthur tilted from the pane, his face obscure in shadow, his hand on the catch. 'Oi! What're you doing down there? Off with you, now, boys, before I sort out the lot of you.'

Nathaniel smiled, daftly, as if to say he was only joshing, and with a lady they both knew to be very pretty.

'Here, now, Mr Stansky. We didn't mean no harm. We were talking to Miss Michalka.'

'Aye. And I'm sure she's had a lovely time talking with you and has had fair enough. Be off with you now, boys. Scram. On you go.'

There was something about Arthur that Nathaniel could evidently not resist. Certainly there were fair few people whom Nathaniel would bow to. 'All right, Mr Stansky, sir. Good night, Miss Michalka. Safe on.'

Nathaniel started whistling some desultory tune, and set off, with the boys following, down the side of Mrs Bingley's, and followed the road the girl had taken. Before he was lost from sight, Nathaniel turned and gave her a crooked grin, before the gang disappeared in the night.

A gull squawked and then the square was empty of noise. Eliza turned back to the window to thank him, but when she opened her mouth Arthur closed the catch and fiddled with the lock. It was as if in closing the glass he had just shut the very entrance to her heart. He had saved her, and then damned her, in the time it had taken to open and close that window. The light went. And the square was once again flooded in darkness.

Tuesday

3. Lynemouth Town

Lynemouth Town was the oldest quarter of the Island. Narrow, curling streets; terraces many times extended; sloping slate roofs: the houses had been built into whatever cranny the steep side of Marley Hill might afford. From aboard a fishing boat the town was said to resemble a crumbling amphitheatre sliding down the hill. There was still the old system of numbering the houses, with the odd number on the landward side, the even number on the seaward. It looked more of a series of fortifications than a town: slats for windows, or windows showing from just under the gables; high walls, shut doors. There was not much colour here, everything carried in the general umber of the terrace roofs; it had none of the bright awnings of Maiden's Square or Arthur's iced fishes. Some way off, further east and higher up, a burned-out church topped the town, where, roofless, moss had crept over the stones for thirty-six years without much remark.

Eliza's brothel, the Grand, was a large terraced house down the side of a back alley, behind the more insalubrious of taverns that kept late hours. The Grand was not in a good state. Columns were blackening with dirt. Slabs of flagstone were missing from the steps leading up to the door. Behind the house there was a scant garden not much used. The windows sat in deep recesses and drainpipes croaked in the Island's high winds.

It was a sorry sight, the Grand, sorrier still that in 1951 it had lived up to its name, the cat-house itself where Jack and Margaret Malraux had once met in the bar, and talked, and laughed, and hatched plans for a grander life away from the churchly eye of England. It was where, so soon after deportation, the new Islanders came to eat and drink and fall in love, and there was a general exultation that somehow, despite their expulsion, they had won the war against the Church. In the fifties, the Grand had always been busy, as a bar and dancing hall, and then in the sixties, when things had turned quiet, it had turned into a brothel, although not very successfully.

Now, the Grand was often empty. It had the smell of the sickroom, as if the new freedom of the Island had somehow set in the rot.

There were several rooms and three girls, including Eliza, employed there permanently. Musa, the proprietor, did not have the money to spend on a renovation of the place. Damp grew, sponging the skirting boards and ceilings. Cobwebs hung woolly from its ceilings. A woody smell came from the rooms – mulchy and sour – which the girls had become used to, but the men could smell distinctly on their entrance. Musa had brought in Eliza this summer to inject something new into the failing state of affairs, which had worked, briefly, until she too had just become old hat.

This morning, at the mirror in her room, Eliza contemplated once again her brow. What words might mark the day? The eyeliner knocked against her teeth. Since coming to the Grand, Eliza had daily kept this small ritual. It was a way to cope, she guessed, with the everyday invasion of privacy that the job brought with it. A man might knock at her door at any time, and though they tended not to, it still prevented her from completely relaxing. And there were so few customers these days that the girls could never refuse them.

Eliza was Mr Carter's favourite, with his high forehead and rather lipless grin, but even then he might only come every fortnight or so. Still, when she had been more popular this summer, she had found this trick a good one to give her some space. Her first word written there had been *Escape*, so that she might imagine the possibility of not working here or living on the Island. Her second word, the next day, was, of course, *Arthur*.

Sometimes, on trips to the grocer's, when she would be faced with the open hostility of one of the Island women in the queue (they looked down on all the girls from the Grand), she reassured herself that on her brow, under her fringe, she had written *sour-faced bitch*, so that when she smiled politely at their cold stares she knew precisely who had won. Often, she wrote his initials, *A.S.*, or his initials and hers, *A.S.E.M.*, in tiny letters along her hairline. Sometimes she chose abstract words, such as *meekness*, which she didn't have, or *plenty*, which she also didn't have, or this word *escape*, even when she had no route to do that. At her pluckiest, she wrote the word *England*: the land to which she dreamed of going. Aye, regardless of what she did, if Arthur did not want her, she wanted out of this place. Whenever Eliza saw another woman with a fringe she wondered whether they might write these words at their hairlines; was tempted too to flick up the flank and scan the brow for words. One day, on walking into a tavern in Lynemouth Town, she almost pushed back the bangs of the barmaid to see if there was a sentence or two. What might it be? *Ale*, perhaps; but on looking at the lined face and slack mouth, perhaps *ailing*.

Perhaps it should say, *Fuck off, Nathaniel Malraux!*, as a statement of defiance to the boys last night. She had been upset by their crabbing of her, down in the square, but she knew they were only bored and getting up to mischief. They would not disturb her so easily.

Alternatively, it was Mrs Page's funeral this afternoon – perhaps it should be in reference to that. Eliza had been the gravedigger since she had left school, and had buried every Islander who had died these past six years. Perhaps she could pen the word *grave*, to mark the solemnity of the day as well as its thrust. Or *Victoria Page*, in memory of the dead woman.

She didn't mind being the Island's undertaker, though the salary was not enough to live on. When her ma had died, in June of this year, Linda had been heavily in debt, and Eliza had practically to give away the baker's she had owned. Once the creditors had been paid, there was very little left (£35, in fact), and, with Arthur grown cold, Eliza had been forced to take the only job that was going: at the Grand.

Across her forehead she decided to pen:

find the girl

Yes. That was the thing; that was the thing. She would do

a good job for Mrs Page this afternoon, but to find the girl was the hidden imperative of the day. Eliza moved the fringe back down and checked that the words were hidden.

With the words now penned, Eliza stepped out early on Tuesday morning. *Find the girl.* Aye. It was even colder than yesterday. Clouds moved fast about her, rushes of grey. She decided to forgo looking in Lynemouth Town, since it was unlikely the girl would have skirted all the way around Marley Hill to here without freezing to death. Instead, Eliza took the steep cobbled road out of the Grand, walking east. The town was not even close to waking up, its fronts shuttered and doors shut. She walked past Linda's old baker's, which had been renamed since Eliza had sold it. She could barely look at the loaves lined up on the shelf.

A few people here and there were getting ready for the day, but this place was poorer than Warkworth Town and few had constant work aside from the gutters at their stations, curing fish. The smell those shops gave off was of salt and seawash, and you could find a fish-curer easily from the yellow colour of his hands. Eliza weaved through the narrow streets. Lynemouth Town was a place for the night, not the broad eye of daylight.

She made it to the old ruined church before catching her breath. She was sure the English girl would look for somewhere remote and secluded, near here, perhaps, or the Eastern Bay, to keep hidden from view. Lynemouth Town spread out below like a fur. The girl would surely avoid the town.

The burned-out church was made of slate without

mortar or cement. It must have stood here for centuries, serving the Island's Christian community before the Movement's arrival in '51, and the godly folk had opted for resettlement in England. A moss had made the old stones nearly completely green. Rocks and other slabs stood at the base of the walls, as if the church were steadily tumbling toward the Sound. Down at the shore the sea sucked at rock. The sky hung low over the roofless walls.

There was little left to indicate it had once been a place of worship: an iron cross at the top, merely, which hadn't burned. Pews were overturned and no books were left. The arches were charred and black. At the entrance Eliza noticed that someone had cut the letters INRI into the bluish moss, and she wondered what it meant. It was probably the work of these boys; some anti-English graffiti.

Eliza wanted to stay a while, she liked the way the wind was stopped at the church's walls, and felt, somehow, as if her agitations were calmed here. But Mrs Page's funeral was at one o'clock and she would have to be at Forrester's by noon. With some of the £5 fee for burying Mrs Page, Eliza might buy herself something new from Buttons. A new scarf perhaps, or some socks. It was freezing cold and it was only to get worse as the December fogs came.

She walked on. There were children about in many of the houses, and Eliza reckoned on it being half-term. The houses were larger up here with bigger gardens, and they looked out rather defiantly over the sea. Few Christian souls had wanted to stay on after 1951 and the houses they had left were taken over by the deportees, and the excess were run to ruin by the Island kids. Eliza stayed five minutes outside one of the empty houses she had found but, after seeing no activity, she walked on toward the Eastern Bay.

She wondered – would a girl of English origin – brought up by the Church and fostered in its teachings – look different to the Island girls here? Would God somehow strengthen the whites of her eyes so that they were brighter than her own? Make her hair more flaxen, her nails less soft, her skin more luminous? Eliza had not seen the girl up close: only the red length of hair and the freckled skin. Eliza thought it wonderful: to be brought up believing in some kind and gently steering presence; to have a much stronger stake in some infinitely wiser thing than yourself. Nothing could be wasted, not in God's eyes; no. Eliza imagined that the girl would be boundlessly positive, since isn't that what the Church made you believe in, in the irresistible rightness of every act? Eliza had never believed in God – how could she, she had never been taught – but she had always thought that – given a different life in England – she would have been a natural at it. But it was too late for that now.

As Eliza walked, nearing the Eastern Bay, she wondered, again, what the girl was doing here. It was hardly a place for a holiday. Perhaps she had come to proselytize. Perhaps the girl had come to rescue her. Maybe she had come to find someone. Eliza made a silent vow to help her, and hide her, if she could.

The Eastern Bay was rough and the sand was scraggy and dark. Its currents made it too dangerous to fish and boats had often run aground here as they aimed for Warkworth pier. Breakers smashed against rocks. Its beach was often clogged with the drift of seaweed, and only birds alighted at the sand. Eliza fancied going down there but it was no time to be a daredevil, not with the girl to find, and Mrs Page to bury.

Eliza continued onward to Sea View Road, checking the houses. John Verger was in his living room, reading. Another man was watching television. One or two women poked their heads out of the curtains, wondering what she was doing sneaking around. They probably thought she was sharking about for another body for Mr Forrester. Eliza smiled nervously and almost retreated before she put her fingers to the words. *Find the girl.* Time was getting on. As she gained Marley Hill and then began footing her way down to Maiden's Square, Caro Kilman, mistress of the launderette, came running after her. She was wearing a big red coat that tied neatly at the waist; she was always well dressed, was Caro. Her auburn hair, set perfectly in a curl, was shown off by the purely grey sky. She said: 'Good day to you, Miss Eliza.'

'And to you.'

'And will you be assisting at Mrs Page's this afternoon?'

'That I will. And yourself? Will you be attending?'

'Aye. Aye.' Mrs Kilman gave her a cool look. 'You're a brave soul to be helping Mr Forrester like this.'

'It's not so bad.'

'Aye, well.'

'He pays me for it. It's not as if I'd be doing it for free, now.'

'No, well,' Caro said, 'I guess we all must pay for our fish. But you know, I haven't seen you much in the monger's these days.'

'Just haven't had the appetite for it.'

'Not since your ma's death?'

'No, not since Ma died, aye.'

'Well, it will return soon enough. Mark me. A fit young woman like you can't be on the tatties all the time now, no.' Caro had that knack of seeming both cold and caring: Eliza had never felt at ease with her. 'You'll be needing some fish inside you. Or you'll risk anaemia, you know.'

Eliza reassured Mrs Kilman she'd go to Arthur's and buy herself some cod with her wages. Mrs Kilman smiled at her but in a sceptical fashion. She gave her an odd look so that Eliza checked her fringe was in the right place and that the words could not be seen.

'Mrs Bingley said she bumped into you after you were at the launderette, last night.'

'Aye?'

'Well. I thought maybe you might be going to Stansky's, after mine, but you didn't. I just wondered what else you were doing, down at the square, when you couldn't get your dress.' Eliza shrugged. She was not in the mood for interrogation, especially not from Caro. 'You and Arthur used to be good friends. More than good friends. We don't see you two together any more. Did something . . . happen?'

'Nothing happened. We broke it off.'

'Oh. It's just . . . it was very abrupt, wasn't it, after your ma's . . . demise? We all thought you two would be together. But then you went to the Grand, and, of course, you can't expect a man like Arthur Stansky to be making his home with someone from the Grand, oh no, dear.'

'Well. That's the choice of Mr Stansky, of course.'

'It's just, well, something must have happened? No need to keep such a big secret, Eliza: you can tell me. I was very good friends with your ma, of course, she always did confide in me.'

With that laughable fact, Eliza said her goodbyes, absolutely wishing to be as far away from her as the Island would permit. She watched Caro descend the hill to the square. There was no one more gossipy than Caro Kilman; and no one she desired to speak with less about that night with Arthur. No one knew what had happened, apart from her, and Arthur, and Musa of course. And that's the way it would stay.

It was now nearly noon. Mrs Page's funeral was at one. Eliza gave up the search for the English girl and headed back to the Grand. She would have to change into something more fitting for the funeral: Mrs Page was to be buried by her today.

4. An English Girl

The girl stood unmoving in the light of the window. Dirt trimmed the bottom of the mattress where she had slept last night. The taps dripped. Half a broken mirror reflected back the room and her red hair, which looked as sumptuous as a gift of God. The house was derelict, but it would be Sarah's home, for her week on the Island.

Last night, after the ten hours she had spent in the hold of the boat, after creeping under the pier and then stealing across the Island, her legs had felt mercifully free, as if unpinned from restraints. The adrenaline too had made Sarah fast, her eye alert to any movement or shadows. She had had the sense of a pursuant, up until the square, at which point, though for no particular reason, Sarah had seemed to lose them. In the dark, she had been able to see very little of the Island, save the chalk-white houses, and occasionally, people in kitchens and lounges. The houses had a look of battleships.

Sarah had walked for an hour in the cold and salty air, footing her way carefully, but going fast if anyone seemed to be approaching. It seemed to take her an age to move through the dark, as if she walked through water, through a flood plain. Coming down the hill, the sea and sky were a block of dark before her, and she couldn't tell where the road might end and a cliff begin. She walked, wary to stop, but knowing she had to rest soon, lest she should freeze to death before she could even begin the search for Laura.

Sarah stopped at a row of darkish houses, with overgrown gardens and no sign of anyone about. All of the houses looked shabby and uncared for, some of the windows smashed and the hedgerow overgrown. She walked until the end of the road, circled back to check no one was behind her, then chose the house closest to the bay.

It was white and small and all of its windows were still intact. Sarah crept into the front garden. Once there had been a gravel path running up to the door but it was now covered with weeds. A track ran along the side of the house and she pushed aside brambles, her hair snagging on thorns. For a moment, Sarah thought someone was there, ahead of her in the back garden, but then a bird took flight and flapped against the branches. She waited moments, holding the knife, now, ahead of her, then she pushed the pine door and went into the house.

There was a kitchen in the first room, which smelled of old bread, empty rooms downstairs, with an upturned sofa and greying curtains. A staircase led to a landing where there were bedrooms and a long-abandoned bathroom with spots of rising damp. There was no one here.

Sarah waited for minutes, up in the bedroom overlooking the road, waiting for someone to appear, but no one did. And then, at midnight, after the exhaustion of the boat trip, during which, out of fear, she had been unable to even doze, she had curled up on the grubby mattress and fallen asleep surprisingly easily, sleeping until morning in the bright green sleeping bag she had brought with her from England.

Now Sarah stood at the window, in the weak stir of light. Over the roofs the sky was slung over them like a greying bed-sheet. She was cold, and had kept all of her clothes on from last night. In her hands, she held the newspaper article, the one that had brought her here. Her mother's mugshot looked out onto the world rather stunned, as if Laura were surprised to see it again.

For most of her life, Sarah had been told her mother had run off with another man. Her father had sat her down at the kitchen table, one warm July evening in 1976, and told her Laura had left them both, to start a new family with someone else. Sarah had learned the word *affair*, Laura had been having an *affair*. He said everyone was very upset with Laura for what she had done, it was a very bad thing to have an affair. Even the police were very upset with Laura, and that's why they had come to visit.

But in this past week, everything had changed. Now she knew the truth. Sarah looked out to the Island's vast sky, the flat long sea. This Island might be her mother's home. This Island might have been her mother's home for the past ten years. Laura Wicks was not an adulterer, but a criminal.

At the window, Sarah opened the article she had found last week, that had been folded these past ten years and kept in the cellar. Along the creases the ink had gone, but there was still more than enough to read. Her mother's eyes stared out from the mugshot, grey and light, her hair in the blonde bob that Sarah remembered. The article was from the *Newcastle Chronicle*, dated July 5th, 1976.

> Laura Wicks, of Trimdon, County Durham, has been arrested on suspicion of aiding the bombing of Saint Gregory's Church in Berwick yesterday. The Minister of Saint Gregory's, Rev Ed Williams, who was at the church early, died this morning from his burns.
>
> Wicks, a mother of one, was found on the scene; the two men she was with, and who launched the missiles, had already escaped by the time the police arrived. All three are thought to be members of the Secular Movement.
>
> It is thought Wicks had no part in starting the fire, but was the driver of the getaway car and alerted the two men to flee.
>
> The Secular Movement today issued a statement of responsibility for the church bombing, demanding the repatriation of criminals from the Island back to England and for the reinstatement of Secular rights.
>
> The Church issued a response saying it would not negotiate with terrorists.
>
> This has been the worst summer of secular atrocities since the emergency powers were issued in 1951, and is the thirteenth church fire in the North-East alone.
>
> After the Unrest in 1950, approximately 500 members of the Secular Movement were deported to the Island. This is the first orchestrated action from the Secular Movement in twenty-six years, and another mass expulsion is likely to follow.

The Secular Movement, which comprises members who use civil and violent protest against Church rule, are demanding the reinstatement of rights for non-religious people in England and the release of all non-religious prisoners on more minor charges. The Movement has called this the Sunday Agreement, but the Church has not yet entered into any negotiations on this matter.

A source from the Party has commented that the Sunday Agreement is looking less and less likely because of the violence this summer.

Ms Wicks, 26, has so far remained silent on the identities of the two male suspects, despite extensive questioning. Wicks will be held under emergency powers until sentencing.

Sarah wondered if her mother's act that July day ten years ago was an act of courage or an act of disgrace; whether it would be forgiven, or merely forgotten. The bruise on Sarah's wrist where, last Sunday, she had fallen on the cellar steps was starting to yellow. Her slipper had disappeared between two of the slats; going down to find it, under the step-boards, into the dark, it was then that she'd found the box of secrets, and found the article that had led her here, to the Island.

Sarah left the window and unpacked her warmest clothes, the socks, the comb, the toothbrush, the empty bottle she had used to pee in on the boat. She unpacked the knife but thought better of it and put it back in the bag. Half the bread was spoiled: last night, waiting for the boat to leave, and under the pier, her bag had lain unnoticed in a pool of water. But there was still margarine and cheese and a tin of corned beef, which she would save for the weekend when the food situation might become more desperate.

Sarah decanted the sopping half-loaf to the bin and saved what she could. She was already hungry but wouldn't let herself eat yet. It would be a week of hunger, she guessed, while she searched the Island for her mother.

She caught sight of herself in the mirror as she went about gathering her things. Silvering at the edges, and with spots of rust, it rendered parts of her invisible, and she was struck by the idea that perhaps she had changed, that coming to the Island had already marked her. She had spent a night here, mostly asleep: she could hardly have changed over ten hours. But she saw something in her eyes, hard, blank, as if she had entrenched her real self much further back, much further away from this new world. She wondered how the Island might have changed Laura, and whether she would even recognize her. She wondered, too, what the people were like here: unshepherded, free, but sad perhaps – they were free only in this patch of earth. Sarah had come from an England where God had swelled the schools and the boardroom and the banks, where the Church operated in sober distinction to the ways of the past. Sarah did not know anything but the croon of Church comfort and the presence of God in her like a second eye. And now she was here, after finding the article on her mother, after journeying to Newcastle and waiting at the docks for hours for the *Saviour*, and after she had stowed herself into the hold of the boat, in this most atheist of Islands.

The thought was terrifying and thrilling both.

Sarah packed a bag with a hastily made cheese sandwich, the torch, another jumper, the knife. At the taps, she washed out the bottle three or four times and then filled it with water; it still had an oily taste.

The path on the carpet was worn as if a multitude, not a family, had at one time taken these steps. The whole house smelled off. In the kitchen, where Sarah had come in last night, there was still crockery stacked at the sink and glassware in the dresser. Yellow scratches marked the length of a long wooden table. A chair was pushed back from the table as if its sitter had only just, violently, departed.

There was a strong smell outside, possibly a pond at the bottom of the garden. Someone with great care had planted a border of stones around the flower beds. A child's toy train had been kicked under the uncleared leaves. She wondered about the child's hand that had once motored the train through the home behind her. The child would be much older than her now. The Christian family that once lived here now probably lived in England, cosy, and church-going, having moved on from the resettlement village in Newcastle to pleasanter neighbourhoods, the memory of the Island merely a shrinking picture. Sarah remembered pictures of resettled families from her history books: their look of palpable relief, after they had cleared the Sound, and come home to England.

At the front of the house, Sarah flattened herself to the side wall. A man was walking past, elderly and bald, wearing tweed. He was talking to a young girl, asking her what she was to do this week, with school off. He kept on saying, 'Aye, aye,' very softly. Sarah looked at the soil around her feet, almost purple in the furrows, convinced that the man, if he found her, would grab and question her, convinced that her strong English scent would be carried on the winds, like a blood-stench, toward him.

When she could hear them no more, Sarah edged beyond the house. Its details she committed to memory: the long white walls, the drainpipe across its front, the loose branches of the hedge and the scruffy gateposts. On the lintel, in a friendly gesture, the words *Swanscott House* were carved.

Sarah tried to keep her eyes only on the path but she kept sneaking looks at the Islanders in their houses. They were doing normal things: laundry, reading the newspaper, cooking, cleaning. Sarah had expected more liveliness, somehow, as if the Islanders' behaviour might always be motivated by their irreligious fury. They had been expelled, after all; and they were all criminals – or the sons and daughters of criminals. As was she, she now supposed: the daughter of Laura Wicks.

At the hilltop, the sea was the colour of silt or ash or something close to it. There were two towns, down below, one light and airy; the other, packed and over-built, somehow making her think of the corned beef she'd brought in the tin. Only the grander one had a jetty, and this was where, she guessed, she had come last night. Behind her was the line of empty houses with Swanscott House, close to the strip of beach, where the breakers splashed against the rocky stacks, and where a slick of grey light winked.

A woman, in red, smiled at her, which made her feel nervous, and Sarah turned and walked much too quickly toward the bigger town, knowing, as she was doing this, that she was only going toward more and more Islanders. Sarah felt as if her blood had a scent, and that its hot spill would carry, somehow, on the wind. As if they might smell the meat she'd had for dinner on Sunday. She knew from her history books the Islanders had no meat: the English thought it would weaken their fortitude – as if the walls of the heart might be thinned by the absence of pork chops, and God might more easily sneak in and lodge Himself there. It was a tactic she had read about in her history books, and Sarah had thought the Church mean for it, as if you could teach God through the lessons of deprivation. It hadn't worked, anyway, the Islanders were no closer to God's bosom than they had been in '51.

Sarah pulled the coat closer to her, much closer, as if it might somehow contain her English reek.

All the grass was scrubby and flat, going down the hill, and mushrooms grew patchily, round and browning at the edges. She wondered, with her half-loaf gone, whether she could pick these and eat them. As she walked the sun came out and the clouds started to move off, and there were patches of blue, though the day became no warmer. With the brightening of the Island she felt better, and resolved to have a look around the town by the bay.

The square looked to Sarah much as a square in England might, without the church, she supposed, at one of its sides. Instead, the fishmonger's was the biggest place here, with the biggest awning, and people hovering about it as if it were the church. Flagstones were washed clean by the sea air; as were the roofs, which were low and slate and shone in winter light. Narrow windows barely broke the masonry. A few gulls wheeled on the winds; their wings massive, their eyes, when she caught them, somehow jealous, as if they envied her the turf.

Sarah pulled her hood closer. A few people came in and out of the shops. Every face she scanned for a likeness to Laura, but she didn't know where to put herself without attracting attention. Not close to the monger's: there were too many people near it. Neither did she have much inclination to be near the funeral parlour. There was a notice on the glass front. A funeral, today, near a place called Lynemouth Bay, at one o'clock, for a woman called Mrs Page. Perhaps she would go there, stand at a distance from the burial pit, to see if Laura might be in the congregation. Perhaps Mrs Page had been her friend.

A woman in a shop called Buttons looked her up and down and then looked away, chatting to another lady of the same age. A boy, with a bruise the size of an apple on his chin, narrowed his eyes and took some steps toward her before his mother called him back. He could only have been about twelve but he looked quite menacing, with his bald head and military garb, as if that mark of violence meant he had the capacity for it. Sarah felt for her knife, and followed the scrape of the sign into the museum.

There was no one inside. Sarah hid for minutes, just in case this boy was to come and cause trouble. When he didn't, she came out of the vestibule and slipped into the room.

The first picture on the wall was a map of the Island, pointing to Warkworth Bay, Lynemouth Bay, and the towns above them. She thought she could make out where Swanscott House would be, above the eastern quarter, which, she was pleased to see, looked rather uninhabited, with fewer houses than the rest of the Island. It had aged pictures of women picking at a quarry, men in old-fashioned clothes, an old 'kirk' above Lynemouth Town, and then the Islanders' resettlement, in England, in 1950.

The narrative continued under the black-and-white photographs, all taken during the Unrest. There was a picture of English identification documents from 1947: light-coloured if issued by the Church; darker if they were from a civil authority. There was a photograph of the elected Minister who had asked the police to do stop-searches; and those with darker papers were given a harder time. The Minister said that Englishmen had gone on too long in the night-time of the Lord. He said every Christian would do well to bring his dark-paper neighbour to Sunday service. He said it was right that better Christians got better jobs. He said it was right that those practising the values of the Lord were rewarded in heaven *and* on earth. The Minister said that Christian folk should pity the Godless. Then he said if they wouldn't respond to charity then the Council had the right to use more aggressive tactics.

A photograph showed a sign above a surgery which said 'No Godless Here'. There was a photograph of a boy with a black eye and one of a policeman with his truncheon poised. After-school clubs were no longer for the dark-papered children. There were two long queues outside a segregated school. Doctors could only treat people of their kind; this was in respect of people's wishes. A map showed boundaries re-drawn along the lines of Church congregations so that the Christian Party won again up north and, said the caption, 'most of the English were pleased with this.'

In the next photograph there was glass everywhere. Secular shops were looted and no one came forward to press charges. There was smashed glass on the roads most days. The Church Youth liked to take cricket bats to knees; the secular gangs liked to use golf clubs so that the altar boys' ears would ring and then they wouldn't hear the babble of God any more. There were photographs of kids bruised and happy as if they craved another beating, their eyes wide and thrilled. English policemen held guns toward a merry gang as they held their dark papers toward the lens. Photographs followed of people throwing rocks through church windows, then nail bombs, then glass-bottle petrol bombs. This was the work of the new Secular Movement, in 1949. A Sunday school was bombed and many children were killed.

In 1950, the Christian Party took government and that was the summer the churches truly burned. There was a sense of siege to the Northern cities. The first thing the Party did was to make the Secular Movement illegal. Anyone left with a darker paper got it swapped, if their family meant more to them than politics, or God, and besides, if you didn't pay a tithe to a church you didn't get a vote, so there was not much good to be done with darker papers.

Riots broke out and the photographs showed an old woman dying with her dark papers still grasped. There were hands nursing bloodied noses; policemen with batons poised midair; noiseless screams; shields braced; heavy boots stamping. Hundreds of protesters died. There were placards saying GODLESS OUT and THE GODLESS ARE WOLVES. There were cars burned out on the roads. The Movement occupied the Newcastle Town Hall and the police made a blockade. When the police took the Hall it was filthy with shit and old food and rats.

A state of emergency was called in London. A policy of containment was discussed, and emergency powers were drawn up. There was a photograph of the Prime Minister signing a paper: the title of it read 'Act for the Displacement of the Secular Movement from Problem Areas'. All members of the Movement were to go.

At the Museum's back wall, photographs showed men and women walking with heavy bags. Some of the women were very smart, in well-cut skirts and coats with fine fur collars, they wore upturned hats, and dark red lipstick. There was a strange look to them, with their flat mouths and pinprick eyes: they seemed faintly bored, as if their indifference were a form of protest.

That January, in 1951, five hundred members of the Movement were deported to the Island. Their families followed later. Some of the photographs were over-exposed but the points of their eyes were shadows. Dark identification papers could be seen falling to the waves.

In the next room, the narrative continued after 1951: England's long happy fifties, sporadic resistance in the sixties, and then suddenly the great wave again of violence in that big year, 1976. Sarah analysed the photographs intently, looking for Laura. There were more church-bombings, riots, the murder of two members of the Christian Party. There were photographs of the Newcastle riots and a summer hot with church fires. A photograph of a man hanging from a tree, neck chafed from the rope, his head lolling. A fat woman lay dead in a pit, her big breasts exposed. A second wave of deportations followed in 1977. This was when Laura would have come. Sarah searched, looking for a photograph of Saint Gregory's, for a burning church at the end of an avenue in Berwick. There were any number of churches with their pulpits burning but none in particular that looked like Saint Gregory's. Sarah searched too for the two men Laura was with that day: but she had no names and no faces to identify them with, and searched instead for the words Saint Gregory's, or Berwick, or Laura Wicks.

There had been no more deportees after 1977. In the last section, it said that the Sunday Agreement, finally signed in 1983, had secured the relaxation of compulsory religious attendance, the carrying of ID cards and the release of minor Secular prisoners given their good cooperation on all crimes still outstanding. The final sentence observed, rather melancholically, that nothing had been achieved insofar as returning the Islanders back to England.

At school, Sarah and her friends had all been told the Movement had gone willingly. It had been a ceasefire, and the members had opted for resettlement, to stop the Unrest. But here there were guns and blindfolds and a man hanging: the Godless on one side, the Church on the other. This had not been the story told to them. Sarah had been fed one story when the truth was very much other. Well, she supposed, Laura's 'affair' was only her father's contribution to the national lie.

Sarah waited there, in the museum, until one o'clock, amongst the walking men, and scared women, and merry policemen with waving guns, waiting for the funeral of this Mrs Page, which her mother might – or might not – be attending.

5. The Grave Courtesan

Heat swelled from the living room's gas-fire. His mam sat in the big old chair, her face as clear as the clock-face above her, wearing her housecoat and slippers. When Nathaniel saw her, nested between the fire and the side table, some block of misery sank him. 'All right, Ma,' he said to her quietly, from the doorway, so as not to give her a fright, 'am off now.'

She batted away the smoke. 'Where you off?'

'Down to the square. And then to Lynemouth Bay.'

'What for?'

'Mrs Page's funeral. You asked me to go. Remember?'

'Is it Tuesday already?'

Nathaniel nodded.

'Aye. Aye. Good lad. Your da would have wanted you to go.' She looked at him and narrowed her eyes. 'You're not going with the boys, are you?'

'No, no.'

'Tell me you're my good lad?'

He told her he was her good lad and then she looked away from him, out of the window to the garden. Nathaniel came to the chair and stroked a lock of her hair. It was so brittle he could snap it. 'All right now, Mammy M?'

'Aye.'

'What's got into you?'

'Nowt.' Her gaze was fixed somewhere in the middle air between the window and her chair. She looked worried.

'Now there's a lie.'

'John Verger was here yesterday, asking for you. About some book you'd borrowed.'

'Oh, aye.'

'D'you know the one?'

'Aye. It's a daft thing he lent me. I'll return it soon enough.'

But Nathaniel couldn't remember where he'd put it. He had tried, in truth, to ignore its existence as much as he could. A book of scripture and paintings, Nathaniel had shuddered as Mr Verger had shown him 'the hidden glories of English faith', and shuddered too, at the tremble of delight in the old man's voice. Verger had delivered a little lecture, telling him about how he had found himself unexpectedly in the church after falling off one of the pews, and describing some miracle act of calling, culminating in this act of theft from the museum. Nathaniel had felt very moody with him, as the old man argued for the consolation the volume might bring 'to someone still grieving'. At this point, Nathaniel had purely wanted to punch him, or gromick up his supper on his lap. But Verger had been his da's best friend, and Nathaniel hadn't had the heart to reject the book. It was a frightful thing, with Christ babied and bloodied on every page, and Nathaniel had no more than taken a few looks before putting it aside in some drawer or cupboard and lost it for ever.

'Well. He'd like to see you,' his ma said, 'and he is a kind man. Your da always talked very highly of him.'

Nathaniel could never seem to persuade his mam of how tiresome Verger was. 'Aye . . . but he's always wanting to talk, always a little sermon about this or that; I can't stand it.'

'You be good to that man, Nathaniel Malraux. He was your da's best friend,' she pointed the cigarette at him, 'just you remember that.'

'Aye, Mammy, aye. I didn't mean anything by it. Let's stop this now. What'll you do today?'

'There's a soap on the box I want to watch.'

'Shan't you go out?'

'Not today, Nath, not today.' He held her wrist; it was tiny. He felt again he could snap it, and felt sorry bad that he kept on thinking of snapping her, his own ma. The poised cigarette was now almost all ash. Nathaniel moved her hand to the ashtray and tapped the cigarette gently. 'Smoke 'em slowly, Ma, I didn't get any more this week.'

'Oh. Did you not?'

'The Boatman wants those pills you get. And you forgot to order them. So no more cigs for a while.'

'I'll get some more. For next week. Commerce with an Englishman, I can hardly believe it sometimes. My own son. Cheeky monkey, eh?'

'Aye, well, let's not complain while we enjoy them, aye?'

Margaret looked up at him and patted his hand gently with hers. 'When'll you be home?'

'Tonight. I'll be here all tonight with you, doll. And we'll have supper together and watch the telly-box. How's that sounding?' Should he chance it now? 'Maybe I could go to Arthur's and buy us fish supper?' His mam didn't answer but looked out again into the garden, her eyes full of vague

alarm. 'No. Well. Not if you don't want to. I'll be here anyway, this evening. All right, doll?' His mam patted his hand
and told him he was her good lad. She put out the cigarette in the ashtray and her eyes slid back to the telly set.

Nathaniel stepped out into the cold air and sucked it up by
the lungful, glad to be shot of the warmth. A few trees here
and there, but everything had the look of being dwarfed by
the sky. He felt happy to be setting out. An edgeless cloud
topped the hill this morning and, making his way to the
top, now surveying the harbour and houses and the men
working down at the herring stations, Nathaniel felt more
than ever the happy king of this dark isle.

Within the half-hour he was down at Maiden's Square
to meet Jake as they had planned. Nathaniel had hoped to
interview Mr Forrester about Mrs Page and her anaemic
demise, but when the boys walked into the parlour, Mr
Forrester was fast asleep, his narrow back facing them,
snoring gently. The two boys crept past and Forrester did
not wake.

Behind the shop there was the mortuary and garage.
The mortuary was a tiled room of white enamel; cool and
very clean, with a chemical smell, flat and strong like chlo-
ride. A window was built into the back, though it was
seldom that a person looked either out or into the colour-
less room. The garage, next to it, kept the Island's only car,
a black old rattlebox whose creaking chassis could be heard
over the whole measure of the Island. Petrol was delivered
by the English boat once a month and the car was used
sparingly, in emergencies, and for those whose emergencies had emerged with less than happy outcomes. It had a

long bonnet and at the tip a logo that meant nothing to those born here. The garage, to Nathaniel, smelled of his da's garage where Jake and he had first shorn their scalps: a mixture of turpentine, grease, paint, oil.

The car looked as if it were waiting for them. Nathaniel got into the front seat and made Jake get in the back, and he pretended he was a taxi driver, just as he'd seen on the telly, and Jake told him where to go and they chatted as they saw the English people on television did. They put on funny voices to imitate them. Nathaniel made Jake bob up and down as if the English road they travelled was a rutted one. When the boy paid from a book of invisible notes Nathaniel said that he would give him a reduction on the price since Jake was a friend.

Jake thought it was the nicest time they had had together in a long time, probably since the summer, before things had turned strangely fraught between them.

A single door joined the mortuary and the garage. When Jake had paid, and after they had swapped places so that Jake was the taxi driver and Nathaniel the chatty customer, the boys shut the cab doors quietly and crept into the mortuary.

It was very still in there, and cold enough that Mrs Page gave off no smell. 'Can you believe it, aye?' said Nathaniel, staring wide-eyed at the closed casket. The two boys were as immobile as Mrs Page and stood together away from the coffin, their shadows no larger than them on the glossy walls. 'Mrs Page, Mrs Page. I remember her giving me a shilling if I ever came to visit.'

'Are you off to Lynemouth Bay for the funeral?' asked Jake.

'Aye. My ma asked me to, like.'

'Is it Eliza still doing the Tongue?'

'Aye,' said Nathaniel.

'Wouldn't mind dying so much if it meant going on her Tongue,' said Jake. 'Me on the tip of her Tongue, oh yes, I could see that all right, though I shouldn't hope for it, I suppose.'

The light coming in at the window was grey and the boys' skin was grey too. 'Go on, then, Jake, open the box.'

'On your way!'

'Why? Scared?'

'No. Just don't want to.'

The boys stood there looking at the coffin, both unmoving.

'Scaredy cat.'

'Am not.'

'Y'are so. It's not nailed or anything. Eliza will be doing it in an hour or so, anyway. You're more fearful than a woman, then, is that what you're saying? More fearful than the doxy herself?'

Sullenly, Jake went to the casket. His hands had a tremor to them but he wouldn't show the other boy. He told himself Mrs Page was dead and couldn't do anything to him now. The wood was surprisingly heavy but soundless in its springs. Jake could not make out much more than a body recumbent in the dark. He brought the lid up further, the underside of it rougher than the top. A sweet smell rose as the lid came to rest on the hinge.

Mrs Page was dressed in Buttons' finest: a plaid skirt, tan stockings and sensible shoes for the lower half; for the top, a plain shirt and woollen cardigan. Everything in her outfit, all the separates, seemed so stiff that if she were flipped over there might be nothing covering her undersides. Jake imagined her bottom squashed fatly against the coffin base. Her skin had a waxy look and her eyes were closed as if they had been sealed with glue. Her lips too had lost their colour. Mrs Page's hands, with knuckles gleaming, held each other over her middle.

'Oh my,' said Jake, and then he burst out laughing. 'She looks just like your ma.'

Nathaniel came round to the box, viewing Mrs Page over the tips of her brogues. 'She looks nothing like my ma,' he said, rather tonelessly, as a sadness pulled at him, because she did, she did, she had just the look of Mammy Malraux! He felt almost like he might blub. He'd come here with Jake to have a lark and be thrilled by the pathos of it, but now an awful spreading sorrow came over him, so that his lids scalded and his cheeks burned. He said something like, 'She looks more like *your* ma,' but she looked nothing like Mammy Lawrence and they both knew it.

Nathaniel closed the lid and then slapped Jake very hard on the back of the skull. 'You say nothing of that ilk again, Jakob Lawrence.' The boy rubbed his head and gave Nathaniel a narrow look, but did not push it.

With some urgency, and without closing the box, the boys left the room, suddenly spooked. Mr Forrester was still facing Marley Hill, but now reading a newspaper spread over his knees. At his crown, he had a bald spot the size of a penny piece. He turned on his swivel chair as if he'd always known they were in there, but laughed at them as they tried to make excuses. Mr Forrester asked what they were doing, and the boys spoke at the same time, until Mr

Forrester gave up, and, after some pressure from Nathaniel, he measured them up for a coffin apiece, until Jake mentioned something about stinky Gots, and how he'd liked to bury a bleeding Englishman in one of these coffins, and Mr Forrester got huffy. The two boys left to play Belly-Up and Shark before he had time to deliver a bigger sermon.

Eliza watched the boys come out of Forrester's, but chose not to comment. She was having a hard enough time snaking around the square so that Arthur would not see her. Last night had been such an embarrassment, with Arthur having to come to her rescue, and then not uttering a word to her. Aye, he had made it quite clear he wanted nothing more to do with her.

Arthur had been her mam's friend, really. Linda had always had a great deal of time for Arthur Stansky. But in the time between Eliza's ma having her first heart attack, and then the second, it was Eliza and Arthur who had become inseparable. It started when Arthur began calling round to the flat, above the baker's, offering some brill or bass wrapped in an oilcloth, his face shiny in the pool of lamplight. Eliza would watch him from her window, as if he were under a lens, a small thing, like an insect of particular curiosity.

She had felt things happening. They would sit at the table, after her ma had gone to her sickbed, talking, until very late, sometimes holding hands, sometimes there would be a kiss. He never smelled disagreeable, despite his profession, and his hands, so roughened by his job, always seemed marvellous to her. Aye, things were developing, gently, gently. They would go out for long walks up and around the Island, he'd sometimes take her out on one of the fishing boats, or guide her hand as he showed her how to gut herring. It was an exquisitely lovely time, wrapped up, as it was, with the grief for her ma, as well as the tender thrill of being with him. She liked the way the Islanders looked at her when they were together, that June: knowing that she had bagged the best man on the Island, and she was proud.

But then her ma died, and their little relationship – that hadn't even started yet, not in earnest – had suddenly collapsed. And the worst thing was, Eliza couldn't even work out whose fault it was.

Maiden's Square was busy at lunchtime. There was a queue of people outside Kilman's launderette and a shuffling line outside the fishmonger's and the grocer's. All around the square there was a reek of fishbait and seawater.

Mrs Bingley was standing with another woman and nodding toward the two boys settled now on the stage. 'I hear,' she said, 'they are sharking about the Island, looking for English spies. For anyone they suspect, you know, of having some English connection. A sorry state of affairs. Not in this day and age. You'd think we've had enough, after thirty-six years, without being persecuted by our own, aye.' The other lady was nodding vaguely and stole a look at them. Eliza took heart that if they were talking about the boys, that meant the English girl was not yet known to them. Mrs Bingley would surely have words about this were she to have seen her, this flame-haired foreigner. Eliza wove past them, avoided Nathaniel and Jake, and found herself at Forrester's.

Forrester's office was warm and musty. Everywhere there was disarray, with old books, notes and newspapers stacked above one another, though it looked necessary, as if the dead's dispatch depended on misrule. Forrester looked up and closed his paper. 'Eliza! How's business?'

'Grand, thank you, Mr Forrester. And yourself?'

He looked about the room, and lowered his voice. 'Between you and me, Mrs Page is a jolly good turn-up for the books. Business was looking rather glum; not enough dead.' He issued a finger urgently toward her. 'Not that I'd wish anyone to go, that's not what I'm saying. But I run a business, aye, love, and I need the money. A funerary home needs its dead as Arthur needs his fishes.' A raised eyebrow. 'And someone needs to feed his fish. Get my ken?' He closed the book of accounts on the desk. 'And I'd always rather see more of you, Miss Eliza. We don't see much of you any more at Maiden's Square.'

'No. I . . . I've been very busy.'

'Business must be very good.'

'Business is business. Other things have been distracting me.'

'Ah! Men, then; boys.'

'No,' she smiled; a sealed, sad, smile. 'Not that either.'

'Ah,' he sighed. He looked down at the chewed pipe. He applied a handkerchief, frowning. 'I always thought of you and Arthur, maybe . . . one day. You used to enjoy stepping out together when your ma was . . . in decline.'

'Not any more.'

'He had such a penchant for you, you know, and now he mopes around the monger's like a lost fish. I can't fathom it. I never see him anywhere but the square, and you're always in Lynemouth Town.' Forrester shrugged, then stuffed some loose shag into the pipe, poking it down with a blunt digit. 'He sleeps and eats and drinks in that pokey attic, you know, above the fishery. Being with all that trout, day in, day out, it can't be good for a man.'

'No. I can't imagine it is. Well, anyway, he's not interested. He barely says a word to me.'

Forrester's eyes flicked back up at her. 'No. Well. No, he doesn't *seem* to be, but perhaps he's only shy, perhaps—'

'Y'are sweet, Mr Forrester, but Arthur Stansky hasn't said a word to me in quite a while now.'

'Well, I hope you haven't quarrelled. He used to have such a soft spot for you.' Memories flooded her: a warm day spent on Marley Hill, when Arthur had carried the picnic in his shrimp net; swimming at the beach in Warkworth Bay when his lips had tasted of kipper. For a moment, the memory was so strong she thought her limbs were in water. 'He sometimes asks me if you're ever around the square.'

'He does?'

But she stopped herself asking more. It was impossible. Nonsense. Arthur only asked Mr Forrester so that he might know how best to avoid her. 'Look, Eliza, dear, tell me. Did something happen? You don't have to keep it to yourself, you know, if you want someone to talk to.'

Eliza cleared her throat and offered her hand. 'Can I get the keys, Mr Forrester?'

'Aye, aye. Oh, I'm sorry: Alison's always telling me not to meddle. Here,' he said, and he gave her the ring of keys, but did not let go. 'These lads. Over there.' He nodded over to Nathaniel and Jake, who were chasing each other about the square. 'Are they much trouble?'

'Not to me,' she said, wondering why she had so quickly lied.

'Well, they do say some funny things. About Gots and spies on the Island. A load of old nonsense, of course. Who out of any of us would want union with England? In this day and age!'

'I don't know.'

'Whipping up trouble for the sake of it. What nonsense. Well, well. Let's press on, eh?' He dropped the keys in her palm. And then he kissed her on the forehead, as a father might. 'Dear, Eliza. You're a good woman, a good woman. Your ma would have been proud.'

Away from the bluster of the square, the mortuary was always very quiet and very still. Whenever she was called here, Eliza would stop a little while in the back room, which seemed so luminous a spot as to render the rest of the Island shadowy and dark. Eliza put her hand down flat on the cool wood. A perilous job, this; burying the dead.

The Pages had chosen a dark, heavy wood, and she was pleased that they had spent a little more of their money. It always made her job easier. Mrs Page's features were damp and yellowy like a bread pudding. Her clothes were probably her best, washed and laundered by Caro Kilman. Mrs Page had not been a slender woman, and her body went right up to the clothy bulges of the box's padding.

Something in Eliza seemed to flag at all this. The memory of her ma's funeral that summer came back to her.

Mr Forrester had arranged all the sundries but it had been Eliza who had clothed her, pinned Linda's hair back into the soft waves she liked and brushed a rouge on her cheeks. Eliza had been burying the Island's dead since she had left school at sixteen, but it had been Mr Forrester who had pushed the Tongue's button that day; this was, finally, a job she was spared.

Since that June, it had been a bad year. The loss of her ma, the poor sale of the baker's, then Arthur's rejection, and the terrible job at the Grand . . . At every step, Eliza had expected a redress to her lot. The world had turned so ungenerous! In six months, she had lost nearly everything, and the Island now seemed a sorry little dump. Eliza thought of her future here: each day played out in long similitude to the last, amid the encroaching winter, when the snow would come to the Island, and would not shift, not for months, and she would stand outside Arthur's fish shop, waiting like a rag-picker, like a beggar, come to scavenge off him what she could.

Mrs Page looked on, calmed of all agitations.

With some envy, Eliza closed the lid.

It was warmer outside. The clouds had gone now, and the sky was blue and high. When enough people had gathered behind the car as was respectable, Eliza gunned the engine. It was a quarter to one. She drove slowly and the cortège followed. From their homes, people watched the car, as it went, rattlingly, to Lynemouth Town.

Eliza kept an eye on Mrs Page but let those gathering proceed as they wished. She took the opportunity to keep an eye out for the girl, expecting her to rear, unexpected and russet-coloured, amongst the Islanders. There was no one at Warkworth Bay, where she had seen the girl last night. Eliza doubted herself for a moment, wondering if she had dreamed of the girl between the beach and the square. Waves collapsed at the sandbar. She remembered the words on her forehead, that she had penned this morning – *find the girl* – and she knew she had not made the stowaway up.

Then the cliffs began swerving crazily inward, gouging gaps of enormous air, and Eliza concentrated on the road until Lynemouth Bay.

The air outside the car was a briny slap. Eliza checked the distance between the boot and cliff edge. Her heart lurched. How the waves scissored the light from up here! Her mother had told her that they bury their dead, over there; over there, she guessed, looking out, lay England. Eliza thought it crude and unromantic, to stop up a mouth with earth. She would much rather be buried at sea, to let her hair open and close like the skirt of a jellyfish. The Sound's beauty – though it was barbarous, aye, she knew that enough – calmed her. She forgot momentarily of her troubles, of Arthur, her dead ma, the English stowaway, and thought of the task ahead. Mrs Page was to be buried by Eliza today.

The Islanders had caught up with her at Lynemouth bluffs. In the congregation, she noticed Nathaniel was there, though the other boy, Jake, was not. Eliza positioned herself some way away from him. He raised an eyebrow to her but she had no desire to speak to him. The rare November sun brought a lovely light to the scene, and the grass on the cliff looked almost polished. It had its moments, this Island.

By half-past one the congregation had fully arrived. There was Caro from the launderette, Mrs Bingley from Buttons, John Verger's bald head poking out like a par-boiled potato. No Arthur to be seen. The reflection from Mr Forrester's round spectacles occasionally caught the Islanders in the eye and they squinted after him. He motioned for quiet.

'Now we are all here, I would like to thank you for coming, to celebrate the life of Mrs Victoria Page and to say goodbye. Mrs Page, as we all know, was a kind, caring woman. She was always trying to do right by people. It is a great loss to us, and to our little state, to have her leave us. Often, life might be said to be hard for us.' He looked down to his feet. 'Whether or not we believe' – and here he looked squarely at Nathaniel – 'we are all exiles now. We came from the Unrest – whether it was 1951, or '77 – and many of us did things, in those days, which we now might regret; which we may even regret every day. It was a very bad time, but in the light of everything else, we acted how best we could, in the name of progressive, not regressive, ideas.

'Now, in 1986, we find ourselves on this rock, and we do not seek any more unrest upon our heads. As part of the Movement, we fought for freedom, and that is what we have here. Freedom. It is not much, not enough to feed our children with or provide for our families,' he smiled, 'not enough to weave a banner with, but freedom is a good thing, and we would not have it, even now, in England.

'But enough of politics. We lead small lives. Over

quickly. Mrs Page's conduct was good and generous. In the midst of private hardship, we might remember her example, and remember Mr Page, who will need his neighbours now, more than ever, in these dark days. I cannot give you the reassurance of the priest at the casket, no promise of sweetness nor of light after we're gone, but I can say that goodness does not go unremarked. Not at all. To Mrs Victoria Page, then.' And the congregation dipped their heads, as if in prayer.

Mr Forrester gave a nod to Eliza. She broke from the rest of the group and went to the back of the car, opened the trunk, and unfolded the stretch of metal. It was topped by a belt of red cloth and nominally, amongst the Islanders, it was called the Tongue.

Mr Page came to the back of the hearse and drew a sprig of heather from the coffin's bouquet. He laid a hand down on the coffin, his palm down. The gesture did not last long. He rejoined the congregation with the flower still grasped.

Eliza gripped the pulley handle. With the grease cold in the cogs, it was always difficult to begin, but the coffin started moving out of the trunk, along the Tongue's conveyor belt. Eliza took the handle with two hands, drawing it round and round, watching the congregation, blackly rapt, as the pointed coffin emerged out of the boot. She kept on going, her forearms made strong from the brothel now strong for the Tongue. The casket edged along the belt, inching along, so it seemed as if the waves frothed about its end. Her forehead was licked with sweat.

With Mrs Page now a third down the Tongue, Eliza stopped to get a breath. Looking up, she saw – she was sure of it – the English girl, standing far away, right at the back of the crowd, unseen by anyone else. The girl was small and thin but her hair fell in brassy locks. In the sun, the red hair had a yellow glow to it. Under the freckles her skin was white as bone.

Eliza's heart sank; she could hardly stop the wheel now! Her grip slipped from the handle and the wheel did one revolution before she was able to reclaim it. Forrester looked at her alarmed. She managed a few more turns, going faster, really, than she should have done. When she was able to look up again, the girl had evidently noticed she had been caught, and had once again disappeared.

The coffin had, by now, travelled most of the Tongue and its top, pointed like a sword, weighed down at the end so that the car started to creak. Mr Page gave a moan. The car looked as if it should toss the box, like a horse wanting to buck its rider. Eliza gave the handle three quick cranks and the coffin was now halfway out into the air and the car groaned madly, and the weight of the box was beginning to tip, and then it teetered at the edge, and then was almost diagonal, until Eliza felt the car give, as the box and body of Mrs Page toppled into the Sound.

Moments passed and Eliza wondered if she really had just dispatched Mrs Page so brutally, and then there was a great splash, and the congregation sucked in a collective breath of air.

Gingerly, Eliza tiptoed over to the cliff edge to check the rocks. She had missed them. No leg or limb could be found kicking into the air. The coffin was nowhere to be seen, and the Sound was sliding around but more or less flat again.

Eliza had always taken great pride in her funerary duties, but Mrs Page had been dispatched in a shockingly brisk manner. Had the Islanders noticed her inattention, her unseemly haste? The English girl had captivated her. But no one seemed any wiser. Mr Page wept a little, others gathered around him; Nathaniel was smoking a cigarette – she wondered how he procured them? – and women huffed and puffed at the sight of him. Eliza folded up the Tongue back into the trunk, and shut the car doors.

Mr Forrester came over and gave Eliza the envelope with her fee. He put the pipe in the corner of his mouth. 'Were you all right there?'

'Aye,' she said, smoothing out her shirt.

He said: 'You just seemed distracted, that's all.'

'No. I'm sorry. A few things on my mind.'

'Well. Not to worry. No one noticed.' Forrester leaned in closer. 'Let's hope we might get a lick of someone else soon, Miss Eliza. My bets are on Mr Kilman. He has bad blood, the old anaemia, I hear.' He gave Eliza a peck on the cheek and a squeeze of her shoulder. 'And sorry about this morning. I didn't mean to harp on about Arthur. It's a private matter, and I understand that you're not wanting anything there.'

'Aye,' she said weakly, into the sun.

When the crowd had gone, Eliza drove the car back to the garage. She kept a lookout from the cab window, but the English girl did not appear to her again.

6. The Woman

Sarah woke that morning in the disused bedroom. Light slanted into the room but made it no warmer. In the chill, which leaked in draughts under doors and between panes, it felt as if her skin were bluing; as if the cold were a colour rubbing off on her. Dirt was building in the nail-beds. The strands of her hair clumped and gave off a brownish tang, but the water from the taps was too icy to think about. She was too warm in bed to move, and the room too cold.

Sarah felt for Laura's article, which was still in the pocket of her jeans. Folded and unfolded so many times in the course of this week, it was now soft and limp, like a worn piece of cotton. The now-familiar photo still shocked her. Sarah mouthed the word 'Laura', as if speaking the word might better her chances of finding her. All this time she had felt so angry with her, that Laura had felt so easily able to abandon the family, on a romantic whim, and never contact them. Now, things were so different.

Sarah had found the article a week ago last Sunday, while the meat from the butcher's was on the kitchen counter, and her father, folded into the sofa, was snoozing after church. The meat – it was pork – had been cold in her hands, as she laid out the medallions in the oven dish, when the boiler pipe had started clanging again. Sarah didn't like to go down to the cellar – it was dark in there, and frightening – but it wouldn't stop until she had levelled a kick at the barrel.

There was dust everywhere down there, thick as a fur, and the bulb only gave a weak light. Vaguely she could hear her father's snores and the sound of the afternoon television; the races, perhaps, at York, or another Sunday service, gone long into the afternoon. At the foot of the stairs, growing through a crack in the floor, a mushroom was struggling into the dark, round and glossy as a blind eye. Sarah thought there was something eerie down here, and frightening, as if someone might lock her in, and choose to forget about her.

She took the steps two by two, but on the fourth or fifth – she wasn't sure – she lost her footing and fell sharply on her knee, her wrist scraping the stair-board. She put her mouth to the cut and the blood was warm. Her slipper was lost between the stair slats. Sarah climbed down and pressed herself between the banister and the wall, so that her hand went groping into the dark. She touched dust and cobwebs, but could reach nothing.

Eyeing a broom propped against the opposite wall, Sarah swept the handle over the stone floor. It brushed against her slipper, and then knocked against something else, boxlike and hollow.

Light and airy, in the arc of the broom it came quickly toward her. There was almost no weight to it. Sarah handled it carefully, like she would that mushroom should she have grasped its stalk. Dusty Sellotape sealed the box; and it was this that made her mind race. For so long, Sarah had asked her dad about Laura, asked about where her mother was and how she could get in contact. What was this box doing, sealed and secret under the stairs? Her father would never answer her straight, not directly, and neither would anyone else in Trimdon. Sarah carried the box carefully upstairs and then, wordlessly, as if nothing had happened, she proceeded to make dinner. Pork medallions. Apple sauce. They went to church and the butcher's every Sunday; the ritual was important to them, to the little family; her and her dad.

After dinner, while her dad was washing up, she cut away at the box's tape. Folded into squares, a newspaper cutting lay flat at the bottom of the box. Sarah's mind leapt to the contents. How many times had she found resemblances in women along the High Street, or trips to cities, her eyes keen to find Laura's blonde bob and freckled cheeks and nervous smile? Every Christmas she had hoped for a letter, or a soundless telephone call in the middle of the night.

Suddenly, there, on the newspaper sheet, there was her mother's face, looking up from the grey-and-white wash of print. It was a delicate portrait, though it wasn't intended as such: Laura's head tilting, the eyes shy, and the lips slightly open as if she had just spoken, or was about to speak. Unguarded and expectant, she looked as if she could be waiting for a blessing; her lips waiting for the host. This woman, though; this woman. Where had she been for ten years?

Sarah's eyes raced through the story, as she learned of Laura's crimes, which were not, as Sarah had understood them, crimes of the heart, but crimes of the Church. For ten years, the news of the mother had been kept from her. And here was the truth: her mother had been working for the Movement, and had driven these two nameless men to a chosen church in Berwick, on July 4th, 1976, and helped them set fire to it. A Minister had died because of them. Sarah imagined Laura in the cold car with bloodless knuckles holding the wheel, ready to drive at the first sound of sirens. But then she'd been caught, and the other two hadn't. *If found guilty,* the report said, *she will be deported to the Island.* But how was Sarah to know if this had happened? Was there a ledger, somewhere, a great English account of those who had and had not been expelled?

There were sounds of footsteps. She pocketed the article as her dad came in. He said goodnight and kissed her on her forehead. Her and her dad. It felt as if it had always been like this.

Out of the warmth of the sleeping bag, Sarah dressed rapidly in her old jeans and jumper. The article she folded neatly into her back pocket. She would need evidence, were she questioned, of who she was, and what she was doing here. At the mirror, she washed her face and rubbed it down with a towel. It, too, could do with a wash; it smelled of bread, somehow; of old dough.

But then, everything smelled of food. Her stomach was knotted, as if it were being squeezed in the claw of some big beast. There was a faintly sour taste, as if the duct between her stomach and mouth was filling with old food in protest at not being fed. Bread and bread and bread, that's what she had eaten since leaving Trimdon on Sunday, but it didn't seem to fill her up. The tin of corned beef glinted at the bottom of her rucksack: she had intended to keep it until at least the weekend, but now she was starting to weaken. Her hunger seemed constantly there, weightless and floating, like a net on water. She had to save the food; she could not predict how this week would go.

Sarah had been hungry since the funeral yesterday. Laura had not been in the congregation. She had had a good long look at the people there, before that woman, with the blunt fringe and yellow hair, operating that strange car, had clocked her head on. The woman had not looked at her menacingly, and Sarah wondered if she could seek her out, if this hunger continued, and beg of her something to eat. There'd been a boy, too, handsome, tall, whose polished skull had fairly winked at her in the winter sun. Perhaps he might be worth asking. There seemed a kindness to his eye.

Sarah had eaten plain bread last night for dinner, before falling asleep early in the grubby room. Hunger made her tired. She had dreamed of Laura, standing in the hallway, just a shadowy figure but Laura all the same, holding the door frame, tense, as if ready to flee. Her mother had been saying her name, over and over, and the tone was scalding, as if the shame of the crimes belonged to the daughter, and not the mother. And then, dreamlike, there had been the image of a man, pawing lamely at the windows of a burning church, and two faceless men running away. Sarah had woken early, cool with sweat.

This morning, in the room, Sarah spooned the beef into her mouth, though she knew she should not, knew these were her reserves until it got really bad. After two or three bites she closed the can again and put it into her bag, guiltily, as if she were ashamed, and left the house immediately, with the smell of the meat on her breath.

Sarah took another route, this time, walking up a coastal road past the bay, toward Lynemouth Town. She had been here yesterday but had fled the funeral so quickly that there had been no time to look, not properly. If only she might find a woman, bearing herself with all of Laura's qualities, in one of these cold stone terraces, she could ask her the question and then spend the week deep in conversation. There was so much she would give to talk to her, merely to say that she had missed her, greatly, and that she wished Laura could be at home with them. Aye, another hunger altogether had filled her these past ten years.

There was a large building with a sign saying the Grand, and then a string of houses, tighter and closer together than the ones she had seen in Warkworth. Cloudier than yesterday, the Island looked dun; as if, without the sunlight, it was left browned, and in need of a lick of paint. The houses, too, looked squashed and somehow grievous. Sarah tried to peer into windows but everything was mostly shuttered, and the winding terraces and tall flats meant it was impossible to spy.

Meat was oily on her breath from the beef she'd had that morning, tasting pink and wet, tunnelling down her nose and on her lips, as if she were a movable abattoir.

As Sarah walked toward the summit of the hill, her hunger seemed to set in motion a loop of images from the museum. The nude boys with their blindfolded eyes. The man hanging, shot in lancing light. The big woman in the ditch. Sarah had never seen pictures like this before.

The photographs from the Unrest shown at school had been of well-presented ladies and gentlemen lining up in an orderly fashion for the deportation boat. Lessons had taught her the Secular Deportation had been an agreeable compromise between the Church and the Movement. None of this violence had been aired. Sarah took the road downhill that would take her to the square, where she would have to find something to eat.

She had already begun to feel affection for Maiden's Square: its cool, autumnal colours, rich smell and familiar shops. Aye, this could almost be England, if you looked at it in slanted fashion.

She aimed for the grocer's, between the launderette and Buttons. There was a customer being served, the grocer, in green overalls, just like at home, weighing what looked to be old vegetables. The shelves were full enough with produce, though it was all cans and nothing much fresh. All the tins were brands she knew from England; they must have come over with her on the benefaction boat. The shopkeeper gave her a funny look and the other man behind him turned around too and she felt herself warming under their gaze. She smiled weakly, and as soon as the other man turned around, she grabbed three old carrots and left the shop.

So that she wouldn't be seen, Sarah walked fast down to the beach. Finding her home from Monday night, in the sheltered bit under the pier, she started on the carrots. She pulled the scarf tighter about her neck and let her hair down, so that it might provide her skin with more of a buffer to the wind. The Trimdon cold was nothing compared to here. These winds. That sea. The taste of the carrots, orange and metallic, was perfect, and their crunchiness felt as if they had cleaned her teeth.

Sarah had walked for a few hours more, looking into houses and avoiding the gazes of Islanders, when she came to the house. It was as if, in the grey and dying landscape, her eye had landed on an exceptional flower, though pale and hard to see.

A woman stood in the kitchen.

Dressed in blue and grey, with freckles over the bridge of her nose and her hair in a blonde bob, the woman stood reading a newspaper on the kitchen table. The skin about her eyes was drawn, and her hair was a little darker than it should have been.

The house was not remarkable, though the roof was rather small for a house this size. Nothing could be seen through the upper windows, though the curtains were unclosed. A chimney, lined with lichen, rose into the air and a trace of smoke was piped there. It didn't look warm, or inviting.

In distinction to the rest of the Islanders – none of the yellow fluorescence of the woman down at the funeral, or the tubby man of the monger's, or the polished sleekness of the boy at the cliff – here was a woman, slender and small, who had such a likeness to Laura that it stopped Sarah there for minutes. Pegged between the gateposts, she then noticed a boy at the kitchen table. His eyes and cheeks were rather sunken, his hair flat and crudely cut. The woman and boy – her son? Sarah's half-brother? – did not talk much, the occasional mouthed syllables here and there as the boy asked for more tea, or the toast. The woman poked a fish slice into a frying pan, turning only to the voice of the boy behind her. Brown and oily and curved, the fish looked like a kipper, and Sarah's memory of its smell filled her nose and her mouth grew wet, looking at the distant food.

Even with Sarah's own distrust, even while Sarah persuaded herself that she wouldn't just stumble upon her, she knew this woman, ahead of her, was familiar. And if it were Laura? What would she ask her? How should she announce herself? Sarah had schooled herself, manfully, she had thought, in coping with her mother's absence. But how would she cope, she wondered, with her reintroduction back into her life?

She had been there for a few minutes or so when the woman looked toward the garden, and Sarah panicked. She did not want to be caught here, not yet. She launched herself down the road, back to Swanscott House, resolving to come back tonight, in the dark, when it would be safer to watch this woman, who might be Laura.

7. Arthur and Eliza

Aye, things had been going well with Arthur, until her mother had died, and Eliza had found out the true scale of her family's bankruptcy.

On the discovery of the debt, Eliza had sold off the baker's, and the apartment above it with her ma's few bits of furniture. She had managed to pay off all the debtors, but there was nearly no money left, and Eliza, in the coming few days, would soon have nowhere to live. She had traipsed down to Warkworth pier when the fishing boats came in, and asked one of the fishermen for a job, but was very quickly laughed off. She went to the curing stations too, in Lynemouth Town, but was told, also unequivocally, there was nothing here for her. And then, one night, at a pub in Lynemouth Town, Mr Musa had offered her a job at the Grand. Privately, she had balked – she was hardly desperate enough for that.

With a few drinks in her, and wobbling down the Island paths, Eliza had gone straight over to Arthur's, convinced that he would, of course, let her stay. And so she had gone to him and asked if she could move in. Though she had not meant – move in – more like, a temporary stay, a few nights on his sofa. She was sure he would say yes . . . and yet, what he said, was no. She wondered if, drunkenly, she had not explained herself very well, because he had gone bright red, really very warm in the monger's cool light, and said, 'But this is all too soon! Move in together? You mean live together? But . . . ' his eyes had gone searchingly around the monger's, to the countertops, chopping boards and knives – 'Eliza. I'm sorry, no, we can't live together, not yet. I'm sorry.'

Eliza had been too embarrassed to tell Arthur about the state of her finances. Thirty-five pounds to her name! She would not ruin Linda's good name. Rejected by Arthur, she had gone straight back to the pub that night, and then, with more drinks in her, shots bought for her by Musa, she had gone, sobbingly, rashly, to the Grand.

When Arthur had found out she'd taken Musa's job he had refused to speak to her. The relationship was off. Both were smarting with the other's rejection and no communication was made for some weeks.

But if their relations were cool when Eliza had started at the Grand, they all but froze when Arthur came to her, one hot summer night, to engage her, not in conversation, but in business.

The Grand did bad business on the Island but it meant this morning she had the time to escape and look for the English girl. She went through Lynemouth Town, passing the old baker's on the way, and down to the bay where she had dispatched Mrs Page rather hurriedly yesterday. No one was there. Eliza walked on toward Warkworth Town, gathering a few of the wild flowers she found along the path. She searched the square and the museum and contemplated going up to the cop shop and declaring a missing person. But how could she declare a missing person who was not even registered as being here? Eliza circled round the Island back to the ruined church (perhaps the girl's religious sentiment might lead her back here?), and then went home to the Grand, the gorse now wilting in the warm palm of her hand.

Forlorn in her room, Eliza mooched, putting the flowers in water, wondering what she might pen under her hair today. The room had a petulant air to it too, as if it were also sulking about having nothing to do. Eliza held the fringe back toward her crown, regarding her brow. Perhaps she might take something sharper to it; a knife, perhaps, and tattoo herself there. Hours passed. She counted her money in the side drawer. With the fee from the Tongue as well, there was now £40 in total. What might she do with it? There was so little to do on this Island.

Eliza wondered what England was like and what it might be like to live on an island not so much an island as a long, seemingly boundless country with hills and rivers and meadows and cities. The postcards she had of the countryside fascinated her: the tall trees, and grazing cows, and big castles. Linda had sometimes told her of London. Lon-don. It sounded mad, purely hectic: the traffic, the dance clubs, the parks and bedsits. All that, though, had been before the emergency powers. It might be somewhat more sedate, now.

Eliza thought, much, of England: because she craved seeing anywhere that was not here. She thought everyone in England would be marvellous and warm and caring toward each other. She thought that they had it all figured out: surrendering this fruitless freedom for some infinitely gentler authority. Aye. That's what Eliza craved. She just wanted someone to tell her what to do. Not. It wasn't that; not really. She just wanted someone to talk to.

She hoped dearly that the English girl was alive and safe. If only she could find her she would offer her haven here, in the Grand; Musa might not notice. But along the tricksome Island paths, curling terraces and long bays, the empty houses and lump of Marley Hill, Eliza had no idea where the girl was, and, faintly, her hope of finding her was beginning to fade.

Musa showed up later at around two that afternoon.

'Where have you been all morning?'

'At Maiden's Square.'

'Well, thank your lucky stars, girl, you're off there again.'

'Why?'

'I'm hungry.'

'So?'

'You're to buy me my fish.'

'But that's Janey's job.'

'Janey's bloods are up. She can't go out. She's ill.'

'Pony. She's always complaining. Harking on this or that. She's so meaty herself she'll never get close to anaemia.'

'Eliza. Are you currently working? Are you otherwise engaged? Are you, might I venture, busy with the delicacies of a man's heart? I don't think so. Here. Now. Two shillings. A kipper. Make it two. No complaints, girl, you get it easy enough already.' His manner suggested more than fish was at stake. And he was right – she didn't have anything else to do – not in the manner of work – and there'd been no customers all day. 'Give my regards to Arthur,' he said, leaving the room.

By the time she reached Maiden's Square, Eliza was terribly nervous. The square was empty, aside from a gull fatly perched on a rooftop or two. Above the monger's she saw the window into Arthur's living quarters, but the curtains were closed. Eliza squeezed back her shoulders, cleared her throat. Without being entirely conscious of what she was doing, and with less than a flicker of consent, her legs took her into the shop.

Dark, wide-winged skate lay flat next to narrow trout. Monkfish gawped. There were purple octopus, rusty crabs, orange lobster, and a box of roe bubbling close to the glass. A salmon was spliced down its middle. A hundred filmed eyes stared at nothing. Everywhere, the smell of cold fish, ice and brine, and everywhere, the sight of moist skins and scales. Red plastic chains hung between Arthur's station and the back room.

Eliza hid behind the slow queue of women. Mostly older women, with thick ankles and set curled hair. With their bulging bellies and toothless frowns, the fish looked at her with wet disinterest. There was no one in the line she knew, and no one behind her, so at least the inevitable embarrassment might be kept between themselves.

Minutes stretched, and each customer in front seemed to have an endless list of requirements: herring with its head off or on, a plaice with a less brown skin, a sprat that didn't have quite such a feral look to it – the woman's voice was a whisper here – since this was where their uncle had died; in those exact waters, and they really shouldn't be eating it because – what if they were eating Uncle Roger? But the children couldn't live off turnips the whole time, now, could they?

Why not, thought Eliza, *I go without fish, day in, day out; I do not eat of Arthur's bounty.*

Two women spoke in quiet voices about the gang of boys and whether they should be afraid again; it was not new, this harassment. People always got het up about the threat from the English, about God being imposed again on their small Island. People – men, normally, and teenagers, mostly – always had it in their heads to create a little police force to check themselves of Gots. But it wasn't necessary. No one had gone back to the old faith.

Arthur prepared the fish for dead Roger's niece. The woman talked to him of the weather, and what he thought of Mr Verger's new sprightly ways, and did he think Beatrice Spenser should get out more, and might salmon help the constitution with all that protein? Arthur nodded amiably. And then, with the fish in her bag, the woman left, but only very grudgingly, because every Islander wanted to talk to Arthur for much, much longer. He was a kind man, and much liked.

Now it was her turn. Eliza looked at Arthur. The air stiffened. A hot wave came up her face. She managed a smile though she couldn't stop biting the side of her cheek. Arthur too had gone completely red. Had his forehead had that lick of sweat minutes ago? His eyes, though, were fixed on hers. 'Yes?' he said.

'Hello, Arthur.'

'Miss Michalka.'

The surname made her wince. 'How are you?'

'Fine.' He hadn't yet blinked. A thousand fish eyes seemed to be staring at her. 'Thank you.' He turned his broad back on her and cleaned his knife in sharp little strokes. Why was it she imagined that blade puncturing her throat and her blood puddling in his palms, he weeping over her dying frame? Her ma had always said she had a melodramatic streak. 'And yourself?'

'Very well, thank you.' Arthur looked about to say something else – opening his mouth, but shutting it again with a horrible snapping sound – and instead went back to cleaning the blade.

Eliza did not know what else to say. 'Well, two kippers then, please.' All joy was knocked out of her. Arthur placed the brown fish in paper and he wrapped it without looking at her.

'Grand,' she said. His eyes rounded. 'I mean—'

'That's fine.'

'I meant, fine, thank you.'

'No need to thank me.' He gestured to the space around him. 'It's my job.' Eliza slipped the coins over the counter top and wished she could place them in the shallow of his palm. Likewise, the bag of fish he slid directly over the plane of glass.

'Arthur, I've never felt angry because of—'

'No. Of course. Goodbye, now.'

She had been dispatched. Eliza whispered what she could manage – a weak *goodbye* – more into her collar than to him – and left the shop, to hear the bell trill her departure.

Eliza managed to get to Warkworth Bay before bursting

into tears. Oh, a fine victory; a veritable triumph! She kicked at the beach as if this might help. What a misery he had made her! She grabbed a handful of sand and threw it, ridiculously, into the air, and it came to rest immeasurably against the rest of the frozen beach. She wanted to open her lungs and scream, but somebody might overhear and think her mad. The grey breakers came ashore. It was stupid, the sea, with its stupid rhythm, its stupid sand and briny water, all for miles around and all for nothing!

Only two nights ago she had been on this beach, with such excitement, watching that brave English girl steal off Monday's boat. If only she had some of that courage herself. Wherever the girl was on the Island, Eliza hoped she was all right. She had so many questions to ask her. How had she come here? How had she stowed herself away on the boat? What was England like? What did the stretch of a meadow amount to? What did voices sound like climbing the walls of a church? And what was it like not to find the sea, staring at you from every which way, with all the dispassion of a dead man's eye? Yes, that was it, the sea: a great big eye, fogged and grey, and this Island nothing more than a piece of grit in all its salted juices.

Arthur's eyes, as well, too, too blank. When she'd walked in, she thought it might have gone well. She had even been rather pleased when Musa had asked her to go. A détente, perhaps. Not for the first time did she wish that she might be one of those fish nestling the ice-chips and awaiting the knife. How much she regretted that August night when Arthur had paid his visit to the Grand.

Furious that Arthur had rejected her, Eliza went at her

job with as much dignity as she could manage, and thence-forth they both avoided each other assiduously. Arthur was angry with her for accepting the job; Eliza was raging that he hadn't bothered to help when she had most needed it.

And then he had come one night, in hot early August, all breathy and half out of his wits, and bedded her, paying her beforehand. Never had she received a sum of money with so little heart. When he put the £5 note on the bed-side table he said, slurringly, 'I heard from all the other men what great fun you are, Eliza,' with something of a leer. He was a big man and must have drunk a boat-load to be that far gone. But when she lay down for him, tears dripped from his cheeks onto hers. And he asked her why, why, why was she here, as if it weren't completely obvious, that on her mother's death, she had been completely, and utterly, broke.

Eliza lay there all night, stony-eyed, while Arthur slept off the booze. Something in her hardened, and when he woke, he looked at her as if he were surprised to see her. 'Nice of you to come, Arthur Stansky.'

'Eliza. I— What happened?'

'You know what happened.'

'I— What have I done! Oh, what have I done!'

'Get out.'

'I'm sorry, Eliza. I'm so sorry.'

But Eliza was having none of it. 'It's all your fault I am here! When Ma died I thought we might be together! Did you not love me? And now I am here, in this,' she could hardly say it, 'brothel, because I have no money, and because you refused to help me!' Her voice softened and she held the bed-sheets in her fists. 'What happened? When

I came to you after Ma's death I asked for your help and you—'

'Eliza! I thought you were asking to move in with me!'

'I meant for a few days! A week! On the sofa! I had nowhere to go! I had no money, no home, no roof over my head—' Arthur did not say anything but looked sightlessly into the blue room. The light in there, from off the Sound, was like a wash of writing ink. 'Shame on you, Arthur Stansky, for the way you've acted. You're a disgrace. Coming in here, to bed me for that beggar's sum.' She pointed to the door. 'Out of my sight. I never want to see you again. I never want to talk to you again!'

Arthur held her wrists and said sorry, over and over. Then he said those words, 'Forgive me, Eliza,' but she threw his £5 out of the door and asked him to leave. She watched his broad shape weave down Lynemouth's alleys and wept in bed for the rest of the morning.

For months, in respect of her wishes, Arthur avoided her. At one point, in September, Eliza told him all was forgiven but he smiled at her politely, in rather a forced manner, and told her he couldn't be with her. He was cold and distant: every time she tried to engage him in conversation, he refused. Now, in November, he barely said a word to her. Nor she to him. She wanted to tell him his apology was enough, that her love had let her forgive him, but could not. She could only think that everything that had happened had ruined his feelings for her. She should probably move on, but felt she could not.

Eliza shook the sand off her shoes and stockings. Rock pools teamed with kelp and crab. The remains of three carrot tops lay powdered in sand; she kicked at them and buried them with her shoe.

At the cliff's headland, she stopped and looked out at the Sound. Musa's kipper she considered throwing back to the sea. Without quite knowing what she was doing she took a step forward. She saw above her the still clouds, and then down by her shoes, the grass so short and bald. She thought of her ma, and Arthur, and Nathaniel, and the English girl. *How the mind wanders*, she thought, *when it senses rest*. It was only a great shame that in dying one had to forfeit every minor keepsake; not the ghost of a memory, not the slender remembrance of a lover's face; not a breeze passing the hair on your neck. There would be nothing left of him for her. Nothing. And the relief of the pain stopping wouldn't even be felt; or at least, not for very long.

Eliza turned from the cliff, because it still meant an awful lot to her; this awful bold world. At least she had been loved, though she was loved no longer. Eliza turned back to the road. Musa was waiting. She at least might do something right, today, and rather than jump down into the comfort of the waves, she would deliver Musa his fish.

8. The Scrap

Jake did not want to hear this story again.

A few plants in the outhouse stood on the shelf, dry and dying. In there, when the tumble dryer was on, a warm mist filled the room and Jake imagined it would be like being in a jungle. Beyond the outhouse, the night was coming down, a block of mauve on blue.

It was too warm in the living room to think.

The gas-fire pumped heat. Its grille was as bright a blue as the sea at summer noon. When you turned the plastic knob sometimes it failed to ignite and the gas would leak and then when it did, the fire went up with a *woomph!* Jake wondered if Mammy Malraux's hair ever caught on the flames. It would light easily, her hair, coarse and dry as tinder-sticks.

Mrs Malraux's armchair was big and flowery and pitted with fag burns. The flowers now were vague as if her rump had smudged them. Even when she was not in the chair, it bore the shape of her hindquarters. Four worn points in the damson carpet took her weight. A bottle of buttercup syrup was on the side table, with pens, old lighters, and completed crossword puzzles. Little porcelain ornaments stood on the mantelpiece, and a golden brass bell, missing its clapper.

NAOMI WOOD

'Och, Nathaniel, you've heard it clear enough. I shan't tell that story again.' Mrs Malraux put the cigarette so far into her lips that when it came out the tip was wet. The big armchair made her as squabby as an infant. Her big calves glittered in the stockings; her bosom rested on the waist-band. Pointing to Nath's boots, and gesturing with the cigarette, she said, 'They were your da's, you know.'

'Aye.'

'Have you filled them out yet?'

'Ma!' the boy said, looking quickly at Jake, who didn't respond.

'Only asking.'

'Go on, Ma, tell us now of the boat.'

'No. Not now. You've heard it clear enough.'

There was silence for a while and then, with no more prompting, Mrs Malraux began. 'Aye. Well. It was about '47. I was fourteen, two years younger than you, now. There was all this bother around, about whether they were religious or civil papers you carried. When my da heard of the Unrest he got very upset. Ma too. Suddenly the police started asking you to show your papers, and it would say, you know, whether you were a member of a church or whether you were non-affiliated. Some people we knew started going to church just to avoid the hassle – and it was hassle, just name-calling, before it got rougher. I asked my ma if we could go to church and she said no. I wanted to go because my friends went, aye, and so people would stop picking on me.'

'But you didn't go?'

'No.'

'Aye. Good, good.'

'Anyways. The police started giving people a hard time, too, especially the boys, who were easy to pick on.'

'How?'

'Stealing things. Beating them up. My cousin came over to ours once with a huge black eye and we didn't need to ask, we already knew. I remember soon after Da left, someone threw a rock through my window. Ma was terrified. Da was working for the Movement by then, all of us knew it but we didn't say anything and we knew we weren't allowed to say anything. Things were hard at school. We started to be taught separately. We couldn't go to games after school with the other kids. I missed my friends, more than anything else. But they were told by their own parents not to talk to me.

'Gangs started up, there were beatings on either side, with cricket bats and golf clubs; anything they could lay their hands on. It was happening in America, too. Then it got worse, because the Movement started to fight back. Suddenly a church was attacked. Nothing like that had happened before. People had thought most of it was going on between teenagers, you know, and some bad police. Then another one, another church, the next week, and then another, the week after, was burned down almost to rubble and people were blaming it on the Movement.

'That was when Mammy moved us out of Newcastle but we were too late. People knew of my family 'cause of Da's sudden disappearance. You could tell a Movement family by their daddy's absence on the weekends. Da was involved in the Newcastle sit-in, in the town hall. That was where he was caught.

'They started talking about expulsions, deportations of

the worst offenders. About a loophole involving the Church and its powers. Emergency powers.' Margaret sniffed a little, here. 'We were served with the papers for the boat, and we were told Da would join us there. All the families were told that, I think. My mam believed them, I suppose. But there were lots who never made it. My da never made it. Someone from the Movement told us he'd died in a holding cell in Sunderland. My ma didn't leave the cabin for the ten-hour trip. Not once.'

Margaret stared at some dead point in the air. 'We smuggled a hand-gun in my drawers all the way across the waters and I was going to put it to the heads of one of the English police when I found out my da had died in one of their prisons. But when I saw my mam's face, I couldn't do it. I couldn't do it.' Margaret's eyes were glassy now, but then she smiled, a sad sort of smile. 'So we ended up here. And Mammy made everything very nice for us, as nice as she could. And then I met your da.'

'And?'

'Another story, aye. On with you, now. There's telly I want to watch.'

Nathaniel could never tire of this story. He loved to hear it. Jake was playing idly with a bowl of potpourri, his fingers digging down into the scented dust. His soft bulk loomed in the evening. 'Did you hear that?' Nathaniel asked. 'The story of my ma?'

'Aye.' Jake wiped the brownish powder on his jeans. It let out a hot flowery stink. The sky had turned violet now as the sun dropped amongst cloud.

'Up to, then, surly Turk.'

'What's that?'

'Need to get changed, aye, be ready for tonight.'

'Where are you off?' Margaret asked, with some alarm.

'To see the boys.'

'Better not be up to no good.'

'No, Mam. Are you to watch the telly-box, now?'

'Aye.'

'And what are you to eat?'

'There's a pie in the freezer.'

'You need some fish, Mam.'

'Don't harp on that now.'

'Your bloods. You've got to think about your bloods. You'll get anaemia.'

'On with you. I'm going nowhere fast. Now give me a kiss and tell me you're my good lad.'

He went over to his mam and planted a kiss softly on her bony brow. 'I'm your good lad, Ma.'

She leaned back into the armchair; contented. 'But you'll be here tomorrow, aye, when I wake up?'

'Aye, Mam,' he patted her hand, 'I'll be sitting at my chair when you walk in here.'

'Then I shall set the porridge for you tonight.'

Nathaniel's bedroom was colder than the living room but less pressing. A single bed with a plastic headboard was in the corner, and covered in a bedspread of purple flowers. A large brown wardrobe was wearing away to a lighter colour at the top, the wood flaking like a callus. It had all of Nathaniel's costumes in it, and it was a cherished thing indeed.

Nathaniel was nearly naked in not much more than pants, and the light gave his skin a mollusc gleam. There was some elegance of manner to Nathaniel that Jake envied, the long-tipped fingers, perhaps, or his lean stature; the way there seemed so little in the way of excess. Jake felt a little plump around him, as if merely Nathaniel's presence wadded him again in baby fat. Nathaniel looked very good with his hair like that, the bristle just showing, as if a match could be lit on the scratch. Jake had re-shaved his scalp last night, after Nathaniel had asked, and his mam had given him what-for, complaining again that he looked 'a victim of summat'.

Nathaniel was talking to him about the girls from school. He said he fancied Bridget, thought she was a looker. Jake said, 'What about Charlotte?'

'Nicholas's sister? A pudding!'

'Aye,' said Jake, 'I think she's lovely.'

'Tell you who *is* lovely,' said Nathaniel.

'Who?'

'Eliza.'

'The doxy from the Grand?'

'Aye,' said Nathaniel. 'But she's the prettiest girl on the Island. One day, Jake, I shall be the first of our boys to have her, and I shan't pay, mark my words I shan't. Och, she is a brass looker!' He pulled on his trousers and a shirt, which was so starched Jake could hear it unfolding like a box. Nathaniel looked to the mirror. 'I would love to fuck Eliza. Eliza Michalka! Doesn't bother me that others have had her. I think she's rum. I think she wants some of this, too.'

'Aye? What makes you think that?'

'Just the way she looks at me, like. Appraising me of my boyish wares.' He pulled on the red braces. 'Pass me a hanky, Jake. Make it two.' He turned back to the mirror, inspecting either side of his face. 'D'you know,' he said, watching the handsome chops go at the words, 'you can tell if a girl's shaved or bushy or whatever by the sound of their piss? If it's just one long stream it means she's still got a bush on her but if it's a spray you know she's shaven as your scalp, Jakob Lawrence. As shaven as your scalp *today*, that is.'

The other boy was standing with the chest lid open, staring down. Nathaniel had expected Jake to laugh but the boy said nothing and did not turn. The upturned lid reminded Nathaniel of the coffin they had opened yesterday, and a thrill rolled down him as if some damp corpse like Mrs Page might be in the chest. Imagine that, Mrs Page softly slumbering the night away as Nathaniel dreamed in bed. He remembered the dead woman's skin, with its film like the mushrooms up on Marley Hill. Had the water started its seep into the coffin yet? Surely now the old woman would be completely submerged; just like his da, he guessed, wet as a fish.

Jake did not move. In his hand two red handkerchiefs bunched. He gave a laugh, and there was something crowing in it. 'What's this?'

'What?'

'This.' Jake turned. A book was held between two fingers. Jake looked directly at Nathaniel, his eyes knowing, as if he had thoroughly crabbed him. He flicked through the pages. 'A book of paintings? Of godly paintings? Look, with verses running down the sides of them.' He turned back to the first page. 'And with the Museum's stamp on it? Now, now, now, Nathaniel, I didn't know you were one for such wares.'

'Look, it's not mine.'

'Aye. Whose is it, then?'

Nathaniel didn't say anything.

'Because it's in your room, in this chest. Which would all suggest, you know, that it's yours.'

'It's John Verger's,' Nathaniel blurted, without thinking.

'Mr Verger's?'

'Aye, look,' said Nathaniel, striding over, 'Verger gave this to me a while back. When he'd just lost his job, and he was all sad and messed up. He was trying to help as I was upset about my da. He was my da's friend. No need, now, to be picking on Mr Verger.'

'But, Nathaniel. He's a Got. Look at this stuff. There's God on every page.'

'It's just a book, Jake, it's nothing.'

'And how did he get it?'

'He took it from the museum. In a fit of boredom or misery or whatever. It's just a book, as I said, put it back now.'

'Just a book! Their whole system is *just a book*. Just a book is what sent us across the waters.'

'John Verger gave me it when he was in a bad place in his head. Listen to me: he's over that now.'

But Jake was no longer listening. 'I bet he's praying every night, asking for a big squelchy kiss from God on his for'ead!' Jake's eyes danced. '*He* should be tonight! Not Mrs Richards! He's even more of a threat than her!'

Nathaniel tugged the book away from him. 'Now listen to me, John Verger is not to be touched. He—'

'Why?'

'He was my da's friend! My da's best friend. Are you not listening? It means he's got immunity.'

'Immunity?'

'He's no spy – he burned churches to be here! He loves this Island!'

'How do you know?'

'Just because! You wouldn't understand, ken. He was my da's best friend. Your da's at home. You get to see him every night. Mine's dead.' His voice went quiet, choked on a hearty love for his dead da and the fact he would never ever see him again. *Never*; the thought crabbed. Quietly, now, he said: 'John Verger was the man who introduced my mam and my dad. Without him, there'd be no me! He's not to be touched. D'you hear me? He's done with this book. He's no believer, he's no spy, and he certainly doesn't work for the English. Look, we can burn it if you like, or throw it in the bin, I don't care; but we don't touch him. Ken?'

Nathaniel dropped the book into the chest and closed the lid. It slammed with more of a noise than he had hoped. He took the handkerchiefs and was surprised to find them so warmed from the boy's hands. All night his feet would be resting on the damp sweet cloth. Nathaniel shoved them into his boots. 'No more of it now. We don't touch Verger, you hear?'

'Aye,' Jake said, but he didn't move: he was looking out, flatly, toward the sea. His eyes seemed to be full of a new kind of knowledge.

With their pockets full of rocks, the gang ran up the steps of Warkworth cliffs and along January Road, with Nathaniel leading the charge. They went up the steep side of Marley Hill to Mrs Richards' house. It was an old house with small windows and a long enough box hedge to hide behind. Since Monday night the Malades had been doing sorties here, watching for when Mrs Richards came in and out, and when she went to bed. Nine o'clock was figured the best time, since that was when Mr Richards often went down to Lynemouth Town for a drink or two at the tavern, and Mrs Richards was alone. At this time, Sammy Carter reported, Mrs Richards liked to read the Bible and copy maps of the Island, intended for the English when they eventually arrived on the warships.

A light was on in the kitchen. The house was broad and low, beetled to the ground; the upstairs, low-ceilinged, warrenish. A light was on in a bedroom. 'Now,' said Nathaniel, 'listen. Sammy, you're to stand guard at the top—'

'What? I always miss out on the good stuff!'

'Don't whine, boy. You've got to help.' Nathaniel's eyes flicked toward Jake, remembering the flat look of the boy at the window that evening. 'Jake did it last time. On your way.'

Sammy sloped away to the top part of the road. The other boys waited, giggling by the hedge, glad it had been Sammy who'd been sent for lookout.

On Nathaniel's signal, they started launching rocks, their wrists flicking toward the walls. Rocks ricocheted from the plaster and the drainpipes. One hit the lintel and splintered the wood. All the boys laughed soundlessly. Nathaniel borrowed a rock from Sammy and threw it hard, imagining that there was a real-life Got in there, or imagining the policeman's face, the one who'd escorted his mam here, the one she'd wanted to shoot. Nathaniel knew that before the boys were men the Island might be reclaimed again into the English Ministry. Perhaps they *should* crab Verger, Nathaniel thought, as he threw another, perhaps he was an English agent, working for the church. His da's friend or no, he couldn't protect Verger forever.

Nathaniel watched them, his Malade boys, the whites of their eyes flashing wet and silky, their arms going like mad trying for the window, until a rock found the upstairs glass and there was a sound of smashing, sounding blameless, and fairy-tale, in the winter night. They all ducked down behind the hedge, their shoulders rolling with the pleasure of it. Jake couldn't control himself and a long loud laugh escaped him.

A woman's voice, afraid, cried out: 'What was that?'

The shadow disappeared; a face appeared at the window. It must be Mrs Richards. Nathaniel imagined her in maths class and here she was, cold at the broken window and scared. 'Who's there?' The laughter was louder now from the four boys crowded behind the hedge. 'Tell me who's there!'

'We want to know,' said Nathaniel, still squat, his back facing the hedge, 'if you're a Got, Mrs Richards?'

'What are you talking about? A Got?'

'Don't get narky with us, we're not getting nasty with you. We just want to know.'

'What are you talking about?'

'Whether you have a babble with God on occasion? A little prayer? A little word with him up top?'

Their teeth and grins were wet in the darktime.

'A babble?'

'Aye,' said Nathaniel, 'a babble, babble, babble.' The boys repeated him saying 'babble, babble, babble' over and over again. 'Do you think to heaven when Master's at it, Mrs Richards? Was it your first time with Master on the marriage bed, seen as you're Got, or were you a naughty girl before he got his paws on you? You're a Got, c'mon, stop denying it! We know this about you!'

'On your way now, boys,' she leaned out of the window, craning to see them, 'before I come down there and crab you myself!'

'Tell us, Mrs Richards. We want to know. What do the English ask you to do? How do they ask you to spy on us? In what manner will you tip the Island back to 1950? Is it maps you're drawing for them, late at night? Or is it propaganda you're writing, is that it?' Nathaniel was coming along, warming to his speechifying, when Jake stood, quietly, unexpectedly, and launched a rock straight toward her face. It struck Mrs Richards on the cheek and she wheeled away, aghast. 'Jake!' Nathaniel said, but the boy was laughing and the other boys were laughing with him. In the shadow, you could see Mrs Richards clamp her hand to her face and then a violent sob.

Nathaniel told them all to scarper. The gang made off, but, since the cut of the jeans had once again stopped the juice at their knees, they ran like idiots, yelping for their needled feet in the moonlight. Sweat pricked on their bulbed skulls and down the sides of their faces. In the corner of his vision, Nathaniel saw Mrs Richards' pink nightgown flapping about, as she came out of her house and onto the road. She grew ever smaller behind them, and all around him the boys' eyes, wet and keen, followed him steadily down to the darkness of the Eastern Bay.

When he was sure they had lost her, they shared a smoke to get some calm into their blood, and each boy went his separate way; rum, and a little bit scared, too, lest they should be found out for this unexpected violence. Had they really crabbed a teacher for an English spy? It was best now that all boys should be at home and watching telly, so their mams could all happily lie for them if the police came calling. They'd meet all together again on Friday night. Jake went larking off with Sammy, and Nathaniel watched them, waiting for them to leave the Eastern cliff before he too set off for home.

The sea below him kept up its steady croon as he walked along the bluffs. The night was low and still. It had been wrong to throw the rock at Mrs Richards, and he hadn't given Jake permission for it, but it was a bit of a rollicky thrill, too. Now he felt cool and calm, as if his whole body had risen up a purer thing from some claggy bog.

He pushed away the thought of Verger's book, and shared a cigarette with himself, jets of smoke joined the Island night. Though he enjoyed the scrap, he often faced the end of the night with a sad feeling that it was all, somehow, not worth it. Even, although it was harder still to admit this, that there might be no English spies on this Island, and that worse than coming to invade, the English might have pure forgotten about them. Out of sight; out of mind. He had started this gang with such a clear idea of revenge for his da's death in the English boat; and yet he seemed no closer to satisfaction. Still, the boys would meet one last time this holiday then that would be it for the week. Then they would be back at school, and they could enjoy a more leisurely pace of harassment.

The night was dark and quiet. He wondered about turning back, to Lynemouth Town, contemplated scaling one of the walls up to Eliza's bedroom, but this lonely finale, that greeted every night like this, was dragging him down, and all he wanted to do was go home. To his mam, aye, his old mam.

It was on walking up Fairview Road that he saw the figure crouching down behind the hedge. At first sight, he thought it was a boy, come to launch rocks against the windows of a Got, but then he saw a flash of long red hair. He stepped on the cigarette and hid behind the cold bricks of the long terrace. The girl crouched by a hedge. A small amount of light was let out from the kitchen, but then, minutes later, the light was snapped off, and it was dark again. He saw the shape of the girl move away from the hedge. Who was the girl watching, at this hour?

Nathaniel kept at a safe distance. She had replaced her hood so that the brass colour of her hair was obscured. When Nathaniel passed the house, he peered into the kitchen but could see nothing – nor could he remember who lived here. The eastern bit of the Island, uninhabited, more squalid than the rest, was not a place for a boy like him.

He followed her onward. The girl walked purposefully, but there was something in her manner that suggested she was frightened. Panicked. She seemed to be making wrong turns, ending up in dead alleys, roads he would not follow her down because he knew they went nowhere.

The wind was flat now, and the trees stood, stirless, in the night. Nathaniel was sure he had never seen her before. He would have remembered a girl such as this. She was beautiful, aye, he could see that, even from the distance.

She walked on; quick, despite herself. She stopped above the eastern beach where the boys had gathered not an hour ago. The sea was a great black bowl before her. She turned back and walked until she came to a house. It was one of the derelict ones, one of the old Islanders' which hadn't been lived in for years. What was she doing, staying here?

Nathaniel waited behind the hedge as she went in and climbed the stairs. In the front bedroom, she came into view. She had a mane of hair; brass and ginger: as if she were a girl coined from something else; a metal, not flesh. She appeared sometimes at the window: the rare shadow, the skin seldom seen behind the glass. Her skin was so freckled it was as if she could have been born in a bowl of dust.

After a while, she came to settle at the sill. A tree obscured her and all that was visible was her fingers. She was reading a piece of paper, it might have been a newspaper. She breathed into her hands, and then rubbed them together. They looked pinky-white but he supposed if he were there standing above her they would be all mottled brown. At one point, she spread her fingers across her whole face and she began to cry, lightly at first and then a whole shake-and-heave, her shoulders joining in with the dance. Her mouth must have been a real twist of it. Even from the garden, down below here, Nathaniel could see how pink she became under the freckles on her neck. It looked winsome, all that pink. After that, he couldn't see her for minutes, and then the light snapped off, and the dark hung about him, loose as a silk.

9. Sarah's Story

Home, now, if it could be called that. Sarah sat by the glass, looking down into the inky depths of the garden, her breath fogging the pane. There was no streetlamp on the road; neither sky nor house nor sea could be seen. In her hands, she held Laura's article.

For some hours this evening Sarah had stayed behind the box hedge. The woman read a book by the fire, the pans above her shiny and brass, her eyes skipping over the words and glancing, occasionally, into the garden, with a look somewhere near dread. Sarah ate two slices of bread by the gravel and thought about the corned beef in the can then stopped herself. Only Wednesday. She had five more days of this. The boy – the woman's son – was nowhere to be seen.

The woman ate dinner alone and then washed the dishes.

She settled again by the fire, with the book on her lap, when some birds suddenly took off from the tree, and startled her. The woman looked out toward the garden as if she suspected someone of being out there, and left the room abruptly, leaving the kitchen in darkness. Sarah, taking this as her cue, left immediately.

*

From the sill, now, in her own room, Sarah contemplated a prayer. For years in England, she had given up on this. At church, she bowed her head as everyone else did, but she didn't believe prayers would do any good. Assuming the posture, she thought about patience and peacefulness and God's good grace, but then her mother was still absent, the fact was immutable, and what words Sarah did launch into countless mornings and soundless nights had always seemed so unanswered.

In church, while everyone else was praying, Sarah studied a portrait of Christ that hung above the altar. Hardly any of the cross could be seen under the lit skin. His fingers, crisped in pain, curled inward to his palms. The loincloth billowed as if a wind disturbed it. A slick of darkness clove the narrow thighs, the knees were pressed together; as were the calves. Blood loosened from a colossal nail. The toes, like the fingers, were curled, holding on to the wood. The eyes looked tired, not boastful. The mouth was open, a plug of black.

Sarah had always held Him as an example of patience. Waiting for her mother, she might try to be as patient as Him. She could try. But it had been a long time. And she had almost given up.

And then it had come, this stroke of luck, this losing of a shoe, and then the way to find Laura had become clear.

After the trip in the cellar, the discovery under the stepboards, Sarah didn't go to school. Every day, instead, she made a clandestine journey to Newcastle Library, to the room with the archives. Sarah didn't tell her dad what she was doing and went to the library in her school uniform.

In the first few days, Sarah checked the newspapers: the

Evening Post, the *Chronicle*, the *Morning Daily*. In that July week of 1976, there were numerous articles about Laura and Saint Gregory's. Sarah found the article in the *Chronicle* but with stories all around it, and advertisements, for toothpaste, amongst other things. It was always the same picture they used: of Laura looking up, curious, somewhat bashful, as if there were a hand hovering over her holding holy water. There were photographs, too, of the Minister, the one who had died in the church, one of his eyes swollen closed, and his skin, blackened between crisp hospital sheets.

Sarah read the other stories from that summer in 1976: more church-burnings, a riot in Doncaster, more protests for the Sunday Agreement. Sarah thought she detected some public sympathy toward the Movement, but then a Sunday School was bombed, again, as if the vileness of 1950 was obliged to repeat itself, and the calls for expulsion seemed to get louder. Rubble was pictured in a scorched-looking street, and a line of policemen stood with shields braced. There were scores of arrests. Burned-out cars looked like bees, dead in summer.

Around Christmas, all stories of Laura disappeared. There was nothing else. The two men Laura was with had not been named anywhere in the press, they were called 'the unidentified suspects of the Saint Gregory fire'. But by December, all mention of them, too, disappeared, so that the trio of Saint Gregory's seemed to have vanished from all reports.

In the first days of March, in 1977, there were court reports from the Movement's trials. There were several groups asking for leniency, others demanding expulsion.

The Church in London insisted on another expulsion, arguing there was no difference between the severity of the crimes in 1950 and 1976. Sarah read through the trials, expecting at any moment to get to Laura's, but again, there was no mention of Saint Gregory's. It seemed as if Laura had dropped as easily out of the public narrative as she had her own family's life. Days in, Sarah found a list of those expelled in 1977. There were a hundred or so names written on the sheet, but the name Laura Wicks was not there.

Later in the week, Sarah changed course. This time, she checked English prison records. She checked all the way from July 1976 to the present: all the female internees under 'W'. Still nothing. No Wicks. Sarah then found all those imprisoned for minor secular crimes and then all of those discharged under the Sunday Agreement, which had made its difficult way into law by 1983. Laura was not on either list.

On Friday, just as Sarah was beginning to give up, as she scrolled the microfiche and yellowing records, she happened upon another picture. It was of the deportation boat, the last one, in the spring of 1977. The title read: 'The Last Boat: England Prays for Peace'.

And there she was, unmistakably, on the boat, her blonde hair thrown by the wind, her eyes, this time, retreating, defensive, cast down. Choppy waters surrounded the hull. Laura's face was the only one really picked up by the photographer. She was hunched into the wind. Two men stood behind her, and Sarah wondered if they might be the two men, the 'two unidentified suspects' of Saint Gregory's.

Sarah copied the photograph twice: one for herself, and one for her dad. Perhaps there had been some official oversight, and her mother's name had been left off a list, or some necessary secrecy which meant her case had not come to court, but she had been deported anyway. A mistake had been made – evidently: because Sarah was sure it was her mother, staring out, bleakly, into the gun-metal top of the Sound.

That Sunday, they went to church, her and her dad. Sarah had not yet mentioned anything about her discoveries, and she didn't know if she would. She didn't want to be dissuaded from what she was going to do. Sarah looked at the portrait of Christ as the rest prayed; His expression seemed encouraging.

After church, they went to the butcher's, as they always did. It was called Wroxham's. In its window, there was a luxurious display of cuts. The smell of the meat outside the red-brick house was a suggestive stink: the display was grand, even a little obscene. Pork medallions ringed in fat, brassy lamb shanks and red steaks were all laid out on a red-and-white chequered cloth, garlanded with parsley. Geese hung on low-slung hooks from their bluing throats; beaks downturned as if coy. In a lozenged line, sausages hung, diced fat near skin. The slick dark liver seemed to hint of some unnameable pleasure. This was God's meat.

Church-people queued up in hungry silence, eyeing slabs of turkey breast, mauve kidney, countless chipolatas. The knife by Wroxham's block was already bloodied. A sign at the shop front said *Pickled Tongues in Freezer*. Eggs nestled in straw.

Sarah said something about the smell, told her dad to order the lamb at the window's front, and went down the butcher's side alley. Out in the yard, there was a smell of warm blood and bone. Sarah lit a cigarette. In the pantry, pigs hung from big hooks. Unhoused of their innards, their bristled ears flapped over their skulls. Sarah sucked harder on the cigarette to block out the smell. The pigs looked like children on their first day at school, their heads hung in snouty commiseration. The front trotters, still muddy from the last-touched field, dangled from airy stomachs. All that space in what was once stomach and heart and bladder; the ribs curved now around empty air. What vessels these once were, wobbling little lives of fat and food, mud and udder, until they had come to the butcher's knife and all life had leaked from the wound.

She remembered from her history books how there was no meat on the Island. Did her mother miss this? The butchers? The slabs of all the red and white meat? She wondered what she was like, Laura: living alone, on this Island, in that sea, with no meat in her for the decade.

Sarah crushed the cigarette out under her boot. She would go to the Island, before her courage fled her. She would go and try and find her. With a sidelong look at the hogs, she went back into Wroxham's.

That night, Sarah made the dinner. They ate the lamb in companionable silence, and her dad went to bed early. He suspected nothing.

Sarah packed a bag: warm clothes, some stocks from the kitchen (corned beef, water, margarine, bread), and, at the last minute, she slipped a knife into the bag. She left out the extra photograph of her mother on the boat, and drew a long arrow to Laura, writing underneath it – 'I've gone to find her. I'll be back as soon as I can.'

That night, by way of three buses, she made her way to Newcastle, down to the docks, with her backpack heavy against her shoulders. Behind a red crate of fish tackle she waited, then watched the Boatman go to and from the depot with these boxes and sacks, netted bags of food, heaving and sweating in the cold November air, unloading them into the hold of the boat which was the *Saviour*. Then he left the boat unattended, for a piss or a pint she didn't know, and Sarah knew it was time.

She left the shadows. She walked down the steps to the boat, put her hand to the cargo clasp. She looked at her own freckled hand and withdrew it very quickly, as if scalded. She was scared. She would be back in a week. The next boat was Monday, but there wasn't another one for the winter. She had to go; now; she had to make sure. Footsteps sounded from the back of the depot. Sarah pulled open the hatch and bundled inside to the dank and rooty smell of potatoes. Minutes later the front cabin was unlocked and Boatman stepped in, the boat lowering under his weight.

The engine gunned.

She was on the boat. In ten hours, she would be on the Island.

Thursday

10. Introductions

Nathaniel woke early. On his bed, a box of sunlight from where he had left the curtains unclosed. Through the window, branches shook in heatless light. Without its leaves, there was something bare and pure about the tree, like one of his boys. Nathaniel liked things scraped of fuzz if they could be. His own scalp could do with a razing; the bristle rasped against the pillow.

The duvet was lumpy in places and flat in others; he was warm only if he did not move. Nathaniel would lie in bed like this, on schooldays, until the last moment possible when he would have to rush and wolf down his porridge, so as not to be late for the bell. He did moderately well at his lessons, but something about their big silences made him lustful, on leaving the school gates, for something rotten. And it was a pleasure, of an evening, to tramp about in big boots with his funny boys, though when he came home he always felt sorry bad that his mam sat up and waited for him alone.

Now this girl was on his mind. Following her last night, her strangeness coming off her like a stink, he had no clue as to who she might be. Her face had been ghostly, shrouded by the hedge and then the hood. Nathaniel would've thought she was one of the boys, crouched and ready to smoke out a spy, had she not been so fully possessed of all that hair. When she had walked away, she hadn't been confident; he could tell that the Island paths were unfamiliar to her. And when he had come to her house, and seen of her what the window would give – the flash of hair and the skin so white it could have been bone – Nathaniel settled on the fact that he had never seen her before; never once in his Island life.

It was *possible* she was some Island girl, born a baby at the Grand, perhaps, and kept in a drawer, and only just let out to roam the Island in the inky parts of the night; or that she was some fisherman's daughter, come off the herring boat; or maybe even that she was some sort of mermaid washed ashore, which would explain the phosphorescence of her skin. He imagined her emerging from the sea, half-naked and faintly fishy, with her hair pelt-like and dark, the little breasts dropping beads of the Sound's cold water. He might stay in bed for much longer, just thinking of the girl like that.

She could, of course, be a new deportee. But they hadn't had anyone since '77. Not a soul. And besides, there would have been some announcement, and people would be talking about the extra boat, you wouldn't be able to escape the gossip about a family moving in. And besides, new Islanders didn't just end up in old squats by the Eastern Bay.

Mermaidy and lushly wet, her skin glossed in salt, he thought of her limbs slipping between his underneath the purple flower-print.

But her provenance, that's what he should think on. No new deportees, no fisherman's daughter, no girl of the

Grand, so what was she? And who was she? Why was she not at school with the rest of them? And why was she staying in that abandoned house?

He thought on anything unusual he'd seen lately. Jake had been narky these past few days but there was not much unusual there. Verger had given him the odd book but that had been months ago. Apart from that, he'd heard nothing new.

But he remembered how agitated Eliza had been at the square on Monday, how distracted, even before the boys had crabbed her. What time had that been? It couldn't have been more than ten minutes after the boat had gone. And then he began thinking, really putting his noggin to it: what if the girl had been on Monday's boat? What if she were a stowaway, unknown to the English and Islanders both? And if she *were* a stowaway, it was possible too she was an English spy, come on a mission to report on the Island! Perhaps the English were truly coming back to reclaim the Island, just as he'd told Jake when they'd set up the gang. If she *were* a spy, if she *had* come on a mission to report in the Church's interest, Nathaniel would need to think about what to do. There might be so much God in her veins he would have to beat it from her. He imagined her now, not as the lustrous mermaid, but as a bloodied girl on the sands of Warkworth Bay, with all that orange hair fanned about her like a crown. Aye, if she were a spy, Nathaniel and his boys might find out the truth with their fists. And what a rollicky lot of scrap that would be.

When he rose, he dressed quickly; it was so cold. Lean all the way to his chops, in the northern light his skin was almost blue. He put on one of his da's old shirts and found new handkerchiefs to stuff down the boots. In the chest he saw the silly book of John Verger. It had been a mistake to keep it. He should burn it, or bury it, before any of the other boys found it. Or just take it back to the museum and no one would be any wiser. He didn't like the fact that Jake now had leverage on him. But he ignored it for now, pressing as it was to find this girl before anyone else did.

He ate breakfast. The toaster's grid lit up red and he warmed his bony fingers on the heat; when he drank his tea he warmed his nose in the cup's steam. He wondered whether he should call round to Jake's and tell him he had found this girl, but his heart sank at the prospect. Wherever he took him, the boy drained a thing of its sweetness. Aye, that was Jake, with his big humpy ears, observing the world with bland insolence. No, Jake would not get the spoils of the girl; not yet. Whoever she was, she was Nathaniel's, for the while.

The toast snapped; the jam was raspberry and sweet. He shoved the crusts in the bin. Not for him, curly hair.

The boy made his way over to Swanscott House. He was fair excited to see her, and so he stepped lightly across the Island, though he knew he could not be caught, not when it was barely eight o'clock. All the boys would be softly kipping at their mam's; getting in their rest before school started again.

As he turned at the top of the hill, the full light showed the Sound at its best, almost so that he thought he might detect England, faint as a smudge, across the way. *Are you from there?* he almost asked the waiting air. *Are you a spy?*

Four roads went down the hill in four directions and he took the one leading to the Eastern Bay. From some way up he saw a slick of oil or light near the rocks at the beach and wondered if some treasure or some such thing had come aground there. He would take a look later. Perhaps the little toy boat she had arrived on. He came off Marley Hill to the abandoned road of houses, and, finally, to her house.

In the window of the upper room he saw that the girl too was awake. Her shadow slid across the wall, crisp in the cold sunshine. There was something a little slower about her today, her features flatter. Nathaniel crouched by the hedge, the jeans nipping. Strange, a little, that in his fists he did not hold any rocks. The shadow of smoke curled on the far wall. Was she smoking cigarettes? If she had cigarettes, did that confirm her Englishness?

At the back of the garden, a pond let off a muzzy smell. With still green algae on it, he thought of his da's boat covered in the same slime then pushed the thought away. He tried, instead, to think who had lived here before, in this house, but he thought perhaps it had always been empty, at least, since he'd known it. The whole street, in fact, was empty, and going to ruin. The back door was in a bad way and open on the latch. There was a yeasty smell inside the kitchen and dirty crockery stood by the sink's side. Cabinets and drawers were still open. Little thought had gone into abandoning it, rushing as the family probably had been, in the Christmas of 1950, to escape the incoming tribe. He checked the other rooms were empty, catching himself in a mirror, surprised at his scalp's dark cap of hair. Aye, it could do with a razing.

His da had not looked fast enough for a house, if this was the kind of home which had been on offer in '51: it was big and grand, if dirty, but that could be helped. There was no chance, however, of moving his ma out of their house: she would never leave it. Not even for a trip to Maiden's Square, never mind packing up for better quarters.

He stopped at the window and smelled it, dimly, on the air. It *was* cigarette smoke. How had the girl procured them? Neither he nor the boys would have sold on cigarettes. It was clearly against the rules. Or perhaps Jake had found her here already, and was sharing cigs with her and chatting. Perhaps they were already at the old gromicks, his big hands pawing at the freckled breasts, and the thought stopped Nathaniel cold.

He turned from the glass and suddenly, like a phantom, she was there, looking at him, from the landing. Her face was still. Her skin was very white, as it had been last night, but in the breadth of a second she had blushed so deeply that the freckles were now surrounded by the colour of blood. He'd like to put his hand there to feel the warm rush of it. Her eyes flashed.

The girl was wearing a rucksack, jeans, heavy boots, heavy anorak; no Island girl might be wearing garb as bad as this.

'Who're you?' she said.

Nathaniel did not answer; surprised as he was that it had been her to ask the first question. He continued to the landing and she went back, a little, toward the room he'd seen her in last night. Behind her, clothes sat in uneven piles and the room was a mess. Now, he blocked the stairs and any exit down. The girl said again, but this time in a whisper, 'Who are you?'

'How is it now,' Nathaniel said, moderating his tone to one of kindness, 'you don't know my name?' And he edged closer to her, coming up to the last step. He was right, he thought, she *was* foreign to here; he had a feeling about it. Something about her voice, her accent, and the cigarettes as well. Pink ringed the girl's eyes; maybe she had cried the night through; maybe she'd been at the old shake-and-heave since he'd left her. It was freezing in here, enough to make the tears come to any man's eye, never mind a doxy such as she. The girl was tiny, really, one quick move and he could have her by the wrist or the hair. And he got that feeling, like how it was after school, when he wanted nothing more than to move, to do something, in order to shake off some vague and unknown sadness.

She said: 'I don't know. I don't know you. What are you doing in this house?'

'I saw you here last night, lamb, I saw you outside that house. Then I followed you here.'

'You followed me here? I didn't see you.'

'Aye. Aye.' He took a step closer. Still kindly, kindly: 'And these cigarettes. Who did you get them from, now? I didn't give you any, and none of my boys would have sold them on.'

'I wasn't smoking any.'

The girl looked adrift, out of her depth, as if her head was bobbing along the Sound's grey water.

'I smelled it.'

'From a shop. I bought them in a shop.'

'Did you now?'

'Yes. Yes I did.'

Despite the cold he saw her brow was damp. Her nerves excited him. 'And you know, now, you can't buy them in a shop, like; you know that, surely.'

Her blue eyes flicked to the side of the room. 'Someone gave them to me.'

'Who?'

'A man,' she said, 'down at the square.'

'Who?'

'I don't know.'

'Who, doll? I didn't catch that.'

'I said *I don't know*.' Nathaniel took another step toward her. He'd crabbed her now. She was all flushed about the skin as if she really was terrified, her eyes flitting about the landing, looking for another exit. She had less and less space now in which to move, and she looked to the back window, as if to gauge its distance from the ground.

'Who are you? If you're not from here, where are you from?' The girl said nothing. 'Look, I've never seen you in the square, nor at school, nor at Lynemouth Town. Are you a baby from the Grand only just discovered? Or have you just come in from the sea, washed up in a boat wreck, a mermaid perhaps?'

The smell of smoke hung in the room like a premonition of her confession. Cigarettes! No Malade would have given her a cigarette, not without crabbing her first. Now she would have to admit it, that she was on Monday's boat, that she was some Evangelical spy on an English mission! What would he do with her? Bundle her up and lock her in the room? Alert the boys to the great English danger within these walls? What a scrappy week it would be, if she were a spy!

The girl stepped back so that she was against the wall, and then suddenly, as if with a sleight of hand, she held something out toward him. Nathaniel couldn't identify it at first, so quick had been the gesture, but she moved it toward him and he saw what it was. Light caught the tip of the blade; its length was grey. It was neither a big knife nor a long one, but it was there, held between them like a torch. There was quiet in the room for a bit as they regarded each other and they wondered who might win this. She held it very still; her hands did not shake; her eyes did not move from him. The blush, which had fairly soaked her face moments ago, had disappeared. No one had ever pulled a knife on him before; no one. He wouldn't be so afraid were he not certain the girl was scared enough to use it. His blood did its surge, as if fairly *he* were the one being crabbed for a spy. He should have played this softly; he'd gone at her too hard.

The girl made a jabbing motion with the blade. 'You come no closer. I've heard of you, all right. I know who you are.'

He held up his hands. 'I'm sure you have. Nathaniel Malraux, miss.'

'Aye. Nathaniel. Yes: I know you.'

'Put the knife down, miss. I promise I won't hurt you. I was as surprised as you were, that was all.'

'You don't intimidate me,' she said, with no sign that she would lower the blade. 'I don't want to be intimidated, you hear?'

'Aye, aye. I hear.'

Slowly, she lowered the knife, but did not put it away, instead, she held it loosely by her side. She said again: 'I just don't want to be intimidated.' Then she did something quite unexpected; with the knife still there, she patted her bag and brought out a pack of smokes, expertly flipped the top with one hand, and offered him one. The tips were lined up perfectly, and smelled good: earthy. Nathaniel took one, as did she, and she lit both of the cigarettes, then put the knife back into the side pocket. Two curling lines of smoke rose.

The girl slid down the wall and sat at the skirting. He joined her there: smoking, watching her smoke. The cigarette tasted unbelievably fresh, without the taste that it normally had of an old brown piece of furniture. There was something leathery and strong to the smell of it, like his da's old tin of Pomade Divine. The girl did it well, the smoking, like she was mistress of it. Lots of practice, he supposed, back in England, where you might buy a pack for merely a cherry. And then she smiled at him, so that he knew she wouldn't bring out the knife again.

'A fine cigarette,' he ventured.

She didn't say anything. Something moved in the garden, and he followed it; when he looked back she was still watching him.

'So you don't have cigarettes here? That's what I'm to learn from this?'

'Aye. You're right about that.'

'Oh,' she said, 'I see. So you want to know where I got these from.'

'Aye.'

The girl looked at the lit end and sighed through her

nose. 'Well. I'm guessing you might know this already.' She took a deep breath. 'I'm from England. I came on the boat. On Monday night.'

'How?'

'I hid myself in the cargo hold. When the Boatman wasn't looking.'

'I knew it! A stowaway, aye, that makes sense! I knew I'd never seen you before, not at school, nor down at the Square.'

'And you saw me last night?'

'Aye. Spying on someone – outside their house.'

'A woman. A woman's house. Do you know whose house that is?'

'No idea. The light was off by the time you left, remember? Why? Want me to make enquiries? I could go have a looksy – I'd know her by name, if I saw her.'

'No. No, don't do that.'

The girl looked down toward her lap, almost guiltily, and he remembered himself as a Malade, and what he was here to do. He made his voice gruffer. 'Why were you spying on her?'

'I wasn't spying.'

'What were you doing outside her house?'

'Watching. Looking. She's someone I might know.'

'Oh, yes. I see. Have they contracted you, is that it, to watch my isle? To spy on us and get us back to God's acre?'

Her eyes were quizzical, confused. 'A spy?'

'Aye. Come to watch the Island, and report back to the Church.'

'No,' she said, 'no. I'm not here to do that.'

'Oh, really? And how am I meant to trust you on that?'

'I give you my word.'

'An Englishman's word is worth nothing.'

'I'm not an English man.' The girl pulled a piece of paper from her bag and handed it over to him. 'Here,' she said, 'read this.'

Nathaniel read the article quickly; it was like any you might find in the museum. Churches burned; the Movement arrested; the promise of expulsion was made. 'And bravo, bravo to them; but what is this to me?'

Her voice was small. 'My name is Sarah. I'm Laura Wicks' daughter.' As she smoked she narrowed an eye against the sunlight. 'Mum was accused of Saint Gregory's ten years ago. And then she disappeared,' Sarah clicked her fingers, 'like that, without a trace. So I've come here, to try and find her.'

'Oh, aye, and why now? Ten years on?'

'I found the article by accident. In my home. In England.' She laughed, but quite mirthlessly. 'For ten years, my dad's kept up this lie, that she was with another man, with another family. But that's not true. I found article after article on her in newspapers from that year. And I'm convinced she was sent here, in 1977, when the last of the Movement were taken here.'

'Your ma, aye? 1977. A lot of people came that year. A lot of people.'

'Have you heard of her?' she asked.

'I can't say I have. But it doesn't mean she's not here.' Nathaniel pointed to the article. 'Mind if I keep hold of it?'

'This isn't a story. I swear. I'm here only to find my ma.'

'Aye, aye. No need to protest. I just want to have a look at it, think on it a bit more.' Nathaniel tucked it into his jacket pocket. 'And this woman, whose house you were outside last night, you think that was her? Laura Wicks?'

'I've looked over the whole Island. She's the closest, so far. But I don't know if it's her. She's the one that's nearest, yes.'

Nathaniel stood, and walked over to the banister. His grin stretched from one ear to the other. 'Are you hungry?'

'Yes,' she said, 'starving.'

So this is the way he'd master her. 'I'll come back tonight with something to eat.' He flicked the cigarette to the back of the landing and it smoked thinly under the windowpane. 'In the meantime, I have some advice for you, which I suggest you ken. If you see any dandies dressed like me,' he gestured toward his clothes, 'it'd be best to avoid them. For your sake, merely. If my boys find out you're English they'll go for your throat.'

'But my ma, she's part of the Movement, she worked to help—'

'Hush now, Sarah. Listen. I shan't tell a soul if you manage not to get yourself discovered. I've read the article,' and he patted his jacket here, 'and, according to you, you've come to look for your long-lost mother who was part of the Movement. Which is interesting, very interesting. But what scant evidence you have for this makes me uncomfortable. Aye. And you don't want to know what Islanders do with unwanted Englishmen. Or women, for that matter. So keep a low profile. Don't talk to anyone. I'll come back tonight. I'll bring you some food. I give you my word.'

She squashed the last of her cigarette onto the carpet. 'And what's the worth of an Islander's word?'

'A bucket of fish; I don't know. You're just going to have to trust me.' He gestured again to his costume. 'As I said, if you see anyone dressed like me, don't talk to them. You'll only find yourself in trouble. And that knife won't help you; not with my lot.'

'I'm not lying,' she said. 'I've got no other business here. No business of spying, I swear.'

He'd been a fool to be scared of her. She was, most likely, soft as anything, with all her English comforts. But she was a peach if ever he'd seen one! A peachy pleasure! He took the stairs two by two. Not a spy then, but a daughter of the Movement. That made things better.

Or perhaps, just more complicated.

11. Bream

Later that morning, Nathaniel sat in the living room, which was so warm he felt as if he were being cooked. Porridge bloated him. Beside him, the oats were still glued to the bowl. He resisted looking at the newspaper article, now folded in his jeans pocket, but he thought of the girl often, that challenge to her eyes, the neat long line of smoke from her cigarette, that knife between them. Her skin and freckles; milk and mud! Poor old thing, how frightened she was! He felt something fold within him: a softening. Aye, he'd expected to feel a jolly fury, a merry rage, on discovering she was an Englisher, but instead, sitting here now, watching the telly-box with his ma, he felt a long, light curiosity. Cowled in her Englishness, that much was true – and yet she was a daughter of the Movement. So it was a noble lineage, like Nathaniel to his Jack Malraux was Sarah to her Laura Wicks.

What a week this could be, with no school, and with little Sarah Wicks in tow!

He'd done a few hours of telly-watching already, with the heat sending him into a soft loop, thinking of the girl. The gas-fire creaked, its bars blue. His mother's pink jumper – with a diamond of small holes at the breast, revealing here and there a greying brassiere – had stains down the front. What had happened to his mam? She would move her leg to and fro, saying she had to dance to keep the blood in it, it tended to deaden. And she laughed, empty sort of, and it was then that Nathaniel wanted nothing more than to leave the house.

'All right, Ma.'

'Monkey.'

'Take a step out with me, Ma.'

'No, Monkey. Not now. Another day. Baneful tired today.'

Boredom made him hanker for something rotten. Sarah was in his mind and blood. When could he go back to her? This evening? This afternoon? He didn't like to leave his mam for so long alone, when he wasn't at school. Mammy changed the channel and an English copper in a navy suit ran after a young man. 'Time is it?' she asked.

'Noon.'

'Aye. Shall have my lunch soon, then. You hungry?'

'No, Mam, just had my porridge.'

'Oh, aye, so you did.' Margaret took a swig of the syrup. 'Aye,' she said again, smacking her lips then leaning back into the chair. 'Are you all right, Nathaniel?' she asked him, giving him an eyeful. 'You're ever so restless.'

'Aye.'

'Why don't you visit Mr Verger? He'd like to see you. He called around again for you yesterday. Asking about that book you'd borrowed.'

'I told you, Mam, I can't find it.'

'The book?'

'Aye.'

'Always was a very good friend to your da. Jack always

said how much he liked him. Well, you best tell him you've lost it, since he seemed to be sore for it.'

'He's always crabbing me, asking me to visit him, asking me to—'

'He was very good to your dad. I don't think you should be complaining that he enjoys your company. Jack wouldn't've liked that.' On the telly, a boy ran from two coppers, barely escaping them. Two cars collided and one of the bonnets was smashed up. Nathaniel wished he were there to see it: the roll and lurch of the metal. Oh, to be that boy! Exhausted and roughed up! And free to do what he pleased! 'And tonight, Nath, what'll you be doing?'

'Off out. Don't know.'

'With the boys?'

'No,' he said, 'that's tomorrow night.'

Sighing, she turned back to the set. The policeman programme finished and another started. It was a game show. A woman spun a big wheel. His mam turned back to him with a youthful look suddenly in her eyes. 'Nathaniel, my son, why don't you buy me a bream? A whole sea bream. I'll give you the shillings. Give you the money for it. Would you like that? You'll have to be in, mind, for tonight. It won't be ready b'fore seven.'

Nathaniel looked at her. 'Seriously?'

'More than the day.' She added, her head cocked: 'As long as you stop in for the night.' His mam fished out her handbag and pulled out three shillings and some pennies. 'A whole sea bream, now, mind,' and as she placed it in his palm she looked up with a timid smile, 'and mind it's from the Norwegian waters, good boy now.' Her hand had a tremor to it. 'If Mr Stansky offers you a fish from the Sound, you say no, love.'

Nathaniel kissed her on the cheek and was out into the hall pulling on his jacket before he had time to think, before he had time to say goodbye, going at a jaunty pace along Blackett Place, feeling the air cut his lungs. He started up Marley Hill. The first fish in months! Were the Islanders full of fish or were the fish full of them? This Island produced some tricksome questions!

No more veggies and po-tat-ies, he sang to himself.

The cold always did this for him; where in the living room he went lollygag in the heat, as soon as he set out he felt all of his boyish years. Perhaps he would take a detour and look in on Sarah and see if she was still there. He'd let her roam about a bit; he knew she wouldn't talk to anyone, and that the boys, warm in their mams' living rooms, wouldn't leave unless they were called out by him. And even if they did see her they were too thick to see her for what she truly was. Exotic and English and oh . . . quite lovely.

And tonight Nathaniel would bring her a bream sandwich and impress on her what a civilized lot they were. He felt happy. Maybe this is what England did to you; made you all oiled up, like a fish, as happy as a herring!

Still, he sobered himself – he was right to be suspicious of her. He'd have to investigate this story, just in case it was figs. Because what if she were a threat, what if this mother story were a pack of lies and what if she were here to fatten the Islanders with tales of God? He imagined his lean body turning into the soft babyness of Jake. No. Aye. He was right to be suspicious of her.

*

At Maiden's Square, Nathaniel smiled at some of the girls going into the grocer's, proud that today it was not vegetables he would buy, but fish, for there was to be *no more veggies and po-tat-ies*. He heard the fishmonger's bell and as he looked around, smiling as he was at the girls in the square, the two almost collided. Nathaniel's heart sank. Bream! The Island! The girl! The gang! Anything but John Verger!

'Nathaniel!'

'Mr Verger.'

A moment passed as they stood watching each other. Nathaniel couldn't help his dislike of the old man. He gave off a sweet smell like some old swelling fruit. Verger asked, 'How are you keeping?'

'Well.'

'And your mam?'

'Fine,' he said, 'you saw her yourself yesterday.'

'Good, good.' Verger's eyes were eager; his voice dropped to a whisper. 'And the book. Did you like it?'

'The book?'

'The book I lent you.' Verger took a little step toward him. 'Of the paintings.' His bag bulged with fish. The dicky bow, spotted and clipped, was fast to his throat.

'Oh aye, the paintings.' Nathaniel moved toward the shop. 'I seem to have lost it.'

The old man's eyes had lost their jig. 'Oh,' he said. His whole aspect seemed to sag.

Now the boy felt sorry for him, but it wasn't his place to be out socializing with an old man. Would his da be this old now? Or older? When Jack died he was still the broad fisherman. Not like this girlish old man, even if his da *was* marbling the seabed. 'I don't know, but I'll have a look, right?' Nathaniel pushed the handle, stopped, and turned back to him. 'Though you were a friend of my da's, which I understand, and I respect, all I'm saying is that you might be careful with a book such as that. Wouldn't want anyone to assume, you know, you were a Got.'

'No, no; preposterous,' said Verger, biting the side of his cheek.

'Aye. I know it. But the others mightn't. And I don't want you to get in trouble with the boys, ken? They've a wild eye for anyone who seems to be harking for the Church. My mam is very fond of you. All I'm saying is: use some discretion.' Then, louder, and with much stiff politesse, he said, 'Good day to you, Mr Verger,' and with the door open, he was hit presently by the salty waft of Arthur Stansky's fishes.

Arthur emerged through red plastic chains. He had been his da's boss – or buyer, really, of Jack's catch – and Nathaniel loved him as an uncle. The monger made him feel shy and excited, as if he were in the presence of some-one cut materially from the same cloth as Mr Malraux. Arthur had evidently forgiven the boy for Monday night, when he'd crabbed Eliza, or forgotten clean about it, or purely never cared in the first place. 'Nathaniel, boy! A pleasure! It's been awful long.'

'That it has,' Nathaniel said, somewhat uncertainly.

'What have you been eating? Stuff of the earth?'

'Aye. Potatoes. Endlessly.'

'How is your ma keeping, then?'

'As usual.'

'Ah. Not getting out much, then? She always was a greatly sensitive soul.'

'Aye. I can't remember the last time she left the house. She has a gromicky fear of the outside.'

'The sea especially, I imagine. It happens to all of us, aye, who've lost one to the Sound. It's difficult ever to go near it. Even to dip a toe in it.' Arthur laughed into his chin, a svelte, kindly laugh. 'Or to eat the fruit of it. Aye, well the Sound will feed and kill us both.'

'And are you well, sir?'

'Aye. Business is doing well. As well as one can hope.'

Arthur looked down into the counter. At five that morning he had gone to Warkworth pier to pick up the catch. Back at the monger's, he laid out the fish on the ice chips, pretending he was a painter setting up a still-life. The fish were cold in his hands, sea-soaked, and the smell of brine and seaweed filled the shop. He laid out split herrings, sea trout and brill, monkfish and flounder, and a catch of rock-fish on the chips. Paying attention to the orange scale, the rainbow shine, the dark wet lids, he placed each fish in the counter with regard to hue and luminescence. A hunk of blood-red tuna he placed at the heart of the display. Arthur loved his fishes as he loved Miss Michalka: generously, instinctively.

Arthur had been hoping Eliza might come into the shop today, after the ham-fisted job he had made of everything yesterday. Now, he was prepared, and ready, and had made a beautiful display, and he'd practised being nonchalant and charming. But it was past one o'clock, and still she had not come. The lonely monger felt a rising desire to cry into the fish hearts and spleens because he was hopelessly in love with Eliza and she didn't care for him. Not any more.

How disastrously he had coped with her coming to him that night in June. With her ma's death, Arthur had felt suddenly, overwhelmingly responsible for her. He felt plunged into a crisis of commitment. They weren't even official. His immediate reaction to her request – to move in with him! – was a quick, bowled-over 'no'. He didn't have to live with her if he didn't want to. She had been too fast; far too fast. But he hadn't meant for her to join the Grand; not this; not at all. When he'd heard she'd done that he wondered if it was out of revenge. And then, righteous with envy, he'd gone to the Grand in August, because his friends had been talking about how enjoyable she was . . . what great fun . . . and in the morning she'd cried, telling him how broke she had been – and! Only begging from him a sofa! – he'd felt terrible; so ashamed.

And now she wouldn't speak to him, and he had promised himself he wouldn't get involved with her. He couldn't hurt her again; and he had resolved to stay away from her. And she would stay away from him, or made every effort to. It was agony.

Yesterday had been horrible; her face cold, her words polite; only her eyes soft and unable to be unkind. Oh, she was the Island's saint! When he had passed the kipper over to her he had thought that perhaps their hands might touch and he might feel the warm quick pulse of her skin. But she had placed the coins on the cold counter and then she had said it – the word 'grand' – and it had set them both off in disarray.

Aye, around her he was boorish and indelicate; over-weight, and reeky of fish. She, however, was a great white dart of ice that would not melt. Oh, it was his entire fault: from the moment she had asked him for shelter, to the night at the Grand; the glare of the salmon only seemed to confirm this.

Still, he saved up his shillings and his pounds – for what, he didn't know, perhaps to buy a new shop that might enamour her to him, buy out Forrester's, or put a deposit on a house, where she might envision setting up a family with him. He would handle the fishmonger's and bring home what they had left of a day to feed the three or four little Stanskys who had by some good grace inherited their mother's looks, and ditched their father's nose. Or perhaps he might buy her something from Buttons – and present it to her on her birthday. When was her birthday, he would have to find out, but who could he ask? He couldn't ask her. Oh, would she ever forgive him? Could he ever forgive himself?

'Mr Stansky?'

The boy was looking at him.

'Sorry, son. Miles away. What'll it be, then? The eel makes a great spitchcock, Mrs Spenser was telling me. Or the ginpike, she has a lovely bite on her.'

'The ginpike?'

'Peachy fish. Something like trout.'

'No, Mr Stansky, sir, just the bream, please.'

When Arthur held the fish, tip to head from hand to elbow, the ice chips melted on his skin. 'That's an eight-ouncer. How's that for you?'

'Perfect.'

'For Mammy Malraux is it now?'

'Aye,' Nathaniel nodded and grinned. 'She hasn't cooked fish in months.'

'Ah. A special occasion?'

'No,' he shrugged, 'she seems to have it in her today, that's all. She seems to be feeling better, that is.'

'Well, she'll enjoy this one, that's for sure.'

'Mr Stansky?'

'Yes, son?'

'Is it from the Norwegian waters?'

'That she is.'

'Good. 'Twas what Mammy M requested.'

'Nowt wrong with that, son. Your da was a marvellous man. She must miss him. It was a great shame; and it happens too often, aye, that we lose one to the Sound.' Arthur wrapped the fish in paper, closing the fins into the package. 'Well, for you that is three and fourpence.' Nathaniel slid the coins over the counter. 'Enjoy it, then, son, it should be a good feast after your fast.'

The bell behind the boy rang and they both turned to Mrs Bingley, pulling a tartan trolley. 'Hello, Mrs Bingley,' said Nathaniel.

'Well,' she said, 'good morning, Nathaniel,' rather primly, but she hardly looked at him and started instead talking to Mr Stansky, rattling on about some theft from the grocer's. Well, if carrots were the only thing on Mrs Bingley's mind it meant the girl hadn't been found by anybody yet. And it meant Mrs Richards had not complained too widely of the crabbing she had received last night. A relief, on both counts.

Not a fish in months! And now it was this big fat fish

with its head and its fins and its tail! As the bag swung from his fingers and Nathaniel made his way from the square back home, he thought of Sarah's eyes on him and that ludicrous knife. She would never use it. She was too scared. But it had thrilled him, really, when she'd pulled it on him. Such an outrageous manoeuvre! He liked her better for it. He'd bring her some food tonight and win her over, so by the end of the week all she'd be looking for was cuddles and caresses.

12. Tea

In the late afternoon, Margaret prepared Arthur's fish. The slack-jawed bream fell easily from the paper and onto the oven tray. Margaret studied him and his deep frown. She didn't really want the fish to be in the kitchen. If it had come from the same place as Jack lay now . . . what if it had swum through his bones? My husband is a fish, she thought, or his bones are their beds.

Margaret Malraux did not know whether to weep into its gills or rip its head off.

She had developed this antipathy maybe a year or so after Jack's death. In the first year, her grief made it difficult to be squeamish, and when people came around (prim Mrs Bingley, or dear Mrs Page), with cod pie or clam casserole, she was not going to refuse. She knew, vaguely, that her boy needed to be fed and what he left she would eat without much pleasure. But as the bones of her bonny fisherman became, most likely, strewn along the seabed, Margaret developed a pure antipathy to the sea. She would not eat of its waters, not from the Sound, where the boat went down, nor, increasingly, from the Norwegian waters. No; she would not eat of the sea. She imagined Jack's molecules like plankton in its currents. Aye; now he was nothing more than mulch drifting in water, ready to be siphoned by mollusc or whale.

They had a fishless diet, Margaret and her son, because to eat fish was to entertain the possibility they might be eating him. And in the past few years she had stopped leaving the house so much, always afraid that the sight of the sea would send her racing back toward that grief.

But when John Verger came round yesterday night, he talked to her, in a worried fashion, of her son. He said that people were talking about some hooliganism in the square on Monday night. He said another boy had become involved in the gang – a Nicholas Carter, who wasn't older than twelve, and who now bore a bruise on his chin, supposedly from its connection with Nathaniel's fist. Verger said that the violence, and the intimidation, had to stop. Margaret told him how difficult she found it without Jack, mastering this boy of such wilfulness. Verger said he would be here to help, and he had held her hand in his, and that was when she had made her resolution to cook her boy a fish. It would be a way to keep him at home.

After all, that was what Nathaniel was always asking her, always saying that he could pick up something at Arthur's if she wanted. She would cook the fish for him, which would encourage him to stay at home, and keep him away from these boys. This would be the first step. Aye. Better meals had to be had. The Malrauxs would no longer eat potatoes.

Tentatively she slipped her finger into the wet body. Underneath his gills, the pouches of his cheeks, the tip of her finger touched the vertebrae, so sharp they almost pricked her finger. The backbone snapped between its head and tail, and Margaret moved its head to a plate. Its eyes, filmed and black, looked blankly at the ceiling. She regarded the flesh under the grey skin. How to make sense of her husband's death? Their love had been the only good thing about the Island. And now. Now there was so little to be consoled by. She couldn't understand it. Nothing could be extrapolated from the sea, from its tough opacity; its unerotic charge. The sea had devoured her husband! He had only wanted to suck up the air!

The Sound had taken away all comfort.

Margaret wiped the blade on her pinny. She pushed the knife in and spliced the fish open. Its translucent ribs left indents in the flesh. Margaret bent down to smell the seawater on its scales. *Were you near him,* she wanted to ask, *Were you near my Jack?* and then, *I can't do this, I'm frightened; I'm frightened of eating him!*

She stayed a while near its skin, breathing, slowly, slowly, until she regained composure and reminded herself that she was doing this for her boy. For he was the purpose, the meaning. She would feed her boy the fish to keep him from this gang.

Into the bream's belly she stuffed tinned anchovies and bottled capers. Margaret dropped the fish-head into the bin. The rest of the bream she put in the oven, and kicked the door shut.

If Jack were here he would know what to do. Was Nathaniel a terror? A hooligan? She just couldn't think it; he was such a bonny boy; he was not a boy who would harass, not a boy to terrorize. He was a lovely boy with eyes so blue. The pinafore she put back to where it always hung and she moved to the sink to scrape the scales from her hands. The flakes fell, sparkling in the water.

Margaret checked her hands were free from scurf and looked out into the back garden, with the clothesline, the bare trees and garage. Nathaniel was in there, fixing up Jack's workstation. There had been a time when she would pick the long red rhubarb stalks and make jam for husband and son. There had been a time when, home from a trawl, Jack and she would go out to watch the aeroplane fly over the breadth of the Island. It came on the last Sunday of the month and they liked to watch it and imagine the pilot's sense of freedom up there in the big air. They remembered, too, their once-cherished sense of freedom; which hadn't been freedom really, not in England in the late forties, but a sense of boundlessness, a sense that they could travel and go anywhere. But England had gone, disappeared in the wash, and with it, its roads and cities and ports, and though that sense of freedom too had disappeared, it had been replaced with their love for one another. It had been enough to sustain them; just. And now Margaret had her boy, and her boy only, and she would do anything to keep him from himself.

The plane would come this Sunday, she guessed, but she wouldn't go out to watch it.

The doorbell rang. It was unusual for Margaret to receive anybody at home, never mind two visitors in two days. She hoped it wasn't Verger again, at any rate; sometimes she couldn't bear his concern. Her hands she checked again were free from fish scale before opening the door.

Caro Kilman. There she stood, her auburn curls round

against the grey sky, wearing a plush red coat. As sturdy and polished as a first-class train carriage, next to Caro was a sleek creamy Labrador, with wet eyes and panting tongue. Directly, the snout was at Margaret's crotch. Caro pulled the dog back to her side with a smart snap of the leash. Margaret noticed the fine gloves. 'Hello, Margaret. Sorry about that. A nose on him.'

'It's fine. Hello, Caro.'

Margaret smoothed down her green plaid skirt and tried to give her hair a little volume at the crown. She always felt bad about herself next to Caro, who always looked very well put together, as she should do, being mistress of the Island's launderette. She had always wondered if Caro had held a little flame for Jack.

'Margaret.'

Margaret led her through the vestibule and into the hall, and Caro removed her coat, though it was not much warmer than outside. Underneath was a purple frock, cinched at the waist with a matching belt. The scooped neck showed a lovely oval of skin, quite pearlescent. Her perfume, something of roses, breasted the air, and made Margaret's nose itch.

The parlour was rarely used and cooler for it. Caro sat herself in the armchair, moving her hand over the dog's glossy coat. Margaret lit the fire. Underneath the parlour's window was the veneered box where Margaret kept Jack's letters. *Maggie*, they would start, invariably, and then some sentimental little thought – *I'm at sea without you.* She knew bits off by heart but tried hard not to read them. *Y'are a bag of cockles to warm any sailor's heart.* On long missions, when he would be out at sea for a month or so at a time, the ferry, that brought the catch back to the Island every Thursday, would bring her a letter too. But Margaret tried hard not to read them; they tended to make everything worse.

Caro put her ungloved hands toward the fire.

'Would you like some tea, then, Caro?'

'Please.'

When Margaret returned with the tray of tea and biscuits, Caro was staring anxiously at the ceramic cockatoo on the mantelpiece, as if afeared it would jump onto her lap. Margaret left the door open so that Caro could smell the baking fish and know that she kept a good house, and also so that the room wouldn't warm and Caro wouldn't be inclined to stay. Steam piped from the teapot's spout.

The dog had by now fallen asleep, snoring gently in front of the fire. Margaret placed the tray on the side table and then sat herself on the sofa. 'And Morris? How's his anaemia, if you don't mind me asking?'

Caro held her head up high as if stretching her neck. 'It does give him an ache.'

'Aye. I imagine.'

'Right pale, he is, with very little colour in his lips. And under his eyes, you know.' She pulled the skin down underneath her eye. 'All round here very pale pink; not red, like you or I. And his heart is shaky, too, what with the iron, you know, and not having enough of it. Me, I've never suffered from it. Have you?' Caro did not stop to hear the reply, instead flattening the dress over her knees, saying, 'I told Morris to eat more salmon. Arthur says this might help.'

'It's a chronic ache, then, the anaemia?'

'No, not as such; it doesn't affect him all the time.'

Margaret looked at the pot and wondered if she could hazard now to pour the tea, but it would be an embarrassment if it came out as bathwater. Margaret did not want to be embarrassed, not in front of Caro. Caro looked at an exact point on the carpet with a washed-out look in her eyes; when she looked up she was somewhat flushed. 'I'm scared for Morris. Seeing Mrs Page buried like that. She was quite young, you know, only sixty-five. It was a heart attack but she was very weak, very weak already from the lack of iron.'

'You can't die from anaemia, Caro—'

'You can if it gets really bad. Morris is sweaty, at night, like a radiator in bed with me. I've heard it causes heart palpitations. Palpitations!' Caro's eyes rounded alarmingly. 'That's a heart attack!'

For moments, neither woman spoke. Caro looked mournfully at the dog, Margaret looked mournfully at the picture of Jack and Jack looked at the sea, and, unbeknown to him, into the lonely soul of Margaret Malraux. 'Of course, it wasn't something my Jack was affected by. Anaemia. He was always a big healthy man. It must be hard for you, I can't imagine.'

'I expect,' Caro said, re-crossing her legs and smiling tightly, 'it is the same feeling as when you lost Jack in the accident. It is hard, sometimes, to get to the pity of another's suffering, but not impossible.'

Margaret stood and splashed the hot tea into the cups. She poured too much milk into Caro's cup and hoped it would make it cold, passing the cup and saucer over to her, while the dog snoozed by Caro's feet. 'Mrs Bingley is the same with Gordon. Washed out with worry, day in, day out, for his bloods. Aye, it is hard for us women. If we're not hard enough on this Island, oh aye, if there's softness left in us on any account, then the anaemia comes. Very cruel; life.'

Margaret drained her cup of tea, though it was quite hot, hoping Caro might do the same and leave with her fat dog. But she was evidently in no rush.

Caro coughed and then said: 'And Nathaniel?'

'Yes?'

'He was in the launderette last week. Acting very strange.'

'And?'

'And then I saw him outside in the square on Monday. With his friends. They were larking about in a queer manner.'

'Perhaps, as we didn't grow up on this Island, it might be hard for either of us to imagine what is normal, and what is queer.'

Caro placed her cup and saucer on the carpet and put her hands on her lap, neatly, like two hands carved of soap. The corners of her lips twitched briefly upward toward her eyes and then her expression became markedly more sober. 'Yes, well. Mrs Richards had a hard time of it last night.'

'And what is that to me?'

'It was reported to me that these boys were involved. Nathaniel, and his ilk.'

'Reported to you? Are you the new policewoman of the isle, then, Caro? Strange, I thought we already had a force fit for that purpose.'

Caro simpered. 'Mrs Bingley told me.'

'My boy does not parley with those hooligans. You can take that from me.'

Margaret looked out onto the street. Caro drank her tea.

'How is business? Nathaniel tells me he spends nearly all of his pocket money at your launderette. Keeping his fineries spruce.'

'Well, I'm not here to discuss Nathaniel's sartorial choices—'

'I didn't assume you were.'

'No.' Caro stood, as if being at the level of the cockatoo might confer her with some degree of authority. 'That I didn't. But what I do want to discuss with you, Mrs Malraux, is the issue of this gang. They're sharking about the Island for Gots or English spies or who knows what and I think it's a bad business. We hardly need thugs like that around, not any more, not after our troubles. Not in 1986, for goodness' sake. They're vandalizing things, harassing people—'

'Rubbish.'

'Poor Mrs Richards was hit last night by a thrown rock.'

'Are you implying my boy—?'

'Well, was he here?'

'Of course.' Margaret lied with ease: 'He was watching the telly with me.'

But Caro pressed on. 'Are you talking to him? Finding out the problem? He's a menace, Margaret, and people are scared.'

'How dare you tell me how to raise my child! He's a good lad. You just don't see it. You have no proof he was there; none whatsoever.'

The muscles in Caro's neck squeezed. 'Fine.' She stood and picked up her gloves, and with the tip of her brogues nudged the dog's belly. The Labrador woke and yawned. 'I only came to warn you, Margaret, out of a good sense in my heart. That Nathaniel should be—'

'Yes?'

'I only thought I might be a help. I care. And without Jack—'

'Thank you.'

The dog gave a bark and they both looked at him as if they wondered how he had got there.

Caro said quietly, 'Do you even know where he is now?' After the pronouncement of Jack's name, moments ago, Margaret assumed Caro was now talking about her husband. *Did she know where he was now?* What kind of question was that? Margaret imagined Jack's limbs dancing in the tide; the fish swimming between his bones. Her heart ached. Caro raised an eyebrow, persisting, leaning toward her as if Margaret were deaf, or at least incapable, saying: 'Nathaniel. Your son, Margaret. Do you know where he is?'

'Yes.' Margaret laughed. 'He's in his da's garage. Do you want to check up on him? Lend him a hand to saw through an English spy?'

Caro was now evidently fuming though her face remained expressionless. She turned neatly on her heel and walked swiftly to the hall. The dog followed lazily. Caro vigorously buttoned the coat with one gloved hand. It was dark in the hall and Margaret felt ashamed of the carpet. 'I only came as a friend, as I said.'

A waft of bream escaped from the kitchen.

On the front steps a broad wind hit the two women. The row of pebbledash houses gleamed, their slate roofs slick in evening rain. Margaret wrapped the cardigan closer; this was as far as she would come out. 'Enjoy the plane on Sunday, if you're to see it, Mrs Malraux.'

'My regards to Morris,' Margaret replied, but Caro had already set off, the dog trotting behind her. 'And his bloods,' Margaret added, but with very little voice.

From behind her, the oven bell rang out.

In its warm chamber she saw the fine skin blackening.

13. Fish Supper

There were cases of anaemia on the Island, but fewer than the Islanders thought. In the early fifties, when the deportees had arrived, a rumour had circulated that the lack of meat would drive them all mad, and it had become a long-term concern of the terrorist mothers to keep their children on a surfeit of iron.

Ever since then, preoccupied with nearly nothing else, not fighting the English nor petrol-bombing churches, the Islanders became obsessed with the imminent danger of anaemia, convinced that it was the fastest path to pack your child in a little box off Lynemouth Bay. The danger of the disease also furnished them with ample opportunity to visit the fishmonger's, which the late Stansky and now his son, Arthur, both handsomely presided over, in order to get their store of protein. But the only thing in their blood was a persistent and inter-generational hysteria, which brought down men and women who, in their previous lives, had brought down the sturdy brick walls of churches.

Further rumours circulated in the early sixties that the *Saviour* was taking back to England the very worst cases, for blood transfusions, in English hospitals. Rumours followed of patients fed up on pork chops and gammon. They said that to think of England was to teach a man despair;

to think of meat, suicide. But people talked in the square, outside Stansky's, working out if they could get back to England on the boat, for this was the decade when the boredom had crept in, when the age of the revolution was well and truly over, and the Islanders had to live within the bounds of their freedom.

The Island children didn't have the same hang-ups, they hungered for nothing, the taste of meat never once having passed their lips.

And though the craze for meat fizzled in the middle of that decade, the fear of anaemia never left them. When people died of heart failure, like Mrs Page, a rumour always spread that it was the anaemia that got them, even if they'd been the most loyal customers of Arthur Stansky. Mrs Page had had the spoon-shaped nails and yellow under-eyes and pale skin that had sent the rumour mill going, but she had died of a heart attack, last week, pure and simple.

Still, it was a bad mother who kept a household without fish.

Tonight's dinner, in the Malraux house, had been a grand feast, one Nathaniel hadn't been used to. For the months of eating tatties and turnips, Nathaniel would never have allowed himself to dream of this meal of bream.

Mammy Malraux was a wonderful cook, and it seemed to make her happy. He only wished she would do it more. The way she sat, smiling to her ears, when she saw him eat, he wished he could see that face more. It was a kind of joy that would stop a clock or crack the flagstones. She had looked awful sad of recent times. She always grew more melancholic in winter. But tonight she had even asked him to move the table into the parlour, so that they could sit at the chairs and not in front of the television. On the mantelpiece, Jack grinned down from the photograph.

Nathaniel ate as if he had not eaten in days. His mother watched him, her blue eyes (like his own, he knew) fixed on him. At one point she looked at him, panicked, and then looked at the bream. It was her first bite of the fish, but when she swallowed it looked painful, as if it had been a mouthful of bone. 'It's hard, aye, for me, this fish.' She prodded its side then dropped the fork noisily. Her pale yellow cardy bagged until her wrists. 'I can't eat. Because what if. Oh.' Her eyes flitted to the photograph of his da. Then she composed herself, and gave a weak smile. 'Don't much fancy it. Not tonight. But you go ahead. You eat. Have mine.' She slid her plate over to him and then rested her cheek on her fist. 'My good boy, isn't that right?' She ruffled the short spikes of his hair with her palm. 'My good bald boy, aye?'

And he swatted her away and said, 'Ma!' but that was the thing: she made his heart a rollicky softness when she spoke to him like this. He'd like his mam to put her arms about him; she squeezed his hand across the table. He felt a little bad, because he'd banked on her lack of appetite, and banked on her portion being available for Sarah. In fact, he'd even eaten his whole plate, so sure was he that his ma would eat nothing. 'That I am, Mammy M.'

'And you've got nothing to do with this gang?'

'No, Mam, I told you. Don't believe a word of what Mrs Kilman was saying. She's only out to get me since I stopped using the launderette.'

'Oh.' Margaret was surprised. 'Caro didn't say that. She said you were in last week.'

'Nope. Haven't seen her in a month. Thought I could do my vesties better myself, and she took exception to that. She's nursing the slight, that's all, and she probably misses the,' Nathaniel stopped, searching for the right word, 'revenues.'

'Ah,' Margaret said, softly laughing, in a sad sort of way. 'I see. I see. Caro didn't mention that. No, she didn't mention that.' She looked again at the photograph of Jack. The cockatoo grinned with birdish menace. 'Nathaniel, love, will you do something for me?'

'Aye, Mam, anything, anything you ask.' He would, he would, he'd drop off Lynemouth Bay if she asked him!

'Will you put that bird in the bin?' She tipped her head toward the china on the mantelpiece. 'I'm sick of it looking at me.'

'Aye, Mam, of course. I've never much liked it myself.'

In the kitchen, Nathaniel put his mam's portion in a roll, spreading it with a thick yellow layer of margarine. Nothing could beat a fish sandwich and he bet Sarah would be sore for it. He wondered when she'd last eaten something proper; and he wondered what this bream might win him.

He considered telling his ma the truth – that he was off to see a girl – but she wouldn't believe him and would assume he was out with the boys. Besides, it was only for the hour, just to give the girl a fright to her gilly-high shoes, before he'd back off and be sweet to her. He needed to know, definitively, that her story was no fib. So he could eventually tell the boys. And reassure himself, that he was bedding no Godly girl.

His mam was snug now, in front of the telly, and he'd

done the washing up like the good son he was to her. 'I'm off to the garage, now,' he said, and she nodded, gently, as he slipped out of the too-hot house.

Nathaniel walked east, over Marley Hill, and then skirted round past Mrs Richards', where he ducked down and walked close to the hedge lest she should crab him for last night. He smacked his lips of the left-over fish oils; rubbed them up a bit to make them soft as if it were Pomade Divine they had been treated with. He could still taste the dinner on his lips. A perfume of a most peculiar character: Essence de Bream. He took the scree carefully down the hill, lit a cigarette, caught something, some dead mushroom now slimed to the bottom of his boot, and scraped it off on the side of the pavement. The slow cadence of the Sound coming up from the shore was a winter music to his ears.

Aye, he had decided to act tough with Sarah tonight; give her a bit of a fright, and smoke out the lie if it was there. If she was spying, he'd discuss it with Jake: he would share the news reluctantly, but he needed another boy's ear to bend on this. It was too important to keep to himself. It was his duty, he supposed. What rotten luck if a cherry such as this one was a spy for English soil! A rotten lot, indeed.

When he reached the row of empty houses he paused to catch his breath; he'd come at quite a jog. The last house, at the end of the road, looked threatening to fall into the sea. All around it looked marshy and habitually overgrown, as if it had been built on waste-ground. It would be a wicked place, devilishly cold, in this month of November.

*

In the bedroom, the girl was all soft snorting rhythms, a small shape in the corner. Asleep, at nine o'clock! This Island must tire her English eyes.

The room was dark but he saw that the clothes had been tidied up since he'd glimpsed the room this morning. This, he approved of; he would have never treated his vesties like that, casting them about as if she took no care of her possessions. Before waking her, Nathaniel looked for maps or notes or photographs or anything that might give the girl away as a spy. There was nothing but clothes and the last of a loaf.

He had expected her to wake, but her breath was steady and her eyelids still closed. Her hair was all coppers and rusts. Her mouth was open, and he saw how her lips were lined white before the freckles started. The boy crouched down to her. He wanted to put his hand on her skin to see if it put out the lovely warmth that all girls seemed to have. She breathed softly, like an infant.

But he stood suddenly, as if her breath was rank, remembering himself. This girl was English. It was very likely she had come on some mission to spy on them. He thought of his da drowned in the flimsy English boat. Aye, the Island could never be second to a girl, even if she was a cherry such as this. He nudged her shoulder with the tip of his boot. Half-asleep, her eyes darted about the room in panic. 'What?'

'I brought you some food. Tea. Here.' Nathaniel switched on the light and saw that the rucksack, with the knife, was by the sink at the corner. 'Drink some tea.' Sarah sat up, blinking against the hard light. Her face had lost some colour. *Oh, Sarah*, he thought, *you're to be frighted tonight, and though it is for your own good, I'd just as well do this to my own mam.* Nathaniel poured the tea into the top of the cap and handed it over. 'Is that a uniform?' she asked him, her breathing louder, pointing with a finger. 'You were wearing it this morning, too.'

'Part of a group I'm in.' He ledged himself at the sill; the glass, at his back, was cold.

'Are you part of a police? I've heard there's a police here, and that they dress in strange clothes.'

'Part of the police, in a way. We police the Island, that's true.'

'For what?'

'For English spies. For people who want us to join back with England.'

'And there are people like that, here?'

'Oh, aye. Of course. People are bored of being alone. They want back into God's land. And the English want us back, too.'

'I don't think the English care.'

'What? Of course they do. We're a threat. And they've set up a network of spies on the Island in order to convert people. And with each prayer they send out, each hand they hold, each piece of scripture they read, they're building up the Church in their minds. Until the whole Island will tip back to the old way. And if the Islanders go back to faith they'll want union with England, and we'll all be lost!' Sarah leaned her head against the wall, looking at him. Something curiously blank about her blue eyes. Like his, perhaps. 'Oh, aye, you can never be too careful. See, what if they sent an Englishman who they *said* was part of the Movement, but really worked for the government? What if they were tricksier indeed, and they planted a girl who no one would suspect?'

The expression on Sarah's face didn't change.

Nathaniel stepped from the sill and took the fish sandwich from his satchel. He kept his eye on the bag by the sink. He came close to her, her head near the ball of his knee, the roll offered in his palm. She didn't take it, and her mouth was flat. He gestured a little with his wrist. She stared, sightlessly, somewhere in front of her. Perhaps he had crabbed her at the heart of the lie and she would now confess everything. But he knew she would not refuse the food and a moment later she reached up for the roll.

Nathaniel went back to the sill where the branches drubbed the glass. They didn't talk for a while as Sarah ate the buttered bread and bream, and she washed it down with tea. 'I went to the museum,' she said. 'I know what went on. I saw the pictures; I know what the Unrest did to your families.'

'Aye.'

'It was sad. Very sad. What happened. What the English did.'

'What you did.'

'No. Not me. Not my family.' She threw the foil to a corner of the room. 'My family have been just as broken by the Unrest. You read the article, so you know what my mum did for you.'

'Tell me it's not a lie, Sarah.'

Her blue eyes were as cold as the sea and just as sad. 'I told you. I told you the truth. I'm looking for her, for Laura Wicks. Nothing else. I promise.'

And it felt as if his heart were pure about to break its banks, so sure was he of her sincerity.

'Bet you were hungry?' he said, warmth now coming into his voice.

'Starving.' Sarah stood and stretched, and went over to the bag. He tensed, but she brought out the pack of cigarettes again and offered him one. With a match she lit his and her own. 'We tend to eat meat, back home, me and my dad.'

'Oh,' he said, 'my ma talks of that.'

'You don't have meat here, do you?' She leaned against the sink.

'Oh, no. Just the fishes. I'nt a finer thing than a fish, when you want that.'

'So you've never had pork? Or beef?'

'If it's not of the wet, I've probably not had a taste.'

'It must be strange. This Island. To live here.'

'No. I don't know anything else, it's not strange to me,' he said. 'Tell me of your ma, now. Tell me more of the story.'

Sarah tapped her ash into the sink. She observed herself in the glass, somewhat warily, then watched his reflection. 'When I was seven, my mum left. She was having an affair, Dad said. He said she'd run off with another man. For months I asked if she was coming home, if we could go and visit her, but my dad always said no. Looking back on it, I suppose, knowing what I do, it was an odd situation. People don't just disappear like that: there are arguments, and angry telephone calls. But Mum just disappeared.

'When I was a teenager, maybe thirteen or so, I began asking the neighbours about her, but there was a wall of silence. No one in the village remembered her, or they said they didn't know her, or they said they had lived somewhere else when Laura lived in Trimdon.'

'Your town?'

'Aye. My town. There's hardly any family on my mum's side and the ones there were wouldn't talk anyway. When I pushed Dad on it, he said he'd found love letters, and correspondence, but he said he wouldn't show them to me, said they were private, which I understood. I didn't really even want to see them. He said Mum and her lover were in hiding, because the Church wouldn't let them live openly, which would explain why we couldn't contact her. And so I accepted the story, I couldn't provide another explanation. And either way, Mum was gone, and I couldn't do anything about it.'

'And then?'

'And then I found out about the fire. Last week. I was down in the cellar. Our boiler, it makes this noise, the pipe's loose. I went down to fix it, but I lost my footing and fell and lost a slipper.' A weary smile. 'Who would've thought that losing a slipper might get you here?

'Anyway, the shoe fell between the boards and I couldn't reach it. It was too dark for me to see. So I took a broom and it pushed against a box. A shoebox. Just a normal shoebox, but it was sealed with tape.' Sarah lit the next cigarette with the one she was smoking and paused, pulling her fingers against the enamel of the sink. The wind outside was less fierce, now, against the glass. She coughed, and then continued: 'I didn't look inside. Instead, I made dinner. It was pork medallions, with apple sauce, but I bet you have no idea of what that is, do you?'

The boy shrugged.

'Later that night, I read the article, about my mum, and the church fire. I couldn't believe it. There was my mum's name: Laura Wicks, and her photograph, calling her a terrorist. A murderer. All this time I thought she was off making families with someone else. And there she is, on the front page, a political dissident.'

'Aye. Go on.'

'I didn't say anything to my dad. Not a word. Instead, I went to the archives up at Newcastle. I tried to find anything I could on her. Anything that would give me an extra clue. But I came to a dead end. I read deportation lists and prison lists but I couldn't find her name anywhere. I was about to give up. Then I found this.' Sarah bent over to her bag again and brought out another folded piece of newspaper. She handed it over to Nathaniel.

He held it out and looked at the photograph, brow furrowing. 'What's this?'

'That's her. The one in the middle, on the last boat here.'

'But there's no mention of her. Nowhere that names her.'

'Do you think I wouldn't be able to recognize her?' she snapped. 'That's her. I'm sure of it.'

'But it was ten years since you last saw her!'

Sarah snatched the paper from his hands. 'It's got to be her. Or else where can she be?' She was desperate-sounding, now, and knew it. 'They must have missed her off a list. Mistakes were made. Things happened so fast. She's got to be here. She isn't anywhere else.' Nathaniel came over to where Sarah stood at the sink. He moved some hair from her face and put it back to the gingery mass. Her eyes welled. 'I miss her,' she said, then, 'Sorry,' even quieter.

What empty houses they lived in, he and Sarah both! Here she was, one parent down, just like himself. He felt a stabbing bit of grief for his da, who had deserted him too, but not half as willingly. Then he got lost a bit thinking about his mam and how she had pushed the plate of fish over to him, patting his hand, unable to eat. He was about to bring Sarah closer when he saw her eyes slide to the bag and the knife.

He dropped his hand from her face.

'Aye, well, I haven't heard of Laura. But, as I said, people don't go out, people get scared, people stop in away from the sea.' He remembered his specific resolve to lay it on mean so that he could test her. What kind of Island boy would he be if he didn't have it in him? And what kind of Malade? He put his hands to her jaw and cupped her face. 'Or maybe your ma got so sick of the Island she threw herself to the Sound.' He laughed. 'You never know. Whether it's us who're full of the fishes or them that are full of us. Ha!'

Sarah looked up at him, her eyes flashing. Her cheeks too had that red rush to them, just the same as when he'd seen her this morning. 'And this mother story,' he said, 'I don't know. Could all be bollocks, aye, Sarah Wicks? Maybe she's in England making house with her fancy man. Have you considered that? That she may actually be fucking this man!'

'But the photo—'

'Who cares about the photo? There aren't even any

names underneath it! Who knows why you're here!' Suddenly he took a boot to whatever he could find, kicking over a plastic chair by the mattress, then stamping about a bit, mad with the thought that she might have made her grief up. 'Could all be a right load of bollocks, aye, Sarah Wicks!'

His breath was ragged now as he calmed himself. 'I shan't tell the boys of your being here, yet. But I wouldn't push it.'

Nathaniel had given her the bit of terror, as he had intended, but he didn't feel good for it, as he normally did after a bit of the scrap. Oh, but it was problematic, aye, the possibility of love with an English girl! As if embarrassed, he turned away from her and without looking round he said over his shoulder, 'Tomorrow. I'll come back for you at lunchtime. With some food. And as I said: don't talk to anybody.' And then he left without saying goodbye.

14. Maggie

All morning, Margaret had been upset about the bream. She'd barely eaten a mouthful; even watching Nath had been painful. How could she be his mother, cook for him, provide for him, ask him to stay at home, if it took so much energy and grief merely to make him supper?

For the past few days she'd barely got up out of her chair for anything more than a meal or the relief of her bowels, watching her boy swan in and out of the house. Knowing he was up to no good, perhaps, but not having the energy, either, to say or do anything. Aye, Caro Kilman was a gossip, and a pain in the neck, but perhaps there was some truth to her words.

It was just after breakfast. Margaret Malraux put a hand to the buttercup syrup then stopped herself. Instead, she walked into the cooler air of the hallway, where the phone was on the trestle mute. In the parlour, where she had sat with Caro yesterday, she twisted the blind so that the light of the day came. The room was not much brightened for it. Under the window were Jack's letters.

Margaret handled the box attentively. She did not do this often, but she was allowed, today, given how upset the fish had made her last night. She sat where Caro had sat, telling her limply of her child, and laid out the piece of paper on her knees. The paper, even flattened, sprang at the folds. She supposed, really, that she shouldn't read this. Not today. Letters were hard. His letters were hard. She supposed, if she were sensible, she should spare herself the pain of all these memories. But the bream had been so difficult to manage, and she wanted merely minutes of comfort.

March, 1977: The Sound

Maggie,

I was sitting here staring out to sea and I thought of you. The sea has been wild these past few days and it has given us no respite. This evening it has finally quietened, and I have the opportunity to write.

The catch has been tremendous, despite, or because of, the storms: the fish have fairly leapt into our nets, so sick are they of the sea below. Mackerel, haddock, even cod; the boat groans with the heavy loads. Whiting comes out of our ears! Peter has insisted we stay out for days further; hence the letter. I won't be home as promised, dearest Maggie, but a few days later; perhaps even a week. I wish it wasn't this way, but there's little I can do, what with the price of fish bringing in such a profit. Surely, they slip into the nets faster than you jumped into bed with me.

There, I was feeling melancholic, and even just writing to you has cheered me. Last night I thought about our first encounter. I don't know why. Sometimes these things transpire from nowhere. It seems to happen when I am at sea: the mind is left to wander, and here I am, with you, in 1951, at the Grand, remembering.

The Grand – that old cathouse, of all places! We were in the great dance hall (do you remember?), when everything was jubilant, and we celebrated every night, that we had, in some way, won the war – though, of course, we hadn't. But the triumph was there, and we were playing up to it: us, drunken, thrilled infidels.

You were drinking, what was it? It must have been gin; as always. You were sitting underneath the great leafy palm in the corner of the room. Your lips were red, I remember, and your dress green; fancy, with a big skirt on it. I remember thinking – this woman, this Margaret Malraux – for I had heard of you, heard about a ferocity that gave you the reputation of a lioness – I remember thinking that you were the loveliest mouse I had ever laid my eyes on.

You didn't hold my gaze for long, but carried on your conversation with your friend. Was it Frieda? I think it was. I said to Verger, should I talk to her? Should I offer to buy her a drink? He told me to take a flower from the vase and offer it to you. And so I did. My heart was in my mouth. I brought out a carnation, snapped off its end, and walked over. I tried to put it in your hair. I was drunk, drunk enough to try such a manoeuvre – I wouldn't have sober, that's for sure – and you turned around and swiftly slapped my hand away.

But then you danced with me. How can I thank you for dancing with me? I, who dance as if always aboard a boat, I should not have dared this, this of all things, to win your heart! It was a foolishness – but you forgave me, and these culpable left feet. Was it a waltz, or a polka? It could have been a jive, for all I knew. You said some words to me. Some words. Maggie, you said your name was, and I thought it the prettiest thing on the whole Island.

Maggie, dancing with you, feeling your head rest against me, you, you were the land of plenty. Even on this tiny island in the middle of the North Sea, which I felt had surely imprisoned me, I felt a sense of boundlessness. When I saw you, I knew I should happily live out my gaol term – a thousand-fold – with you here by my side.

Dearest Maggie. It is growing dark. I will have to stop soon.

It pains me still to leave you, early in the morning, in the darkness, when the sun hasn't even come up yet. I hope you know that. In the summer I close the window, before I leave, to shut out the sound of the sea, for I know you are jealous of it, and I do not wish you bad dreams. But it is good for me to be on the boat, to leave the Island sometimes – it's important to me, and of course you know that. The Island would strangle me if I didn't have a release from it. I find it, occasionally, stifling, and our Godless polemic – well, I have grown tired of it, and I do not care whether my neighbour believes in goats or sheep or flying fish.

At least, out here, on the wide open sea, I am free from all of that – out here, I contend only with the waves. The waves decide on everything I do: when I eat, when I sleep, even when I think about you. I am fastened to them, I suppose; they are my God, if there is one.

Do you see, the sea has made your Jack into quite the

philosopher. Indeed, it has seduced me into so many things – letter-writing, drawing, philosophy – I promise I shan't let it seduce me into its bed. For that, I am yours alone.

The sky! A stab of light has emerged from what I thought was surely night. I wish you could see it. But moments have gone, and it has already disappeared. When I write I feel as if you are here with me now, and I do not want to leave the page. I will see you soon, give a kiss to Nathaniel – I miss you, Maggie.

All my love, all my life,

Jack

Margaret placed the letter back on her knees, putting the first page on top of the second. The fire roared beside her. It was not right to make a habit of this; it was too hard, but November was nearing its end, as it must. And the bream was in her belly. And Jack was in the sea.

Tenderly, she restored the letter to the box. There were more letters there, and they were all beautiful. She shouldn't read these; not too often. They consoled her and saddened her at the same time. Where was the last one he had sent, she wondered, she had put it somewhere for safe keeping and then lost it – if only she could find that last letter, perhaps it might draw these matters of grief to a close!

Footsteps ran down the stairs and she heard the doors bang. There was a faint whistling, a high, chirpy tune. Anxiety flooded her. Margaret snapped up the blinds and wrenched the window from its jamb. It gave with a cracking sound of paint. 'Where are you going?' she shouted to the retreating form heading up Blackett Place.

'Over to Mr Verger's!' and Nathaniel gave her a wave.

Margaret could tell, just from his voice, even yards away, that he was lying. How could fish be the only possibility, and yet be so impossible! Oh, what was she to do with her son!

15. Bloom

Nathaniel was there, at her adopted home, waiting for her, just as he had promised. He sat smoking on the sill, watching the front garden. All bristles and blue eyes, when he saw her he grinned. She felt herself warm under his gaze.

Sarah was glad to be home – she had spent the morning at the woman's house, this time creeping closer to the kitchen and crouching down near the garden wall. Yesterday, she had stayed away, telling herself it was prudent to search the rest of the Island for further possibilities of Laura. As Nathaniel had advised, she had talked to no one, and kept a low profile. And, as she had promised – this time to herself – Sarah traipsed the Island paths in search of another candidate. But everywhere she went, no woman was as persuasive as this one here, and, this morning, she had sat and watched, for hours, looking for all of her likenesses to Laura. But it was cold and lonely, and slightly perverse, she knew, spying on this woman, and it was a relief to be back at home, and talking to someone; no longer hiding.

'Where's your bag, Sarah Wicks?' She took it off and left it by the sink. 'I always have to be careful, you see, of that knife.' From his satchel he pulled out a foil square. 'Come with me,' he said, 'we can go somewhere we won't be seen by anybody else.'

There was not much sun, today, a spoonful or so in the sky. The two walked, mostly in silence, through the purple heather to the edge of the Eastern cliff. 'Down here,' he said, 'we'll be hidden. We won't be seen by anybody.'

The sea was rougher here because of the rocks. They made the waves choppy and big and when the sea came tumbling up toward the beach, and then sucked back, the pebbles made a grinding sound as if they were chains rattling against pavement. There were no houses around the Eastern Bay; only the thinnest stretch of beach could be seen from its cliff-top. 'Keep to the rocks, at the side,' he said. 'We're not supposed to go down here, but at least it'll be private, aye, and there'll be no one around.'

Sarah started footing her way down the rocks. 'C'mon, then,' she said, 'unless you *want* to be seen with an English girl!'

Nathaniel began his way down, but it was made harder by his tight jeans, which hampered his movement, so that she was much faster than him. It was irritating, how quick she was, descending like a topsoil come off in rain, when all he could do was place his boots carefully down the wet cliff face.

Level with the sea, a salty breeze met his face. If they kept away from the sandbar they would be fine. On a rock big enough for two, Sarah ate her sandwich and Nathaniel watched her, cautiously – he thought – so that she wouldn't notice. It was just a marge sandwich; there'd been no more fish left from yesterday night. He hoped she wasn't too disappointed.

Sarah was close enough so that he could feel her jacket against his own. It was surprising, how blue it got underneath her eyes; how orange the lashes were when she looked down to the sand. Dusted in freckles, they were hectic and went purely everywhere. He'd kill to see her angry again, like when she had coloured scarlet earlier on. When he saw her – no, when he thought about her – a warmth rolled in his blood. It was like the time he'd tried his ma's sedatives and felt his whole body go slack and calm but somehow strong; that was how she made him feel. Though she did not, exactly, send him to sleep; or hadn't, anyway, last night.

He sensed an affinity between them, that his empty bits were her empty bits too. But he was annoyed at her too. There was something aloof about Sarah, as if she thought her Englishness made her better than the Island's mob. Still the thought nagged at him, about how he should talk to his boys, of what he should do with her. He couldn't let them see her; not yet. They would assume her to be a spy; as he did; as he had. He imagined Jake placing a punch, and the blood gushing from her nose and lips. But to keep her a secret was somehow to admit her culpability. Still, he'd managed to postpone the meeting tonight, and that had bought him some time.

'Look,' she said, 'over there.' Tiered on the wind, gulls circled at the other end of the beach and wings flapped between the rocks. Sarah stood and started walking, as if she didn't have a fear of anything. Was she so undaunted by anything put in her way? Perhaps this was a very

English trait, as if God watched for every rock you might fall over and gave you a surging sense of confidence.

On her approach a gull launched into the air, its orange claws dangling as it flew. Nathaniel followed her toward the rocks, the wind turning with a foul smell, like a sewage, and it made him nearly bring up a reflux of Mammy's porridge.

Yards away, a fish's black eye stared up at them. The tail was silver-yellow, its body plump. Its gills were powdered in sand and its pink mouth gaped. Further on, there was another fish, its threaded fins striking the air. Sarah nudged it gently, so that you could see its heavy lids and snout flecked in sand.

She kicked it back to the sea, so that slowly, in the tide, it was carried off toward the Sound. The boy and girl watched the floating fish and it made them feel sad, indirectly, about their own lives.

By the rocks the smell was stronger still. All the birds had flown off now but were still close above them. A whole boat-load of fish were sunning themselves on the cold grain. Slipshod over one another, the fish were everywhere, a spill of organs and bones and scale. Some of the flesh had been eaten as far as the spine. A purplish air hung. Their greasy remains reminded him of the bream they'd had last night, and Nathaniel felt he would gromick at merely the thought of it. Razorous teeth grinned upward.

With each swill the Sound tried to carry them off but there were too many for that. 'A bloom,' he said.

'What? What's that?' Sarah looked up at him, then back, surveying the puddled graves. 'What's that, then?'

He pointed way out across the Sound. 'There's a band

of algae out there choking the fish. They can't get enough air, aye.' He walked downward to the water's edge. 'They drowned in the water and then were carried to the shore.'

'It's horrible.'

'Aye,' he said, 'but it happens. The Sound is a nasty business, at times.'

'Is it dangerous?'

'No. I mean. Not really. Just have to fish from the other side of the Island. Go into the Norwegian waters, like. Means less fish for the winter.' He saw in the sea the shadows of things: weeds, and rocks, before the sandbank veered. An uninterrupted stretch, the sea went right out to meet the sky, a line of the horizon jammed in between. Were he to close his eyes, he would know this Island from end to end. It was a grey sea today, bluish under its top. It looked so long, as if it were impossible that land could be found after it. 'My da's boat's out there.'

'He's a fisherman?'

'Was a fisherman. He's dead now.'

'I'm sorry,' she said.

'But this would be where his boat was. Across the Sound, aye, between here and England.'

'I'm sorry,' she said again. 'It must be hard.'

'Aye, well. Can't be changed.' The lump was so sore in his throat he thought he might be about to do the shake-and-heave. What an embarrassment, to be blubbing in front of an English girl! But still the big hot tear came and it came with a sense of weariness and gratitude. 'Sorry. I shouldn't be crying. I'm man enough now to take it. 'Twas a long time ago.'

'How long?'

'I was seven. Nine years ago.'

Neither said much, for the while.

'Thank you, for the food, for the sandwich, last night,' Sarah said. 'I thought you were angry. I didn't know if I would see you again.'

'You were lucky to get the bream, aye. My mam's not in the way of cooking much.'

'She's poorly?'

'No, not that.' It was all he could say and Sarah held his hand. When he brought it to his lips it smelled metallic, like tin. He wondered, again, just what he was meant to do with her. The light, obliquely from the sea, had turned her blue eyes grey. 'Ma doesn't get out much. Not after Da died.'

'Why?'

'She's scared, I guess, though I don't know what of. If I could only get her to move, to go out just a little bit. She sits in her chair all day, day in, day out, and I don't know what to do with her. If only I could get her to move! Just a few steps, perhaps, even out to the garden. But she won't leave, you know. She just won't do it. There's no point in even trying to persuade her.'

Another floating fish came on the next wave, eyeing the sky dreamily, as if lovelorn. Very gently, Sarah picked it up and put it next to the rocks. 'There's so many of them,' she said and they both watched the dead fish for a bit as if they expected something else to happen.

Suddenly, Sarah started to run up the yellow beach, her ginger hair flying in the huge wind off the sea. Her squawks made the gulls go crazy above them. Nathaniel gave chase, trying to catch up with her. They circled back and found themselves at the rocks. He cornered her so that he was very close, maybe a stride or so away. Sarah backed off then stood still and they held each other's gaze. She picked up a fish and thrust it out between them. The slime on it caught in the light. 'Be careful,' she said. You couldn't tell if her eyes were grave or playful.

'I'm more scared of that fish than I am of your knife.'

'I shouldn't be so sure, if I were you.'

The fish flopped, bending backward, and they both laughed, but she thrust it out again, jabbing. Nathaniel ran back a few paces down the length of the beach and then felt the hard pressure of it against his back. It landed with a wet slapping sound and then dropped to the sand. 'You're dead!' he shouted, and he raced back toward her, to the pool of fish, and grasped a fat one by his boot, and immediately threw it at her, catching her neck. Sarah fell dramatically as if she'd been shot and then turned over, belly-up, her laughs ringing out in the big sky.

He lay down next to her on the freezing sand. 'Sorry,' he said, still laughing.

'Aye,' she said, breathing heavily.

'Sarah?'

'Yes?'

'Are you to leave on Monday's boat?'

'Aye,' she said. 'That's the plan.'

'And your ma? You think you'll find her before then?'

'That woman. In the house. I think it could be her.'

Nathaniel cast his mind back to Wednesday night and the blackened kitchen. 'Do you want me to come with you? To see who she is. I'd know who she is, if only I saw her.'

'No,' said Sarah, 'I want to do this alone. I'll ask her in my own time. Tomorrow, perhaps. Aye. Tomorrow.'

'And if it is her, what will you say?'

Sarah laughed a little. 'You know, I don't know. I haven't thought of the questions, yet.'

They lay watching the birds watch them. The sand around them smelled of old seawater; the breakers were close, on the steep beach, not yards away. He imagined the bones of his da washing up on this shore, or glistening in the nets of Arthur's friends as they pulled in the trawl. 'Tell me about England, Sarah.'

'What do you want to know?'

'What it's like. My da used to tell me stories, about where he was from. But my ma won't speak of it; not much anyway.'

'Well, it's bigger than here, and busier.'

'And the Church? What do they do in your life?'

'You go to church on a Sunday. You say prayers at school. You have Bible lessons. You learn about Christ.'

'And you believe in it? All that stuff.'

'I did. And then I didn't. Not for a while. I don't know. When I thought about Mum leaving, it didn't seem to be right; it didn't seem to make any sense. And you? Despite yourself? Despite the Island.'

'No! Never.'

Sarah turned over on her side and rested her head on her palm. 'Never even thought it might be worth your while putting out a word or two?'

'No,' his voice straining here. 'Never. Do I believe in ghosts? Or spirits? Or magic? No. And I don't believe in God.'

Sarah smiled and closed her eyes.

'What's that on your wrist, there?'

She opened her eyes and explored the bruise with her fingertips. 'It's where I fell, on the cellar steps, last week. My lucky wound.'

'Why d'you think your da kept it? The article? I mean, if he'd lied to you all this time?'

'Maybe it was all going to come out at some point. Some grand revelation on my eighteenth birthday. I don't know. I don't know.'

Nathaniel stood, and then helped her up. 'Here, you can have it back,' he said, handing over the sheet from the *Chronicle*.

'Does that mean you believe me?'

'Aye,' he said, nearly managing a laugh, 'but don't push it.' He checked his watch. 'I have to go. Have to check up on my mam. Make sure she's OK. But I'll come back for you. Later this afternoon. Be at Swanscott House, aye, at about four or so, and I'll come back for you then.'

Birds circled overhead, waiting for them to leave. There was a boy, too, up at the cliff edge, watching Nathaniel and the girl at their larks. He wore the epaulettes and scarf and boots of the boy down at the beach, though he wasn't half so handsome, and he left before he was seen by them.

16. At the Malrauxs'

When the Secular Movement came to the Island, it was as
if they vanished from the sight of an eye surveying them.
All it took was the breadth of the sea to dispossess them of
English standards. The new Islanders were disinherited of
God and free to do as they pleased. They smoked and
drank and made love as if everything they did was a fist up
to that surveying eye (though they said they did not believe
in it, aye, this eye). They hated God though they would not
believe in him. They had parties in the bar at the Grand,
drinking, drinking, there was so much drinking in those
days, and couples would shack up in the rooms at the back,
or walk down to the beach to the cold sand and look out
across the waters to an imperceptible England. Those days
were fabulous; if hinged, a little, on a feeling near despair.

The Sound was so long; other land, so far away.

In the sixties things turned quiet; and life returned to
normal, back almost to the way it had been in England. It
had become tiring, and boring, the novelty of being reck-
less, and people settled down to work. The Island became
another little England, with its petty gossip, and harmless
feuds, and small kindnesses, and it might have been England in all but name had the burned-out church not been
left to nature's creep.

Lynemouth Town, was, by the late sixties, a place of ill repute: of dark pleasures, of taverns, and brawls, and brothels, and its bay was the place where the Islanders buried their dead. Most of the Islanders avoided Lynemouth, if they could, lest one might see a leg or limb knifing into the air from the rocks. In 1977, with the second wave of migrants come from an even more evangelical England, Lynemouth Town had done well again, peddling all of its naughty pleasures, but then history had repeated itself, and into the eighties the brothels and bars had emptied as people settled back to ordinary life.

But to Eliza's ma, Lynemouth Town had always been a place of toil and pleasure: where the prostitutes would stop, early in the mornings, and they would drink black coffee and eat the hot sweet rolls just fresh. Eliza thought them all remarkable women, with their thin red lips and arched brows, and she knew that Linda had loved their company too. They talked, with mouthfuls of the hot bread, about the previous night's happenings, while Linda vigorously kneaded some dough for loaf or bagel, and Eliza always felt slightly ashamed, though her ma had given her no instruction not to listen. Then again, her mother probably hadn't imagined Eliza going into the profession, leaving her daughter, as she thought she had done, in the capable hands of Arthur Stansky, fishmonger.

Eliza missed her ma. It didn't look as if time would help this. She had woken this morning and written the word *Linda*, high up near her hairline, and then smoothed the fringe down against her brow, holding back the desire to weep. There was so little to be done. What use mourning on this draughty Island with the sea like a rope around its neck? One lived and one died here. One hoped for respite, often it was absent, and when it did come, with the warmth of a summer's day or a gift of fish, one might believe this was evidence of some felicitous eye keeping care of you. But then the joy soon bottomed out, and life went on, just the same. No, there was not much respite on the Island; not here; not for them.

That afternoon, and all of yesterday, Eliza had been looking for the English girl but once again she had found dark houses, a busy square full of Islanders, and people on the roads, milling about the baker's or Caro's, or down at the pubs, but none by the English girl's description.

Up at the church she saw the breakers of the Sound. Eliza wondered what the iron cross might mean to someone who was not her; what it might mean to the heart of this English girl. This was His station of sacrifice, Eliza knew that much. She sat for a while in its shelter, thinking that if the English girl were feeling homesick, she might come here for some consolation. The Islanders had been wrong to shove so much of faith away, and now they were stuck in the great loll of the sea like dead sailors on a ship. It was pride, nothing else, keeping them from asking the English for more help. They could ask them for more fishing equipment, tools to build more boats, more books for the school. They might order new clothes and furniture. If an extra boat was laid on, a ferry, perhaps, the Islanders could come and go as they pleased. How many lived here? Fifteen hundred or so? All of them – even to think about it made Eliza smile – could re-join the world!

But it was 1986, still too early, and the Islanders still too sore, to hope for this.

There was still a faint smell of carbon, in here, though the church would be about thirty-six years burnt by now. She wondered who had done it, this last act of defiance against England. Eliza put her hands on her knees and cocked her head, as if she were listening to a service. How grateful she would be to hear some words of guidance right now. She just needed someone to talk to. The Sound sparkled invitingly.

On Monday night, watching the girl sneak from the boat, Eliza had imagined talking to her about railways and Walkmans and churches and all manner of English things. But now, Eliza knew that if she found her, she would not ask questions of England, but tell the girl about her own life: of her time growing up here, of her ma's death, of her job at the Grand and as grave-mistress, and she would, finally, unburden herself of the secret of Arthur. But now the hope was lost, since the girl was lost, and what secrets she had were to be kept inside, or written in inconsequential letters on her brow.

By two o'clock she reckoned she would go home. Back to the Grand. Oh, but that hollow little room; those thin little curtains. *Linda.* Linda could at least say, on her deathbed, that she had had a rich life. Her mother had grown up in England and seen America before God had swelled across the globe. At least her ma had stood up for something. Now the Islanders were free to do what they wanted, and they did very little.

Eliza had come all the way round to the school-house; she must have been walking for hours, now, to get from the Eastern Bay to the north tip of the Island. The school-house was empty and a little eerie without the sounds of children. Too cold to carry on, Eliza walked up the hill and along Blackett Place and stopped, seeing Margaret Mal-raux's house.

The blinds in the parlour were closed flat. No slats of light came from within. Poor Margaret, with no Jack to help her with the boy, and Nathaniel such a terror. He was only bored; Eliza knew that, knew that the Island was as much a noose for him as it was for her; knew that he did not necessarily want to frighten, but only to break up the endless grey days. Eliza moved on, but stopped in her tracks.

She remembered, suddenly, the scent of his cigarette, the one he was smoking at Mrs Page's funeral. And the idea came to her with no effort, or forethought, but suddenly it was quite clear what she should do. If Nathaniel got those cigarettes, somehow from the Boatman, perhaps he could . . . Eliza rapped the door. Slow footsteps approached.

Margaret poked her head out from within. 'Oh, dear. I thought you were Mrs Kilman.' She opened the door wider and pulled the shawl closer to her neck. Margaret's blue eyes were sunk but sharp. 'How pleased I am it's you.'

'Hiya, Mrs Malraux.'

'It's been too long, eh?'

'Aye. Sorry about that.'

'Not at all. Not to worry. You look well.'

'As do you.'

'You lie.' Margaret cocked her head toward the living room. 'In with you, now, for a cup of tea, before I catch my death.'

It was just as Eliza had remembered: the brown-dia-monded carpet, the yellowy walls, the telephone on the trestle, the stairs curving to the first floor. In the living room, there were little ornaments all over the place, stacks of magazines and a radio. The cushions of Margaret's arm-chair dipped with the phantom weight. 'Eliza, dear, I hope you don't think I'm rude, can you bear to make the tea? My leg is sore and I can't stand on it.' Margaret dropped her-self into the chair with a sigh. Her breath came out rattled.

'Of course.'

In the kitchen there were tea stains on the counter-tops and rusty lids on tin cans and a smell of grease from the cooker. Crumbs gathered about a toaster, which was prob-ably as old as Eliza. Limescale flecked the kettle's insides and Eliza washed it out at the sink and put it to the boil. Everything – the floor, the spoons, the glassed cupboard fronts – had a slight tackiness to it, as if something sweet had spilled, and no one had bothered to mop it up. Eliza made the tea, giving the kitchen a bit of a clean as she went.

She brought Margaret her tea and took her own mug to the armchair opposite. She wondered if this was where Nathaniel sat. 'How are you, dear? Are you well? You look peaky,' Margaret said, steam curling around her nose.

'Fine. A little worn-out.'

'Aye. Work does that to you. How are you coping?'

'All right. It's hard sometimes.'

'Of course. Well, we all have to work. Until you get to my age, I suppose.'

'What did you do? When you were younger?'

'I worked at the herring station, but not for long. Jack

brought in more than enough, so I stopped that, as soon as I could.' Margaret looked down at her lap. 'My hands are still a little yellow from it, you know.' She tittered and then said again, 'And Jack brought in more than enough.'

'Of course,' said Eliza, 'of course.'

On the mantelpiece was a bell Eliza bet had been stolen from the church. Surely Nathaniel would be home soon. Margaret lit a cigarette and Eliza pretended not to notice. 'How's Nathaniel?' she said.

'Keeping out of trouble. Just. Do you know anything about this gang?'

It was then that Eliza fully understood what she was to do, otherwise she would have sat there and said yes, I know about this gang, she would have said that they had crabbed her on Monday night. She would have said: your son is a good-for-nothing, Mrs Malraux, and you should intervene before these larks turn into something terrible. But to say that would not help herself whatsoever, in what she had suddenly come here to do, and so, without hesitation, Eliza said, quite boldly: 'No. What gang?'

Margaret sighed. 'Mrs Kilman was in here yesterday telling me tales of this gang, that Nathaniel is the ringleader, and is leading them all into trouble. I said he's an Island lad, he's bored; he gets up to mischief. They shouldn't be so hard on him. They don't know what it's like. She doesn't even have any kids, so how would Caro know how they're meant to behave? And on this Island, of all places. They're bored, these boys, just a wee bit bored, and causing mischief.'

'Aye, of course. Of course. It's probably just games. It will pass, I'm sure. A phase, merely.' The tea was steaming in her hands and though Eliza had been cold all day, traipsing along countless roads in search for the lost girl, she was now intolerably hot. Perhaps this is what pushed Nathaniel to crabbing people, this great swell of heat. She removed her coat. 'And he's not mentioned anything? Of anyone?'

'No, should he have?'

'No, not at all, not at all,' said Eliza. 'But you know Nathaniel, always knows the most about Island gossip!'

'Aye, aye, I suppose,' said Margaret.

'Where is he now? Nathaniel. Is he around?'

'No,' Margaret said, her eyes drifting back to the telly. 'But he'll be back soon. He promised me that.'

Eliza ventured: 'I grew up here. It was hard. There's not so many children of your own age. Not many things to do. He'll turn out fine.' She was surprised at the finesse of the lie. 'He's just got extra energy and he doesn't know what to do with it.'

'Aye. That's exactly it.'

'Boys have so much energy,' Eliza continued blandly. 'If it's not girls then it's just some other trouble.' Margaret's eyes were now fixed on the set. It might be easier to do it like this, to catch her off-guard. 'These cigarettes, though, do you know where he gets them from?'

Margaret stared down at the one lit in her hand. There was something almost merry about the way she said it: 'Will you not tell anyone?'

'I shan't tell a soul.'

'He swaps them with the Boatman, for my pills. Oh, it is a naughty affair, but one that won't harm anyone, aye.'

'And what pills are they, now, Mrs Malraux?'

'Sedatives. They just make you sleepy, and so you can't

think about things. I get them at the doctors in Warkworth. But a cigarette's better, doesn't make you so tired after.'

Eliza laughed; so, it was as she had assumed. 'Very entrepreneurial of him. Very.'

'Aye. I know. A very entrepreneurial boy. He's a good lad.'

Margaret put out the cigarette and raised the volume of the television. She began to nod off. If Eliza did not do something this would be her, in forty years' time, dozing off, next to the fire, unable to hold or finish a conversation. Margaret would sit here like this, for thirty more years, this human engine covered in fat. Eliza did not want to grow old and alone on this Island. She could not allow it. If Nathaniel had this connection to the Boatman just as Margaret had said, then Eliza would try and use it as best she could. She allowed herself to begin hoping.

Margaret woke with a start, and smiled at her, flicking over a channel. Her jaw she cupped again in her palm. The television babbled. Eliza stood and went into the kitchen. Water spilled over her fingers as she rinsed the cup. Then a door slammed, out front, and then the inner door. The boy. Nathaniel. Eliza felt the cold air brought with him as he came into the warmth of the living room. Eliza's heart started to race. She would have to insist on his secrecy. But what if he told his gang? What if they came after her down one long and dark Island alley, for being a traitor?

'Nathaniel!' Margaret said.

'Hiya, Mam.'

'Did you see Mr Verger?'

'Aye.' Plainly a lie, Eliza thought, from the sound of his voice.

'And you gave him back his book?'

'Aye. That I did, Mammy M. He was right pleased with me.'

Eliza looked in on the room from the space between door and frame. The boy was pink about the chops and his blue eyes were dancing. He was in all that get-up again. He caught her spying; she blushed, and came back into the living room. The boy's eyes slid over her breasts and down her trousered legs. Nathaniel almost managed a blush himself. 'Why, hello, Miss Michalka, I didn't know you were here.' His mother's hands were in his. 'To what do we owe this pleasure?'

Eliza gathered her coat and fiddled with the collar. 'I was passing. You reminded me, on Monday night, that I hadn't seen your ma in a long time. I thought I would pop in.'

Without missing a beat the boy replied: 'Very kind of you.'

'Aye,' said Margaret. 'We had tea. Did I doze off now?'

'Aye. But I was beginning to as well. It's very warm in here.'

'Oh. I don't feel it. My feet are always cold.' Margaret wiggled her stockinged feet in the airless room. 'The toes are near purple in the winter. That's why I have the fire on. Because I don't feel it. The warmth.'

'Well, I think it's best I'm off now,' Eliza said.

'I'll see you out,' he said.

'Good afternoon, Mrs Malraux,' Eliza put out her hand and held Margaret's fingers, and they were indeed cold, just as she said. 'You keep well,' she said to her, although by now Eliza realized this might be the last time she would ever see her.

'Aye. Goodbye, duckie.'

Eliza squeezed her hand. Linda used to call her that.

Nathaniel's step was close to hers as they walked into the hall. 'You know you're welcome any time, any time, now.' He helped her on with her coat. 'Though best when my ma's asleep,' and he gave her a squeeze of both shoulders. He glanced up toward the second floor. 'Or I could visit you at the Grand? At your invitation, of course,' he laughed. 'I'm not a boy to pay for these wares.'

'Right.' Eliza smiled tightly. 'Can I have a word with you? Outside?'

Nathaniel opened the door and waved her on.

A cold skiff rose from the Sound but it was a welcome blast. Someone had gritted Margaret's pavement in the hope that she might ever move outside. There was no one on the road but still Eliza lowered her voice, and she came a little closer to him. 'Look, Nathaniel, your ma told me how you get these cigs.'

'And?'

'Well. What I'm saying is this.' Eliza cleared her throat and did not quite know where to start. It was imperative that he would agree and fundamental, therefore, that she said it in the right words. 'You exchange those pills for cigarettes, am I correct in thinking this?'

'Yes.' The boy surveyed the road. 'But it wouldn't be to your advantage to start spreading that, ken?'

'No. I realize that.'

'You didn't say nothing to my ma?'

'Nothing. Only what your ma told me. She knows you're using her pills, but that's it.'

'Aye. And she's a good woman who deserves a few good things. A few cigarettes will harm no man.'

'Aye. Aye. Right.' Eliza dipped her head toward him. Her heart felt fair near her throat but all she thought was: *I cannot end up like Margaret Malraux! Nor like my own mam!* 'But what I'm saying is this, Nathaniel. If you get these pills on the boat, then maybe you can get me on it too? Can you have a word with the Boatie? Get me on Monday's boat, sweet man.'

The boy's expression switched rapidly from astonishment to anger: he seemed affronted, as if she had insulted him. 'I am not in the business of getting people off the Island.' His voice was stiff. 'This Island is a place of beauty. Plenty! You have more than enough here.'

'I need to leave. I want to leave. I need to leave before I go mad here.'

'You'd be leaving us; me.'

'I know. I know.'

'Why? Why go?'

'Because I want to go somewhere that isn't here.'

The muscles in his jaw moved. 'Why?' he said at last. 'This freedom's a hard thing to ape. You won't get that in England. The land of God and Fury.'

Eliza thought of Margaret Malraux dozing near the fireplace. She thought of Mrs Page's coffin sliding into the waves. She thought of Arthur's face, and Mrs Bingley's, when they saw who was walking into the fishmonger's. 'Because I am unhappy here,' she said, looking squarely at the houses opposite. 'Because I don't have any friends, and I'm lonely. Because I'd like to see some place that isn't here, and talk to people not from here.'

'If you're lonely, doll, I'm here.' He hooked a thumb on the belt of her coat, pulling her closer. He smelled of soap and cigarettes; she saw his face, round and lovely: a thug and a beauty both.

Eliza disentangled herself. 'No,' she said, quietly, 'I need more.'

'And England? *England?* You want to go there? Why?'

Eliza shrugged. 'Because there's nowhere else to go, of course. I just want to get out of here.'

'Not this week. I've got a lot on my mind, doll.'

'But then the fogs will come. There's no other boat till spring. I can't wait that long. I'm scared of what I might do.' Eliza put her hand on his jacketed arm, stroked up and down a bit. 'I'm desperate, Nathaniel, you've got to help me.'

The boy sucked the air between his teeth. He warmed his fingers on his breath and then stuck them in his pockets. They did not speak for a while, then he said, 'It will cost you. I shan't do this for free.' He narrowed his eyes, calculating. He cleared his throat. 'If I get you passage on that boat, I want fifty pounds. At least.'

'Pony!'

The boy licked his lips. 'How much do you have?'

'Forty. And that's what's left of my ma's money.'

'Well,' he smiled, 'I'm sure you'll enjoy your winter to come.' The boy made a little bow and made to go inside.

'Forty-five! That's all I can offer. The Grand is quiet. I don't even know how I can make that. Only a few punters come any more. But I can try.'

'Then try you must. If it's there, the full fifty, you've got a place on Monday's boat. I can guarantee it. If not, get used to it; you won't be leaving. At least, not till next spring.' At this, he smacked a large wet kiss full on her lips. 'Won't charge me for that, will you?' And then he turned his back on her and shut the door, right in her face.

17. Jakob Lawrence

The summer of '86 had been warm. Jake and Nathaniel had spent each day building sandcastles and swimming in the sea. For the whole warm week they didn't stop larking about on the beaches, as if the summer had untied them from the imperative of being men, and the creamy wash of the Sound was lovely on their skin. They knew they were acting too young for their age but they enjoyed it even more because no one was there to observe and criticize. They weren't the Malades, then, and Nath wasn't the chief; and they didn't have the costumes, nor the cigarettes, nor the scalped pates. And in the sky the Northern sun was like a burst yolk. It was a very happy week and Nathaniel treated Jake with so much care.

One day, it was the best day really, Jake and Nathaniel were fishing with stick and bent pin and raw limpets at the bay. The rock pools that summer were busy with buttercrab and stickles and the most enormous amount of seaweed. When the boys failed to catch anything they started making castles, swiftly kicking them over, sending the sand exploding into the scorching air. They bronzed all afternoon. Heat was everywhere. By the end of the day they were pink.

As night fell late, they left the beach, with their towels slung over a shoulder, wearing knitted jumpers against the cool, heading over to the Malraux house. Warming up by the fire and licking their lips of salt, Mrs Malraux fed them margarine sandwiches and cups of tea with a topskin of milk. She fussed about so much Jake thought she was lovely and was allowed to call her *Mammy M*. And then she brought out some ginger nuts she'd been saving just for wee Jake and Nathaniel on a day such as this.

In summer, darkness came at midnight.

They were like brothers, that night, Jake and Nathaniel, and Mrs Malraux fussed over them as if they were both her sons. And Jake talked to old Mammy M, and told her how he was doing at school, and she said what a grand pair of boys they both were. It wasn't half as good as Jake's house, what with there being no rollmops, but being around Mammy Malraux herself more than made up for this.

But after that summer, Nathaniel changed. He started acting queer, visiting the museum a lot. At the start of school, in September, he brought Jake up to the nook on the west side of Marley Hill, pointing with his finger at the space he thought his da's boat kept under the waves. They came back again and again after school, to this place, Nathaniel talking of his da's death as if the English had murdered him with that boat.

Nathaniel harked on and on about how his ma was forced here, and made Mammy M tell the boys over and over how her family had been served with their deportation papers – as if she was any different from anyone else! Nathaniel started to talk about English spies, a network of them, operating on the Island at a buzzing frequency you couldn't quite hear. It scared Jake, the pictures he'd drawn, of English boats coming over and planes passing and dropping bombs. Nathaniel called it a crusade. He said it would happen if they didn't act soon. And so they had formed the gang one night after school, the Malades, for the protection of the Island.

The garage was very dark, that September night, when they first did it. Half-filled jars lined the shelves with nails and stops and hooks and hundreds of other things Jake didn't know the names of. There were smells of turpentine and solvents. This was a place indeed for a man like Jack Malraux.

Jake did Nath's scalp first. They spread out newspaper under their boots, and watched the shorn float down, big tufts of it, until Nath's scalp was completely bald. 'We'll get rid of them now, Jake. Any Englisher or spy on this Island. My da's memory deserves it, aye.' Nath then started off around the curve of his ear, and Jake laughed because it tickled with those trailing fingers and the buzz of the razor. He wriggled like a fish but Nathaniel didn't mind. He supposed Nath was the first Malade, officially.

When they came out of the garage Mammy M gave them what for and they stood there guffawing as she gave them slaps over their scalps for being so daft. But really she had no true idea of what being a Malade was about. Neither, it seemed, at times, did her son.

Nathaniel was nowhere to be seen tonight. Old Baldie Boots had cancelled the meeting, showing up at Jake's house this morning, saying he was poorly. He was probably at home, agog with Verger's book. It should be Verger for tonight, and Nathaniel knew it. It was just like Nathaniel to deem who was and who wasn't a spy, given some crazy rubric only he knew how to read. It wasn't fair. That was probably why he'd bottled it tonight, scared that Jake would choose Verger as the next target, and Nathaniel wouldn't have the balls to disagree with him in front of the lads. Well, he would see about that.

Jake squatted among the rocks, in the shadow of Warkworth pier, where the wind couldn't get such a lick on him. He watched Sammy ahead of him, skipping pebbles, and he watched Sammy's jacket, making sure the sea didn't get to it. Jake thought himself a kind boy, one who would do this type of thing for his friends. Sammy walked up toward the rocks and sat down beside Jake, closer than he would have thought necessary, since there was so much length to the beach.

'I have something to tell you, Jake.'

'Oh, aye?'

'Something important,' he said. 'D'you have a cig?'

'You know only Nath has those.' The boy sighed and looked uncomfortable, biting his lip and worrying at his shoelace. 'Out with it, then.'

'I saw something.'

'What?'

'I saw Nathaniel with someone, this morning. A girl.'

'From school?' Jake's heart began to race. 'Was it Charlotte?'

'No. That's the thing. She wasn't from school.'

'Eliza, then?'

'No. No. Not Eliza.' Jake's relief was palpable. 'You don't understand,' Sammy said, digging at a furrow of sand, 'I've never seen her before. Never in my life.'

'Oh, aye, and how can that be?'

'Dunno,' Sammy said. 'But I swear to you she's a stranger to me. But not to Nathaniel.'

'Go on, then.'

'They were walking along the bay, the rough one down at the eastern end. Calm as anything. I thought I could smell a bloom, and I wanted to have a looky. That's when I saw her – the girl, and Nathaniel, walking along the beach. I can't fathom where she's from. A grozzly girl like this, and I mean a real grozzly: she's a cherry! And there she was, larking about the bay with Nathaniel, and she was laughing all the time, and he was looking dead syrupy for her.'

'Who is she?'

'No idea, as I've said.'

'And then what happened?'

'So I followed them. At a distance, like, so they wouldn't crab me. And I followed her, and her lovely carroty hair, all the way to one of those houses, the empty ones near the eastern cliff.'

'Aye, aye. The row of them?'

'Aye. Called Swanscott House.'

'So where d'you think she's from?'

'She's not from here, that's for sure. I've never seen her at school. Nor down at the square nor down at Lynemouth. And no new boat has come with another family, has it?'

'No.' Jake scratched his scalp. He smelled onions on himself from dinner. 'I don't know. Perhaps a new family's come, maybe, in time for school starting again next week?'

'Nah! We would have heard of it.'

'P'raps she was on Monday's boat, come over from Newcastle!' Sammy's eyes were wild. 'An English spy! A missionary come over the waters to turn us Malades back!'

Jake laughed. 'Do you think so? And how would she have got on Monday's boat, then, clever clogs?'

'I don't know. Maybe she bribed the boatman, or sneaked herself into the hold. Whatever. All I know is she's not from here.' Sammy leaned closer toward him. 'And she's a cherry, or did I tell you that already?'

'Yes, Sammy, a "grozzly", as you said. What happened after that, after they got to the house?'

'I hid behind the hedge for a while. Maybe an hour or so, just watching them, like.' He coughed. 'Nothing much happened; they were just chatting, at the old chin-wag, like old friends, though he's never mentioned her before. So, you see, I don't know what his game is. She's a secret, if he hasn't mentioned her, and that makes me think, what if she is? What if she is truly English? Or what if she were a stowaway, even, forbidden cargo on Monday's boat? I wonder what we might do to smoke Christ out of her! I didn't know whether I should say anything, like, seeing as Nathaniel's the chief.'

'Nathaniel's not the chief. That's never been established.'

Sammy stood up suddenly. His bald head bobbed in the dark and his eyes looked the same inky colour as the sea. 'Let's see her now! Bet she'd like a bit of Malade, wouldn't she? Bet she's bored of English boys! Bet she's come to the Island for a sort-out! Couldn't find any slug' – at this he grasped his crotch – 'and wanted some of ours. I'd give the carrot some of what she wants, sure I would.'

He began to sing, crooning to the Sound, wheeling round and round.

> *Oh lovely, my peacheroo,*
> *Open up, see what I can do;*
> *Miss Carrot, open up the leafies,*
> *And let my Slug through.*

'Oh,' Sammy shouted to the brilliant dark, 'she is all ginger-fizzed loveliness!'

'Aye, aye,' said Jake, laughing.

'Shall we go and have a looky? Then we can tell the boys about it tonight. It's a Friday night – it *should* be a night for the scrap, just as Nathaniel promised. Just because he's getting syrupy with the girl doesn't mean we have to stay mooning about at the beach. Who knows? Maybe we can even have a bite of the crab ourselves.'

'Where's Nicholas?'

'Tucker? Don't know.'

'Is there anyone else we can take with us? In case we need, you know . . . ' Jake searched for the word. 'Reinforcement.'

'They've all stopped in with their mams.'

'Lazy biters. Well. The spoils will just be for us two, then.'

Swanscott House was white in the November dark, like a bone in soil. It rose thinly from the brambles and high grass; a fence hung broken from the hinge. Aside from the waves breaking at the eastern beach the road was quiet. Jake hadn't said anything since they'd left Warkworth Beach. He wondered what it meant if Nathaniel kept a secret like this.

Surely she should be interrogated, and yet here she was, supposedly coddled by the leader of their gang.

Sammy and Jake stood behind the hedge, watching and waiting.

After some minutes, Nathaniel appeared overhead. It was a shock, to see him in this room, though they'd known he might be there. He stood at the window with his hands on the leading looking out. Jake and Sammy giggled, knowing they were both thinking what it would be like to crab him as a spy. Jake wondered if he might find a rock here, and throw it at the window; wondered whether he could clip the cheek of Old Baldie Boots, as he had done Mrs Richards. He could have him for consorting with an Englisher. He only wanted to give the boy a bit of a fright.

Through the leaves, Jake saw the girl appear, rust-coloured about the hair, and freckled, as Sammy had said. He'd never seen her before, at school, nor down at Maiden's Square, and she was too young to be working the taverns or brothels of Lynemouth Town. Aye, he would have clocked a girl such as this. Sammy whispered: 'That's her.'

'I've never seen her before in my life.'

'Nor me.'

Jake's voice was full of longing. His breath clouded as he spoke. 'Oh, she is a cherry!'

'Is she not just?'

Nathaniel and the girl went away from the window; who knew to what long bed they might have descended? To what deep and lovely nest? There was something different about the boy, something darker about the skull. His scalp could do with a razing, that was for sure. The light snapped off though they had not left the room. The boy, in there, with the secret girl, with the light off? It only seemed to confirm that something wrong was going on, that she was a secret to be kept to the shadows. 'And you definitely think she was on Monday's boat?' Jake said. 'Did anyone see her coming off it?'

'No. No one *saw* her come off it – but it doesn't mean she didn't.'

'Aye, I suppose.'

'What's the alternative explanation?' Sammy was whispering and talking fast. 'Why, I know all the doxies on the Island. Stowaway or not, she came off Monday's boat, I'm sure of it. Lest she were washed up to sea in a shipwreck, I don't know. But I've never seen her before on this whole solly Island. I swear it.'

Sammy suggested that they confront him but Jake shook his head, and waved him on down the road. He said that they would ask him about the girl tomorrow at the postponed meeting. 'To crab him better,' he said, 'and in front of the gang.' It was a sorry business, not to be involved in your gang's affairs, and Jake and Sammy left the house with a hump of displeasure.

But Jake's face broke into a smile as he contemplated what they might do next. 'Now we know where he is, he won't know where we are.' Sammy asked what this meant, but Jake didn't answer. Instead they ran over Marley Hill and trotted down westward, where the Norwegian sea was like a big black bowl before them, and where the schoolhouse was silent, waiting for the boys' return on Monday, before they swung into Blackett Place.

*

Mrs Malraux's house looked as empty as Swanscott House. Jake told Sammy to stay outside, and that if he saw Nathaniel coming he was to come in immediately and start talking to Mrs Malraux in a very loud voice, and then Jake would walk into the living room as if he'd just come from the toilet. Mrs Malraux wouldn't know what had happened.

The door gave without a noise. The vestibule smelled of old lino. Jake pushed aside the next door, with the swirls of glass that magnified some bits of the stairs and shrank other bits, then shut it back to. A sound of light snoring came from the living room. Slow and steady under the thick bosom. Jake poked his head round the pane; there Mammy was, and, he'd guessed rightly, completely asleep. He checked the clock above the gas-fire. Nine thirty.

Jake came back to the hall, unsure of what he was doing here. Old Baldie Boots would kill him if he found him here. The peg on the wall waited for Nathaniel's jacket. He'd never been here when that peg held nothing.

Jake took the stairs. Nathaniel's room was quiet and cold. He crept quickly to the chest and opened the lid, rifling through the clothes until he hit the hard boards of the book. Jake had felt sick when he'd first seen these paintings of Christ. To be so *coddled*, he thought, with blurry distaste, to be so *watched*, was as abhorrent to him as his rare imaginings of what went on in England, with its damp and girlish God, and its feeble, pandering folk. Aye, the book only confirmed to Jake how much he loved the Island, with its electric air and dark seas and lightless winters, how little he wanted to do with the old faith.

Immunity? For Verger? Bollocks to that, aye.

Jake shoved the book in his bag and closed the lid of the chest.

Mammy's snores continued from the living room. Jake went cautiously downward. How long had he been here? Five minutes? Fifteen? In the living room, Mammy slept and the clock's long hand had hardly moved. He readied himself to leave, but he'd had so little time to luxuriate in Nathaniel's house alone.

The slat of darkness from underneath Mammy M's room was inviting. He'd never been in there. If Baldie Boots found him, he'd have his guts. He'd kill him. He'd tell everyone he was an English spy, and the boys would be at his throat before he might have a chance to defend himself. But it was there, the room: dark, cosy, inviting.

A sweet smell met him, on entering her bedroom, similar to his own mam's room. Moonlight, cut by the windowpanes, fell on the bedspread. The wadding of the duvet was lumpy, you could tell it was old. Could tell it might have seen a rollicking, all those years ago when Pappy Malraux was about. 'Jack Malraux,' the boy said, and then again: 'Jack,' to the moonlit bedroom, exultant in his sense of ownership in the dead man's room. There was a photograph of Nath's da on the dressing table with some old bottles of perfume and other pictures of Nath acting cutesy, twirling round with his da's ears when he was a baba. Mr Malraux looked a nice man, with that smile, and the fisherman's hands gripping tightly the ankles of his wee boy. And here he was, in Mr Malraux's space. The thought thrilled him in his body: to be like Nathaniel's da, master of the bedroom, and the sea, and his son.

Jake opened the vanity-table drawers. There were folded jumpers and blouses, all pastelly colours of wintry thickness, some looking bobbled and stained. No matter what they said or did, they couldn't get their mothers to dress better. Despite the suits their sons wore with such aplomb, the mothers seemed not to notice, and wore whatever drab thing came to hand, or whatever old English thing they might buy at Buttons.

More blouses yet in the second drawer, but this time he plunged his hands right in, hoping he might catch on to something secret. His hand touched a silky thing and something wiry. It was a beige brassiere; he wished it were black. He could put that in his pocket and use it for something, but he couldn't think what, so he let it go, shut the drawer and opened the third. Yellowing letters and old bills. Mammy M's original identity papers. On a darker paper, in a bold neat print, was the word NON-AFFILIATED; the word that had led them all here. It looked like it was written an age ago. Jake tossed it back to the pile.

He put his hand right down to the bottom, felt the cardboard edge and then there was something else, completely unexpected and cold in his grip. After all of the silks and slips, it felt hard and definite, very foreign to ladies' under-things. Jake turned it over in his hand, then put it to his nose to smell. Peppery, almost, and cold against his cheek. It was squat, littler than he would have thought. Mammy Malraux's handgun, smuggled here over thirty-six years ago; the one she had wanted to use against the English policeman. He might shoot her just to never hear that story again.

The front door banged. Jake stood frozen, with the gun

in his hand and the drawer wide open. Nathaniel's voice in the hallway shouted, 'Mammy!'

Sounds of disrobing. Jake pictured the peg where Nathaniel would hang the jacket. The shout again, *Mammy!*, a little more panicked this time, and then Mrs Malraux saying, *Aye, through here*. A light snapped on in the hall, and then there was talking.

Jake put the gun in the bag, with Verger's book. Crab-like, he edged out of the room, his back sliding along the walls, the diamonded carpet now a mess near his boots. The door was half-open and he saw through to the kitchen: Nathaniel, his back turned, the tensed cotton of his shirt and the 'Y' of the red braces. Jake's heart felt fair near his throat and sweat seemed to spill from him. He moved along the wall not taking his eyes off the boy. He found the gold handle of the inner door.

The outer door closed with no more than a clicking sound. Outside, Sammy was crouched behind the wall, looking sick with nerves. Motioning to him urgently, Sammy ran down Blackett Place, and Jake followed as quietly as he could, not saying a word, knowing how close they had come to the boy's full fury, until they were at Marley Hill. They stopped for breath. Sammy explained something about freezing in fright and being unable to speak the lie he had meant to say, but Jake didn't care. He was too relieved to care.

They went down Marley Hill quickly, their hearts keeping time with their boots. At Warkworth Bay, their lungs felt as if they were bleeding, they had run so fast. And at the cold sand, the air was like iced wedges and the sea was a long black lump with the pebbles grinding the night.

Realizing how close they had both come, Sammy and Jake laughed and laughed as the broad white birds wheeled in the sky.

And then, into the big open night, Jake fired the gun and the bullet went whizzing and his wrist flexed at the power of it and they did not hear the bullet come back down but they laughed and laughed and wiped clean from their minds the sight of Nathaniel and the English girl. They were high on everything they had seen, but more than that, the boys were high on having escaped.

18. A Bath

'Say that again, Mammy?' he said, shouting over to her from the kitchen. Nathaniel wolfed down the marge sandwich in not much more than three bites.

'I said I heard something, in the house.'

'And what was that, Mammy?'

'Something, I don't know.'

Nathaniel wandered into the living room. 'No, no, now, I told you, it was me. In the garage. I'm fixing up Da's garage, remember? Remember I came back this afternoon? After Eliza was here?'

'Aye, aye.'

'And then I went to the garage to do some work. I said I'd be there the whole evening, like, remember?'

'Aye. I forgot. I am daft. Sorry, love.' Margaret smiled, wearily, and switched off the television; it closed with a popping sound. 'It's best when you stay at home. You're a good lad, Nathaniel. Your da always liked being in that workshop. He said he liked the smell of it. It always smelled greasy to me.'

Nathaniel chewed at the next sandwich. Its yellow taste was bland, but he'd been nearly all day with Sarah, and was just about famished for anything. He didn't like to lie to his mam but he could hardly tell her the truth, pent up, as he had been all day, with an English girl.

'And did you get much done?'

'In way of what?'

'Whatever you were doing.'

'Much, much,' he said; and, in a way, he had.

Margaret looked around the living room, her eyes not stopping on anything in particular, then she started to nod along to some thought or other. 'And how about another fish, aye, for next week? Maybe after school Monday? A good feast after your first day back?'

'That would be grand, Mammy M, just grand. I think it's just ace you're back to cooking again. And then, soon enough, you'll be eating all the fish of the sea again. You'll see.'

'A bream? Or a sea bass?'

'Serious?'

'As the day.'

'Aye,' he said. 'A sea bass.'

'Good, well.' Margaret heaved herself up from the seat. 'I'm off to bed. You don't stay up too late. School's starting again on Monday. You don't want to be too tired. You're a good lad stopping in with me on a Friday night. I do appreciate it, son.' She kissed him goodnight.

Nathaniel sat by the fire as he heard his mam in the bathroom: the sound of the flush then the cranking of the taps. He wondered if she would wash her face. He was glad, finally, to be in the warmth. Sarah's house was such a block of ice. *Sarah's house*; those words were now familiar to him. That evening, after the strange little chat with Eliza, he'd brought Sarah over a marge and jam sandwich – it was all he could muster from the fridge – to talk to her, of Laura, and her home, and of England. Hours in, he'd noticed the lilac flush of her skin, and, holding her hand in his, he'd felt how cold she was. He'd smelled, too, a brackish waft from her; she had probably not washed since she had come from England. And so he'd brought her back home. Or had nearly brought her home; all that was stopping him was Mammy Malraux getting into bed.

Nathaniel went into Mammy's room, where the moonlight fell in oblongs on the quilt. He checked Mammy was not smoking in bed. He closed the drawers of the vanity table and then the curtains, so that the room turned dark. He sat with her until, minutes in, he heard the snores comb the air. A dreadful thought came to him, of Mrs Page, still in the casket, and Nathaniel left the room.

In the hall, he could smell everything intensely, as if he were a stranger here: the yellowy smell of nicotine was everywhere; on the wallpaper, on the carpeted stairs, in the mouthpiece of the telephone, in the fibres under his boots. What would Sarah think of his house? How could they go on living here? How could his mam never leave this house!

Nathaniel left with barely a sound, and jogged to the end of the road. 'Sorry,' he said, 'I was so long. Mam took a while to go to bed.'

'Can I not meet her?'

'No,' he laughed. 'Of course not.' He laughed, but this time gently. 'I told you that! I have a reputation to keep intact! Me! With an English girl? I don't think so. My ma might put a gun to your head if she knew you were English. Though I wouldn't let her. C'mon, now, come inside.'

They went a few paces and then she stopped. 'Nathaniel.' Sarah pressed his forearm. 'I didn't know whether I should say this. But I thought I saw someone. Running away. From your house, just after you walked in. I heard someone talking to someone else and then I heard footsteps running, but it was too dark to see. I couldn't see a thing.'

'I'm sure it was nothing,' he said.

'Sometimes I'm scared here,' she said. 'Sometimes I don't know what to think. I've seen your boys around. One with a bruise, he looked at me. Do they know I'm here?'

'No.'

'Should I be afraid? I don't know. I don't know how this Island works.'

'Sarah, Sarah. They don't know you're here. Only I know you're here. And if you see one, dressed like me, you don't look at them. Don't talk to them. Promise me you won't talk to them.'

'I won't, I've told you I won't. But I'm scared, some-times.'

'No need, now; no need. You're with me now. And I'm the king of this isle, as I've said.'

Sarah did not look displeased with his home. At a theatri-cal creep, she followed him into the living room, where he set the gas-fire to full. She looked around the room, and then from the window into the garden. When she sat in his mam's chair she closed her eyes for a while. Odd: to see Sarah there, and not the constant form of Mammy. He let her rest as he made her up a sandwich. When he glanced over to her, she had closed her eyes, and was beginning to look better for the warmth.

'It's so nice,' she said, when he woke her with the jam roll. There had not been much left, even though he'd only had marge in both of his sandwiches. He'd ask his ma for some money for groceries tomorrow.

'Aye, too hot, normally. Most of the time I can't stand being here. Gets rid of my vigour. Holidays are the worst for that, when you're stuck inside, being gassed by the fire. Sometimes I think I'm going mad, sitting in here. Although you're sitting in my ma's chair.'

'She stays in here, all the time?'

'Aye,' he said. 'I can't get her out of the house. Not for nothing. Not for shopping, not for fish, nor for the plane.'

'The plane?'

He sat opposite her. 'Aye. It comes on the last Sunday of every month. Flying over from England. I think it might be some surveillance project, some way of spying on us. Others think it's off to Norway. Still, it's what people do; look at it, as it goes across the sky. It's a spectator's sport, to watch it fly across.'

'Oh,' she said, with her fingers pressing into the white loaf, and the red jam squeezing out just. She barely suppressed a laugh and giggled into the sandwich.

'An Island delight, aye, looking at the aeroplane,' and Nathaniel laughed at himself, at the silliness of it. 'We have such larks, here, you know. I'll be able to show it you in a couple of days. It's coming this Sunday.'

When he returned from the bathroom, Sarah was washing the plate, looking sort of dreamy as she watched the hot water and soap slip over her hands. The bath was running. 'I've put in extra bubbles,' he said.

Steam curled in the bathroom and the mirrors were already clouded. Nathaniel had laid out a towel and a flannel near the short green bath. He closed the curtains, though no one would be in the garden looking in. The bath was now nearly full.

'Here's your towel. And some shampoo. And a bar of soap. Sorry it's so cracked, like. I'm sure you're used to much better provisions in England.'

'Thank you.' Sarah looked around the room and he couldn't detect any signs of displeasure. Perhaps this wasn't so bad, compared to English standards. Her eyes darted one way, coy. 'Well?'

'What?'

'Are you going to leave?'

His face broke in two with his grin. 'Now what would my mam think if I was having a bath and not in the bathroom?'

'Your mam's asleep!'

'But if she were to check!'

'She's not going to check. She's asleep.'

'I'm sorry, Sarah. You either have a bath with me in the room, or no bath at all.'

'You're blackmailing me!'

'Aye. But I shan't look. Promise.'

Sarah sighed and he saw the red flush behind her freckles once again. Oh, what a cherry she was! How beautiful when angry! He wondered how far down the freckles went. He wondered if all English girls were like this, and, if they were, whether the Malades should really be crabbing them all for spies, or looking at them with somewhat more gentler intentions. 'Turn around, then,' she said.

The steam was thick and sweet and warm. Nathaniel looked at the wallpaper, starting to peel off, leaving a yellow underside. He traced the amber-coloured glue with a finger, wondering how on earth he could persuade Sarah to stay. Monday. Monday. Monday was far too soon.

Then he found the bit of mirror he was looking for so that he could watch her undetected. He caught her just as she dropped into the bathtub, managing to see a scrap of breast. Nearly – but not quite – a nipple. There was a suck of water and then the water went still. 'Can I turn around now?'

'Of course not! But you can sit there. On that stool. Facing the wall.'

Extra bubbles! Extra bubbles! What an idiot he was. What a chaste layer of foam covered her! In the mirror, all he could see was her head, with her ginger hair now tied in a topknot. A strand had escaped and curled on her neck like the fish-hooks you could see at Arthur's. She'd smell a whole lot sweeter now, though there had been something faintly thrilling about her before, and he had often, these past couple of days, day-dreamed of her taste as something like the seabed.

Sarah began to soap her arms and then scrubbed at her fingers with the nailbrush. She went at them hard and he worried about her skin going raw. As she leaned toward her toes, he saw her breast just coming out of the water, but he could hardly look, for fear he might jump into the bath with her. Her skin was pink with the heat; her eyes squeezed against the fog.

Then suddenly, like a seal plunging for food, she sank under the water. When she emerged her hair was glossy and black like a pelt. The water, which had heaved about her, now lapped gently the enamel sides. In her palm she poured the shampoo and then lathered it against her crown. Could he ask to soap the bubbles in her hair? To follow the line of her neck to the twin weights of her breasts? What a rollicky softness was rolling in his blood, what a terrible ache she provoked in him!

Sarah plunged into the hot again. She came up, all rinsed, and puppish again. Breathing the steam close to the waterline, she stayed like that for moments longer, then rose and said, 'Tell me about these boys.'

'The Malades?'

'Your gang.'

'What do you want to know about them?'

'Why are you frightened of them?'

'Frightened of them! Are you mad?'

'OK. Frightened of them for my sake.'

'You're the one that should be frightened. A gang like mine don't take nicely to English girls.'

Sarah stared straight ahead, her toe on one of the taps.

'Well. There's Jake. He's my second man. And then there's Sammy and Nicholas, he's a Freshcut.'

'A Freshcut?'

'Aye. He's the one you saw with the bruise. We made him a new member on Monday night.'

'And how did you do that?'

'Nicholas made some promises to us. He promised to always rid the Island of Gots. He promised to always report anyone he thought might be going back to English faith.'

'And how do you do that? Find someone who's gone back to faith?'

'Well, say if they're found with Church things, like a Bible, or scripture from the museum. Or say they coo at you, saying, "God bless," or you see them praying or rolling their eyes to heaven. Something like that. Then we'll go and investigate. Then we'll go and look for photographs or maps they've taken of the Island to send back to England.'

'And have you found people doing this? Drawing maps, taking photos?'

'We haven't found the maps, per se, or the photographs either, but that doesn't mean there aren't people here working for the English.'

'But if you haven't found any evidence, doesn't that mean they're innocent? I mean, they were deported because they were working for the Movement, I can't understand why they'd suddenly want to go back to the Church.'

'Because you don't know what loneliness can do to a man's heart. Your old English gentleman thinks he can do just fine without God and he goes round bombing the church in 1950 or '76. But the real test is not in England, but when they get here. They had to have a whole heap of courage when they drove up the church path to throw the petrol at the pews; but nothing like what you need to live here. This Island will make you meek and mild, if only for the promise that you may once in your life see somewhere that isn't here. Within days a Newcastle gent might give up his soul to God. And that's a fact. The Church knew something of loneliness, aye, how quickly it might draw us back to the homeland. That's why they sent us here. My boys, we're here to stop that.'

'And me? How do I fit into this?'

'You?' Nathaniel stared at the peeling wallpaper. 'You.' He couldn't see her at all but he could imagine her in his mind. 'I have to find some way of telling them that you're neither Got nor spy. That you came on Monday's boat as a stowaway and are looking for your ma. Jake will be the difficult one in this. He sees things in black and white. He can't understand the subtlety of being English and yet being no Got. That's why I don't want you to talk to him. He's thick as two planks sometimes but it doesn't mean he's not curious. And he has a nasty streak in him that I can't seem to temper. So you keep away, you hear?'

'Yes, sir! Don't worry. I can handle him myself.'

'No, you can't. And you don't even know that.'

He held the towel out in front of him to its full length.

'Close your eyes,' she said.

He heard the suck of the water again and then, as her back was turned, he saw the scissoring of her legs and a red foot the colour of blood. 'OK,' she said, 'I'm done.'

In his bedroom, Sarah wore a pair of his jeans and one of his shirts. From the look of her, you could tell she would be clean-smelling. If she wore his braces, she could almost be a Malade. He laughed to himself, imagining her with a bald shiny pate and bovver boots.

'I'm not taking any clothes off.'

'OK,' he said, 'neither will I.'

'Promise?'

He didn't say anything, and she gave him a dig in the

ribs. She sat, leaning against the bed. She brought out the photograph of the boat from her bag. 'I couldn't believe this when I saw it. My mum, just like that, staring up from this photo.'

'And you're sure?'

'It's her. She's here. I just know it.' Sarah looked up at him. 'This woman in the photograph. I'm going to ask tomorrow if she's Laura.'

'Do you want me to come with you? I might be able to help.'

'No,' she said. 'I want to do this alone.'

When they turned in for the night, they lay together like two chaste babies, and the heat radiated off her as if she were still in the tub.

'Sarah,' he said, quietly, 'I don't think you should go on Monday.'

'I have to,' she said. 'I can't stay. I came to find her. Then I've got to go back.'

'But Monday's too soon.'

'I know. But my dad's at home. Alone.'

They held each other tight as if, around the bed, there was the depthless Sound they could both so easily fall into.

19. Questions and Answers

The Island, then, was still fending off winter's fog. A heat-less summer's day had arrived, the sky massive and blue, though the air was Novemberish and cold. White morning light pulled at the walls of the Malraux house.

Sarah's skin had lost the warm colours of last night. She was still asleep when Nathaniel brought her up a jam-sandwich breakfast, looking newly minted, fresh as a brass coin. 'Here, Sarah,' he said, squeezing a shoulder, 'I'm sorry it's not much, like.'

'I slept so well,' she said, blinking, and then devouring the sandwich as if she hadn't eaten anything in months.

When she rose she dressed again in his clothes. As she moved about the room the shadow on the wall matched hers, shape to shape. Light folded along the lines of the shirt. Nathaniel even put her in a pair of red braces. He clipped the metal mouth to the middle of her jeans and then brought the 'Y' shape up over her back and then brought them over her shoulders, his fingers quickly running over her breasts. He brought the metal mouth to bite at the waistband of her jeans. He did it twice, which made her laugh. She coloured warmly but smiled and held his fingers with her own.

'Now all you need is some boots. I could lend you some of mine but they're still too big for me, never mind a doxy like you.'

Lolling on the bed, he watched her put together the last of the outfit. Lit by the winter sun, he saw the velvety hairs on her cheek. All night he'd cradled that body, as if she were some ship's treasure washed up on the shale. He felt somehow special, as if he had been the one marked out to shepherd this girl in the ways of the Island. His da would have liked her. That was for sure. He'd introduce her to Mammy M, later in the winter, and they could reminisce about England.

'There,' she said, when she was done dressing: 'I look a fine Malade.' Then she did a funny bow, her hand wag-tailing in the sheer light, her mouth easy, laughing still.

But he couldn't think of the Malades now. He didn't want them to botch this for him. And he stood and kissed her, with her laughing eyes still going in the daylight, but it was as if the boys were already prowling, down there in the garden, with rocks in their hands, waiting for her; as if their shadows, behind walls and hedges, had spilled over the Island's strong daylight like an ink, because she had merely said their name.

When they crept downstairs his mam called out to him and he said, 'Morning, Mam!' and then, silently giggling, they left the house to the Sound's winds, and Sarah remembered how cold the Island was, despite the sun. She should prob- ably not have mentioned the boys. Nathaniel seemed to tense whenever they talked about them. This gang; she wondered if they were really a force to be reckoned with, or some band of bored boys with nothing to do.

On the steps was a grit someone had laid down, in readiness for snow. Light glinted off the drainpipes. 'You seem happy,' he said to her, as they set off.

'Aye,' she said. 'It's just. I'm ready to know.'

'About your mam?'

'Aye. Yes.' She smiled at herself. 'Do you think your mum heard us? Last night? This morning?'

'No,' he said, 'no.'

They began the walk up Blackett Place. Ahead, the road curved toward the square or up to Marley Hill. Over the way, there would be the woman's house, looking out, she knew now, over the Norwegian waters. 'Does it ever get warm here?' she asked. 'I can't imagine it.'

'Sometimes. For a few weeks. We had a hot summer, this year.'

At the end of the lane, he said: 'You know, I read somewhere that this road was occupied by crofters, before the deportees came. That they went to church every Sunday, and that Blackett Place was where the vicar used to live. Funny, to think of the people living here before us. And these people, too, with such a Churchly bent.'

He held her hand in his for a while.

Sarah thought of Nathaniel as a blessing, as if, several leagues from church, she suddenly understood what that word meant.

He dropped her at the foot of Marley Hill. Sarah wanted him to stay, so that she could see his reaction on viewing this woman, but he insisted he had to leave to the square, for 'some business needs sorting'. He said he would come back to Swanscott House that afternoon, and asked her to return there to meet him, later this afternoon, 'for your safety', he said to her, 'No one knows you're there.' And he walked away, down the long slope of road that led back to Warkworth Town.

Sarah stood at the hedge, alone, for half an hour or so, before the woman entered the kitchen. This woman who could be Laura. Sarah folded out the photograph, and the article from the cellar. She looked from one to the other. Moments passed; minutes went; Sarah kept attempting to go to the house but as soon as she took a step in the right direction her confidence fled her. Laura Wicks, who had been an adulterer for so much of her life, now, in a couple of weeks, transformed into a distinguished criminal. Sarah had longed for this moment for so many years, and now she couldn't work out what she would ask her. She wanted to know and yet not knowing was so much easier. Finally, she tucked the papers into her pocket and managed the long gravel path to the door.

The doorbell trilled. Then the sounds of footsteps came: measured; flat. The woman said something to the boy but Sarah couldn't make out the words behind the door. A chain rattled along the latch and the door opened so that the hem of the dress skimmed the porch and the woman's head poked out; like a bird with its ringed fingers around the door-frame. 'Yes?'

The red door narrowed. The boy appeared at her side, reaching a hand through her legs, bunching the cloth of her dress in a fist. His hands were still wet with soap. Sarah's mind emptied; what were the appropriate words to say? *Are you my mother? Am I your daughter? And is this, then, my brother?* The boy stuck the loose thumb of his other hand in his mouth and gave Sarah a sullen stare, stroking his nose with his finger. Some surge of disbelief threatened to send her back to the gates. 'Hello,' Sarah said, although to which one, she didn't know.

The woman scanned the garden from corner to corner and then craned her neck to see the hedge. 'What do you want?'

'I'm . . . looking for someone. Her name is Laura Wicks. Mrs Laura Wicks. She was deported here. In '77.'

The woman pushed the boy away from her; he squealed in protest. She guided him into the hallway, shoulder-ways, and shut the door behind her, so that the red door was flat again. Her hand came to rest gracefully on the knocker. Lilies; she smelled of lilies. 'Who're you?'

'Sarah. Sarah Wicks.'

'And who is that?'

'I'm her daughter.'

The woman took a big breath and her small chest puffed out. She was small-ribbed and sinewy, with very little skin or fat or muscle or anything between the air and her veins. Blonde and freckled, just like Laura, but there was something sharper about her, as if she had turned pointier in the cold. The woman strode past Sarah, down the gravel, to the gateposts. Suddenly she began to kick the hedge as if she were trying to beat out rodents from within it. 'Who're you with? Are you here alone?'

'Yes . . . of course. I'm not with anyone.'

'Don't lie to me, girl. I know you're with this gang.

What's your game? I don't know what you're doing, snooping around, but I don't like it. You stay away from this house. What are you up to? Hmm? Searching for English spies? Or just the faithful? I'm neither. Don't give me this lie of looking for someone.' The woman stood taller and said, rather defiantly: 'I shan't end up as another Mrs Richards,' then, narrowing her eyes, 'although I didn't know they had a girl in the gang.'

The woman marched past her, almost shoving her to the side as she regained the step.

'I'm looking for my ma, that's all, for Laura Wicks. She was deported here in '77. I came here to find her, to tell her—'

But it was obvious now that the woman wasn't even listening. 'Look, girl, I don't know who you are or what you want, but I want you to leave. For three days you've been out there watching me! Skulking behind the hedge, looking for the right time to come back, at night, is that it, to crab me? I have a son inside. What can I tell you? That I don't believe? That I am a woman of the Movement? I am all of these things. Do you not know how scared people have become of even leaving their own homes at dark? What a broken Island! What a place you've made this to live! The Island's a prison! There aren't any spies here, do you hear me? None are at this address. So leave me alone! In broad daylight, for goodness' sake!'

Sarah was at a loss about what to say. She kept her voice toneless and calm. 'I don't know what you're saying. I'm not involved in any gang. In fact, I'm English, as I've just said. I just wanted to know your name. Because I've been searching this Island for the past week, for this woman, my mother, and you . . . you look like her. Her name is Laura Wicks.' The woman's eyes looked out toward the sea and then returned to Sarah. 'Just tell me. Please. Look at this photograph. It's of the last deportation boat. Do you recognize the woman in the photograph?' The woman's lips bunched and then sagged. For a moment, you might believe she had softened, because something in her eyes seemed fluid and compassionate, almost as if she were about to weep. 'Or at least tell me your name.'

'My name is Beatrice Spenser,' she said, thinly, and then re-composed her features. 'I don't know what you're talking about. I don't know about Laura Wicks. Please leave me and my son alone. I can't help you.'

'Mrs Spenser?'

'Aye.'

Sarah put a foot on the step and the woman stared down at it as if suddenly outraged. 'I'm looking for an Englishwoman, who might—'

'There is no Englishwoman here. I am an Island woman now! And if you don't leave me alone, I shall go to the police – I will not be as silent as the others!' With her boot, Mrs Spenser kicked Sarah's foot off the step, and pulled the door shut.

The red door was flat again to the house-front.

And the woman waited, one arm across her belly, in the shaded kitchen, waiting for Sarah to leave. Sarah put the photograph back into her bag, and set off, as Nathaniel had told her, back to Swanscott House. Beyond the loss that this woman said she was not, in fact, Laura, Sarah was astonished: she had never, at any point, expected fury.

20. John Verger

John Verger had come over on the boat, like most of the others, in 1951. His had been low-level work for the Movement: scouting out weak clerical locations, passing on information between Movement members, advising on some of the more tactical legislation in the courts. But the police still had his number and he was duly escorted out of England with his dark papers and case. On the boat, he'd met Jack Malraux, and they had become firm friends, Jack working at the docks and then out at sea; Verger picking the quarry, quite a happy toiler at the rock. He had always enjoyed the difficulty of the work. In England he'd fancied himself as an intellectual; a radical objector; on the Island, he was surprised at his delight for the pick. He'd lost too many friends to the waters to think this a bad job.

How things had changed in these years. Verger had grown quiet when Jack had died, years ago. Jack Malraux had been his best friend on this Island; perhaps, his only friend. After Jack died, Verger carried on at the job but without much delight, and then he had stopped altogether.

Retiring had been hard. Days would pass so slowly. A wave might take a decade to break; night-time, a century. He tried to busy himself because he knew he was becoming bored, which was dangerous; that a man should not be without his labours. He hadn't brought a sweetheart from England and he hadn't met anyone on the Island either, despite Jack's best efforts. He hadn't minded so much, then; he hadn't felt much of a drive, for that. He seemed to miss, now, the presence of this woman: this imaginary wife with whom he might grow old, as if she had once existed, and had gone, as if she had left a clearance of ground which he now trod alone. Jack, too, was too absent.

In his retirement, Verger started walking the Island. He would begin at the Eastern Bay, to watch the waves rear and break on the skerries; then go down to Lynemouth Town, to watch the men in the pubs, and women slip into brothels, and children play on the roads, wondering which Islander might be expecting the next eternal salted bath – Morris Kilman, most likely, from all reports – and then he would go up to Maiden's Square to watch Arthur Stansky cut and quarter his fish; a man treasured, and adored.

Verger could not find on the Island the delight he had once, daily, experienced here. Perhaps, somewhat, he savoured this steady withdrawal, and though he knew it was bad for him, he did little to stop it. He walked with a sense of commitment to his nervous crisis, but still wondered when it would break. A weary curiosity came with him, on his walks, for his new-found depression, though it always finished, at night, in a much more serious case of bleakness.

Aye, nothing seemed as it had been. He longed for his job. He could not seem to lift his spirits.

It had been getting warmer – the ground no longer wintry and hard but damp and boggy – when he had seen the old church above Lynemouth Town and decided to pay it a visit. Perhaps he had not been here since early '51. The church was in a sorry state: the moss and lichen spreading, the beams stubbed and charred. Nearly roofless, nature had crept in, and, between the stones, the hill was visible, though there was neither clump nor clod of tree to see.

In the cool church John touched the stones, greened by the creeping plant. The moss was coarser than he had expected. He put one foot on an upturned pew, one on the skirting, pulling himself up to view the clouds: most of the sky was visible from here. A cross still rose at the steeple, it was wedged into the rock so deeply that had any man tried to pull it out, surely they would have met with failure. The iron cross had gone unburned. Wetted, now, by days of rain, the beads hung motionless from the bar. In the distance, the horizon sealed sea and sky together. And he noticed the letters INRI, at the centre of the bars, and he placed his fingers within the letters' troughs. *Iesus Nazarenus, Rex Iudaeorum; Jesus of Nazareth, King of the Jews.* He remembered that from school. He retracted his hand, though, as if the cross still burned from when Jack Malraux and John Verger set a match to this place, in the spring of 1951.

Abruptly, John felt his foot travel into the air where he had thought he would find stone. His hand scrabbled at the moss. His nail-beds filled with earth. His boot sought the pew again but this time it tipped, knocking him backward, so that he gashed his knee, and his head rushed with a sudden surge of blood.

The smell of the burned church was intense as if the

knock to his head had provoked a sudden sensitivity to the memory.

John sat himself on the cold ground. His breath came quickly; it sounded like a crab scuttling on pebbles. His knee was cut deeply and the pain started to thud in the joint. John's vision clouded. He felt himself sweating, despite the chill, and his fingertips burned. A great load of guilt rose in him. From somewhere, far off, he heard a bell, like the sacring bell he remembered from his school's chapel, which held him, stilled him, so that he did not think of his knee. Where could the sound be coming from? He looked toward the sky and the unmoving clouds. John thought of the little bell in the fishmonger's, and the bells of the police, and that bell of the church at home, in England, ringing in the body of Christ.

And then, on this day in May, in 1986, he heard the bell again, invisible yet ringing, pealing and rippling, and the epiphany was marvellous.

Verger did not feel in possession of himself. He felt very thirsty. The bell rang madly as if children played at the clapper. And a great, furious warmth rose up his face. Then his vision broke, in that he was able to see again, quite perfectly, and he sat there for a long time, searching for what wonder of bells he had heard.

How quickly time passed as he sat there. Jolts of pain from his knee bothered him only occasionally. Cloistered in the moss, Verger felt all the depression of that year lift off; he was impervious to the cold that night. There was a breadth of stars: their lights pulsed; the sea shone; everything seemed to tremble. Christ's presence was all around him. Verger felt touched by grace, and delivered.

John felt himself God's new servant, one who had been taught kindness, to himself above all things, in His roofless office. And, oh, it was a magnificent grace. The old man, now, felt enormously free; the guilt had fled him.

That week, he went to the museum to read scripture and prayers from the English newspaper. When he had conjured up enough courage, he stole the book of paintings from one of the museum's displays. There was an ecstatic thrill to the theft. But Christ, the man, up on that cross, knew something of the Sound, knew something of what it was like to endure the hardship of this Island – who was in some way the Island embodied. Verger wondered how the Islanders could not see that God suffered as they suffered – that He did not judge, nor censor, but loved, only, from afar. Nathaniel's blue eyes too, held in them this shock of love, as if his eyes too were made of the same stuff as Christ's eyes.

When he had given Nathaniel the book, the boy had resisted, and he had sulked. Finally, he had relented, though the boy was resisting still, saying he had lost it, but Verger would carry on schooling him, until he saw God's Message. It took one who believed in Him to be so angry with Him, Verger could see that, and he wouldn't allow Jack's boy to throw away his life as he had.

It seemed, to Verger, that he now understood a world he had never truly known before. It seemed he now knew this Island absolutely; as if he had uncovered the Island for its true, vast acreage, with the columned light of its long afternoons, pale breadths of sandy beaches, and this humane, rich muck under his step; this place where he would school Nathaniel into faith, then, at long last, he would lie down, and though his body would slip into the wash, his soul would be at rest here, in the earth, on the Island, at the church he had burned by the bay.

21. Stansky & Son

Nathaniel waited for him at the back of the monger's. The red chains, between the shop and the outside, swung lightly, bringing with them the smell of the sea. From here you could see the long slope of Marley Hill and its bald sides. You could see, too, the garage at the back of Forrester's, over the partition wall, and you could just see into the enamel-tiled room where Mrs Page had, on Tuesday, lain in state. Nathaniel remembered how Jake had compared dead Mrs Page to his mam, and how much he had fair hated him for it. The boy had such gall in him; such poison, to be saying things like that about a fine woman as Mammy Malraux.

He fancied a cigarette, but he wouldn't smoke out here, lest he should show any disrespect to Mr Stansky.

Nathaniel caught the reflection of himself in the windowed door: all throat and hairy scalp. His blue eyes looked as black as coals. What had happened in the past week, what a change had come over him! He'd barely had time, between waking and leaving, to dress properly. The eyelets of his boots sagged as if in disappointment. He pulled the laces fast, but he'd forgotten the handkerchiefs and the boots were far too big. He would have to spruce himself up before the scrap tonight.

The scrap. The thought failed to thrill him, but the boys would be down at the square, chumming about, playing Belly-up and Shark, waiting for him to come and have done. He hadn't heard a peep from the gang since they'd crabbed Mrs Richards. Their silence left him with a sense of disquiet. Surely one of them had seen her? Seen the brass flash of hair along the Island paths? No, no, no; this silence was troubling enough. And if they had seen her, why were they not talking of her to him?

Suddenly Nathaniel felt too old for this; these games; these boys.

Arthur chatted away genially to a customer and Nathaniel wondered when he would leave so he could come back to the pantry and talk to him of this girl! Sarah Wicks, soft in the bath. Oh, she was a rollicky sight! Coming out frothed from the tub! He wouldn't be able to stand seeing the blood ream from her mouth, maybe a tooth knocked loose, or a punched eye socket, all in the name of finding out if she was an English spy. He had to keep the boys away from her; at any cost, any cost whatsoever!

The talking came to an end and the monger's bell rang. Through the chains' big red links, Nathaniel saw someone leave; it might have been John Verger, or maybe Mr Tucker. Mr Stansky washed down a long knife, and replaced it at the magnetic strip, so that it joined the other knives, dove-grey and flashing in the clouded light. Mr Stansky's apron was spattered in so much blood and guts it must have a reek to it. Sucking on that apron would give a man protein enough for life; enough, even, for Morris Kilman to spring from his sickbed.

Still grubbing his hands against the pinny, Mr Stansky

came out the back and took a good lungful. 'Hello, our Nath,' Mr Stansky said, giving the boy a grin. Once again, Nathaniel felt that curling joy, as if he stood next to the emblem of all fishermen. Nathaniel liked to think that some briny lineage ran from Jack to Arthur to Nathaniel, though they were in no way related. He wondered how – professionally, like – he might get his hands on Arthur's knives. 'Hello, Mr Stansky, sir.'

'A fine morning.'

'Aye, that it is. Have you been down to the fish-boats today?'

'Oh no, that's Thursday for you.' Arthur put his hands under the pinny. 'That's when the catch comes in, on a Thursday.'

Nathaniel nodded, and mouthed the word 'Thursday' soundlessly, as if committing it to memory. 'It's a nice life, eh, running the fish shop?'

Arthur shrugged and looked down at the boots he wore for the monger's. 'It's harder than it looks.'

'What do you mean? You could have fish pudding every night of the week if that was your wont!'

Arthur did not say anything but stared off distantly in the direction of Marley Hill. Arthur's black hair parted perfectly at the centre; the quills were gelled hard. After some moments, the older man spoke. 'What can I do for you, lad? Is it Mammy Malraux? Are you needing a hand?'

'No, no. Mammy's fine. She even cooked your bream on Thursday.'

This brought a smile to the monger's face. 'And did she enjoy it?'

Nathaniel looked sheepish. 'Nah. She didn't eat a

mouthful. It's still too hard for her, she says. No reflection on you, mind. Nor your fish.'

Arthur picked some stray bit of gut or slop from off the apron. 'Well. You don't know how hard for her it's been; how hard. You must be understanding. Your mam's in fine fettle, you know, there's no need for her to eat the fish if she doesn't want to.' Arthur chuckled lightly, giving him an extra bit of chin as he looked down at the gutters. 'This fear of anaemia. It keeps me in business. Keeps my fingers skinning and gutting all day, you know, but it's nothing to worry about. You can survive without fish. It's just fear that keeps everyone coming back.' He leaned in toward Nathaniel. 'Though I'd like you not to spread that, ken?'

'Aye,' said Nathaniel, laughing. 'Your secret's safe with me.'

'So,' said the monger, still laughing into his bib, 'what can I do for you?'

Some moments passed as Nathaniel tried to get at the right words and tone. On such a delicate matter, he had to get it right. He put together the words in his head, rearranged them and then put them in a different order. Then he gave up, and said, quite simply: 'There's a girl.' And he felt like even on his scalp he was blushing.

'Oh, aye.'

'And she is a cherry.'

'Go on.'

'But she is not the right one for me. Not the right kind; not at all.'

'Not the right kind?'

'Aye. Not the right kind at all! I'll never be able to walk out with her, or share her with the boys. And I don't know what to do about it. I can't tell the lads about her; I can't even tell my mam. But, oh, she has me agog!'

'Is she from school?'

'Aye . . . sort of. But it's as if I didn't pay attention to her before. Like before this week, she didn't even exist; like I've only just noticed her. And I can't remember what it was like *not* to know her. And I can't remember what it is I'm meant to be bothered about with the lads. Ah, it's ruined me.' Nathaniel caught himself in the glass and saw again his scalp, now all fuzzed and dark. 'I'm half the man I was!'

'Ruined you? What are you talking about?'

'Aye. Ruined me. I'm in love.'

'And? Love's better than a whole month of summer.'

'The boys, they won't like her.'

'Who cares about the boys?'

'They're my lads, Mr Stansky. My gang!'

'No, no, no, Nathaniel. You've got it purely the wrong way round. They're your lads now, and you may think they're important, which they are, by all means, but this girl's got to go first. What's her name?'

Nathaniel coughed, looking a little strangled about the neck. 'I can't tell you. Just in case it comes out.'

'Being embarrassed of her, of what she is, of what she does, will only make things doubly – triply – worse.' Mr Stansky picked at some dirt underneath a nail. It was then that Nathaniel saw how tired he looked, how slumped about the shoulders. 'Trust me on that one.'

'She's going to leave me.'

'Leave you? How? She doesn't live with you, does she?'

'No, no, I don't mean that. Leave me; stop loving me. She might as well be across the waters in England by

Monday, for all she will remember me next week.' The boy slumped against the wall, his lips pouting his sorrow. 'You need to tell me how to persuade her to stay!'

'Is she so lovely?'

'Aye, Mr Stansky. She's all ginger about the hair, and lips so red it's like she's been guzzling berries.' Arthur laughed. 'And I don't want her to go.'

'Now, now, now. Enough of this. She's not going anywhere. Don't you worry, boy. You tell her how you feel and she'll stick right by your side. I promise you. It's the only thing to do. Forget all your fear and do the right thing, lad. Tell her how you feel, while you've still got the chance. I certainly wish I had.'

'How's that?'

Arthur sighed. He readjusted the belt under his apron as if to make better room for his guilt. 'I was in love with a woman once, and I loved her, as you said you loved this girl. But I too was scared and fearful of what people might think. Being the fishmonger, on an Island such as this, it gives you a higher sense of yourself than your worth. It makes you too proud, too proud, when you should be far more humble. It's fish mouths we have our fingers down, most of the time, remember,' he gestured with his hand, 'this is not the reek of the brothel.' Nathaniel laughed and then stopped himself, seeing the watery look in Mr Stansky's eyes. The monger looked back at the shop, and the wind brought with it a hearty stench of the sea.

'I loved this woman. But when it came to making a decision, I bottled it. We were courting a little before her mam's death, but when her mam died, and when she asked if we could be together, I said no. I didn't realize the consequences then.' He laughed mirthlessly into his chin. 'I didn't realize how broke she was. And then, because of my decision, she decided to do something which I became embarrassed over. By then, I didn't want to tell my friends I was involved with her; I didn't want anybody to know I had anything to do with her. And then I lost her.' Arthur clicked his fingers. 'Like that. In an instant. I was drunk, and angry, and I went to her and . . . oh. I wish I could take back that night! I'm such a fool,' he said, though Arthur's words were barely audible now.

It must be Eliza, must it not? The whole Island had a suspicion that he mooned about the Square longing for her. What a sorry state, Nathaniel thought, to be in love with someone who had no care for you. And for a man like Arthur Stansky! The fishmonger himself! There was no dignity to it, no, for a man like Mr Stansky to fall in love with a doxy like Eliza, and for her not to love him back. Mr Stansky would be better off without her. He'd be better off with her gone, settled in England, severed from the Island like a chopped tail. And there was no doubt of her uninterest: Nathaniel had seen that, plain on her face, when she'd shown up at his house, threatening to blub, telling him how much she wanted out of here. You simply wouldn't leave the Island if you were in love with some-one here; no, the logic didn't work.

Meanwhile tears were welling up in Arthur's big brown eyes. Nathaniel too noticed the grey creep of stubble. How they were all sprouting, these men, he and Arthur both, with too much hair! 'I am sorry, Mr Stansky, I didn't mean to make you sad. There, there. I'd forget about her now.' Suddenly Nathaniel felt the father, and Arthur, his awkward son. 'No doxy's worth your tears, now. You should move on to another. One more pliant to your needs. You don't want to be troubling with a doxy like Eliza.' And then he said it, braved the awful truth: 'She doesn't care about you, Mr Stansky. The whole Island knows it. And I don't say that to harm you, in any way, aye, just to help you, that is, move on.'

Arthur wiped the tear away with the big fist of his hand. 'Aye, aye, I know. It's just, I'm always hoping that maybe . . .' He sniffed. 'One day . . . Well. You're right. It's over now.'

'I'm sorry,' Nathaniel said.

'No, no, no. Hark at me, all mawkish. Forgive me.' Arthur breathed deeply, steadying himself. 'It's been a strange week. I heard there's a bloom come in, and I'm worried about winter stock. That's all. No. You're right. It's right to forget about her; sometimes it gets to me, that's all. It's the bloom that's worrying me. Aye. There's reports of it on the eastern beach but I'm worried it will belt the Island and there'll be nothing to eat all winter. We can't live from provisions only. And I'm among those who don't want the Island to starve to death.'

'Will it be OK?'

'Of course, of course. We'll have enough to eat. I promise you.' Arthur dabbed now at his eyes with the corner of his apron, and then turned to Nathaniel, his face full of passion. Light glinted from the planes of his nose. 'Now you go tell your girl to stay. Don't mind your boys – they'll settle soon enough. But don't let her wriggle from you. They're slippery like that. First chance of escape and she'll take it. With both hands. D'you hear me, son? You do anything to make her stay.'

'Anything?'

'Anything, aye . . . within reason, that is.'

Anything. Anything. Nathaniel could, he thought, do something, something that would ensure Sarah would stay until spring. It was a little mischievous, but she'd come round to the logic of it, once she saw how much sense it made, and what a rollicky winter they'd have together. Especially, it seemed, now so obvious, that with Eliza's money, he'd be such a lord of it all! And when Nathaniel looked at Mr Stansky, wet-eyed and in need of nursing, Nathaniel knew he couldn't live the winter without his girl. To tumble into a depression such as this was surely death for a man! 'Thanks, Mr Stansky.'

'Well,' the monger said, 'I have a shop to run. I have to be off.' They shook hands. 'Oh, and Nathaniel? I like your pate. It suits you, a bit longer. Will you watch the plane tomorrow, with your mam?'

'That I will, if I can get her out. And yourself, Mr Stansky?'

'Aye. I'll watch it from the beach.'

But Arthur did not continue serving customers. Instead, he shut the shop at lunchtime, which was a rare thing, and much commented upon by passers-by. Instead, he went up to his apartment, took off his apron, his boots, and all of his clothes, and went to bed: overwhelmed by this morning's conversation, and, overwhelmed, above all, by his own true stupidity, at ever having let Eliza go in the first place. He slept solidly for the whole afternoon, and woke up feeling no better.

22. Money

Winter now, but then it always was. The day had started off looking sheer and bright like the first day of spring, but the afternoon had lustily rushed into cloud and grey, and then the whole pretence of day had collapsed into little more than night at barely three o'clock.

Already Saturday. Eliza still didn't have enough money for the boat. And here she was, enveloped in shadow, watching the fish shop. How many times that night had she watched a fish brought to the waxy light, and filleted by the man's deft hand? And not just tonight. Long autumn nights had been spent here, with the branches drubbing the museum's windows. The time the trees were in leaf seemed so brief . . . But from autumn to winter to summer, there would be Arthur, a constant pain and pleasure both. He would always be there to torment her: his belly canting forward from the belt-hoops, chatting amiably to anyone who was not her, amongst his treasured fish.

Eliza had waited in at the Grand all day for a customer and nobody had come. Not even Mr Carter. She kept looking in her bedside drawer for the banknotes but no amount of counting would conjure any more. It still amounted to £10 less than she needed. How could she make £10 in two days? It seemed an impossibility, but so too did spending another winter on the Island.

That afternoon, at the mirror, Eliza had pulled back her fringe and contemplated writing something. How about, *I'm staying here and there's nowhere to go*? How about, *My heart's too heavy to carry on*? Eliza had dropped the pen, fed up with the game, and her brow had been left blank. She contemplated going out to look for the English girl, but that hope, too, seemed dead. Nathaniel had stopped by the Grand and, like a cheerful hangman, had told her that unless she had the £50 for the boat on Monday, he could assure her she was not going anywhere. On his way out from her room, he had said, 'Feels awful to be so alone, doesn't it just?' but he was gone before she could ask him what on earth he meant by that.

Eliza imagined the fishmonger's to be like a church: a place of ritual, and uninterruptible silences. Aye, it was a sacrosanct place, even if it was for the butchering of fish. This was the holy place of the Island: the fish with their sheen and iridescence, flake and scale, fogged and bright eyes; the armoured crustacean and the slippery eel; this was where people came to talk, and be fed, and be reassured, by the wise and clerical silences of Mr Arthur Stansky. And here she was, the constant spy of the Island, unloved by him.

Eliza watched the bend and heft of the man at work. She thought: if I don't make enough money, and Arthur does not want me, I shall take myself off the cliff at Lynemouth Bay so that I may no longer have to live here. She would swallow all the brackish waters as easily as a liquor. She imagined her coat billowing behind her and the electric shock of her bones meeting the hard flat sea. Aye. She might be glad of that enough. And she'd spare the Island the expense of a funeral.

But rather than drumming up business or thinking of a way to earn the ten missing pounds, here she was again, watching Arthur move about the fishmonger's as if administering some office of grace. But he looked sad, or weary, drawn about the eyes. He had dropped Mr Tucker's fish, which was very uncharacteristic of him, and seemed to chat with little pleasure to a rather harried-looking Beatrice Spenser. Eliza wondered why he was so out of sorts. How dearly she wanted to steady his arm, to guide him to the ripened trout or gelatinous roe, and let him scrape his hands on her rank and grubby pinny. Then she imagined his hand clamped between her fleshy thighs, but she put that thought out of her mind immediately. Every erotic thought of him was barbed.

It was not to be. It was over. England called for her now. If only she could somehow make the £10.

Arthur said goodbye to a customer and turned the lock in the door. He looked out into the square, his face shadowed. *Oh, Arthur, if only you might love me*, she thought, *then this Island might prove a little richer, because right now, oh, what a pit of poor earth it is proving to be!* Eliza sighed, gathered her coat about her, and left the museum.

Caro Kilman was finishing up at the launderette. Eliza popped in to pick up the dress she had come in for on Monday. It was cosy in here, and the room was full of an odour that was not far from the smell of the mortuary. Eliza liked the scent of the powders and the liquids, and the sight of the clothes on the hangers. Everywhere, there was that smell which made the nostrils burn – well, everyone save Caro, with her nose and eyes that couldn't smart at bleach. The Islanders were poor in most things but liked their fineries treated just so.

'How are you, Caro?'

'Aye, well, well.'

'And Morris?'

'Keeping up as well he can, poor wee man.'

'Is it the anaemia?'

Caro moved her chin to the heel of her palm. 'Aye, his blood! Such a problem with his blood.'

The launderette also did shoes and there were open boxes piled on top of one another. They reminded Eliza of the boys' boots. A notice of goods for sale was pinned to the wall; herring lines and fish tackle. 'I imagine it's very hard.'

Caro said nothing but pressed her lips into a thin line and touched her generous auburn curls. She turned and Eliza watched the lavender dress dip slowly in between the racks of clothing. Caro hummed a faint tune, occasionally saying, 'Now where is it? Where've you got to?' Her voice was bright from behind the back of the shop. 'Found it! It's a lovely dress, Eliza, such a blue.'

Caro handed it over and the film squeaked on the counter. Eliza asked, hazarding the favour: 'Can you add it to the tab?'

'Aye,' she said, 'but you'll have to be paying this back soon.'

'No doubt, no doubt.'

Caro's bosom seemed heaving fairly near her throat. 'Did you hear about Mrs Richards on Wednesday night?'

'No?'

'A sorry story, aye.'

'What happened?'

Caro cocked her head to the side. 'Nathaniel and his boys. Looking for spies. Again. They threw rocks at Mrs Richards' window and then she was struck by one on the cheek. Had to have stitches.'

Eliza was dumbfounded. 'You're joking. I had no idea. I was only at Mrs Malraux's yesterday. She didn't mention it.'

'Aye, well, she wouldn't, would she? That boy's all she's got. She'd hardly condemn her own son. And she is very fierce of him.'

'They threw a rock! At her face!'

'Aye. Mrs Bingley said there was blood everywhere. And that Mrs Richards had a real fright of it. Ten stitches, she had, at the doctor's.'

'My. I didn't know it was so bad.'

'And I can hardly think who's going to have a word with him to put a stop to his behaviour, what with Jack no longer with us.'

'The police?'

'What are they going to do with them? They're not much older than the boys.' Caro leaned her bulk against the till. 'Some people shouldn't be allowed to be parents, you know. Letting Nathaniel roam about the Island, just as he likes! Those boys frighten the life from me,' she said.

'Aye, but you've got Morris. I shouldn't worry.'

'Oh, Morris. Morris is in bed all the time. You know I feed him up with whatever I can afford at Stansky's but it's still so bad. His bloods never seem to get any better. He's fair yellow, he's missing that much iron. And his nails: so weak and soft! And so pale underneath the eyes! Oh, seeing the sight of him near kills me! You know he hasn't been out of bed for weeks.' Caro looked up at Eliza, her eyes round and wet. 'I'm so scared for him!'

'I didn't realize it was so bad, Mrs Kilman. What will you do?'

Caro looked at her, suddenly alarmed, and her whole demeanour froze. Mrs Kilman sat up straight and gripped the bagged dress. Her voice was suddenly edged: 'Don't you come sharking about here, doll. Morris is going nowhere, d'you hear me? He's in fine fettle. Now I know it's winter and times are tight but you don't come round here trying to pick up another fare for the Tongue. It shan't be Morris, d'you hear me?'

'I would never— I wouldn't have come—'

'I don't care. You can say this or that but I know when you're sniffing about for money. The shame! Get you gone, now. Do you wish death upon my house? So you can make a fiver! My Morris is in good shape; fine shape. The shame of you, Eliza Michalka. What would your mother have thought!'

'No. I never said that, I would never—'

'Aye, and I know someone sniffing for business when I see one.' Caro pushed the dress across the counter, and then folded her arms over her bosom. Her gaze flicked to the door. 'I shan't add it to the tab. You can have it for free. But I shan't launder another thing for you, not on your life, d'you hear? Sharking about the Island, looking for fares for the Tongue! The shame!'

Eliza took the bag wordlessly and slipped out of the shop.

Shame curled in her breast. It was true. If anyone was ready for the Tongue, it was Morris, and it would have meant an extra £5 if he could – somehow – die before Monday. Eliza hated herself for thinking of it. But it had been worth a shot. She sloped away home, feeling hopeless.

23. The Burning Book

Night-time now was as lustrous as glass.

Nathaniel walked from Sarah's house, hands shoved deep into his pockets, the wind drying out his eyes. He couldn't remember the last time he was so cold; his neck was frozen. He felt unkempt: his hair needed shaving, he needed a wash, he'd smoked so many of the girl's cigarettes he felt sick. The boys were waiting, for their Saturday night thrills, as he had promised them, a big Malade meeting before school started again, and yet the anticipation that had once rallied him was now gone. Something in him had gone slack. Even when he'd made the quick trip over to Eliza's, to give her a bit of a scare, he'd felt so undelighted by his own threats. When he left, he could barely look at her.

The boy walked, fixed to the path. Grey trees were the faintest marks against the night sky. He hadn't been home enough; he should go home and see his ma, make sure she was all right. There was no point in doing anything if his ma was not all right; the woman of his life, aye. He'd like to turn and go back to Blackett Place, to be near the warmth of the fire, but he couldn't cancel another meeting. He walked on.

All afternoon, Sarah had been at the shake-and-heave. Nathaniel probably could have told her that that woman wasn't Laura Wicks. That he'd never heard of a Laura Wicks on this Island. And, if he'd really put his mind to it, that the woman down at the Eastern Bay was none other than Beatrice Spenser. But what good would it have done? Tomorrow they would go to the museum and check the log-book for Laura's name; and then Sarah would know, finally, that her ma was not here, and settle down to their winter of pleasure.

Nathaniel was tired. The afternoon had tired him. He wanted always to be with her, but it was as if all that brassy hair, the sheer colour of it, fatigued his eye. And if he couldn't be with Sarah then he wanted to be with his ma, not sharking about the Island with these bald infants.

Jake was waiting for him at the Warkworth bluffs. Nathaniel wanted nothing more than to go directly to the boys; he had no desire for a private chat. He nodded at him and tried to walk on to the square but Jake quickly caught up with him, and Nathaniel was forced to slow down, then stop.

'Where were you?' Jake said.

Nathaniel stopped. 'What?'

'We were meant to meet this afternoon.'

Everything about the boy aggrieved him: the pearly big ears, the slabby cheeks, the tubby middle. The big bland eyes.

'We were?'

'To plan for tonight, remember, you said that yesterday.'

'Aye.'

'To plan our target.'

'I get it.'

'So where were you? I called round to yours, and your mam said you weren't there.'

Nathaniel looked out over the bay. The sand was flat and the tide was out. The sea smelled off; or perhaps there was a westerly wind coming off the bloom. 'I was out,' he said, without looking at Jake.

'I know that already.'

'I was with—'

'That English girl? The one at Swanscott House?'

So the boy had seen her. Jake knew about Sarah. Of course he did. You couldn't keep one secret on the Island to yourself, not with Jake sniffing around, bored, and ready to spoil your fun.

'C'mon, Nath. I've seen her with my own eyes. I know she's not from here. I would be able to recognize a doxy such as that! Go on. Tell me. Give her up.' The big night air filled the bay. Could he push the boy from here and pretend it was an accident? What might he give to never see Jake on these Island paths again! 'Tell me who she is, Nathaniel.'

'She's from Lynemouth Town. You've never seen her before?'

'That's not true. I know that's not true. Tell me the truth, Nath.'

'Why! Why should I?'

'Because I'm your second man, Nathaniel. I started this gang with you on the same night. We share everything, remember?'

Nathaniel felt himself relenting: he would give the boy the minimal amount of information, just so he could get past tonight. 'You promise not to tell the boys anything?' Jake nodded. 'The girl. She's off Monday's boat. She hid in the hold. She's a stowaway, but she has no business of spying. Her ma was deported here on the '77 ship, for burning a church in Berwick. Sarah's come to find her.'

'Sarah? Sarah who?'

'That's her name. That's the girl's name. Sarah Wicks.'

'And her ma's name?'

'Laura Wicks.'

'Laura Wicks? Never heard of her. There's not a Laura Wicks from here to Marley Hill. It's pony, Nath, it must be, it must be, she's obviously making up lies. There must be some other mission she's on!'

'No. I believe her. She has a newspaper article, and a photograph of her ma on the boat. She can prove it.'

'But that could be anyone! Anyone at all. It's a story, Nath, a story, just so she can crab you and learn about the Island! And an English girl, in our midsts, we should be crabbing her for a spy!'

It was an odd feeling, not having the energy for a fight. Nathaniel looked at him blankly, curious about what part of his personality had deserted him this past week, knowing that if Jake had been like this on Monday, surely he would have swung the boy out to the Sound. 'Leave it out now,' he said, quietly, nodding over to the square. He cupped the back of Jake's neck with his hand. To his touch, the boy felt much warmer than himself. 'Listen, now, Jake, the boys are waiting. We'll talk about her – about everything – later, OK? Tomorrow, or something. Just not now, Jake, I don't have the energy for it. We've got all winter to find out what she's about; just let me find my way with her, at the beginning.'

'I *want* to see her.'

'No. You'll do so when I say you can.'

'No, Nath, now.'

'Listen to me.' Nathaniel squeezed his eyes; he felt a headache coming on. 'You can see her when I say. Not before. You're not the leader of this gang. I am. And I say not now. So leave it out.'

Nathaniel walked toward Maiden's Square and left Jake standing by the cliff edge.

It had been a long, disappointing week for any boy who was not Nathaniel. There was no mention of the boys' stay in their mothers' warm living rooms. They had been promised nights of thrills and all they had got was Nicholas at the start of the week and Mrs Richards in the middle. Tonight had to make up for this.

Nobody mentioned Nath's cap of hair although the others were all distinctly bald, aside from Sammy, who'd done something odd with his pate. The hair was shaved on either side so that the fuzz was in a central line. 'What's with the hair, Samuel?' Nathaniel asked. 'You look like your scalp's grown a cunt.' A nervous titter went through the group. Sammy stood next to Jake and tried to come up with a response. 'A fur, Samuel Carter, is what you've got. And we don't accept ladies in our circle, you know that rule very well. So get rid of it, lad.'

Nathaniel saw them cower a little, and the tiredness began to go. Aye, he could knock two heads together and watch them smash like eggs. Oh, he murdered for something. Was it the girl? Or these boys? Or the scrap indeed? He just needed to stop thinking. Really he'd be happy to be down at the bay, alone, in the dark, skipping stones, smoking cigarettes. Or at home with his ma. Sarah had ruined things, and perfected things, at the same time.

'Who's on, then, for tonight? I've an eye on Caro Kilman. She was around at my ma's the other night, telling such stories of us.'

'Caro Kilman's at my mam's,' Jake said, 'having tea.'

Nathaniel saw the challenge in the other boy's eyes.

'Did you not think, boy, did you not think it politic to try and dissuade Mrs Kilman from suppering with your ma? Surely better to nurse old Morris back to health!'

'How was I to know she was the target for tonight? I've not heard any English words from her. And I haven't heard anything from you, these past few days.'

The other boys exchanged glances and there was the sound of boots shuffling; edging away, a little, from the two boys.

'Don't answer back, Jakob Lawrence. The point is, you shouldn't have let her in! You should have said your ma was ill! So we could have had someone for tonight!' Nathaniel tried to relax himself. 'So who's next? Who's got a bright idea?'

'John Verger?'

'What?' Nathaniel stared at Jake. His mouth was dry but he kept his voice level. 'I have told you about this. About him.'

'Nicholas saw him down at the old church.'

'Is this true?'

Nicholas nodded his head vigorously.

'When?'

'This morning,' Nicholas said shyly. The bruise on his chin had greened in the past week.

Jake continued: 'Mooning about, sitting by the church walls. He looked to be having a molly time of it. And I think he's the one doing the graffiti, the ones that say INRI, or something like that.'

'I told you,' Nathaniel said, 'he's my da's pal.'

'Aye, aye,' said Jake. 'But I can't think of anyone else, aside from maybe the girl—'

'What girl?'

'I haven't seen her before,' Jake said. 'Copper-coloured hair.' He clicked his fingers, as if he were hoping for recall. 'What's her name?'

'I told you not—'

'Up at Swans—'

'Stop it, Jake.' There was silence in the square for a while. Nathaniel's scarf, as if oblivious, danced about in the Island's wind, jigging and whirling, as if a part of him were determined to escape. And then there was a terrible moment, really very terrible, when the boys congregated saw the eyes of their leader go brighter and wetter and sharper too, and there was a fear that Jake had upset him so much, that Nathaniel was about to cry. No one wanted that; not even Jake.

When Jake resumed, it was amiably, as if he were chattering to his mam. 'Aye. So Verger. And I'm not saying he's a bad man, no, but Nicholas saw him down at the church this morning and there's no denying it's a sure sign of faith.'

Nathaniel didn't want this. He didn't want things to get too deep. What would his ma say, if they went after John Verger for a spy? What would his da have said? 'Who else saw him at the church?'

'I did,' said Samuel, tracking a hand over the fuzz.

'And me,' said Nicholas.

'Aye! I know about you already, Tucker.' Nathaniel was in no mood for this. It was as if his gang was suddenly turning brutish beyond even his own ken. 'Fine,' he said – because better John Verger than the English girl, and what were a few rocks anyway? Or a few smashed windows? And what were the boys but purveyors of a violent sort of goodness – though Verger shouldn't be the target; not at all.

Nathaniel smiled at them, and, most importantly, Jake. 'All right, boys. A good spot, Jake. Verger it is. As you wish.'

Verger's house, up on Heath Rise, not much further from where Nathaniel had looked out over the Sound on Monday night, had an ill-tended character. Trees obscured most of the bottom floor's rooms. Branches scraped the glass. It was a typical Island cottage, not much looked after. 'I wonder where he is,' one of the boys said, at a faint whisper, as if in the presence of something to be revered.

'Down at the Grand!' Jake cried.

'Fucking Eliza!'

'Down on his hindquarters having his fill of God.'

Nathaniel had been to this house many times as a boy, with his hand in his da's hand, but never here, to do this. But if he couldn't let on about the girl, then Verger it would be – and maybe it was the right thing to do. It was idiotic for Verger to have given him the book, and he supposed the old man should be punished for it. Then there were the pep talks, and the reminiscences of England, and the lectures on his da – oh no, this all had to stop.

Rocks were thrown. Most of the boys were a bad aim,

most ricocheted off the plaster. Nathaniel saw how their eyes grew wide with it: the good generous violence. They threw their stones hard. 'The oldest Got on the isle!' Nathaniel shouted, joining in with the rest of them, and he felt the old pure love for his boys return. The boys were beauties, like babies; even Sammy, with his line of fuzz, looked a winsome sight. So this was goodness! This was right! It had a reek to it, but so must everything worth fighting for.

A window smashed. Jake had thrown the winning stone. The boys cheered and clung about him, rubbing his head with their fists. 'All right, Jakey!' 'Yes, Jakey-boy!' they said.

Jake was laughing and jumping about and pointing at the hole in the window. Where had the boy assumed this new power? Jake bent over to his bag and reached down into the satchel. The rest of the boys too had gone very quiet. Rising in Nathaniel was the knowledge of what it would be. His heart sank at the prospect.

'John Verger's been found with this book. A book of paintings of Christ! A real Got living on our Island, a Got more than all the others.' Jake flipped the pages and the boys gathered round to see. 'Look!' he said, pointing. 'For shame! The glory of Christ splashed on every page!'

'That isn't your book, Jakob Lawrence.'

'No. Aye. Whose is it?'

'It isn't yours.'

Sammy looked at Nathaniel, eyes wide and distressed. 'Have you seen this, Nath? Have you seen these pictures? Wow!'

'Gives me the gromicks!' said another.

'Give me a bucket, I need to heave! The rot's in my blood!'

'Aye,' Jake said, watching the boys turning the pages. 'A man so sweetened by the coddle, I bet he doesn't sleep without muttering a prayer.' The boys were quiet, softly abuzz. They'd never seen such pictures. 'A man. With a book such as this.' He looked directly at Nathaniel. 'I hate to think what he believes—' He stopped, brought out a lighter and put it to a page. 'Or what length he'll go to, to get the English back here. If the English aren't already here.'

Oily green flames jumped high in the night.

A sadness fell upon Nath as he remembered the old man outside Arthur's, grinning at merely the sight of him. He should stop Jake, but he couldn't. Not now; not any more. He thought of Sarah. No; he could not.

The burning book went straight into the dark hole of the room. For moments, all was darkness, as the boys stood and watched, rapt by this sudden escalation of violence. An acrid smell sliced the air. A curtain, clasped to a bracket on the wall, caught, and with a huge noise, the room filled with bright orange light.

24. Grace

Eliza applied the needle to the blue flame. Her hand was shaking; the needle quivered. It was four o'clock in the morning. The match went out, the needle turned from red to black. Eliza hesitated, then pushed up her fringe and stuck the needle in. She steeled herself against the pain, then pushed it in further, and began to write. Starting with the letter *V*, she punctured the skin down to the dip and then began the shoot upward. The letters seamed in blood as she began the *e* and *r*. Eliza felt as if she might faint but dug the needle in harder. In minutes, the name, finally, was cut into her skin. *Verger*.

Eliza had been sleeping lightly, at about ten o'clock last night, still waiting for a customer to grace her door with a £5 note, when she had been woken by what sounded like an explosion. From the window she saw the orange flames up near the viewing station at Marley Hill. Pulling on her coat, she winched up the glass, jumped onto the flat roof and rattled down the iron staircase. When she reached the road she ran as quickly as she could to the burning house but then hung back, yards away. A black net of boys idled by the house, but she did not stop them. One of them threw another flaming missile. She stood by and then the boys scattered: some down to the beach, some up the hill.

The fire was mounting, and smoke escaping through a smashed window. Eliza went up to the house, as close as she could get, and shouted Verger's name through the door, but the heat was tremendous and the smoke thickening. She wondered if she should go inside and look for him. What if the old man was in there, inhaling all that smoke? Eliza left the house blazing as the Islanders showed up with water pails and buckets, and a hose from the main taps.

Verger emerged, minutes later, a shadowy figure at the end of the road. Eliza thought he looked tiny, but as she neared him he seemed to get no bigger. When he looked at the burning house, he sagged. He asked her if it was his house and she said that it was. Eliza held him by the elbow and brought him back to the Grand. He asked her who had done it and she merely shrugged. 'I don't know,' she lied.

Eliza passed an inked swab over the bloodied letters and felt the sting. She had chosen black ink, the better for it to show. She should have stopped the boys from doing what they did. How wrong to think the boys were merely bored, merely playing games! Was that not what she'd told Margaret? And now here they were, the brutal lot of them, assaulting people, and burning down houses! But to turn them in would have meant no escape!

Eliza put the swab back in the inkpot. There it was now, his name, her guilt, tattooed on her brow.

'Eliza! Here!' Musa called, from some way away. She mopped up the word with a ragged piece of tissue, bringing off blood and ink together, and flattened the wing of hair against her forehead. 'Coming,' she said, wiping away her tears with the bloodied rag.

Rain came on Sunday morning. Verger stood at the window, watching the sheets of it, imagining parts of his house that had never before seen water grow damp, then sodden. There was something of the dirge to the fat heavy drops breaking against the roof of the Grand; something funereal to the slow spray against the window. The world out-side was nothing more than a blur. His shirt, which the previous evening had been ironed crisp, was crumpled; there was an air of surrender to it. His dicky bow wilted at the edges. His hands hung, and the veins rose swollen within them.

The night spent – at a brothel! – had been fitful. A woman had guided him here last night, steering him by the elbow, when she had found him sobbing outside the burn-ing house. He had felt out of his mind. He had felt as if he couldn't see. She stopped when he stopped, told him to mind his footing when the path became rutted. His house was gone, burned and gone. She had pulled him along, half-dragging him, when he had stiffened on seeing the Grand.

In the reception he smelled unusual smells. The woman was arguing with the man he knew as Musa. Verger pulled some pounds from his wallet and this made him quiet. Musa led him down a corridor and opened the door with a gold spiked key. Musa said, 'Ha, ha, should I send in a girl to see you, sir?' but Verger shut the door without a reply.

This room, he supposed, was a spare; blue, functional, little about it was decorative. In here, he was out of the way. Yes, he thought, leaning his shoulder against the window, listening to the squeaks of the Grand's sign in the wind, there was little to be done. His house was gone; Nathaniel lost. Long strings of rain slid down the window. Further out, it dripped off the terrace eaves across the street. The day, at least, in glum camaraderie, is in mourning for me, Verger thought; for what I have lost. A small comfort. The water soaked what it could.

Verger was brought tea and some porridge for breakfast. He sat and ate by the window. It was eleven o'clock, he must've been by the window for hours. He felt as if he hadn't slept at all.

The rain was letting up now, coming gentler. Verger opened the window; the air felt rinsed and crisp. He felt himself a slow servant of God – defeated, already, and by a mere child, at that. His Message was a low throb; a distant pulse. He had carried the Message to the boy and this was his recompense! Must he get down on his knees and thank God for his loss? How ungenerous was His reward! Oh, he could push his fist into the boy's face, and watch the blood ream about his lips, and feel it, just for a second, a moment of justice; of reprieve; of pleasure, even, and power. The smooth scalp he could claw in his hands.

The world did not make sense: not like this.

There was a tapping at the door. Verger feared, if it were the woman again with the tea, he might take this violence to her soft body. The door opened. Eliza. She looked just as she had on the day of the funeral, with that smart length of fringe, and the strong able body. Swollen eyelids gave her a hooded look, as if she had been crying for some time. So, it was Eliza who had brought him here last night. 'I hope I haven't disturbed you.' Her hand was still at the door knob, as if she were about to shut it once again and flee. 'I came to see if you were all right. If there was anything I could do.'

'No, no. You have not disturbed me. Please. Do take a seat.' Verger gestured to the armchair. He sat neatly on the edge of the bed, conscious he was sitting on a well-used mattress. He gave her a rueful smile, and she smiled back; this Eliza, this woman of kindness. And yet a whore, he knew that; they both knew where they were. Eliza played her fingers through her hair.

'How are you feeling this morning?' she asked. 'It must have been a shock.'

'Oh. Well. You know. My house – it's gone.'

Eliza looked down at her lap where her hands lay flat. 'Yes. Yes, I know.'

'So, my house is burned. Gone completely. That, I must accept. Everything is rubble, I suppose.'

'Do you,' she began, then faltered. Her voice was thin: 'Do you have any idea who did this?'

'No,' he said softly, 'I don't.'

She took a deep breath. 'I know who—'

'Eliza. It's funny how we haven't really met before. I mean, I saw you at Mrs Page's, and you did a very good job, but we haven't actually spoken, before now, have we? What is your surname, Eliza?'

Her eyes widened in confusion. 'Michalka.'

'Michalka. A Jewish name?'

'Yes.'

'So you weren't one of the deported, then? If you were a religious family?'

'No.' She adjusted the tone of her voice; she had evidently not come expecting this conversation. 'Ma came here voluntarily. She had had a hard life, she thought the Island might be a refuge. And it was, in a way, for her.'

'Germany?'

'No,' she smiled, 'London.'

'Lucky thing.'

'I . . . ' Eliza started, and swallowed, and then looked at him levelly. 'I know who. No. I know who did this.'

'Speak up, my dear,' he said softly.

Her voice was barely more than a whisper. 'You are a good man, I understand.'

'A good man?'

'Aye.'

'If I am a good man, then you are a good woman. If I had stayed outside my house I would have frozen to death. You took me back here. You rescued me. And now I am here, in this room, warm, at least, and alive.'

Her eyes were brimming with tears. 'I could have . . . I could have stopped them . . . but . . . those boys, I need to get out of here.'

'Come now.'

'It was wrong. I should have—'

'Aye,' he said, but gently. 'Wrong of them, not you.'

'But if I had reported them, on Monday, there would be no . . . oh!' Verger moved to the chair, kneeling, and put his arm around her. Her shoulders shook as she began to cry. 'I am a bad woman! Selfish. And nothing but a whore! Do you not see where I had to bring you back to? Of all places to drag you to, in your state of tears! I wish I could be finished with it all! To be done with it all! And I didn't stop them. I'm sorry, Mr Verger, so sorry. It's just that I want to get out of here.' She looked at him with her wide brown eyes and it was as if the light of God was singing in them. Yes! Singing from the iris itself. 'I want to leave so very badly.'

'My child! My child! Hush now. You are a spotless creature. You do not deserve anyone's blame. You couldn't have done a thing about it.' The woman fairly shook in his arms as if she were quarrying out all the misery. This woman, who opened men like clams, getting to their filthy spots of pleasure – it was this woman who so badly needed the Light! This woman, who sent the men off to the fish, the squid, the sharks, without so much as a mention of God's name! This was the very soul that needed grace!

The rain started again and they both looked toward the window from the blue pale room. Eliza pushed a tissue to her nose, her tears spent now. 'I *must* get out of here.'

He said: 'It will come. You will not be here for much longer, I promise you.' He cupped her face with his hands and she gave him a weak smile. With her other hand she swept her fringe from her eyes. Written on her forehead was his name. Fresh blood scabbed the letters. 'My name,' he said. 'You have my name upon your skin.'

'It was a penance. For not helping you. For not stopping the boys.'

'Oh, unnecessary. You cannot earn grace by punishing yourself.'

'I'd like that to be true, but I don't think it is.' She dissolved into tears again. 'Sometimes I think someone is punishing me!'

'Why?'

'Because everything I ask for – companionship, love, family – is denied to me. And I can't understand it. I think of myself as a good woman. One who thinks of others. And yet I never seem to get what I want!' She stopped sobbing and looked flatly out of the window. 'He is so distant with me, sometimes I think he barely knows I exist.'

'God?' John ventured.

'Arthur.'

'Ah,' he said, 'so we are talking of a man here?'

She sniffed. 'Arthur Stansky. He came to me every night when my ma was ill. And when she died, I went to him, and he rejected me. It was too soon, perhaps, but I didn't have a choice! I was broke. And I loved him, I really did. Then he came here, to the Grand. It was a very bad thing to do. And we haven't spoken since. Not really. I forgave him for that night, long ago, but he won't talk to me.'

'Dear, dear. He's ashamed. It doesn't mean he doesn't like you.'

'But I said I had forgiven him!'

'Aye, but the heart is a difficult thing to understand. We act contrary to how we feel, and we feel contrary to how we act. He is just ashamed of himself. I promise.' He laid his hand down on the crown of her head, as he imagined a minister might, and felt all the good love for this world that he thought, this morning, he had lost forever. 'You are too fine a woman to punish yourself like this.'

'Thank you,' she said to him, and took his hand and put it in her own. It was soft, her palm, and it suddenly reminded John of where he was. He retracted it quickly, although he didn't mean to.

'Sorry,' he said, quite ashamed of himself.

Eliza shrugged. 'What will you do today?'

'Salvage what I can. Begin again. Eke something of goodness from this thing.'

'You seem almost happy about it.'

'What else can I do. And you?'

'I am planning my way out of here. But it's a secret.' She smiled weakly. 'Don't tell anyone.' She seemed about to say something further but then stopped herself.

'Well, I wish you luck. You are too fine, too good a woman to be stuck here.' Eliza smiled thinly and turned in the eave of the door. 'Sorry,' she said, 'you know, about the tears. I've reduced the rate at the reception desk as you weren't . . . seen to. Don't let Musa crab you for more.'

'I won't.'

'Oh, and Mr Verger? Please don't tell anyone that Arthur came here. To the Grand. It was wrong of him, but I wouldn't want the whole Island to know.' Verger nodded his head. 'Then it is goodbye.' She smiled and said, 'And thank you.'

John returned to the window. Outside, the rain had stopped and a hole had found its way in the white mesh of the clouds, and what was left of the winter trees were streaked with sunshine. Aye, the whole world had seemed to give up its sulk. He remembered last May's epiphany and the feeling of God's friendship swelled his breast. He could burst with it, there was such a pride to this feeling, that he was so small and yet deemed so instrumental to the world!

And what was the burned lot of his house but merely the companion to the charred loveliness of the church. John had more than he needed, and was thankful for it.

25. An Article of Faith

They walked up the hill in silence: Sarah and the boy.
Nathaniel's skull was all stippled, it looked almost like a
spillage, too much of himself grown from what had been
purely skin. He had been so . . . what was the word?
Peeled, when she had first seen him; his forehead almost
vergeless. 'Come down with me to the museum,' he had
said to her, at home in Swanscott House. Sarah had looked
up to watch him dress, the braces stretched and then
snapped, the shirt as stiff as paper. He was grinning, urging
her out of the warmth of the sleeping bag.

Yesterday, she had returned from the fruitless visit to
Mrs Spenser and spent the afternoon crying and feeling
foolish. What an idiot she had been to think that of all
these people here she could merely pluck her mother out
from within them! She had been a fool not to sweep the
Island further; not to look for other possibilities. Nathaniel
managed to calm her down, but when he left that evening
she was weeping again: childish grief gripped her, all the
misery she had felt on Laura's absence suddenly returning, ten years later. A failure; the whole trip had been a
failure. Laura was lost to her; she was lost in newsprint
and photographs; neither on the Island nor in England.

Laura had disappeared; and Sarah couldn't explain it.

She had been asleep when Nathaniel had tiptoed in, late last night. When he came down to the sleeping bag, he smelled, improbably, of soot. She found grains of sand in his ears and in his hair. She wondered if he was drunk and asked him that. He said he had never touched a tipple in his life. He fell asleep within minutes, his breath slowing, a carbon waft about him, the smell of fire on his clothes.

As they rounded the first bit of Marley Hill, Sarah saw the sea. The sun was high, heatless and white. Odd, how it gave no warmth. The rain had stopped but a fog was closing in at the bay. They walked in silence: Sarah, plonking along, ungainly in her walk; she hoped Nathaniel wouldn't notice. The boy's eyes ferreted the hill – watching for this gang, these boys. He was scared, she could see that much, though he carried himself as someone who knew nothing of fear. At the hilltop she saw the little town with its big houses and the square and the bay with the black pier. Tomorrow, she would walk back down it, knowing nothing more about her mother than when she had arrived. Nathaniel followed her line of sight down to the jetty. 'And you're serious about going? Tomorrow?'

She looked up at him, surprised. What else could she do? 'I can't stay. My dad'll be waiting for me.'

'Not even for the winter? Just for a few months?'

'No. Not even for the winter.'

'It's baneful hard, Sarah, hearing you say that.'

'Aye,' she said, 'and it's hard to say it. But England's my home.' He swallowed and looked out across the sea. 'I'll miss you, Nathaniel. And I'll remember you. I promise.'

He avoided looking at her. 'Come on, then.'

They headed to Maiden's Square, taking the steep of Marley Hill. Low and doleful, the trees up here were so thin it was a wonder they stood up to the Island winds. Sarah couldn't think of this Island in summer, couldn't imagine that its earth had, months ago, known something of warmth. No fierce heat; no warmth in the waters; no lambent light of summer at rest on the sea-top. No – she would always imagine it like this: wintry and November-ish, a difficult place for comfort. Nathaniel traced the bones of her spine as she walked. He was the Island's warmth, and that was all.

At the flat, he led her to the square, to the places Sarah always wanted to remember: the launderette, the grocer's, the fishmonger's, that shop down there called Buttons. In her mind's eye too she sketched a portrait of him. There was something to this picture of Nathaniel, or the antici-pated memory of him when she would be back in England, that was fragile, as if, at the windy mount of Marley Hill, he had been nothing more than a statue of ash.

He'd not yet told her what they were here for. The mu-seum's door was hidden by the stage and its sign banged the stone wall, plangently, insistently, as the wind swung it. Sarah asked what they were doing here but Nathaniel didn't reply and led her on, pushing the door, and bringing her into the low-beamed room. In the museum he cupped her jaw so that her mouth was close to his. 'No one's here,' he said. He kissed her and his tongue darted into her mouth, the hand straying, scooping a breast.

She broke away from him. He watched her, alarmed, suddenly.

In the photographs, in the next room, there were black eyes and nostrils and slit mouths. Their fatigue came off the mob like a stink. Had he brought her here to shame her again? To teach her a lesson in her country's fine narrative? She felt, now, that she could not be shocked: some hardness of the Island had become part of her and she could not be moved or shamed.

'I think there is a logbook, here; I think they kept a log, of who came here and when.' Nathaniel stooped down to a cabinet, reaching for a thick red book, pulling it from the shelf and mounting it on a lectern. The book cracked as he opened it: the pages were rough-hewn, the paper heavy. At the top of the column *January 1951* was written. On the first page there were dates of birth and home towns, mostly from the North: Manchester, York, Newcastle, Sunderland. Lots of young men; at the beginning. The next date was that year's summer: more women, this time, and children: she saw the name Margaret Firth (he pointed here, and said, 'That's my mam, aye,') and then flicking through the pages she saw the dates went further and further apart. Until they came to a stop, in 1977. He said to her, very tenderly, and quietly, as if she were a child: 'And it's 1977 you're looking for? Am I right?'

'Yes,' she said.

Nathaniel turned the page. Sarah looked to the other room and her country's history seemed completely absurd – to get rid of people like this, and photograph them, to boot, in their Godless march to exile. She felt proud of her mother, for Saint Gregory's, for burning down a house of cold and moral probity. One could not just let it all happen. There were other things to account for, aside from God.

There was a long list of deportees in the summer of 1977: mostly those who had been convicted of the church-burnings in '76. She remembered some of the names from the deportation lists she had read in the Newcastle Library. There were a hundred or so names here until they came to a stop. 'But no Laura,' she said. 'No Laura. I don't understand. These would have been her contemporaries in the Movement. Laura was arrested for one of these church-burnings. I don't understand. How is it she's not on a prison list, and not on a deportation list either?' Sarah began to admonish herself, again, just as she had done all day yesterday: 'I see a stupid photograph then leap on the first boat out of England. I'm an idiot. A real idiot.'

Nathaniel scanned each name in the column until he came to the last name. 'Sarah? Who was the woman you talked to yesterday? Mrs Spenser? Beatrice Spenser?'

'Aye.'

'Well, look at that,' he said, pointing to the last name in the column. 'Looks like she was on the last boat too. Perhaps she knows something about your ma. Perhaps she's worth another try.'

'She doesn't want to talk to me.'

'So?'

'She made that quite clear, Nathaniel. That she knows nothing about Mum, and even if she does, she doesn't want to tell me anything.'

'C'mon, Sarah. She's the one most likely to know something. Your photograph shows the last boat that came here, correct? Well, turns out Beatrice *was on that boat*. She might know who that woman is. She might know who your ma is. Come on, now, doll.' He brought his arm around her and let the boards of the book hit the pages softly.

Hundreds of captive eyes seemed to follow her as she left the museum with him. Nathaniel almost had to pull her along. So Mrs Spenser was on the last boat here. It didn't really mean anything. And she wasn't up for probing her any more. She just wanted to go home, and be done with the whole thing – consign it to memory, and misadventure. Laura was lost.

Mrs Spenser's house looked tired, as if one more blast of wind could powder it back down to sand and stones. The jolly red door was fooling no one. For the first time, Sarah noticed the slight list of the house, how it seemed to lean toward the cliff and the suggestion, in the marshy front garden, of neglect. Loosened, the house might fly from here, with very little force whatsoever.

'She won't speak to me,' she said to Nathaniel, tugging at one of his cuffs, and eyeing the steep hedge warily. 'She doesn't know anything. Let's go, let's go back to the house.'

'She could have chosen a better lodging,' Nathaniel said, ignoring her. He gave a short, nicking laugh. ' 'Tis worse than my abode.'

He walked the gravel path; she followed, lagging. Nathaniel rang the bell when he saw she was not going to do it. There were the sounds of slippers and mumbled warnings, probably to the boy, and then the door unlocking. When Mrs Spenser saw who it was, she came out of the house and shut the door flat behind her. 'Yes?' the woman snapped, eyeing Nathaniel, then turning back to

Sarah. 'I told you, young lady, I didn't want to speak to you again.'

'Please, Mrs Spenser, I need to talk to you.'

'I have nothing more to say.'

Sarah gathered her courage. 'I saw your name in the logbook in the museum. You were one of the last ones here in '77. Which meant you were on the last boat, which means you might know something about that woman in the photograph.'

'That means nothing,' she snapped, and though her voice was full of conviction, Mrs Spenser reached out to the door handle, as if to steady herself, and her eyes flitted nervously down the trunk of Nathaniel's jacket.

'It means you might have been on the boat with her. It means you might know what happened to her after she came here. Laura seems to have disappeared. Please, if you know anything, it would be a great help to me. A great help.'

Beatrice pulled her dressing-gown closer to her throat. Between the hem and her slippers, the thin ankles were mauve with cold. 'Fine,' she pointed a finger to Sarah. 'You can come in.' She flicked her hand toward Nathaniel. 'But you can leave him out of it.'

'Fine,' he said. 'I'll wait out here, freezing to death.'

'I won't be long,' Sarah said.

'No,' said the woman to Nathaniel, and boldly, here, she took a few steps toward him: 'I don't want you outside the house. I *know* about Mrs Richards. Is your memory so short you can't remember Wednesday night? Wait at the end of the road. Not here.'

*

Sarah walked through the cold hall, Mrs Spenser followed. The kitchen was just as it looked from the outside, with the brass skillet pans on the hooks, the small fireplace and big stove. Nothing could be cleaner, or more polished. It was strange, for Sarah, to be inside, looking out; like being in a different world, the room untouched by sunshine, on account of the high hedge. 'Your son,' Sarah said, 'he's asleep?'

'Aye.'

'You brought him with you? From England?'

'No. I had him here. He's five.'

Beatrice filled the kettle and put it on the gas. The black iron looked heavy in her grasp. The stack of newspapers was taller than it had looked from the outside, and yellower, too, as if they had been there for some time. Damp and finely layered as a pastry, Sarah wondered why she kept them. 'You've been watching me for days,' Beatrice said, by the oven, choosing not to turn. Steam started to pipe from the spout, and she put her hands toward the heat. 'How did it enter your mind that this was an acceptable thing to do?'

'I'm sorry. I didn't mean to scare you.'

Beatrice turned, her eyes lively with anger. Blue and accusing, they reminded Sarah of her mother's eyes when she was annoyed. An angry blush had come up around the freckles. 'Well, you did. Those boys! They crabbed Mrs Richards on Wednesday night, and I thought you were coming for me. When you were outside – oh! I was so frightened! You have no idea!'

So that was it: Beatrice had assumed, yesterday, that Sarah was part of Nathaniel's gang. Hence her rage, yesterday, at being called on – not rage, however, but fear: Mrs Spenser was scared of her. Sarah said gently: 'I have nothing to do with them. I met Nathaniel by accident. He's fed me, these past few days, and given me shelter, and without that, I don't know, I might have been very ill. Whatever he has done in the past is not my business. I apologize, if I scared you. But I can tell you, quite certainly, that I have nothing to do with this gang. Nothing.'

The kettle whistled. Cups hung neatly from a rack above the oven. Looking no more pleased than when she had opened the door, Beatrice poured powdered milk into a jug and added water. She stirred it inattentively for some moments, the hood of the spoon clinking against the jug's sides, doing circles and circles, the other hand holding the small of her back as if she suffered from an ache. 'So where are you from? In *England*, as you said.' Her tone was mocking.

'Near Newcastle.'

Beatrice set the steaming cup down. Tiny flecks of milk floated on the tea's top. She smirked. 'Near Newcastle? And?'

'It's called Trimdon, just outside it.'

She looked at her quickly. Her expression had changed completely. 'Trimdon?'

'Yes.'

'And that's where your mother was from as well?'

'Yes. Look. I don't want to take up any more of your time, Mrs Spenser. But I need to know if you've ever heard of Laura Wicks.' Sarah took out the article and spread it on the kitchen table. Laura looked out, vague, her features smudged by wear. 'Here. Saint Gregory's. This is what she was arrested for. That's her, there.' Sarah indicated the date. 'That's the day after she disappeared. July 5th, 1976.' Sarah delved down into her bag, and produced the photograph of the last boat. 'And here is the picture of the last boat, in '77. There she is. And you were on that boat too, somewhere. I saw your name in the logbook. I know that you were on this boat. But I can't seem to find Laura anywhere. Not here, on this Island; and not on any documents either.'

Beatrice sat opposite her at the long wooden table. The tabletop was worn smooth, as if it had come, like driftwood, from the sea. 'I will talk to you, if you promise that you have nothing to do with this gang. Promise me. Mrs Richards had such a hard time of it the other night, I couldn't bear it if anything happened to my son. Promise me.'

'I promise.'

Beatrice held the edge of the table so that her knuckles showed white. She shook her head as if she disagreed with some thought or feeling in passing. 'Sarah. In this photograph, that's me. I remember that coat. I still have it, somewhere. It was so long ago. Nearly ten years, now, aye. They always said we looked alike. Me and Laura. You've mistaken me for your mother.'

'That's you?'

'Aye.' She tapped at the face Sarah had assumed to be Laura's. 'That's me.'

'That's *you*?'

'Aye. But Laura – your mum – didn't come here with the rest of us.'

Sarah's voice was little more than a whisper. 'Why? Why not?'

Beatrice stood and piled more logs into the grate and then warmed her hands against the flame. Without turning her back, she said: 'Laura was a friend, though we didn't know each other for long before I was deported. She was a kind woman. Very kind. I liked her very much. But we were different. She was a lot stronger than me.'

There was a moment or so of silence and then a log cracked. 'I arrived a little later than she did, in August, after one of the Movement's burnings in Preston. Laura and I, amongst other women from the Movement, were held in a female prison, in Sunderland. That was '76. When the police started interrogating me, about people I knew, deals I'd be willing to make, Laura kept on saying, *Don't believe them, they're lying, don't give people up*.

'But there was months and months of this. We'd be taken to a bare room, one of the "interview rooms", and asked the same questions, over and over again. The police kept on saying that if I gave them a name, of anyone higher up, they would get me a lenient sentence, in an English prison. They said that I wouldn't have to go to the Island. One of them hit me. But there wasn't much violence. They knew I'd give in – they recognized something in me, I guess.'

Beatrice turned: her face was rather haggard – as if this confession was going to be painful. 'And eventually, I did give in. I blabbed and blabbed, about any names, of anybody in the Movement I could remember. And I remember how your mother wasn't angry with me when I did it. She held me, when I wept, and told me everything would be OK. I couldn't be as strong as her. I just couldn't.'

'How do you mean?'

'Laura was so steadfast. She wouldn't give up the names of the two men she was with at Saint Gregory's. But there were consequences to this. Laura would come into the cafeteria with black eyes and fat lips. I think things happened to her that I wouldn't like to say. But she remained silent, no matter what they did to her. I admired her, very much, but I didn't have the same strength.

'When it came to the trials, though, in '77, Laura was excluded. Hers was still an open case. And when it came to the expulsion that summer, Laura was not on the deportation list for the Island. Finally, we all saw Laura's strategy. In keeping the secret, she had kept the case open, and saved herself from deportation. Of course, I regretted confessing. The promise of a soft sentence was not kept. We were all duly packed off on the boat, just as they'd always planned. And here I am,' Beatrice turned and gestured to the photograph of the boat, 'wondering if it might not be better to jump into the waves.'

Beatrice's face had cleared, as if by talking she had removed some weight of history pressing on her. In fact, she looked teary, as if she might be about to cry. 'Oh, I am sorry, dear, it's always difficult talking about the past. We avoid it, here, you know. It might drive us mad if we talked about nothing but England all the time.'

'Mum's in an English prison?'

'Aye. You know, I've been watching out for her. In the newspapers that come across on the boat. I thought that, maybe, with the Sunday Agreement, in '83, she might have confessed. They were letting people go, by then, "minor" members of the Movement who were cooperating. Still she didn't give up any names. When they announced the list of prisoners who were to be released, hers wasn't on it. I couldn't believe it. I couldn't believe her tenacity, her determination.'

'So she could have come back to us? Three years ago? And she chose not to?'

Beatrice shrugged and smiled at her sadly. 'Aye. Well. Your mother always had a very deep sense of honour, I think. Perhaps it was misplaced. I don't know.'

'Where is she? What prison?'

'She was in Sunderland. But she's not there any more.' She took the cups from the table and poured the cold tea down the sink, despite Sarah having had none of hers. The taps went on with a flourish as Beatrice rinsed the sink. Then she sat, and she smiled at her, quite warmly. The pans above her gave the woman a beatific look – there was a sense, perhaps, of atonement: as if speaking about Laura had comforted her. 'Now, Sarah. I am going to show you something. It may be shocking to you. It was a shock to me, too. I picked up the newspaper on Tuesday morning from the museum, as I always do, and for the rest of the day I couldn't think about anything else. It's concerning your mother. And her whereabouts. Take the top newspaper from the pile, Sarah. There's news in there for you.'

News? It was news enough that Laura was in an English prison. Sarah rose and took the top newspaper from the pile. The paper was thin in her hands, and damp. As Beatrice had said, the date was last Sunday, and it had evidently been brought to the Island on last Monday's *Saviour* with Sarah herself. There were mugshots of two men at the top of the article. The headline was *Justice for Saint Gregory's*. Sarah began to read.

> These are, finally, the identities of the two men responsible for the church-burning at Saint Gregory's in Berwick on July 4th, 1976, which killed the parish Minister, Rev Ed Williams.
>
> During a raid of a Movement house in Whetstone, North London, Christopher Ware and Thomas Hemming were shot and both killed after they refused to give up their weapons.
>
> For ten years the case has remained unsolved.
>
> The driver of the getaway car, a Mrs Laura Wicks, who was apprehended at the scene, has never revealed the two men's names, even when offered release as part of the terms of the Sunday Agreement.
>
> On hearing about their deaths, Mrs Wicks, now 36, confirmed to the police yesterday that Ware and Hemming were the two men she was with who set fire to the church and murdered Rev Williams. Mrs Wicks, given her cooperation, and time in police custody, will now be released as part of the prisoner roll-out instigated by the Sunday Agreement in 1983.

Sarah stopped reading. There was no photograph of the woman. Just her name.

Laura Wicks.

Beatrice smiled. 'You see. She kept her word. When she told the police their names, it couldn't hurt Tom and Chris. Not any more. She kept her promise right until she had to.'

'Did you know them? These two?'

'No. I never met them. They were very lucky to have Laura as the driver that day. Anyone else would have given them up for a song. And now she's to be released. How lucky she is. Or at least, not lucky. But clever. She was always very clever, your mum.'

Sarah re-read the article. Here it was: the evidence, finally, of Laura's whereabouts. And it had been shipped over in one of the boxes on the boat! All this time, Sarah had been so close to the answer and yet completely unaware of its whereabouts. If only she'd stopped at the newsagent's after the butcher's last Sunday, or watched the television before sneaking off to Newcastle! If only she had opened one of the boxes on the boat that night!

'How old are you now, Sarah?' Beatrice asked.

'Seventeen,' she said, as she re-read the article again.

'Aye, aye,' Beatrice said softly. 'God knows it must have broken her heart to think she might never see you again. And now she's coming home; you might even see her before Christmas.'

'But I'm on the Island.'

'And she's in England. Aye. Well,' Beatrice almost gave a chuckle, 'stranger things have happened. No harm in it now. You'll see her when you're back. Can I ask, Sarah, how it was you managed to come here?'

Now it was time for Sarah to smile. 'I smuggled myself on Monday's boat.'

'A stowaway!'

'It wasn't very hard, you know. Newcastle docks – they're not policed, or anything, I sneaked in when no one was looking. You could do the same, I bet, from the pier, creep in when the Boatman wasn't looking—'

'No,' the woman said, firmly, 'it may not be much, but the Island's home now, aye. I can't go back to England; not after they chucked us out. It wouldn't feel like home, there, not any more. And I have a life here,' she smiled sadly, 'I think.'

Sarah looked at the article again. 'But the whole street thinks she was having an affair with someone from York!'

Beatrice laughed. 'Well. There'll be some issues to iron out, certainly.'

Sarah was tempted to ask Beatrice about her crimes, ask why she was here on the Island, but she stopped herself. She didn't look like she wanted to go over these things. Sarah said thank you, and asked her if she might convey a message to anyone in England.

'No,' Beatrice said. 'But recommend me to Laura. You have her likeness, now that I can see it.'

'And so do you,' Sarah said, almost laughing. 'May I keep this?' she asked, pointing to the paper.

Beatrice nodded, held her hand, and said, 'Goodbye, Sarah Wicks.'

'Thank you, again, for talking to me. I know it was hard.'

From the hallway, putting the newspapers back into her bag, Sarah heard the woman shout after her. 'And you tell those boys to stay away from this house!'

Sarah didn't know whether to laugh or cry. The answer all along had been in one of the boxes in the boat – she might have even been sitting on it. For ten hours, at least, Laura's whereabouts had been under her nose. Under her bottom, in fact. And soon she would meet her. Really meet her. Laura Wicks was coming home. Sarah raced out of the house to tell Nathaniel the news.

26. The Aeroplane

At midday on Sunday, Margaret had fixed herself a decent lunch of baked potato with piccalilli; and had even managed a crossword, going only twice to the dictionary. As the day went on, she sat there happily, ready to cook more fish tomorrow, ready to bring her baby boy back home. Her monkey. He was a naughty boy to be sharking the Island like this, but that's all it was. Mischief – Eliza had said. Tomorrow night, at supper, she might even try a mouthful or two of her meal. Jack would think she was being silly, not eating fish for this long.

After the crossword, Margaret laid the newspaper on her lap and took a small sip of the buttercup syrup. She wouldn't re-order the pills. They were bad for her anyway; she shouldn't be taking them. She would insist on no further cigarettes in the house. And Jake too: he would be banned from supper, or, for that matter, from coming around at all; aye, he had the devil in his eyes.

Margaret closed her eyes. She thought of Jack's letters. *In the summer I close the window, to shut out the sound of the sea, for I know you are jealous of it.* She opened her eyes but it was all right that he was not there because she could not change it and she had to go on for her son. The pen rolled away from her lap. Such a sense of peace in the house today. For most of her life, a Sunday had been a time for burning churches – but how happy she was that all of that was over now. What else was it that he had written? *I'm in love with you, Margaret Malraux – I tell the fishes it every day.* Her eyelids dropped again.

A metallic hum woke her minutes or hours later. She squinted toward the window; there was still some daylight outside. Margaret raised herself from the chair. She did not feel scared about what she was about to do. From behind the chair she brought out her big shawl for warmth. Doubtless, it would be cold outside. Outside.

Margaret opened the first outhouse door and man-oeuvred herself down the step. Holding on to the ledge with the plant pots, she made it to the back door. She managed the next step with a little hop, and then the pavement, which led on to a rhubarb bush, the garage, and a tree of unknown name. When Jack had brought her mackerel home from the catch, she would peg the fish up on the clothesline with the socks, to let them dry out in the sun.

The noise was behind her, now, and growing. Evening was coming and with it a great rolling mist that might obstruct her view. The last time she had done this – she knew, quite specifically – was autumn, nine years ago, because Margaret and Jack had not seen another plane together again. They had always come out on the last Sunday of the month, when some plane, on its way to Norway or some other destination, crossed the Island. Perhaps it went somewhere special, or maybe it had come, specifically, to watch them. They didn't know and they didn't care. All Islanders, without exception, loved the plane: suggestive, as it was, of Elsewhere.

In the garden, before it arrived, Jack and Margaret would talk about what they missed from England.

'Spare ribs,' he would say.

And she: 'Steak!'

'Red wine.'

'Nail polish. Nice lipstick.'

'Constant electricity.'

'Cigarettes.'

'More women.' An elbow in the ribs. 'Less men.'

'Fewer. Fewer men.'

'Women who don't correct my grammar.'

And then the plane would come, from nowhere, the sound drilling into the clouds, low and near. They would watch in awe, as if it imparted some vision of the world that was now impossible to imagine.

'How small are we to him?' she asked.

'Can he even see us?'

Margaret and Jack would jump up and down flapping their arms like children. 'Hallo!'

'Can you see us?'

'Yell if you can see us!'

They both wanted to see some passenger's hand flash in the window, or for the pilot to give a debonair salute. Anything to acknowledge they weren't in this alone.

Margaret had not seen the plane since Jack's death, bound, as she was, in the yellowing walls of her house.

She craned her head upward and waited. It emerged,

moments later: its body slipping in and out of the low-banked cloud. It's so beautiful, she thought, this machine, its shape stitching the cloud. How could it be held up like that? Margaret imagined herself in it, racing through air, with a great aerial view of the world, peering down at their tiny Island. She wondered if under the crests of waves the pilot could see shipwrecks and caves and hidden mountains. She wondered if he could see Jack's lost boat or the palace of his bones. She wondered if the plane travelled not just through air and space but time as well, so that the pilot knew what she had just done, as well as what she would do next.

The grey spike tipped out of sight. The sound faded. The shape flashed once or twice in the gaps between the clouds. Margaret stood in the garden until she was sure it had gone. Evening came.

Inside, in the kitchen, Margaret tossed away the last of the cigarettes. She had a moment of doubt, then redoubled her efforts and broke the cigarettes in two, tipping them into the kitchen bin where Thursday's head of bream still eyed her miserably. She would not smoke; no, she would not. She could do this as well, for her son.

They would have a fish supper tonight, just like they did when Jack was here, when he would emerge in his yellow fisherman's trousers, cold and big and starving, and they would eat together and he would jump Nathaniel on his knee. Margaret went to the purple room off the hallway and opened the wardrobe. Her fingers moved gently down the arm's lengths of her coats and dresses, vaguely embarrassed, as if someone might catch her. The fabrics were heavy and well-made, not like what was to be had any more. A box on top of the wardrobe held silk scarves, her old favourites. She tied an orange one at her throat. In the mirror she looked better for it; it gave her some colour in the cheeks, and hid some of the chin.

At the shelves, full of old boy's adventure stories and some philosophy books – they were all Jack's – her recipe book sat on the lowest rung. She hadn't looked at this book since she had given up cooking. In their early married years they had eaten enormously well: Margaret had made a feast every night, and she had been a good cook; still was. The smells of the food came to her, the weight of the dishes she would cook them in, the feeling of sweat escaping squashed breasts under her pinny. She had run a hot kitchen.

There were even, she found, some recipes from before the deportation, which she remembered jotting down – lamb shank roast, pork belly stew – in Newcastle. There was a picture of suet pudding. A small triangle had been cut from the pie, and tallow and kidney spilled onto the plate, steaming in perfection. Margaret tied the knot of the orange scarf tighter.

As she decided on the dish – Arctic char with parsnips – she snapped the book closed and a piece of paper fell from its flush pages. In her hands, the folds were sharp, they had been firmly pressed over the years. Margaret could not believe it. Here, in this book, all this time. So here it was; Jack's last letter, stored here safely and then, in the final negligence of grief, forgotten about.

Margaret read it quickly in the fading evening light.

October, 1977

Dear Maggie,

> *Hello my dear. A short note that should
reach you tomorrow. I will be back the day after that,
so I really shouldn't write, and save us the expense, but
I like to think of your face when you have received a
letter, and I imagine you will go and sit out in the
garden (if it is fine), on the stripy deck-chair, and sit
there for ten minutes or so, reading my words.*

*How is Nathaniel? Is he behaving himself for his
mother? I hope he is not giving you too much trouble.
He is as naughty as I was at that age.*

*It is night-time now, and I am sitting in my cabin,
using candle-light to see by. The generator is down again
but I do not mind – it makes much less of a noise.*

*By day I wonder what it is you do when I am on
the boat. I think about what you might think about;
I wonder what you do – even when you have told me,
repeatedly, all that it is you do on a normal day. I think
about you taking Nathaniel to the square, to the
launderette, to the beach – I think about you putting
him to bed and singing that wee song for him.*

*But somehow I cannot quite grasp together every
little moment of your day. I want to know what it is you
are doing when I am casting the nets, or pulling in the
trawl. Whether you are gardening, or perhaps doing the
washing, looking up at the aeroplane without me, or
whether you are buying your bream at Stansky's.*

*But then, even knowing the monuments of your day,
I still desire more. It is the long stretches in between
buying the fish and cooking it that I most desire to know*

about. These bits, shall we call them your lost time, when you are walking home or simply sitting in your armchair, these moments fall out of my scope, and they fall out of memory, out of remembrance. They are precious. I wish I could somehow keep them, because I know that these moments are lost, irretrievably, in and amongst more important things.

My favourite way to imagine you is to think of you at your armchair. Suddenly, your gaze has fallen into nothingness, and you stare at nothing. Whatever has alighted on the bonny shores of your mind has captivated you, and I know, during these instances, I do not exist for you. It does not make me anxious. We all of us have these moments of deep meditation. I wonder where you are. Are you thinking of Newcastle? The Grand? Your Pa? Wherever your memory has taken you, it has bound you fast to the longest minute.

If I could make a narrative out of every one of these lost moments I would be a happy man. I would read such a book from morning to night, so that I might ken you better. All the dross: that's what I'd like to know of you. And in the margins, because isn't that how far we get in, when we try to map out our lover's mind, only to the margins – never the heart, no, not really – I will pen my notes on you. And all of these lost chapters I will weave into a narrative, and I shan't let a soul read it. And I will call it, In Search of the Lost Time of Margaret Malraux. Who would not fall to their knees to hear the majestic and muddied thoughts of my wife? You're an irresistible woman – impossible at times.

Maggie. The candle is sputtering and I am nearly out

of wax. I will put down my pen, and then I will think of you. Who would have guessed you'd married such a sap? But there you are. I'm in love with you – I tell the fishes it every day.

All my love, all my life,

Jack

Margaret folded it back to. She carried the recipe book to her armchair then laid out the letter on the bottom stair in the hall. Nathaniel should read his father's words. How beautiful; how sonorous. It might teach him something of kindness.

She gathered her coat and her purse, checking there was enough money for the char. And then she did it: walked out of the front door, and made her way over to Mr Stansky's.

27. The Fog

Fog filled the garden. Rich with the smell of fish and the sea, fog rolled down the streets and hung about doorways. At first, the air was tissuey, easily broken by the hand, no more than a mist, and then, as the early afternoon tipped quickly into darkness, it thickened into a fog, near the bay at first, as if the salt on the cliffs better attracted it, then it had gone cottony in the streets, and in the square, and up above to Warkworth Town and down into the crowded streets of Lynemouth, so that by evening the fog had come so low it skirted the hill, leaving Marley Hill exposed, the mount poking itself out of the cloud like a leg from a fussy girdle.

Down in the garden of Swanscott House, Sarah and Nathaniel had watched the aeroplane as it flew through the low-banked cloud. It was always sad for Nathaniel to see it: he remembered the times when his mam and dad would watch it together, and he remembered the odd feeling too, of being excluded from the ceremony. He remembered once going out into the garden to join them, and his da saying to him, quite kindly, but firmly, 'No. This is for your mam and dad, just now,' and his parents had cuddled up to each other only when they were sure he was gone. From what English ceremony did they keep him? And is this what they did in England, in Hartlepool and Newcastle, in the places of his parents' birth, stand and whisper to each other and watch aeroplanes? He'd been embarrassed, watching them get syrupy in the garden below, at the way they were acting like kids – despite this evidently being an adult ceremony, from which he was excluded.

Nathaniel had watched it with Sarah, today, although the sense of occasion had been somewhat lost on her, which he didn't mind. It was an Island thing to do, and, more specifically, a thing for old English people to do, like his ma, and his pa; he understood that now, was old enough to understand the significance of what they had lost. When the plane appeared in sight, Sarah had been about to say something, and Nathaniel had wondered if she was about to tell him she had actually been on a real plane. He was glad, if this were true, that she hadn't said anything. He didn't like to think of her gallivanting so far away from him.

As the plane had sounded over the Island, Sarah had, instead, talked of an Englishwoman who was nowhere near the Island, who had remained on English soil all this time. Sarah had looked thrilled, when she'd come back to Swanscott House, after talking with Mrs Spenser, purely talking a mile a minute about her ma being discovered in England, something about the deaths of two men and the confession of their names, the Sunday Agreement, and her mother's release from an English jail. Nathaniel didn't listen so much as watch her: the warmth of her cheeks, the sudden sharpness of her eyes. She was excited. The news of her ma's return had made her buoyant.

*

But Sarah saw how her private happiness seemed to dull him. Nathaniel had watched the plane fly its course overhead with a longing look, and she was aware that his father was not missing, was not waiting to be discovered. Distantly, as she was talking of Laura, and her mother's confession, Nathaniel was toeing the grass with his boot, so that it was almost bald in that patch, and fiddling with one of the studs on the jacket.

Tomorrow, she would go back to England on the boat. And maybe even tomorrow night her mother would be at home with them.

And if she could stay, would she? He was unlike any English boy she had ever met. When they slept in the bed, together, on Friday night, she wondered how it was she had ended up here. Not just on this Island, but with him. And yet it felt right, as if by knowing him she might better know the Island, as if Nathaniel were a kind of map.

Beatrice had seemed frightened by him, which had shocked her, since Sarah had suspected his gang were really only nuisances, not the menaces Nathaniel had tried to impress on her in the beginning. And Beatrice had mentioned something or other, a – what was the word – *crabbing* – that was it – of a Mrs Richards on Wednesday, and only yesterday night he descended to the sleeping bag with the stink of fire on him.

And yet, here he stood, with the aeroplane banking slowly, tipping, at an angle, greyly flying from them, his blue eyes looking sightlessly toward the sky, an emblem of all the good she had found on the Island.

No, she thought, though Beatrice was right about her

mother, she wasn't right about Nathaniel. She couldn't be. He was a good boy; a kind boy.

Sarah stopped talking, all of a sudden, and ran up into the house, past the kitchen with the pushed-back chairs, past the long staircase and up into the bedroom looking out onto the garden. Her fingers knocked the window. Nathaniel looked up at her. All week, she had viewed him as some boy of rebellion and grace, but now she knew him for what he was. Lonely and sad, a boy made from the cold wash of the Sound. She waved down to him. His eyes rounded in delight. A strip of teeth grinned up at her. 'Hello,' she said and Sarah heard her own little voice in the room. He took steps toward the house but she gestured for him to stop. Sarah unlatched the window and removed her jumper, brought the white T-shirt off so that she sat crouched in the pale bra. At her spine she unclipped it. The bones of her ribs curved white; the pink tips of her breasts were hard in the cold. A gamey scent came off her skin, her skin which was the same coolness as the air. She laughed, naked in the fog.

Downstairs, she heard his boot-steps, the sound was now familiar to her. He began on the stairs. Soon he would be at the landing, then at the door. She would stay by the window. She would let him find her.

The boots were behind her now. He must be inches away from her. There was silence for moments but she did not move. Then there were his lips on her neck, a tongue kissing toward her ear. She felt a surge of calm, and pleasure, that she had come here – wrongly, perhaps, but still she had managed to find the truth – and the thought of

Laura returning was perfect, and the thought of the boy, here with her now, was perfect too.

A hand moved her jaw toward him though she didn't turn her hips. She felt the hard plates of his teeth and pressed him closer to her, the buckles of the braces hard against her hips. His fingers came up her thighs and then to her breasts, thumb thumbing a nipple, the other hand bringing her around to face him, so that she saw his whole face in the moonlight. A hand grasped down to her, waiting, she moved against the sill, his finger quick, rounding her. Her legs sided his hips; his skin under his shirt was so white it was almost a glare. She held on to his shoulders.

He looked suddenly bashful and shy, biting his lip. A blush had come up his cheeks. 'Nathaniel?' she said, as he sat down next to her, his knees against her knees. He smelled of apples, and she remembered how, last night, he smelled of soot. 'I want to ask you something.'

'Aye. Go on.'

'When I talked to Mrs Spenser, she said something bad had happened with Mrs Richards, on Wednesday, and that she didn't want it happening to her. What happened, Nath? I think you should tell me.'

He didn't say anything for a few moments. 'Something bad happened with Jake. He did something which I didn't give him permission to do. We were just playing about, and then he took it too far. He always takes it too far.'

'She was scared, Nath. I don't think you should go around the Island frightening people.'

Nathaniel unwrapped her arms from around him. 'Look. I didn't tell you before because you were excited about the news of your mam. But Jake, the one who crabbed Mrs

Richards – he knows about you. He's seen you. He knows you're not from here. And I'm worried about it, about him – he can be such a menace, as I said. He knows you're English, and he'll think you're a threat, and he hates to be left out of things.'

'What does it matter, now, Nathaniel? I'm away tomorrow.'

'Aye. It's just worrying me a bit, that's all. Though it shouldn't do; I know that.'

'It's over now, Nath. I'll stay in all day. Today and tomorrow. And then I'm off. And I'll be far away from him.'

'And from me.'

Sarah brought him back, kissing him. The boy unlaced his boots, took off his socks, and pulled out some handkerchiefs. 'Why've you got hankies in your boots, Nathaniel?'

'They were my da's. Still waiting to fill them.'

Sarah laughed.

When they made love they did it gently as if they were swimmers plumbing the depths of a bay.

28. After the Fire

After the fire last night, Nathaniel had stomped away, unwilling to talk to Jake or give him any further information about the English girl. Oh aye, Jake was in Nathaniel's bad books, but he didn't much care. It had been a triumph, last night, and though Nathaniel still had the English girl under his wing, Jake had won with Verger.

That afternoon, when Sammy questioned him about the English girl, Jake was forced into some amount of lies about where he had spent the day. He told Sammy he'd been down to Swanscott House earlier to talk to Sarah. *Sarah*, he said, as if he were on familiar terms with her. He told Sammy that he'd touched her long copper hair and how she had blushed when she saw him. 'Oh, she is a dolly,' he said, 'despite her Gottery!'

He told Sammy how Old Baldie Boots had stood by mute as Jake laid down the law to her about how they did things on this Island. He told him how she'd bossed Nathaniel about, as if she was his own mam. How he had interrogated Sarah and how he thought this mother story was a cover-up for a much more menacing plan; he told him how frightened she'd become.

The two boys laughed gleefully in Sammy's bedroom as

Mr Carter shouted at them to keep it down – he was waiting for the aeroplane and didn't want to miss it.

None of this was true – Jake had not laid eyes on her since Friday night with Sammy himself – but Sammy seemed to believe him, and they hatched plans for what they would do with Sarah next. Stick her up on a cross or leave her cold in the church or parade her about town pinned in English newspapers. Somehow she would be punished for her English provenance.

No, Jake had not seen Sarah, but, last night, he had dreamed of her.

He dreamed he had been at the mortuary with her. There was no casket in the room; he had thought Mrs Page would still be here, but that was the bad logic of dreams, since he knew in real life that she was already under the waves. The enamel walls gleamed like a bathtub with room enough for two. Seated, Sarah held his hand while he looked down at his lap and tried hard not to laugh. He noticed the tenting of his trousers as the girl's chest heaved up and down and then she looked at him, and smiled, and kissed him softly on the lips. Sarah held him tightly against her bosom, which flattened against him and was as lovely as pudding. He put a finger down the passage between each bosom and then gave each one of them a squeeze. The bulge gave to his clambering hand. His finger strayed to a cold hard nipple. He felt a burst of delight. The girl held him closer. He peered down the black vest and glimpsed there the bra-less epiphany of one of her nipples. The freckles ringed the cool brown tip. He felt a surge of shame and delight, and he wondered, consciously, if he had wet the bed.

Then suddenly, Jake and Sarah were down on a beach and there was nothing but the sea; the North Sea Sound just as it always was. Jake looked down and in his arms he was carrying the girl and her white limp arms were as floppy as a fish. Her ginger hair fanned about her like a crown. She was so lovely and cool and clean and tasted of salt. He was taking her somewhere but he did not know where; he just knew she was an enormous weight, far heavier than she should have been. And then he woke.

Aye, last night's dream was bothering him. He wanted to see Sarah for himself again, to cleanse himself of the image, despite Nathaniel's warnings not to. He left Sammy's house, saying a polite goodbye to Mr Carter, and skirted around Marley Hill toward the Malraux house to see if Nathaniel was in. Mrs Malraux was in the parlour, reading, which was unusual for her; he'd never known her not to be encushioned in her armchair by the fire. She came to the door and looked at him narrowly with a handwritten paper still clutched, and told him Nathaniel was not here. Jake had begun to walk away when she took a step outside and said, 'You be careful, boy, sharking about these parts. You're not as welcome as you might think.' Jake thought back to the summer, when everything had been hot and scratched, the beach like a warm cracked bone, when Mammy Malraux had fed them up on biscuits and tea, and purely he thought she had cared for him, and him for her. He'd even called her Mammy. Well, this was how the Malrauxs turned on you; theirs was a fluid treachery.

But Jake said nothing and set off from the house. He walked quickly, shamefaced by Mammy Malraux's comment, and aware that, despite the dark, he should not be found here along Island paths. People would be looking for them, to hold them to account for Verger's fire. But he thought the silence would stick days longer, and Verger, old and unliked, wasn't likely to grass on them. Perhaps the Malades would never be caught for it; another blameless deed in the anonymity of night! But he walked to Swanscott House, urgently now, wanting to see Sarah just so that he might erase the dreamed image from his mind.

The light was on in the upper room but no one could be seen. He hoped he could crab her alone. At the back, in the garden, the air smelled of pond water. Into the house, the smell continued. Jake checked the rooms but no one was there. Very quietly, he took the stairs. The house was freezing. He heard nothing.

He checked the bathroom and the master bedroom, then pushed at the door of the room he had seen her in on Friday. It gave easily, without a noise. Into the small slot of air he let his eyes fall.

It was them. Together. They were kissing. They were making little sopping noises. They were lying on the bed, naked, the fog, outside, playing on their skin. A shapeless anger spread in Jake. Here it was indeed, for anyone to see, the toppling of a Malade! The English girl's hair was as shiny as a metal. In the light her limbs were almost lavender. Nathaniel moved his hands over her haunches to her breasts, repeatedly, as if he were reminding himself, again and again, that he could. Jake felt a hot, overflowing grief.

He idled by the door. To look away was pure loneliness; but to gaze upon them was agony.

In the last few minutes they'd stopped their wet squelching and fallen into what looked a deep and peaceful sleep. For some reason their stillness panicked Jake more than their smooching. They would be cold like this; naked.

Jake took Margaret's gun from out of his bag and held it out into the quivering air. He put the nozzle to the keyhole, liking the fact it might tunnel through the hole and into the air without splitting the frame. The gun knocked against the wood: the girl stirred but did not wake. Why wouldn't they move, why wouldn't they wake up, so that Jake could be outraged on behalf of the gang? Fog danced on them. He heard her gentle breathing and wondered, *Would it have the same sound on my chest?* From nowhere, a tear came into his eye and his heart felt fit to bursting. Though he knew, as a Malade, he shouldn't, his shoulders started the shake-and-heave, and his nose ran, and he felt the hot tears start to fall unstoppably. Jake thought of their smells together, mingling; he too would like to be inside her stinky crevices; inside, where she'd be as soft as the seabed.

Jake wiped his tears and took a good lungful. He couldn't stand this; not any more. He put the gun back in his bag and rapped on the door. 'Nathaniel?' he whispered. He shook his head to let some cold in. 'Nathaniel?' His voice sounded reedy from the blubbing. No answer, so he hit harder and harder, until Nathaniel shouted, 'Coming!' in an exasperated voice, and Jake stepped away to the banister, where he waited, uselessly, for minutes.

The boy emerged in nothing more than black jeans, doing up the fly with a cig in the crook of his mouth. Boyish skin crested over bones. The light of the match caught all the angles of his face. 'All right, Jakey. To what do I owe this pleasure?' He shut the door behind him, obscuring all view of her.

Jake couldn't quite look at him. 'I came to see the girl.'

'Oh, aye?'

'You promised me you'd show me her. Before the meeting last night, you said that.'

'I said we could all meet, some time. I didn't promise you anything. And I think you've had a good enough grozzly, for tonight, as it were.'

'I haven't even talked to her. This English girl. Found out what she's about.'

'You've had more than a good look. In flagrante, as we were.'

'In flagrante?'

'Aye. Good you didn't catch us actually at it. That might have raised a blush or two.' Nathaniel looked philosophical and smiled, wagging a finger at him. 'It does go to show, though, this theory on Gots and marriage, as we asked Mrs Richards Wednesday. See if she were a Got, Jake, it'd be no bonanza before marriage, get my ken? It's a good test. We're going to have to fuck all the girls on the Island! For the sake of our cause! Ha, ha!'

Jake found his throat very dry. 'Is she a goer, then?'

'Oh, aye,' Nathaniel said. He curled his hands over the banister and leaned back. 'A real cracker-jack.'

'Look.' Jake wouldn't lose this; not yet. 'I haven't told the other boys yet but I will if we don't see more progress. We need to interrogate her, find out what she's really about! Find out what secrets she may be gathering about the Island!'

'In a while. She's here for a while. The whole winter now, if I can get my way. It'll happen in the next few days. Then all the boys will meet her. But on my say so. We need to break them in, slowly, slowly.'

'Aye, aye,' said Jake, 'and we can talk about what sort of thing we should get up to with her. What sort of talking we should do. We might find the stinkiest things in her.'

Nathaniel gave him a curious look. 'That's the right thing. That's the right thing. You're a good boy, lad.'

'I'd do anything for the Malades. Anything you ask. And with the fire we really showed who—'

Nathaniel's face darkened. 'I told you before. It wasn't your place. Listen, Jake. It wasn't your place to suggest Verger. As I said, *immunity*, it was for me to suggest or not to suggest Verger. Do you understand that yet? Thick as two planks, sometimes!'

The girl, and Verger again? Who else might the boy defend? Christ himself could walk the Sound and he would be just as much Malade as they! 'I hate this. I hate what's happened to us! You've changed so much this week it's like you're barely a Malade now!'

Nathaniel looked as if he was about to fly at him, really sock a punch, but instead the boy sighed and asked him to sit on the stairs. He even passed the cigarette over so Jake could have the last draw. 'I know it's hard, Jake, but we've got to remember where we've come from on this. We're brothers, aye, we want the same thing.' There was a sense of weariness to Nathaniel and his voice softened even further. 'Remember, aye, when we had long hair, like a girl's, before we scalped ourselves this summer? Remember how much came off onto the garage floor, and how my ma yelped when she saw us? She said, "Och, look at you, you look like two big babies!" And what your ma said, as well, remember what a bollocking she gave us? Remember, Jake. We're brothers in this.' Nathaniel put his arm around him. The weight was good. 'But I've got to sort out this girl's business, aye, before we give her a galling. And you, out of everyone, should know what these boys are like, they've got no gentleness, they'll be after her like a pack of dogs. No, no; the policy, toward her, stands. The other boys can't ken yet, or else they'll want a looky and then they'll want some scrap and it will end in hardship for everyone. You know this, don't you lad? It'll be our secret, aye, just for this while, between you and me – like old times.' Nathaniel smiled. When the boy was kind and gentle like this, it was like Jake's own da had come back for a month of Sundays. 'I promise to show and share, Jake, once everything's ready. But not before. You need to trust me on this one.'

'Aye, aye, I do.'

Jake squashed the end of the cigarette out, and Nathaniel stood. 'I'll see you tomorrow night after the boat. Gather the boys in the square for nine o'clock or so. But no sooner, aye. I'll have an announcement to make. Of some money we'll see ourselves earning.'

'Money?'

'Aye. A whole lot of it.'

'From what?'

'A shipment. We're shipping out a new product. Forty pounds at least! Can you imagine?'

'What product?'

'Now, now Jake; that's not for your ken. Not right now. But I'll tell you tomorrow. In the square. At nine or so.'

Jake felt a flicker of irritation – *to be left out of the plans again!* – but he told himself to forget about it, while things were going so well. Now he had the boy back in his camp. He was about to suggest a trip to Maiden's Square, with rocks and stones which could be flung at any house, just for the two of them – like old times – but Nathaniel was walking back to the room. Or he thought they might set an agenda for the meeting tomorrow night; anything so that Nathaniel wouldn't descend to the mattress and to the girl, but the boy walked away, and shut the door firmly behind him. That feeling of calm, as if everything had been settled back to the normal way, suddenly broke. Jake stayed for a while, alone on the last stair-board, listening to the soft words of Nathaniel waking her, then the slopped sounds of kissing. And his blood gave that urgent ache again, and Jake ambled outside, into the freezing fog.

The Sound was purely hectic in his ears as he walked back up Marley Hill. Jake thought of the room where they lay rolling atop each other, Nath's black scalp where once it had been beautiful and bald. Cavorting like this with an English girl! Jake should tell Mammy Malraux and watch her blush rise. She would pronounce her son a traitor for this!

There was no one in Maiden's Square: the gang were all in hiding after the fire and cosying up to their mams and watching telly, no doubt. All they wanted was for school to start again tomorrow and for everything to go back to the way it was. But the way it was did not exist, not any more.

Jake was freezing but he went down to Warkworth Beach, his hands balled against the cold, watching the waves draw toward him, wishing for Sammy, or Nicholas; the loneliness in him a barbarous ache. He thought of Nath and Sarah in bed. Jake had wanted nothing more than to join them, that was all; to close himself into the narrow nest of those two exquisite bodies, to put either hand in their hands, and fall asleep with them, as the fog banked silently about the house.

Over the way, the dark roofs in Warkworth Town were beginning to float in the fog. He felt that he must have release or else he too would be lost. Goading himself with the thought of them, he refused to go home until he had shed this feeling.

Men in taverns were drinking and laughing while he stood alone on the cobbled streets. Above the town would be Verger's house, blackening, still hot. He'd like to visit it, to see what the Malades had done, but it was too danger-ous, not while the smell of soot was still in his clothes.

Jake walked deeper into Lynemouth Town. He heard a scraping sign and followed the noise. He found the source down a narrow alley and onto the terraced street. The Grand. Promises of kissery and prickery. The expectation of pleasure suddenly lengthened and loosened his spine, flick-ing his head upright, as the tail of a snake flicks its head. He walked taller as he went in. And the girl and Nathaniel slipped from his thoughts.

*

Supine on the mattress, long-legged, older than the girl; the woman looked toward the window. Her hair was a strip of blonde falling down her back. When she turned, it looked to Jake like she had been crying: all red-rimmed around the eyes, a little wet under the nose. But she was enough to make the heart aloft; enough to give his mind the sense of sailing right out across the Sound.

'Hello,' Jake said, in all quiet tones, remembering how they had crabbed her on Monday night. He'd have to go soft with her, in order not to frighten her.

Her eyes slid up and down the length of him. She didn't say anything, nor did she stand, and Jake stood looming, not quite knowing what to do, or where to place his boots. The silence hung between them until she said: 'What do you want?'

'Eliza,' he said. 'Eliza.'

'Aye,' she said, and still didn't look back: 'That's my name.'

'Eliza—'

'Please go away.'

Jake didn't move.

'I said, go away.'

'Eliza, I've come here . . . ' He didn't know what to say. He thought of Nathaniel in his bedroom, boasting how he, the leader of the Malades, would be the first boy to have her. He remembered the look of complete self-assurance. Tonight, there was something limp about her, but still as lovely. 'I've come here to—'

'I'm sick of the sight of you boys.'

'I'm here alone.'

'I don't care. You're too young. Please go away.'

'I've got the money, I could pay—'

'I said no.'

Nathaniel would expect him to be skittish, like this, frightening at the first task. Jake was scared enough, all right. 'I have five pounds.' Eliza did not say anything but turned to him, stony-eyed. 'Here. Look.' He thought the money would get her. Jake took out the notes, soft as cotton, holding them in his palm. He was pleased to see he did not shake much. Eliza looked at him, something blank about her gaze, like Nathaniel's eyes too when he was lost in the scrap, voided of something important.

She looked at the money as if he were very far away. 'Is it your habit to carry about this amount of money?'

' 'Tis a fortnight's food allowance. Guess my mam will have to be content with tatties for a while.' He smiled at her and expected some warmth but she didn't give any.

She said: 'Ten pounds or nothing.' Her gaze did not leave the money as she picked it up, between forefinger and thumb, as if it was somehow filthy. 'Tomorrow. Come at six. No earlier, and no later. And bring the extra five pounds.'

'I—'

'I don't care. It's ten pounds or nothing.'

'Why? Why do I' – he corrected the whine of his voice to something more gentlemanly – 'have to pay more?'

'Because,' she put the money in the side table by the bed, 'you're a hooligan, Jakob Lawrence. Because you burned down Mr Verger's house. Because you're a child. Because I'd do anything not to do this. But I can't. So bring the ten pounds. Or you get nothing.'

'How'm I meant to find an extra fiver?'

Eliza shrugged. 'Ask your mam for more fish money. I don't particularly care.'

He said, 'Well.' He tried to think of some way of salvaging his triumph. 'It's ten pounds for the whole night. Or there isn't a deal.'

Eliza shrugged her consent. 'How old are you, boy?'

'Fifteen,' he said.

Eliza closed her eyes for just a moment, and then led him to the door. For the second time that night, it was shut right in his face. But this time, Jake was too elated to care. Aye, somehow, tonight, he had won.

29. The Deal

Verger's house was not, of course, the first case of arson on the Island. It was Jack Malraux and John Verger who set their matches on the church's pews in March of '51, and the small blaze rapidly grew, as the Islanders came to observe the last church-burning they would ever see. They watched, the sum of England's Secular Movement, most knowing it was not the church going up in flames, but each person's former life, and it was with a mixture of sorrow and triumph that they observed the fire. It was a last act of defiance, but to whom? No one of clerical consequence saw it. But it still felt deeply necessary. And then soon the bells rang from the cop shop, sirens ringing, telling them to scatter, but not before the church's loot had been divvied up, ready for mantelpieces, tablecloths, and a special place above the telly. And Jack Malraux and John Verger had never – officially – been named as the arsonists.

The culprits of the second fire on the Island, the ones who had set fire to Verger's house, had not yet been found.

Verger was ensconced at Caro Kilman's, who was fussing over him as she did Morris. The police, a volunteer group based nominally in Lynemouth Town, were slow in their investigation. People spoke to them of these boys, this gang – they called themselves the Malades – but when Verger had been quizzed about Nathaniel Malraux or Jakob Lawrence, he hadn't said a thing, merely turning a gold ring round and round his index finger. Caro tried to push him into implicating the boys but Verger would say nothing. The policeman asked whether a politic visit to Mrs Malraux would be in order but Caro sighed bullishly and said 'no chance'. The policeman had gathered neighbours' suspicions but, as yet, there were neither witnesses nor evidence.

'Come now,' Caro cajoled Verger, 'try and remember.'

'I do remember, Mrs Kilman. I remember that I saw no one.'

'No one at all?'

'No one.'

Mrs Kilman looked at the chinless policeman with some sense of despair. Verger was wrapped in a tartan blanket, having caught a chill on Saturday night. 'Well,' she said, raising her eyebrows, 'looks like no one saw anything at all. Isn't *that* surprising.'

'In fact, come to think of it, I do recall one thing now,' said Verger. Mrs Kilman's eyes lit up. 'That I might have left the stove on. And what if the kitchen had caught fire, and then the rest of the house? Perhaps it was my fault?'

'Your fault, sir?' the policeman said.

'Aye.'

'But your bedroom was the first room to go up. Not the kitchen. And there was a broken window, as if someone had thrown a missile,' said the policeman. 'A burning missile, sir.'

'Oh. Well. Yes, yes, of course.'

'Can I ask, Mr Verger, where you were last night, when the house first caught fire?'

The old man looked at him frankly, as if he thought this was the first good question the policeman had managed. 'I was down at the church. The ruined one at Lynemouth Town. I was,' he wetted his lips as if they had been scorched from the blaze, 'praying. I was praying.'

Mrs Kilman blushed and looked away, and suggested, in a tactful manner, that the old man was suffering from shock. She suggested the policeman pay a visit to Eliza Michalka, who had picked Mr Verger up outside his home and given him a place to stay for the night. The policeman looked rather pleased at this. 'And I am sure,' Mrs Kilman continued, 'she did it purely out of good thoughts and not out of a general sense of lucre.'

'She profited not a shilling from my being there,' Verger said.

'Aye, well. I doubt she'll implicate anyone,' Caro said, 'now that we have all assumed this rather thick veil of silence.' And she walked off with a cross look and went to see after Morris.

The policeman went round to the Grand, as bidden, to question Musa and Eliza. Neither of them gave up much more than Verger or Mrs Kilman. Eliza admitted picking up Verger outside his house, but she said it was already half-burned by the time she got there, and that she saw no one run off, or acting suspiciously. Musa said he merely provided Verger a safe place to sleep for the night. The policeman asked if the old man paid him for the pleasure, and Musa looked offended: 'Oh no, sir; I don't think we've lost all of our sense of charity.' Eliza raised her eyebrows.

Both were instructed, were they to see either Nathaniel Malraux or Jakob Lawrence, to get in touch with him.

The policeman left with rather a longing look at Eliza.

'Well, well, well,' said Musa, 'looks like the boys are in trouble.' Eliza said nothing. How might she broach the small matter of Jake? Verger's tattoo throbbed. 'And did you really not see anything? Down at his house?'

'I said no. I was telling the truth.'

Musa shrugged. 'Poor Verger. 'Twill be hard with winter coming. And the fog has come so early this year. Well, the Grand is a good place to lick your wounds, so to speak. Still, he was very particular about having no lady visitor *whatsoever*. "Whatsoever!" he said.'

'Come on,' she said. 'He was hardly in a fit state.'

'Aye, well. I would never refuse a lady like you, Miss Eliza. I was always surprised you never did do better here.' Musa looked down at the paper on the desk. 'Ah, well. He will survive. There are provisions enough, I suppose. The pier will be full tonight of English charity and we will see how much can be siphoned off for the old man. 'Twill be a long winter.' Musa sat and studied a paper. 'But then they always are. Well, well, the *Saviour* will be back in February.'

'Aye.'

'And do you feel ready for the winter, Eliza? Have you stored up provisions? Ready for the long hard months?'

'As well as can be expected.'

'You eat like a bird, anyway.' He was still looking down at the paper. 'I'm surprised you haven't come down with the anaemia, you eat so little fish.'

'Went off it, aye, after Mam's death.'

Musa looked up, tipping his head, as if looking at her for the first time. 'Aye. I suppose you did.'

'Well. I'm off to my room. I'm expecting someone.'

He looked surprised. 'Are you?'

'Yes. I am.' Eliza stood to go back to her room. 'Send him through. He'll be here at six.'

'Good, good, good. Some business at last!'

Eliza took a good long breath. 'It's Jake. The boy. It's Jakob Lawrence. The one the policeman was asking after.'

Musa shrugged. 'Just leave my commission.' He said slowly: 'I really don't want to know.' And he turned the leaf of the paper.

Yes, it was the last *Saviour* of the winter. And Eliza would be on it. And Musa didn't have a clue she was escaping. How many times had she traversed this passage from the reception to her room, wondering if there was ever to be an escape from this tread of hall?

Her room was closeted away at the back of the house, with a big window halved by the sea and sky. The sea, this evening, was capped by the approaching fog. She sat and watched. It had not been so bad, really, this Grand life. During that summer, in her fury with Arthur, she had schooled herself into almost enjoying this place. But then time had gone on, and only Mr Carter came now, and she'd grown quite dull, just like the other girls, who grazed and mooched with much the same insolence she had seen of cows on the telly, their eyes full of the same bovine vacuity. Eliza could understand why the Island men shunned the great trough of them. No wonder the Grand was quiet, with girls such as Janey ruling the place.

But now England. Eliza was going to England. She was overjoyed; or thought she should be. It was five o'clock. Eliza passed the brush over her teeth and the comb through her hair. The boy would be here in an hour. Jake, with his babyish mouth, and his constant tic of licking his lips. Jake, who had launched the torch – she was sure it had been him, balder as he was than Nathaniel – on Friday night. Jake, who had terrorized Mrs Richards. Aye, she saw the gang's slug-trail from one spot of terror to the next.

But to refuse Jake meant she would not escape. Eliza had spent the past six months hectoring the thin stiff air asking for respite and here it was: a chance to leave. She reasoned that if there were a God, as Verger had seemed to insist, then this act forthcoming would be squeezed into some dark and unheeded chamber of His heart where it would be, instantly, warmly, forgotten.

In her mind, in the early evening light, it was a much pardonable felony.

Eliza began to pack a bag: a few dresses, jumpers, socks, tights, a pair of good shoes; a newspaper article of London her ma had given her with a map on it, as well as three English banknotes. That afternoon she had sneaked some bread rolls from the kitchen and now she stuffed them in the side pockets of the bag, where the Sound couldn't get a lick on them. Zipped and closed, there was something neat and absurd about the case, as if all the folded clothes were taking her, and not being taken, to a place she had no clear idea of. England. It was a joke, really, for her to go there, a prostitute, from this Island, to the holiest place in the world! But to stay here was another joke, and a miserable joke at that.

Eliza kicked the bag under the bed. Perhaps she should do the right thing and refuse the boy. She should give him back his money and stay. He was a child! A child and an arsonist and a hooligan! But Eliza had not reported the fire, nor stopped the gang when she could have, so what use was it to make her stand of goodness now?

In the mirror, the tattoo of *Verger* was scabbed and raw. How might she mark this? Should she tattoo the word *Jake*, too, on her skull, cosy next to *Verger*, so that she might have victim and criminal squashed together on the same brow? Eliza jammed her fingers into the cut to make it bleed. For moments she nursed her outrage but then gave up and tearfully mopped her forehead with a tissue. Not much point in feeling sorry for herself, since it was not going to stop the crime itself.

There was now half an hour left. The lamp gave off the sallow light of the sick ward. Eliza moved her fingers across her brow, feeling the warm throb of the cut, and then across the walls, trailing them to the contours of the room. She had loved and hated this place; that sea out there; this silence, in here. She remembered Arthur's face that summer, the colour of leather, how the arc of wrinkles fell from his eyes. Leaving, of course, meant leaving him. *Oh, Arthur*, she thought; *the loss of you is the worse part of leaving.*

Eliza had decided she would not say goodbye to him: she would leave silently. She had not been shrewd enough in her life; it was shrewd now, to leave quietly.

At the door, she noticed an envelope. Eliza checked the corridor but there was no one. Might it be from Arthur? A parting note, somehow? Or from Jake? Saying he had changed his mind? Was her passage on the boat less secure than she had hoped? At her bed, she split the top of the envelope and began to read.

Monday 1 December, 1986

Dear Miss Eliza,

I must thank you for the kindness you showed me last night. Without you, as I said, I may have frozen to death outside my house, with such rain as we had early Friday morning. If I could I would offer you some token of my appreciation, but as you know, I have nothing left. Now I am staying at the Kilmans' while I get my things together, which is very kind of them, especially given Morris's ill health.

So instead I would like to give you this prayer, which you may not have ever heard, which is famous across the waters, and which is, to all of us, happily free. It is most of all about forgiveness. I hope in all of this you might forgive yourself. Know that I have. And know that you are loved regardless of anything you might do, or not do. This is what we call Grace, and it is God's dearest gift to us.

What I didn't mention to you yesterday, out of shame (see, we all have it), is my reason for forgiving the boys so quickly after their setting fire to my house. You may not know it, but once I – and another conspirator, namely Nathaniel's father, Jack – set fire to the church down at Lynemouth Bay, back in 1951. It was foolish and childish. We did it to impress the other Islanders, and it did impress some of them. But now we are left with no place for our community to gather, and we are poorer for it. And I will have to carry this guilt with me forever.

A few months ago, I found myself at the church during a particularly hard time, and it was there that I knew things had come full circle. I found God, there, Eliza, or should I say; He found me . . . or perhaps, just that I had never truly been Lost. I heard bells again, as if they were the bells of the police come to get me, like in '51, but I knew they weren't: they were soft church bells, ringing soundlessly, ringing for me.

Just as God forgave me for setting fire to His house, I must forgive the boys for setting fire to mine. We must, as it says, 'Forgive those who trespass against us.'

As I get my feet on the ground, and as you formulate your plan to leave the Grand – I admire your bravery in this, very much – perhaps we could meet some time soon, to discuss things. And don't worry about Arthur, dear: I'm sure it will all work out for the best.

With all best wishes, to you,

And my thanks,

J.V.

I trust you will not show anyone this letter.

She read the prayer at the end. *Forgive us our trespasses*, she read. *As we forgive those who trespass against us.* It must have been exactly six. Verger's letter slipped neatly into her suitcase as she told the boy to come in.

Jake's eyes swung from corner to corner. Here he was, with his sleek skull and hooligan's clothes. His jacket was boxy and gave him the look of someone hung from a scaffold. He smiled. Eliza said his name. All gone was the nervy regard of last night. Had he taken something, one of Mrs Malraux's pills, perhaps?

'I brought you the money,' he said. The money, aye. The money, that tarted up this deed from crime to necessity. 'The last of it,' he said, putting a five-pound note in her hand. She was terrified of what was happening, and what was happening so rapidly, but wordlessly she stuffed it into the cabinet drawer. £50 was there: complete. Before she had even turned, he put his arms around her.

The boy was kissing her neck. So it had started already, with so little as a flicker of consent . . . though who was she fooling, she'd invited him in, had taken his money; she'd barely simpered, though she had planned a doggish digging-in of heels! Something about the air had shifted. Was it a sense of triumph? Aye. All £50 lay crumpled in the drawer. She was going. She almost smiled. England. *England!*

So quickly they were on the mattress and she could smell the must of one hundred men who'd been on this bed in years past. She felt his teeth and tongue and gums and the rise and fall of his breath. Almost erotic; the smell of his hair, this pomadey smell, and the pressure of his ribs on her, and the stiff jeans against her thighs. What a girlish mouth he had, kissing her, squashing her lips with his. Sheened in sweat, his palms were slick too. The boy was nearly naked now (how had he managed that so quickly, in all his trappings?), and he was beautiful and thuggish, like some god or devil, come down to shame and gratify her both.

Eliza heard a bang as the jeans hit the floorboards. She

tried to work out what the noise was, a metallic, heavy sound, but he was clambering on top of her now and a bead of sweat had fallen into her eye and was making it smart.

As he started what he had come for, she watched the window. She couldn't bear to look at him. She thought instead of John Verger and his hopeful prayer. She thought of Margaret in her armchair and her chin jogging along with her words. She thought of Linda in her brogues in the coffin. She thought of the Sound, and how surely she had contemplated jumping into it.

A hand, silhouetted in the dark, delved to her breast; he pinned it down with his mouth, a roguish nuzzle.

With doleful grunts, Jake began. It was neither better nor worse than any other customer. He had strangely plump hands, keying them into her mouth. She couldn't do this; but she must! And didn't Verger say the trespass would be forgiven! Jake made boyish mews of pleasure, then with a brute, joyful grunt, the job was over, the deed done, the awful money made.

The boy collapsed. She scooped him off her so that he lay flat next to her. The smell coming off him was as pungent as onion.

Fog banked. Under the flank of her hair she traced the tattoo: *Verger*, it said, and here she was bedding the culprit. How expertly the mind dodged the law when offered a way out of a dilemma! How quickly she had known she would bed him for this sum!

The boy started to snore. Eliza rose and dressed. She put the £50 in her purse, put on the big coat with the fur collar, and her ma's gloves. It was a silliness to write her words in a grave situation such as this, but she couldn't resist. The word Verger was there, now mangled and red. In blue ink, underneath that word, she wrote:

Now I go across the waters.

She screwed in the full stop with some degree of purpose: the little dot was the Island, and she was going far beyond it. Soon the world was about to crack open.

Eliza coaxed out the bag from under the bed and winched open the window. She threw her case and herself over the side onto the flat roof below. A moment of hesitation as she looked back to the room: what if the boy caught a cold, sprawled naked and unguarded on top of the bedspread, with the window open like that? But she had to rush. There was very little time.

30. Foreign Tastes

They'd made love all day in the back bedroom upstairs. The fog was as thick as cotton, and they felt a sense of weightlessness and suspension, as if they were alone on the Island. Exquisite and together, there seemed to be nothing beyond the room but the Sound. And every hour or so a sense of joy burst in them, more intense still for the little time that was left to them. Occasionally, Nathaniel went down to the front garden, to smoke, and watch for Jake. An air of anxiety followed him when he returned up the stairs. Sarah teased him about being scared but he'd looked at her quite seriously and said that he was.

Now, in the early evening, they sat in the kitchen in Swanscott House. It was full of the same metallic light as the bedroom. The tablecloth, which they had found in one of the chests of drawers, was worn and threadbare, with rings of coffee stains and pan marks. The flowers at the bottom of the cloth were fraying at the hem. Sarah had spread it out across the table so that they could eat their last dinner together, and Nathaniel had found a candle, and put it in a glass bottle and lit it for her, so they could eat by the light of the flame. 'I wonder who it was who lived here,' she said. 'Before us.'

'Some Island family.'

'Now English.'

'Aye. Now English, like you.'

'And now we can both remember it as our home. You can visit it and I can think of it. Swanscott House; where I met you. Where we had this.'

Sometimes, panicked, he looked at the kitchen glass, convinced Jake had edged through the overgrown garden and crept up on them without a noise. He had told her Jake had come last night, while she was sleeping, wanting a look at her. He did not want the boy here. Or any of the boys.

She said, 'I'm sure he won't come back. He's feeling abandoned. That's all.'

'Him and everyone else.'

Sarah looked down on the plate. 'I told you. I have to leave. My mum's coming home. Maybe before Christmas.' Her eyes were excited and keen. 'She may even have been released by now. She may be waiting in England. And I couldn't stay anyway. My dad. He's at home, alone. Imagine if I asked you to come back with me. Would you leave?'

'But, Sarah,' he knew his voice sounded syrupy, but perhaps that might help his cause, 'I need you here with me.'

'We can't do it,' she said, with some firmness.

Sarah's skin was soft and lovely in the light. She wore his shirt and braces and her big anorak over the clothes with the red scarf he had given her. It was as if, in here, in the kitchen, the windy kingdom of the Sound had all but disappeared. 'You do have some strange garb,' he said to her, tugging at the end of the scarf. He sighed. 'How can I convince you to stay?'

'You can't. The boat's tonight. I've got to be on it,' she said. She traced one of the tablecloth's flowers. 'You know, I always imagined finding Laura in a grand house. With an open fire and books everywhere. Or on the beach, walking along the bay. I always imagined that when I saw her she would recognize me completely.' She bit at her lip. 'I've no idea who she is. No idea whatsoever. Even if she is back home, I can't think about what I'll say to her, or what she'll say to me. She's a stranger to me, just as you were. And I feel ashamed, at what she did.'

'They didn't do it out of enjoyment. It's not right us being here, stuck on this rock. It's the right cause, Sarah.'

'I know; I know,' she said. 'But a man died for it.'

'Many died for it. On both sides.'

The fog was thickening, so that the landscape looked as if covered with virgin snow. His mam would be alone now, in the living room, waiting for him, but he couldn't bear the thought of Mammy suffering on account of him, and he turned to Sarah and kissed her across the table. Being with Sarah, it was like . . . It was like after hours of the scrap, coming into a warm hot bath where he might stretch out his limbs and enjoy relaxing, because though there was nothing he wanted more than to feel the dark breath of the Island's night air and watch the smash of a window, above all this he wanted to come back home to Sarah, to the neat basin of her lap and the softness of her cheek. Aye, above all, when he was with Sarah, he forgot even what the scrap meant to him.

And the satisfaction of her staying with him far out-weighed the guilt of what he was about to do. Obedient to his love as Arthur was to his, he would not let her go. He could not. And Arthur had advised him on this; and Arthur always kept good counsel.

Nathaniel stood. 'What's this you've got for me?' He read the tin. 'Corned beef? Beef, that's cow, isn't it? It's beef with corn in it?' Nearly three-quarters had already been eaten. 'You didn't leave much for me,' he said. It was moist inside the can, with a strong smell.

'Aye, well, it was my only food, before you arrived.'

'Before I arrived and everything changed.'

'That's right.'

'It smells of old shoe.'

Sarah stood and cut the square loaf he'd brought from home. The meat went lumpishly onto the bread, and she spread it thinly. She hadn't ruled out that he might have some sort of reaction to it. What if it were a kind of poison to his system? The flakes were pink and moist. The smell of it made her salivate; though the sight of it wasn't appetizing. Nathaniel sniffed it warily. 'Or foot, aye, it smells of foot,' he said.

'Just try it.'

Nathaniel took a bite. There was something leathery about the taste, and very brown, as if he chewed a piece of particularly expensive furniture. 'It's OK,' he said, 'but not up to much. Still,' he grinned, 'the first Island lad to have the flesh of a cow in me! I was always one for firsts!'

Nathaniel kissed her and he could taste the salt in his own mouth. He felt purely joyous. 'Here, let me make yours.' Sarah sat down at the long kitchen table, the light from the candle playing on her hair. 'You do look lovely, there, Sarah. A real treasure,' he said. She combed the hair back from her face and smiled at him.

Nathaniel spread the last of the beef thickly on the slice. He talked to her, asking her about her dad, and what she'd do when she got back to England, and what she'd tell him about where she had been. He laughed as she imagined all of the stories she could tell them. While she was talking, Nathaniel crushed the sedative in his fingers and spread it thinly onto the chopped tinned beef. With a fork he mashed it in until it couldn't be seen, and then he folded the bread over, just as she'd done. He'd been lucky; there'd only been one left in the small amber bottle in his Mam's bathroom cabinets. It would last the few hours or so that he needed. Sarah would be happy with him, once she saw reason. Once she'd spent the winter here she would realize what a good idea this was, and she could see her ma in good time in the spring. Maybe even let her mam and dad have some quiet time on their own this winter. Tonight, he would persuade the Boatman to take Eliza and he'd come back to the house, as Sarah woke from the love-coma, and he'd be able to show her the money he'd spend on her this winter.

'Here,' he said, passing the plate over to her.

When she ate, she ate heartily. 'Last meal,' she said, but her laugh was quiet, as if the fog had come indoors and muffled her voice.

31. Eliza and Arthur

It was seven o'clock by the time Eliza reached Maiden's Square. Propped in the museum's alcove, that hour bound with every other hour she had spent there, she stood and waited, though she knew it was too late for Arthur to appear. Too late, as well, to say goodbye.

She thought of the English girl. It filled her with regret that she hadn't managed to find her again, that she had slipped out of sight after Mrs Page's funeral. A certain note of anxiety struck her. Eliza wished, dearly, that the girl was well, and being looked after by someone. Perhaps Mrs Malraux had taken her in – or, goodness forbid, Caro Kilman. Or maybe the girl was planning to sneak herself back on the boat tonight, just as she had done last Monday, and they could talk at length while they both hid in the cabin for England.

Eliza could barely see the shop's frontage for all the fog. No shadows to be seen; nothing but this milky swell. Between the folds of her bag Eliza felt for her purse. The money was still there: £35 from her mother's inheritance; £5 from Mrs Page, and a further £10 from Jake. £50 in total. Just as Nathaniel had asked. Her mind emptied. Everything would be fine. The boat would come and take her away to England. And she would be rid, forever, of this Island. But she couldn't leave quite yet. Not without saying a goodbye to Arthur, even if it were just, in effect, a gesture.

Eliza crossed the square and cupped the sides of her temples, peering into the dark room. This window had kept her at the longest distance for so many nights. The gutting knives flashed. Could a message be scrawled on the glass, in the condensation, and might it last till morning? What might it say, but *I love you*, and *goodbye* and *I'll miss you* and *I'm sorry*.

A fluorescent light blinded her for moments. She squinted into it. A lumbering shadow grew larger on the tiled wall, going toward the knives. It had to be Arthur. *He is going to kill me!* was her first thought, but she told herself not to be so melodramatic. Presently, his face was no more than an inch from the other side of the glass, as hers was; straining into the dark and light both. Arthur withdrew; the lock snapped twice. He was locking it against her, she was sure, keeping the slattern on the cold side of the square, but then the door opened and he was standing there: warm, real, breathing, his hands tucked under his arms. Arthur said, 'Hello.'

Her breath left her mouth before she too said hello and then looked down at her shoes.

'Eliza.' It was the first time she had seen him here without the bloodied pinny. He said, 'Come in. Please. There's something rank in that mist tonight.'

She followed him into the shop. The clock at the wall read a quarter past seven. Arthur lifted up the counter and put it back to, so that he was on one side, and she on the other. With a lurch of horror, she wondered if he had assumed she was a late customer and was about to sell her a bream. 'Arthur, I—'

'Eliza.' He turned his back on her, regarding the knives, and she truly did wonder if he was contemplating which one to pluck from the magnet and sink into her heart. But when he turned back to her it was as if his face had aged ten years in the moments just passed. 'Eliza. I've never known how to say sorry. About that night. That night in the Grand this summer. It was unforgivable. Just after your ma's death. It wasn't right, aye.'

'You don't need my forgiveness,' though her voice was surprisingly stern, 'I forgave you a long time ago.'

'Aye, but I've been angry with myself ever since. When your ma died, things moved so fast, and I got scared. And then I got so, so incredibly jealous of you working in the Grand, and I was so angry that you were there . . . I didn't think for a second of your financial situation. And then I came to you, and we . . . I couldn't be sorrier. I'm still so ashamed.'

Eliza didn't say anything.

'And after that, I resolved that I would keep myself to myself and not interfere in your business.' His eyes climbed the walls. 'But I couldn't – I can't – stop thinking about you. Every day when I make up the display, I wonder if it's you who will come and admire the colours. And it's always Mrs Kilman or Mrs Bingley, come to tell me of their husband's bloods, or they fret that the fish were caught where a loved one was lost. I don't say much, I never do, apart from now, it seems, I can't stop talking . . . ' He laughed. Arthur had sounded almost jolly, but now his voice went sort of tone-less and flat. 'Every day my heart is as cold as these dead fish. Every day, as I go about my butchering, I seem to get further and further from you, until it's my heart under the knife that I gut and quarter. I can't stand this life without you. I love you.'

'What?'

'I love you.'

'What? Why do you say this now?' Her voice wasn't really much more than a whisper.

He coughed, as if he were embarrassed. 'Mr Verger was in here this morning.'

'Mr Verger?'

'Aye. Talking of you. Saying you had a fair place in your heart for me.'

'No,' she said. 'I'm afraid you're mistaken. He must have been disturbed, perhaps, upset, from the fire. Did you hear, the old man lost his—'

'What do you mean?' Arthur lifted the swing so that he was on her side. The skin by his eyes was dark and she noticed he had not shaved in a while. 'I love you, Eliza. I'll do whatever it takes to make amends. Eliza; dear Eliza.'

She looked at him blankly, as if she had too perfectly managed the art of feeling nothing. Arthur moved to take hold of her arm but she shrugged him off. She would not let him undo her. She had to leave. 'No,' she said again, 'I don't love you.'

'Mr Verger said—'

'Mr Verger got it wrong. Mr Verger was mistaken.'

'He said that you had always wanted to say something, that both of us, we were stuck in shame and I was so—'

'*I'm leaving*, can't you hear me?'

'What?'

'I'm leaving the Island.'

'You can't. I mean. How?'

'I've paid Nathaniel. He'll pay off the Boatman. I've passage on the *Saviour* tonight.'

'How much?'

'Fifty pounds.'

'Fifty pounds! Why? Where are you going?'

'Where else? To England. There's nothing left for me here.'

'But I love you. We could be happy together here, dear Eliza—'

'Why do you have to say this now? Why do you say this tonight, of all nights? I have to go, Arthur.' She hit her palm against the glass case. 'Why could you not have told me before? It's not fair you are saying this to me now!'

Arthur's voice, too, turned flinted. 'Because Mr Verger only said it this morning. *I* had no idea you had plans to get on the English boat. How was I to know?' He stopped. He was quieter now. 'Is your mind made up?'

Eliza saw him, pinny-less, in the glass-and-enamel shop. Here he was in his palace of fish. It would not be a difficult life here. No longer would she be the rag-picker come, in the late nights at the museum, to scavenge off him what she could. She wanted to look after him; wanted to be looked after by him. But she thought of the Island and the Sound and the gossiping women and marauding boys and the thought of Arthur, maybe, failing her again. It would take twenty steps to get off that pier. Twenty steps to England.

The lamp sputtered. It turned dark, and light, and dark again, and all the counters, glass tops and knives were lost completely in the black. 'Arthur?'

'The bulb's gone.' He sounded sad, and faraway. 'A sign, perhaps.'

The light gave a last flicker and they saw each other again, their faces as close as they had been moments ago, though there was no glass between them now, just an inch of air. Then, finally, darkness came: thick, luxurious, depthless. She touched his neck. He gave a sigh. They held each other, willing the other to let go, and he said sorry again. She hushed him and they stood like that for some moments, no more than a statue of an embrace, amongst the sheer tops and polished glass.

He said to her, tell me you will stay with me, tell me you will stay with me here.

And then he kissed her.

She whispered, 'Goodbye,' and fled.

Now, so thick as to be a bog, fog filled the square. Despite herself, despite her twenty-four years here, Eliza could not quite remember which way was which. In an objectless stride she set out. She felt quite dizzy, and freezing cold, and half-blind, and half-witless for losing him. *Arthur!* Aye, here was the sting: here was her punishment enough for Jake, for that merry felony, and it was murder enough.

The air was like a clod of earth. The scrape of the museum sign was somewhere, but she could not tell if it was close or far. Surfacing in her mind came the picture of the deportees, gathered at Newcastle pier, waving their dark documents. And was that where she was going now? To England? What madness did England hold!

She was close enough, now, to see the stonework of the Museum. If she walked away, from this point, she would pass Buttons and the grocer's and Mrs Kilman's, past the surgery and the hardware shop, and if she walked on she would come to the cliffs and the steps down to the pier. Eliza moved herself toward the sound of the sea. This fog held a ratty stink.

'Eliza!' Arthur's voice: where was it coming from? 'Eliza!' There was a lag now, and his voice was thin, as if he was heading down to the cliffs. 'Eliza!'

'Wait,' she said, 'I'm here!'

'Eliza!' he said: he was further off, heading toward Warkworth Bay.

'I'm here!' but she could not throw her voice; not like him, and she knew he was getting further away. She took the narrow path from Maiden's Square out toward the headland, thinking that if she could get to the top of the cliff, the fog might be thinner near the water's edge. She had no idea about the time, or whether she had missed the boat: it seemed like it had been hours between the boy and Arthur.

At the cliff, she saw him: walking toward the pier. How solitary he looked! She scrambled down the cliff steps. 'Arthur!'

He turned and saw her.

'Eliza!' He held something up in his pale hands. 'I'm coming with YOU!' he shouted, as she ran down the last few steps and onto the beach, past the rocks where she had hidden last Monday night. As she came closer she saw more distinctly what it was. Money. 'Arthur!'

He stood there. Smiling. The money outstretched.

'Why on earth have you all this money?' she said, getting the breath back up her.

'Saving up,' he said, 'for a rainy day.'

'Oh, Arthur.'

He brought her closer toward him.

'You know what Mrs Malraux said to me today?'

'What's that?'

'I haven't seen her for years, and you know the first thing she said to me? It was – why are you and Eliza Michalka not hitched already? And I honestly couldn't think of a reason why. Marry me, Eliza, in a big church, in big old England, with a vicar, and music, and plenty of space outside. Will you?'

'Of course, Arthur,' she laughed, and almost couldn't stop, 'of course I will.'

And when he held her for the second time that night, there was no more sadness to speak of. 'England,' he said, 'we're going to England.'

32. The Fugitives

Jake had lost her, briefly, at the square. She had disappeared as surely as if the fog had swallowed her. Then she had emerged at the headland, squawking, *Arthur, Arthur*, into the night. And now here they were, man and woman, Arthur and Eliza, clasped together, all tender embraces at the pier, even while her smell – like sardines on toast – was rich on his fingers.

The fog, with the moon on it, was purely white. It was knuckling cold. Jake squatted down amongst the rocks at Warkworth Bay, hearing the rattle of crabs by his boots. He thought of last night: Nathaniel and the English girl in that room, and the long blue lines of their bodies embracing. Pent in the fog, Eliza and Arthur continued at their love-making, all kisses, cuddles, caresses. How was it that everyone so easily betrayed their promises? Barely a day had passed before Nathaniel had given up on every Maladey principle to bed this English girl! Not an hour had passed between Jake's going to Eliza's bed and her leaving it for this fishmonger!

Jake had skipped school today to get the extra £5, which he had smuggled out from his mam's savings. A policeman had called round to the Lawrences' late that afternoon but Jake had merely watched him from the bedroom and his mam had lied, saying she didn't know where the boy was. There'd been hell to pay after, but he knew he could rely on his mam, what with his da gone fishing, and her pure dependence on him for the next two weeks, if only for company. No, his mam had not given him up for Verger's fire, and he was ever so proud of her for it. But it did mean he had to spend the day hiding in his bedroom upstairs, with the thoughts of Eliza circling over the anticipated shapes of her hips and breasts.

Oh, this evening, Eliza had made him ache! And now she was here, in the time he had paid for, with this man!

Without a thought, he had followed her here, down to the flat roof and through the winding cobbled streets of Lynemouth Town, over the cliff-tops to the square. All the time, jogging along, yards from her, he could taste her taste, peculiar as a mollusc. Then he had come down to the rocks, witnessing some reconciliation he had no care for, his knees bent and sore against the sand.

And now the fishmonger and Eliza stood at the pier, canoodling and smooching, and Jake was nowhere in her thoughts. He'd paid for the whole night! £10! Eliza had tricked him. She had stolen from him. Last night's ache returned, the one he thought he had quashed. Careless and coquettish, Eliza laughed close to the fishmonger's neck.

The gun was a cold lump at the small of his back.

Jake contemplated breaking them up and demanding Eliza should come back with him to the Grand, just as he had paid for, but the monger was a big man and Jake didn't fancy his chances arguing him down. He didn't know what to do, aside from wait, and watch.

*

There was a sound of footsteps coming down the cliff. A long whistle arced into the cold. The fog was too thick to see anything until Nathaniel emerged at the beach, his skull like a black ball. He waved over to Arthur and Eliza and they waved back to him. Not surprising that Nathaniel should have something to do with her presence here. It would be just Nathaniel's kind of joke to embarrass Jake like this. Perhaps they had planned it together; Nathaniel and Eliza colluding to spoil the night and make him look like the fool.

What was it that the boy had said last night? *We're due to make some money, on a shipment.* What were they shipping? Fish? Seafood? Was this why Arthur was here? But why was Eliza here too? Perhaps she had a cut of the profits, or – and this made Jake gag – perhaps she was a present for the Boatman.

Jake ducked lower behind the rocks as Nathaniel strode toward the pier. The boy looked intolerably cheerful. The scarf was a new addition; he hadn't known Nathaniel to feel the cold and now it flapped redly in the fog and wind. Perhaps Jake could steal back to Swanscott House and finish the night off with the English girl, if Nathaniel was to spend his night here doing business at the pier.

From the rocks, Jake watched the company – the fishmonger, the whore, the leader of the Malades – unable to imagine what on earth they were talking about, or what product they were shipping, until he gave up, and walked, slowed by the sand, toward the waiting pier.

No one turned or heard him coming; they carried on talking in whispers. When would they look? Hadn't they heard him yet? The fog was filling the bay. The *Saviour* would be here soon, and after whatever product had been swapped, he might drag Eliza back to the Grand to have his money's worth. Promises were promises. At the very least, Jake wanted half of his money back. Blondly standing on the pier, her hands clasped about a case as if she were off on holiday, Eliza was nodding her head at Nathaniel, her smile oily and distant.

Yards from the pier, Jake shouted up at them: 'What's going on?'

Nathaniel turned. His eyes slid down Jake's costume, appraising him. It was always on the tip of his tongue for Nathaniel to suggest a corrective, to pull at an escaped shirt-tail, or to point to a scuff on one of his boots. It seemed, though, that the boy couldn't think of a reprimand tonight, because Nathaniel opened his mouth and then closed it again with a snapping sound. Still no one had said a thing. Jake looked at Eliza: she flushed and looked away, narrowing her eyes against the fog. He closed the yards between them and took the steps up to the jetty. 'What's going on here? Why this meeting?'

'Here, Jakey, hallo. Have a cigarette.'

'No. What's going on, Nathaniel?'

'No cigarette? You've changed your stripes, Jakey-boy.'

Eliza's face was ashen now, and she was concentrating on the sea.

'I don't want a cigarette. What's this, then?'

'That shipment. The shipment I was telling you about.' Nathaniel leaned toward him, as if business made them chums again. In a low whisper he said, 'We're due to make a cracking lot of money just now.'

A broad low hum began, though the boat itself could not be seen. 'Ah, the *Saviour* indeed,' said Arthur and everyone looked toward him, then out to the bay. The sound of the engine grew louder. The tide started to rush in toward the water's edge, the scud white in the night. Gulls squawked overhead but neither wing nor beak could be seen. Eliza put herself further into Arthur's shadow.

Nathaniel pulled Jake toward him. 'Look here, Jake: Miss Michalka and Mr Stansky have given us a hundred pounds for their safe passage on the boat.'

Miss Michalka? Mr Stansky? A hundred pounds? This was the shipment? People? Jake could countenance fish or medicine as trades for cigarettes or whatnot, but not people, not when people were the most precious cargo on the Island. 'No. But they can't. No one gets off this Island. Where are they going?'

'Africa, Jake, where do you think? To *England*, of course. Where else would you expect?'

Jake did not know what to say. To England? Surely they hated the English; surely the point was to preserve the Island, not get people over to join them! The leader of the Malades, helping people on their safe passage to England!

'A hundred pounds, Jake, a hundred pounds!' The boy unfurled his fingers, stuffed with banknotes. 'We're rich. Now we can do what we please.' And Jake had effectively put the money directly into Nathaniel's pocket; oh, he had been a foolish lad to bed Eliza for that sum!

'Nathaniel: we can't do this. It's wrong. What'll we tell the lads? We're meant to be stopping the English, not getting people to join them. Nath, it's against everything we believe in, and you know it.'

'Look, even if we give fifty of these to the boatman, we'll be princes of this isle for the whole winter. Don't be crabbing me now with morals, when we've got all this money!' Jake opened his mouth to speak but Nathaniel gave a snap of the notes. Money from the fishery and brothel both. 'Stop your mouth now. This is business. Nothing more. *Enough*, Jake. Your morals tire me out, aye. In fact, they always have.'

'Morals! Morals that *you* gave me. Morals that *we* work for! And what will you spend it on? Your English girlfriend! What a mess, aye, what a fucking hash.'

A horn boomed sadly in the white air. A bow wave carried the waves faster to the beach, spilling over each other in foamy slop. The boat was a smudged shape, in the fog, then more definite, and bigger, then it loomed toward them as it came to the pier. The engine churned the water as the *Saviour* docked at the pier.

When it stopped, the Island felt strangely quiet, though the waves knocked against the boat's hull. The Boatman appeared, large and bald.

'You can't do this, Nath, it's wrong,' he said, but Nathaniel was already halfway down the pier.

Nathaniel shook hands with the Boatman as if they were old friends. They talked for some minutes, then Jake saw money exchanged, and then the boy was waving over to the waiting couple.

The lags between the waves had begun to slow.

Eliza did not look at Jake as she and Arthur began the long walk. He remembered how she had held him, hours ago, and he felt as if his heart were breaking. Maybe he could shout over the fog and tell Arthur what had happened. That would have broken up the little romance. That would have stopped it short. But he had the feeling, indistinctly, that he would not be believed, and they were too far away now, at the end of the pier, chatting aimlessly to the Boatman. Eliza stood laughing, as if she hadn't wronged him, as if she hadn't reneged completely on her promise.

And here it was: the English benefaction; boxed provisions for the hard winter to come when the freezing fog would envelop the Island. The Boatman had each one in hand as Nathaniel followed him counting his money. How the Islanders would grovel and snap at their heels and coo their thank-you's for English charity. England; aye, what had England ever done for them but expel them then throw them the scraps? And now they were putting two on the boat to join them. This was a nasty business.

There was a vague buzzing in his ears. The money went *snap, snap, snap* in Nathaniel's hands.

With the boxes now at the end of the pier, the Boatman beckoned toward Eliza and Arthur and they were installed up at the driver's section, closeted within. That whore and her man were probably squashed up tight against each other; and Nathaniel, here, was probably only just let loose from his English girl's bed. Long-limbed in the blue light, she'd be at Swanscott House peacefully sleeping and waiting for him, until they could spend the money over the winter and be the Lord and Lady of this isle, dining on bream and scallops and who knew what, with more cigarettes to boot.

'He says he'll use the money in the brothels, Jake! Says

there are none to be found in Godly England, so I don't know how Eliza shall ply her profession. But imagine that, an Englishman in the Grand! They'll have him for breakfast before hell might have a chance. And he didn't even ask for the pills! Just gave me the cigs with a very wide grin. Here, Jake, have one. Have one, our Jake, and get smoothed out. You're all agitated, now.'

'I said I don't want one.' The cargo door was now flush with the rest of the boat. The boatman took the rope from the bollard, grinning insanely, piling the length of rope in his wide fat hands, his bald head greenish in the fog. And then, just as suddenly, the Boatman was inside, and starting the engine, and readying to leave.

Waves lapped gently against the yellow letters of the *Saviour*.

'Are we letting every man and child have his passage to England, then? I thought a Malade such as yourself might feel differently.' Nathaniel only sighed and looked away to an indefinite point. Jake abandoned any fear he had and went at him as if he were not Nathaniel, as if he were just another boy: 'We are the Malades! We're meant to be doing what's right for the Island! Not move people off it! Not so they can abscond to *their* way!'

Nathaniel shoved him in the chest, the force knocking Jake to the pier. The nose of Margaret's gun struck his pelvic bone. The boy stood over him, with that absurd shock of hair. 'Enough,' Nathaniel shouted, the word punctuating the night. 'If only I could tell you how much I've had enough of you! Out of my way, Jake! You're no leader here. You're no man. You're just a boy. A stupid boy who doesn't understand anything!'

Jake looked at him, unable to say anything. The engine gunned.

The sound of steps came from off the cliff. Sarah was quick. She jumped from the steps and ran the length of the bay in very little time at all. The colour of her hair was deeply copper. She gained the pier with a wild look; the freckles flush and dense around her nose, her hands clasped tight to the bag's straps. Nathaniel's face had fallen; lost slack like an old boot.

About the boat there was an upswell so that the waves came quicker to the shoreline. The sound of the engine was convulsive at first, then flattened to a hum. The *Saviour* was readying to leave.

Nathaniel said, 'Sarah.' He held her by the hands and pulled her up to the pier. A gull wailed above the sound of the engine.

She looked around, her skin soft with sleep. She laughed mirthlessly. 'What did you give me, Nathaniel? It sent me to sleep. It knocked me out; I could barely stand.' She squinted over to the end of the pier. 'Is that the boat there?'

'Aye,' he said, but quietly.

Jake gave a whoop, his eyes raking Nathaniel's. 'Another bird to fly the Island, then! Well, miss, I can tell you, you can't, because the boat is all full up, all full up with the others. Did your boyfriend not tell you? He's filled it with a whore and a fishmonger.'

The girl looked from one boy to another. To no one in particular, she said, 'I have to go home. I have to go home.

My dad's waiting for me, and my ma too, when she gets there.'

'*My dad, Nath, my dad!*' Jake mimicked. 'It's to be winter on this isle for you, doll.'

The sound of the engine rose.

'Go on, then,' said Nathaniel. He brought Sarah toward him – just as Jake had brought Eliza toward himself and felt the long sagging in his chest which was love – and kissed her. 'There's still time. He didn't lock the cargo hold. You can still get in. I'm sorry,' the boy said, 'I couldn't bear you going.' Nathaniel looked toward the sea, the hand with the banknotes now loose by his side.

The girl lurched toward the boat, the sound of her shoes smacking the pier. Jake took off behind her. Not paces down the road, he caught up with her and twisted her wrist into the small of her back. He could no longer see Nathaniel behind him. 'No, no, no. Now, Sarah, an Island life isn't so bad!' His feet widened so that he was a scaffold around her, so that he could talk directly into the pleasantly dusted ear. He felt the button of his jeans at her hip, could he be as close to her as Nathaniel had been? His voice coaxed at her: 'We want you here, we want to talk to you. Give up the struggle and it won't hurt so much. That's the truth of it. That'll ease you through. Come now, give up the fight, doll!' Sarah thrashed against him. 'I'll show you how, it's a lovely thing, this Island, when you know it.' He felt his blood, rum and warm, rush about him. The girl wheeled, her body tense in struggle; her face stricken. Jake held both wrists now fixed. Oily smoke joined the mist.

'For God's sake, let me go!'

'No, no, no; no God to help you now.'

NAOMI WOOD

The girl turned around and her face was a red blur, all freckles and a blush of fear. Jake felt a wet spray against his face – he thought he had been caught by a wave – but it was her spit, a thick scud. He looked at Nathaniel. The boy stood there, immobile. Why was he not doing anything? Why did he not defend his boy, his Malade? Nathaniel stood there, absolutely still. Jake let go of the girl's wrist.

As soon as he let the gun off, the air about him was hot and sprayed with a smell of pepper. The gun kicked and his hand shook with it. Jake walked toward her fallen shape: twisted, like a downed bird. Distantly he heard the trailing sound of the engine so the boat must have gone now. The girl was flat to the pier, with her thick red hair roping the platform. There was a bone bit visible in her shoulder which made him pure want to gromick. The boy crouched and turned her over so that her face was a white disc; her eyes skipped around the place.

Behind him he heard Nathaniel running up the pier.

She was a thing of beauty amongst the waves, breaking against the pier in the wake of the *Saviour*. The eyes were wild and flashy blue, the black rounds getting bigger and bulging; silky, almost. Jake gave another squeeze of the trigger and her lips opened in an 'o' and about the wound blood pooled. Her breath caught. 'Aye,' he said. He kicked her to the Sound.

As if she were crowned in copper, her hair spread in the water.

Nathaniel, wet-eyed, limp, scrabbled down to the beach and sat nursing her. There were strange sounds coming from his mouth. Yowling softly as if he were a bleeding baby. With the freezing sea up to his chest, he combed back and forth her crown of red hair.

Jake threw the gun to the Sound. Then he ran from them, from the pier, and from the cliffs, back into the impossible light of the Island.

England

Wherever there had been moisture was now frozen. It was early, and the sun had not yet come up far enough to melt the frost. Above her, ragged cloud was breaking away to light.

The fog had lifted, leaving behind a world spun in frost. She heard the stiff iced leaves crack underfoot. She saw the new shops and the old fruit-stalls, selling their mounds of winter fruit. Occasionally people passed her, none whom she recognized, but she did not look for long.

Everywhere in the windows there was an abundance Laura was not accustomed to. Perhaps Trimdon had come into some new source of wealth, though from what, she couldn't imagine. She passed a delicatessen where there were bags of pistachios and berries; a shop, next door, of showers, neat sinks, polished taps and Plexiglas. Light pulled over rooftops. A plane flew under the last of the moon.

Laura passed the butcher's: shoulders of lamb next to the dark mess of liver. She'd probably had meat once a year, at Christmas, since she'd been gone: even then it was only a dry slice of turkey. She was hungry, moved on, passed the grocer's and the pub on the corner.

At the cafe, newly named, a woman in a paper hat

prepared for the day; a man sat in the window, a bald man eating breakfast, the jaw working all the muscles in the gleaming cheeks. He was reading a newspaper: the headline read *A Good Sunday Agreement?* and it showed a picture of Laura, next to the reverend who had died, as well as the mugshots of Thomas and Christopher, the two dead men who she had – finally – been able to name as her accomplices. When she had heard of their deaths, on a quiet news bulletin broadcast in the women's cafeteria, Laura had pushed back her chair and walked straight to the inspector's office. Uttering their names had been like saying obscenities, so skilfully had she schooled herself in the art of silence. In days to come, she had been read her rights from the Sunday Agreement, and, after preliminaries – facts checked, names corroborated, the general closing of the case – preparations for her release had been made.

The date of the newspaper was December 3rd, 1986. More than ten years had passed since the bombing of Saint Gregory's. Her daughter would be a woman, now, she supposed.

Ice cracked under her shoes. Laura followed the stone wall on the sunny side of the street, leading out of the valley, where her boots could find the tarmac and no longer any frost. She thought: if I put my boots down harder the whole world will smash like a glass and I will find that this is a dream.

Laura opened the gate and checked her watch. Her house looked no different. Sarah's curtains were open upstairs;

perhaps her girl was an early riser. At the house, she put her arms up to the doorframe to steady herself. Just a moment to collect, feeling the sun on the back of her neck. The shadow behind her was cruciform in winter light. She remembered the last time she had been here, stepping out into the cool July morning in 1976, though she did not regret Saint Gregory's.

The lock turned the key easily, and why wouldn't it? Did she expect them to have shut up shop without her? The room, then, was just as she had left it, messier perhaps, the dresser still cluttered with things, an old bag of onions, the telephone on its cradle. Green glass bottles near the bin, ready for the bank, a half-litre of whiskey at the table. She was ready to climb the stairs but turned.

There was a bowl of oranges on the side. At the table she put a finger into the seam of the flesh, pulled, felt the skin give.

Into the morning air, the scent spilled. Laura turned to the stairs.

With deep and affectionate thanks to my agent at WME,

Cathryn Summerhayes,

who found this book in a very different form four years ago,

and to my editor at Picador,

Sam Humphreys,

who turned it into what it is today.

picador.com

blog
videos
interviews
extracts

EVALUATION IN EDUCATION AND HUMAN SERVICES SERIES

Editors:

George F. Madaus
Boston College
Chestnut Hill, Massachusetts, USA

Daniel L. Stufflebeam
Western Michigan University
Kalamazoo, Michigan, USA

Previously published books in the series:

Kelleghan, T., Madaus, G., and Airasian, P.: THE EFFECTS OF STANDARDIZED TESTING
Madaus, G. (editor): THE COURTS, VALIDITY, AND MINIMUM COMPETENCY TESTING
Brinkerhoff, R., Brethower, D., Hluchyj, T., and Nowakowski, J.: PROGRAM EVALUATION, SOURCEBOOK/CASEBOOK
Brinkerhoff, R., Brethower, D., Hluchyj, T., and Nowakowski, J.: PROGRAM EVALUATION, SOURCEBOOK
Brinkerhoff, R., Brethower, D., Hluchyj, T., and Nowakowski, J.: PROGRAM EVALUATION, DESIGN MANUAL
Madaus, G., Scriven, M., and Stufflebeam, D.: EVALUATION MODELS: VIEWPOINTS ON EDUCATIONAL AND HUMAN SERVICES EVALUATION
Hambleton, R., and Swaminathan, H.: ITEM RESPONSE THEORY: PRINCIPLES AND APPLICATIONS
Stufflebeam, D., and Shinkfield, A.: SYSTEMATIC EVALUATION
Nowakowski, J.: HANDBOOK OF EDUCATIONAL VARIABLES: A GUIDE TO EVALUATION
Stufflebeam, D.: CONDUCTING EDUCATIONAL NEEDS ASSESSMENTS
Cooley, W., and Bickel, W.: DECISION-ORIENTED EDUCATIONAL RESEARCH
Gable, R.: INSTRUMENT DEVELOPMENT IN THE AFFECTIVE DOMAIN
Sirotnik, K., and Oakes, J.: CRITICAL PERSPECTIVES ON THE ORGANIZATION AND IMPROVEMENT OF SCHOOLING
Wick, J.: SCHOOL-BASED EVALUATION: A GUIDE FOR BOARD MEMBERS, SUPERINTENDENTS, PRINCIPALS, DEPARTMENT HEADS, AND TEACHERS
Worthen, B., and White, K.: EVALUATING EDUCATIONAL AND SOCIAL PROGRAMS
McArthur, D.: ALTERNATIVE APPROACHES TO THE ASSESSMENT OF ACHIEVEMENT
May, L., Moore, C., and Zammit, S.: EVALUATING BUSINESS AND INDUSTRY TRAINING
Abrahamson, S.: EVALUATION OF CONTINUING EDUCATION IN THE HEALTH PROFESSIONS
Glasman, N., and Nevo, D.: EVALUATION IN DECISION MAKING: THE CASE OF SCHOOL ADMINISTRATION
Gephart, W., and Ayers, J.: TEACHER EDUCATION EVALUATION
Madaus, G., and Stufflebeam, D.: EDUCATIONAL EVALUATION: CLASSIC WORKS OF RALPH W. TYLER
Gifford, B.: TEST POLICY AND THE POLITICS OF OPPORTUNITY ALLOCATION: THE WORKPLACE AND THE LAW
Gifford, B.: TEST POLICY AND TEST PERFORMANCE
Mertens, D.: CREATIVE IDEAS FOR TEACHING EVALUATION
Osterlind, S.: CONSTRUCTING TEST ITEMS
Smith, M.: EVALUABILITY ASSESSMENT
Ayers, J., and Berney, M.: A PRACTICAL GUIDE TO TEACHER EDUCATION EVALUATION

Advances in Educational
and Psychological Testing:
Theory and Applications

edited by
Ronald K. Hambleton
Jac N. Zaal

Kluwer Academic Publishers
Boston/London/Dordrecht

Distributors for North America:
Kluwer Academic Publishers
101 Philip Drive
Assinippi Park
Norwell, Massachusetts 02061 USA

Distributors for all other countries:
Kluwer Academic Publishers Group
Distribution Centre
Post Office Box 322
3300 AH Dordrecht, THE NETHERLANDS

Library of Congress Cataloging-in-Publication Data

Advances in educational and psychological testing : theory
   and applications / edited by Ronald K. Hambleton, Jac N.
      Zaal. p.   cm.—(Evaluation in education and
      human services series)
   Includes bibliographical references.
   ISBN 0-7923-9070-9
   1. Psychological tests.   2. Educational tests and
   measurements.
I. Hambleton, Ronald K. II. Zaal, Jac N. III. Series:
Evaluation in education and human services.
BF176.A42   1990
150'.28'7—dc20   90-31493
                                        Rev. CIP

Printed on acid free paper.
Printed in the United States of America.

Contents

Preface

Over the last 20 years there have been a large number of technical advances and changes in the field of educational and psychological testing. According to Anne Anastasi,

> The decade of the 1980's has been a period of unusual advances in psychological testing. Technological progress, theoretical sophistication, and increasing professional responsibility are all evident in the fast-moving events in this field (A. Anastasi, *Psychological Testing*, Sixth Edition. New York: Macmillan, 1988).

On the psychometric front, advances in topics such as item response theory, criterion-referenced measurement, generalizability theory, analysis of covariance structures, and validity generalization are reshaping the ways that ability and achievement tests are constructed and evaluated, and that test scores are interpreted. But psychometric advances, as substantial and important as they have been, are only a fraction of the major changes in the field of testing. Today, for example, the computer is radically changing the ways in which tests are constructed, administered, and scored. Computers are being used to administer tests "adaptively." That is, the sequence of questions an examinee is administered depends upon his or her performance on earlier administered items in the test. Tests are "adapted" to the ability levels of the examinees who are being assessed. One result is shorter tests with little or no loss in measurement precision. Computers are also being used to store or bank test items. Later, items of interest can be selected, and the computer is used to print copies of the test.

The field of cognitive psychology is also having a major influence on testing practices. Researchers such as Robert Sternberg, Robert Glaser,

Richard Snow, and Susan Embretson in the United States have highlighted the importance of new types of cognitive variables in instruction and assessment as well as new ways for identifying important cognitive variables (i.e., through cognitive task analyses). Development of tests to measure these variables proceeds from a theory-based orientation unlike the more common pragmatic test development approaches that require extensive validation work after tests are constructed.

Also, test results are increasingly being used to address policy questions. National and state assessments, for example, which exist in many countries, are now being used to monitor the quality of educational progress and direct financial resources to areas of concern.

In view of the recent rapid, extensive, and important developments in educational and psychological testing, the International Test Commission (ITC) felt that it could further its mission by organizing a collection of papers from researchers in several countries which focused attention on the technical advances, advances in applied settings, as well as emerging topics in the testing field. The result was this book which contains 14 chapters from 22 contributors. A brief description of the ITC itself follows this preface.

The book is divided into three main parts. Part I—*Methodological Advances*—contains six chapters. Ronald Hambleton and H. Jane Rogers, from the University of Massachusetts at Amherst in the United States, describe the concept of criterion-referenced measurement and how it is reshaping assessments in schools, industry, and the military. The testing focus is on assessing what it is persons know and can do rather than on how persons compare with one another. The latter testing focus is central in norm-referenced measurement. David Weiss and Michael Yoes, from the University of Minnesota in the United States, describe a new theory of measurement, item response theory (IRT). IRT has become immensely important as a new measurement framework for test construction and test evaluation. It provides descriptors of test items that do not depend upon the particular samples of persons used in item calibrations, and provides ability estimates that do not depend upon the particular choices of test items from the domain of items measuring the ability of interest. Both measurement features are very useful in the hands of measurement specialists. Dato de Gruijter and Leo van der Kamp, from Leiden University in The Netherlands, and H. Swaminathan, from the University of Massachusetts at Amherst in the United States, prepared chapters on generalizability theory and analysis of covariance structures, respectively. Both chapters address research concerning the analysis of data for test validation purposes. Generalizability theory represents an extension of classical test theory, while covariance structure analysis is an extension of factor analysis methods. Wim van der Linden, from the University of Twente in The Netherlands, describes some of his research involving testing and decision making in the presence of uncertainty and different consequences associated with errors in classification decisions. Finally, John Hunter, from Michigan State University, and Frank Schmidt, from the University of Iowa in the United States, have addressed issues and methods of meta-analysis or validity generalization, as it is often called. This line of research has become important in industry and the military as attempts are made to make strong statements about test validity in the presence of many small sample studies with different predictor tests, criterion measures, test designs, and groups.

Part II—*Developments in Applied Settings*—contains five chapters. Robert Roe and M. Greuter, from the University of Delft in The Netherlands, have addressed many of the current issues and methods associated with personnel selection. With the need to improve job performance in industry as well as to prepare for lawsuits brought by rejected applicants clearly in mind, current research on personnel selection is substantial and important. From inside the Dutch government, Jac Zaal describes some of the current research that is focused on the uses of assessment centers in performance evaluations and personnel selection. Stan Scarpati, from the University of Massachusetts at Amherst in the United States, reviews some of the current practices and assessment issues confronting professionals who work with handicapped children and adults in public settings. Testing of the handicapped is common in the United States, but a large number of problems and technical issues need to be overcome to insure that it is done well. Fons J. R. van de Vijver and Ype H. Poortinga, from Tilburg University in The Netherlands, provide an overview of the problems of test administration in a cross-cultural context and focus considerable attention on the detection of biased test items. The issue of item bias or fairness has become an important topic for test development. Currently, there appears to be a considerable amount of misunderstanding about item bias definitions and approaches for identifying it. Katherine MacRury, Philip Nagy, and Ross Traub, from the Ontario Institute for Studies in Education in Canada, provide a review of the concept of large-scale assessment programs and their expected effects. In view of the newness of large-scale programs as well as the substantial interest that exists worldwide, they also offer an agenda for further research.

Part III—*Emerging Topics*—contains three chapters. The first chapter, by Ronald Hambleton, Jac Zaal, and J. P. M. Pieters—the latter, from the University of Nijmegen in The Netherlands—introduces readers to computerized-adaptive testing (CAT). It appears that CAT can reduce testing time and examinee frustration without any loss in measurement precision. These authors also address both hardware and software issues as well as guidelines for evaluating CAT. Robert Sternberg, from Yale University in the United States, provides an introduction to cognitive theories and their role in building new psychometric instruments. Finally, Walt Haney and George Madaus, from Boston College in the United States, review the important developments over the years that have influenced the current ethical and technical standards for test construction and test usage.

The ITC is grateful to the contributors for their willingness to give of their time, experiences, and scholarship to this book. We hope that educational researchers and psychologists around the world will find the book useful in their work.

Ronald K. Hambleton
Jac N. Zaal

INTERNATIONAL TEST COMMISSION
COMMISSION INTERNATIONALE DES TESTS

Goal

The International Test Commission (ITC) is a collection of national psychological societies, test commissions, test publishers, and other organizations who use tests. ITC's goal is to assist in the exchange of testing information among member and affiliate organizations on matters pertaining to the construction, distribution, and uses of educational and psychological tests. To achieve its goal, ITC carries out the following activities on a regular basis:

- organizes symposia at international psychology meetings
- publishes a journal addressing testing issues and developments
- encourages and/or directs research studies and reviews on important testing issues and developments.

Current Projects

Presently, ITC has several projects under way which should provide important information on tests and testing practices to countries all over the world:

- The extent to which tests are adapted and used in foreign countries.
- Copyright abuse of tests.
- Survey of test legislation.
- Organization of a symposium on adapting tests for uses in different cultures at the 1990 meeting of the International Association of Applied Psychology in Kyoto, Japan.
- Collection of national society ethical and technical standards for test use.

ITC reports the findings from its projects at international meetings of psychologists, in its journal, and in other publications.

Benefits from Membership in the ITC

Several benefits accrue to members from participation in the ITC:

- communication with other organizations involved with tests to discuss problems, issues, needs, and possible solutions
- opportunity to influence the specific directions and research program of the ITC
- opportunity to contribute to a Commission whose goal is to improve the quality of testing practices around the world

History of the International Test Commission

The idea of setting up an international body as a central stimulus for better use of tests worldwide was first raised by Professor Cardinet in Switzerland in the late 1960s. Through correspondence with national societies and meetings of interested individuals during international conferences in 1969 and 1971, the initial idea for an organization began to take shape. The International Test Commission was formally established and, by 1974, 15 countries were represented at a general meeting held during the Montreal conference. At that time, the Netherlands Committee on Testing Affairs accepted responsibility for administration of the ITC, an international Council was appointed, and Dr. Ype Poortinga was elected President and Editor of the Newsletter. Although initiated with encouragement from the International Association of Applied Psychology, the ITC was established as an autonomous body—primarily because delegates to the Commission were to participate as representatives of their national societies, or test commissions, unlike the IAAP, whose membership is on an individual basis. At the 1975 IUPsyS Conference in Montreal, the Council prepared a draft constitution and by-laws which were amended and provisionally accepted in Paris in 1976, then formally ratified at the quadrennial business meeting held during the IAAP conference in Munich in 1978. The constitution of the ITC was based on the document "Recommendations Concerning the Construction, Distribution, and Use of Psychological Tests" which was approved by the IAAP general assembly in 1971.

Memberships

There are two types of membership possible in the ITC, *full* and *affiliate*. A *full* member of the ITC will be a national commission, a national psychological society, or other national body which has been recognized by the association(s) of psychologists in a country and is working towards the following objectives:

- to advance professional test development and to raise the standards of psychological tests
- to protect the public against the personal and societal consequences of the use of inadequate or inappropriate psychodiagnostic procedures and of the use of tests by unqualified persons or in a manner objectionable on scientific or ethical grounds.

Currently, 13 national societies are members of the ITC, and three other national societies have filed for membership.

Affiliate membership is open to other organizations with an interest in tests, such as test publishers, units of government, hospitals, or universities (i.e., departments) involved in psychometric work, or groups of psychologists who work with tests. Affiliate members do *not* have voting powers. Currently, there are 20 affiliate members of the ITC, with four other testing organizations having filed for membership and awaiting admission decisions.

The ITC Bulletin (Bulletin de la Commission Internationale) which is bilingual (English and French) is published biannually and sent to all full and affiliate members, and subscribers.

Application for Membership

National psychological societies, test commissions, test publishers, and major test users who are interested in joining the ITC may obtain an application for full or affiliate membership from the ITC by writing:

Ronald K. Hambleton
ITC President (1990–1994)
University of Massachusetts
Hills South, Room 152
Amherst, MA 01003
U.S.A.

The fees for full membership are related to the number of members in the national organization. For affiliate members, there is a fixed fee.

Full Members

1 to 100	members	£ 15.00	($ 26 U.S.)
101 to 1,000	members	£ 35.00	($ 60 U.S.)
1,001 to 10,000	members	£105.00	($180 U.S.)
10,000+	members	£225.00	($380 U.S.)

Affiliate Members

National or international organizations	£105.00 ($180 U.S.)
Other organizations	£ 35.00 ($ 60 U.S.)

Membership Applications

Applications for membership are usually confirmed at a general meeting of the ITC. The Council calls such a meeting at least once a year. Postal votes of the ITC Council Members are also used to process applications for ITC membership.

ADVANCES IN EDUCATIONAL AND PSYCHOLOGICAL TESTING: THEORY AND APPLICATIONS

I METHODOLOGICAL ADVANCES

1 ADVANCES IN CRITERION-REFERENCED MEASUREMENT

Ronald K. Hambleton
H. Jane Rogers

One of the major changes in the testing field over the last 20 years has been the increased interest in and use of criterion-referenced tests (CRT). Criterion-referenced tests provide a basis for assessing the performance of examinees in relation to well-defined domains of content rather than in relation to other examinees, as with norm-referenced tests. Criterion-referenced tests are now widely used (1) in the armed services, to assess the competencies of servicemen; (2) in industry, to assess the job skills of employees and to evaluate the results of training programs; (3) in the licensing and certification fields, to distinguish "masters" from "non-masters" in over 900 professions in the United States alone; and (4) in educational settings such as schools, colleges, and universities, to assess the performance levels of students on competencies of interest.

The primary purpose of this chapter is to provide an introduction to the field of criterion-referenced measurement and to several of the technical developments that provide the measurement framework for constructing, evaluating, and using these tests in a wide number of educational settings.

A Brief History and Some Central Ideas

One of the first references to criterion-referenced testing appeared in a three-page paper by Robert Glaser in *American Psychologist* in 1963.

Over 900 papers have been published on the topic since that time, and the direction of educational testing has been changed dramatically. Glaser (1963), and later Popham and Husek (1969), were interested in an approach to testing that would provide information necessary for making a variety of individual and programmatic decisions arising in connection with specific objectives, skills, or competencies. The Popham-Husek article was especially effective in stimulating educational measurement specialists to take up the challenges associated with criterion-referenced measurement. Norm-referenced tests were regarded as limited because they could not provide the desired kinds of information.

Standard procedures for testing and measurement within a norm-referenced framework are well known to psychologists, but these procedures are far less appropriate when the questions being asked concern what examinees can and cannot do or what levels of proficiency examinees have attained in relation to a set of objectives or skills of interest (Glaser, 1963; Hambleton & Novick, 1973; Popham & Husek, 1969). Norm-referenced tests are constructed principally to facilitate the comparison of individuals (or groups) with one another or with respect to a norm group on the trait measured by the test. In contrast, criterion-referenced tests (or, as they are sometimes called, "proficiency tests," "domain-referenced tests," "mastery tests," "competency tests," "credentialing exams," or "basic skills tests") are constructed to permit the interpretation of individual (and group) test scores in relation to a set of clearly defined objectives, skills, or competencies.

Many definitions of criterion-referenced tests have been proposed in the literature over the last 20 years (see, for example, Nitko, 1980; Popham, 1978a). In fact, Gray (1978) reported the existence of 57 *different* definitions! At present the most widely accepted definition comes from Popham (1978a): "A criterion-referenced test is used to ascertain an individual's status with respect to a well-defined behavioral domain" (p. 93). Four points about the definition are worth noting. First, terms such as *objectives*, *skills*, and *competencies* are now used interchangeably in the measurement literature and by persons working in the testing field. Second, each objective measured in a criterion-referenced test must be *well defined*. The emphasis for this requirement goes back to work by Popham (1974). Well-defined objectives facilitate the process of writing test items and enhance the validity of test score interpretations. Item writing is improved because well-defined objectives provide a framework within which item writers and item reviewers can work. Validity is enhanced because of the clarity of the content or behavior domains to which test scores are referenced. The breadth and complexity of each domain of content or behaviors defining an objective can (and usually do) vary, but the domain *must* be clearly defined. Domains are clearly defined when test users and item writers can agree on the content that is appropriate for test items. The appropriate breadth of the domains depends on the purpose of the test. For example, diagnostic tests are usually organized around narrowly defined domains (e.g., the student will identify the meaning of a word consisting of a root word and a prefix). Year-end assessments, on the other hand, will normally be carried out with more broadly defined objectives (e.g., the student can comprehend the meaning of scientific passages).

Third, when more than one objective is measured in a criterion-referenced test, test items are usually organized into nonoverlapping subtests corresponding to the objectives, and examinee performance is reported on *each* of the objectives. Fourth, the definition does *not* include reference to a cutoff score or standard. It is common to set a standard of performance for each objective measured in the test and/or on the overall test, and interpret examinee performance in relation to it. But descriptive interpretations of scores such as "Examinee A answered 70 percent of the items correctly in the domain of content that addresses knowledge of capital cities of states" are frequently of interest, and standards are *not* needed in this type of score interpretation.

That a standard need not be set on a criterion-referenced test may come as a surprise to some people who have mistakenly assumed that the word *criterion* in *criterion-referenced test* refers to a standard or cutoff score. In fact, *criterion* is a word used by both Glaser (1963) and Popham and Husek (1969) to refer to the *domain of content or behavior* to which test scores are referenced.

Four other requirements for CRTs might also be highlighted at this point:

1.   The number of objectives measured in a criterion-referenced test will (in general) vary from one test to the next.
2.   The number of test items measuring each objective and the value of the minimum standard will (in general) vary from one objective to the next.
3.   There is *no* requirement that multiple-choice items be used. A review of currently available CRTs would clearly highlight the frequent uses of multiple-choice items, but this says as much about the versatility of the format as anything. Performance-assessments and other objective formats are also appropriate.
4.   One common method for making a mastery/nonmastery decision

involves the comparison of an examinee's percent (or proportion-correct) score on the objective in question with the corresponding standard. If an examinee's percent score is equal to or greater than the standard, the examinee is described as a "master (M)"; otherwise, the examinee is described as a "nonmaster (NM)." But, more complicated models for decision-making, which consider the relative seriousness of the two types of decision errors (false-positive and false-negative errors), are available for use and many of these methods were reviewed by van der Linden (1980).

In summary, there is no "rule book" that (1) prescribes the optimal number of test items per objective, number of objectives in a test, or item format; (2) requires a common cutoff score across objectives; or even (3) describes how mastery/nonmastery decisions are made. These test specifications are set to accommodate the needs of the testing program and its practical constraints (such as limits on the available testing time). What is not optional for valid criterion-referenced testing, however, is (1) the existence of a set of clearly defined objectives and (2) a statement of the intended uses of the test scores. Within the framework provided by these two requirements, tremendous scope exists for the construction and use of tests to assess examinee performance in relation to a body of content.

The testing literature has reflected some confusion over the differences among three kinds of tests—*criterion-referenced tests, domain-referenced tests* (DRT), and *objectives-referenced tests* (ORT). The definition for a criterion-referenced test offered earlier is similar to one Millman (1974) and others proposed for a *domain-referenced test*. If Popham's definition (or a similar one) of a *criterion-referenced test* is adopted, there are no essential differences between *criterion-referenced* and *domain-referenced* tests. However, the expression *domain-referenced test* is less likely to be misunderstood than the term *criterion-referenced test*. Why continue then to use the term *criterion-referenced test*? Popham (1978a), one of the leaders in the criterion-referenced testing field, offers one excellent reason: there is considerable public support for criterion-referenced tests, and therefore it would be undesirable and a waste of time if another campaign had to be initiated by psychologists and educators for domain-referenced tests.

On the other hand, ORTs are different from CRTs *and* DRTs. The primary distinction is as follows: In a CRT or DRT, the items are organized into clusters with each cluster of items serving as a representative set of items from a clearly defined content domain measuring an objective. With an objectives-referenced test, *no* clear domain of content is specified, and items are *not* considered to be representative of a content domain. Differences between the two types of tests on the matter of "content domain specification" have one very important implication for the type of test score generalizations that can be made from each test. With ORTs, unlike CRTs or DRTs, score interpretations must be made in terms of the *specific* items included in a test.

There are a number of excellent sources of technical information about criterion-referenced tests. Berk (1984a), Hambleton (1980), Hambleton (1990), Popham (1978a), and Roid and Haladyna (1982) are among the most useful because they cover multiple topics within the criterion-referenced measurement field.

Over its short history, the field of criterion-referenced testing has been hampered by some confusing terminology and some faulty methodological contributions. At the same time, fortunately, substantial progress has been made toward the establishment of a practical and usable criterion-referenced testing technology (Berk, 1984a; Hambleton, 1990; Popham, 1978a). There is now sufficient technical knowledge to (1) construct criterion-referenced tests, (2) assess their psychometric properties, and (3) use and report test score information. In fact there are probably thousands of examples of successful CRT programs in education, industry, and the military (see, for example, Hambleton, 1990; Popham, 1978a).

Norm-Referenced Versus Criterion-Referenced Tests

The primary purposes of norm-referenced tests and criterion-referenced tests differ substantially, and so approaches to test development, test evaluation, and test score usage will differ as well. Some individuals have mistakenly argued that there is only one type of achievement test from which both norm-referenced and criterion-referenced interpretations are made. It cannot be disputed that norm-referenced interpretations may be drawn from scores on a criterion-referenced test, though, because score variability may be restricted, reliability of score rankings may be low. Also, "weak" criterion-referenced interpretations (interpretations without generalizations) or objectives-referenced interpretations can be made with item scores from a norm-referenced test. But neither of these two interpretations is optimal (see, for example, Carver, 1974).

Because NRTs and CRTs use similar types of test directions, draw upon the same item formats, and require the same types of cognitive processing on the part of examinees, it is not always possible to distinguish one type of test from the other simply by looking at them. The differences between the two tests are significant, however, and far greater than just the way in which scores from these tests are interpreted.

There are four main areas of difference between norm-referenced tests and criterion-referenced tests (Hambleton, 1985): (1) test purpose, (2) content specificity, (3) test development, and (4) test score generalizability.

The difference in purpose between norm-referenced and criterion-referenced tests can be characterized as "the basic distinction" (Popham & Husek, 1969). Norm-referenced tests are designed and constructed to provide a basis for making comparisons among examinees in the content area(s) measured by the test. Since the number of items used to assess performance on specific objectives is often small (recall that norm-referenced tests are really *survey* tests), and therefore of limited practical value, criterion-referenced interpretations drawn from norm-referenced test scores generally have limited validity and reliability. Criterion-referenced tests, in contrast, are constructed to facilitate a sharper interpretation of performance in relation to the set of objectives covered by the test. They are somewhat analogous to what have been called *diagnostic* tests in the literature. Scores can be used to (1) describe performance, (2) make mastery/nonmastery decisions, and/or (3) evaluate program effectiveness. Just as criterion-referenced interpretations are possible from norm-referenced tests, norm-referenced interpretations may be made with criterion-referenced tests. However, comparisons of examinees based on criterion-referenced test scores may be somewhat unstable when test scores are relatively homogeneous, as they might be before or following instruction on the objectives measured in the test.

The second difference is concerned with content specifications. Construction of both norm-referenced and criterion-referenced tests begins by developing test blueprints or specifications that define the content, characteristics, and intent of the test. Although norm-referenced tests may use objectives to define and limit the content domain of interest, the use of well-defined objectives is *central* to the development of good criterion-referenced tests. Popham (1984) suggested that one way to define rigorously the item domain for each objective measured in a criterion-referenced test would involve specifying four aspects: (1) description, (2) sample test item, (3) content description, and (4) response description. Stringent adherence to domain or item specifications, as they are called, is essential in constructing criterion-referenced tests because the resulting scores are referenced back to the item specifications at the interpretation stage. Clear "targets" for test score interpretations are essential with criterion-referenced tests. This point will be expanded in the next section of the chapter.

The third difference between norm-referenced and criterion-referenced tests lies in the area of test development. Norm-referenced tests are designed to "spread examinees out" so as to increase the stability of the rankings of the examinees. To accomplish this task, norm-referenced test score variance must be increased, which is done by selecting items of moderate difficulty (p-values between .30 and .70) and high discriminating power (point biserial correlations of over .30). In general, the increased score variability of norm-referenced tests will improve test validity and reliability, but it can also result in tests failing to contain the test items that "tap" the central concepts of a particular area of achievement (Popham, 1978a). For a full review of norm-referenced test development methods, readers are referred to Linn (1989). Criterion-referenced test interpretations, on the other hand, do not depend on score comparisons among examinees. Criterion-referenced test scores are interpreted "directly" by referencing scores to the appropriate domains of content (Hambleton, 1982, 1990). Test item pools are formed by preparing items that conform to test specifications and measure the objectives. Items that do not meet content specifications, are poorly written, or have statistics suggesting they are flawed, are removed from the item pool at the outset.

The fourth major difference is score generalizability. Norm-referenced performance is interpreted best in relation to a "norm" group. It is of limited value, and rarely appropriate, to generalize student performance to a body of content because of the way in which test items are selected for inclusion in a norm-referenced test. In contrast, test score generalization is a valuable attribute of criterion-referenced measurement. Because performance on a specific set of test items is rarely of interest and because of the fact that items can be matched to domains of content, test score generalizations beyond the specific items on a test can be made to the larger domains of content, measuring each objective assessed by a criterion-referenced test.

Test Development

Basic Steps

Twelve steps for preparing a criterion-referenced test are presented in figure 1–1. The intended purpose of the test will dictate the degree of attention to detail and thoroughness with which the steps are carried out. A few brief remarks on each of the test development steps follow:

Steps in Preparing Criterion-Referenced Tests

1. Preliminary considerations
   a. Specify the purposes of the test.
   b. Specify the objectives to be measured by the test.
   c. Specify groups to be measured, special testing requirements resulting from student age, race, sex, socioeconomic status, linguistic differences, handicaps, etc.
   d. Make initial decisions about item formats (i.e., objective-vs. performance-oriented).
   e. Determine time and financial resources available for test construction and production.
   f. Identify and select qualified staff (note individual strengths and role in test development).
   g. Specify an initial estimate of test length (include number of objectives and items, as well as approximate time requirements).

2. Review of objectives
   a. Review the descriptions of the objectives to determine their acceptability.
   b. Select final group of objectives to be measured by the test.
   c. Prepare item specifications for each objective and review them for completeness, accuracy, clarity, and practicality.

3. Item writing
   a. Draft a sufficient number of items for pilot-testing.
   b. Enter items into a (preferably) computerized item bank (to facilitate revision process and retrieval).
   c. Carry out item editing.

4. Assessment of content validity
   a. Identify a group of judges and measurement specialists.
   b. Review the test items to determine their match to the objectives, their representativeness, and their freedom from bias and stereotyping.
   c. Review the test items to determine their technical adequacy.

5. Revisions to test items
   a. Based upon data from 4b and 4c, revise test items (when possible and necessary) or delete them.
   b. Write additional test items (if needed) and repeat step 4.

6. Field test administration
   a. Organize the test items into forms for pilot testing.
   b. Administer the test forms to appropriately chosen groups of examinees.
   c. Conduct item analyses and item bias studies.

Figure 1–1. Steps for Preparing Criterion-Referenced Tests

7. Test item revisions
   a. Using the results from 6c, revise test items when necessary or delete.

8. Test assembly
   a. Determine the test length, the number of forms needed, and the number of items per objective.
   b. Select test items from available pool of valid test items.
   c. Prepare test directions, practice questions, test booklet layout, scoring keys, answer sheets, etc.
   d. Specify modifications to instructions, medium of presentation or examinee response, and time requirements that may be necessary for special needs examinees.

9. Selection of a standard
   a. Determine if descriptions of examinee performance or determination of mastery status is most appropriate for test purpose(s). (If descriptions are the primary use, go to step 10.)
   b. Initiate (and document) a process to determine the standard to separate "masters" from "non-masters." Alternately, more than one standard can be set, if needed (for example, "honors," "acceptable," and "minimum").
   c. Specify considerations that may affect the standard(s) when applied to handicapped examinees (i.e., alternative administration or modification to accommodate special needs).
   d. Specify "alternative" test score interpretations for examinees requiring modified administrations.

10. Pilot test administration
    a. Design the test administration to collect score reliability and validity information.
    b. Administer the test form(s) to appropriately chosen groups of examinees.
    c. Identify and evaluate administration modifications to meet individual special needs that may affect validity and reliability of tests.
    d. Evaluate the test administration procedures, test items, and score reliability and validity.
    e. Make final revisions based on the available technical data.

11. Preparation of manuals
    a. Prepare a test administrator's manual.
    b. Prepare a technical manual.

12. Additional technical data collection
    a. Conduct reliability and validity investigations.

1.   Step 1 ensures that the test development project is well organized. The early articulation of test purpose(s) and factors that might affect test quality will help manage resources. Also, identifying special groups—handicapped examinees, for example—ensures that when the test is administered, it will measure examinees' achievements rather than reflect their special testing needs.

2.   Domain specifications are invaluable to item writers when they are carefully prepared. Considerable time and money can be saved in the test development process by not having to revise test items extensively due to the lack of detailed directions given to the item writers.

3.   Some training of item writers in the proper use of domain (or item) specifications and in the principles of item writing is often desirable, particularly if novel item formats are to be used in the test.

4.   This step is essential. Items are evaluated by reviewers to assess their match to the objectives, their technical quality, and their freedom from bias and stereotyping.

5.   Any necessary revisions to test items can be made at this step and, when additional test items are needed, they should be written and Step 4 repeated.

6.   The test items are organized into booklets and administered to a sample of examinees like those for whom the test is intended. (The desirable sample size will depend on the importance of the test.) Necessary revisions to test items can be made at this stage based upon the field-test results. Item statistics are used to identify items that may need revision.

7.   Whenever possible, malfunctioning test items should be revised and added to the pools of acceptable test items. When substantial revisions are made to test items, Step 4 should be repeated.

8.   Final test booklets are compiled at this step. When parallel forms are required, and especially if the tests are short, item statistics should be used to ensure that matched forms are produced.

9.   A standard-setting procedure is selected, implemented, and documented. If a description of examinee performance is used in place of, or to supplement, a standard, its interpretability and relation to the test's purpose should be explained.

10.   Test directions are evaluated, scoring keys are checked, and the reliability and validity of scores and decisions are assessed. Sometimes, many of these activities are carried out on the data provided by the actual test administration. Whenever possible, though, these activities should be carried out using a second field test (the first is step 5). An item bias study is also carried out at this step (Scheuneman & Bleistein, 1989).

11.   For important tests such as those used for credentialling, a

test administration manual and technical manual should be prepared.
12. No matter how carefully a test is constructed or evaluated initially, reliability and validity studies must be carried out concurrently.

Norcini and associates (1988) provided an excellent application of the above steps to the construction of a criterion-referenced performance test to measure physician competence. The Department of the Army (1986) described a similar set of steps (with considerably more detail) for the construction of criterion-referenced job competency tests.

Objectives

Mager's (1962) classic book on preparing behavioral objectives had a tremendous impact on psychology and education in the 1960s and 1970s. Few psychologists at one time or another have not read the book or at least had the opportunity to write a few behavioral objectives. Instructors have been trained to write them; curricula have been defined by them; and objective-referenced tests have been constructed to measure them. Behavioral objectives are relatively easy to write and have contributed substantially to the organization of curricula, but, as emphasized by Popham (1974, 1978a, 1984), they do *not* lead to unequivocal determination of the domain of content or behaviors that describe the objectives. For example, consider the following: "The student will identify the tone or emotion expressed in a paragraph." Whether someone planned to teach the objective or to write the test items to measure it, several points would need to be clarified first. Which tones or emotions? How long should the paragraphs be? At what readability level should the paragraphs be written? What is the best way to approach the assessment? Also, a test item writer might wonder about the "fineness" of discriminations that are to be required of an examinee. Popham (1974) referred to tests built from behavioral objectives as "cloud-referenced tests." This description seems appropriate.

The production of test items to measure objectives cannot be handled efficiently when the content domains are unclearly defined. Also, when the domains of content are unclear, it is not possible to insure that representative samples of test items from each item domain are drawn.

As was mentioned earlier, domain specifications are one important development in criterion-referenced testing (Popham, 1978a, 1984). A domain specification can be prepared to clarify the intended content or

Sample Mathematics Domain Specification

Objective

The student will be able to find the name of a point between 0 and 1 on the number line.

Directions and Sample Test Item

Read the problem carefully and choose the correct answer. Place the letter beside your answer on the answer sheet next to the number of the problem.

Find the numeral which correctly replaces the pointer in the number line above.

a. 3   b. 1¾   c. ¾   d. ¼

Content Section

1. The student is given a number line with the endpoints labeled zero and one using rational numbers with the same denominator.
2. The divisions on the line shall be equally spaced.
3. The number of divisions on the line will be a multiple of the given denominator.
4. A pointer is used to identify the unknown point on the line.

Response Section

1. There are one correct and three incorrect responses.
2. The responses are given in ascending or descending order.
3. The distractors shall include
    (a) the numeral which represents the ordinal position of the point in question;
    (b) the numeral which represents the length of each division on the number line; and
    (c) the numeral which is one more than the correct response

Figure 1–2.   A Sample Domain Specification in the Mathematics Area

behaviors specified by an objective. (Other approaches are described by Nitko, 1980, and Roid & Haladyna, 1982.)

Domains come in at least two varieties (Gray, 1978; Nitko, 1980). In an *ordered domain*, the subskills that describe an objective are arranged in some meaningful way, such as in a learning hierarchy. One of the advantages of an ordered domain is that statements of examinee performance in relation to the domain can be made from a test that may only measure a few of the subskills (see, for example, some of the current research by Bergan and his colleagues). In an *unordered domain*, and this is the more common of the two types of domains, the content or behaviors defining the domain are specified, but relationships among the component parts are not specified.

Popham suggested four steps for the preparation of a domain specification. The first involves the preparation of a general description. This description can be a behavioral objective, a detailed description of the objective, or a short cryptic descriptor. Next, a sample test item is prepared. The sample item will reveal the desired format and help to clarify the appropriate domain of test items. The third step is usually the most difficult. It is necessary to specify the content or behaviors included in a domain. Occasionally, for the purpose of clarification, it is also desirable to indicate which content or behaviors are *not* included in a domain specification. Characteristics of response alternatives or response limits are specified in the final step. Examples of domain specifications in the areas of mathematics and science are shown in figures 1–2 and 1–3, re-

---

Sample Science Domain Specification

Objective

Examinee will be able to apply Ohm's Law in various word problems.

Directions and Sample Test Item

Read the word problem below and answer it by circling the correct answer. All the answer choices have been rounded to the first decimal place.

A current of 4.2 amperes flows through a coil whose resistance is 1.4 ohms. What is the potential difference applied at the ends of the coil?

(a)   .3 volts   (b)   3.0 volts   (c)   5.6 volts   (d)   5.9 volts

Content Section

1. All problems will be similar to but different from the ones presented in instruction.
2. In the directions the examinees will not be told to use Ohm's Law nor should they be given the mathematical formula.
3. The directions will also specify how the answers have been rounded off.
4. The examinee can be asked to calculate any of the variables in Ohm's Law.

Figure 1–3. A Sample Domain Specification in the Science Area

5. The variables given in the word problem will always have correct units and contain a decimal form (i.e., 2.5 volts not 2½).

Response Section

1. Alternatives will be placed in a numerical sequence from smallest to largest number.
2. The alternatives will be of the correct unit and a decimal form.
3. The alternatives will include the correct answer and three plausible distractors:

Calculating current:

correct answer: $\dfrac{\text{voltage}}{\text{resistance}}$

plausible distractors: $\dfrac{\text{resistance}}{\text{voltage}}$, resistance × voltage
resistance + voltage

Calculating voltage:

correct answer: current × resistance

plausible distractors: $\dfrac{\text{current}}{\text{resistance}}$, $\dfrac{\text{resistance}}{\text{current}}$

Calculating resistance:

Correct answer: $\dfrac{\text{voltage}}{\text{current}}$

plausible distractors: $\dfrac{\text{current}}{\text{voltage}}$, current × voltage
current + voltage

Figure 1.3. (Continued).

spectively. Additional guidelines for preparing domain specifications and a variety of examples are provided by Hambleton (1990) and Popham (1978a, 1984).

To date, most of the domain specifications that have been prepared utilize objective item formats (e.g., multiple choice). Several examples of domain specifications that are not, are presented in Hambleton (1990). Two matters that require special attention when nonobjective item formats are used are (1) clear directions for administering the test, and (2) a clearly developed plan for scoring examinee performance and/or products produced.

Test Items

Perhaps the most critical task in criterion-referenced test construction, following the preparation of domain (or item) specifications, is generating test items that measure the objectives while conforming to the constraints outlined in the domain specifications. Specifying relevant examinee skills and behaviors in the domain specifications will facilitate the item-writing process. Nevertheless, translating specific tasks into test items that conform to the objectives and allow test users to make valid diagnostic or mastery interpretations about examinee performance is a difficult process. The difference of purpose between criterion-referenced and norm-referenced tests renders many traditional psychometric item analysis and selection measures inappropriate for criterion-referenced test construction. For example, norm-referenced test developers can use item difficulty and item discrimination indices in order to select effective items (i.e., those which discriminate between examinees with varying degrees of knowledge). Criterion-referenced test developers, on the other hand, should be less reliant on these measures and should select items on the basis of their ability to assess examinee knowledge or instructional effectiveness (see, for example, Hambleton, 1985). Therefore, criterion-referenced test item construction and selection rely heavily on domain specifications and the skills of item writers to construct valid items. It is well documented, too, that item writing training will usually improve test quality (see, for example, Wieberg, Neeb, & Schott, 1984).

The most widely used criterion-referenced test item format over the years has been the multiple-choice question. This format is familiar to most item writers, and the features required of a "good" multiple-choice question are well known to test developers (e.g., Haladyna & Downing, 1989a, 1989b; Haladyna & Shindoll, 1989; Roid & Haladyna, 1982). Carlson (1985) and Gulliksen (1986), however, have offered useful examples and insights into the use of alternative item formats that, although not necessarily new, receive infrequent use. Millman and Westman (1989) have recently addressed the use of computers in the item-writing process. Expanding the array of item formats and approaches to item writing should promote more accurate measurement and interpretation of examinee performance.

Content Validity

According to the *Test Standards*, establishing content validity requires reviewers to "assess the degree to which the sample of items in the test is representative of some defined domain of content." Expert judgment is the main mode of investigation of a test's content validity, or related concepts, curricular validity and instructional validity. The difference among the three approaches to validity determination is the particular domain of content to which test content is matched: In assessing content validity, test content is matched to the content specifications for the test; in assessing curricular validity, test content is matched to a domain of content defined by the curriculum of interest; and finally, in assessing instructional validity, test content is matched to what is actually taught in a program where the test will be used. Content validity evidence seems important regardless of the test use. On the other hand, curricular evidence seems most useful in choosing norm-referenced tests or conducting curriculum evaluation studies. Instructional validity evidence is especially useful with what are known as "high-stakes" tests (Popham, 1987).

Determination of content validity involves a consideration of three features of the test items: (1) item validities (i.e., the extent to which each test item measures some aspect of the content included in a domain specification), (2) technical quality, and (3) representativeness (Hambleton, 1984a). These three factors will be considered next.

Item Validity. The quality of criterion-referenced test items can be determined by the extent to which they reflect, in terms of their content, the domains from which they were derived. Unless one can say with a high degree of confidence that the items in a criterion-referenced test measure the intended objectives, any use of the test score information will be questionable.

Two approaches are currently used to establish the validity of criterion-referenced test items. One approach involves the collection and use of judgmental data (Hambleton, Swaminathan, Algina, & Coulson, 1978; Rovinelli & Hambleton, 1977). For example, Hambleton (1984a) offered this set of directions:

> First, read carefully through the lists of domain specifications and test items. Next, indicate how well you feel each item reflects the domain specification it was written to measure. Judge a test item solely on the basis of the match between its content and the content defined by the domain specification that the test item was prepared to measure. Use the five-point rating scale shown below:

Poor	Fair	Good	Very Good	Excellent
1	2	3	4	5

With this procedure or other variations, a measure of the perceived match between items and the objectives they were written to measure can be obtained along with an indication of the agreement among reviewers' ratings.

The second approach requires items to be pilot-tested on a group of examinees similar in characteristics to those for whom the test is intended. The examinee item response data are analyzed to determine item difficulty levels and discrimination indices. An item that has a difficulty level that varies substantially from the difficulty levels of other items measuring the same domain specification should be studied carefully to determine if the variation is the result of a content or technical flaw. Items with very low or negative-valued discrimination indices should also be studied carefully for flaws. Readers are referred to Berk (1984b), Millman (1974), Popham (1978a), and van der Linden (1981) for discussions of additional item statistics and their usefulness in building criterion-referenced tests.

The use of item analytic techniques is important in the content-validation process. In situations where at least a moderate-sized sample of examinees is available and where the test constructor is interested in identifying aberrant items, not for elimination from the item pool but for correction, the use of an empirical approach to item validation will provide important information with regard to the assessment of item validity.

In summary, obtaining content specialists' ratings is the method to use for assessing item validities; empirical procedures should be used for the detection of aberrant items in need of correction. An excellent review of item statistics for use with criterion-referenced tests was prepared by Berk (1984b). Readers are also referred to Hambleton (1985) and van der Linden (1981) for other reviews.

Technical Adequacy of Test Items.   The technical adequacy of test items is usually established at the same time as test items are reviewed for the appropriateness of their content. Measurement specialists can be asked to review the test items to identify flaws in items such as grammatical cues, awkwardly worded item stems, and nonrandom distribution of correct answers across the answer positions. Sample item technical review forms are given by Hambleton (1984a; 1990).

Representativeness of the Test Items.   Reviewers are asked to evaluate the representativeness of items measuring each objective. From a grid developed to describe the content or behaviors in a domain specification, reviewers can judge the degree of item representativeness. For example, a group of reviewers can be asked, "How well does the set of test items sample the domain of content or behaviors defining the objective?" When representativeness has not been achieved to some desired level, new test items should be added and/or items deleted to obtain the desired level of representativeness.

Item Selection

The item selection process is straightforward provided that the criterion-referenced test developer has been careful in defining objectives and in constructing test items. Larger domains require special attention to insure that representative samples of test items are drawn. With large domains especially, it helps to prepare a grid to organize the relevant content or behaviors. A test is usually constructed by taking either a random or stratified random sample of items from each domain of interest.

The consistency of mastery/nonmastery decisions over retest or parallel test administrations can be increased by selecting test items in a different fashion. Of course, increasing the number of test items is effective but often it is not feasible to do so. When the primary purpose of a testing program is to make mastery/nonmastery decisions, a more reliable and valid set of test scores will result if test items are selected from the available pool of items measuring each objective on the basis of statistical properties. For example, suppose a standard is set at 80 percent correct in the domain of test items measuring an objective. Test items that discriminate effectively in the region of the cutoff score (80 percent) on the test score scale will contribute most to decision consistency and validity. A test constructed in this way will have maximum discriminating power in the region where decisions are to be made; therefore, more reliable and valid decisions will result. One possible drawback is that scores derived from the test cannot be used to make descriptive statements about examinee levels of performance because test items measuring each objective will not necessarily constitute a representative sample. There is at least one way to make descriptive statements about examinees' level of performance when nonrandom or nonrepresentative samples of test items are chosen: by introducing concepts and models from the field of item response theory (Hambleton, 1989; Hambleton & Swaminathan, 1985). Although the feasibility of such an approach has not been fully tested, the interested reader is referred to Hambleton (1989) for a discussion of item response theory.

Test Length

A large body of literature exists on the topic of criterion-referenced test length (Hambleton, 1984b; Hambleton, Mills, & Simon, 1983; Wilcox, 1980). Only a few of the more practical contributions are cited in this subsection.

When the primary use of the scores is description, a well-known formula for the precision of domain score estimates, based upon the binomial test model, is useful:

$$\text{Precision}^2 = \frac{\hat{\pi}(1 - \hat{\pi})}{n}$$

By simple algebra, an expression for test length (n) in terms of precision of domain score estimates and domain scores can be obtained:

$$n = \frac{\hat{\pi}(1 - \hat{\pi})}{(\text{precision})^2}$$

By specifying a typical value for π (domain score estimate) in the group of examinees of interest, and the level of precision required of the domain score estimates, the appropriate test length can be found. Suppose the desired level of precision = .15 and π = .75. The value of n is 8.3. Therefore, 9 test items are needed to ensure the desired degree of precision in the domain score estimates. When in doubt about a typical value of π, set π = .50. This will ensure that a conservative test length is obtained, that is, a test length longer than one that will be needed is used.

When criterion-referenced test scores are to be used to make mastery/nonmastery decisions, there are a number of aids for selecting test lengths. Millman (1973) prepared a set of tables to predict the likelihood of examinees being misclassified as a function of domain score, test length, and cutoff score. Wilcox (1976) prepared tables that allow the user to study relationships among test lengths, cutoff scores, and minimally acceptable probabilities of correct classifications for examinees.

Eignor and Hambleton (1979) developed an approach to choosing test lengths in which test developers select a probable domain score distribution (from five that are available for the group to be measured) and then refer to tables that connect useful group test score summary statistics such as decision consistency, kappa, and decision accuracy (relation between decisions based on a test and decisions evolving from a criterion measure such as teacher ratings) to test length. (The tables are limited to cases where the standard is 80 percent.) Other methods based upon IRT models are reviewed by Hambleton (1984b).

Psychometric Issues and Methods

Reliability Issues and Methods

Criterion-referenced test scores are used principally in two ways: (1) to make inferences about levels of proficiency, and (2) to make mastery/ nonmastery decisions. With the first use, of interest is the precision with which domain scores are estimated. Of interest with the second use is the test-retest decision consistency or parallel-form decision consistency.

Unfortunately, the usual approaches for assessing test score reliability (test-retest reliability, parallel-form reliability, and corrected split-half reliability), which are routinely applied to norm-referenced tests, do not address directly the two main criterion-referenced test score uses, and therefore they are of limited value in the context of criterion-referenced measurement (Hambleton & Novick, 1973). It has been argued that classical reliability indices are not useful with criterion-referenced tests because the scores often are fairly homogeneous and so classical reliability indices will be low. But this is not the main problem with classical indices. If low reliability indices were the problem, the problem could be resolved by interpreting reliability indices more cautiously in light of homogeneous test score distributions or designing reliability studies to ensure more heterogeneous score distributions. Actually, norm-referenced test reliability indices are not useful with criterion-referenced test scores because they fail to provide useful information about individual score and decision consistency.

Reliability assessment has probably received more attention from psychometricians than any other in the criterion-referenced testing field. The interested reader is referred to Berk (1980) for reviews of the main contributions. A few of the more practical contributions to the topic will be considered next.

Reliability of Domain Score Estimates.   The standard error of measurement associated with domain score estimates (proportion-correct scores) can be calculated easily. It is useful in setting up confidence bands for examinee domain scores. Fortunately, it is not influenced to any considerable extent by the homogeneity of examinee domain score distributions (Lord & Novick, 1968). One disadvantage is that a constant level of error is assumed across the full range of test scores. One advantage of working within an item response theory framework is that error estimates unique to each proficiency level are available (Hambleton, 1989; Weiss & Yoes, see Chapter 3).

Another approach for determining the consistency of domain score estimates was reported by Millman (1974). He suggested that the standard error of estimation derived from the binomial test model given by the expression $\sqrt{\hat{\pi}(1 - \hat{\pi})/n}$, could be used to set up confidence bands around domain score estimates. In the expression, n is the number of items measuring the objective and $\hat{\pi}$ is the proportion-correct score for the examinee on the set of items measuring the objective. Variations on the binomial error model were described by Berk (1980).

Reliability of Mastery Classifications. Hambleton and Novick (1973) suggested that the reliability of mastery classification decisions should be defined in terms of the consistency of decisions from two administrations of the same test or parallel forms of a test. Hambleton and Novick suggested the formula below to measure the proportion of examinees who are consistently classified on the two administrations:

$$p_o = \sum_{j=1}^{m} p_{jj}$$

where p_{jj} is the proportion of examinees classified in the jth mastery state on the two administrations and m is the number of mastery states. In practice, m is usually equal to two. The index p_o is the proportion of decisions that are in agreement. Among the factors affecting the value of p_o are test length, quality of test items, choice of cutoff score, group heterogeneity, and the closeness of the group mean performance to the cutoff score. The p_o statistic has considerable appeal and is easy to calculate. For important tests such as those used for awarding high school diplomas or licenses to practice in a profession, a level of decision consistency over 90 percent has become the goal. Decision consistency levels between 70 percent and 90 percent are often acceptable for teacher-prepared or commercially prepared criterion-referenced tests that are used to monitor performance on a day-to-day basis (see, for example, Subkoviak, 1988).

Swaminathan, Hambleton, and Algina (1974) argued that the statistic p_o has one limitation: it does not take into account the proportion of agreement that occurs by chance alone. For example, suppose examinees were assigned to one of two mastery states based on "coin flips." Heads are masters and tails are nonmasters. By chance alone, 50 percent of the examinees will be classified into the same mastery state on "two administrations." Decision consistency is assessed to be 50 percent, and this is due to chance factors only! In assessing the consistency of decisions resulting from the use of a test, it would seem to be desirable to account in some way for the agreement due to chance. Therefore, Swaminathan and colleagues (1974) suggested using coefficient k (Cohen, 1960) as an index of decision consistency that is corrected for the agreement due to chance alone. This coefficient is defined as

$$k = (p_o - p_c)/(1 - p_c)$$

where

$$p_c = \sum_{j=1}^{m} p_{j\cdot} \cdot p_{\cdot j}$$

The symbols $p_{j\cdot}$ and $p_{\cdot j}$ represent the proportions of examinees assigned to mastery state j on the first and second administrations, respectively. The symbol p_c represents the proportion of agreement that would occur even if the classifications based on the two administrations followed a strictly random process. Thus, in a sense, it can be argued that k takes into account the composition of the group, and that, in this sense, it is more group independent than the simple proportion of agreement statistic, p_o. The statistic k can be thought of as a measure of decision consistency that is over and above the decision consistency due to chance alone.

The coefficient k depends on all factors that affect the decision-making procedure: the cutoff score, the heterogeneity of the group of examinees, and the method of assigning examinees to mastery states. Therefore, it is useful to report all of these factors when reporting k since this information contributes to its interpretation.

The concept of decision consistency is a useful one with criterion-referenced tests, but the approaches described above require the administration of a single test twice, or the administration of parallel forms of a test. In both cases, testing time is doubled. This approach is often difficult to implement in practice because of limited testing time. One way to avoid the extra testing time in assessing reliability with norm-referenced tests involves the use of the split-half method to determine the reliability of scores from a test that is one-half as long as the one of interest. Then, the Spearman-Brown formula is used along with the split-half reliability estimate to predict the reliability of scores with the test of interest. Unfortunately, the approach used with norm-referenced test scores cannot be applied to the problem of assessing consistency of decisions emanating from a single administration of a criterion-referenced test because there is no "step-up formula" analogous to the Spearman-Brown formula. Different approaches for estimating decision consistency from a single administration were developed by Subkoviak (1976) and Huynh (1976). While the mathematical development of the formula is not comparable, Subkoviak's formula and the more complicated one by Huynh are the analog of the corrected split-half reliability index which is used with norm-referenced tests to estimate parallel-form reliability from a single test administration. Most recently Woodruff and Sawyer (1989) have advanced two other methods that show promise but they will not be discussed further here.

Subkoviak defined a coefficient of decision consistency for an examinee i, denoted $p_c^{(i)}$, as the probability of the examinee being consistently classified on two test administrations (with either the same test or parallel forms). For the case of two mastery states, this probability is given by

$$p_c^{(i)} = \text{Prob}(X_i \geq c, Y_i \geq c) + \text{Prob}(X_i < c, Y_i < c)$$

where c is the cutoff score on the objective and X_i and Y_i are the scores for the examinee on the two administrations. The two terms represent the probability of examinee i being consistently assigned to either a mastery or a nonmastery state. A measure of decision consistency for a group of N examinees is easily found:

$$p_o = \frac{\sum\limits_{i=1}^{N} p_c^{(i)}}{N}$$

In order to determine p_o, it is necessary to estimate $p_c^{(i)}$, $i = 1, 2, \ldots,$ N. Estimates can be obtained if two assumptions are made: (1) examinee scores on the two administrations are independently and identically distributed; and (2) for a fixed examinee, scores on the two parallel tests are binomially distributed. Of course, the appropriateness of the estimate of $p_c^{(i)}$ will depend on the validity of the two assumptions. The first assumption is quite reasonable. Assume there exists a sampling distribution of possible test scores for an examinee with a given true score. Variation in scores across occasions is due to errors of measurement. The first assumption is satisfied if the sampling distribution applies equally well to the examinee for both test administrations, and if the scores are randomly drawn from the distribution. The second assumption is less reasonable because it cannot be true when item difficulties vary, and, in general, they will. Fortunately, Subkoviak has shown that violations of this second assumption have only a modest effect on the results.

With only the two assumptions, Subkoviak showed that

$$p(X_i \geq c) = \sum_{X_i=c}^{n} \binom{n}{X_i} \pi_i^{X_i}(1 - \pi_i)^{n-X_i}$$

and

$$p_c^{(i)} = [p(X_i \geq c)]^2 + [1 - p(X_i \geq c)]^2.$$

Once an estimate of an examinee's domain score (proportion-correct score), denoted $\hat{\pi}$, is obtained, $p(X_i \geq c)$ and $p_c^{(i)}$ can be obtained easily. The average of $p_c^{(i)}$ for $i = 1, 2, \ldots, N$, is calculated next. The average serves as an estimate of the consistency of mastery decisions between two test administrations. The estimate is obtained from a *single* administration and depends on the chosen standard of performance. Subkoviak's estimate of decision consistency is very popular because the computational formula is straightforward and the assumptions on which it is based are reasonable.

It is also possible to obtain an estimate of k using Subkoviak's method. The only additional information needed is the proportion of examinees assigned to each mastery state on the single test administration. By making the reasonable assumption that these proportions would be the same on a retest or a parallel-form administration, the proportion of agreement expected by chance (p_c) can be obtained by the method introduced earlier ($p_c = p_1 \cdot p_{\cdot 1} + p_2 \cdot p_{\cdot 2}$). Therefore, if $p_1. = .20$ and $p_2. = .80$, then $p_{\cdot 1} = .20$ and $p_{\cdot 2} = .80$, $p_c = .20^2 + .80^2 = .68$. With a value of p_c and with the p_o estimate from Subkoviak's method, k can quickly be calculated. The proper reliability information (whether one is discussing domain scores or mastery classification decisions) should be provided for each reported score to aid in criterion-referenced interpretations (Hambleton & Novick, 1973).

Validity Issues and Methods

Many contributions to the criterion-referenced testing literature have been made since the late 1960s, but the important topic of criterion-referenced test score validity has received limited attention from researchers. Often measurement specialists have assumed the validity of criterion-referenced test scores rather than make a concerted effort to establish the validity of the scores in any formal way. The argument seems to be that, if the appropriate test development steps are carried out, a valid criterion-referenced test will necessarily result. But the validity of the resulting scores will depend on their intended use in addition to the care with which the test was constructed.

There are a number of signs that the situation is changing. First, several articles are now available to describe the nature of the validity questions and how they should be approached (Fitzpatrick, 1983; Kane, 1982; Haertel, 1985; Hambleton, 1984a; Linn, 1979, 1980; Madaus, 1983; and Messick, 1989). Second, there have been several exemplary validity studies in the literature (Kirsch & Guthrie, 1980; Livingston, 1989; Ward, Frederiksen, & Carlson, 1980).

Many criterion-referenced test developers have argued that, in order to "validate" their tests and test scores, it is sufficient to assess "content validity." Usually judgments are obtained from persons with content expertise concerning the match between test content and the objectives a test is designed to measure. Since these judgments focus on test content, the expression *content validity* is used to describe the nature of the activities carried out by the content specialists; but it should be clear that content validity refers to certain characteristics of the test content. The content validity of a test does not vary from one sample of examinees to the next, nor does the content validity of a test vary over time. However, any use of a test (whether *norm-referenced* or *criterion-referenced*) is ultimately dependent on the scores obtained from a test administration, and the validity of the scores depends upon many factors (most especially, the intended use of the scores) in addition to test content. It is possible that examinee item responses and resulting test scores do not adequately reflect or address the skills of interest even though the test itself was judged to be content valid.

Fortunately, there is a wide assortment of methods that can be used to gather validity evidence relevant to the intended uses of a set of test scores:

1. *Intra-objective methods* include item analyses, the evaluation of test content (determination of item and content validity), and score reliability;

2. *Inter-objective methods* include what are often called "convergent" and "divergent" validity studies—studies to determine whether test scores correlate with variables they might reasonably be expected to relate to, and studies to determine if test scores are uncorrelated with variables they should not be related to;

3. *Criterion-related methods* include prediction studies and studies of the relationships between (say) mastery classifications and independent measures of performance such as those that might be obtained from teachers, instructors, or supervisors;

4. *Experimental methods* include determining the sensitivity of test scores and mastery classifications to the effects of instruction on test content; and

5. *Multitrait/multimethod studies* address what it is that a test actually measures.

Accumulating validation evidence can be a never-ending process. The amount of time and energy that should be expended on the validation of test scores and mastery classifications should be directly related to the importance of the test use.

In the brief section that follows, several validity investigations that are unique to criterion-referenced tests will be described.

Construct Validity Investigations. Construct validation studies have not been common in criterion-referenced measurement (see, for example, Haertel, 1985). This may be because criterion-referenced test score distributions are often homogeneous. (For example, it often happens that before instruction most individuals do poorly on a test and after instruction most individuals do well.) Correlational methods do not work well with homogeneous score distributions because of problems due to score range restrictions. But, as Messick (1975) has noted:

> Construct validation is by no means limited to correlation coefficients, even though it may seem that way from the prevalence of correlation matrices, internal consistency indices, and factor analysis (p. 958).

Construct validation studies begin with a definite statement of the proposed use of the test scores. A clearly stated use will provide direction for the kind of evidence that is worth collecting. A few investigations that could be undertaken to estimate the construct validity of a set of criterion-referenced test scores are described next.

Factor Analysis. Factor analysis is commonly employed for the dimensional analysis of items in a norm-referenced test, or of scores derived from different norm-referenced tests. It can be used, too, in construct validation studies of criterion-referenced test scores. One reason for its lack of use is that the usual input for factor analytic studies are correlations, and correlations are often low between items on a criterion-referenced test or between criterion-referenced test scores and other variables because score variability is often not very great. Also, inter-item correlations are often low because of the unreliability of item scores. However, the problem due to limited score variability to some extent can be reduced by choosing a heterogeneous sample of examinees—for example, a group including both masters and nonmasters. Another strategy would be to work with objective scores rather than item scores.

The research problem becomes a problem of determining whether the factor pattern matrix has a prescribed form. The prescribed form is set by the researchers, and is based upon a logical analysis of the objectives and other research evidence concerning the structure of the objectives measured in the test. Evidence that the estimated structure among the variables matches the prescribed form will support both the research hypotheses and the validity of the scores as measures of the desired objectives.

Experimental Studies. There are many sources of error that reduce the validity of an intended use of criterion-referenced test scores—for example, clarity of test directions, test speededness, and level of motivation. Experimental studies of potential sources of error to determine their effects on test scores are an important way to assess the construct validity of a set of test scores. Logical analysis and observations of testing methods and procedures can also be used to detect sources of invalidity in a set of test scores.

Multitrait-multimethod approach. The category of construct validation would also include "multitrait-multimethod" validation of objective scores (Campbell & Fiske, 1959). Multitrait-multimethod validation includes any techniques addressing the question of how much examinee responses to items reflect the "trait" (objective) of interest, and how much they reflect methodological effects.

Criterion-Related Validity Investigations. Even if scores derived from criterion-referenced tests are descriptive of the objectives they are supposed to reflect, the usefulness of the scores as predictors of, say, "job success" or "success in the next unit of instruction" cannot be assured. Criterion-related validity studies of criterion-referenced test scores are no different in procedure from studies conducted with norm-referenced tests. Correlational, group separation, and decision accuracy methods are commonly used (Messick, 1989). Also, selection of reasonable and practical criterion measures that do *not* themselves require extensive validation efforts remains as serious a problem for conducting validation studies with criterion-referenced tests as it is for norm-referenced tests. There are, however, two important differences: first, test scores are usually dichotomized. (Examinees above a cutoff score are described as masters and, otherwise, nonmasters.) Second, and related to the first, instead of reporting correlational measures as is commonly done in criterion-related validity investigations with norm-referenced tests, readily interpretable validity indices reflecting the agreement between decisions based on the test and an external dichotomous criterion measure are often reported. For example, in industrial settings, the two categories on the criterion might correspond to "performers" and "non-performers."

Criterion-referenced test scores are commonly used to make decisions. In instructional settings, an examinee is assumed to be a master when his or her test performance exceeds a minimum level of performance. Decision validity, which is simply a particular kind of criterion-related validity, involves (1) setting a standard of test performance, and (2) comparing the test performance of two or more criterion groups in relation to the specified standard.

One advantage of decision validity studies is that the results can be reported in a readily interpretable way (percentage of correct decisions). Alternatively, the correlation between two dichotomous variables (group membership and the mastery decision) can be reported and used as an index of decision validity. Other possible statistics are reported by Hambleton (1984a) and Popham (1978a). Finally, the validity of a set of decisions will depend on several important factors: (1) the quality of the test under investigation; (2) the appropriateness and size of the criterion groups; (3) the characteristics of the examinee sample; and (4) the minimum level of performance required for mastery. All four factors will impact on decision validity. Clearly, since a number of factors substantially influence the level of decision validity, it must be clearly recognized that what is being described through a summary statistic of interest is *not* the test but the *use* of the test in a particular way with a specified group of examinees. The same point applies equally well when interpreting norm-referenced reliability and validity indices.

Standard Setting

One of the primary purposes of criterion-referenced testing is to make decisions about individuals. This requires a standard or cutoff score on the test score scale to separate examinees into two categories, often labeled masters and nonmasters.

At the outset it is essential to stress that *all* of the standard-setting methods in use today involve judgment and are arbitrary. Some individuals have argued that arbitrary standards are not defensible and, therefore, they should not be used (Glass, 1978). Popham (1978b, 1978c) countered with this response:

> Unable to avoid reliance on human judgment as the chief ingredient in standard-setting, some individuals have thrown up their hands in dismay and cast aside all efforts to set performance standards as arbitrary, hence unacceptable.
>
> But *Webster's Dictionary* offers us two definitions of arbitrary. The first of these is positive, describing arbitrary as an adjective reflecting choice or discretion, that is, "Determinable by a judge or tribunal." The second definition, pejorative in nature, describes arbitrary as an adjective denoting capriciousness, that is, "selected at random and without reason." In my estimate, when people start knocking the standard-setting game as arbitrary, they are clearly employing Webster's second, negatively loaded definition.

But the first definition is more accurately reflective of serious standard-setting efforts. They represent genuine attempts to do a good job in deciding what kinds of standards we ought to employ. That they are judgmental is inescapable. But to malign all judgmental operations as capricious is absurd (p. 168).

Popham (1978a, 1978b, 1978c) stressed that many of the decisions that are made by society to regulate our lives are made arbitrarily, but in the positive sense of the word. For example, fire, health, environmental, and highway safety standards, to name just a few areas in which standards are set, are set arbitrarily. And in educational settings, *arbitrary* decisions are made by educators about such matters as curriculum and instructional methods. It is certainly true that sometimes standards are set too high or low. Hopefully, though, through experience and with careful evaluations of the test score results, standards that are not "in line" with others can be identified and revised. The consequences of assigning a nonmaster to a mastery state (false-positive error) or a master to a nonmastery state (false negative error) on a credentialing exam, however, are considerably more serious than errors made on (say) a classroom test; therefore, more attention must be given to the setting of standards on the more important testing programs.

Many of the available standard-setting methods have been described, compared, and critiqued in the literature (Berk, 1986; Glass, 1978;

Table 1–1. A Classification of Methods for Setting Standards

Judgmental Methods	*Empirical Methods*	*Combination Methods*	
Item Content	*Data-Criterion Measure*	*Judgmental-Empirical*	*Educational Consequences*
Nedelsky (1954)	Livingston (1975)	Contrasting Groups and Borderline Groups (Livingston & Zieky, 1982). Criterion-Groups (Berk, 1976)	Block (1972)
Angoff (1971)	Livingston (1976)		
Ebel (1972)	van der Linden & Mellenbergh (1977)		
Jaeger (1978)			
Guessing	*Decision-Theoretic*	*Bayesian Methods*	
Millman (1973)	Hambleton & Novick (1973)	Hambleton & Novick (1973) Schoon, Gullion, & Ferrara (1979)	

Hambleton, 1990; Hambleton & Powell, 1983; Hambleton et al., 1978; Meskauskas, 1976; Millman, 1973; Shepard, 1984). Table 1–1 lists many of the popular methods. The methods are organized into three categories labeled "judgmental," "empirical," and "combination." The judgmental methods require data from judges for setting standards, or require judgments to be made about the presence of variables (e.g., guessing) that influence the setting of a standard. The empirical methods require examinee test data to aid in the standard-setting process. The combination methods use both judgmental data and empirical data in the standard-setting process. Livingston and Zieky (1982) and Popham (1978b) have developed helpful guidelines for applying several of the methods. Several of the popular judgmental, empirical, and combination methods are described next.

Judgmental Methods

In these methods, individual items are inspected in order to judge how well the minimally competent examinee would perform on the test items. Judges are asked to assess how or to what degree an individual who could be described as minimally competent would perform on each item.

Nedelsky Method. Judges are asked to identify distractors in multiple-choice test items that they feel the minimally competent student should be able to eliminate as incorrect. The minimum passing level for that item then becomes the reciprocal of the number of remaining alternatives. It is the "chance score" on the test item for the minimally competent student. The judges proceed with each test item in a similar fashion, and, on completion of the judging process, each judge sums the minimum passing levels across the test items to obtain a standard. Individual judges' standards are averaged to obtain a standard for the set of test items.

Ebel's Method. Judges rate test items along two dimensions: relevance and difficulty. There are four levels of relevance in Ebel's method: essential, important, acceptable, and questionable. Ebel uses three levels of difficulty: easy, medium, and hard. These levels form a 3×4 grid. The judges are asked to do two things:

  1. Locate each of the test items in the proper cell, based on their relevance and difficulty.

2. Assign a percentage to each cell, that percentage being the percentage of items in the cell that the minimally qualified examinees should be able to answer.

The number of test items in each cell is multiplied by the appropriate percentage (agreed on by the judges), and the sum of all the cells, when divided by the total number of test items, yields the standard.

Angoff's Method. When using Angoff's method, judges are asked to assign a probability to each test item directly, thus circumventing the analysis of a grid or the analysis of response alternatives. Each probability is to be an estimate of the minimally competent examinee answering the test item correctly. Individual judges' assigned probabilities for items in the test can be summed to obtain a standard, and then the judges' standards can be averaged to obtain a final standard.

Empirical Methods

Two of the typical methods in this category depend upon the availability of an outside criterion, performance measure, or true ability distribution. The test itself, and the possible cutoff scores, are observed in relation to these criterion scores. An "optimal" cutoff score is then selected. For instance, Livingston's (1975) utility-based approach leads to the selection of a cutoff score that optimizes a particular utility function. Livingston suggested the use of a set of linear or semi-linear utility functions in viewing the effects of decision-making accuracy based upon a particular cutoff score. A cutoff score is selected to maximize the utility function.

On the other hand, a method by van der Linden and Mellenbergh (1977) leads to the selection of a cutoff score that minimizes "expected losses." A test score is used to classify examinees into two categories: masters and nonmasters. Also, an external criterion, specified in advance, is used to dichotomize the examinee population into "successes" and "failures." Then the expected loss (the quality to be minimized) is specified, and the cutoff score that minimizes expected losses over the sample of examinees is chosen. Essentially, expected losses occur when examinees who score high on the external criterion (successes) fail the test, or when low-scoring examinees (failures) on the external criterion pass the test. The goal is to choose a cutoff score to minimize the expected losses which is accomplished by locating the cutoff score on the test so that essentially the maximum number of successful persons on the criterion pass the test and unsuccessful persons on the criterion fail the test.

Combination Methods

With these methods, judgments are made about the mastery status of a sample group of examinees from the population of interest. Choice of method determines the nature of the required judgments. Next, one or more groups for whom mastery determinations have been made are administered the test. Details are offered next for analyzing the judgmental data and the test scores.

Borderline-Group Method. This method requires that judges first define what they would envision as a minimally acceptable performance on the content area being assessed. The judges are then asked to submit a list of examinees whose performances would be so close to the borderline that they could not be reliably classified as masters or nonmasters. The test is administered to this group, and the median test score for the group may be taken as the standard. Alternately, it may be decided to pass more or less than 50 percent of the minimally competent examinees.

Contrasting Groups Method. Once judges have defined minimally acceptable performance for the domain specification being assessed, the judges are asked to identify those examinees they are certain are either masters or nonmasters in relation to the specified domain of content or behaviors. The test is administered to the groups, and the score distributions for the two groups on an objective-by-objective basis are then plotted, with the point of intersection taken as the initial standard. The standard can be moved up to reduce the number of false-positive errors (examinees identified as masters by the test, but who have not adequately mastered the objectives) or down to reduce the number of false-negative errors (examinees identified as nonmasters by the test, but who have adequately mastered the objectives). The direction to move the standard will depend on the relative seriousness of the two types of error. If the score distribution overlaps completely, no decisions can be made reliably. The ideal situation would be one in which the two distributions did not overlap at all. The validity of this approach to standard setting depends on the appropriateness of the judges' classifications of examinees.

Summary

In summary, probably the most difficult and controversial problem in criterion-referenced testing concerns setting cutoff scores or, as they are sometimes called, the standards, on the test score scale to separate examinees into mutually exclusive groups. It is now well recognized by most criterion-referenced test users that there are no magic test score points waiting to be discovered as the standards. Rather, setting standards is ultimately a judgmental process that is best done by appropriate individuals who (1) are familiar with the test content and knowledgeable about the standard-setting method they will be expected to use, (2) have access to item performance and test score distribution data in the standard-setting process, and (3) understand the social and political context in which the tests are being used. A set of guidelines for designing and implementing a defensible standard-setting process was prepared by Hambleton and Powell (1983).

Guidelines for Test Evaluation

CRTs are presently receiving extensive use in schools, industry, and the armed services because they provide information valued by test users which is different from the information provided by NRTs. But CRTs, like other data-collection instruments used in educational decision-making, are of variable quality and lesser quality tests are not going to meet fully the informational needs of users.

Most of the major test publishers in the United States have available a wide assortment of criterion-referenced tests for assessing reading, mathematics, language arts, and other content areas. In addition, many local school districts, state departments of education, and smaller test publishers have produced their own criterion-referenced tests. Many of the available tests, however, fall far short of the technical quality necessary for them to accomplish their intended purposes (see, for example, Hambleton & Eignor, 1978). When tests lack sufficient technical quality, there are a number of plausible explanations: for one, many of the available criterion-referenced tests were developed before an adequate testing technology was fully explicated. Fortunately, an adequate technology exists for constructing criterion-referenced tests and using criterion-referenced test scores (Berk, 1984a; Hambleton, 1990). Guidelines can now be produced by which criterion-referenced tests and their manuals can be evaluated. The recently published *Standards for Educational and Psychological Testing* (1985) for evaluating tests and test manuals prepared by a joint committee of the American Educational Research Association, American Psychological Association, and National Council on Measurement in Education were helpful, too, and were used in preparing 25 content and technical questions. The following questions should be addressed when evaluating criterion-referenced tests, commercially prepared or otherwise:

Content Questions

1.   Do the competencies measured by the test cover the content domain of interest?
2.   Are the competencies themselves well written so that the appropriate domain of content for each competency is clear?
3.   Is there a capability for adding to or taking away from the test content so that the final test provides a suitable match to the content domain of interest?
4.   Is an appropriate rationale offered for the selection of competencies measured in the test?
5.   Is the test item content appropriate to measure the competencies?

Technical Questions

6.   Do the test items meet the standard item-writing principles?
7.   Are the test items free from bias and stereotyping?
8.   Is each group of test items measuring a competency *representative* of the domain of content spanned by the competency?
9.   Was the item review process in test development carried out properly?
10.   Was a suitable sample of examinees used to pilot the test items?
11.   Were item statistics used correctly in building the test?
12.   Do the test directions address important information such as test purpose, scoring, time limits, the standard(s), and marking answer sheets (or test booklets)?
13.   Are the time limits sufficient for examinees to complete the test?
14.   Are the test administrator's directions complete so as to insure a proper test administration?
15.   Are the print size, quality of printing and artwork, and page layouts appropriate for the examinees?

16.   Are the reliability and validity studies conducted with sufficient-sized samples of examinees for whom the test is intended?

17.   Are useful reliability indices such as "decision-consistency" and "kappa" reported for the test scores?

18.   Are the reliability indices high enough to justify the use of the test in the intended application?

19.   Are personal and environmental factors that influence test performance addressed in the test manual?

20.   Is a test manual available that addresses test purposes, test development, administration, scoring, psychometric properties of the test scores, and test interpretations?

21.   Is there justification offered (and is it appropriate) for the choice of standards (or cutoff scores)?

22.   Is the process used to set standards fully documented in the manual and is it appropriate?

23.   Is there acceptable and fully documented validity evidence for the intended uses of the test scores?

24.   Are there cautions in the technical manual about the size of errors of measurement and/or misclassification errors and the role of these errors in score interpretations?

25.   Are the test scores reported fully and clearly for the intended users of the test scores?

Clarification and expansion of many of the questions above can be found in Berk (1984a), Hambleton (1990), and Popham (1978a).

Identifying well-constructed, reliable, and valid criterion-referenced tests is essential for insuring that the purposes of a testing program are accomplished. The importance of the 25 individual questions above will vary somewhat from one test to another. Still, some attention to each question in criterion-referenced test evaluation would normally be desirable.

Conclusions and Areas for Additional Research and Development

In this chapter, current technology for constructing and evaluating these tests was discussed along with a comparison of norm-referenced and criterion-referenced tests. Given the extensive use of criterion-referenced tests, it is fortunate that there now exists a well-developed technology for building criterion-referenced tests and evaluating test scores. On the other hand, because of the newness of the area and the rapidity of developments, the technology is not widely known or used and, as a result, many criterion-referenced tests do not achieve levels of quality that one might wish for (Hambleton & Eignor, 1978). But the situation has improved and will continue improving now that many of the important contributions have been identified (Berk, 1984a); textbooks and instructional materials have become available (e.g., Berk, 1984a; Hambleton, 1990; Popham, 1978a); and there is a greater need for technical information among practitioners because of the wide use of criterion-referenced tests. It is worth repeating that the technology presented in this chapter, if followed carefully, can contribute substantially to the assessment of examinee knowledge and skills and the proper use of criterion-referenced test score information.

At present, research is still under way on (1) methods for setting standards, (2) formats for reporting scores to maximize test score usefulness, and (3) approaches for describing objectives. New studies that offer potential for the improvement of criterion-referenced testing practices include (1) research on microcomputers for storing, administering, and scoring tests and (2) studies with item response models for developing continuous growth or developmental scales to which objectives, test items, and examinees can be referenced.

References

American Educational Research Association, American Psychological Association, & National Council on Measurement in Education. (1985). *Standards for educational and psychological testing.* Washington, DC: APA.

Angoff, W. H. (1971). Scales, norms, and equivalent scores. In R. L. Thorndike (ed.), *Educational measurement*, 2nd ed. Washington, DC: American Council on Education, pp. 508–600.

Berk, R. A. (1976). Determination of optimal cutting scores in criterion-referenced measurement. *Journal of Experimental Education* 45:4–9.

————. (1980). A consumer's guide to criterion-referenced test reliability. *Journal of Educational Measurement* 17:323–349.

————. (ed.). (1984a). *A guide to criterion-referenced test construction.* Baltimore, MD: The Johns Hopkins University Press.

————. (1984b). Conducting the item analysis. In R. A. Berk (ed.), *A guide to criterion-referenced test construction.* Baltimore, MD: The Johns Hopkins University Press, pp. 97–143.

————. (1986). A consumer's guide to setting performance standards on criterion-referenced tests. *Review of Educational Research* 56(1):137–172.

Block, J. H. (1972). Student learning and the setting of mastery performance standards. *Educational Horizons* 50:183–190.

Campbell, D. T., & Fiske, D. W. (1959). Convergent and discriminant validation by the multitrait-multimethod matrix. *Psychological Bulletin* 56:81–105.

Carlson, S. B. (1985). *Creative classroom testing: 10 designs for assessment and instruction.* Princeton, NJ: Educational Testing Service.

Carver, R. P. (1974). Two dimensions of tests: psychometric and edumetric. *American Psychologist* 29:512–518.

Cohen, J. (1960). A coefficient of agreement for nominal scales. *Educational and Psychological Measurement* 20:37–46.

Department of the Army. (1986). *Skill qualification test and common task test development policy and procedures* (TRADOC Reg. 351–2). Fort Monroe, VA: U.S. Army Training and Doctrine Command.

Ebel, R. L. (1972). *Essentials of educational measurement.* Englewood Cliffs, NJ: Prentice-Hall.

————. (1978). The case for norm-referenced measurements. *Educational Researcher* 7:3–5.

Eignor, D. R., & Hambleton, R. K. (1979). *Effects of test length and advancement score on several criterion-referenced test reliability and validity indices* (Laboratory of Psychometric and Evaluative Research Report No. 86). Amherst, MA: School of Education, University of Massachusetts.

Fitzpatrick, A.R. (1983). The meaning of content validity. *Applied Psychological Measurement* 7:3–13.

Glaser, R. (1963). Instructional technology and the measurement of learning outcomes: Some questions. *American Psychologist* 18:519–521.

Glass, G.V. (1978). Standards and criteria. *Journal of Educational Measurement* 15:237–261.

Gray, W. M. (1978). A comparison of Piagetian theory and criterion-referenced measurement. *Review of Educational Research* 48:223–249.

Gulliksen, H. (1986). Perspective on educational measurement. *Applied Psychological Measurement* 10(2):109–132.

Haertel, E. (1985). Construct validity and criterion-referenced testing. *Review of Educational Research* 55(1):23–46.

Haladyna, T. M., & Downing, S. M. (1989a). A taxonomy of multiple-choice item-writing rules. *Applied Measurement in Education* 2(1):37–50.

————. (1989b). Validity of a taxonomy of multiple-choice item-writing rules. *Applied Measurement in Education* 2(1):51–78.

Haladyna, T. M., & Shindoll, R. R (1989). Item shells: A method for writing effective multiple-choice test items. *Evaluation & the Health Professions* 12(1): 97–106.

Hambleton, R. K. (ed.). (1980). Contributions to criterion-referenced testing technology. *Applied Psychological Measurement* 4(4):421–581.

————. (1982). Advances in criterion-referenced testing technology. In C. R. Reynolds & T. Gutkin (eds.), *Handbook of school psychology.* New York: Wiley, pp. 351–379.

————. (1984a). Validating the test scores. In R. A. Berk (ed.), *A guide to criterion-referenced test construction.* Baltimore, MD: The Johns Hopkins

University Press, pp. 199–230.

————. (1984b). Determining test lengths. In R. A. Berk (ed.), *A guide to criterion-referenced test construction.* Baltimore, MD: The Johns Hopkins University Press, pp. 144–168.

————. (1985). Criterion-referenced assessment of individual differences. In C. R. Reynolds & V. L. Willson (eds.), *Methodological and statistical advances in the study of individual differences.* New York: Plenum Press, pp. 393–424.

————. (1989). Principles and selected applications of item response theory. In R. L. Linn (ed.), *Educational measurement,* 3rd ed. New York: Macmillan, pp. 147–200.

————. (1990). *A practical guide to criterion-referenced testing.* Boston, MA: Kluwer Academic Publishers.

Hambleton, R. K., & Eignor, D. R. (1978). Guidelines for evaluating criterion-referenced tests and test manuals. *Journal of Educational Measurement* 15: 321–327.

Hambleton, R. K., Mills, C. N., & Simon, R. (1983). Determining the lengths for criterion-referenced tests. *Journal of Educational Measurement* 20(1):27–38.

Hambleton, R. K., & Novick, M. R. (1973). Toward an integration of theory and method for criterion-referenced tests. *Journal of Educational Measurement* 10: 159–171.

Hambleton, R. K., & Powell, S. (1983). A framework for viewing the process of standard-setting. *Evaluation & the Health Professions* 6:3–24.

Hambleton, R. K., & Swaminathan, H. (1985). *Item response theory: Principles and applications.* Boston, MA: Kluwer Academic Publishers.

Hambleton, R. K., Swaminathan, H., Algina, J., & Coulson, D. B. (1978). Criterion-referenced testing and measurement: A review of technical issues and developments. *Review of Educational Research* 48:1–47.

Huynh, H. (1976). On the reliability of decisions in domain-referenced testing. *Journal of Educational Measurement* 13:253–264.

Jaeger, R. M. (1978). *A proposal for setting a standard on the North Carolina High School Competency Test.* Paper presented at the Spring meeting of the North Carolina Association for Research in Education, Chapel Hill.

————. (1989). Certification of student competence. In R. L. Linn (ed.), *Educational measurement,* 3rd ed. New York: Macmillan, pp. 485–514.

Kane, M. T. (1982). The validity of licensure examinations. *American Psychologist* 37:911–918.

Kirsch, I., & Guthrie, J. T. (1980). Construct validity of functional reading tests. *Journal of Educational Measurement* 17:81–93.

Linn, R. L. (1979). Issues of validity in measurement for competency-based programs. In M. A. Bunda & J. R. Sanders (eds.), *Practice and problems in competency-based measurement.* Washington, DC: National Council on Measurement in Education, pp. 108–123.

————. (1980). Issues of validity for criterion-referenced measures. *Applied Psychological Measurement* 4:547–561.

————. (ed.) (1989). *Educational measurement,* 3rd ed. New York: Macmillan.

Livingston, S. A. (1975). *A utility-based approach to the evaluation of pass/fail testing decision procedures* (Report No. COPA-75-01). Princeton, NJ: Center for Occupational and Professional Assessment, Educational Testing Service.

—————. (1976). *Choosing minimum passing scores by stochastic approximation techniques* (Report No. COPA-76-02). Princeton, NJ: Center for Occupational and Professional Assessment, Educational Testing Service.

—————. (1989). *New Jersey College Outcomes Evaluation Program: A report on the development of the general intellectual skills assessment.* Princeton, NJ: Educational Testing Service.

Livingston, S. A., & Zieky, M. J. (1982). *Passing scores: A manual for setting standards of performance on educational and occupational tests.* Princeton, NJ: Educational Testing Service.

Lord, F. M., & Novick, M. R. (1968). *Statistical theories of mental test scores.* Reading, MA: Addison-Wesley.

Madaus, G. (ed.). (1983). *The courts, validity, and minimum competency.* Boston, MA: Kluwer Academic Publishers.

Mager, R. F. (1962). *Preparing instructional objectives.* Palo Alto, CA: Fearon Publishers.

Meskauskas, J. A. (1976). Evaluation models for criterion-referenced testing: Views regarding mastery and standard-setting. *Review of Educational Research* 46:133–158.

Messick, S. A. (1975). The standard problem: Meaning and values in measurement and evaluation. *American Psychologist* 30:955–966.

—————. (1989). Validity. In R. L. Linn (ed.), *Educational measurement*, 3rd ed. New York: Macmillan, pp. 13–104.

Millman, J. (1973). Passing scores and test lengths for domain-referenced measures. *Review of Educational Research* 43:205–216.

—————. (1974). Criterion-referenced measurement. In W. J. Popham (ed.), *Evaluation in education: Current applications.* Berkeley, CA: McCutchan Publishing, pp. 311–397.

Millman, J., & Westman, R. S. (1989). Computer-assisted writing of achievement test items: Toward a future technology. *Journal of Educational Measurement* 26(2):177–190.

Nedelsky, L. (1954). Absolute grading standards for objective tests. *Educational and Psychological Measurement* 14:3–19.

Nitko, A. J. (1980). Distinguishing the many varieties of criterion-referenced tests. *Review of Educational Research* 50:461–485.

Norcini, J. J., Hancock, E. W., Webster, G. D., Grosso, L. J., & Shea, J. A. (1988). A criterion-referenced examination of physician competence. *Evaluation & the Health Professions* 11(1):98–112.

Popham, W. J. (1974). An approaching peril: Cloud-referenced tests. *Phi Delta Kappan* 56:614–615.

—————. (1978a). *Criterion-referenced measurement.* Englewood Cliffs, NJ: Prentice-Hall.

—————. (1978b). *Setting performance standards.* Los Angeles, CA: Instructional Objectives Exchange.

—————. (1978c). As always, provocative. *Journal of Educational Measurement* 15:297–300.

—————. (1978d). The case for criterion-referenced measurements. *Educational Researcher* 7:6–10.

—————. (1984). Specifying the domain of content or behaviors. In R. Berk (ed.), *A guide to criterion-referenced test construction*. Baltimore, MD: The Johns Hopkins University Press.

—————. (1987). Preparing policy-makers for standard-setting on high-stakes tests. *Educational Evaluation and Policy Analysis* 9:77–82.

Popham, W. J., & Husek, T. R. (1969). Implications of criterion-referenced measurement. *Journal of Educational Measurement* 6:1–9.

Roid, G. H., & Haladyna, T. M. (1982). *A technology for test-item writing*. New York: Academic Press.

Rovinelli, R. J., & Hambleton, R. K. (1977). On the use of content specialists in the assessment of criterion-referenced test item validity. *Tijdschrift voor Onderwijsresearch* 2:49–60.

Scheuneman, J. D., & Bleistein, C. A. (1989). A consumer's guide to statistics for identifying differential item functioning. *Applied Measurement in Education* 2(3):255–275.

Schoon, C. G., Gullion, C. M., & Ferrara, P. (1979). Bayesian statistics, credentialing examinations, and the determination of passing points. *Evaluation & the Health Professions* 2:181–201.

Shepard, L. A. (1984). Setting performance standards. In R. A. Berk (ed.), *A guide to criterion-referenced test construction*. Baltimore, MD: The Johns Hopkins University Press, pp. 169–198.

Subkoviak, M. (1976). Estimating reliability from a single administration of a criterion-referenced test. *Journal of Educational Measurement* 13:265–275.

—————. (1988). A practitioner's guide to computation and interpretation of reliability indices for mastery tests. *Journal of Educational Measurement* 25: 47–55.

Swaminathan, H., Hambleton, R. K., & Algina, J. (1974). Reliability of criterion-referenced tests: A decision-theoretic formulation. *Journal of Educational Measurement* 11:263–268.

van der Linden, W. J. (1980). Decision models for use with criterion-referenced tests. *Applied Psychological Measurement* 4:469–492.

—————. (1981). A latent trait look at pre-test-post-test validation of criterion-referenced test items. *Review of Educational Research* 51(3):379–402.

van der Linden, W. J., & Mellenbergh, G. J. (1977). Optimal cutting scores using a linear loss function. *Applied Psychological Measurement* 11:593–599.

Ward, W. C., Frederiksen, N., & Carlson, S. B. (1980). Construct validity of free-response and machine-scorable forms of a test. *Journal of Educational Measurement* 17:11–29.

Wieberg, H. J. W., Neeb, K. E., & Schott, F. (1984). Empirical comparison of trained and non-trained teachers in constructing criterion-referenced items. *Studies in Educational Evaluation* 10:199–204.

Wilcox, R. (1976). A note on the length and passing score of a mastery test. *Journal of Educational Statistics* 1:359–364.

————. (1980). Determining the length of a criterion-referenced test. *Applied Psychological Measurement* 4(4):425–446.

Woodruff, D. J., & Sawyer, R. L. (1989). Estimating measures of pass-fail reliability from parallel half tests. *Applied Psychological Measurement* 13(1): 33–43.

2 GENERALIZABILITY THEORY

Dato N. M. de Gruijter
Leo J. Th. van der Kamp

An ongoing problem in the field of educational and psychological testing is that all measurements are contaminated by error. Consequently, measurements in this field are inaccurate, so it is of prime importance to assess the extent to which the measurements are contaminated. Classical test theory was developed in order to deal with this problem of measurement error. A central role in this theory is played by the concept of *reliability*, i.e., the extent to which observed variation reflects true variation in measurements or, more technically, the ratio of true to observed score variance. For the estimation of reliability, parallel measurements are needed—measurements with identical true scores and error variances. The correlation between two parallel measurement instruments in a sample from the population of interest, r_{xx}, estimates the population reliability.

The concept of parallel measurements, however, is problematic. For one thing, how do we know that our measurements are parallel in the sense of classical test theory? It is quite possible to construct several tests that seem parallel with a first test, but that differ among themselves, as Guttman (1953) demonstrated. Furthermore, parallel measurements are not always available. Raters considered as measurement instruments might, for example, be nonparallel. In other test situations the very construction of parallel tests would seem incorrect. In achievement testing, for example, subsequent tests should not be parallel to the first achievement test, but all tests should reflect the subject matter as adequately as possible. These and other examples show the concept of parallel measurements to be the Achilles heel of classical reliability theory.

Generalizability theory (Cronbach et al., 1963, 1972; Shavelson & Webb, 1981; Shavelson, Webb, & Rowley, 1989) can be viewed as an extension of classical test theory. The strict assumption of parallel measurement of classical theory is dropped in favor of so-called sampling assumptions. Generalizability theory hypothesizes a *universe* or *domain* of *admissible* observations, and the actual observations (i.e., the measurements) are seen as a sample from this universe. The aim of measurement is to *generalize* from these observations to the whole domain of admissible observations. To illustrate this approach, take the case of achievement testing. In achievement testing the domain consists of all conceivable items with respect to the subject matter, and a particular test is a sample of items from this domain. The test administrator wants to infer the examinees' achievements in the relevant item domain from the responses to the sample of items at hand. In order to be able to make some inferences, the sample should be representative of the domain. In generalizability theory it is usually assumed that the sample is random. In some applications this is actually the case: i.e., when a large pool of items is available, it is possible to select a number of items at random from the pool. In general, however, the random sampling assumption is not substantiated by a random sampling mechanism because the universe of generalization is hypothetical. Nevertheless, the assumption of random sampling can be a practicable one for a description of the relation between samples and universe. Sometimes, however, a refinement is needed. Random sampling does not seem to give an adequate description of the work of a test constructor who tries to make well-balanced test forms. *Stratified* sampling (Rajaratnam et al., 1965) seems more realistic here. In stratified sampling the universe is divided into strata, and a number of items is randomly selected from each stratum.

In the previous example the universe consisted of items, and any of the items constitutes an admissible condition of measurement. A set of similar conditions of measurement is coined a facet. In general, the universe contains more than one set of similar *conditions* of measurements: i.e., a universe can be multifaceted. A universe might, for example, have, two *facets*, raters and items, and the universe of admissible observations might consist of combinations of raters and items. The size of a facet can be finite. It is possible that all conditions of a facet are represented in a study, in which case the facet is *fixed*. With a fixed facet a generalization to more conditions is clearly not intended. In general, a generalization to other conditions, similar to those in the study, *is* intended, and the facet has more conditions than those in the study. For convenience the number of conditions in such a situation often is taken to be infinite.

Associated with the facets are sources of variance or *variance components*. The primary goal in generalizability theory is to estimate these components. This is done in a G study (generalizability study). A D study (decision study) collects data for making decisions or interpretations.

Variance Components in a One-Facet Universe

Let us take, as an example, a universe with one facet: items. All combinations of items and persons are possible, and the universe is called crossed i(items) $\times$ p(persons). The score X_{pi} of person p on item i can be decomposed according to the ANOVA decomposition

$$X_{pi} = \mu + (\mu_p - \mu) + (\mu_i - \mu) + (X_{pi} - \mu_p - \mu_i + \mu), \qquad (1)$$

where μ is the grand mean, $(\mu_p - \mu)$ the person effect, $(\mu_i - \mu)$ the item effect, and $(X_{pi} - \mu_p - \mu_i + \mu)$ the residual. The residual can be decomposed further into an interaction term μ_{pi} and a random error e_{pi}. If there are no replications, these two components cannot be distinguished: they are confounded and one can denote the residual with pi,e.

The expected score of examinee p in the item universe, the examinee's universe or domain score, is μ_p. This score, or the person effect $(\mu_p - \mu)$, is frequently the value of interest when a generalization from observational data is intended.

It is appropriate here to notice that the ANOVA decomposition is only one of the possible score decompositions. Another decomposition of the observed score is in terms of linearly related true scores,

$$X_{pi} = a_i + b_i\tau_p + e_{ip}. \qquad (2)$$

Equation (2) specifies the congeneric test model, where τ_p is the parameter of interest. When model (2) holds, the ANOVA decomposition results in interactions μ_{pi} which are correlated with universe scores, a point which will be addressed later.

Let us return to equation (1). With each source of variance in this equation a variance component is associated. The variance component for persons, $\sigma^2(p)$, is the variance of μ_p or $(\mu_p - \mu)$. Further, there is a variance component for items, $\sigma^2(i)$ and a residual variance, $\sigma^2(pi,e)$. The variance of observed scores equals

$$\sigma^2(X_{pi}) = \underset{pi}{EE} (X_{pi} - \mu)^2 = \sigma^2(p) + \sigma^2(i) + \sigma^2(pi,e), \qquad (3)$$

where E is the symbol for expectation.

With the crossed universe, there are several possible observational designs. One can administer all items in the study to all available persons. In this case the design is *crossed i x p*, with an observed score X_{pi} for every person p and every item i in the study. An alternative design is the nested *i:p* design, in which every person responds to a different set of randomly selected items. The *p:i* design is also possible. In the latter design each item in the study is answered by a different random group of persons. This design would seem to be of limited value, but it is not. First, the nested *p:i* design could be employed when one is interested in items instead of persons. In generalizability theory there is no reason whatsoever to treat persons differently from other facets, a point which has been stressed repeatedly by Cardinet and associates (1981, 1982, 1983). Second, such a nested design might look different when items are replaced by raters: aren't there many situations in which persons are rated by different raters? With these "standard" designs the whole gamut of possibilities is not exhausted. In incidence sampling (Sirotnik & Wellington, 1977), items and persons, or, more generally, two different aspects, are combined in possibly more complicated ways. Matrix and incidence sampling are related to generalizability theory, but there are also some differences. The conventions for defining variances are, for example, different from those of generalizability theory (De Gruijter & Van der Kamp, 1984). So, in order not to complicate the exposition of generalizability theory, incidence sampling will not be discussed further (See Sirotnik & Wellington, 1977).

An analysis of variance for the crossed *i x p* design is given in table 2–1. There are n_p persons in the study and n_i items. The dot notation in the formulas of table 2–1 is used to indicate that the mean is taken over the relevant subscript. The expected mean squares (*EMS*) in the last column are based on the assumption that the persons are randomly sampled from an infinite population and the items are randomly sampled from an infinite domain of items.

Estimates of the variance components can be obtained by setting the *EMS* equal to the obtained *MS*. One then obtains

$$\hat{\sigma}^2(pi,e) = MS(pi,e) \qquad (4a)$$

$$\hat{\sigma}^2(i) = (MS(i) - MS(pi,e))/n_p \qquad (4b)$$

$$\hat{\sigma}^2(p) = (MS(p) - MS(pi,e))/n_i. \qquad (4c)$$

Table 2–1. ANOVA for the Crossed Design (Random Model)

Source of Variance	df	SS	MS	EMS
Persons (p)	$n_p - 1$	$\sum_p n_i (X_{p.} - X_{..})^2$	$SS(p)/df(p)$	$\sigma^2(pi,e) + n_i\sigma^2(p)$
Items (i)	$n_i - 1$	$\sum_i n_p (X_{.i} - X_{..})^2$	$SS(i)/df(i)$	$\sigma^2(pi,e) + n_p\sigma^2(i)$
Residual	$(n_p - 1)(n_i - 1)$	$SS(t) - SS(p) - SS(i)$	$SS(pi,e)/df(pi,e)$	$\sigma^2(pi,e)$
Total		$SS(t) = \sum_i\sum_p (X_{pi} - X_{..})^2$		

Table 2–2. ANOVA for the i:p Design (Random Model)

Source of Variance	df	SS	MS	EMS
Persons (p)	$n_p - 1$	$\sum n_i (X_{p.} - X_{..})^2$	$SS(p)/df(p)$	$\sigma^2(i,pi,e) + n_i\sigma^2(p)$
Residual (i,pi,e)	$n_p(n_i - 1)$	$\sum_i\sum_p (X_{pi} - X_p)^2$	$SS(i,pi,e)/df(i,pi,e)$	$\sigma^2(i,pi,e)$

When the number n_p and n_i are small, the estimates are imprecise. With the computational scheme exemplified in equation (4), however, it is possible to obtain negative estimates of variance components! So, whatever the purpose of the study, it is important to obtain confidence intervals for components as well. Brennan (1983) provides a valuable reference on the computation of point-estimates and variances and covariances of variance components. He also discusses the computer program GENOVA for generalizability analyses. The computations he gives are all based on obtained mean squares. Other possibilities for obtaining confidence intervals for estimated variance and covariance components are bootstrapping (see, e.g., Efron, 1979), jackknifing (see, e.g., Gray & Schucany, 1972), and Bayesian estimation (see Box & Tiao, 1973).

The second design to be discussed for the one-facet universe is the $i{:}p$ design. With this design, different persons answer different items. In order to keep the discussion simple, let the number of items be fixed to n_i for all persons. The ANOVA is given in table 2–2. The variance component $\sigma^2(i)$ is confounded with $\sigma^2(pi, e)$ in this design. Therefore, the notation $\sigma^2(i, pi, e)$ is used in table 2–2, instead of $\sigma^2(i) + \sigma^2(pi, e)$. The variance of components for persons, $\sigma^2(p)$, can still be estimated.

Generalizability Coefficients for the One-Facet Design

In classical test theory the reliability of a test is defined as the squared correlation between observed and true scores. In generalizability theory one is not interested in the true scores of a particular test, but in the universe scores defined by the universe of admissible observations, i.e., tests. The squared correlation between observed scores on a particular test and the universe scores μ_p or person effects ($\mu_p - \mu$) is relevant. Cronbach and associates (1963, 1972) discuss the estimation of such generalizability coefficients for particular tests, or, more generally, conditions.

In the theory of generalizability, the estimation of such a coefficient for particular conditions is not emphasized, however. In many applications, for example, one wants to generalize to future studies with other conditions. The intraclass correlation

$$\rho^2 = \frac{\sigma^2(p)}{\sigma^2(p) + \sigma^2(pi, e)} \qquad (5)$$

is chosen instead as a measure of generalizability. (Cronbach and colleaques use $E\rho^2$ instead of ρ^2 in order to indicate the fact that the intraclass correlation estimates the expected squared correlation between

observed and universe scores, the expectation taken over conditions.)
Here $\sigma^2(pi, e)$ corresponds to the error variance in classical test theory.
The variance components in equation (5) can be estimated by means of a
study with a crossed i(tests) x p(persons) design (not with a nested design!).

Equation (5) gives the relative size of universe score variation to be
expected with an arbitrarily chosen condition. However, when there are
n_i conditions in a study, it might be more adequate to obtain the
generalizability of an average score based on n_i conditions. From table 2–1
it is clear that $MS(p)$ equals n_i times the variance of mean scores. The
expected value of the mean score variance is obtained by dividing $EMS(p)$
by n_i. The intraclass correlation for mean scores, a so-called stepped-up
intraclass correlation, can be expressed as

$$\rho^2 = \frac{\sigma^2(p)}{\sigma^2(p) + \sigma^2(pi, e)/n_i}. \tag{6}$$

It can be estimated from the data of the crossed i x p design as

$$\hat{\rho}^2 = (MS(p) - MS(pi, e))/MS(p) = \frac{n_i}{n_i - 1}\left(1 - \frac{\Sigma s_i^2}{s_t^2}\right), \tag{7}$$

where s_t^2 equals the total score variance or n_i^2 times the variance of mean
scores. In other words, the generalizability is estimated by Cronbach's
coefficient alpha (Cronbach, 1951).

It is well known that coefficient alpha is a lower bound to reliability in
classical test theory. In general it also underestimates generalizability. This
happens whenever interaction correlates with universe scores. This is the
case, for example, with binary items when the proportions correct differ.
Cronbach and his associates were well aware of this fact. The bias becomes
small for at least moderate n_i, however, which then makes alpha a useful
coefficient despite it. An alternative is to stratify the items with respect to
difficulty and use coefficient alpha stratified, as suggested by Rajaratnam
and associates (1965).

Equation (6) gives the generalizability coefficient for mean or total
scores based on n_i components. It is clear that the generalizability can be
estimated for each value of n_i' when the variance components $\sigma^2(p)$ and
$\sigma^2(pi, e)$ have been estimated. In other words, it is possible to estimate the
generalizability of n_i'-item tests from data obtained for an n_i-item test
$(n_i' \neq n_i)$. The estimate can be written in the form

$$\hat{\rho}^2(k) = k\hat{\rho}^2/\{1 + (k - 1)\hat{\rho}^2\}, \tag{8}$$

where $k = n_i'/n_i$ and $\hat{\rho}^2$ equals the generalizability estimate of the n_i-item
test. This equation is identical to the Spearman-Brown formula for

lengthening a test, derived within the framework of classical test theory.

Next, consider the $i{:}p$ design, where i stands for items. The *EMS* in the row for persons in table 2–2 again equals n_i times the variance of average person scores, or the variance of total scores divided by n_i. So, the stepped-up intraclass correlation is

$$\rho^2 = \frac{\sigma^2(p)}{\sigma^2(p) + \sigma^2(i, pi, e)/n_i}. \tag{9}$$

This coefficient differs from the one in equation (6) in that $\sigma^2(i)$ is added to the error variance. This is as it should be: different persons answer different items and observed score differences between them arise partly from differences between the difficulties of the item sets. When the items are dichotomously scored, the estimate of equation (9) equals—apart from a small correction factor—Kuder-Richardson formula 21 (Rajaratnam et al., 1965). It is consistent, in contrast to KR-20, coefficient alpha for binary variables, in the crossed design.

The $i{:}p$ design with dichotomously scored items is an interesting case. Without further assumptions than those of independence of item responses and random selection of items from an unlimited item pool, the binomial error model, a strong true score model frequently used in criterion-referenced measurement, is valid. So the strong results of this model can be used instead of the more general but weak results of generalizability theory.

It is also possible to estimate the generalizability for the nested design on the basis of data from a crossed design (Rajaratnam, 1960). This is relevant in the case that decisions are made according to the nested design, e.g., employees are rated by their respective supervisors (Rajaratnam, 1960), while the G study uses a crossed design.

There is more to say about the generalizability coefficient defined in equation (9), but that will be postponed until the section on types of error.

Universes with More Than One Facet

Where more facets are involved, the possibilities for different designs increase. Let us take the two-facet $i \times j \times p$ universe as an example. Here p stands for persons, and i and j might stand for items and raters, respectively. Apart from the crossed $i \times j \times p$ design, several designs with (partial) nesting are possible like: $(j{:}i) \times p$, $i \times (j{:}p)$, $j{:}(i \times p)$, $(i \times j){:}p$, and $i{:}j{:}p$. The $(j{:}i) \times p$ design then is the design in which every person responds to every item, but each item is rated by a group of different raters. Clearly,

Table 2–3.   *EMS* for the *i* x *j* x *p* Design (Random Model)

Source of Variance	EMS
Persons (*p*)	$\sigma^2(pij,e) + n_j\sigma^2(pi) + n_i\sigma^2(pj) + n_in_j\sigma^2(p)$
Items (*i*)	$\sigma^2(pij,e) + n_j\sigma^2(pi) + n_p\sigma^2(pj) + n_pn_j\sigma^2(i)$
Raters (*j*)	$\sigma^2(pij,e) + n_i\sigma^2(pj) + n_p\sigma^2(pj) + n_pn_i\sigma^2(j)$
Interaction (*pi*)	$\sigma^2(pij,e) + n_j\sigma^2(pi)$
Interaction (*pj*)	$\sigma^2(pij,e) + n_i\sigma^2(pj)$
Interaction (*ij*)	$\sigma^2(pij,e) + n_p\sigma^2(ij)$
Residual	$\sigma^2(pij,e)$

such a design is relevant when rater time is sparse and expensive. Such a design becomes degenerated when each item is rated by only one rater: item and rater effects become confounded. Cronbach and colleagues (1972) use a special symbol for complete confounding. With only one rater per item $(j{:}i) \, x \, p$ is written as $(j,i) \, x \, p$ or $(i,j) \, x \, p$, where i,j means "i joint with j."

The *EMS* for the crossed design with random facets "items" and "raters" is given in table 2–3. The coefficient for each component in table 2–3 equals the frequency of each value of a component. For example, each interaction term for the interaction between p and i occurs n_j times in the total of $n_p \, x \, n_i \, x \, n_j$ observations. In more complicated designs the determination of the *EMS* becomes more complicated, but in books on ANOVA and generalizability theory rules for the derivation of the *EMS* are given (see, e.g., Kirk, 1982; Winer, 1971).

The variance components again can be obtained by equating observed *MS* with *EMS*:

$$\hat{\sigma}^2(pij,e) = MS(pij,e) \tag{10a}$$

$$\hat{\sigma}^2(ij) = (MS(ij) - MS(pij,e))/n_p \tag{10b}$$

$$\hat{\sigma}^2(pj) = (MS(pj) - MS(pij,e))/n_i \tag{10c}$$

$$\hat{\sigma}^2(pi) = (MS(pi) - MS(pij,e))/n_j \tag{10d}$$

$$\hat{\sigma}^2(j) = (MS(j) - MS(ij) - MS(pj) + MS(pij,e))/(n_pn_i) \tag{10e}$$

$$\hat{\sigma}^2(i) = (MS(i) - MS(ij) - MS(pi) + MS(pij,e))/(n_pn_j) \tag{10f}$$

$$\hat{\sigma}^2(p) = (MS(p) - MS(pj) - MS(pi) + MS(pij,e))/(n_in_j). \tag{10g}$$

The stepped-up intraclass correlation or generalizability based on n_i items and n_j raters equals

$$\rho^2 = \frac{\sigma^2(p)}{\sigma^2(p) + \sigma^2(pj)/n_j + \sigma^2(pi)/n_i + \sigma^2(pij,e)/(n_in_j)}. \tag{11}$$

The denominator of this equation equals the *EMS* for persons in table 2–3, divided by n_in_j. The generalizability coefficient is estimated as

$$\hat{\rho}^2 = \frac{MS(p) - MS(pj) - MS(pi) + MS(pij,e)}{MS(p)}. \tag{12}$$

So far only random effects models have been discussed, while the coefficient in equation (11) is also based on the random effects models. It gives the expected correlation between scores based on n_i items and n_j raters, and scores based on a different set of n_i items and a different group of n_j raters. It is possible, however, that one wants to generalize over raters, holding items fixed. The generalizability coefficient then becomes (Maxwell & Pilliner, 1968):

$$\rho^2 = \frac{\sigma^2(p) + \sigma^2(pi)/n_i}{\sigma^2(p) + \sigma^2(pj)/n_j + \sigma^2(pi)/n_i + \sigma^2(pij,e)/(n_in_j)}. \tag{13}$$

The interaction variance for the interaction between persons and items now has become part of the true score variance, in the terminology of classical test theory. The possibility of defining and redefining the universe of generalization, as demonstrated here, is one of the central issues in generalizability theory.

The redefinition of universe scores, reflected in equation (13), is a convenient result. This redefinition means that one of the facets, the facet "raters," is considered fixed. This would seem to necessitate a new ANOVA for the $p \times i \times j$ design, the old analysis being based on random facets. Equation (13) shows that such a re-analysis is not needed. This is due to the fact that the variance components for the random model and those for a mixed model, a model with some fixed facets, or a fixed model are simply related. Writing $\sigma^2(p|I)$ for the variance component for persons defined for the universe with a fixed set of items, it can be demonstrated that

$$\sigma^2(p|I) = \sigma^2(p) + \sigma^2(pi)/n_i. \tag{14}$$

The generalizability coefficient in equation (13) is readily estimated on the basis of the observed mean squares in the crossed $i \times j \times p$ design. Simpler yet is to compute sum scores by summing over the fixed items and to do an ANOVA on the resulting $i \times p$ design for raters and persons, but with such an analysis, however, one can miss interesting information.

A similar generalizability coefficient can be computed for a generalization over items, holding raters fixed. Fixing both facets is possible without problems only when the second-order interaction $\sigma^2(pij)$ is zero and $\sigma^2(pij, e)$ is pure error.

Another possibility is to estimate the generalizability coefficient for the random model with other numbers of items and raters, n'_i and n'_j. This is done by using equation (11) with estimated variance components and with n_i and n_j replaced by n'_i and n'_j. The estimation of the generalizability coefficient for other numbers of items and raters than used in the study, is a generalization of the one-facet Spearman-Brown formula. This generalization is quite useful for practical purposes. In a G study one might have chosen values of n_i and n_j that are thought to be sufficient for a reasonably accurate estimation of variance components. In practical applications, in a D study, costs might be prohibitive with these values. On the basis of G study results one might then search for an optimal combination of number of items (n'_i) and raters (n'_j): a combination that gives an acceptable generalizability according to equation (11) and that is realistic in terms of costs and time demands.

The discussion on multifacet universes is not complete without a discussion of designs. For illustrative purposes, let us analyze the $(j{:}i) \times p$ design and compare it to the $i \times j \times p$ design. In the $(j{:}i) \times p$ design one has, for example, administered n_i items to n_p persons. All items are rated by n_j raters, but different raters do the job for different items. The EMS for this design are given in table 2–4. Only five different variance components can be estimated in this design, compared to seven components in the crossed design: the components for pj and pij, e and those for j and ij are confounded. An analysis of a $(j{:}i) \times p$ design is less informative than an analysis of a crossed design. The generalizability coefficient in a nested $(j{:}i) \times p$ design with n_i conditions from the facet "Items" and n_j conditions from the facet "Raters" is

$$\rho^2 = \frac{\sigma^2(p)}{\sigma^2(p) + \sigma^2(pi)/n_i + \sigma^2(pj, pij, e)/n_i n_j}, \qquad (15)$$

which can be estimated from the data in such a nested design, but also from a crossed $i \times j \times p$ study. One should notice that it is not always possible to go the other way around, i.e., from a less informative design to estimates relevant for a more informative design.

It is important to know what the possibilities of different designs are. It is not always possible, or feasible, for example, to use a crossed design in D studies. A less informative design even can turn out to be quite efficient. This is easily seen by comparing equation (15) with equation (11) for the crossed design. The contribution of $\sigma^2(pj)$ to the denominator is smaller in

Table 2–4.   *EMS* for the (*j:i*) x *p* design (random model)

Source of variation	EMS
Persons (*p*)	$\sigma^2(pj, pij, e) + n_j\sigma^2(pi) + n_i n_j\sigma^2(p)$
Items (*i*)	$\sigma^2(pj, pij, e) + n_p\sigma^2(j, ij) + n_j\sigma^2(pi) + n_p n_j\sigma^2(i)$
Raters within items (*j:i*)	$\sigma^2(pj, pij, e) + n_p\sigma^2(j, ij)$
Interaction (*pi*)	$\sigma^2(pj, pij, e) + n_j\sigma^2(pi)$
Interaction (*pj:i*)	$\sigma^2(pj, pij, e)$

the former design. So, when the number of items and the number of raters per item are fixed, it is better to distribute the items among a larger group of raters than to let the work be done by a few raters. This effect is more pronounced as the interaction variance $\sigma^2(pj)$ increases.

Absolute, Relative, and Other Errors

In the previous sections the computation of correlational type generalizability coefficients, i.e., the squared correlation between observed scores and a well-chosen universe score, has more or less been stressed. Such correlation coefficients are relevant when one is interested in people's relative positions in some group or population of interest. This is the case, for example, in intelligence testing when one wants to estimate the relative position of a person within a well-defined population of persons for which test norms have been obtained.

In other situations, one may be interested in the absolute universe score μ_p of a person irrespective of whatever population. This is the case in criterion-referenced measurement. Here an estimate of a person's universe or domain score is compared with a standard or criterion on the domain score scale. Variation in test difficulty becomes relevant now.

In order to analyze the problem further, consider a one-facet design, with tests as conditions. Condition means μ_i are expected to vary, and the more they do, the more that measurements X_{pi} are expected to vary over test forms. Observed scores can be inaccurate estimates of universe scores due to variation in test difficulty, and this variation between test forms should not be overlooked by using a correlational measure for describing measurement accuracy.

The difference between the two situations can be exemplified by the distinction between *relative* errors and *absolute* errors. *Relative* errors are made when the deviation score for a person is used as an estimate of the person effect ($\mu_p - \mu$):

$$\delta_{pi} = (X_{pi} - X_{.i}) - (\mu_p - \mu). \tag{16}$$

When the sample of persons is large, $X_{.i}$ is an accurate estimate of μ_i and δ_{pi} can be equated to

$$\delta_{pi} = X_{pi} - \mu_p - \mu_i + \mu, \tag{17}$$

i.e., δ_{pi} is the sum of the confounded interaction and random error contribution. Notice that the relative error δ_{pi} is relevant when the deviation scores are not divided by some scaling factor, like the test standard deviation. So, the standard deviations of different tests should be quite similar. It would also be possible that the universe and observed scores μ_p and X_{pi} are defined after an initial rescaling of the raw scores. The variance of δ_{pi} equals $\sigma^2(pi, e)$, and the generalizability coefficient from equation (5) seems an adequate measure for the accuracy of measurements.

When the observed scores X_{pi} are used for estimating μ_p, the relevant error is the *absolute* error defined as

$$\Delta_{pi} = X_{pi} - \mu_p = (\mu_i - \mu) + (X_{pi} - \mu_p - \mu_i + \mu), \tag{18}$$

which equals δ_{pi} plus the condition effect of condition or test i. The expected variance of the absolute errors equals

$$\sigma_\Delta^2 = \sigma^2(i) + \sigma^2(pi, e). \tag{19}$$

In absolute measurement the size of the error variance is generally more important than the size of the generalizability coefficient, because the purpose of measurement is not discrimination between persons as such, but the assessment of the error in absolute measurements. Nevertheless it might still be useful to find the corresponding generalizability coefficient appropriate in this situation

$$\rho^2 = \frac{E(\mu_p - \mu)^2}{\underset{i\ p}{EE}(X_{pi} - \mu)^2} = \frac{\sigma^2(p)}{\sigma^2(p) + \sigma^2(i) + \sigma^2(pi, e)}. \tag{20}$$

In the nested $i{:}p$ design, where the main effect for i is confounded with the residual, a distinction between relative and absolute measurements cannot be made (cf. equation (9)). In a crossed $i \times p$ design with n_i items, such a distinction certainly is relevant. A score on the n_i-item test is an imperfect measurement of the relative true score on that test and, more indirectly, an imperfect measurement of the universe score. Actually, with respect to absolute measurement, the crossed design can be viewed as a small piece of a larger design as demonstrated in figure 2–1.

Each test is administered to a (sub)sample of persons. Viewed on its own, this gives a crossed $i \times p$ design for each test. Srivastava and Webster (1967) derive a generalizability coefficient relevant for the estimation of

test		1				2			
	item	1	2	3	. . .	$n_i + 1$	$n_i + 2$	$n_i + 3$	. . .
person	1	x	x	x					
	2	x	x	x					
	3	x	x	x					
	.		.	.	.				
	.		.	.	.				
	k + 1					x	x	x	
	k + 2					x	x	x	
	k + 3					x	x	x	
	.					.	.	.	
	.					.	.	.	
	.								. . .
	.								. . .
	.								. . .

Figure 2–1. Observation Scheme with Several Tests, and Each Test Consisting of Different Items Administered to Different (Sub)Samples of Persons

absolute universe scores when the design of figure 2–1 is used. The coefficient equals the coefficient for the nested $i{:}p$ design in equation (9). The available data are *not* $i{:}p$, however. When one test has been administered, the variance components, needed in equation (9), can be estimated using the estimation equation for the crossed design (equation (4)). The result equals the one for the generalizability coefficient of a nested design with crossed data, as derived by Rajaratnam (1960) and mentioned in the section on generalizability coefficients for the one-facet design.

Another kind of error is the error of estimation. In classical test theory a person's true score is estimated as

$$\hat{\tau}_p = \rho_{xx'} (x_p - \mu) + \mu, \tag{21}$$

where $\rho_{xx'}$ is the classical test reliability; this regression estimate (21) is known as Kelley's estimate. The error of estimation is defined as the difference between this regression estimate of the true score and the true score itself. The variance of estimation errors is smaller than the variance of measurement errors.

In generalizability theory it is not so easy to apply regression estimates. One possibility to estimate the universe score μ_p in connection with condition i is

$$\hat{\mu}_p = \frac{\hat{\sigma}^2(p)}{\hat{\sigma}^2(X_{pi}|i)} \hat{\rho}(X_{pi}, \mu_p) \, (X_{pi} - \hat{\mu}_i) + \hat{\mu}, \tag{22}$$

where the problem then is to estimate the correlation between people's observed scores on i and their universe scores, $\rho(X_{pi}, \mu_p)$. In equation (22) μ_p is estimated, but when only people's relative positions are of interest, $\hat{\mu}$ can be dropped from the equation. Alternatives to equation (22) have been suggested. Cronbach and colleagues (1972) suggested to estimate the universe score μ_p by

$$\hat{\mu}_p = \hat{\rho}^2(X_{pi} - \hat{\mu}_i) + \hat{\mu}, \tag{23}$$

where $\hat{\rho}^2$ is the generalizability coefficient, the estimate of the average condition-specific generalizability. The use of equation (23) is troublesome when conditions are not equivalent, when, for example, the universe score scales of the various tests differ (cf. equation (2)). With a one-facet universe there is one design in which such problems do not show up, i.e., in the $i{:}p$ design. Here the same population quantities μ and ρ^2 are estimated with each sample. In the $i{:}p$ design similar to figure 2–1, for example, all samples should be pooled in order to obtain one estimate $\hat{\rho}^2$ and one estimate $\hat{\mu}$.

The estimation of μ_i and μ will be discussed separately in the next section. A further discussion of the problems of regression estimates can be found in Cronbach and colleagues (1972). They also discuss the logic of using such estimates. Their use of such estimates, however, is not without problems: different subpopulations have different regression estimates, and it makes a difference for a person whether a common regression estimate is used or subpopulation regression estimates, and, in the latter case, to which subpopulation the person is allocated.

The Estimation of Condition Means

In regression equations (22) and (23), estimates of condition means were needed. But also when the use of those equations is not considered, it can be useful to have estimates $\hat{\mu}_i$. This can be elucidated by means of the problem of estimating universe scores μ_p. In the previous section, before the introduction of regression estimates, μ_p was assumed to be estimated by the raw score X_{pi}, obtained with some condition i. The discrepancy between X_{pi} and μ_p was called the absolute error. For the moment assume that μ_i and μ were known. Then a better estimate of μ_p is

$$\hat{\mu}_p = X_{pi} - \mu_i + \mu. \tag{24}$$

Here the troublesome condition effect is eliminated from the raw score. In practice μ_i and μ should be estimated, not only in connection with equation (24) but also in connection with the regression estimates mentioned in the previous section. One possibility is to estimate μ_i by the average observed score in condition i, and to use the average of the estimated condition means $\hat{\mu}_i$, as an estimate of μ. When sample size is small, $X_{.i}$ is an imprecise estimate of $\hat{\mu}_i$, however, and when the number of conditions for which estimates $\hat{\mu}_i$ are available is small, μ can not be accurately estimated. In this section more adequate estimates $\hat{\mu}_i$ and $\hat{\mu}$ will be derived.

The derivation of the estimates is motivated by the idea that Kelley estimates can be adequate for the estimation of condition means μ_i as well. A simple model

$$X_{pi} = \mu + (\mu_p - \mu) + (\mu_i - \mu) + e_{ip} \tag{25}$$

is assumed. In other words, there is only an additive condition effect ($\mu_i - \mu$). It is further assumed that the observed scores for each condition are normally distributed with a common variance $\phi = \sigma^2(p) + \sigma^2(e)$, and that the condition means are normally distributed with a mean equal to μ and with variance $\phi_o = \sigma^2(i)$. The estimation equations for the μ_i given these assumptions have been derived by De Gruijter and van der Kamp (1984) on the basis of work by Bayesian statisticians such as Lindley (1971). The normality assumption, however, is not strictly necessary (Lindley, 1969). The estimation equations are:

$$\hat{\mu}_i = \rho_i^2 x_{.i} + (1 - \rho_i^2)\hat{\mu}, \tag{26}$$

with

$$\hat{\mu} = (\Sigma w_i)^{-1} (\Sigma w_i x_{.i}), \tag{27}$$

$$\rho_i^2 = \phi_o/(\phi_o + n_i^{-1}\phi), \tag{28}$$

and

$$w_i = (\phi_o + n_i^{-1}\phi)^{-1}. \tag{29}$$

In this context, n_i is the number of persons measured under condition i. The condition mean μ_i is estimated as a weighted average of the observed condition mean and an estimate of the grand mean. The estimate of the condition mean is regressed more to $\hat{\mu}$ when the error variance, ϕ, is larger, the condition variance, ϕ_o, is smaller, and the number of observations, n_i, is smaller. When n_i becomes very small, $\hat{\mu}_i$ approaches $\hat{\mu}$, and $\hat{\mu}_p$ should be estimated by X_{pi} (cf. equation (24)). This extreme can be called the absolute approach to the estimation of μ_p. When, on the other hand, n_i becomes large, μ_i can be estimated correctly by $X_{.i}$. The universe scores are then estimated by computing deviation scores $X_{pi} - X_{.i}$ and adding an estimate of μ. This extreme could be called the relative approach to the estimation of μ_p. In general, the best solution is between the two extreme solutions.

In order to make a practicable procedure, reasonable estimates of ϕ_o and ϕ should be obtained. A possibility, based on a suggestion of Jackson (1973) for the $i{:}p$ design with unequal n_i for different persons, is

$$\hat{\phi} = \left(\sum n_i - m\right)^{-1} \sum_p \sum_i (x_{pi} - x_{.i})^2 \tag{30}$$

and

$$\hat{\phi}_o = s_{x.}^2 - m^{-1} \left(\sum n_i^{-1}\right)\hat{\phi}, \tag{31}$$

where in this context n_i is again the number of persons measured under condition i, m is the total number of conditions and

$$s_{x.}^2 = \sum (x_{.i} - \bar{x})/(m - 1) \tag{32}$$

with

$$\bar{x} = m^{-1} \sum x_{.i}.$$

When estimates $\hat{\mu}_i$ and $\hat{\mu}$ are available, equation (22) might be used for a regression estimate of an examinee's universe score. It is interesting to note that the equation which can be derived by combining equations (22) and (26) with μ known, is identical to Jarjoura's equation (40) with $K = 1$, which was derived without the intermediate step of estimating the condition effect.

Multivariate Generalizability Theory

Measurements in psychology and education often involve multiple scores describing individuals' intellectual functioning due to various aspects of, for example, cognitive and other skills, achievement motivation, aptitudes, personality, and the like. Each of the multiple scores may be interpreted by itself, taking into account the conditions of measurement. Instead of treating each variable separately, multiple scores can be conceived as vectors, and be treated simultaneously within a generalizability framework. The main motive to do so is that a multivariate generalizability approach may well be more informative than a univariate approach, because it considers the mutual dependence of the multiple scores and also allows for the construction of composite scores from the multiple scores at hand.

Several lines of development in multivariate generalizability may be distinguished. The first line of development may be exemplified by the following example taken from Cronbach and colleagues (1972). Both intelligence test batteries, the WISC and the WAIS, have two separate domains of tasks. Each of these domains could be treated in its own right by a univariate generalizability analysis for each of them leading to two separate universe scores. The question is, however, whether this is the most elegant way to treat them. It would be more informative to consider a universe score dimension in which the mutual dependence of the verbal and the performance scales are expressed. This implies that the universe score of one of the domains is considered to be estimated in a more accurate way if this universe score estimate is based on the observed scores for both kinds of tasks. The optimal estimation equation for the verbal score $\hat{\mu}_{p(V)}$, for example, is a regression equation

$$\hat{\mu}_{p(v)} = a_V x_{p(V)} + b_V x_{p(P)} + c \tag{33}$$

where a_v, b_v, and c can readily be obtained from regression theory (see de Gruijter & van der Kamp, 1984, p. 109).

Instead of being interested in the universe scores themselves, one may also emphasize their difference if, for instance, gain scores are at stake. This kind of problem as well as the one where a potentially relevant combination of different universe scores is an additive combination can also be solved by regression techniques (see Cronbach et al., 1972).

A second line of development stresses composite scores obtained from tests developed according to the same table of specifications. In the model considered by Jarjoura and Brennan (1983), each examinee is presented with only one form, and each examinee has as many universe scores as there are fixed categories in a table of specifications (i.e., a number of items are nested within each of several fixed categories). For the measurement procedure implied by the table of specifications, variance and covariance components for categories are estimated, resulting from the analysis of a single test form. As in the univariate generalizability approach, variance and covariance components can be obtained using mean squares and products of the observations. For tests developed according to a table of specifications, the multiple scores, i.e., an examinee's profile of scores over all categories, is of prime interest. A composite universe score can also be obtained from these multiple category scores, using, for example, a priori proportional weights (see Jarjoura & Brennan, 1983).

A third line of development in multivariate generalizability theory emphasizes the interpretation of variance and covariance components in the first place, while a derivation of a multivariate generaliability co-efficient analogous to the univariate coefficient, as well as the construction of composite scores using optimal weights for subtest scores, come second. The tests are not considered to be developed from tables of specifications, whereas the weights provided are a posteriori weights that may have limited relevance for the intended use of the test. Essentially, the weights for combining observed subtest scores are defined to maximize the generalizability of the composite score.

To illustrate the latter approach to multivariate generalizability, suppose that we have a crossed $p \times i$ one-facet study with n_i conditions, and a vector of $r(=2)$ measurements for each person p. The decomposition of the variance-covariance matrix for total scores in this one-facet design is:

$$\begin{pmatrix} \sigma^2(_1X_p) & \sigma(_1X_p,_2X_p) \\ \sigma(_1X_p,_2X_p) & \sigma^2(_2X_p) \end{pmatrix} = \quad \begin{array}{l} \text{observed score} \\ \text{variance-covariance} \\ \text{matrix} \end{array}$$

$$n_i^2 \begin{pmatrix} \sigma^2(_1p) & \sigma(_1p,_2p) \\ \sigma(_1p,_2p) & \sigma^2(_2p) \end{pmatrix} + \quad \text{persons}$$

$$n_i \begin{pmatrix} \sigma^2(_1res) & \sigma(_1res,_2res) \\ \sigma(_1res,_2res) & \sigma^2(_2res) \end{pmatrix}. \quad \text{residual} \qquad (34)$$

where
$_1X_p$ = observed score on variable 1 for person p,
$_2X_p$ = observed score on variable 2 for person p,
$_1p$ = abbreviation for $_1\mu_p$: person p's universe score on variable 1.
Clearly, in equation (34), $\sigma(_1p, _2p)$ is the covariance between universe scores of variables 1 and 2.

Analogous to univariate analysis of variance to obtain estimated components of variance, multivariate analysis of variance provides estimates of components of variance and covariance. In the multivariate case, instead of scalar values for the sums of squares and mean squares of ANOVA, we have matrices of sums of squares and cross products, and mean squares and cross products. Also analogous to the univariate situation, equations can be derived to relate mean squares and cross products to components of variance and covariance for the universe scores (see Webb et al., 1983, for an example). Multivariate generalizability coefficients have been given by Joe and Woodward (1976) as an extension of the univariate generalizability coefficients.

The treatment of multivariate generalizability given above had to be rather elementary out of necessity. For one thing, the relationships between univariate and multivariate generalizability have not been pursued. In addition, generalization to more complex designs and specific problems in multivariate generalizability have not been treated. In the multivariate case even less is known concerning, for instance, the sampling variability of variance and covariance components, the computation of relevant components for unbalanced designs, and other problems. Problems that need to be addressed are summarized by Webb and associates (1983), who also give further references to research in this field.

Applications of Generalizability Theory

Generalizability turned out to have many possible applications in psychological and educational measurement. In the following, only a brief sketch will be given of several applications.

Test scores can be interpreted as being criterion, or content, or domain referenced. That is to say, an observed score is considered to be a representative sample of a well-specified content domain. In such criterion-referenced interpretations the primary question is how a person's universe score with respect to the criterion set in advance may best be estimated. Here, the focus of measurement is on absolute decisions, as Cronbach and colleagues (1972) call them. In criterion-referenced measurement a criterion is set in a well-defined behavioral domain. The test user is interested in the difference between a person's universe score and this criterion, λ. This leads to the following error in estimating a person's universe score from observed score

$$\Delta_{pi} = (X_{pi} - \lambda) - (\mu_p - \lambda) = X_{pi} - \mu_p. \tag{35}$$

And an index of dependability for a criterion-referenced or domain-referenced test, $\phi(\lambda)$, is

$$\phi(\lambda) = \frac{\underset{p}{E}(\mu_p - \lambda)^2}{\underset{i}{E}\underset{p}{E}(X_{pi} - \lambda)^2}$$

$$= [\sigma^2(p) + (\mu - \lambda)^2]/[\sigma^2(p) + (\mu - \lambda)^2 + \sigma^2(i)/n_i + \sigma^2(pi,e)/n_i]$$

$$= [\sigma^2(p) + (\mu - \lambda)^2]/[\sigma^2(p) + (\mu - \lambda)^2 + \sigma_\Delta^2]. \tag{36}$$

More information on the application of generalizability theory to criterion-referenced measurement may be found in, e.g., Brennan (1983), Kane and Brennan (1980), and De Gruijter and van der Kamp (1984).

Generalizability theory has also been used to conduct investigations on cross-level inference in psychological and educational research. Such an approach facilitates multilevel analysis and cross-level inference to test external validity of measurement results. In this vein of research, Fyans (1983) proposed a model that generates sequential tests of alternative hypotheses to assess the veridical level of generalizability empirically using Bayesian techniques of inference.

In the field of personality assessment, observational techniques loom large; the applicability of generalizability theory in this field of research has been described by Wiggins (1973). An extensive use of the generalizability paradigm in the context of personality research is made by Van Heck (1988), who studied anxiety as a trait by a self-report inventory. In this research, the generalizability of self-reports and observational data across situations has been investigated, among others (see also Endler & Magnusson, 1976; Magnusson & Endler, 1977). Coates and Thoresen (1978), and Cone and Foster (1982) give an application of generalizability in the field of behavioral therapy.

Concluding Comments

Generalizability theory's main contribution to measurement is that it provides a conceptual framework for research enabling an investigator to ask better questions. In combination with its technical apparatus, generalization theory offers a unique approach to psychological and educational measurement problems. In this sense, generalizability theory is a general measurement procedure in which the following four stages can be distinguished:

1. *The observation stage*—the choice of a research design is made (i.e., facets and conditions are chosen), and relevant mean squares are computed;

2. *The estimation stage*—decisions are made whether the facets are finite or infinite and random or fixed, and variance components are estimated;

3. *The measurement stage*—specifies which facet (or combination of facets) is the focus of measurement and which facets may limit the generalization of the measurement (i.e., sources of error); in this stage estimation of error and generalizability are obtained;

4. *The optimization stage*—specifies the recommended population of differentiation and the universe of generalization.

These stages of generalizability analysis (see Cardinet & Allal, 1983, for a more elaborate description) parallel the general stages of the empirical research cycle, but in addition to the latter cycle the necessary computational procedures are pinpointed.

On the one hand, generalizability theory's stages of analysis parallel the general empirical research paradigm. On the other hand, generalizability theory as a theory of test scores belongs to the domain of test theory per se. It has been mentioned already, that generalizability theory elaborates classical test theory, viz. liberates classical reliability. There are also relationships of generalizability theory with other psychometric approaches: the analysis of covariance structures and item response theory. Both topics are addressed in subsequent chapters.

With covariance structure analysis, the relationship has to do with the multivariate extension of generalizability theory. Both generalizability theory and covariance structure analysis aim at obtaining estimates of variance components from the variance-covariance matrix. The difference between the two is that "the assumptions in covariance structure analysis are almost always stronger than those in generalizability analyses" (Brennan, 1983, p. 121).

Item response theory or latent trait theory is, in principle, a scaling theory aiming to assign scale values to items as well as to persons to whom the items are presented. The individual items are, essentially, the basic units of measurement and as such considered as fixed entities. No specific conditions of measurement, hence no universes, are considered. And although item response theory is judged by some workers in this field as a promise for the future of educational and psychological measurement, to the extent that alternative approaches have to be considered as outdated, in our view such a conclusion would be incorrect. Each approach has its merits and demerits: it depends upon the typical question a researcher has to answer. There is no one true measurement approach in testing.

References

Box, G. E. P., & Tiao, G. C. (1973). *Bayesian inference in statistical analysis.* Reading, MA: Addison-Wesley.

Brennan, R. L. (1983). *Elements of generalizability theory.* Iowa City, IA: American College Testing.

Cardinet, J., & Allal, L. (1983). Estimation of generalizability parameters. In L. J. Fyans, Jr. (ed.), *New directions for testing and measurement: Generalizability theory.* San Francisco: Jossey-Bass, Inc., pp. 17–48.

Cardinet, J., Tourneur, Y., & Allal, L. (1981 and 1982). Extension of generalizability theory and its applications in educational measurement. *Journal of Educational Measurement* 18:183–204; and 19:331–332.

Coates, T. J., & Thoresen, C. E. (1978). Using generalizability theory in behavior observation. *Behavior Therapy* 9:605–613.

Cone, J. D., & Foster, S. L. (1982). Direct observation in clinical psychology. In L. Kendall, & J. N. Butcher (eds.), *Handbook of research methods in clinical psychology.* New York: Wiley.

Cronbach, L. J. (1951). Coefficient alpha and the internal structure of tests. *Psychometrika* 16:297–334.

Cronbach, L. J., Gleser, G. C., Nanda, H., & Rajaratnam, N. (1972). *The dependability of behavioral measurements.* New York: Wiley.

Cronbach, L. J., Rajaratnam, N., & Gleser, G. C. (1963). Theory of generalizability: A liberalization of reliability theory. *British Journal of Statistical Psychology* 16:137–163.

De Gruijter, D. N. M., & Van der Kamp, L. J. Th. (1984). *Statistical models in psychological and educational testing.* Lisse: Swets & Zeitlinger.

Efron, B. (1979). Bootstrap methods: Another look at the jackknife. *Annals of Statistics* 7:1–26.

Endler, N. S., & Magnusson, D. (eds.) (1976). *Interactional psychology and personality.* Washington, DC: Hemisphere.

Fyans, L. J., Jr. (1983). Multilevel analysis and cross-level inference of validity using generalizability theory. In L. J. Fyans, Jr. (ed.), *New directions for testing and measurement: Generalizability theory.* San Francisco: Jossey-Bass, Inc., pp. 49–66.

Gray, H. L., & Schucany, W. R. (1972). *The generalized jackknife statistic.* New York: Marcel Dekker, Inc.

Guttman, L. (1953). A special review of Harold Gulliksen's "Theory of Mental Tests." *Psychometrika* 18:123–130.

Jackson, P. H. (1973). The estimation of true score variance and error variance in the classical test theory model. *Psychometrika* 38:183–201.

Jarjoura, D. (1983). Best linear prediction of composite universe scores. *Psychometrika* 48:525–539.

Jarjoura, D., & Brennan, R. L. (1983). Multivariate generalizability models for tests developed from tables of specifications. In L. J. Fyans, Jr. (ed.), *New directions for testing and measurement: Generalizability theory.* San Francisco: Jossey-Bass, Inc., pp. 83–102.

Joe, G. W., & Woodward, J. A (1976). Some developments in multivariate generalizability. *Psychometrika* 41:205–217.

Kane, M. T., & Brennan, R. L. (1980). Agreement coefficients as indices of dependability for domain-referenced tests. *Applied Psychological Measurement* 4:105–126.

Kirk, R. E. (1982). *Experimental design: Procedures for the behavioral sciences.* Belmont, CA: Wadsworth.

Lindley, D. V. (1969). Bayesian least squares. *Bulletin of the International Statistical Institute* 43:152–153.

——————. (1971). The estimation of many parameters. In V. P. Godambe & D. A. Sprott (eds.), *Foundation of statistical inference*. Toronto: Holt, Rinehart and Winston.

Magnusson, D., & Endler, N. S. (eds.) (1977). *Personality at the crossroads: Current issues in interactional psychology*. Hillsdale, NJ: Erlbaum.

Maxwell, A. E., & Pilliner, A. E. G. (1968). Deriving coefficients of reliability and agreement for ratings. *British Journal of Mathematical and Statistical Psychology* 21:105–116.

Rajaratnam, N. (1960). Reliability formulas for independent decision data when reliability data are matched. *Psychometrika* 25:261–271.

Rajaratnam, N., Cronbach, L. J., & Gleser, G. C. (1965). Generalizability of stratified parallel tests. *Psychometrika* 30:39–56.

Shavelson, R., & Webb, N. (1981). Generalizability theory: 1973–1980. *British Journal of Mathematical and Statistical Psychology* 34:133–166.

Shavelson, R., Webb, N. M., & Rowley, G. L. (1989). Generalizability theory. *American Psychologist* 44:922–932.

Sirotnik, K., & Wellington, R. (1977). Incidence sampling: An integrated theory for "matrix sampling." *Journal of Educational Measurement* 14:343–399.

Srivastava, A. B. L., & Webster, H. (1967). An estimation of true scores in the case of items scored on a continuous scale. *Psychometrika* 32:327–338.

Van Heck, G. L. M. (1988). Modes and models in anxiety. *Anxiety Research* 1:199–214.

Webb, N. M., Shavelson, R. J., & Maddahian, E. (1983). Multivariate generalizability theory. In L. J. Fyans, Jr. (ed.), *New directions for testing and measurement: Generalizability theory*. San Francisco: Jossey-Bass, Inc., pp. 67–82.

Wiggins, J. S. (1973). *Personality and prediction: Principles of personality assessment*. Reading, MS: Addison-Wesley.

Winer, B. J. (1971). *Statistical principles in experimental design*. New York: McGraw-Hill.

3 ITEM RESPONSE THEORY

David J. Weiss
Michael E. Yoes

During the past 30 years or so, a new theoretical basis for educational and psychological testing and measurement has emerged. It has been variously referred to as latent trait theory, item characteristic curve theory, and, more recently, item response theory (IRT). Although this new test theory holds considerable promise as a successor to classical test theory, it has been underutilized by test practitioners. One important reason for this underutilization is that many test developers have not had sufficient time to devote to the study of the technical and mathematical intricacies involved in this new test theory and its mathematical models. This chapter is intended as an overview of IRT for individuals with some background in the basic methods of classical test theory. Readers are referred to Hambleton (1989) and Hambleton and Swaminathan (1985) for other overviews of IRT.

Classical Test Theory

For many years, classical test theory (CTT), sometimes called "true and error score" theory or "number-correct score" theory, was the only practical theoretical basis for measurement available in the behavioral sciences. CTT is based on a measurement model which states that each individual has some unobservable (i.e., latent) quantity, called a "true score," which can never be measured directly. Instead, in CTT, an "observed" number-correct score is measured with the understanding that this measure contains some amount of error as an estimate of the "true" score.

CTT is based on four major concepts: item difficulty, item discrimination, reliability, and number-correct test scores. The model assumed by classical test theory is typically represented as

$$\text{Observed Score} = \text{True Score} + \text{Error}. \tag{1}$$

This is a linear model, specifying that there is a linear relationship between a person's observed number-correct score on a test and the error-free true score that it estimates.

Throughout the long history of CTT as a model for psychological measurement and testing, it has become obvious that there are many technical problems presented by CTT which it cannot overcome. It is at least partly in response to these recognized inadequacies of CTT that IRT was developed.

A major problem with CTT stems from the definitions of the test item parameters—item difficulty and item discrimination. Item difficulty is defined in CTT as the proportion of examinees who answer a specified item correctly. This is commonly referred to as the "p-value" of the item. Low p-values are associated with difficult items and high p-values are associated with easy items. Item discrimination in CTT is typically defined as the correlation between a dichotomously coded item score (0 = incorrect, 1 = correct) and total (number-correct) test score, usually using either the biserial or point-biserial correlation coefficient. A low item discrimination indicates that a correct response to an item has little or no relationship with total score. Items that have low or essentially zero item discriminations, as defined in CTT, are usually removed from a test to improve its measurement characteristics.

Test item parameters thus defined in CTT are dependent upon the sample in which the items were administered. For example, if a set of test items were administered to a high-ability group of examinees, the item difficulties (and probably the item discriminations) would be very different than if the same items were administered to a group of examinees of moderate or low ability. IRT resolves this problem of sample dependency by providing item parameters (to be discussed below) which are invariant (in a specific sense); that is, they are not dependent on the ability level of the group upon which the item parameters were developed.

A second major problem with CTT concerns the scoring of individuals. Test scores in CTT are usually total number-correct scores, or some function thereof. Because individuals are scored based on the number of items to which they respond correctly, test scores are dependent on the difficulties of the items in the test selected for use. In contrast, IRT provides scores for individual examinees which use information available on the items administered, but which are not dependent on the specific set of items administered. In IRT, examinees do not even have to receive the same items in a test. This can be accomplished because the score for an individual is not only based on the number of correct responses but also takes into account the statistical characteristics of the items answered correctly as well as incorrectly by the individual.

A third major problem with CTT involves the concept of reliability. "True" scores cannot be directly measured, and must be estimated from observed scores. Point estimates of true scores are derived from the "index of reliability," which in turn is based on the reliability coefficient. Reliability coefficients are also used to create confidence intervals around the estimated true scores—these are referred to as "standard errors of measurement" (SEM). These concepts are defined in CTT as

$$\text{reliability} = 1 - (\text{error variance}/\text{total score variance}) \qquad (2)$$

$$\text{index of reliability} = \sqrt{\text{reliability}} \qquad (3)$$

and

$$SEM = SD_x \sqrt{1 - \text{reliability}} \qquad (4)$$

where SD_x is the standard deviation of the total test scores.

Because reliability involves the total (i.e., observed) score variance, both the estimate of an individual's true score and its confidence interval are dependent upon the particular sample of examinees involved in the total score distribution. In IRT, the computation of reliability is not necessary in order to compute the SEM. Moreover, in IRT, procedures are provided for computing SEMs that can differ for different individuals.

Historical Background of IRT

The historical roots of item response theory lie in the study of psychological scaling. Charles Mosier (1940) described the relationship between psychophysical scaling and psychological measurement. In psychophysical scaling the psychological response is observed, and from this response an inference is made about appropriate levels of the physical stimulus. Item response theory is an adaptation of this idea wherein a behavioral response is observed and an inference is made about the psychological trait assumed to underlie that behavior.

Paul Lazarsfeld (1950), a sociologist, developed one of the early forerunners of IRT, which was applicable only to the classification of an individual into a group. Lazarsfeld called this approach "latent structure analysis."

Louis Guttman (1944) developed an error-free (i.e., deterministic) model of IRT, although he did not refer to it as such. Guttman developed the idea of the "trace line," which was later called the item characteristic curve in IRT. While it may be unrealistic, in most instances, to assume an error-free model, the placement of parameters describing the person and the items on the same scale represented a major step forward toward the development of more sophisticated IRT models.

In 1952, Frederic Lord wrote his Ph.D. dissertation in which the groundwork was laid for the application of IRT to dichotomous test items (Lord, 1952). Lord has since remained one of the most important and prolific contributors to the IRT literature (e.g., Lord & Novick, 1968; Lord, 1980). He helped to develop the two-parameter logistic model and was influential in Birnbaum's (1968) development of the three-parameter logistic model for IRT.

Another very influential person in the IRT literature was Georg Rasch, a Danish mathematician, who independently developed and refined the one-parameter IRT test model (Rasch, 1960/1980). This model is often referred to as the Rasch model in recognition of his contribution to the field.

Many other individuals have made important contributions to the development and implementation of IRT. Hambleton and Swaminathan (1985) provide a more detailed account of the historical development of IRT. Hambleton (1989) provides an excellent overview to the field of item response theory.

Assumptions of Item Response Theory

As a test theory based upon a family of mathematical models, there are certain assumptions that must be made about the data, or conditions, under which the model can be assumed to hold. There are four basic assumptions which must be made when using IRT as a model of test behavior.

The first assumption is seemingly trivial. Under both IRT and CTT an assumption must be made that if the examinee knows the correct answer to a test item, he or she will probably answer it correctly. This could be referred to as the "know-correct" assumption. It is often useful to phrase this alternatively—that if an examinee answered an item incorrectly, then he/she probably did not know the correct answer.

The second assumption of IRT involves the dimensionality of the latent space. In general, IRT assumes that the probability of a correct/keyed response by an examinee is attributable to his/her standing on some specific number (k) of latent traits or abilities. In geometric terms, an individual's position on each of the latent traits can be conceptualized as a point in k-dimensional space. For most applications of IRT, it is assumed that the latent space is unidimensional. Unidimensionality implies that examinee performance is attributable to a single latent ability/trait. In common terms, unidimensionality means that the items measure one and only one variable (knowledge, ability, attitude, personality trait). Most tests (and hence test items) currently in use are designed to measure a single ability or trait, so the unidimensionality assumption is not unduly restrictive.

When a test is administered under speeded conditions, it must be recognized that there are at least two dimensions involved in examinee performance: response speed and the latent ability/trait being measured. For these reasons, most of the common IRT models are not appropriate for speeded tests. Although most IRT models currently in use involve unidimensional domains, the development of multidimensional IRT models has progressed significantly in recent years and promises more generalized IRT testing models to be available to the test practitioner in the near future. Factor analysis of the item intercorrelation matrix can be used, for example, to check the dimensionality assumption (Hambleton & Traub, 1973).

The third assumption of IRT, which is sometimes discussed along with the dimensionality assumption, has to do with local independence. Local independence means that the probability of a correct/keyed response of an examinee to an item is unaffected by responses to other items in the test. Technically, local independence means that items are uncorrelated for individuals *with the same ability/trait level* (statistical independence). In reality, this assumption is violated if, for instance, the content of an early item in a test provides clues as to the correct/keyed response for a later item; in that case, the two items will correlate more highly than they should just based on the trait that they have in common. Local independence is a crucial assumption in IRT because, as will be seen, items are combined based on this assumption. Factor analysis can also be used in an attempt to demonstrate local independence. After removal of the k specified dimensions (based on the dimensionality assumption) from the item intercorrelation matrix, all of the remaining item intercorrelations should be essentially zero (McDonald, 1985).

The fourth and final assumption of IRT has to do with the assumed shape of the item characteristic curve, or, as it has been more recently called, the item response function (IRF). This assumption involves the particular mathematical form of the IRF. Some of the current IRT models are based on the form of the normal ogive. This function is approximated by the logistic ogive, which is mathematically much easier to work with. In general, with the common IRT models, the number of parameters in the mathematical function used to describe the item dictates the form of the IRF, resulting in what has been generally referred to as the one-, two-, and three-parameter models.

Basic IRT Concepts

The Item Response Function

Item response theory is, in a sense, a generalization of classical test theory. Many of the concepts in IRT bear some similarity to their CTT counterparts, and some of the terminology is very similar. For instance, the concept of parameters that describe a test item—item difficulty and item discrimination—is used in both IRT and CTT, and although they are defined differently, some of the same basic ideas are similar.

Let's say that we have a test item on which a high-ability group of examinees (e.g., those 1.5 standard deviations above the mean) scores 85 percent correct, whereas in a low-ability group (e.g., examinees at −1.5 standard deviations) only 33 percent of the examinees answer the same item correctly. If a line is drawn between the two CTT p-values, as was done in figure 3–1, we note that the line has a sizable slope. In other words, this item differentiates very well between people who are high ability and people who are low ability. In CTT, the item would have a high point-biserial correlation with the proportion-correct total score.

If a large enough sample was available—or a population—it would be possible to break the ability/trait continuum into many trait level group-ings, from very low to very high, and plot the proportion correct for each subgroup. The dashed line in figure 3–2 is an example of how the data might look. This line shows observed proportion correct for 100 people at each trait level from +3 to −3 on a standard score scale, at intervals of .25. The curve frequently takes on an S-shape. This S-shaped curve, based on observed proportion-correct scores for trait level groupings, can be called an empirical item response function (EIRF).

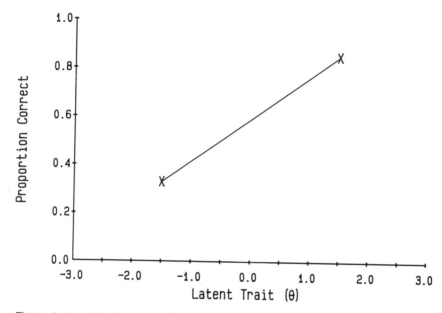

Figure 3-1.   Item Discrimination in Classical Test Theory

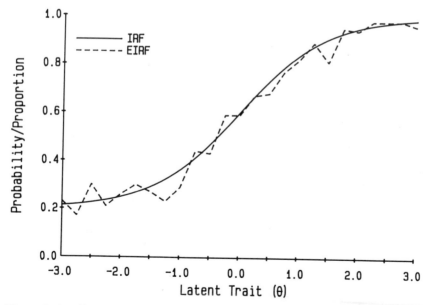

Figure 3-2.   Empirical Item Response Function (EIRF) and Estimated Item Response Function (IRF)

Because interest is centered on what happens in a population, and not just in a sample (even though it might be very large), the shapes of the curves for the population must be estimated. In a population, however, we no longer speak in terms of proportion-correct but substitute the concept of probability of a correct response. Also, the graphs are not based on total test score (which is usually standardized), but rather the graphs use the (unobservable) latent trait that the test items measure. The latent trait is frequently called ability, since IRT has mainly been applied to ability testing, although it can be any trait or construct that is being measured by the test. It is usually symbolized using the greek letter theta—θ.

The population graph that plots the probability of a correct response at varying levels of the latent psychological trait for a single item is at the center of IRT; it is the item response function or IRF. The IRF, shown by the solid line in figure 3–2, is fitted to the empirical response function in the process of estimating the parameters of each test item.

There are several parameters, or numerical values, that describe different aspects of an IRF. The difficulty of an item, as defined in IRT, is defined at the center of the IRF. If we mathematically find the center of the fitted IRF and read down to the standard score scale of the horizontal axis, the *difficulty* of the item is identified as the location on the trait scale of the center of the IRF.

The center point of the IRF is also the point at which the acceleration of the function changes from a positive acceleration to a negative acceleration. It is at this point that the slope of the curve is maximum. The item *discrimination* in IRT is proportional to this maximum slope.

The third parameter that usually describes an IRF is the probability associated with the lower (left-hand) end of the curve. This parameter represents the probability of a correct/keyed response for individuals with very low trait levels; it is, therefore, sometimes referred to as the *"pseudoguessing" parameter*.

The three parameters that usually describe the IRF are referred to in many applications as the "b, a, and c" parameters of the items, referring to difficulty, discrimination, and lower asymptote parameters, respectively. Figure 3–3 shows several test items that differ in difficulty, discrimination, and their c parameters. Item 3 is the least difficult (easiest) while item 5 is the most difficult. Item 3 is also the most discriminating item and item 2 is the least discriminating. Item 3 also has the lowest c parameter and item 4 has the largest.

When a test item is described in terms of all three parameters, a three-parameter model is used. If it is assumed that the c parameter is 0, and

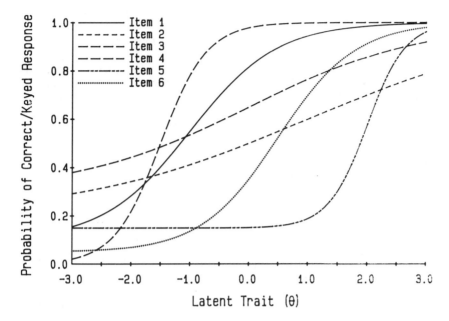

Figure 3–3.   Item Response Functions for Six Items

only the a and b parameters are used to describe the IRF, a two-parameter model is being used. When the items are described only in terms of their item difficulties, assuming that all the discriminations are the same (equal) and that the c parameters are all 0, a one-parameter (or Rasch) model is being used.

References to IRT models are typically made in terms of the mathematical forms that describe the IRFs. There are two general mathematical forms for these ogive-shaped functions. One uses the function for the cumulative normal ogive, resulting in the normal ogive model. The other general family of IRT models uses a logistic function, which is another kind of mathematical function that is very similar to the normal ogive curve but has a different equation. The equation describing the logistic ogive is much simpler to work with. For this reason, most applied work in IRT uses the logistic ogive models to describe the IRFs. Equations (5), (6), and (7) are the equations for the one-, two-, and three-parameter logistic IRFs, respectively.

$$P(u = 1|\theta) = [1 + e^{-D(\theta-b)}]^{-1} \qquad (5)$$

$$P(u = 1|\theta) = [1 + e^{-Da(\theta-b)}]^{-1} \tag{6}$$

$$P(u = 1|\theta) = c + (1 - c)\,[1 + e^{-Da(\theta-b)}]^{-1} \tag{7}$$

The D value is a constant set equal to a value of 1.7 to maximize the agreement between the normal-ogive and the logistic test models. (For an expanded discussion, see Harris, 1989.)

Combining IRFs

Thus far, only IRFs at an individual item level have been considered. A useful property of IRFs (based on the local independence assumption) is that they are additive. Consequently, the IRFs for the items in a test can be added together at each level of θ. This is accomplished by taking the probability of a correct response for each item at each θ level and summing these probabilities. The result, when plotted, will be essentially an average of the IRFs involved. This curve, created by summing the IRFs, is called the *test characteristic curve* or *test response function* (TRF).

The horizontal axis for a TRF is still θ, the trait measured by the test.

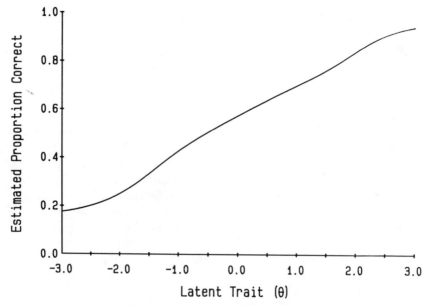

Figure 3–4.   Test Response Function for a Six-Item Test

The vertical axis is the sum of the probabilities of a correct response for each of the test items. When these probabilities are added together, the result is called an estimated number-correct score (sometimes called a "true" score). This score is on the same scale, and analogous to, the number-correct scores typically used in CTT. If the estimated number-correct score is divided by the number of items in the test, the result is an estimated proportion-correct score for each θ level. Thus, if we know an individual's θ estimate, his/her number-correct or proportion-correct score for the test can be estimated, too.

The TRF, therefore, provides a link between the type of scoring (i.e., number-correct) common in CTT testing applications and the IRT-based scoring methods which score the individual in terms of his/her estimated θ level. Figure 3–4 shows the TRF based on the six three-parameter items.

Information

The concept of information is, like the concept of the IRF, central to IRT. Information in the psychometric or statistical sense has to do with how precisely something is being estimated. Sir Ronald Fisher (1922) defined statistical information as the reciprocal of the precision with which a parameter can be estimated. In IRT it is possible to determine how much information an item provides at each point along the θ continuum. Thus, the more (i.e., higher) information there is at a given θ level, the more precise the measurement will be at the θ level. Consequently, one advantage of IRT is the capability of determining which items measure best at specific θ levels. CTT does not provide any easy means to accomplish the same feature.

The slope of the IRF at any point along the curve reflects how well the item differentiates contiguous θ levels. Mathematically, this slope can be described by the slope of a line tangent to the IRF at that particular level of θ. In calculus, this is known as the first derivative of the function that describes the IRF. In general, the amount of information provided by an item at a given level of θ can be represented as

$$I(\theta, U) = (\text{Squared IRF Slope})/(\text{Conditional Variance}). \qquad (8)$$

Since the slope of an IRF can be (and usually is) different at each level of θ (see, e.g., figure 3–3), item information also depends on θ level and is also a function. Thus the amount of information that an item provides at every possible θ level can be computed and the resulting values can be plotted graphically.

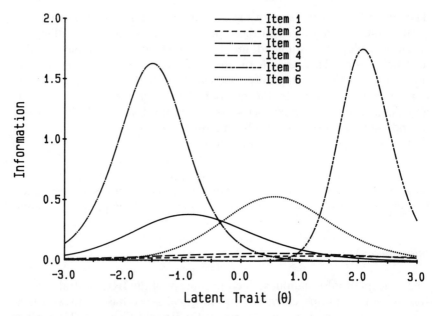

Figure 3–5.   Item Information Functions for a Six-Item Test

Figure 3–5 shows the corresponding item information functions (IIFs) for the items whose IRFs are shown in figure 3–3. Note that the IIF reaches its peak at the point where the slope of the IRF was maximum (i.e., at the item difficulty). Also note that items which have higher item discriminations (e.g., items 3 and 5) produce IIFs that are much more peaked than those items with moderate or low discriminations (e.g., items 1, 2, 4, and 6). For the items with low discriminations (e.g., items 2 and 4) the range of the θ continuum over which the information is spread is much wider.

This illustrates an effect known as the bandwidth-fidelity paradox (McBride, 1977). Because highly discriminating items provide more information, it is desirable in constructing a test to have highly discriminating items to achieve precise measurement (fidelity). The problem with using highly discriminating items is that they only provide information over a narrow range of θ (e.g., items 3 and 5 in figure 3–5), and little or no information outside that range. Less discriminating items provide information over a much wider range of θ (bandwidth), but not as much information at any one level of θ (e.g., items 1 and 6). Thus, sometimes a compromise must be made between the total information provided (fidelity) by the item and the range (bandwidth) over which that information is available.

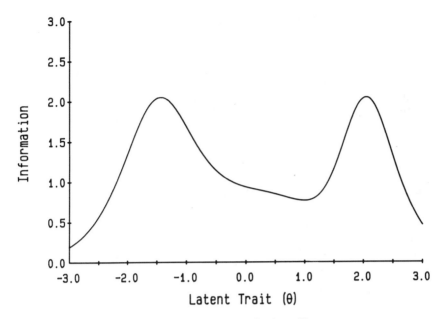

Figure 3-6.   Test Information Function for a Six-Item Test

Since the IIF is a transformation of the IRF, the same rules apply to its use. Specifically, the assumption of local independence allows the IIFs to be summed for the set of items that comprise a test. The resulting function is referred to as a test information function (TIF) and shows the relative amounts of information provided by the test at each level of θ. Figure 3-6 shows the TIF which would result from a test composed of the items whose IRFs are shown in figure 3-3 and whose IFFs are shown in figure 3-5. This provides a means to evaluate the ranges of θ in which a test is measuring best, and where it may need further development. One of the most interesting uses of information in IRT is the fact that the IIFs and TIF can be developed before the test is constructed (more will be said about the use of IRT information in test construction later).

The TIF shows the maximum amount of information that is available from a test composed of those particular items. To achieve this maximum information, the items must be scored in a way that optimally weights them. If a computer program is used to estimate θ levels using a maximum likelihood or Bayesian method (explained below), then these estimates are already optimally weighted and you can use the TIF directly as an indicator of the amount of information available at each θ level. It is possible, however, to use other scoring methods (e.g., number-correct) to estimate the θ level of an examinee. In this case, the amount of information provided by the estimated scores which are not optimally weighted is called the test score information function (TSIF). The TSIF will have the same general shape as the TIF but will provide less information at all values of θ, reflecting the fact that a number-correct score does not (except in the case of the one-parameter logistic model) account for all the information in an examinee's responses to a set of test items (see Lord, 1980, p. 74, for examples).

Conditional Standard Errors of Measurement

The IIF is defined as the squared slope of the IRF over a conditional variance. As such, it is on a squared metric. To return the information index to the original unsquared metric, it is necessary to take the square root of the IIF. Also, remember that statistical information was defined as

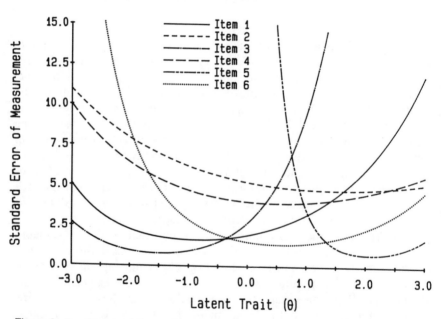

Figure 3–7.   Standard Error of Measurement Functions for Six Items

the *reciprocal* of the precision with which a parameter (in this case, θ) can be estimated. Consequently, to obtain an estimate of the error of measurement of each θ level it is necessary to take the reciprocal of the square root of the information available at that θ level. The function produced by this process is referred to as the conditional standard error of measurement function (CSEM).

Examples of CSEM functions are shown in figure 3–7 for the items from figure 3–3. Interpreted in an opposite manner from the information function, these functions show the amount of *error* associated with each θ level. Thus, where the function is lowest is where the item measures most precisely. This function can also be computed for a test as a whole, by computing the reciprocal square root of test or test score information. The interpretation is the same as for the item CSEM, except that the resulting test standard error function indicates how accurately various θ levels can be measured by the test as a whole. Figure 3–8 shows the conditional standard error of measurement curve for the test information function shown in figure 3–6.

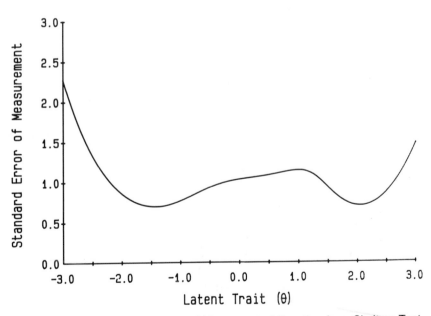

Figure 3–8. Test Standard Error of Measurement Function for a Six-Item Test

Estimating Ability

There are two common methods for estimating θ levels of examinees. These methods are *maximum likelihood estimation* and *Bayesian modal estimation*. To understand both of these methods, however, it is necessary to introduce briefly the concept of the likelihood function.

The purpose of either of the θ estimation procedures is to take into account all of the information in the examinee's entire pattern or vector, as it is sometimes called, of responses to the test items. If an examinee answers an item correctly, then his/her response is scored as a "1." If the examinee answers an item incorrectly, then his/her response is scored as a "0." The response vector for each examinee, therefore, consists of a string of 0s and 1s which indicate how he/she responded to the test items.

Recall that the probability of a correct response was represented by the IRF (denoted $P(\theta)$; see equations (5)–(7)). In a similar fashion, the probability of an incorrect response can be conceptualized as an IRF in which each probability is $[1 - P(\theta)]$, producing a function that is monotonically decreasing. The probability of an incorrect response is usually referred to as $Q(\theta)$.

Probability theory states that the probability of independent events occurring together is equal to the product of their separate probabilities. Because of the assumption of local independence, it can be assumed that the probability of responding correctly to any item in a test is (statistically) independent of the probability of responding either correctly or incorrectly to any of the remaining items. The function described by the multiplicative product of the appropriate probabilities (the "correct" or "incorrect" IRFs probabilities at each level of θ) corresponding to the examinee's response pattern is known as the *likelihood function* (LF).

The LF for a single item is simply the IRF for a correct response, if the individual answers the item correctly, or its complement $[1 - P(\theta)]$, if the individual answers the item incorrectly. With two items, the LF is the product of these two IRFs which reflect the correctness/incorrectness of the examinee's responses. The LF, therefore, gives the conditional probability of a response pattern given θ. When more than two items are involved, the multiplication of the "correct" and "incorrect" IRFs is simply continued across all of the items that an individual has answered. Figure 3–9 shows the likelihood functions for two different response patterns to the items whose IRFs are shown in figure 3–3. For response vector 1 (RV1), the six items were scored 101101, respectively; for response vector 2 (RV2), they were scored 101000.

Having obtained the likelihood function for a given string of correct and incorrect responses made by an individual to test items for which IRF

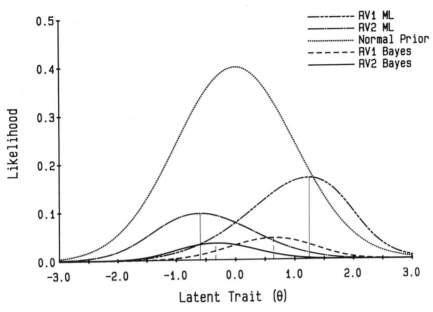

Figure 3–9. Likelihood Functions and Bayesian Posterior Distribution Functions for Response Vector 1 (RV1) and Response Vector 2 (RV2)

parameters have been estimated, the question becomes one of determining what value of θ most likely gave rise to that response pattern. For maximum likelihood estimation, the most likely θ level is that level of θ which is associated with the highest value (the maximum) of the likelihood function. The solid vertical lines in figure 3–9 show the θ estimates of $+1.23$ and -0.60 for the two response patterns.

One problem with ML estimation, however, is that if an examinee responds to all of the items either correctly or incorrectly (sometimes called perfect or zero response vectors, respectively) then the likelihood function does not have a single identifiable peak and the maximum likelihood estimation procedure cannot provide estimates of θ for those individuals. This problem is partially solved by Bayesian θ estimation.

For Bayesian estimation one additional step must be added beyond that of maximum likelihood estimation. Bayesian methods presume that if the distribution of θ is known or can be assumed for the population, then that information can be used in making more accurate estimates of θ. The assumed distribution of θ is referred to as the prior distribution. The likelihood function is then weighted (i.e., multiplied) at each level of θ by the density (height) of the prior distribution at that same level of θ.

This process of multiplying the likelihood function times the assumed prior distribution results in a new (weighted) likelihood function called a *posterior distribution*. The most likely estimate of θ for the particular response pattern is then taken to be that level of θ associated with the modal (highest) value of this posterior distribution. Figure 3–9 also shows the Bayesian posterior distributions for the same two response patterns, assuming a normal prior distribution of θ centered at 0. Note that the resulting Bayesian θ estimates (the vertical dashed lines) differ from the ML estimates.

A problem with Bayesian θ estimation is that if the assumption regarding the distribution of θ is not valid, Bayesian estimation will result in poor estimates of θ. One advantage of the Bayesian estimation method, on the other hand, is that perfect or zero response vectors can be scored and an estimate of θ determined, whereas this is not possible for maximum likelihood estimation.

Estimating IRF Parameters

Because all applications of IRT are dependent upon the item parameters (i.e., the b, a, and c values of the IRF), it is important that these parameters be estimated as accurately as possible. The problem in item parameter estimation is one of determining the parameters that describe an ogive-shaped function which best fits the observed data (i.e., the EIRF). The process of item parameter estimation, sometimes referred to as item calibration, is mathematically very cumbersome and beyond the scope of this chapter (for details, see, for example, Hambleton, 1989; Hambleton & Swaminathan, 1985, ch. 7; Harwell, Baker, & Zwarts, 1988; and Swaminathan, 1983).

Item parameter estimates are typically obtained from computer programs designed to estimate them. The methods and differences of each of the programs is, again, beyond our scope. Some of the computer programs available for computing item parameter estimates are LOGIST, BILOG, ASCAL, and BICAL. (For a current review of BILOG and LOGIST, see Mislevy & Stocking, 1989).

The selection of a program for estimating the item parameters is dependent on the form of the IRF selected (one-, two-, or three-parameter model) and the type of estimation procedure desired (maximum likelihood, marginal maximum likelihood, or Bayesian). Some of these programs are available for use only on a mainframe computer, others operate only on microcomputers, whereas some programs are written for both types of computers. What they do share in common is that they are all computationally intensive and require a great deal of computer time. If a mainframe computer is used, the programs can be quite costly to operate.

LOGIST (Wingersky, Barton, & Lord, 1982) is a maximum likelihood estimation program that will estimate the parameters of the one-, two-, and three-parameter logistic IRF models. If a one-parameter (Rasch) model is used, BICAL (Wright & Mead, 1976) is also a maximum likelihood procedure. ASCAL (Assessment Systems Corporation, 1989) implements two-and-three-parameter model estimation on a microcomputer, using a modified maximum likelihood method with some Bayesian priors. A related program, RASCAL (Assessment Systems Corporation, 1989), estimates item parameters for the one-parameter logistic model in a manner similar to that of BICAL. BILOG (Mislevy & Bock, 1982) uses marginal maximum likelihood (which requires that some assumptions be made about population distributions) to estimate parameters of any of the three models on either a mainframe or a microcomputer.

One characteristic common to all IRT parameter estimation programs is that they must all arbitrarily define the zero point (i.e., center point value) of the θ/b continuum. In the two- and three-parameter models, the zero point is (typically) defined as the mean of the abilities of the sample whose data are used in the item parameter estimation. In the one-parameter model, sometimes the zero point is defined as the mean of the item difficulties of a set of items. This leads to a slight modification of the statement made earlier that the item parameters are invariant. Actually, the item parameters are invariant within a linear transformation.

If item parameters are estimated on two separate groups, then the resulting estimates in each group are centered on the mean ability of that group. Invariance within a linear transformation leads to the capability of transforming the item parameters in one group to the scale of another group, which is generally referred to as the linking problem (Vale, 1986). Similarly, the estimates in one group of individuals can be transformed onto the same scale as those of another group, thus facilitating the equating problem (Angoff, 1982) that has been the focus of much research in classical test theory applications.

Applications of IRT

Test Construction and Development

As was mentioned earlier, one of the primary advantages of IRT is that the theory provides explicit methods for test design and construction. To use IRT principles in test construction, first item parameter estimates must be obtained for each of the items that might potentially be used in a test. With item parameter estimates in hand, the information can be used to (1) aid in constructing a measuring instrument with the desired statistical properties and (2) assess the test's performance prior to its administration. Because a test is simply a collection of items, experiments can be carried out with different combinations of items until a test with the desired statistical characteristics is obtained.

The TIF (and its related function, the test response function) provide very powerful tools to the test constructor for the purpose of evaluating the properties of a test in terms of how well it measures across the latent continuum. The TIF is useful since it provides a measure of the precision at which the test will measure at each level of the latent trait; it can also be converted into a standard error of measurement function for the test.

Using this methodology in test design, items added to the test are items that will contribute more information in the areas along the latent continuum where that information is needed. Items that do not contribute to the desired test characteristics can be deleted from the test. The TIF can be examined after the addition or deletion of individual items, or subsets of items, to evaluate the effect on the resulting TIF.

Although it is not possible to convey here a detailed explanation of how TIFs can be used to construct a test with specific properties, a general idea can be given by explaining how to create a peaked test, a common form of test used in many achievement settings.

A peaked test is one in which the test needs to be constructed to measure well in a particular region of the latent trait continuum. Normally this situation arises when a cutoff score exists for sorting examinees into two categories—for example, masters and nonmasters. Such a test might be used to classify examinees on either side of a cutoff or mastery score. In developing a peaked test, an attempt should be made to produce a test whose TIF has its maximum value of information (i.e., provides the maximum precision or the smallest standard error of measurement) at, or very near, the cutoff score. In selecting items to create such a TIF, items are selected that have item difficulty values near the cutoff score (the cutoff score can be converted to the IRT scale through the test characteristic curve). The item discrimination values for selected items should be as large as possible since this will add to the test information in the vicinity of the cutoff score, and the lower asymptote parameters (c) should be as small as possible since large values of the c parameter tend to reduce information. Readers are referred to Hambleton and Swaminathan (1985), and van der Linden and Boekkooi-Timminga (1989) for a longer discussion of test development using item characteristic curves.

Equating and Linking

Equating is necessary when two forms of a test are available (e.g., Form A and Form B), which were not explicitly made to be parallel, and the scores from both tests need to be placed onto the same scale. When the scores from the two tests are referenced to the same scale, examinees may be compared though they may have taken different tests.

There are generally two kinds of equating—horizontal and vertical. Horizontal equating involves equating scores from tests of approximately the same difficulty level—for instance, tests within a single grade level. Vertical equating, on the other hand, involves equating scores from tests of different difficulty levels—for instance, across different grade levels. Classical test theory is replete with equating methodology (see, for example, Angoff, 1982) since the scores obtained for individuals are so dependent on the particular set of items used in a test. Because of this dependency, equating in CTT is difficult and sometimes requires that questionable assumptions be made about test scores.

In theory, IRT item parameters are invariant, which is to say that scores resulting from the administration of one set of items (e.g., Form A) are already on the same scale as scores resulting from the administration of a second set of items (e.g, Form B) and, therefore, no equating is necessary. In reality, this is not entirely true, because the true item parameters are unknown. Estimates must be used instead. In the process of item parameter estimation, the zero point (center) of the scale for item difficulties is arbitrarily centered on the mean of the θ estimates, or in the case of the Rasch model on the mean of the item difficulties, for the group of examinees whose data were used in the item parameter estimation process. In practice, therefore, the item parameters are invariant within a linear transformation. Thus, if two tests are composed of items whose item parameters were estimated separately, it cannot be certain that the item parameters are on the same scale because of possible ability level differences in the two groups on which item parameters were estimated.

To insure that the scores from the two tests are on the same scale, constants must be determined that provide the linear transformation by which the item parameters of one test can be shifted onto the same scale as the item parameters of the other test. Once this transformation has been applied, the scores from the two tests (based on the transformed item parameters for one of the tests) are on the same scale. Once the item parameter estimates of two sets of items are on the same scale, no score equating is necessary, since the estimates are on the same scale as the item difficulties.

Because equating is not technically a concern in IRT, a special term has been applied to the methodology for determining the constants for the linear transformation necessary to place two sets of parameters (and hence their scores) onto the same scale. In IRT terminology, *linking* refers to this process. (See Vale, 1986, for a discussion and examples of linking.) In general, linking procedures require that something be in common between the two tests. Either the two tests must share some common items, or some subset of examinees must have taken both tests or a third test which measures the same trait (referred to as an anchor test).

The capability of linking items onto a common scale in IRT, in turn, sets the stage for the development of item banks. In an item bank, large numbers of items measuring the same variable are stored together, along with their (linked) IRT item parameters. To construct a test from such a bank, a test constructor merely needs to select items according to the test specifications desired. When a second test is needed, for example to measure the same examinees at a later point in time, a new subset of pre-calibrated items is selected from the bank. This process can be repeated as needed for additional measurements.

The use of pre-calibrated item banks eliminates the need for the construction of parallel forms of tests, and makes possible the measurement of individuals at multiple points in time to measure change and growth. Van der Linden and others (1986), in a special issue of *Applied Psychological Measurement* on test item banking, explore a number of issues concerning the development and use of such item banks.

Adaptive Testing

An adaptive test is one in which a subset of items is selected from an item bank for administration to a particular individual based on his/her performance during the process of testing. In an adaptive test, an item (or set of items) is administered, a score is calculated, and another item (or set of items) is selected, based on the score from the previous item(s).

The first adaptive test was Alfred Binet's well-known test of intelligence (see Weiss, 1985), now known as the Stanford-Binet IQ test. Binet's test had all of the characteristics common to an adaptive test, namely, (1) a variable starting point, (2) an item selection rule, and (3) a termination rule. Adaptive testing (also called tailored testing) did not begin to emerge as a viable measurement alternative to the conventional paper-and-pencil test, however, until the advent of the computer age coupled with the development of IRT. The computer can be programmed to act as a test administrator—selecting an item, presenting the item to the examinee, evaluating and scoring the examinee's response, and selecting the next item based on the information obtained from the previous responses—a process that continues until some termination criterion is reached. Adaptive testing, when controlled by a computer, is usually referred to as computerized adaptive testing (CAT).

IRT-based CAT is based on the principle that items are to be selected that best measure a person at his/her ability level. In general, an item is selected that provides the most information at the examinee's current ability estimate. Then, based on his/her pattern of responses (correct/incorrect), including that item, his/her ability level is re-estimated and a new item is selected at the newly estimated ability level. This process is continued until some specified degree of precision of the examinee's ability level is reached (see Weiss & Kingsbury, 1984, for examples).

Most work involving CAT to date has been directed at ability tests with highly developed item pools. But, as microcomputer costs have declined, many CAT applications are spreading into other areas, including achievement testing and mastery (classification) testing (see, for example, chapter 1). Many more IRT-based computerized adaptive versions of existing instruments can be expected in the years to come. More details on CAT are presented in the Hambleton, Zaal, and Pieters chapter and Wainer (1990).

One of the major advantages of adaptive testing is a reduction in the number of items that need to be administered to an examinee in order to achieve an estimate of ability with some specified level of precision. This results from the fact that conventional tests present many items which provide little or no information about the examinee's ability level. By using adaptive item selection procedures, it is common to reduce the length of most tests by 50 percent or more (Weiss, 1985). Because items are selected to measure optimally the examinee in question, it also becomes possible to approximate equiprecise measurement—measurements that are of equal high quality—for all examinees. This is not possible with a conventional test in which all examinees take the same fixed set of items.

IRT-based adaptive testing procedures can also be used in classification or mastery testing by establishing a confidence interval around the examinee's ability estimate after the administration of each item. Items are administered to the examinee until his/her confidence interval (standard error band) no longer overlaps any cutoff score(s). Common use involves a 95 percent confidence interval around the estimated ability level (see Weiss & Kingsbury, 1984, for examples).

Other IRT Models

Nondichotomous Models

All of the IRT models discussed thus far (i.e., the one-, two-, and three-parameter models) are based on dichotomous item response data; that is, the items are scored *correct* or *incorrect*. There also are nondichotomous IRT models that can be used with multichotomous responses. These models are likely to be useful in work with rating scales (e.g., Likert scales), as well as in interest and attitude measurement.

A considerable amount of work on nondichotomous IRT models has been done by Fumiko Samejima. The three principal nondichotomous IRT test models are:

1. The nominal model (Bock, 1972; Samejima, 1972), which uses categorical item responses that are not on an ordered scale, such as the response categories of a multiple-choice test item.
2. The graded response model (Samejima, 1969), which can be applied to categorical item responses that can be ordered along a continuum, such as the responses to a five-category Likert rating scale.
3. The continuous model (Samejima, 1973), which is based on item responses that are numerical ratings on a continuous scale, such as a number from 0 to 100.

What results, in general, from these models are item category response functions, similar to IRFs, for each of the possible response options/alternatives. These response functions are then used in maximum likelihood procedures to estimate individual trait levels. The major advantage of these models is that they provide a coherent basis for the efficient design and scoring of a variety of different kinds of measuring instruments.

Multidimensional Models

All of the models referred to previously (including the nondichotomous models) assume the existence of a single latent trait that underlies performance on the test items. If an examinee's response to a test is a function of more than one trait, other models must be developed. This situation might occur in an arithmetic word problem in which the examinee must be able to read and comprehend the text of the word problem (verbal ability) and also be able to formulate and solve the computational aspects of the problem (numerical ability). A correct answer to such a problem likely implies high levels of both of the component abilities. An incorrect answer, however, can result from different combinations of ability levels on the two (or more) latent traits involved.

To date, the work in IRT has focused on constructing unidimensional instruments, partly because those models are sufficiently well developed that it is now practical, and also partly because most measurement instruments can be refined to meet the requirements of the unidimensional model. Reckase (1983, 1985) and others have developed multidimensional IRT models which assume that the response of an individual is dependent on his/her location on several latent traits. In general, these models result in an item response function which can, at least conceptually, be thought of as an item response surface located in $k + 1$ dimensions, where k is the number of latent traits assumed to underlie performance. Thus, the unidimensional model is really just the special case where $k = 1$ and the item response function can graphically be depicted in two dimensions (θ and the probability of a correct/keyed response). With two latent traits, the item response function is a surface which can be graphed in three dimensions (Trait 1, Trait 2, and the probability of a correct/keyed response). When the model moves beyond two dimensions it is no longer possible to depict the item response function graphically. Much more about multidimensional IRT models will be forthcoming in the coming years.

Summary

IRT comprises a family of measurement models that can be used for the design and analysis of a variety of psychological and educational measurement instruments. Although these mathematical models of test behavior have their roots in classical test theory, the strong assumptions they make provide the psychometrician with powerful models and methods capable of solving a variety of applied measurement problems. As research on these models and their estimation procedures continues, additional models and procedures will be developed, and a better understanding of the limitations and applications of the models and their technology will emerge. The net effect will be better practical tools for the measurement specialist and the solution of other applied problems that are as yet intractable.

References

Angoff, W. H. (1982). Summary and derivation of equating methods used at ETS. In P. W. Holland & D. R. Rubin (eds.), *Testing equating*. New York: Academic Press, pp. 55–69.

Assessment Systems Corporation. (1989). *User's manual for the MicroCAT Testing System*, (3rd ed.) St. Paul, MN: Author.

Birnbaum, A. (1968). Test scores, sufficient statistics, and the information structures of tests. In F. M. Lord & M. R. Novick, *Statistical theories of mental test scores*. Reading, MA: Addison-Wesley.

Bock, R. D. (1972). Estimating item parameters and latent ability when responses are scored in two or more nominal categories. *Psychometrika* 37:29–51.

Fisher, R. A. (1922). On the mathematical foundations of theoretical statistics. *Philosophical Transactions of the Royal Society of London (A)* 222:309–368.

Guttman, L. (1944). A basis for scaling qualitative data. *American Sociological Review* 9:139–150.

Hambleton, R. K. (1989). Principles and selected applications of item response theory. In R. Linn (ed.), *Educational measurement*, 3rd ed. New York: Macmillan, pp. 147–200.

Hambleton, R. K., & Swaminathan, H. (1985). *Item response theory: Principles and applications*. Norwell, MA: Kluwer Academic Publishers.

Hambleton, R. K., & Traub, R. E. (1973). Analysis of empirical data using two logistic latent trait models. *British Journal of Mathematical and Statistical Psychology* 26:195–211.

Harris, D. (1989). Comparison of 1-, 2-, and 3-parameter IRT models. *Educational Measurement: Issues and Practice* 8:35–44.

Harwell, M. R., Baker, F. B., & Zwarts, M. (1988). Item parameter estimation via marginal maximum likelihood and an EM algorithm: A didactic. *Journal of Educational Statistics* 13:243–271.

Lazarsfeld, P. F. (1950). The logical and mathematical foundation of latent structure analysis. In S. A. Stouffer, L. Guttman, E. A. Suchman, P. F. Lazarsfeld, S. A. Star, & J. A. Clausen (eds.), *Measurement and prediction: Studies in social psychology in World War II, Vol. IV*. New York: Wiley, 1966. (Originally published by Princeton University Press, 1950.)

Lord, F. M. (1952). *A theory of test scores* (Psychometric Monograph, No. 7). Psychometric Society.

——————. (1980). *Applications of item response theory to practical testing problems*. Hillsdale, NJ: Lawrence Erlbaum Associates.

Lord, F. M., & Novick, M. R. (1968). *Statistical theories of mental test scores*. Reading, MA: Addison-Wesley.

McBride, J. R. (1977). A brief overview of adaptive testing. In D. J. Weiss (ed.), *Applications of computerized adaptive testing* (Research Report 77–1). University of Minnesota, Department of Psychology, Psychometric Methods Program.

McDonald, R. P. (1985). *Factor analysis and related methods*. Hillsdale, NJ: Lawrence Erlbaum Associates.

Mislevy, R. J., & Bock, R. D. (1982). *BILOG: Maximum likelihood item analysis and test scoring with logistic models for binary items.* Chicago: International Educational Services.

Mislevy, R. J., & Stocking, M. L. (1989). A consumer's guide to LOGIST and BILOG. *Applied Psychological Measurement* 13:57–75.

Mosier, C. I. (1940). Psychophysics and mental test theory: Fundamental postulates and elementary theorems. *Psychological Review* 47:355–366.

Rasch, G. (1960/1980). *Probabilistic models for some intelligence and attainment tests.* Chicago: University of Chicago Press. (Originally published by The Danish Institute for Educational Research, Copenhagen, 1960.)

Reckase, M. D. (1983, April). *The definition of difficulty and discrimination for multidimensional item response theory models.* Paper presented at the meeting of the American Educational Research Association, Montreal, Canada.

————. (1985). The difficulty of test items that measure more than one dimension. *Applied Psychological Measurement* 9:401–422.

Samejima, F. (1969). Estimation of latent ability using a response pattern of graded scores (*Psychometric Monograph No. 17*). Psychometric Society.

————. (1972). A general model for free-response data (*Psychometric Monograph No. 18*). Psychometric Society.

————. (1973). Homogeneous case of the continuous response model. *Psychometrika* 38:203–219.

Swaminathan, H. (1983). Parameter estimation in item response models. In R. K. Hambleton (ed.), *Applications of item response theory.* Vancouver, BC: Educational Research Institute of British Columbia, pp. 24–44.

Vale, C. D. (1986). Linking item parameters onto a common scale. *Applied Psychological Measurement* 10:333–344.

van der Linden, W. J. (1986). The changing conception of measurement in education and psychology. *Applied Psychological Measurement* 10:325–332.

van der Linden, W. J., & Boekkooi-Timminga, E. (1989). A maximin model for test design with practical constraints. *Psychometrika* 54:237–247.

Wainer, H. (Ed.). (1990). *Computerized adaptive testing: A primer.* Hillsdale, NJ: Lawrence Erlbaum Associates.

Weiss, D. J. (1985). Adaptive testing by computer. *Journal of Consulting and Clinical Psychology* 53:774–789.

Weiss, D. J., & Kingsbury, G. G. (1984). Application of computerized adaptive testing to educational problems. *Journal of Educational Measurement* 21:361–375.

Wingersky, M. S., Barton, M. A., & Lord, F. M. (1982). *LOGIST User's Guide.* Princeton, NJ: Educational Testing Service.

Wright, B. D., & Mead, R. J. (1976). *BICAL: Calibrating rating scores with the Rasch model* (Research Memorandum No. 23). Chicago: Chicago Statistical Laboratory, Department of Education, University of Chicago.

4 ANALYSIS OF COVARIANCE STRUCTURES

H. Swaminathan

Research in the social and behavioral sciences often involves the formulation of theories that explain or predict phenomona of interest. These theories are operationalized in terms of models that specify relationships among the observed and hypothesized variables or constructs. Once a model is constructed, empirical evidence regarding the validity of the theory can be obtained by testing hypotheses based on the model. The validity of the theory is supported (but never proved) by the extent to which the hypotheses are confirmed. Similarly, the validity of psychological measures is assessed by constructing and testing hypotheses regarding relationships among variables and the underlying constructs.

When studying the relationships among *observable* variables, regression analysis may be appropriate. For example, if, in a validity study, it is hypothesized that variable A is related to variable B but not to variable C, then regression models relating variable A to B and variable A to C may be formulated, and the hypothesis that $\beta_{AB} = 0$ and $\beta_{AC} = 0$ tested to determine if the hypothesized relationships hold. (Here β_{AB} and β_{AC} are the regression coefficients for predicting A from B and A from C, respectively.) These hypotheses may also be tested in terms of the correlation coefficient, i.e., $\rho_{AB} = 0$, $\rho_{AC} = 0$. If it is determined that $\rho_{AC} \neq 0$, an explanation that variables A and C are not directly related but related through a common variable D may be forwarded, and this hypothesis tested.

This simple regression or correlational approach is not appropriate if more complex relationships are postulated. In a validity study reported by Muthen (1986), it is postulated that mathematics achievement for high school students in the spring is directly related to the mathematics achievement in the fall, while mathematics achievement in the fall is influenced by such background variables as family background, demographics, class type, and opportunity to learn. Two regression equations are needed to model these relationships; the first regression equation relates spring mathematics achievement to the fall mathematics achievement; a second regression equation relates the fall mathematics achievement to the background, demographics, and classroom variables. A simple approach in this case is to fit a regression equation for predicting fall mathematics achievement from the background variables, predict the fall mathematics achievement, and then use the predicted fall mathematics achievement scores as scores on the regressor for predicting spring mathematics achievement. Such two stage procedures are not strictly proper in this case since the regressor for predicting spring mathematics achievement, the predicted fall mathematics achievement, is measured with error. Analyses of such complex relationships require the formulation of "path models" and simultaneous estimation of all the parameters involved.

Regression or path analysis procedures described above are also not applicable when *unobservable* or *latent variables* are involved. In such situations, a "regression model" that relates the observed variables to the unobservable variables must be constructed, the coefficients estimated, and by studying these coefficients and testing hypotheses about them, appropriate conclusions are drawn. Since the "regressor" variables in this case are not observable, the variance-covariance matrix of the observable variables must be expressed in terms of the unknown "regression coefficients" and the variance-covariance matrix of the unobservable regressors. The unknown coefficients or parameters are then estimated and conclusions drawn about the appropriateness of the model that is postulated.

The factor analysis model is probably the most well-known example of a model in which relationships between observable variables and unobservable "factors" are of interest. In factor analysis a linear model is formulated that relates the observed variables to the underlying factors or constructs. These relationships are often stated in terms of the number of underlying factors or in terms of factor loadings which should be zeros. A factor analysis of the observed correlation matrix is carried out, the factor solution is rotated, and the rotated solution is examined to determine if the specified hypotheses are tenable. The hypotheses of interest are tested in a variety of ways; if the hypotheses relate to the number of factors, then the number of factors that explain a "sizeable" proportion of variance is examined to see if the hypothesis can be retained; if the hypothesis is stated in terms of factor loadings, then an arbitrary cutoff value (such as .3) is set, the loadings below this cutoff value are taken as zeros, and the tenability of the hypothesis is assessed.

The importance of factor analysis in testing stems from the fact that it is the most widely used method for assessing construct validity. For example, suppose that a test of spatial ability contains items that are purported to measure the constructs of spatial orientation and spatial visualization. It can then be hypothesized that a factor analysis of the matrix of inter-item correlations should yield two factors corresponding to the constructs of interest. One way to test this hypothesis is to follow the factor analysis procedure outlined above, i.e., examine the proportion of variance accounted for by the first two factors, and if this is considered sufficient, then proceed with the rotation of the factors and examine the magnitude of the factor loadings to determine if the first factor loads only on the items that measure spatial orientation and the second factor only on the items that measure spatial visualization. Such an approach is clearly not very satisfactory since subjective decisions are involved in every stage. A more reasoned approach is to postulate a linear model that relates the items only to those constructs measured by the items (items that do not relate to a construct are *restricted* to have zero loadings on that construct) and test the hypothesis that the model fits the data. This procedure is analogous to the path analysis procedure described previously.

While the "confirmatory" approach described above was suggested by Anderson and Rubin (1956) and Lawley (1958), it was not until Jöreskog (1966, 1967, 1969) and Jöreskog and Lawley (1968) provided a more systematic treatment of the approach and an efficient numerical procedure for the estimation of parameters that the method became practicable. Since then, as a result of the works by Bock and Bargmann (1966) and Jöreskog (1970, 1973), factor analysis has been recognized as a special case of covariance structure analysis. In covariance structure analysis, a model that specifies linear relationships between the observed variables and the latent variables is formulated; the parameters of interest are then estimated, and conclusions drawn by testing hypotheses concerning these parameters. A researcher who is concerned with validating a theory or a test can formulate models, dictated by the theory, that relate observations to underlying constructs, and, through an analysis of covariance structures, establish the validity of the theory or the test.

The purpose of this chapter is to provide an introduction to the analysis of covariance structures, review the various models, outline procedures that are currently available for the estimation of parameters, indicate procedures for testing hypotheses of interest, and, finally, demonstrate how various parametric specifications of the models can be used in investigations of test validity.

Linear Structural Relations Models

Linear structural relations (LISREL) (Bentler, 1980) models are the building blocks on which models for the analysis of covariance structures are based. These models consist of two components: a measurement component and a structural component. The measurement component specifies how the latent variables or hypothesized constructs are related to the observable variables. The structural component specifies the relationships or causal paths among the hypothesized constructs. Structural relations models are most clearly described using path diagrams. In drawing path diagrams, the following conventions prevail: (1) directly observable variables are enclosed in squares; (2) unobservable variables are enclosed in circles; (3) one-way arrows lead from "causes" to "effects"; and (4) double arrows represent noncausal relationships.

As an illustration, consider the well-known true score model, where the unobservable true score τ gives rise to the observable score y in the following manner:

$$y = \tau + e. \tag{1}$$

Here e is the random unobservable error (Lord & Novick, 1968). In terms of a path model, the relationship given in equation (1) can be diagrammed as in figure 4–1.

In the figure, the variable τ is a "causal" variable. Hence the arrows lead from τ to the observable variable y. The numbers above the arrows are the structural coefficients, assumed to be known in this case. If we extend the model in equation (1) to the more general model

$$y = \lambda\tau + e \tag{2}$$

the path diagram becomes that given in figure 4–2, with structural coefficient λ.

We now extend the model in equations (1) and (2) to the well-known common factor model, where $y_1, y_2, \ldots, y_p$ are p observable variables, $\eta_1, \eta_2, \ldots, \eta_r$ are the r common factors, and $e_1, e_2, \ldots, e_p$ are the unique factors. Then

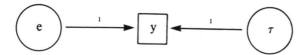

Figure 4–1.   Path Diagram for the True Score Model

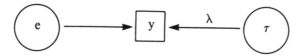

Figure 4–2.   Path Diagram for the Generalized True Score Model

$$y_i = \lambda_{i1}\,\eta_1 + \lambda_{i2}\,\eta_2 + \ldots + \lambda_{ir}\,\eta_r + u_i\,e_i, \qquad (i = 1, \ldots, p). \quad (3)$$

The common factors, $\eta_1, \eta_2, \ldots \eta_r$ and the unique factors, $e_1, e_2, \ldots, e_p$, are unobservable. If we assume that the common factors are orthogonal to each other and to the unique factors, then the model in equation (3) can be diagrammed as shown in figure 4–3.

The fact that there are no paths connecting $\eta_1, \eta_2, \ldots, \eta_r$ indicates that these causal variables are unrelated to each other. This situation corresponds to the common factors being orthogonal. If it is assumed that the factors are correlated, then the path diagram is modified by drawing double arrows from one factor to another.

In validity studies, it may often be necessary to postulate causal models where one set of observable variables $(y_1, \ldots, y_p)$ has $\eta_1, \ldots, \eta_r$ as causal variables, while another set of observable variables $(x_1, \ldots, x_q)$ has $\xi_1, \ldots, \xi_q$ as the causal variables. In addition, it may be appropriate to take $\xi_1, \ldots, \xi_q$ as the causal variables of $\eta_1, \ldots, \eta_r$. For the purposes of illustration, we will assume that there is only one η causal variable and only one ξ causal variable. The path diagram for this model is shown in figure 4–4.

According to the model given in figure 4–4, the measurement model for the observable variables $y_1, \ldots, y_p$ is

$$y_1 = \eta + \epsilon_1, \qquad (i = 1, \ldots, p). \quad (4)$$

Similarly, the measurement model for the x variables is

$$x_j = \xi + \delta_j, \qquad (j = 1, \ldots, q). \quad (5)$$

Thus η and ξ can be thought of as true scores, and the set i_1 and δ_j as errors. In addition, a causal relationship between the true scores η and ξ is postulated:

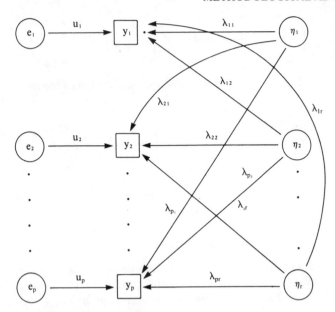

Figure 4–3.   Path Diagram for the Common Factor Model

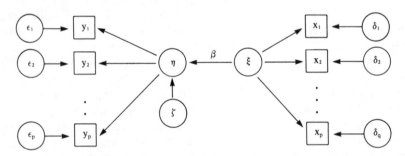

Figure 4–4.   Causal Model for a Validity Study

$$\eta = \gamma\xi + \zeta. \tag{6}$$

This last equation resembles the regression model for predicting η from ξ with regression coefficient γ and error ζ. In this case, however, η and ξ are not observable; they are related to the observable variables $(y_1, \ldots, y_p)$ and $(x_1, \ldots, x_q)$ in the manner described by equations (4) and (5). The fact that η and j are not observable makes regression analysis inappropriate. Note that in equations (4) and (5) the coefficients of η and ξ are unities, and this specification may be too restrictive. This restriction may be relaxed by introducing path coefficients in equations (4) and (5), and, if of interest, the hypothesis that these coefficients are unities can be tested.

Illustrations of the use of causal modelling in validation studies are given by Bentler and Speckart (1979) and Wheaton, Muthen, Alwin, and Summers (1977). An excellent example of a causal model is given by the theory of attitude-behavior relations of Fishbein and Ajzen (1975). In this model, the constructs Initial Behavior (B_1), Future Behavior (B_2), Subjective Norms (SN), Intentions (I), and Attitudes (A) are related in the manner shown in figure 4–5. Thus, in the measurement part of the model, the constructs B_1, B_2, SN, I, and A are considered to be factors. However, in contrast to the exploratory factor model (figure 4–3), not all observed variables are hypothesized to be related to each of the factors or constructs. Thus, the measurement model can be thought of as a confirmatory factor analysis model (Jöreskog, 1969). The hypothesized causal relationships among the constructs, however, impose a structure on the constructs, and hence a straight confirmatory factor analysis is inappropriate. The entire model, involving both measurement and structural components, must be tested. The goodness-of-fit of this model to the data provides evidence of the validity of the theory as well as the construct validity of the instruments. We shall return to the issue of statistical fit later.

The study carried out by Wheaton and associates (1977), while not intended as a construct validation study, serves to illustrate the use of causal modelling in validating an instrument. In studying the relationships among Anomie, Powerlessness, Education, and Socioeconomic Index, the authors postulated the model given in figure 4–6. (It should be noted that the model presented is a simplified version of the more elaborate model given by Wheaton and associates, 1977.) According to the measurement model, Anomie and Powerlessness are measures of the construct Alienation, while Education and SEI are measures of the construct SES. According to the structural part, Alienation has Socioeconomic Status as a causal variable. These relations are diagrammed in figure 4–6. In the absence of the structural relationship between Alienation and SES, the construct validity of the measures Anomie, Powerlessness, Education, and SEI can be assessed through confirmatory factor analysis. With the inclusion of the structural component, the goodness-of-fit of the model to the data serves as partial evidence of the construct validity of the instruments and also the validity of the theory.

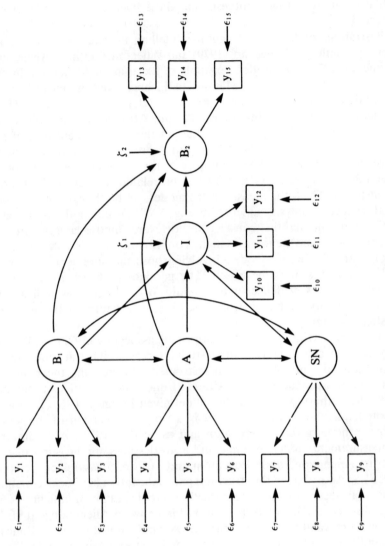

Figure 4–5. Model for Attitude-Behavior Relations

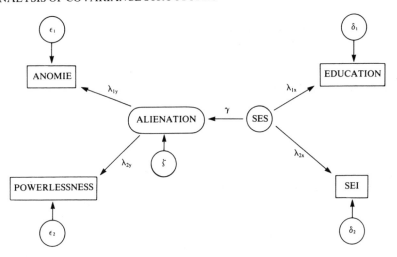

Figure 4-6.   A Causal Model for Relating Alienation to SES

Specification of the Covariance Structure

The models specified in figure 4-1 through 4-6 express the relationships between observable and unobservable variables. The parameters of interest are the path coefficients, which are indicators of relationships within and between the observable and unobservable variables, and the variance-covariance matrix of the unobservable variables. In order to estimate the parameters, the models given in the last section must be expressed in terms of the variance-covariance matrix of the observable variables.

The true-score model given in equation (1),

$$x = \tau + e,$$

gives rise to the variance structure

$$\sigma_x^2 = \sigma_r^2 + \sigma_e^2, \tag{7}$$

where σ_x^2 is the variance of the observable variable x, σ_r^2 is the variance of the true score, and σ_e^2 is the error variance. In deriving equation (7), we have assumed that the covariance between τ and e is zero, i.e., $\text{cov}(\tau, e)$ $= E[(\tau - \mu_r)\,(e - \mu_e)] = 0$. Here $\text{cov}(\tau, e)$ indicates the covariance between τ and e, $\mu_r = E(\tau)$, and $\mu e = E(e)$. The problem is that of estimating σ_r^2 and σ_e^2 when σ_x^2 is given.

In the model given by equation (2), τ is replaced by $\lambda\tau$, where λ is a fixed but unknown constant and not a random variable. If we denote the variance of a random variable u as $V(u)$, where

$$V(u) = E[u - E(u)]^2,$$

then using the well-known relationship

$$V(ku) = k^2 V(u),$$

we have

$$\sigma_x^2 = \lambda^2 \sigma_r^2 + \sigma_e^2. \tag{8}$$

The parameters that must be estimated are λ, σ_r^{22}, and σ_e^2.

The factor model given by equation (3) is the multivariate analog of the model given in equation (2). In order to derive the equations necessary for estimating the parameters, we must express the variance-covariance matrix of the vector of observable variables in terms of the parameters that specify the relationships between the observable and unobservable variables. Let $V(u)$ be the variance-covariance matrix of the $(kx1)$ random vector u. By definition,

$$V(u) = E[u - E(u)] [u - E(u)]',$$

where $'$ indicates the transposition operation. It follows that

$$V(a'u) = a'V(u) \, a,$$

where a is a $(kx1)$ vector, and

$$V(Au) = AV(u)A',$$

where A is a (mxk) matrix of rank m.

The factor model given by equation (2) can be expressed using matrices as

$$y = \Lambda f + e. \tag{9}$$

If we assume that f and e are uncorrelated, i.e., the covariance between f and e is zero, then

$$V(y) = \Lambda V(f) \Lambda' + V(e).$$

Denoting the variance-covariance matrices $V(y)$ as Σ and $V(e)$ as Θ, where Θ is a diagonal matrix whose elements are the unique variances, and setting $V(f) = I$, the covariance structure for the orthogonal factor model becomes

$$\Sigma = \Lambda \Lambda' + \Theta. \tag{10}$$

In the oblique factor case, the assumption that $V(f) = I$ is relaxed. If we denote $V(f) = \Phi$, the variance-covariance matrix of the factors, then the covariance structure for the oblique factor model is

$$\Sigma = \Lambda\Phi\Lambda' + \Theta. \tag{11}$$

Clearly, model (10) is a special case of model (11), and model (8) is a special case of model (10). Thus the model given by equation (11) is a model of some generality.

To derive the covariance structure for the models given in figures 4–1 through 4–6, the relationships between observable and unobservable variables must first be specified. To illustrate the principles involved, the model in figure 4–5 is considered. In this model, the observable variables $y_1, \ldots, y_{15}$ are related to the unobservable variables $\eta_1, \ldots, \eta_5$ (where $\eta_1 = B_1$, $\eta_2 = A$, $\eta_3 = SN$, $\eta_4 = I$, and $\eta_5 = B_2$) in the following manner:

$$
\begin{bmatrix} y_1 \\ y_2 \\ y_3 \\ y_4 \\ y_5 \\ y_6 \\ y_7 \\ y_8 \\ y_9 \\ y_{10} \\ y_{11} \\ y_{12} \\ y_{13} \\ y_{14} \\ y_{15} \end{bmatrix} =
\begin{bmatrix}
\lambda_{11} & 0 & 0 & 0 & 0 \\
\lambda_{21} & 0 & 0 & 0 & 0 \\
\lambda_{31} & 0 & 0 & 0 & 0 \\
0 & \lambda_{42} & 0 & 0 & 0 \\
0 & \lambda_{52} & 0 & 0 & 0 \\
0 & \lambda_{62} & 0 & 0 & 0 \\
0 & 0 & \lambda_{73} & 0 & 0 \\
0 & 0 & \lambda_{83} & 0 & 0 \\
0 & 0 & \lambda_{93} & 0 & 0 \\
0 & 0 & 0 & \lambda_{104} & 0 \\
0 & 0 & 0 & \lambda_{114} & 0 \\
0 & 0 & 0 & \lambda_{124} & 0 \\
0 & 0 & 0 & 0 & \lambda_{135} \\
0 & 0 & 0 & 0 & \lambda_{145} \\
0 & 0 & 0 & 0 & \lambda_{155}
\end{bmatrix}
\begin{bmatrix} \eta_1 \\ \eta_2 \\ \eta_3 \\ \eta_4 \\ \eta_5 \end{bmatrix} + e. \tag{12}
$$

Using matrix notation, we obtain

$$Y = \Lambda\eta + e, \tag{13}$$

so that $\Sigma = V(y)$ is given as

$$\Sigma = \Lambda V(\eta)\Lambda' + V(e) \tag{14}$$

$$= \Lambda V(\eta)\Lambda' + \Psi. \tag{15}$$

The covariance structure model given above resembles the factor model given by (11). However, the structural component in figure 4–5 introduces the following relationships among the variables:

$$\eta_4 = \gamma_{41}\,\eta_1 + \gamma_{42}\,\eta_2 + \gamma_{43}\,\eta_3 + \zeta_1$$

$$\eta_5 = \gamma_{51}\,\eta_1 + \gamma_{52}\,\eta_2 + \gamma_{54}\,\eta_4 + \zeta_2. \tag{16}$$

Thus

$$
\begin{bmatrix} \eta_1 \\ \eta_2 \\ \eta_3 \\ \eta_4 \\ \eta_5 \end{bmatrix}
=
\begin{bmatrix}
0 & 0 & 0 & 0 \\
0 & 0 & 0 & 0 \\
0 & 0 & 0 & 0 \\
\gamma_{41} & \gamma_{42} & \gamma_{43} & 0 \\
\gamma_{51} & \gamma_{52} & 0 & \gamma_{54}
\end{bmatrix}
\begin{bmatrix} \eta_1 \\ \eta_2 \\ \eta_3 \\ \eta_4 \\ \eta_5 \end{bmatrix}
+ \zeta, \tag{17}
$$

or, equivalently,

$$\eta = B\eta + \zeta. \tag{18}$$

Alternatively, the model given above can be expressed as

$$(I - B)\eta = \zeta, \tag{19}$$

or

$$\eta = (I - B)^{-1}\,\zeta \tag{20}$$

$$= H\zeta, \tag{21}$$

where

$$H = (I - B)^{-1}.$$

Hence, the variance-covariance matrix of η can be expressed as

$$V(\eta) = HV\,(\zeta)\,H'$$

$$= H\,\Psi\,H'. \tag{22}$$

The variance-covariance matrix of ζ is a (5×5) matrix, assumed to be diagonal. As a result of the relationship among the η's,

$$V(\zeta_1) = V(\zeta_2) = V(\zeta_3) = 0.$$

Thus Ψ is a diagonal matrix with two nonzero elements corresponding to the values of ζ_4 and ζ_5. Substituting $V(\eta)$ given in equations (22) and (15), we obtain the covariance structure

$$\Sigma = \Lambda(H\,\Psi\,H')\,\Lambda' + \Theta. \tag{23}$$

Clearly, the model given in equation (23) is more general than the factor model given in equation (11). In fact, the factor model in equation (11) is a special case of equation (23) and is obtained by setting $H = I$, the identity matrix, and letting $\Psi = \Phi$.

For the model given in figure 4–6, we derive the covariance structure by denoting Anomie as y_1, Powerlessness as y_2, Education as x_1, SEI as x_2, Alienation as η, and SES as ζ. Thus,

$$\begin{bmatrix} y_1 \\ y_2 \end{bmatrix} = \begin{bmatrix} \gamma_{1y} \\ \gamma_{2y} \end{bmatrix} \eta + \epsilon, \tag{24}$$

$$\begin{bmatrix} x_1 \\ x_2 \end{bmatrix} = \begin{bmatrix} \lambda_{1x} \\ \lambda_{2x} \end{bmatrix} \xi + \delta, \tag{25}$$

and

$$\eta = \gamma \xi + \zeta. \tag{26}$$

The variance-covariance matrix Σ_y of y_1 and y_2 is

$$\Sigma_y = \Lambda_y \, V(\eta) \, \Lambda_y' + \Theta_\epsilon, \tag{27}$$

while for x_1 and x_2,

$$\Sigma_x = \Lambda_x V(\xi)\Lambda_x' + \Phi_\delta. \tag{28}$$

From the relationship between η and ξ we obtain

$$V(\eta) = \gamma V(\xi)\gamma' + \Psi$$
$$= \gamma\Phi\gamma' + \Psi. \tag{29}$$

Finally, the covariance matrix of x of y, Σ_{xy}, is

$$\Sigma_{xy} = \Lambda_x \, \text{cov}(\xi, \eta) \, \Lambda_{y'} + \text{cov}(\epsilon, \delta). \tag{30}$$

Now

$$\text{cov}(\eta, \xi) = V(\xi)\gamma + \text{cov}(\zeta, \xi). \tag{31}$$

If we assume that $\text{cov}(\zeta, \xi) = 0$, and $\text{cov}(\epsilon, \delta) = 0$, then

$$\Sigma_{xy} = \Lambda_x\Phi\gamma' \, \Lambda_y'. \tag{32}$$

although γ is a scalar in the above expression, it is treated as a matrix for the sake of generality.

Combining all the results, we obtain

$$\Sigma_y = \Lambda_y \, [\gamma\Phi\gamma' + \Psi] \, \Lambda_{y'} + \Theta_\varepsilon, \tag{33}$$

$$\Sigma_x = \Lambda_x\Phi\Lambda_x' + \Theta\delta, \tag{34}$$

and

$$\Sigma_{xy} = \Lambda_x\Phi\gamma' \, \Lambda_{y'}. \tag{35}$$

It is consistent and customary to write the variance-covariance matrix of the observable variables y and x as the variance-covariance matrix of the joint set, y, x. In this case,

$$\Sigma = \begin{bmatrix} \Sigma_y & \Sigma_{yx} \\ \Sigma_{xy} & \Sigma_x \end{bmatrix} = \begin{bmatrix} \Lambda_y[\gamma\Phi\gamma' + \Psi]\Lambda_y' + \Theta_\epsilon & \Lambda_y\gamma'\Phi\Lambda_x' \\ \Lambda_x\Phi\gamma'\Lambda_y' & \Lambda_x\Phi\Lambda_x' + \Theta_\delta \end{bmatrix}. \quad (36)$$

The covariance structure model given in equation (36) can be combined with that given in equation (23) to yield a model of great flexibility. The purpose of defining a model of such generality and flexibility is to allow the development of a unified method for the estimation of parameters and for testing the fit of the model to the data. There are, however, several general models for the analysis of covariance structures; these models are reviewed in the next section.

Models for the Analysis of Covariance Structures

For some 40 years, the principal model for studying the relationships between variables has been the linear factor analysis model stemming from the work of Pearson, and further developed by Spearman, Burt, Thurstone, and others. Since the work of Bock and Bargmann (1966), and the work of Jöreskog (1970, 1973), this model has come to be recognized as a special case of a class of models for the analysis of covariance structures. The pioneering work of Bock and Bargmann (1966) was an attempt to provide a model that expressed the relationship between one or more observable variables and a linear combination of unobservable random variables, and to develop a general procedure for the estimation of the parameters associated with the model.

In developing their model, Bock and Bargmann (1966) assumed that the $(nx1)$ vector of observed scores y_i of the i'th subject takes the form

$$y_i = \mu + Ax_i + e_i, \qquad (i = 1, \ldots, N), \qquad (37)$$

where μ is a vector mean of the variables in the population of subjects. A is a (nxr) matrix of known coefficients of the linear functions that express the relationship between the manifest and the latent variables, x_i is the $(rx1)$ random vector of the "latent" scores of the i'th subject, with mean vector O, and e_i is the random vector of measurement errors, with mean vector O and (nxn) dispersion matrix Γ.

The structural model for the dispersion matrix Σ implied by the linear relationship (37) is assumed to be

$$\Sigma = A\Phi A' + \Gamma, \qquad (38)$$

where Φ is the (rxr) dispersion matrix of x_i.

Bock and Bargmann specify three distinct cases of equation (38), as follows:

Case 1

The latent variables are uncorrelated, i.e.,

$$\Phi = \text{Diag}[\phi_1, \ldots, \phi_r],$$

and the errors are uncorrelated and homoscedastic, i.e.,

$$S = \gamma I,$$

where I is the $(n \times n)$ identity matrix and ξ is the common error variance. Thus,

$$\Sigma = A\Phi A' + \gamma I. \tag{39}$$

Case 2

The latent variables are uncorrelated and the errors are uncorrelated but not assumed to be homoscedastic, i.e.,

$$\Gamma = \text{Diag}[\gamma_1, \ldots, \gamma_n]. \tag{40}$$

Case 3

The latent variables are uncorrelated, and the errors are uncorrelated and homoscedastic; however, the observations are assumed to be multiplied by unknown scale factors represented by a $(n \times n)$ diagonal matrix G, so that in this case the covariance matrix of the observations has the structure.

$$G\Sigma G = G(A\Phi A' + \gamma I)G. \tag{41}$$

In each of these three cases, A is known and the elements of Φ, Γ, and (in the last) G appear as parameters to be estimated.

Although general in nature, the models (39), (40), and (41) are not flexible enough to contain a wide range of covariance structural models as special cases. In generalizing models (39), (40), and (41), Jöreskog (1970) and Wiley, Schmidt, and Bramble (1973) have suggested a model of greater flexibility and generality. The structural model suggested by Jöreskog for the dispersion matrix assumes the form

$$\Sigma = B(\Lambda\Phi\Lambda' + \Psi)B' + \Theta. \tag{42}$$

The $(n \times m)$ matrix B, the $(m \times p)$ matrix Λ, the $(p \times p)$ symmetric matrix Φ, the $(m \times m)$ diagonal matrix Ψ are the parameter matrices, either prescribed or to be estimated from the data.

The generality of equation (42) is evident when, for example, we set $B = I$, the identity matrix; $\Lambda = A$; $\Phi = \Phi$; $\Psi = \gamma I$; and $\Theta = 0$ to obtain equation (39). Similarly, setting $B = I$; $\Lambda = A$; $\Phi = \Phi$; $\Psi = \Gamma$; and $\Theta = 0$, we obtain the model given in equation (40). To obtain equation (41), we set $B = G$; $\Lambda = A$; $\Phi = \Phi$; $\Psi = \gamma I$, and $\Theta = 0$. The common factor analysis model, where the dispersion matrix Σ has the structure

$$\Sigma = \Lambda \Phi \Lambda' + \Psi, \tag{43}$$

with the matrix Ψ assumed to be diagonal, is a special case of equation (42). It is obtained by setting $B = I$ and $\Theta = 0$ in equation (42). In making provision for the parameter matrices to be either hypothesized or estimated from the data, and by providing a procedure for the estimation of parameters, Jöreskog has made the model given by equation (42) extremely flexible and general.

It is possible to conceive of models which cannot be obtained as special cases of the model given by equation (42). The longitudinal factor models given by Corballis and Traub (1970) and Corballis (1973) can be obtained by setting $B = I$ and $\Psi = 0$ in equation (42). However, the matrix Θ specified in these longitudinal factor models is, in general, not diagonal, and hence cannot be obtained as a special case of equation (42). A similar situation prevails with certain structural equation models (to be discussed later) that arise in econometric theory. Thus, models that take into account the nondiagonal nature of Ψ and Θ given in equation (42) are necessary.

McDonald (1969) and consequently McDonald and Swaminathan (1972) presented a covariance-structure model that permits Ψ and Θ to be non-diagonal and outlined procedures for estimating the parameters in such models. Even this model was not general enough to handle the models that combine those given in figures 4–5 and 4–6.

Jöreskog (1973, 1978) recognized that a linear structural equation model of the type

$$\eta = B\eta + \Gamma \xi + \zeta, \tag{44}$$

which arises in the context of econometrics, combined with measurement models for η and ξ, yields a covariance structure model of great generality. The measurement models specified by Jöreskog are

$$y = \Lambda_y \eta + \epsilon \tag{45}$$

and

$$x = \Lambda_x \xi + \delta, \tag{46}$$

where y and x are observable variables. Models (45) and (46) imply that η

and ξ are the "common factors" of the variables y and x. The structural model (44) specifies a "causal" relationship between the variables η and ξ.

As an example of the model specified by equations (44) to (46), consider the model for attitude-behavior relations (figure 4–5). To obtain an alternative formulation of this model, we let the variables B_1, A, and SN be denoted as ξ_1, ξ_2, and ξ_3, and I and B_2 as η_1 and η_2. With this notation, the model in figure 4–5 can be diagrammed as given in figure 4–7.

According to the model in figure 4–7,

and

$$
\begin{bmatrix} y_1 \\ y_2 \\ y_3 \\ y_4 \\ y_5 \\ y_6 \end{bmatrix} = \begin{bmatrix} \lambda_{11y} & 0 \\ \lambda_{21y} & 0 \\ \lambda_{31y} & 0 \\ 0 & \lambda_{42y} \\ 0 & \lambda_{43y} \\ 0 & \lambda_{44y} \end{bmatrix} \begin{bmatrix} \eta_1 \\ \eta_2 \end{bmatrix} + \begin{bmatrix} \epsilon_1 \\ \epsilon_2 \\ \epsilon_3 \\ \epsilon_4 \\ \epsilon_5 \\ \epsilon_6 \end{bmatrix}. \tag{47}
$$

$$
\begin{bmatrix} x_1 \\ x_2 \\ x_3 \\ x_4 \\ x_5 \\ x_6 \\ x_7 \\ x_8 \\ x_9 \end{bmatrix} = \begin{bmatrix} \lambda_{11x} & 0 & 0 \\ \lambda_{21x} & 0 & 0 \\ \lambda_{31x} & 0 & 0 \\ 0 & \lambda_{42x} & 0 \\ 0 & \lambda_{52x} & 0 \\ 0 & \lambda_{62x} & 0 \\ 0 & 0 & \lambda_{73x} \\ 0 & 0 & \lambda_{83x} \\ 0 & 0 & \lambda_{93x} \end{bmatrix} \begin{bmatrix} \xi_1 \\ \xi_2 \\ \xi_3 \end{bmatrix} + \begin{bmatrix} \delta_1 \\ \delta_2 \\ \delta_3 \\ \delta_4 \\ \delta_5 \\ \delta_6 \\ \delta_7 \\ \delta_8 \\ \delta_9 \end{bmatrix}. \tag{48}
$$

The causal relationship between η and ξ can be expressed as

$$\eta_1 = \gamma_{11}\xi_1 + \gamma_{12}\xi_2 + \zeta_1$$
$$\eta_2 = \beta_{11}\eta_1 + \gamma_{22}\xi_2 + \zeta_2.$$

Using matrix notation, the above model can be written as

$$
\begin{bmatrix} \eta_1 \\ \eta_2 \end{bmatrix} = \begin{bmatrix} 0 & 0 \\ \beta_{11} & 0 \end{bmatrix} \begin{bmatrix} \eta_1 \\ \eta_2 \end{bmatrix} \tag{49}
$$
$$
+ \begin{bmatrix} \gamma_{11} & \gamma_{12} & 0 \\ 0 & \gamma_{22} & 0 \end{bmatrix} \begin{bmatrix} \xi_1 \\ \xi_2 \\ \xi_3 \end{bmatrix} + \begin{bmatrix} \zeta_1 \\ \zeta_2 \\ \zeta_3 \end{bmatrix},
$$

i.e.,

$$\eta = B\eta + \Gamma\xi + \zeta.$$

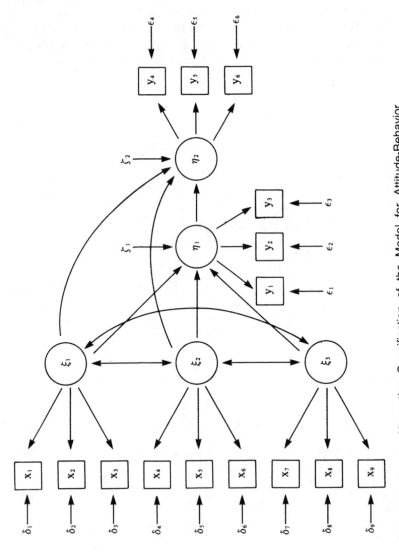

Figure 4—7. An Alternative Specification of the Model for Attitude-Behavior Relations

This alternative formulation of the model in figure 4–5 illustrates (1) the generality of the model given by equations (44) to (46), and (2) the different ways in which a model may be formulated. (Compare the two formulations of the attitude-behavior relations model, equations (13) and (18), with equations (44) to (46).) While one formulation may appear to be more complex than the other, the final results are identical.

The model given by equations (44) to (46) leads to the following covariance structures:

$$\Sigma_x = \Lambda_x V(\xi)\Lambda_x' + \Theta_\delta, \qquad (50)$$

$$= \Lambda_x \Phi \Lambda_x' + \Theta_\delta, \qquad (51)$$

$$\Sigma_y = \Lambda_y V(\eta)\Lambda_y' + \Theta_\varepsilon, \qquad (52)$$

and

$$\Sigma_{xy} = \Lambda_x \left[\text{cov}(\xi, \eta)\right] \Lambda_y'. \qquad (53)$$

Since

$$(I - B)\eta = \Gamma\xi + \zeta,$$

$$V(\eta) = (I - B)^{-1} \Gamma\Phi\Gamma' (I - B')^{-1} + \Psi \qquad (54)$$

and

$$\text{cov}(\xi, \eta) = \Lambda_x \Phi\Gamma' (I - B')^{-1} \Lambda_y'. \qquad (55)$$

Combining these structures, we obtain the general structural model

$$\Sigma = \begin{bmatrix} \Sigma_y & \Sigma_{yx} \\ \Sigma_{xy} & \Sigma_x \end{bmatrix} = \begin{bmatrix} \Lambda_y[A\Gamma\Phi\Gamma'A' + \Psi]\Lambda' + \Theta_\epsilon & \Lambda_y A\Lambda\Phi'\Lambda_y' \\ \Lambda_x\Phi\Gamma'A'\Lambda_y' & \Lambda_x\Phi\Lambda_x' + \Theta_\delta \end{bmatrix}$$
$$(56)$$

where $A = (I - B)^{-1}$. This model is currently the most widely used model for the analysis of covariances structures, or LISREL systems. A computer program for the analysis using the above model is available (see the section on computer programs).

The seemingly simple model for attitude-behavior relations gives rise to the formidable covariance structure model given in equation (56). The matrices Λ_x and Λ_y are those given by equations (47) and (48). The matrices B and Γ are given in equation (49). Thus, to validate the theory relating attitudes to behavior, it is necessary to establish that the variances and covariances among the observed variables have the structure specified by equation (56).

If we let

$$F_1 = \begin{bmatrix} \Lambda_y & 0 \\ 0 & \Lambda_x \end{bmatrix}, F_2 = \begin{bmatrix} (I-B)^{-1} & 0 \\ 0 & I \end{bmatrix}, F_3 = \begin{bmatrix} \Gamma \\ I \end{bmatrix},$$

$$G = \Phi,$$

$$H_1 = \begin{bmatrix} \Psi & 0 \\ 0 & 0 \end{bmatrix}, H_2 = \begin{bmatrix} \Theta_\varepsilon & 0 \\ 0 & \Theta_\delta \end{bmatrix},$$

it can be seen that the model given in equation (54) can be expressed as

$$\Sigma = F_1 (F_2 F_3 G F_3' F_2' + H_1) F_1' + H_2. \tag{57}$$

The model given in equation (57) is intuitively appealing in that it resembles a hierarchical factor analysis model; at the first level, the variance-covariance matrix among observed variables is given by the model

$$\Sigma = F_1 \Phi_1 F_1' + H_1$$

where Φ_1 is the variance-covariance matrix of the factors. At the second level, the variance-covariance matrix Φ_1 itself appears to possess a structure, i.e.,

$$\Phi_1 = F_2 \Phi_2 F_2' + H_2.$$

Finally, at the third level, the variance-covariance matrix of the second order factors appears to have the structure

$$\Phi_2 = F_3 G F_3.$$

With this formulation, it can be seen that the model in equation (57) is an obvious extension of the original model of Jöreskog given by equation (42).

Despite the apparent generality of the model in equation (57), it is not general enough to handle certain applications. Swaminathan (1984) formulated a model for longitudinal factor analysis where

$$\Sigma = F \Delta T \Delta^{-1} \Psi \Delta^{-1} T' F' + U. \tag{58}$$

In this model, F, Δ, Ψ, and U are parameter matrices to be estimated, and T is a constant matrix. Clearly, this model cannot be obtained as a special case of the model in equation (57).

In order to remedy the situation, Bentler (1976) and, independently, McDonald (1978) have presented more general models for the analysis of covariance structures that include model (58) as a special case. The McDonald model for covariance structure analysis (COSAN) is given as

$$\Sigma = \left(\prod_{j=1}^{m} F_j \right) P \left(\prod_{j=1}^{m} F_j \right), \tag{59}$$

where F_j is of order $(n_j - 1 \times n_j)$, P is symmetric of order n_m. The model given by Bentler (1976) has the form

$$\Sigma = \sum_{j=0}^{m} \left(\prod_{i=1}^{j} A_i \right) L_j \left(\prod_{i=1}^{j} \right)' \tag{60}$$

where the matrices A_i are defined like the F_j in equation (59) and L_j are defined like P. McDonald (1978) has shown that the model (60) can be obtained from equation (59) by writing

$$F_j = \begin{bmatrix} A_j & I & 0 \\ 0 & 0 & 0 \end{bmatrix},$$

with identity matrices of appropriate orders, and

$$P = \begin{bmatrix} L_m & 0 & \cdots & 0 \\ 0 & L_{m-1} & \cdots & 0 \\ \cdot & & \cdot & \\ \cdot & & & \cdot \\ \cdot & & & L_0 \\ 0 & & & \cdot \end{bmatrix}.$$

Although these models appear unwieldy, they yield results that are applicable to a greater variety of structural models than that given by the model in equation (57).

It should be noted that the above models are appropriate for studying relationships among continuous variables. More recently, Muthen (1984) has developed a linear structural model, similar to that proposed by Jöreskog (1978), for the analysis of continuous as well as discrete data.

Identification of the Structure

A basic problem that arises with the structural models above is that the parameter matrices $[B, \Gamma, \Phi, \Psi, \Lambda_x, \Lambda_y$ in model (57); F_j and P in model (59); A_i, L_j in model (60)] may not exist such that the relationship given by equation (59) holds. Alternatively, these matrices may exist but not be unique. The second problem, which is the more important of the two, is termed the *identification problem* (Wiley, 1973).

For the sake of simplicity, we shall discuss the problem of identifying the structure in terms of the structural model of Jöreskog (1973) given in equation (46). In this case, the matrix B can be replaced by BT_1^{-1}, Λ by $T_1 \Lambda T_2^{-1}$, and Φ by $T_2 \Phi T_2'$, where T_1 and T_2 are nonsingular matrices. Hence, there is a great deal of indeterminacy in the structural model. In order to remove this indeterminacy and to obtain unique solutions, it is necessary to impose restrictions on the parameter matrices. The total number of equations, as given by the distinct elements of Σ, is $n(n + 1)/2$.

If r is the total number of parameters to be estimated, then a minimal condition for the structure to be identified is

$$n(n + 1)/2 > r.$$

The identifiability of parameters becomes a crucial issue when estimating the parameters. The maximum likelihood estimates, which are consistent under usual conditions, will not be consistent when the parameters are not identified. In addition, the test statistic for testing the hypothesis that the structural model given by equations (57), (59), and (60) is tenable has the x^2 distribution (asymptotically) with $\{n(n + 1)/2 - r\}$ degrees of freedom, where r is the number of identifiable parameters. Swaminathan and Algina (1977) have also shown that in order for the estimates of the parameters to be scale invariant, the identification conditions must also be scale invariant. Thus the problem of identification of parameters becomes a central issue in the analysis of covariance structures.

As an example, consider the model given in figure 4–5. The total number of observable variables is $n = 15$. The number of parameters to be estimated is: 15, corresponding to the λ's; 6 for the paths leading from B_1, A, and SN to I and B_2; 6 for the interrelationships among B_1, A, and SN; 2 corresponding to the error variance for predicting I from B_1, A, and SN, and for predicting B_2 from I, A, and B_1; and 15 error variances corresponding to ϵ_1 to ϵ_{15}. The total number of parameters is, therefore, $15 + 6 + 6 + 2 + 15 = 44$. Since $n(n + 1)/2 = 120$, it appears that the model is identified. However, this is not the case. Since

$$y_1 = \lambda_{11} \eta_1 + \epsilon_1,$$

it follows that

$$\sigma_{y1}^2 = \lambda_{11}^2 V(\eta_1) + V(\epsilon_1).$$

Since multiplying λ_{11} by a constant and dividing $V(\eta_1)$ by the same constant will leave σ_{y1}^2 unchanged, there is an indeterminacy in the model. We therefore must fix five of the λ's to be unities. This reduces the number of parameters from 44 to 39. With this restriction on the parameters, the model is identified.

For the model given in figure 4–6, the number of observable variables is 4. Hence, $n(n + 1)/2 = 10$. The number of parameters is 10 (4 λ's, 1 γ, and 5 residual error variances). The model is clearly not identified; λ_{1y} and λ_{1x} must be restricted to be unities in order to minimally identify the model.

The problem of identification is a very complex one and has not been solved for the general models given in this chapter. Determining if a specific model is identified must proceed along the lines indicated in the examples discussed above. Further examples and some general guidelines are, however, given by Algina (1980), Jöreskog (1973), and Jöreskog and Sörbom (1984), and the reader is referred to these authors for more detail on the problem of identification.

Estimation of Parameters

In order to estimate the parameters in the covariance structure models, we shall assume that a random sample of N observations $Y_1, \ldots, Y_N$ is available. If Y is the sample mean vector, the sample variance-covariance matrix S is given by

$$S = \frac{1}{(N-1)} \sum_{i=1}^{N} (Y_i - \bar{Y})(Y_i - \bar{Y})'.$$

The estimation problem here is to use S to obtain estimates of the parameters of the structure.

We define $\phi(S, \Sigma)$ to be a scalar measure of error-of-fit of the matrix Σ to its sample estimate S, where in all applications below, Σ is given by equations (56), (59), and (60), and we minimize the measure with respect to the parameter matrices or the vector of parameters, θ.

Three widely used measures of distance are

1. The unweighted sum of squares, or the least squares criterion,

$$\phi_1 (S, \Sigma) = Tr(S - \Sigma)^2; \qquad (61)$$

2. ϕ_2, a variant of the likelihood function of the observations, given by

$$\phi_2 (S, \Sigma) = \log |\Sigma| + Tr(S\Sigma^{-1}) - \log |S| - n; \qquad (62)$$

3. The weighted sum of squares, or the generalized least-squares criterion,

$$\phi_3 (S, \Sigma) = Tr\{S^{-1} (S - \Sigma)\}^2. \qquad (63)$$

The values of the parameters that minimize ϕ_1 are known as the least-squares estimates (LSE); those that minimize ϕ_2 are known as the maximum-likelihood estimates (MLE); and those that minimize ϕ_3 are the generalized least-squares estimates (GLSE) (Jöreskog & Goldberger, 1972; Browne, 1982). Thus LSE, MLE, and GLSE are to be found among the solutions of the system of nonlinear equations $\partial\phi/\partial\theta = 0$, where θ is the vector of parameters. In addition to these estimation procedures, Lee (1980) has addressed the problem of estimation of constrained parameters.

The implementation of any one of the three estimation procedures hinges upon the availability of algorithms for the solution of the equations $\partial\phi/\partial\theta = 0$. Solving these equations is equivalent to finding the minimum values of the functions given in equations (61) to (63). There are several procedures that are currently available for the minimization of functions of several variables. The most well-known of these are the Fletcher-Powell procedure made popular by Jöreskog (1967) and the classical Newton-Raphson procedure (Jennrich & Robinson, 1969; McDonald & Swaminathan, 1972). The Fletcher-Powell procedure is a first-order procedure requiring only the first derivatives of the function to be minimized. The Newton-Raphson procedure, on the other hand, requires the vector of first derivatives as well as the matrix of second derivatives. One of the major factors that seems to have hindered the implementation of the Newton-Raphson procedure in general covariance structure models is the difficulty involved in evaluating the matrix of second derivatives. McDonald and Swaminathan (1973), McDonald (1976), Bentler and Lee (1975), and Swaminathan (1976) have developed the appropriate matrix calculus for obtaining the matrix of second derivatives for a general covariance structure model. Since these results are rather complex, we refer the reader to the above authors for details.

Assessment of Model-Data Fit

Once the parameters are estimated, the goodness-of-fit of the model to the data can be determined. The likelihood ratio statistic for assessing goodness-of-fit is

$$x^2 = N \{\log |\hat{\Sigma}| + Tr(S\hat{\Sigma}^{-1}) - \log |S| - n\}, \tag{64}$$

which is the minimum value of the maximum-likelihood criterion ϕ_2 multiplied by the sample size. The statistic has the x^2 distribution with $\frac{1}{2}n(n + 1) - r$ degrees of freedom, where r is the number of parameters. If the computed x^2 value exceeds the tabulated value, the hypothesis that the model fits the data is rejected. No goodness-of-fit statistic is available when the least-squares criterion is used.

The major problem with the likelihood ratio statistic is that it is a function of the sample size, and, with large N, a good fit may be difficult to find.

On the other hand, with small N, many competing models may fit the data adequately, rendering the statistical procedure meaningless. The x^2 statistic is most useful in evaluating the improvement in fit when hierarchically less restrictive models are compared. Clearly the most restrictive model that fits the data is the most parsimonious and, hence, the model of choice. For a more detailed discussion of the issues surrounding model-data fit, the reader is referred to Bentler and Bonnett (1980).

An excellent example of assessment of model-data fit is given by Jöreskog (1979). For this example, we use the full version of the model of Wheaton and associates (1977). The researchers were concerned with the stability of the construct Alienation over time. The indicator variables Anomie and Powerlessness were measured in 1967 and again in 1971. The path diagram is given in figure 4–8.

The measurement model corresponding to the path diagram is

$$\begin{bmatrix} y_1 \\ y_2 \\ y_3 \\ y_4 \end{bmatrix} = \begin{bmatrix} 1 & 0 \\ \lambda_{21y} & 0 \\ 0 & 1 \\ 0 & \lambda_{42y} \end{bmatrix} \begin{bmatrix} \eta_1 \\ \eta_2 \end{bmatrix} + \begin{bmatrix} \epsilon_1 \\ \epsilon_2 \\ \epsilon_3 \\ \epsilon_4 \end{bmatrix}$$

$$\begin{bmatrix} x_1 \\ x_2 \end{bmatrix} = \begin{bmatrix} 1 \\ \lambda_{21x} \end{bmatrix} \begin{bmatrix} \xi \end{bmatrix} + \begin{bmatrix} \delta_1 \\ \delta_2 \end{bmatrix}$$

The structural model is

$$\eta_1 = \gamma_1 \xi + \zeta_1$$
$$\eta_2 = \beta \eta_1 + \gamma_2 \xi + \zeta_2,$$

i.e.,

$$\begin{bmatrix} \eta_1 \\ \eta_2 \end{bmatrix} = \begin{bmatrix} 0 & 0 \\ \beta & 0 \end{bmatrix} \begin{bmatrix} \eta_1 \\ \eta_2 \end{bmatrix} + \begin{bmatrix} \gamma_1 \\ \gamma_2 \end{bmatrix} \begin{bmatrix} \xi \end{bmatrix} + \begin{bmatrix} \zeta_1 \\ \zeta_2 \end{bmatrix}$$

This model is identified; the total number of equations is $n(n + 1)/2 = (6)(7)/2 = 21$. The parameters are: 3 λ's; 3 structural path coefficients $\beta, \gamma_1, \gamma_2$; 1 ϕ; 4 $\theta\varepsilon$'s; 2 θ_δ's; 2 Ψ's. The total number of parameters is 15, so the degrees of freedom for the χ^2 statistic are $21 - 15 = 6$. The computed χ^2 value (using the LISREL computer program) is 71.54, which is significant at the .05 level. Hence, the model-data fit is not acceptable. Jöreskog (1979) reanalyzed the data by permitting the covariance between ϵ_1 and ϵ_3 and between ϵ_2 and ϵ_4 to be nonzero, since these are errors on variables measured over time. With this less restrictive assumption, the number of parameters increases by two, because $\text{cov}(\epsilon_1, \epsilon_3)$ and $\text{cov}(\epsilon_2, \epsilon_4)$

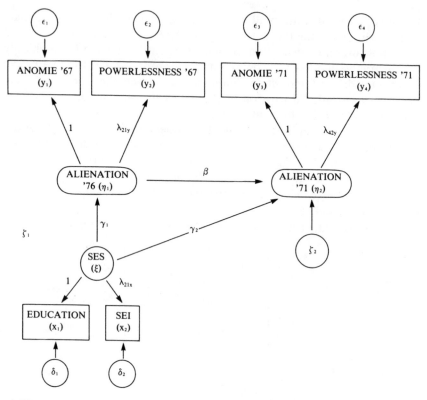

Figure 4–8.   Model for the Study of Stability of Alienation

are now estimated. The degrees of freedom for the χ^2 statistic are then 4. The recomputed χ^2 value is 4.77, indicating that the model fits the data adequately. In further analyses of the data, Jöreskog and Sörbom (1984) fitted a model where only ϵ_1 and ϵ_3 are correlated. With the restriction that ϵ_2 and ϵ_4 are uncorrelated, the χ^2 statistic has a value of 6.33, with five degrees of freedom. This model also fits the data adequately. Jöreskog and Sörbom (1984) based their decision to fit this model on the value obtained for the *modification index*. The modification index is an indicator of the expected decrease in the χ^2 value if a parameter constraint is relaxed. In the example above, the modification index for the covariance between ϵ_1 and ϵ_3, θ_{31}, was the largest. The modification index for the covariance between ϵ_2 and ϵ_4 was not large enough to warrant relaxing the constraint $\theta_{42} = 0$.

Jöreskog and Sörbom (1984) have also introduced several new goodness-of-fit indices. The goodness-of-fit index (GFI) is a measure of the relative amount of the sample variance-covariance matrix that is accounted for by the specified model. In contrast to the χ^2 test, the GFI is independent of sample size and is robust with respect to violations of the assumption of normality. The adjusted GFI (AGFI) adjusts for the number of degrees of freedom in the model. Theoretically, both indices are scaled from zero to one, where one indicates a perfect fit. A root mean square residual statistic has also been introduced: it is a measure of the average residual covariance.

Computer Programs

Several computer programs for the models described in this chapter are available. The most widely used program is LISREL (Jöreskog & Sörbom, 1984) which is based on the Jöreskog model for covariance structures (equation (56)). LISREL is available for both mainframe and personal computers. The program will accept as input raw data, correlation, covariance, or moment matrices. Parameter estimates may be obtained using any of the following estimation procedures: unrestricted least squares (ULS); instrumental variables; two-stage least squares; generalized least squares (GLS); or maximum likelihood (ML). Output includes parameter estimate, standard errors (ML only), t-values for each parameter estimate (ML only), and goodness-of-fit indices (not for ULS).

The McDonald model (1978, 1980) has been incorporated in the COSAN computer program. The estimation procedures available are ULS, GLS, and ML. Input data can be raw scores, correlation or covariance matrices. Output includes the results of the minimization procedure, parameter estimates and their standard errors, and residuals.

The Bentler (1976) model is implemented in the program EQS (Bentler, 1984). The program does not use matrix algebra in formulating equations, but instead uses the convenient convention of regression-like equations. Parameters can be estimated using ULS, GLS, or ML procedures. The program may also use nonnormal theory to obtain parameter estimates for observed nonnormal variables having similar marginal kurtoses. Parameters may be constrained to be equal to other parameters, constrained to be equal to linear combinations of other parameters, or constrained between an upper and lower bound.

Muthén (1984) has developed a LISREL companion program called LISCOMP, which performs covariance structure analysis of dichotomous,

ordered, categorical, and continuous indicator variables. LISCOMP produces ULS and GLS estimators and can compute univariate and bivariate
probit regression by the ML method. The program allows for both single
and multiple sample analyses.

Conclusion

The method of covariance structure analysis outlined in this chapter provides researchers with an extremely powerful tool for the analysis of social
science data. The procedures described in this chapter permit a researcher
to formulate an appropriate structural or causal model, based on theoretical grounds, and test the adequacy of the fit of the model to the data.
Through such an approach, social scientists can examine the validity of
measures or instruments and accumulate evidence regarding the validity
of a theory.

Despite, or perhaps because of, its versatility and power, covariance
structure analysis is a delicate tool that must be used cautiously. The most
critical issue in using covariance structure analysis is that of the identifiability of the structure. Unfortunately, the identification problem has not
been solved for the general model. The identifiability of the structure can
be ascertained in specific cases using the methods described earlier. A
practice used sometimes is to try several structural models and choose
that which, according to the computer program, is identified. Unless the
structural model is identified on logical grounds, the researcher runs into
the danger, after trying several parametrizations, of choosing a model
whose structure is "empirically identified." Bentler (1980) has cautioned
against this practice by noting that identification is a population and not
a sample issue. Moreover, models derived in an empirical manner often
cannot stand up to the rigors of cross-validation. A good check is to follow
the procedure suggested by Cudeck and Browne (1983) for cross-validation
whenever possible.

The steps in carrying out covariance structure analysis can be summarized as follows (Lunneborg & Abbott, 1983):

1.   Define the general structural model.
2.   Construct a path diagram of relations among the observable and
unobservable variables.
3.   Develop a set of theoretically based, hierarchical models which can
be used as alternatives to the null hypothesis.
4.   Translate into matrix equations the hypothesized relations among
variables.

5. Test the system of equations in a model for identifiability.
6. Constrain or fix parameters to achieve a testable model.
7. Assess the goodness-of-fit of the hypothesized models to the data (using χ^2 statistics and modification indices).
8. Choose the most appropriate model that is consistent with theory and the diagnostic information produced in step 7.
9. Return to steps 2 to 8 and cross-validate whenever possible.

By carefully following the steps listed above, the full power of covariance structure analysis can be realized. The recent availability of computer programs for the mainframe as well as personal computers permits this important research tool to take its place among the well-established statistical methods for the analysis of social science data.

References

Anderson, T. W., & Rubin, H. (1956). Statistical inference in factor analysis. *Proceedings of the Third Berkeley Symposium on Mathematical Statistics and Probability* 5:111–150.

Algina, J. (1980). A note on identification in the oblique and orthogonal factor analysis model. *Psychometrika* 45:393–396.

Bentler, P. M. (1976). Multistructure statistical model applied to factor analysis. *Multivariate Behavioral Research* 11:3–26.

———. (1980). Multivariate analysis with latent variables: Causal modeling. *Annual Review of Psychology* 31:419–456.

———. (1983). Some contributions to efficient statistics in structural models: Specification and estimation of moment structures. *Psychometrika* 48:493–517.

———. (1984). *Theory and implemention of EQS: A structural equation program*. Los Angeles: BMDP Statistical Software.

Bentler, P. M., & Bonnett, D. G. (1980). Significance tests and goodness of fit in the analysis of covariance structures. *Psychological Bulletin* 88:588–606.

Bentler, P. M., & Lee, S. Y. (1975). Some extensions of matrix calculus. *General Systems* 20:145–150.

Bentler, P. M., & Speckart, C. (1979). An evaluation of models for attitude-behavior relations. *Psychological Review* 86:452–464.

Bock, R. D., & Bargmann, R. E. (1966). Analysis of covariance structures. *Psychometrika* 31:507–534.

Browne, M. W. (1982). Covariance structures. In D. M. Hawkins (ed.), *Topics in applied multivariate analysis*. Cambridge: Cambridge University Press.

Corballis, M. C. (1973). A factor model for analyzing change. *British Journal of Mathematical and Statistical Psychology* 26:90–97.

Corballis, M. C., & Traub, R. E. (1970). Longitudinal factor analysis. *Psychometrika* 35:79–98.

Cudeck, R., & Browne, M. (1983). Cross-validation of covariance structures. *Multivariate Behavioral Research* 18:147–167.

Fishbein, M., & Ajzen, I. (1975). *Belief, attitude, intention, and behavior: An introduction to theory and research.* Reading, MA: Addison-Wesley.

Jennrich, R. I., & Robinson, S. M. (1969). A Newton-Raphson algorithm for maximum likelihood factor analysis. *Psychometrika* 34:111–124.

Jöreskog, K. G. (1966). Testing a simple structure hypothesis. *Psychometrika* 31:165–178.

————. (1967). Some contributions to maximum likelihood factor analysis. *Psychometrika* 32:443–482.

————. (1969). A general approach to confirmatory factor analysis. *Psychometrika* 34:183–201.

————. (1970). A general method for analysis of covariance structures. *Biometrika* 57:239–251.

————. (1973). A general method for estimating a linear structural equation system. In A. S. Goldberger & O. D. Duncan (eds.), *Structural equation models in the social sciences.* New York: Seminar Press.

————. (1978). Structural analysis of covariance and correlation matrices. *Psychometrika* 43:443–477.

————. (1979). Statistical estimation of structural models in longitudinal-developmental investigations. In J. K. Nesselroade & P. B. Baltes (eds.), *Longitudinal research in the study of behavior and development.* New York: Academic Press.

Jöreskog, K. G., & Goldberger, A. S. (1972). Factor analysis by generalized least squares. *Psychometrika* 37:243–260.

Jöreskog, K. G., & Lawley, D. N. (1968). New methods in maximum likelihood factor analysis. *British Journal of Mathematical and Statistical Psychology* 21:85–96.

Jöreskog, K. G., & Sörbom, D. (1975). *Statistical models and methods for the analysis of longitudinal data* (Research Report 75–65). Uppsala: University of Uppsala.

————. (1984). *LISREL IV: Analysis of linear structural relationships by maximum likelihood, instrumental variables, and least squares methods.* Mooresville, IN: Scientific Software.

Lawley, D. N. (1958). Estimation in factor analysis under various initial assumptions. *British Journal of Mathematical and Statistical Psychology* 34:149–151.

Lee, S. Y. (1980). Estimation of covariance structure models with parameters subject to functional restraints. *Psychometrika* 45:309–324.

Lord, F. M., & Novick, M. R. (1968). *Statistical theories of mental test scores.* Reading, MA: Addison-Wesley.

Lunneborg, C. E., & Abbott, R. D. (1983). *Elementary multivariate analysis for the behavioral sciences.* New York: North Holland.

McDonald, R. P. (1969). A generalized common factor analysis based on residual covariance matrices of prescribed structure. *British Journal of Mathematical and Statistical Psychology* 22:149–163.

————. (1976). The McDonald-Swaminathan matrix calculus: Clarifications, extensions, and illustrations. *General Systems* 21: 87–94.

————. (1978). A simple comprehensive model for the analysis of covariance structures. *British Journal of Mathematical and Statistical Psychology* 31:59–72.

————. (1980). A simple comprehensive model for the analysis of covariance structures: Some remarks on applications. *British Journal of Mathematical and Statistical Psychology* 33: 161–183.

McDonald, R. P., & Swaminathan, H. (1972). Structural analysis of dispersion matrices. Unpublished manuscript, Ontario Institute for Studies in Education, University of Toronto.

————. (1973). A simple matrix calculus with applications to structural models for multivariate analysis. *General Systems* 18:37–54.

Muthén, B. (1984). A general structural equation model with dichotomous, ordered, categorical, and continuous latent variable indicators. *Psychometrika* 49:115–132.

————. *Some uses of structural equation modelling in validity studies: Extending IRT to external variables using SIMS results* (Research Report No. 268). Los Angeles: Center for the Study of Evaluation, University of California

Swaminathan, H. (1984). Factor analysis of longitudinal data. In H. G. Law, C. W. Snyder, J. A. Hattie, & R. P. McDonald (eds.), *Research methods for multimode analysis*. New York: Praeger Publishers.

————. (1976). Matrix calculus for functions of partitioned matrices. *General Systems* 21:95–99.

Swaminathan, H., & Algina, J. (1977). Scale-freeness in factor analysis. *Psychometrika* 43:581–584.

Wiley, D. E. (1973). The identification problem for structural equation models with unmeasured variables. In A. S. Goldberger & O. D. Duncan (eds.), *Structural equation models in the social sciences*. New York: Seminar Press, pp. 69–83.

Wiley, D. E., Schmidt, W. H., & Bramble, W. J. (1973). Studies of a class of covariance structure models. *Journal of the American Statistical Association* 68:317–323.

Wheaton, B., Muthén, B., Alwin, D. F., & Summers, G. F. (1977). Assessing reliability and stability in panel studies. In D. R. Heise (ed.), *Sociological Methodology*. San Francisco: Jossey Bass.

5 APPLICATIONS OF DECISION THEORY TO TEST-BASED DECISION MAKING

Wim J. van der Linden

Historically, the use of tests has its roots in the necessity for selection and placement decisions in education, the army, and public administration. This is demonstrated in DuBois's (1970) historiography of such cases as Binet's pioneering work on developing a test for the assignment of retarded children to special education, the testing of conscripts for placement in the army during World War I, and the examination of applicants for the civil service in ancient China. It is no coincidence that, in each of these fields, decision making is characterized both by high visibility and a massive number of examinees. In such cases it seems logical to use tests on which to base decisions.

Inspired by these early successes, decision makers have been using tests ever since. Nowadays, the use of tests has pervaded such fields as the admission of students to schools, the selection of personnel in public as well as private settings, the assignment of clients to therapeutic treatments, the choice of careers in vocational guidance situations, pass-fail decisions in instructional units, certification, personnel review, tracking decisions in individualized study systems, and the evaluation of training programs. Although their contents and format may vary, it is inconceivable that the use of tests will ever leave these fields.

It is conspicuous that, although the *practice* of testing has its roots firmly in decision making, test *theory* has been developed mainly as a theory of measurements. This was already manifest in Spearman's pioneering work on what is now known as classical test theory. In this theory, test scores are modeled as a linear combination of a true score and an error of measurement, and the concern is primarily in quantities such as the reliability coefficient, the standard error of measurement—as well as in their properties as a function of test length, item selection, and the like. Modern item response theory shows the same concern with measurement (ability estimation), and was not conceived as a theory of decision making either. The history of test theory shows a few exceptions, though, of which the publication of the Taylor-Russell (1939) tables, with their subsequent influence on the testing literature, and Cronbach and Gleser's (1965) *Psychological Tests and Personnel Decisions* deserve special mention. To date, the latter has been the first and only monograph attempting to provide test-based decision making with a sound theoretical basis.

Recently, however, the situation has changed somewhat, and some test theorists are now seriously involved in attempts at modeling and optimizing the use of test scores for decision making. A major impetus for this change has come from the introduction of modern instructional systems such as individualized instruction, learning for mastery, and computer-aided instruction. In such systems, testing primarily serves instructional decision making, and an important task of their developers is to design optimal decision procedures. A seminal paper by Hambleton and Novick (1973) was the first to point at the challenge of these developments to classical test theory.

Although test theory has long ignored decision problems, at a more abstract level the study of optimal rules for decision making has had an extensive tradition in statistics dating back to early publications such as von Neumann and Morgenstern (1944) and Wald (1950). More up-to-date treatments of statistical decision theory can be found in DeGroot (1970) and Ferguson (1967); a short but excellent introduction is given in Lindgren (1976, ch. 8). The primary intention of this chapter is to demonstrate how the various types of decision-making problems in testing can be solved using the framework of statistical decision theory. In particular, in doing so, an (empirical) Bayesian point of view will be assumed.

In the next sections, first some decision-theoretic notions will be introduced. Then, a classification of all possible types of test-based decisions will be given. Subsequently, the main part of this chapter, showing how problems with respect to the various types of decisions can be solved using Bayesian decision theory, is addressed. In the final section, some results will be presented on the application of decision theory to the problem of simultaneous optimization of combinations of different types of decisions in individualized instruction systems.

Elements of a Statistical Decision Problem

Statistical decision problems arise when a decision maker is faced with the need to choose a preferred action; the outcome of the action depends on the state of nature about which only partial information is available. A simple example is the vacationer who has to decide whether or not to go to the beach, but must rely on a forecast for information about the weather; a more sophisticated one is the researcher who has to decide on the basis of sample data which of his/her hypotheses holds for a given population.

The set of all possible states of nature relevant for the decision problem is known as the *state space* in decision theory. This set will be denoted by Ω; whereas a numerical parameter ω will be used to index the individual states in Ω. (When Ω is discrete, ω_s, $s = 1, \ldots, S$, will be used.) Let A be the set of all possible actions from which the decision maker can choose. Technically, A is known as the *action space*. Individual actions will be denoted by a (continuous action space) or a_t, $t = 1, \ldots, T$, (discrete action space). For each action $a \in A$, the decision maker is confronted with certain consequences. These consequences depend not only on the action chosen but also on the (unknown) state $\omega \in \Omega$ nature is in. Some of these consequences may be positive; others negative. It is supposed that the decision maker is able to summarize the consequences of his/her actions given the true state of nature into an evaluation on a numerical scale. Because this scale is assumed to run from negative to positive evaluations, it is what is technically known as a utility scale. So in the following, the existence of a *utility function* $u(\omega, a)$ on $\Omega \times A$ is supposed. For each possible combination of an action and a state of nature, this function indicates how positively the decision maker evaluates the outcomes. When A is discrete, the utility function will be notated by $u_t(\omega)$.

The decision problem would be easy if the true state of nature were known. If nature is in state ω_0, the best action is the one for which $u(\omega_0, a)$ is maximal. In most decision problems, however, nature does not fully disclose its true state; all we have at hand are fallible data—for example, information from a sample, or subjective beliefs. A desirable way of formalizing this is to assume the existence of a *random variable Z* representing the outcome of some experiment or measurement conducted to get known the true state of nature, and whose distribution depends on ω. In the following it is assumed that the family of probability distributions of Z with distribution functions $F(z) \equiv F_Z(z; \omega)$ is known.

If the true state of nature is not known with certainty, the decisions based on A are likely to be less than optimal. A rational approach, then, is to look for a decision rule that optimizes the outcomes across repetitions of the same decision problem, but with nature in possibly different states. The main purpose of decision theory is to find such rules and to study their properties. Formally, a (nonrandomized) decision rule is a prescription specifying for each possible value z of Z which action $a \in A$ has to be taken. Hence, a proper notation is to write the decision rule δ as a mapping from the data Z to the action space A: $A = \delta(Z)$. Due to the fact that Z is a random variable, using δ implies that the actions are also random. At first sight this may seem embarrassing. However, there is no way to escape the random nature of our data about ω. Moreover, the decision maker is free to choose whatever rule we would like to have from the set of possible mappings from Z to A, which gives him/her the opportunity to select an optimal one.

It is obvious that our criterion for selecting an optimal decision rule should have to do with the utilities of the decision outcomes, $u(\omega, a)$. The function $A = \delta(Z)$ implies that these utilities must be considered as realizations of a random variable $U = u(\omega, \delta(Z))$. In such cases it is natural to replace this variable by its expectation. Therefore, we define the expected utility as:

$$R(\omega, \delta) \equiv E[u(\omega, \delta(Z))] \qquad (1)$$
$$= \int u(\omega, \delta(z))dF(z)$$

If nature is in state ω and decision rule δ is adopted, then equation (1) shows the utility to be expected. However, the actual actions still depend on the values taken by Z, so their utility usually will vary about the value of equation (1).

Bayes Rules

It is still not possible to define a criterion for a uniformly best decision rule δ using the expected utility function in equation (1). The reason is its dependency on the unknown value ω. One way out of this problem would be to make a sensible choice for this value, say ω_0, and to select a δ_0, such that the expected utility $R(\omega_0, \delta)$ is maximal. This approach is taken, for instance, in minimax theory where ω_0 is selected as a value of Ω that represents the least favorable state of nature to the decision maker. As a consequence, the decision maker is guaranteed that the minimum expected utility for δ_0 is never smaller than $R(\omega_0, \delta_o)$.

Another approach is not to select one special state ω of nature, but to assume a distribution function $G(\omega)$ over Ω. This may represent the decision maker's subjective probabilities of the possible states of nature or its empirical distribution. For both interpretations $G(\omega)$ is known as the a priori distribution (or *prior*) because it represents knowledge about ω available before the data $Z = z$ are observed. Having $G(\omega)$, we are now able to define the *Bayes utility* of decision rule δ as

$$B(\delta) \equiv E[R(\omega,\delta)] \qquad (2)$$
$$= \int R(\omega,\delta)dG(\omega).$$

In the literature, this quantity is also known as the *Bayes risk* of the decision procedure, although, strictly speaking, this name is only proper if a loss function instead of a utility function is used.

The Bayes utility in equation (2) only depends on the decision rule. It now seems obvious to select from the class of possible rules the one, say δ^*, that maximizes the Bayes utility:

$$B(\delta^*) = \max_{\delta} B(\delta). \qquad (3)$$

Rules satisfying equation (3) are known as *Bayes rules*. Throughout this chapter it will be assumed that the quantities used in the above definition of a Bayes rule exist for the problem at hand (though it will not necessarily be true that the problem has a unique Bayes rule).

Monotone Bayes Rules

For the actual maximization in equation (3) it would be helpful if the (possibly infinitively) large set of all possible rules δ could be restricted to some subset of a tractable form. In addition to this technical consideration, there is a less lofty reason for which the attention sometimes has to be restricted to a subset of possible rules. This has to do with the acceptability of some types of rules among those involved in the decision procedure. In education, for example, students, teachers, and administrators are familiar with selection decisions in which the decision rules have a *monotone form:* students are admitted to a program if their grade-point average or their test score are above a certain cutting point and rejected otherwise. It would be a shock to all parties if some institutions changed the form of their selection rule and started, for instance, admitting students with low or high scores while rejecting those with intermediate ones. However, the restriction to monotone rules is only correct if they constitute an essentially complete class (Ferguson, 1967, p. 55); otherwise rules with a higher expected utility are wrongly ignored.

The conditions under which a class of monotone rules is essentially complete are known (Chuang, Chen, & Novick, 1981; Ferguson, 1967, sect. 6.1). Two conditions have to be met: first, the so-called posterior distribution of ω given Z-z should be stochastically increasing, that is, if $F(\omega|z)$ is the distribution function of ω given $Z = z$, $z_1 \geq z_2$ must imply $F(\omega|z_1) \leq F(\omega|z_2)$ for all ω. Second, there should be an ordering of the actions for which the difference between utility functions for adjacent pairs of actions changes sign at most once. For the decision problems dealt with in this chapter, the conditions will be made more specific below.

A Classification of Test-Based Decision Making

The use of test scores for decision making in education and psychology can be classified in a simple way (van der Linden, 1985a, 1985b). In each of these settings three basic elements can be identified, and each type of decision making can be viewed as a specific configuration of these elements. In general, four different types of decision making can be distinguished. Further, for each of these types four possible restrictions or refinements can apply. This classification of test-based decision making will now be elaborated. In the next sections it is then shown how Bayesian decision theory can be applied to the problems in this classification.

Basic Elements of Test-Based Decisions

Each type of decision making can be identified as a specific configuration of one or more of the following elements:

1. A *test* that provides the scores on which the decisions are based;
2. One or more *treatments* with respect to which the decisions are made;
3. One or more *criteria* by which the successes of the treatments are measured.

The term *test* is used here because of the focus of this chapter. It could easily be replaced by any other measuring instrument or source of data without invalidating the content of this chapter. Likewise, *treatment* is a generic term here, referring to whatever manipulation, experiment, or program is used to change the condition of individuals. Examples of treatments in educational and psychological settings are: instructional programs, applications of audiovisual-materials, or psychological therapies. It should be noted that information about the success of the treatment on the criterion may be provided by any source. In this chapter it is assumed that the information is quantitative by nature. In practice, the criterion is often measured by another test.

Types of Decisions

Four basic types of decisions are distinguished. Each type of decision can be represented by a unique flowchart containing one or more of the above elements.

1. Selection Decisions. In selection problems the decision is the acceptance or rejection of individuals for a treatment. A typical feature of the selection decision is that the test is administered before the treatment but that the criterion is measured afterwards. Well-known examples of selection decisions are selection of personnel in industry and admission of students to educational programs. Figure 5–1 gives a flowchart displaying the structure of the selection decision. Selection research has had a long tradition in educational and psychological testing in which the selection decision was viewed as a prediction problem. Until Cronbach and Gleser (1965), the usual approach was to establish regression lines or expectancy tables to predict criterion scores and to accept individuals with predicted criterion scores above a given threshold value.

2. Mastery Decisions. Unlike selection decisions, mastery decisions are made after a treatment. The content of the decision is whether individuals

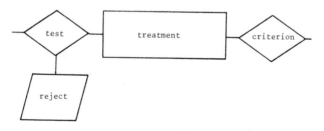

Figure 5–1. Flowchart of a Selection Decision

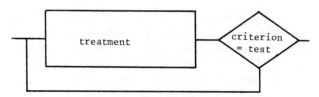

Figure 5–2. Flowchart of a Mastery Decision

who followed the treatment are successful on the criterion. A further feature is that the criterion is internal and not external to the test. It is the unreliability of the test as a representation of the criterion that creates the mastery decision problem. Due to measurement error, the possibility of false-negative and false-positive decisions exists, and it is the task of the decision maker to minimize their consequences. Figure 5–2 shows the formal structure of the mastery decision problem. Examples of mastery decisions are pass-fail and certification decisions in education.

3. Placement Decisions. In placement problems, several alternative treatments are available and it is the decision maker's task to assign individuals to the most promising treatment. The same test is administered to each individual and the success of each treatment is measured by the same criterion. Placement decisions differ from selection decisions by the fact that more than one treatment is available and that each individual is assigned to a treatment. The case of a placement decision with two treatments is shown in figure 5–3. Examples of placement decisions can be found in individualized instruction where students are allowed to follow different routes through instructional units but regardless of routes, the same criterion is appropriate. Aptitude-treatment interaction (ATI) re-

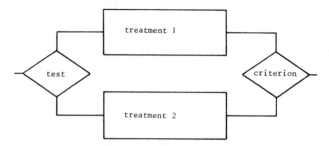

Figure 5–3. Flowchart of a Placement Decision (Case of Two Treatments)

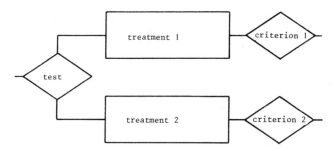

Figure 5–4. Flowchart of a Classification Decision (Case of Two Treatments)

search has given the main impetus to interest in the placement problem. In ATI research, the traditional approach has been regression analysis with a separate regression line for each treatment assigning individuals to the treatment with the largest predicted criterion score.

4. Classification Decisions. As is clear from figure 5–4, the difference between placement and classification decisions is that in the latter, each treatment has its own criterion. Further properties of the two types of decisions are equal. Examples of classification decisions arise in vocational guidance situations where most promising careers or training programs must be identified. The most popular approach to classification decisions has been the use of linear-regression techniques. Each criterion is then mapped on a common utility scale, and the decision rule is to assign individuals to the treatment with the largest predicted utility.

Further Restrictions and Generalizations

It should be noted that the above types of decisions are not always met in their pure forms. These decisions often occur in combinations; also, further restrictions or generalizations may apply. An example of a combination of two types of decisions arises in a selection problem where the criterion is unreliably measured. If success on the criterion is defined by a threshold value, then, in fact, after the treatment a mastery decision has to be taken, and the problem is a selection-mastery decision problem. A combination of a selection and a classification problem is met if more than one treatment is available but not all individuals are accepted for a treatment. In individualized instruction—for instance, as implemented in CAI-systems—decision making can be viewed as guiding students through a network of several of the above decisions. The simultaneous optimization of such networks will be discussed in the final section of the chapter.

For each basic type of decision, one or more of the following restrictions or refinements may apply:

1. Multivariate Test Scores. Instead of a single test, a battery of tests may be used as a basis for the decision. The use of test batteries has had a long history in the practice of personnel selection and vocational guidance. Formally,the use of test batteries implies decision rules defined on a vector of test scores instead of a single score.

2. Sequential Testing. In a sequential testing strategy, test items are administered until a decision can be made with a desired level of certainty (see, for example, van der Linden & Zwarts, 1989). The recent introduction of the computer in educational and psychological testing has stimulated the interest in sequential testing strategies for decision making (see the Hambleton, Zaal, & Pieters chapter). If tests are used in this mode, sequential Bayesian procedures have to be used (Lindgren, 1976, sect. 8.5).

3. Multiple Criteria. In some applications, the success of a treatment has to be measured on more than one criterion. Each individual criterion is then supposed to reflect a different aspect of the treatment. Formally, the presence of multiple criteria implies the necessity to define utility functions on a vector of criterion scores instead of a single score.

4. Multiple Populations. The presence of different populations of examinees reacting differently to the test items may create the problem of "fair" decision making. In education, the problems of fair selection and mastery decisions have been struggled with for a long time, in particular for populations defined by race or sex. Formally, the presence of populations reacting differently to test items implies different probability distributions of test and criterion scores for each population. In addition, the decision maker may have different utilities associated with different populations. As a result, a separate decision rule has to be established for each population.

5. Quota restrictions. So far it has been assumed that the number of vacancies in each treatment is unlimited. Due to the shortage of resources, however, these numbers are often constrained. Consequently, Bayes rules for quota-restricted decisions have to be found by methods of constrained optimization.

Conclusion

The above classification of test-based decisions shows four basic types of decisions that may occur separately or in combination. Furthermore, for each decision one or more refinements or generalizations may hold. In addition, the utility structure and probability distributions may vary from problem to problem. However, the key to finding Bayes rules for each possible decision is still the optimization of its Bayes utility, which will now be illustrated for a sample of decision problems.

Selection Decisions with Linear Utility

In selection decisions, test scores are used to decide on the acceptance or rejection of individuals for a treatment, with success measured on a future criterion. In order to apply the framework of Bayesian decision theory, the "unknown state of nature" should now be interpreted as the individual's unknown criterion score, and the "data" about this state are provided by the test score. For a randomly sampled individual, let the criterion be a continuous random variable Y, with as possible states, success $(Y \geq y_c)$ and failure $(Y < y_c)$. The test score is assumed to be a discrete random variable X with possible values $x = 0, 1, \ldots, n$ (number-right score). The information in X on Y is given by a joint probability function $k(x, y)$. Since the conditions for a monotone decision are assumed to be met, the Bayes rule for the selection problem is a cutoff score x_c, with an acceptance and a rejection decision for $X \geq x_c$ and $X < x_c$, respectively.

Formally, utility is a function defined on the true state of nature with a possibly different form for each action. A moment's reflection shows that in the present problem utility should be an increasing function of the criterion for the acceptance decision, but a decreasing function for the rejection decision: the higher the criterion score of an accepted individual, the higher the utility of the decision; whereas the opposite holds for a rejected individual. A linear utility function that meets this property is given in van der Linden and Mellenbergh (1977):

$$u(y) \begin{cases} b_0(y_c - y) + a_0 & \text{for } x < x_c \\ b_1(y - y_c) + a_1 & \text{for } x \geq x_c, \, b_0, b_1 > 0. \end{cases} \quad (4)$$

This function, which is shown in figure 5–5, consists of two additive components:

1. $b_0(y_c - y)$ and $b_1(y - y_c)$ represent amounts of utility dependent

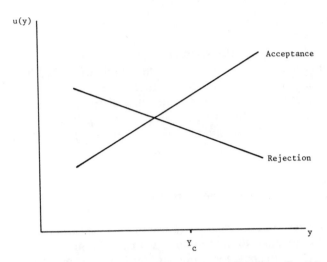

Figure 5–5.   Linear Utility Function for a Selection Decision

on the difference between the criterion score and success threshold y_c with constants of proportionality b_0 and b_1.

2. a_0 and a_1 are amounts of utility independent of the criterion score but dependent on the decision. They can be used, for instance, to allow for treatment costs.

When sampling individuals from the population, the Bayes utility for decision rule x_c is equal to

$$R(x_c) = \sum_{x=0}^{x_c-1} \int [b_0 (y_c - y) + a_0]k(x, y)dy$$

$$+ \sum_{x=x_c}^{n} \int [b_1(y - y_c) + a_1]k(x, y)dy. \qquad (5)$$

Using $k(x, y) = g(y|x)h(x)$, $\int g(y|x)dy = 1$ and $\int yg(y|x)dy = E(Y|x)$, it follows

$$R(x_c) = \sum_{x=0}^{x_c-1} \{b_0[E(Y|x) - y_c] + a_0\}h(x)$$

$$- \sum_{x=x_c}^{n} \{b_1[E(Y|x) - y_c] - a_0\}h(x), \qquad (6)$$

where $E(Y|x)$ is the regression function of Y on X.

Completing the first sum

$$R(x_c) = \sum_{x=0}^{n} \{b_0[E(y|x) - y_c] + a_0\}h(x)$$

$$- \sum_{x=x_c}^{n} \{b_0 + b_1) [E(Y|x) - y_c] - (a_0 - a_1)\}h(x). \quad (7)$$

Since the first sum is now a constant, $b_0 + b_1 > 0$, $h(x) \geqslant 0$ for all x, and the monotonicity conditions guarantee that $E(Y|x)$ is increasing in x, equation (7) is maximal for the value of the smallest value of x_c for which

$$(b_0 + b_1) [E(Y|x) - y_0] + (a_0 + a_1) \quad (8)$$

is not negative. If the monotonicity conditions are not strict or it does not hold that $h(x) > 0$ in the neighborhood of the solution, this value of x may not be unique. Throughout this chapter it will be assumed that conditions like these are fulfilled.

The regression function $E(Y|x)$ can easily be estimated by drawing a sample from the population and administering the treatment.

It should be noted that equation (8) is the difference between the two conditional expected utilities given $X = x$ associated with the acceptance and rejection decision. This is clear from inspection of the bracketed terms in equations (6) and (7). The expectations are known as posterior expected utilities; they can be considered the expected utilities after the observation $X = x$ has been made. For a monotone decision it holds in general that the optimal cutoff score is located at the point at which the posterior expected utilities cross (e.g., DeGroot, 1970, sect. 8.9). In the following, this property will be used without further validation.

A closed-form solution exists if the regression function is linear, that is, if

$$E(y|x) = \beta x + \alpha \quad (9)$$

Then, it follows from equation (8) that x_c is the smallest value larger than

$$\frac{y_c - \alpha}{\beta} + \frac{a_0 - a_1}{\beta(b_0 + b_1)}. \quad (10)$$

An interesting case arises if $a_0 = a_1$. Under this condition the second term in equation (10) vanishes, and the solution contains the regression parameters only. For this and other properties of the linear utility function, see van der Linden and Mellenbergh (1977).

Multiple Populations

As noted earlier, the presence of multiple populations in selection decisions creates the problem of fair selection if each population reacts differently to the test items. In such a case, the test items are often said to be "biased" against one or more of the populations.

The only thing needed to deal with multiple populations in selection decisions seems to include separate probability distributions of test and criterion scores for each population in the model to allow for differential item properties. However, the problem of fair selection often involves the notion of "disadvantagedness" as well, in particular when some of the populations are defined by race or sex. As Gross and Su (1975) and Novick and Petersen (1977) argue, this aspect of fair selection is only a question of utilities. A selection rule is "fair" if those involved in the decision process accept the utility structure underlying the decision rule. Hence, in addition to separate probability distributions, separate utility functions are needed to allow for different utility structures for the populations.

Now the above selection model can easily be adapted to the case of multiple populations (Mellenbergh & van der Linden, 1981). Let $i = 1, \ldots, p$ denote the populations in the selection problem. Then, equation (4) has to be replaced by

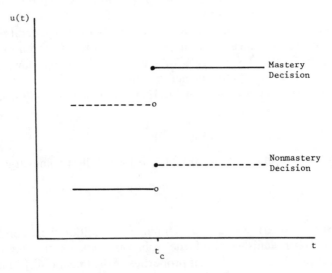

Figure 5–6.   Threshold Utility Function for a Mastery Decision

$$u_i(y) = \begin{cases} b_{0i}(y_c - y) + a_{0i} & \text{for } x < x_{ci} \\ b_{1i}(y - y_c) + a_{1i} & \text{for } x \geq x_{ci}, \, b_{0i}, \, b_{1i} > 0 \end{cases} \quad (11)$$

and the probability functions $k_i(x, y)$, $i = 1, \ldots, p$, are now allowed to vary across populations. The Bayes utility for a random individual is defined analogous to equation (5) as $R_i(x_{ci})$. Let s_i be the relative size of population i. Then, when sampling randomly from the total population under consideration, the Bayes utility is equal to

$$R(x_{c1}, \ldots, x_{cp}) = \sum_{i=1}^{p} s_i R_i(x_{ci}).$$

But this is just a weighted sum of the Bayes utilities of the separate populations. Hence, the decision procedure is optimal if, analogous to equations (5) to (8), for each population a separate Bayes rule is derived. An example of the model with real test data is given in Mellenbergh and van der Linden (1981).

Mastery Decisions with Threshold Utility

In the mastery decision problem, the unknown state of nature is the individual's true score on the criterion variable measured by the test. The data are the observed test scores. The true score is defined as the expected proportion of test items a given individual solves correctly. The true score of a random individual is denoted as T, with possible values $t \in [0, 1]$. A mastery level t_c is assumed, and an individual is considered to master the criterion if $t \geq t_c$, and not to master it otherwise. Unlike the selection problem, there is no way whatsoever to measure the criterion variable directly. Hence, a test model is needed to derive the statistical relation of X to the true score T.

For the purpose of illustration, a threshold utility function is chosen. Although figure 5–6 shows that this function has a jump at t_c that may be less realistic in some applications, it has been studied extensively in the mastery testing literature (Hambleton & Novick, 1973; Huynh, 1976; Mellenbergh, Koppelaar, & van der Linden, 1977; van der Linden, 1980, 1982; Wilcox, 1977). The threshold utility function is defined by the following four constants:

$$u(t) = \begin{cases} u_{00} & t < t_c, \, x < x_c \\ u_{10} & t \geq t_c, \, x < x_c \\ u_{01} & t < t_c, \, x \geq x_c \\ u_{11} & t \geq t_c, \, x \geq x_c \end{cases} \quad (12)$$

However, since the derivation following below holds for any positive linear rescaling of equation (12), it will be assumed for convenience that $u_{00} = u_{11} = 0$.

Let the joint distribution of X and T be given by the probability function $k(x, t)$, and let $g(t|x) \equiv k(x, t)/h(x)$. For the sake of illustration, the optimal cutoff score x_c will now be derived using a comparison of the posterior expected utilities for the mastery and nonmastery decision.

If the mastery decision is taken for a random individual with test score $X = x$, the posterior expected utility is equal to

$$E_1(u(t)|x) = \int_0^1 u(t)g(t|x)dt = u_{01} \int_0^{t_c} g(t|x)dt. \qquad (13)$$

For the nonmastery decision

$$E_0(u(T)|x) = \int_0^1 u(t)g(t|x)dt = u_{10} \int_{t_c}^0 g(t|x)dt. \qquad (14)$$

Suppose x were continuous. Then equations (13) and (14) would cross at the value of x for which

$$u_{01} \int_0^{t_c} g(t|x)dt = u_{01} \int_{t_c}^1 g(t|x)dt$$

or

$$\int_0^{t_c} g(t|x)dt = \frac{u_{10}}{u_{01} + u_{10}}. \qquad (15)$$

However, X is a discrete test score. Therefore, the Bayes utility is maximal if x_c is chosen to be the smallest integer value larger than the solution to equation (15).

It should be noted that this solution holds for any test model providing the probability function in the left-hand side of equation (15), and that it can be calculated only after such a model is specified.

A usual choice in mastery testing is the beta-binomial model (Huynh, 1976; Mellenbergh, Koppelaar, & van der Linden, 1977). In the model it is assumed that (1) the conditional distribution of X given $T = t$ is the binomial,

$$f(x|t) = \binom{n}{x} t^x(1 - t)^{n-x}, \qquad (16)$$

and (2), the marginal distribution of T is the beta distribution with probability density function

$$b(t) \equiv B^{-1}(v, w - n + 1)t^{v-1}(1 - t)^{w-n}, \qquad (17)$$
$$v > 0, \ w > n - 1,$$

where $B(v, w - n + 1) \equiv \int_0^1 t^v (1 - t)^{w-n} dt$ is the complete beta function (e.g., Johnson & Kotz, 1970, ch. 24). The choice of equation (16) is motivated by the fact that the responses of a fixed individual to a series of test items can often be described as a sequence of Bernoulli trials, whereas equation (17) defines a flexible family of distributions on $[0, 1]$ that contains most true-score distributions occurring in practice. Keats and Lord (1962) have shown that moment estimators of v and w exist that are a simple function of μ_X and the KR-21 reliability coefficient. They also found a satisfactory fit of the beta-binomial model to test score distributions ranging widely in form.

For integer values of v and w, it holds that

$$\int_0^{t_c} g(t|x) dt = \int_0^{t_c} f(x|t) b(t) dt$$

$$= \sum_{\gamma = v+x}^{v+w} f(\gamma | t_c) \qquad (18)$$

where $f(.|t_c)$ is the binomial probability function with success parameter t_c (Johnson & Kotz, 1970, sect. 24.6). Thus, a suitable estimate of the integral in equation (15) can be obtained via a table of the cumulative binomial.

A Numerical Example

Using the beta-binomial model, the result in equation (15) was used to calculate the optimal cutoff score x_c for tests of length $n = 20$, mastery threshold $t_c = 14$, and utility ratio $u_{10}/u_{01} = 1$. The data were simulated such that the average true score μ_T and the KR-21 reliability coefficient varied systematically (van der Linden, 1984). Table 5–1 shows how x_c depends on these two parameters. For tests of high reliability, x_c varies hardly with μ_T, but this robustness is lost quickly for tests of lower reliability. For KR-21 = .05, $\mu_T \leqslant 13$ yields $x_c \geqslant 20$, but the optimal cutoff score drops immediately to below zero for $\mu_T > 13$. Only tests of high reliability yield stable cutoff scores.

An unexpected phenomenon in table 5–1 is the opposite direction in which x_c varies with μ_T. If the average true score μ_T goes down, x_c goes up. Hence, for low performing populations the cutoff score should be set high, whereas it should be low for high performers. At first sight, this goes against our intuition. However, it is a logical consequence of our criterion of maximal expected utility. An analysis of equations (12) to (15) reveals the following: for high performing populations, almost all individuals are above the mastery threshold t_c. Therefore, the Bayes utility of the decision

Table 5–1. Optimal Cutoff Scores for Populations Varying in Average True
Score and Tests Varying in Reliability ($n = 20$, $t_c = 14$, $u_{10}/u_{01} = 1$)

KR-21	Average True Score									
	1	3	5	7	9	11	13	15	17	19
.95	16	15	15	15	15	15	14	14	14	14
.80	F	19	17	16	16	15	15	14	14	14
.65	F	F	F	F	17	16	15	14	13	12
.50	F	F	F	19	19	17	16	13	12	P
.35	F	F	F	F	F	20	16	13	P	P
.20	F	F	F	F	F	F	19	11	P	P
.05	F	F	F	F	F	F	20	P	P	P

Note: *F* indicates a cutoff score larger than 20 (all students fail); *P* indicates a cutoff score
lower than 0 (all students pass).

procedure tends to consist only of contributions from true masters and
false nonmasters. Since the proportion of true masters among these two
categories depends on the cutoff score x_c, and the utility of a true master
typically is larger than the utility of a false nonmaster, x_c will take a low
value. This phenomenon was dubbed "the regression-from-the-mean
effect" in van der Linden (1980). It is a reversion of the well-known
regression-to-the-mean effect due to the fact that in the derivation of
equation (15) the conclusion goes from the true score t_c to x_c instead of the
other way around.

Placement Decisions with Normal-Ogive Utility

The typical feature of the placement decision is the presence of more than
one treatment and the fact that each individual is assigned to a treatment.
As before, the unknown state of nature is the individual's criterion score
after a treatment. Hence, although there is one criterion common to all
treatments, each individual has a different unknown state of nature for
each criterion.

Let Y be the criterion common to the treatments $j = 1, 2, \ldots, m$, and
let X denote the test score again. It is assumed that the treatments are
ordered by the strict monotonicity conditions for the placement decision
given in van der Linden (1981), so that an optimal cutoff score x_j exists for
the decision between treatments j and $j + 1$. For the sake of illustration,

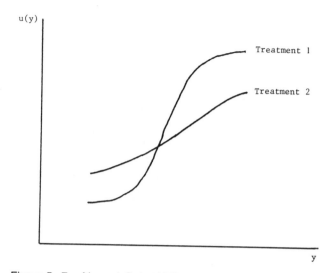

Figure 5-7. Normal-Ogive Utility Function for a Placement Decision

the normal-ogive utility function introduced by Novick and Lindley (1978; see also Berhold, 1973) will be used (see also figure 5-7):

$$u_j(y) = \Phi \left\{ \frac{y - \mu_j}{\sigma_j} \right\}, \tag{19}$$

where Φ is the normal distribution function with parameters μ_j and σ_j.

The relevant quantity is the posterior expected utility for treatment j after test score $X = x$. This will be denoted as $E_j(u_j(Y)|x)$. It is assumed that the conditional distribution of Y given $X = x$ is normal with conditional mean and variance $E_j(Y|x)$ and $\text{Var}_j(Y|x)$, respectively. It follows that

$$E_j(u_j(Y)|x) = \Phi \left\{ \frac{E_j(Y|x) - \mu_j}{[\text{Var}_j(Y|x) + \sigma_j^2]^{1/2}} \right\}. \tag{20}$$

The optimal cutoff score x_j is now the smallest value of x for which the posterior expected utility for treatment $j + 1$ is larger than for treatment j, that is, the smallest value of x for which

$$\Phi \left\{ \frac{E_{j+1}(Y|x) - \mu_{j+1}}{[\text{Var}_{j+1}(Y|x) + \sigma_{j+1}^2]^{1/2}} \right\} - \Phi \left\{ \frac{E_j(Y|x) - \mu_j}{[\text{Var}_j(Y|x) + s_j^2]^{1/2}} \right\} \tag{21}$$

is positive. But this is also the smallest value of x for which

$$\frac{E_{j+1}(Y|x) - \mu_{j+1}}{[\text{Var}_{j+1}(Y|x) + \sigma_{j+1}^2]^{1/2}} - \frac{E_j(Y|x) - \mu_j}{[\text{Var}_j(Y|x) + s_j^2]^{1/2}} \tag{22}$$

is positive. If it is known how the posterior expectations and variances depend on x, the optimal cutoff score can be found graphically or numerically from equation (22).

Suppose now that the posterior expectations are linear and that homoscedasticity may be assumed. That is,

$$E_j(Y|x) = \beta_j x + a_j, \qquad j = 1, \ldots, m \tag{23}$$

and

$$\text{Var}_j(Y|x) = \text{Var}_j(Y.X) \quad \begin{array}{l} x = 0, \ldots, n \\ j = 1, \ldots, m, \end{array} \tag{24}$$

where $\overset{\cdot}{\text{Var}}_j(Y.X) = \{1 - [\text{Cor}_j(Y,X)]^2\}\text{Var}_j(Y)$ and $\text{Cor}_j(Y,X)$ is the linear correlation coefficient between Y and X for j. Substituting equations (23) and (24) into equation (22) yields as a result that x_j is the smallest value larger than

$$[\epsilon_j(\mu_{j+1} - a_{j+1}) - \epsilon_{j+1}(\mu_j + a_j)]/(\epsilon_j\beta_{j+1} - \epsilon_{j+1}\beta_j) \tag{25}$$

with

$$\epsilon_j \equiv [\text{Var}_j(Y.X) + \sigma_j^2]^{1/2}.$$

More theory on placement decisions is given in van der Linden (1981).

Quota-Restricted Placement

In the above placement model, it was assumed that the number of vacant places in the treatments was unrestricted. In practice, however, quota restrictions regularly apply, and then a modification of the decision rule is necessary.

Following Chuang, Chen, and Novick (1981), three kinds of quota restrictions are distinguished:

1. Exactly N_j individuals should be assigned to treatment

$$j = 1, \ldots, m,$$

where $\sum_{j=1}^{n} N_j = N$ (number of examinees);

2. At least N_j individuals should be assigned to treatment

$$j = 1, \ldots, m,$$

$$\text{where } \sum_{j=1}^{m} N_j \leqslant N;$$

3. At most N_j individuals should be assigned to treatment

$$j = 1, \ldots, m,$$

$$\text{where } \sum_{j=1}^{m} N_j \leqslant N;$$

In a (strictly) monotone placement problem, the posterior expected utilities of adjacent pairs of treatments cross at most once in the range of test scores. Therefore, if the N examinees are arranged in decreasing order of test score, the following placement rules maximize the Bayes utility in the above three cases:

1. Beginning with the highest scoring examinee, N_m places in treatment m are filled, then N_{m-1} places in treatment $m - 1$, and so on.
2. Suppose the $(k - 1)$th examinee in the order of examinees has been assigned to treatment j. Then the following rule for k is optimal:
i.   If $x_k \geqslant x_{j-1}$, assign k to treatment j.
ii. If $x_k < x_{j-1}$ and treatment j has not received N_j examinees, then choose from the following rules the one with the larger posterior expected utility: (a) assign k to j; (b) assign k to $j - 1$, reassigning the lowest scoring examinee in $j + 1$ to j (and, if $j + 1$ then has fewer than N_{j+1} examinees, the lowest scoring one in $j + 2$ to $j + 1$; etc.).
iii. If $x_k < x_{j-1}$ and j has received N_j examinees, then assign k to $j - 1$.
3. Again suppose the $(k - 1)$th examinee has been assigned to treatment j.
i.   If $x_k < x_{j-1}$, then assign k to the treatment in $\{j - 1, j - 2, \ldots, 1\}$ with the largest posterior expected utility.
ii. If $x_k \geqslant x_{j-1}$ and treatment j has received N_j examinees, then choose from the following rules the one with the larger posterior expected utility: (a) assign k to $j - 1$; (b) assign k to j reassigning the highest scoring examinee in j to $j + 1$ (and, if $j + 1$ had already N_{j+1} examinees, the highest scoring one in $j + 1$ to $j + 2$; etc.).
iii. If $x_k \geqslant x_{j-1}$ and j has not received N_j examinees, then assign k to j.

Classification Decisions with Threshold Utility

The same notation as for the problem of the placement decision will be used. However, because every treatment now has its own criterion, the criterion variable is treatment dependent and will be denoted as Y_j.

Suppose that for each criterion a success threshold d_j can be defined. Then the following threshold utility function may be a proper choice:

$$u_j(y_j) = \begin{cases} w_j & \text{for } y_j \geq d_j \\ v_j & \text{for } y_j < d_j \end{cases} \tag{26}$$

with

$$w_j > v_j, \qquad j = 1, \ldots, m.$$

The last condition simply states that the utility of a success on treatment j is larger than the one of a failure.

Let $\Phi_j(d_j|x) \equiv \int^{d_j} g_j(y_j|x)dy_j$, where $g_j(y_j|x)$ is the probability density function of Y_j given $X = x$ and treatment j. This quantity defines the probability of a failure on criterion Y_j after treatment j. Van der Linden (1987) shows that the following conditions are sufficient for a monotone Bayes rule in a classification problem with threshold utility:

$$w_{j-1} - v_{j-1} \leq w_j - v_j \qquad j = 2, \ldots, m \tag{27}$$

$$\Omega_j(d_j|x) \text{ is decreasing in } x \qquad j = 1, \ldots, m \tag{28}$$

$$\Omega_{j-1}(d_{j-1}|x) - \Omega_j(d_j|x) \text{ is} \qquad j = 2, \ldots, m. \tag{29}$$
$$\text{increasing in } x$$

The condition in equation (27) indicates that the relevant order of the treatments is with respect to $w_j - v_j$. The other two conditions state that the probability of a failure should be decreasing in the test score, but that the difference between probabilities for two adjacent treatments should increase.

The optimal cutoff score for a decision between treatments j and $j + 1$ is found by comparing posterior expected utilities. If an individual with test score $X = x$ is assigned to treatment j, the posterior expected utility is equal to

$$E_j(u_j(Y_j)|x) = \Omega_j(d_j|x)v_j + [1 - \Omega_j(d_j|x)]w_j. \tag{30}$$

The interest is in the value of x at which $E_j(u_j(Y_j)|x)$ and $E_{j+1}(u_{j+1}(Y_{j+1})|x)$ cross, that is, the value of x for which

$$\Omega_j(d_j|x)v_j + [1 - \Omega_j(d_j|x)]w_j$$
$$= \Omega_{j+1}(d_{j+1}|x)v_{j+1} + [1 - \Omega_{j+1}(d_{j+1}|x)]w_{j+1}$$

or

$$(w_j - v_j)\Omega_j(d_j|x) - (w_{j+1} - v_{j+1})\Omega_{j+1}(d_{j+1}|x)$$
$$+ w_{j+1} - w_j = 0. \tag{31}$$

However, since X is discrete, the optimal cutoff score is the smallest value of x for which the left-hand side of equation (31) is positive. The conditions in equations (27) to (29) guarantee that this expression is an increasing function of x. If it takes the value of zero outside the range of possible test scores, the cutoff score is set at its corresponding border.

An interesting case arises if the utility parameters w_j and v_j do not vary across treatments. Then it follows that $w_j - v_j = w_{j+1} - v_{j+1}$ and $w_{j+1} - w_j = 0$, and the left-hand side of equation (31) reduces to

$$\Omega_j(d_j|x) - \Omega_{j+1}(d_{j+1}|x). \tag{32}$$

This expression reminds us of equation (21). Analogous to the argument following equation (21), it can be shown that for the choice of a normal distribution function for $\Omega_j(.|x)$ together with linear regression functions $E_j(Y|x) = \beta_j x + \alpha_j$ and homoscedasticity, an optimal value of x_j equal to the smallest value of x larger than

$$\frac{(d_{j+1} - \alpha_{j+1})[\mathrm{Var}_j(Y.X)]^{1/2} - (d_j - \alpha_j)[\mathrm{Var}_{j+1}(Y.X)]^{1/2}}{\beta_{j+1}[\mathrm{Var}_j(Y.X)]^{1/2} - \beta_j[\mathrm{Var}_{j+1}(Y.X)]^{1/2}} \tag{33}$$

is obtained (van der Linden, 1987). This quantity can easily be calculated if estimates of the regression parameters and the pooled variances of Y given $X = x$ are available.

Multivariate Test Scores

The use of a test battery instead of a single test was mentioned earlier as a possible refinement of test-based decision making. How Bayes rules can be derived in such cases will now be shown for the problem of placement decisions.

It is assumed that the preceding theory of placement decisions with threshold utility holds. However, in addition to test score X, a second test score Z with information about the criterion variables $Y_j(j = 1, \ldots, m)$ is given. Z is also assumed to be defined by number-right scoring and may take the values $0, 1, \ldots, r$. Let $k_j(x, y_j, z)$ be the joint probability function of test scores X and Z and criterion score Y_j, while $p(z)$ is the probability function of Z. Furthermore, let S_j denote the set of ordered pairs (x, z) for which treatment j is assigned. The expected utility when sampling from the population is defined as

$$R(S_1, \ldots, S_m) = \sum_{j=1}^{m} \sum_{S_j} \int u_j(y_j)k_j(x, y_j, z)dy_j. \tag{34}$$

It follows immediately that

$$R(S_1, \ldots, S_m) = \sum_{j=1}^{m} \sum_{S_j} p(z) \int u_j(y_j) q(x, y_j | z) dy_j, \qquad (35)$$

where $q(x, y_j | z)$ is the probability function of (X, Y_j) given $Z = z$.

Suppose now that equations (28) and (29) hold for each value of z. Then, for each possible z-coordinate, equation (35) can be maximized following equations (30) and (31) with respect to the x-coordinates in S_j. Thus, the optimal sets S_j are defined by a series of $(r + 1)(m - 1)$ cutoff scores, namely, $m - 1$ scores for each of the $r + 1$ possible values of z.

By symmetry, it holds that the z-coordinates if the optimal sets S_j can also be defined by a series of cutoff scores $z_1, \ldots, z_{m-1}$ of the failure probabilities $\Omega_j(d_j | z)$ have the properties in equations (28) and (29) for each value of x. In the testing literature, classification rules that are monotone in two distinct test scores are known as "conjunctive rules." For classification into a given treatment, such rules require that the examinee pass a certain cutoff score on x as well as on y. In other words, it is impossible to compensate a failure on one test by a high score on the other.

Combination of Basic Decisions

As noted before, a well-known example of combination of basic decisions in education is an individualized instruction system. Figure 5–8 shows a simple system in which a selection decision is followed by a module with a mastery decision after which a placement decision guides the students through two possible sequences of mastery decisions. Real-life systems often have a more involved structure.

In systems of more than one decision point, it is possible to optimize decision rules simultaneously. In doing so, more efficient use of the data in

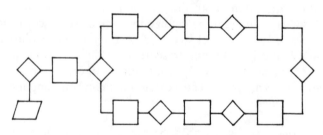

Figure 5–8. Example of an Individualized Study System

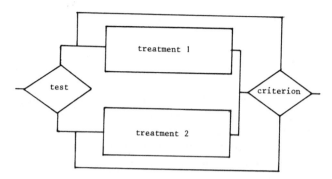

Figure 5-9.   A System of One Placement and One Mastery Decision

the system can be made. Also, more realistic utility structures can be used.
   In order to illustrate the procedure, the simple case of a system with one placement and one mastery decision (van der Linden & Vos, 1986; Vos & van der Linden, 1987) will be dealt with (see figure 5-9). The placement test score is denoted as $X(x = 0, 1, \ldots, m)$, the observed mastery test score as $Y(y = 0, 1, \ldots, n)$, and the true mastery test score as $T(t \in [0, 1])$. Furthermore, the following definitions are made: x_c is a cutoff score on x, y_c is a cutoff score on y, t_c is the mastery threshold on t, $j = 1, 2$ are the two possible treatments, and $i = 0, 1$ are the possible states of nonmastery $(T < t_c)$ and mastery $(T \geq t_c)$, respectively. Without bothering about conditions for optimality, a monotone rule with maximum utility is looked for; that is, from the pairs of cutoff scores (x_c, y_c), the one with the largest Bayes utility will be chosen. The following threshold utility function is adopted:

$$
u_{ij}(t) = \begin{cases}
v_{00} + w_j & \text{for } t < d, y < c \\
v_{10} + w_j & \text{for } t \geq d, y < c \\
v_{01} + w_j & \text{for } t < d, y \geq c \\
v_{11} + w_j & \text{for } t \geq d, y \geq c \qquad j = 1, 2.
\end{cases} \tag{36}
$$

The parameter v is dependent both on the mastery state and the mastery decision, but it is independent of the treatment. In addition, the treatment-dependent parameter w can be used to allow for differences in, for instance, treatment costs. Although this function could be made more realistic by replacing v by continuous functions of the true score t, it nicely demonstrates how in a simultaneous approach a utility function defined on the ultimate criterion of the system (mastery-nonmastery state) can be brought into a previous decision (placement decision).

The Bayes utility for assignment to treatment 1 and a correct mastery decision is equal to

$$\sum_{x=0}^{x_c-1} \sum_{y=0}^{y_c-1} \int_0^{t_c} (v_{00} + w_1)\, \phi(x, y, t)dt, \tag{37}$$

where $\phi(x,y,t)$ is the probability function of (X, Y, T). Combining the two possible treatments, two possible mastery decisions and two possible mastery states, the total expected utility when sampling from the population of individuals is equal to the sum of eight expressions like equation (37). From van der Linden and Vos (1986) it can be verified that this sum can be reduced to the following posterior form:

$$
\begin{aligned}
R(x_c, y_c) = \text{constant} &+ \sum_{y=y_c}^{n} \left[(-v_{00} - v_{11}) \int_0^{t_c} \phi_0(t|y) + v_{11} \right] \kappa_0(y) \\
&+ \sum_{x=x_c}^{m} \left\{ v_{00}\left[\int_0^{t_c} \{\rho_1(t|x) - \rho_0(t|x)\}dt + w_1 - w_0 \right\} \lambda(x) \\
&+ \sum_{x=x_c}^{m} \sum_{x=x_c}^{m} \left\{ \left[(v_{00} + v_{11}) \int_0^{t_c} \pi_0(t|x, y)dt - v_{11} \right] \eta_0(x, y) \right. \\
&- \left. \left[(v_{00} + v_{11}) \int_0^{t_c} \pi_1(t|x, y)dt - v_{11}]\eta_1(x, y) \right] \right\}, \tag{38}
\end{aligned}
$$

with $\phi_0(t|y)$, $\rho_j(t|x)$, $\pi_j(t|x,y)$ being the posterior probability density functions of T given $Y = y$, $X = x$ and $\{Y = y, X = x\}$, respectively, and where $\eta_j(x,y)$, $\lambda(y)$, and $\kappa_j(y)$ are the marginal probability functions.

To obtain the optimal values of x_c and y_c, equation (38) has to be evaluated numerically for all possible pairs of values, whereupon the pair for which equation (38) is maximal can be determined. This can be done as soon as accurate estimates for the three different posterior probabilities of a failure in equation (38) are available. To obtain these estimates, a test theory model is needed.

Conclusion

A review of the applications of Bayesian decision theory to test-based decision making was given. Four basic types of decisions were distinguished, each of which may be subject to further restrictions or generalizations. Decisions may also be made separately or in combination. The test theory literature contains many more results for selection and mastery decisions than were presented in this chapter. The placement and classification decisions as well as some of the possible generalizations and restrictions and the case of combinations of decisions have been largely unexplored. Of paramount importance, however, is research on realistic utility functions for test-based decisions. Such functions should not only yield robust decision rules (Vijn & Molenaar, 1981), but also be supported by empirical evidence of their appropriateness (Vrijhof, Mellenbergh, & van den Brink, 1983). Developments in this field will be decisive for the applicability of Bayesian theory to test-based decision making.

References

Berhold, M. H. (1973). The use of distribution functions to represent utility functions. *Management Science* 19:825–829.

Chuang, D. T., Chen, J. J., & Novick, M. R. (1981). Theory and practice for the use of cut-scores for personnel decisions. *Journal of Educational Statistics* 6:129–152.

Cronbach, L. J., & Gleser, G. C. (1965). *Psychological tests and personnel decisions*, 2nd ed. Urbana, IL: University of Illinois Press.

DeGroot, M. H. (1970). *Optimal statistical decisions*. New York: McGraw-Hill.

Du Bois, P. H. (1970). *A history of psychological testing*. Boston: Allyn and Bacon.

Ferguson, T. S. (1967). *Mathematical statistics: A decision theoretic approach*. New York: Academic Press.

Gross, A. L., & Su, W. H. (1975). Defining a "fair" or "unbiased" selection model: A question of utilities. *Journal of Applied Psychology* 60:345–351.

Hambleton, R. K., & Novick, M. R. (1973). Toward an integration of theory and method for criterion-referenced tests. *Journal of Educational Measurement* 10:159–170.

Huynh, H. (1976). Statistical considerations of mastery scores. *Psychometrika* 41:65–79.

Johnson, N. L., & Kotz, S. S. (1970). *Continuous univariate distributions*, Vol. 2. Boston: Houghton Mifflin.

Keats, J. A., & Lord, F. M. (1962). A theoretical distribution for mental test scores. *Psychometrika* 27:59–72.

Lindgren, B. W. (1976). *Statistical theory*, 3rd ed. New York: Macmillan Publishing Co., Inc.

Mellenbergh, G. J., Koppelaar, H., & van der Linden, W. J. (1977). Dichotomous decisions based on dichotomously scores items: A case study. *Statistica Neerlandica* 31:161–169.

Mellenbergh, G. J., & van der Linden, W. J. (1981). The linear utility model for optimal selection. *Psychometrika* 46:283–293.

Novick, M. R., & Lindley, D. V. (1978). The use of more realistic utility functions in educational applications. *Journal of Educational Measurement* 15:181–191.

Novick, M. R., & Petersen, N. S. (1976). Towards equalizing educational and employment opportunity. *Journal of Educational Measurement* 13:77–88.

Taylor, H. C., & Russell, J. T. (1939). The relationship of validity coefficients to the practical effectiveness of tests in selection: Discussion and tables. *Journal of Applied Psychology* 23:565–578.

van der Linden, W. J. (1980). Decision models for use with criterion-referenced tests. *Applied Psychological Measurement* 4:469–492.

————. (1981). Using aptitude measurements for the optimal assignment of subjects to treatments with and without mastery score. *Psychometrika* 46: 257–274.

————. (1982). Passing score and length of a mastery test. *Evaluation in Education* 5:149–165.

————. (1984). Over absolute en nog relatievere zakslaag beslissingen [On absolute and more relative pass-fail decisions]. *Tijdschrift voor Onderwijsre-search* 9:243–252. (In Dutch).

————. (1985a). Decision theory in educational research and testing. In T. Husen & T. N. Postlethwaite (eds.), *International encyclopedia of education: Research and studies*. Oxford: Pergamon Press.

————. (1985b). Een overzicht van de moderne testtheorie [A review of modern test theory]. *Nederlands Tijdschrift voor de Psychologie* 40:380–389. (In Dutch)

————. (1987). The use of test scores for classification decisions with threshold utility. *Journal of Educational Statistics* 12:62–75.

van der Linden, W. J., & Mellenbergh, G. J. (1977). Optimal cutting scores using a linear loss function. *Applied Psychological Measurement* 1:593–599.

van der Linden, W. J., & Vos, H. J. (1985). Optimale regels voor toetsgebruik in individuele studiesystemen [Optimal rules for test use in individualized study systems]. In W. J. van der Linden (ed.), *Moderne methoden voor toetscon-structie en-gebruik*. Lisse, the Netherlands: Swets & Zeitlinger. (In Dutch)

van der Linden, W. J., & Zwarts, M. A. (1989). Some procedures for computerized ability testing. *International Journal of Educational Research* 13(2):175–187.

Vijn, P., & Molenaar, I. W. (1981). Robustness regions for dichotomous decisions. *Journal of Educational Statistics* 6:205–235.

von Neumann, J., & Morgenstern, O. (1944). *Theory of games and economic behavior*. Princeton, NJ: Princeton University Press.

Vos, H. J., & van der Linden, W. J. (1987). Designing optimal rules for instructional decision making in CAI systems. In J. Moonen & T. Plomp (eds.), *Developments in educational software and courseware*. Oxford: Pergamon Press.

Vrijhof, B. J., Mellenbergh, G. J., & van den Brink, W. P. (1983). Assessing and studying utility functions in psychometric decision theory. *Applied Psycho-logical Measurement* 7:341–357.

Wald, A. (1950). *Statistical decision functions*. New York: Wiley.

Wilcox, R. R. (1977). Estimating the likelihood of false-positive and false-negative decisions in mastery testing: An empirical Bayes approach. *Journal of Educational Statistics* 2:289–307.

6 META-ANALYSIS

John E. Hunter
Frank L. Schmidt

Scientists have known for centuries that little can be proven from single studies. The elimination of alternate hypotheses requires the work of many researchers in many studies. Because of the unavoidable presence of sampling error, this problem is magnified when the basic data in the study are statistical. Yet the dominant pattern of review papers in the behavioral and social sciences has been to review each study on an individual basis with little or no attention to the role of sampling error in producing variation in findings between studies. Instead, variation in results from study to study has typically been taken at face value or ascribed to methodological weaknesses in some of the studies. Most reviews conclude that "more research is needed," although many studies may already be available on the hypothesis in question. The thesis of this chapter is that, in the long run, the only solution to the problem of sampling error inherent in small sample studies is cumulation of results across studies. The subject of the present chapter is methods for conducting such cumulative analyses.

This chapter will consist of three parts: (1) a brief review of two lines of research in the area, research by Glass and his associates and research by Schmidt, Hunter, and their associates; (2) analysis of publication practices necessary to facilitate cumulation; and (3) an argument for substituting the confidence interval for the statistical significance test.

Overview

The work by Glass and his associates and work by us—Schmidt, Hunter, and associates—are quite complementary; where Glass and his associates have focused on the mean of statistics across studies, we have focused on the meaning of variance across studies. Although we have also been concerned with mean effect sizes across studies, our primary focus has been on artifactual variance created by (1) sampling error due to small sample size, (2) variations in the quality of measurement (i.e., reliability of measures), and (3) differences in restriction in range in the samples considered.

The rules for data inclusion in individual published studies dictated by the need for cumulation across studies are simple: there should be complete publication of all *basic* statistics, and a deemphasis if necessary on derived statistics. For each variable in the study there should be reported a mean, a standard deviation, and a reliability coefficient. The complete zero-order correlation matrix among variables should be given (regardless of whether individual correlations are statistically significant). Regression weights, factor loadings, canonical correlation weights and values, and MANOVA weights are not subject to cumulation across studies and are therefore of less importance to publication.

The statistical significance test will be shown to be the primary cause of poor review procedures in the contemporary literature. Although this problem could be partially solved by making more appropriate use of cumulative testing across studies as recommended by Rosenthal (1978, 1979), two other alternatives are much more powerful. The long-run answer is cumulation of descriptive statistics across studies (as is admitted by Rosenthal, 1978, final footnote). For single studies, the best solution is the confidence interval. The confidence interval provides a nondeceptive estimate of the degree of uncertainty in the results in the individual study, and avoids the implication that this uncertainty has somehow been removed by use of statistical significance tests.

Meta-Analysis: The Glass Method

The basic concepts underlying meta-analysis were employed decades ago by Thorndike (1933) and Ghiselli (1949). Both authors cumulated results across studies based on use of average correlations. Thorndike (1933) went further and corrected the observed variance of findings across studies for the effects of sampling error. Neither author, however, advanced such methods as the solution to the general problem of integrating findings across studies to produce cumulative knowledge. More recently, Light and Smith (1971) pointed out the need to cumulate findings across studies to provide a foundation for the establishment of cumulative knowledge and general psychological principles. The methods they advocated, however, were those of secondary analysis of data. These methods require access to original data, and such access cannot often be obtained. As a result, Glass (1976) argued instead for averaging basic effect size and correlation statistics across studies. White (1976, summarized in Glass, 1976) applied this method to the correlation between socioeconomic status and school achievement. Smith and Glass (1977) applied meta-analysis to the evaluation of psychotherapy. Glass and Smith (1979) cumulated studies of the relation between class size and school achievement. Throughout these studies are sprinkled a number of ingenious methods of converting various statistics to a common form for cumulation (Glass, 1978).

Glass' (1976) methods take the variation in findings across studies at face value. These methods attempt to account for such differences by either explicitly calculating averages over subsets of studies (e.g., the mean effect size for psychoanalytic methods is .59 while the mean effect size is .91 for systematic desensitization in Smith and Glass, 1977) or by correlating the statistic with quantified features of the study (e.g., the correlation between effect size and number of hours of therapy is −.02). Schwab, Olian-Gottlieb, and Heneman (1979) used meta-analysis in this way to cumulate studies of employee motivation generated by expectancy theory. The cumulation methods used in these studies give no consideration to sampling error in the treatment of variance in results across studies. Our work, discussed below, indicates that the effect of sampling error is to increase greatly the apparent variability of results across studies. That is, if sampling error is taken into account, it is obvious that there is much less real variation from study to study than appears in their analyses.

Meta-Analysis Methods Developed for Personnel Selection Research

We have been concerned in our research program with variations across studies for some 10 years. For the most part, we have been concerned with variation produced by artifacts of research design such as small sample sizes. Our first study in this area focused on the question of whether employment tests which are valid for whites might be invalid for blacks (Schmidt, Berner, & Hunter, 1973). A number of studies had reported significant validity coefficients for whites but not for blacks. In examining this literature, we found a disparity between the sample sizes for the two racial groups in those studies, with sample sizes typically much larger for whites than for blacks. This fact meant statistical power was much higher for white samples. Our cumulative analysis showed that single group validity findings were a statistical artifact of these sample size differences. This single group validity cumulation study has subsequently been replicated three times (O'Connor, Wexley, & Alexander, 1975; Boehm, 1977; Katzell & Dyer, 1977).

The single group cumulation procedure does not have great power against the differential validity hypothesis, which holds that while tests may be valid for both groups, they are less valid for blacks than for whites. Katzell and Dyer (1977) and Boehm (1977) claimed to have found evidence for differential validity by using a more powerful cumulation, the cumulation of individual significance tests on each pair of correlations for the two racial groups. However, there was a conflict in their findings. While they found a frequency of significant differences higher than the 5 percent expected under the null hypothesis, the mean validities for blacks and for whites were essentially identical. The discrepancy between these findings was explained by Hunter and Schmidt (1978). Both studies had *preselected* the pairs to be tested, and Hunter and Schmidt showed mathematically that this preselection would have the effect of producing a spuriously high frequency (i.e., as much as 20 percent) of significant differences in the subsample of considered studies. In an unselected sample of 1,190 pairs of regression lines, Bartlett, Bobko, Hannan, and Mosier (1978) found a chance level (5.21 percent) of significant differences in slopes. Hunter, Schmidt, and Hunter (1979) have used a variety of more powerful cumulation procedures with the same result; differences in validity between racial groups have now been shown to be the statistical artifact of the use of small sample sizes.

How small must the sample size be in order to be "small"? The answer to this question depends on the size of the desired confidence interval. For a population correlation of .40, the sample size required to estimate the correlation to within $\pm.05$ is 1,085. If the sample size were as low as 400, the width of the confidence interval would be $\pm.08$. If the sample size were as low as the median reported for test validation studies by Lent, Aurbach, and Levin (1971), i.e., as low as 68, then the width of the confidence interval would be $\pm.20$. Since treatment effects in experimental psychology rarely account for more than 10 percent of the variance (i.e., rarely have correlations greater than .33 with the dependent variable), and correlations in correlational psychology are not commonly more than .50, the numbers above appear to be typical for most fields of psychology. Thus any sample of less than 400 or so would be "small" for most purposes, and sample sizes of 1,000 or more would be required for the detection of subtle differences. Only cumulation of results across studies can generate such sample sizes in most areas of contemporary research.

These facts were pointed out by Schmidt, Hunter, and Urry (1976) in the area of test validation studies. That this is no purely theoretical problem can be seen from table 2 of the Lent, Aurbach, and Levin (1971) study of 1,506 correlations in the test validation literature. In that table there is a correlation of .77 between sample size and the proportion of test-criterion correlations found to be statistically significant, i.e., a correlation of .77 between sample size and the probability of labeling the test valid. Indeed, this result suggests that the vast majority of findings of "invalid tests" might actually be an artifact of low statistical power due to use of small samples.

How much of the variability in results across studies is due to artifacts such as the use of small samples? Using our meta-analysis methods, we have sought to answer this question for the cumulative body of test validation studies (Schmidt & Hunter, 1977; Schmidt, Hunter, Pearlman, & Shane, 1979; Pearlman, Schmidt, & Hunter, 1980; Schmidt, Hunter, & Caplan, 1981; Schmidt, Gast-Rosenberg, & Hunter, 1980). On the average, across test-job combinations, we find that about 80 percent of the variation across studies is accounted for by four artifacts: sampling error, variation in criterion reliability, variation in test reliability, and variation in restriction of range. Moreover, it is the sampling error due to the use of small samples which accounts for most of the artifactual variance, about 85 percent. From the frequency of apparent outliers in our distributions, we hypothesized that the remaining variability is largely due to reporting errors: errors in computation, errors in setting up computer runs, errors in typing or copying from computer outputs, and so on. In any case, the degree of variability left in our distributions after we take out artifacts is small enough that the presence of substantial test validity can be generalized across studies, settings, and organizations. These findings showed that test validity was not situationally specific. Our results show that the previously widespread belief that cognitive employment tests are frequently invalid is a myth created mostly by sampling error. For most test-job combinations, our results show that the test is valid in all settings. For a summary of this research, see Schmidt and Hunter (1981).

Today many organizations—including the U.S. federal government, the U.S. Employment Service, and some large corporations—use validity generalization findings as the basis of their selection testing programs. Validity generalization has been included in standard texts (e.g., Anastasi, 1982) and in the 1985 AERA, APA, NCME *Standards for Educational and Psychological Testing.* Proposals have been made to include validity generalization in the federal government's Uniform Guidelines on Employee Selection Procedures (U.S. Equal Employment Opportunity Commission et al., 1978) when this document is next revised. In recent litigation in Canada, the use of validity generalization findings as the basis for the use of a group intelligence test in selecting tax collectors was upheld (*Maloley et al.* vs. *Department of National Revenue,* 1986).

These methods for cumulating findings across studies have also been applied to research literatures other than test validity. For example, Stoffelmeyr, Dillavou, and Hunter (1983) have used the methods developed for the study of the generalizability of test validities to cumulate findings concerning the relation between premorbid adjustment and later severity of illness in schizophrenics. Despite vast differences in formal definitions of variables, in narrowness or breadth of the definition of schizophrenia, and in extent of treatment, they found that sampling error accounted for all the variation in 23 out of 35 of the distributions of correlations. Even in the remaining cases, the residual standard deviation was quite small in comparison to the mean correlation. The researchers have concluded that the "Conflicting results" perceived by earlier reviewers are probably spurious. Some additional examples of application include the following:

1. Correlates of role conflict and role ambiguity (Fisher & Gittelson, 1984; and Jackson & Schuler, 1985).
2. Effects of realistic job previews (Premack & Wanous, 1984).
3. Evaluation of Fiedler's theory of leadership (Peters et al., 1985).
4. Accuracy of self-ratings of ability and skill (Mabe & West, 1982).
5. Relation of LSAT scores to performance in law schools (Linn, Harnisch, & Dunbar, 1981).
6. Relation of job satisfaction to absenteeism (Hocket & Guion, 1985; Terborg et al., 1982).
7. The relation between job satisfaction and job performance (Iaffaldono & Muchinsky, 1985; Petty, McGee, & Cavender, 1984).
8. The relation of job characteristics to job satisfaction (Loher, Noe, Moeller, & Fitzgerald, 1985).
9. The effectiveness of different techniques for changing attitudes and beliefs (Dillard, Hunter, & Burgoon, 1984).

10. Race effects in job performance ratings (Kraiger & Ford, 1985).
11. Relation between employee tenure intentions and actual turnover (Steele & Ovalle, 1984).
12. The effects of nonselection psychological interventions on employee output and productivity (Guzzo, Jette, & Katzell, 1985).

In some of these nonemployment selection applications, the results have been similar to those for employment tests: most or all of the observed between-study variance in effect sizes or correlations has been found to be due to statistical artifacts (principally sampling error). However, in other cases, considerable variance has remained after correcting for the effects of artifacts, indicating the appropriateness of moderator analyses. In many of these cases, the subsequent moderator analysis has provided evidence for theoretically predicted and meaningful moderators.

Generalized Methods for Cumulating Findings Across Studies

The methods that we have used in our validity generalization studies are quite compatible with those used in Glass' version of meta-analysis. Indeed, the results reported in Glassian meta-analyses can be made more complete by the addition of our computations. A critical step in cumulating results across studies is the detection and elimination of artifactual variation due to sampling error. This variation should not only be eliminated by averaging correlations or effect sizes across studies, it should also be removed from the variance across studies. As indicated earlier, Glassian meta-analysis does the former but not the latter. Formulas suitable for this purpose are derived next.

Cumulating Correlations Across Studies

If the population correlation is assumed to be constant over studies, then the best estimate of that correlation is not the simple mean across studies but a weighted average in which each correlation is weighted by the number of persons in that study. Thus the best estimate of the population correlation is:

$$\bar{r} = \frac{\Sigma N_i r_i}{\Sigma N_i}$$

where r_i is the correlation in study i and N_i is the number of persons in study i. The corresponding variance across studies is not the usual sample variance, but the frequency weighted average squared error

$$s_r^2 = \frac{\Sigma N_i (r_i - \bar{r})^2}{\Sigma N_i}.$$

The weighted average above has the advantage that it gives more weight to those values which have the least sampling error. However, if the population correlation is not constant, then the underlying population correlations are arbitrarily weighted by the sample sizes used in studies done on those populations. The formulas can be altered to use unweighted means in cases in which there is reason to believe the population correlation is not constant.

Correcting the Variance for Sampling Error

How much variation in correlations is there across studies? The observed variance, s_r^2, is a confounding of two things: variation in population correlations (if there is any) and variation in sample correlations produced by sampling error. Thus an estimate of the variance in population correlations can be obtained only by correcting the observed variance s_r^2 for sampling error. The following mathematics show that sampling error across studies behaves like error of measurement across persons, and that the resulting formulas are comparable to standard formulas in classical measurement theory (reliability theory).

Let us use error variable e_i to represent the sampling error in the sample correlation in study i, i.e., we define e_i by $r_i = \rho_i + e_i$.

Then the mean error is

$$E(e_i) = 0$$

and its variance is denoted $\sigma^2(e_i) = \dfrac{(1 - \rho_i^2)^2}{N_i - 1}$.

This formula is analogous to the true score and error score formula $X_p = T_p + e_p$ where X_p and T_p are the observed and true scores for person p. In particular, sampling error is essentially uncorrelated with population values across studies. Thus if we calculate a variance across studies, then the variance of sample correlations is the sum of the variance in population correlations and the variance due to sampling error, i.e.,

$$\sigma_r^2 = \sigma_\rho^2 + \sigma_e^2.$$

Since the mean error is zero within each study, the error variance across studies is the average within study variance

$$\sigma_e^2 = \text{ave } \sigma^2(e_i) = \frac{\Sigma N_i \sigma^2(e_i)}{\Sigma N_i} = \Sigma N_i \frac{(1 - \rho_i^2)^2}{\left(\frac{N_i - 1}{\Sigma N_i}\right)}.$$

The fraction $N_i/(N_i - 1)$ is close to unity. If we take this fraction as unity, and we use the approximation that average $(\rho^2) \cong (\text{average } \rho)^2$, then we have the almost perfect approximation

$$\sigma_e^2 = \frac{(1 - \bar{r}^2)^2 K}{N}$$

where K is the number of studies and $N = \Sigma N_i$ is the total sample size. Using s_r^2 as the estimate of the variance of r, we have

$$\text{est } \sigma_\rho^2 = \sigma_r^2 - \sigma_e^2 = s_r^2 - \frac{(1 - \bar{r}^2)^2 K}{N}.$$

A Significance Test for Variation Across Studies

If the corrected variance across studies is positive, then it may still be trivial in size. Indeed it may even be due to sampling error. This section presents a statistical significance test for whether the observed variation is greater than that expected by chance. However, we do not endorse this significance test because it asks the wrong question. Significant variation may be trivial in magnitude, and even nontrivial variation may still be due to research artifacts.

If a sample correlation is drawn from a population in which the variables are approximately bivariate normal (or are dichotomous), then the sample correlation has mean:

$$E(r) = \rho$$

where ρ is the population correlation and a variance of

$$\sigma_r^2 = \frac{(1 - \rho^2)^2}{N - 1}.$$

The following modified squared deviation has a chi-square distribution with 1 degree of freedom:

$$\chi_1^2 = \frac{(N - 1)}{(1 - \rho^2)} (r - \rho)^2.$$

If these squared deviations are summed across studies, then the sum has a chi-square distribution with K degrees of freedom, where K is the number of studies:

$$\chi^2_K = \sum_i \frac{N_i - 1}{(1 - \rho_i^2)^2} (r_i - \rho_i)^2.$$

Under the null hypothesis that all population correlations are equal, i.e., under the assumption that $\rho_i = \rho$ for all i, the best estimate of ρ is $\bar{r}$, the weighted average sample correlation, i.e.,

$$E(\bar{r}) = \rho$$

and the modified deviation statistic using $\bar{r}$ for ρ has a chi-square distribution with $K - 1$ degrees of freedom.

$$\chi^2_{K-1} = \frac{1}{(1 - \bar{r}^2)^2} \Sigma N_i (r_i - \bar{r})^2$$

$$= \frac{N}{(1 - \bar{r}^2)^2} s_r^2$$

where $N = \Sigma N_i$ is the total number of persons across studies. This statistic can be used for a formal statistical test of no variation. However, it has very high statistical power and will therefore reject the null hypothesis even when the amount of variation across studies is trivial in magnitude. Thus a nonsignificant chi square is strong evidence that there is no true variation across studies, but if the chi square is significant, the variation may still be negligible in magnitude.

Correction Feature Correlations for Sampling Error

Suppose that some feature of study i is coded as a quantitative variable y_i. That feature can then be correlated with the outcome statistic across studies. For example, if correlations between dependency and school achievement varied as a function of the age of the child, then we might code average age in study i as y_i. We could then correlate age of children with size of correlation across studies. An example of this method is given by Schwab, Olian-Gottlieb, and Heneman (1979). However, it is important to note that such a correlation across studies is a confounding of the correlation for population values with y and the noncorrelation of the sampling error with y. This is directly analogous to the role of error of measurement in attenuating correlations based on imperfectly measured variables. Thus the observed correlation across studies will be smaller than would be the case had there been no sampling error.

To avoid confusion between the basic statistic r, which is the correlation over persons within a study, and correlations between r and study features over studies, the correlations over studies will be denoted by the symbol "Cor." For example, the correlation between the correlation r and the study feature y across studies will be denoted $Cor(r, y)$. This is the observed correlation across studies, but the desired correlation across studies is that for population correlations ρ_i, i.e., the desired correlation across studies is $Cor(\rho, y)$. Starting from the formula $r_i = \rho_i + e_i$, we calculate a covariance over studies and use additivity of covariances to produce

$$\sigma_{ry} = \sigma_{\rho y} + \sigma_{ey} = \sigma_{\rho y} + 0 = \sigma_{\rho y}.$$

If this covariance across studies is divided by standard deviations across studies, then we have

$$Cor(r, y) = \frac{\sigma_{ry}}{\sigma_r \sigma_y} = \frac{\sigma_{\rho y}}{\sigma_r \sigma_y}$$

$$= \frac{\sigma_{\rho y}}{\sigma_\rho \sigma_y} \cdot \frac{\sigma_\rho}{\sigma_\rho}$$

$$= Cor(r, y) \frac{\sigma_\rho}{\sigma_r}.$$

But the covariance of r_i with ρ_i is

$$\sigma_{r\rho} = \sigma_{\rho\rho} + \sigma_{e\rho} = \sigma_{\rho\rho} + 0 = \sigma^2_\rho$$

and hence, correlation across studies is

$$Cor(r, \rho) = \frac{\sigma_{r\rho}}{\sigma_r \sigma_\rho} = \frac{\sigma^2 \rho}{\sigma_r \sigma_\rho} = \frac{\sigma_\rho}{\sigma_r}.$$

Thus the observed correlation across studies is the product of two other correlations, the desired correlation and reliability-like correlation

$$Cor(r, y) = Cor(\rho, y) \, Cor(r, \rho).$$

The desired correlation is then the ratio

$$Cor(\rho, y) = \frac{Cor(r, y)}{Cor(r, \rho)}$$

which is precisely the formula for correction for attenuation due to error of measurement if there is error in one variable only. What is the correlation between r and ρ over studies? We have the variance of r as estimated by s_r^2. We need only the variance of ρ which was estimated in a previous section of this chapter. Thus the "reliability" needed for use in the attenuation formula is given by

$$\text{Reliability of } r = \{\text{Cor}(r, \rho)\}^2$$

$$= \frac{\sigma_\rho^2}{\sigma_r^2} = \frac{S_r^2 - K(1 - \bar{r})^2/N}{s_r^2}.$$

Correction for Unreliability and Restriction in Range

Variables are never measured perfectly in science. As a result, most correlations are suppressed from their true values by error of measurement in one or both variables. If the amount of error is known in the form of the reliabilities of each variable, then an estimate of the correlation between true scores is given by the formula for correction for attenuation:

$$c = a_1 r$$

where r is the observed correlation, c is the corrected correlation, and

$$a_1 = \frac{1}{\sqrt{r_{xx} r_{yy}}}$$

where r_{xx} and r_{yy} are the reliabilities of x and y, respectively. If error in only one of the variables is to be corrected, then the other reliability is omitted from a_1. The sampling error in the corrected correlation is related to the sampling error in the uncorrected correlation by the linearity of the correction based on

$$\sigma_c^2 = a_1^2 \sigma_e^2 = a_1^2 \frac{(1 - r^2)^2}{N - 1}.$$

It is often the case that observations must be made on populations different from that to which inference is desired. For example, in industrial psychology, job performance can be for utility analyses and other purposes the desired correlation is that for the entire applicant pool. If the selection is based on only one of the variables being correlated (i.e., the selection test in the industrial example), and if the extent of difference between the two populations in standard deviations of the restricted variable is known, then the observed correlation can be corrected for the attenuating effect of restriction in range produced by the selection:

$$c = \alpha_2 r$$

where

$$\alpha_2 = \frac{u}{\sqrt{(u^2 - 1)r^2 + 1}}$$

where

$$u = \frac{\sigma \text{ unselected}}{\sigma \text{ selected}}.$$

The presence of the term r^2 in the denominator of α_2 means that the correction formula is not strictly linear. However, if r is small (in which case r^2 is very small) or if the standard deviation ratio u does not differ too severely from 1, then the departure from linearity is negligible. Thus, to a good approximation, the sampling error is given by the formula

$$\sigma_c^2 = \alpha_2^2 \sigma_e^2.$$

Both the correction for restriction in range and the correction for attenuation due to measurement error are often necessary. The two corrections can be made one after the other, but the order in which the corrections are made is important. If the reliability is calculated on the selected group, then the correction for attenuation should be done before correction for restriction in range. If the reliability is calculated on the selected group, then the correction for attenuation should be done before correction for restriction in range. If the reliability is known for the unselected population, then correction for restriction in range should be made first. In either case, we have

$$c = \alpha r$$

where α is the ratio of corrected to uncorrected correlations, and the approximation

$$\sigma_c^2 = \alpha^2 \sigma_e^2$$

estimates the sampling error of the corrected correlation. If we represent the sampling error in the corrected correlation by e_i, the corrected population correlation by ρ_i, and the estimate of the corrected population correlation by c_i, then

$$c_i = \rho_i + e_i$$

where

$$\sigma_e^2 = \alpha^2 \frac{(1 - r^2)^2}{N_i - 1}.$$

The total error variance for frequency weighted distribution of the corrected correlations is then given by

$$\sigma_e^2 = \frac{1}{N} \sum_i N_i \alpha_i^2 \frac{(1 - r_i^2)^2}{N_i - 1}.$$

If the correction factors α_i vary only slightly from the mean $\bar{\alpha}$, then a good approximation for this sampling error is given by

$$\sigma_e^2 = \bar{\alpha}^2 \frac{K(1 - \bar{r}^2)^2}{N}$$

which is simply $\bar{\alpha}^2$ times the estimated error variance for uncorrected correlations:

$$\sigma_\rho^2 = \sigma_c^2 - \sigma_e^2.$$

If the extent of unreliability and/or restriction in range is not given study by study but can be estimated as a distribution across studies, then more complicated methods can be used for estimation (Schmidt, Gast-Rosenberg, & Hunter, 1980; Pearlman, Schmidt, & Hunter, 1980; Callender & Osburn, 1980; Hunter et al., 1982).

Data Reporting for Cumulation

Consider first correlational studies. If reported study findings are to be usable in cumulative studies, then the mean, standard deviation, and reliability of each variable must be published. The mean is necessary for the cumulation of norms, for the cumulation of regression lines (or the assessment of possible nonlinearity over extreme ranges), or for the identification of very special populations. The standard deviation is necessary for the same reasons, and a further one. If the relation between two variables is linear, then there is little variation in the correlation produced by variation in the mean from study to study. However, this is quite different for the standard deviation. Differences in variability from study to study can have dramatic effects on variable intercorrelations. If a study is being done in a homogeneous population in which the standard deviation is only half the size of the standard deviation in other studies, then in that population the correlations for that variable would be only about half the size of correlations observed in the other populations. Similarly, if the variance is inflated by observing only high and low extreme groups on a given variable, then correlations for that study would be higher than in a population with the middle range included. The reliability is needed for two reasons. First, variations in standard deviation produce differences in reliability. Second, and more importantly, the variable used in the study may not be identical to that used in published norm studies. For example, a study might include a measure of "authoritarianism," but that scale might consist of a subset of eight items chosen by the investigator; the reliability of this subscale may be quite different from the reliability for the whole scale published in norm studies. In the case of new scales, reliabilities may not have been established on large norm populations; in such cases, the reliabilities can be established by cumulating across studies.

It is imperative that the entire matrix of zero-order correlations between all variables be published (note that the means, standard deviations, and reliabilities can be easily appended as extra rows or columns of this matrix). Each entry in this table may be used in entirely unrelated cumulation studies. Correlations that are not statistically significant should still be included; one cannot average a "–" or an "ns" or a "..." or whatever. If only significant correlations were printed, then cumulation would necessarily be biased. This is even more the case for correlations that are not even mentioned because they are not significant.

Moreover, there is a prevalent misperception concerning "nonsignificant" correlations. Many believe that nonsignificant means that no statistically significant finding could be associated with those variables in that study. This is not in fact the case. The size of a correlation is relative to the context in which it is considered, partial correlations and beta weights may be much larger than zero-order correlations. For example, suppose that we had done a study evaluating supervisors and we found a nonsignificant correlation of .10 between performance of supervisor and subordinate performance. If ability of subordinates were correlated .70 with their performance but not with quality of supervision, then the partial correlation between quality of supervision and subordinate performance with subordinate ability held constant would rise to .14 which might then be statistically significant. If motivation of subordinates were correlated .70 with their performance but uncorrelated with ability, then the double partial correlation of quality of supervision and subordinate performance with both ability and motivation controlled would be .71 which would be highly significant. Thus, although quality of supervision might not be significantly correlated with subordinate performance at a zero level, it might be highly correlated when extraneous variables are controlled. To say the same thing another way, even though an independent variable is not significantly correlated with a dependent variable, its beta weight in a multiple regression might be highly statistically significant. This is another important reason why all zero-order correlations should be included in published studies.

What about experimental studies in which analysis of variance is used instead of correlation? In a two-group design, the F value which is conventionally computed is an exact transformation of the point biserial correlation. The significance test on the point biserial correlation is exactly equivalent to the t or F test. In a 2 by 2 by 2 by . . . design, every effect in the analysis of variance is the comparison of two means and could thus be represented by a point biserial correlation. In fact, the square of that point biserial correlation is the "eta square" or percentage of variance accounted for by that effect. In designs with more than two categories for a facet, the categories are frequently ordered (indeed frequently quantitative). In such cases, there is rarely any significant effect beyond the linear trend. In any case, the eta squared (or better the appropriate square root) can be used as a correlation between the corresponding variables. Thus everything stated above, including considerations of restrictions in range and reliability, is just as true of experimental as of correlational studies.

When measures of variables with less than perfect reliability are used, then should the correlations between such measures be corrected for attenuation due to error of measurement? It is clear from measurement theory that the reduction of correlations due to the use of imperfect measurement is purely a matter of artifact. Reliability of measurement is a matter of feasibility and practicality independent of the theoretical and psychological meaning of the variables measured. Thus it is correlations between perfectly measured variables which are of theoretical importance, i.e., it is the corrected correlations which should be used in analysis of variance, multiple correlation, or path analysis, etc. If the reliability of each variable is published, those cumulating findings across studies can analyze the data using appropriate methods. Cumulation should ideally be done on corrected correlations (although, as shown in the work of Schmidt and Hunter and associates, this correction can sometimes be made after the cumulation). As noted above, correction increases the sampling error in the estimated correlation. The formulas for the correction of variance due to sampling error should be those appropriate for correlations corrected for attenuation. These formulas are given above.

Multiple Regression

Many studies focus on the prediction of a critical dependent variable. Such studies frequently report only correlations between predictors and that dependent variable. Reporting practices may have become even worse recently. Some studies now report only the multiple regression weights for the predictors. But cumulation leading to optimal estimates of multiple regression weights requires cumulation of the predictor intercorrelations as well as the predictor-dependent variable correlations. That is, the formula for each multiple regression weight uses all the correlations between the predictors, and hence they must be cumulatively estimated. In the schizophrenia study mentioned above, we found many correlations between social competence measures and outcome, but few correlations between the social competence measures were reported, and as a result, we cannot generate a multiple regression for the cumulated data.

The practice of ignoring the predictor intercorrelations is extremely frustrating even if large samples are used. Given the predictor intercorrelations, path analysis can be used to test hypotheses about direct and indirect causes. If the predictor intercorrelations are not given, one cannot distinguish between a predictor that makes no contribution and a predictor that makes a strong but indirect contribution. In short, one cannot do the desired path analysis unless the predictor correlations are given as well as the predictor-criterion correlations.

Finally, it should be noted that regression weights are not suitable for cumulation. Suppose that Y is to be predicted from $X_1, X_2, \ldots X_m$. The beta weight for X_1 depends not only on the variables X_1 and Y but on all the other variables, $X_2, X_3, \ldots$ contained in the same regression equation. That is, beta weights are relative to the set of predictors considered and will only replicate across studies if exactly the same set of predictors is considered in each. If any predictor is added or subtracted for one study to the next, then the beta weights for all variables may change. While it may be worthwhile to calculate beta weights within a study, it is crucial for cumulation purposes that the zero-order correlations be included in the published study. *After* cumulation of zero-order correlations, a multiple regression can be run using a set of predictors that may never have occurred together in any one study.

For example, suppose that we wanted to predict job performance from three abilities, a, b, c. In order to cumulate beta weights, we would have to find either (1) studies that computed beta weights for the a, b, c combination, or (2) studies that contained a, b, c as a subset and that published the full set of predictor intercorrelations. On the other hand, cumulation from zero-order correlations greatly expands the set of studies which can contribute estimates of one or more of the needed correlations. In fact any predictive study using a or b or c would contain at least one correlation of interest. In order for r_{ab} to be estimated, there must be at least one study with both a and b; estimation of r_{ac} requires at least one study with both a and c; and estimation of r_{bc} requires at least one study with both b and c. However, there need be no study in which all three predictors occurred together.

Factor Analysis

Factor analyses are often published with the zero-order correlation matrix omitted, presumably to conserve journal space. But zero-order correlations can be cumulated across studies while factor loadings cannot be cumulated. First, the factors which appear in a given study are not determined by the single variables that appear, but by the sets or clusters of variables that occur. For example, suppose a study contains one good measure of motivation and 10 cognitive ability measures. Then it is likely that the communality of the motivation variable will be 0, and motivation will not appear in the factor analysis. Factors are defined by *redundant* measurement; no factor will appear unless it is measured by at least two redundant indicators (and preferably by three). Second, the factors in an exploratory factor analysis (such as principal axis factors followed by VARIMAX rotation) are not defined independently of one another. For example, suppose that in the initial output one cluster of variables defines G_1 and another cluster defines G_2 and the correlation between G_1 and G_2 is r. Then if factor scores are standardized the VARIMAX factors will be defined by

$$F_1 = G_1 - \alpha G_2$$
$$F_2 = G_2 - \alpha G_1$$

where

$$\alpha = \frac{1 - \sqrt{1 - r^2}}{r}$$

Thus each orthogonal factor is defined as a discrepency variable between natural clusters. Therefore, the loading of an indicator of G_1 on factor F_1 will depend not only on the other indicators of G_1 in its own set but also on what other factors appear in the same study. Clusters analysis results and confirmatory factor analysis results present a somewhat different picture. If a cluster analysis or confirmatory factor analysis model fits the data (Hunter, 1980; Hunter & Gerbing, 1982), then the factor loading of an indicator onto its own factor is the square root of its reliability and is independent of the rest of the variables and is thus subject to cumulation. However, high quality confirmatory factor analyses are still quite rare in the literature.

Canonical Correlation

Canonical correlation begins with a set of predictor variables and a set of dependent measures, and is thus conceptually a situation suitable for multiple regression. But in canonical correlation, two *new* variables are formed: a weighted combination of the predictor variables and a weighted combination of the dependent measures. These combinations are formed in such a way as to maximize the correlation between them. The question is, is this ever a theoretically or conceptually appropriate analysis? In 20 years we have never seen a situation in which canonical correlation would be a theoretically meaningful analysis. Consider two situations: first, if each variable is a reliable measure of an indpendently defined construct, it is the zero-order correlations among these constructs which are of primary interest (though one may well wish to account for these with a path analysis). If the variables are independently defined but imperfectly measured, then the correlations should first be corrected for attenuation. Second, if the variables are redundantly defined (i.e., different measures expected to assess the same construct) and unreliably measured, then the appropriate first step in the analysis is a multiple groups analysis (or some alternate form of confirmatory factor analysis). This step leads to the replacement of each set of redundant measures by its corresponding factor score. The primary data are then the set of zero-order correlations between the factors. Thus in neither case is the appropriate analysis canonical regression. But the advent of computers has led to the more frequent publication of canonical regression analyses in place of theoretically meaningful analyses.

It is important to note that canonical regression is not subject to cumulation across studies. In multiple regression, each beta weight depends on the dependent variable and on the specific set of predictors. Thus it generalizes only to other studies in which exactly the same set of predictors is used (which is rare indeed). But each canonical regression weight depends not only on the exact set of predictors in the study but on the exact set of dependent measures as well. Thus it will be very rare that the results of canonical regression can be compared or cumulated.

MANOVA

Experimental psychologists frequently include in their studies multiple dependent measures and occasionally even control variables as well. However, such published studies frequently contain only multivariate analysis of variance (MANOVA) regression weights. Hunter (1979) has argued that the appropriate method for analyzing such data is path analysis rather than MANOVA. He noted that Tukey and others have long pointed out that MANOVA is not an "overall test" as has been mistakenly assumed by many users. He showed that MANOVA does not correctly take into account the causal ordering among the dependent measures that experimenters have typically built into their set of measures, and thus produces biased and misleading weights. An example of multiple dependent measures analyzed using path analysis can be found in Boster and Hunter's (1979) study of opinion formation in juries.

Statistically, MANOVA is a canonical regression, with the treatment contrast variables as "independent" variables and with the measured variables as "dependent" measures. Thus MANOVA suffers from all the problems of canonical regression discussed above. In particular, MANOVA does not make sense if there are any causal relations among the dependent variables, and is *not* subject to cumulation across studies. The basic publication record should be the set of zero-order correlations between contrasts, between contrasts and other measured variables, and between other measured variables. Path analysis can then be used with control variables preceding treatment contrasts preceding dependent measures which can be arranged according to the causal relations among them.

A Proposed Moratoriaum on Statistical Significance Tests

Consider the typical review study in the social sciences. Many studies are found relating variables X and Y, with one list of studies finding a significant relation between them and a second list of studies finding no significant relation between them. The conclusion is often that there are "conflicting results" which can only be reconciled with "further research designed to tease out the subtle interactions and methodological deficiencies which must have produced the discrepancies in findings." Our validity generalization studies indicate that such conclusions can be completely erroneous. The unspecified interactions and unproven methodological deficiencies may be ghosts summoned by the use of small samples and the reification of sampling error.

Consider an example. Based on data from 144 studies, Pearlman, Schmidt, and Hunter (1980) showed that the best estimate of the correlation of general intelligence with proficiency in clerical work is .51. If a perfect validity study could be done using the entire applicant population and using a perfectly reliable job proficiency measure, then the expected correlation between intelligence and performance would be .51. But proficiency measures cannot be obtained on applicants; performance can be measured only on those who are hired. Most organizations hire fewer than half of those who apply. Suppose that those hired are those in the top half of the distribution on intelligence. Then because of restriction in range, the expected correlation between test and performance will be .33 rather than .51. But it is also impossible to obtain perfect measures of job performance. Typically, the best feasible measure is the rating of the single supervisor who knows the person's work well enough to rate it. Based on the cumulative review of King, Hunter, and Schmidt (1980), the best estimate of the interrater reliability of a single rating by a single supervisor would be only .31. If the rater were asked to make multiple judgments and those ratings were combined into a composite score, then the expected interrater reliability would rise to .62. In this "best" of cases, the reliability of the job performance measure would be .62 and the expected correlation between test and performance would be further reduced from .33 to 0.26.

Therefore, because of problems inherent in doing field studies, the investigator begins work with an underlying population correlation of .26. What are the implications of conducting such a field study with a small sample? Suppose that Smith does a study with a sample size of 30. Then if the expected correlation of .26 were found, it would not be statistically significant and Smith would falsely label the test as "invalid." But suppose that Jones found the same correlation of .26 using the mean sample size reported in the review by Lent, Aurbach, and Levin (1971), i.e., $N = 68$. Then the same correlation would be statistically significant and Jones would correctly label the test as "valid." Here we have a prime example of artifactual "conflicting results in the literature": the same correlation is labeled "significant" in one study but "nonsignificant" in another. Thus the same evidence is used in one study to label the test as "valid" and used in a second study to label the test as "invalid." Most reviews treat all studies alike and completely ignore the fact that studies with different sample sizes have a completely different meaning for the term *significant*.

But even if all studies were done with the same sample size, reviews would still not find the uniform results we have assumed in our example. In the discussion above, we have assumed that the observed correlations would equal the population correlations; that is, we have ignored sampling error. If all studies were done with 50 subjects, what would the effect of sampling error be? For 50 subjects, the correlation must be .28 to be significant at the .05 level using a two-tail test. Given a population correlation of .26, the observed correlation will have a mean of .26 and a standard deviation of .13. The probability that the observed correlation will be larger than .28 and hence be labeled as "significant" is .44. Thus, across studies, the test would be correctly labeled "valid" 44 percent of the time and would be incorrectly labeled "invalid" 56 percent of the time. Thus the author list in the review on one side of the issue would be just about as long as the author list on the other side of the issue. But of course all studies that conclude that the test is invalid are actually erroneous. That is, the conclusion stated in the majority of studies is wrong. Thus reliance on the "preponderance of data" using accounts of statistical significance can lead to false conclusions.

There are two points to be made here. First, if the null hypothesis is false, then there can be no Type I errors. All errors are Type II errors, and thus the error rate is one minus the statistical power of the study. Thus the error rate for a 5 percent level test is higher than 5 percent, often much higher. Theoretically the error rate for individual significance tests can be as high as 95 percent. Reviewers greatly underestimate error rates due to Type II error. Second, the error rate in many review studies may be nearly 100 percent. Many reviewers have falsely concluded that there are conflicting results in the research literature reviewed.

If the statistical significance test yields incorrect results when applied across studies, then what is a reasonable alternative? As described above, the long-range solution is cumulation across studies. The solution in single studies is the confidence interval. Suppose that in the situation described above Jones obtained an observed correlation of .15 which is not signiicant while Smith obtained a correlation of .37 which is significant. Using significance tests, they would likely conclude that there was some unknown difference in the jobs in their two studies that caused the test to be valid for Smith but not for Jones, a typical false conclusion. Now suppose that, instead of significance tests, each had used confidence intervals. The confidence interval for Jones is $-.13$ to $+.43$ (i.e., $.15 \pm .28$ for $N = 50$) while it is $+.09$ to $+.65$ (i.e., $.37 \pm .28$) for Smith. These confidence intervals have an overlap of .09 to .43 which includes the population value of .26. Using confidence intervals, they could very likely correctly perceive their results as being comparable rather than conflicting.

Many psychologists apparently believe that statistical significance tests are a solution to the problem of sampling error. Actually, as statisticians have long known, there is no solution to the problem of sampling error within single studies. Significance tests are often used in the psychological literature in a way that is a travesty of statistical theory because Type II error—the most frequent type—is ignored. Attempts to point this problem out to psychologists have been made (Cohen, 1962, 1969). But there is little evidence in current review studies to suggest that this problem is understood by most substantively oriented researchers. The time has come to abandon the statistical significance test in favor of the more powerful and more meaningful alternative: the confidence interval.

The use of confidence intervals should have a revolutionary effect on research reporting. On one hand, psychologists will be surprised to find how much uncertainty there really is in the findings of small sample studies. On the other hand, they will also be surprised to find how much uniformity in empirical findings there really is across studies.

Conclusion

Calculation of confidence intervals quickly reveals that there is little certainty in the results found in single studies with typical sample sizes. Statistical significance tests do not control sampling error and do not solve the problem of sampling error; they merely sweep the problem under the rug. The satisfying illusion of definitive findings in individual studies and the disconcerting illusion of conflicting results across studies in our review literature are products of the same cause. It is time to declare a moratorium on the significance test and require researchers to consider their findings in terms of confidence levels.

The only effective way to eliminate sampling error is to cumulate findings across studies. Doing this requires two steps: (1) computing a frequency weighted average of the effect size statistic across studies and (2) using formulas for the sampling error variance of that statistic to correct the observed variance across studies for sampling error. Where this is not the case and there is in fact real variability across studies, and if this variability is to be studied by correlating the effect size statistic with properties of the study, then the sampling error correction takes a form identical to correction for attenuation due to error of measurement in conventional correlations over persons, as given above. Because most of the basic statistics are typically not printed, current publication practices virtually preclude cumulation of results across studies. In our judgment, the major cause of these poor publication practices is a mistaken belief in the efficacy of single studies, that is, an overestimation of the amount of information contained in single studies. Most researchers have never

METHODOLOGICAL ADVANCES

considered the possibility that their results might have meaning only when pooled with the results obtained by others. Contemporary publication practice is based on the myth of the definitive study. The correct alternative is to treat each research report as a technical report designed to submit results to an accumulating data base.

References

American Educational Research Association, American Psychological Association, National Council on Measurement in Education (1985). *Standards for educational and psychological testing.* Washington, DC: American Psychological Association.

American Psychological Association, Division of Industrial and Organizational Psychology (Division 14). (1980). *Principles for the validation and use of personnel selection procedures*, 2nd ed. Berkeley, CA: Author.

Anastasi A. (1982). *Psychological testing*, 5th ed. New York: Macmillan.

Bartlett, C. J., Bobko, P., Mosier, S. B., & Hannan, R. (1978). Testing for fairness with a moderated multiple regression strategy: An alternative to differential analysis. *Personnel Psychology* 31:233–241.

Boehm, V. R. (1977). Differential prediction: A methodological artifact? *Journal of Applied Psychology* 62:146–154.

Boster, F. J., & Hunter, J. E. (1979). *A causal model of the trial process.* Paper presented at the Western Forensic Association.

Callender, J. C., & Osburn, H. G. (1980). Development and test of a new model of validity generalization. *Journal of Applied Psychology* 65:543–558.

Cohen, J. (1962). The statistical power of abnormal-social psychological research: a review. *Journal of Abnormal and Social Psychology* 65:145–153.

Cohen, J. (1969). *Statistical power analyses for the behavioral sciences.* New York: Academic Press.

Dillard, J. P., Hunter, J. E., & Burgoon, M. (1984). Sequential requests, persuasive message strategies: A meta-analysis of foot-in-door and door-in-the-face. *Human Communication Research* 10:461–488.

Dye, D. (1982). *Validity generalization analysis for data from 16 studies participating in a consortium study.* Unpublished manuscript, Department of Psychology, George Washington University, Washington, DC.

Fisher, C. D., & Gittelson, R. (1983). A meta-analysis of the correlates of role conflict and ambiguity. *Journal of Applied Psychology* 68:320–333.

Ghiselli, E. E. (1949). The validity of commonly employed occupational tests. *University of California Publications in Psychology* 5:253–288.

Glass, G. V. (1976). Primary, secondary, and meta-analysis of research. *Educational Researcher* 5:3–8.

Glass, G. V. (1978). Integrating findings: The meta-analysis of research. In L. Shulman (ed.), *Review of research in education*, Vol. V. Itasca, IL.: Peacock, pp. 351–379.

Glass, G. V., McGaw, B., & Smith, M. L. (1981). *Meta-analysis in social research.* Beverly Hills, CA: Sage Publications.

Glass, G. V., & Smith, M. L. (1979). Meta-analysis of research on class size and achievement. *Educational Evaluation and Policy Analysis* 1:2–16.

Guzzo, R. A., Jette, R. D., & Katzell, R. A. (1985). The effects of psychologically based intervention programs on worker productivity: A meta-analysis. *Personnel Psychology* 38:275–292.

Hocket, R. D. & Guion, R. M. (1985). A re-evaluation of the absenteeism-job satisfaction relationship. *Organizational Behavior and Human Decision Processes* 35:340–381.

Hunter, J. E. (1979, September). *Path analysis: Longitudinal studies and causal analysis in program evaluation.* Invited address presented at the American Psychological Association Meeting, New York.

————. (1980). Factor analysis. In P. R. Monge & J. N. Capella (eds.), *Multivariate techniques in human communication research.* New York: Academic Press.

Hunter, J. E., & Gerbing, D. W. (1982). Unidimensional measurement, second order factor analysis, and causal models. In B. Staw & L. L. Cummings (eds.). *Research in organizational behavior*, Vol. 4. Greenwich, CT: JAI Press, Inc.

Hunter, J. E., & Schmidt, F. L. (1978). Differential and single group validity of employment tests by race: A critical analysis of the three recent studies. *Journal of Applied Psychology* 63:1–11.

Hunter, J. E., Schmidt, F. L., & Hunter, R. F. (1979). Differential validity of employment tests by race: A comprehensive review and analysis. *Psychological Bulletin* 86:721–735.

Hunter, J. E., Schmidt, F. L., & Jackson, G. B. (1982). *Meta-analysis: Cumulating research findings across studies.* Beverly Hills, CA: Sage Publications.

Iaffaldono, M. T., & Muchinsky, P. M. (1985). Job satisfaction and job performance: A meta-analysis. *Psychological Bulletin* 97:251–273.

Jackson, S. E., & Schuler, R. S. (1985). A meta-analysis and conceptual critique of research on role ambiguity and role conflict in work settings. *Organizational Behavior and Human Decision Processes* 36:16–78.

Katzell, R. A., & Dyer, F. J. (1977). Differential validity revived. *Journal of Applied Psychology* 62:137–145.

King, L. M., Hunter, J. E., & Schmidt, F. L. (1980). Halo in a multidimensional forced choice performance evaluation scale. *Journal of Applied Psychology* 65:507–516.

Kraiger, K., & Ford, J. K. (1985). A meta-analysis of race effects in performance ratings. *Journal of Applied Psychology* 70:56–65.

Lent, R. H., Aurbach, H. A., & Levin, L. S. (1971). Research design and validity assessment. *Personnel Psychology* 24:247–274.

Light, R. J., & Smith, P. V. (1971). Accumulating evidence: Procedures for resolving contradictions among different research studies. *Harvard Educational Review* 41:429–471.

Linn, R. L., & Dunbar, S. B. (1982, November). *Validity generalization and predictive bias.* Paper presented at the Fourth Johns Hopkins University National Symposium on Educational Research, Washington, DC.

Linn, R. L., Harnisch, D. L., & Dunbar S. B. (1981). Validity generalization and situational specificity: An analysis of the prediction of first year grades in law school. *Applied Psychological Measurement* 5:281–289.

Loher, B. T., Noe, R. A., Moeller, N., & Fitzgerald, M. P. (1985). A meta-analysis of the relationship of job characteristics to job satisfaction. *Journal of Applied Psychology* 70:280–289.

Mabe, P. A., III, & West, S. G. (1982). Validity of self evaluations of ability: A review and meta-analysis. *Journal of Applied Psychology* 67:280–296.

Maloley et al. v. Department of National Revenue. (1986, February). Canadian Civil Service Appeals Board, Ottawa, Canada.

McDaniel, M. A., & Schmidt, F. L. (1985). *A meta-analysis of the validity of training and experience ratings in personnel selection.* Paper submitted for publication.

McEvoy, G. M., & Cascio, W. F. (1985). Strategies for reducing employee turnover: A meta-analysis. *Journal of Applied Psychology* 70:342–353.

McKinney, M. W. (1984). *Validity generalization pilot study* (Final Report). Submitted to the U.S.E.S. Southern Test Development Field Center, Raleigh, NC.

O'Connor, E. J., Wexley, K. N., & Alexander, R. A. (1975). Single group validity: Fact or fallacy? *Journal of Applied Psychology* 60:352–355.

Pearlman, K., Schmidt, F. L., & Hunter, J. E. (1980). Validity generalization results for tests used to predict job proficiency and training success in clerical occupations. *Journal of Applied Psychology* 65:373–406.

Peters, L. H., Harthe, D., & Pohlman, J. (1985). Fiedler's contingency theory of leadership: An application of the meta-analysis procedures of Schmidt and Hunter. *Psychological Bulletin* 97:274–285.

Peterson, N. G. (1982, October). *Investigation of validity generalization in clerical and technical/professional occupations in the insurance industry.* Paper presented at the Conference on Validity Generalization, Personnel Testing Council of Southern California, Newport, Beach, CA.

Petty, M. M., McGee, G. W., & Cavender, J. W. (1984). A meta-analysis of the relationship between individual job satisfaction and individual performance. *Academy of Management Review* 9:712–721.

Premack, S., & Wanous, J. P. (1985). Meta-analysis of realistic job preview experiments. *Journal of Applied Psychology* 70:706–719.

Rosenthal, R. (1978). Combining results of independent studies. *Psychological Bulletin* 85:185–193.

————. (1979). The "file drawer problem" and tolerance for null results. *Psychological Bulletin* 86:638–641.

Schmidt, F. L., Berner, J. G., & Hunter, J. E. (1973). Racial differences in validity of employment tests: Reality or illusion? *Journal of Applied Psychology* 58:5–9.

Schmidt, F. L., Gast-Rosenberg, I., & Hunter, J. E. (1980). Validity generalization results for computer programmers. *Journal of Applied Psychology* 65:635–642.

Schmidt, F. L., & Hunter, J. E. (1977). Development of a general solution to the problem of validity generalization. *Journal of Applied Psychology* 62:529–540.
————. (1981). Employment testing: Old theories and new research findings. *American Psychologist* 36:1128–1137.
Schmidt, F. L., Hunter, J. E., & Caplan, J. R. (1981). Validity generalization results for two job groups in the petroleum industry. *Journal of Applied Psychology* 66:261–273.
Schmidt, F. L., Hunter, J. E., & Pearlman, K. (1982). Progress in validity generalization: Comments on Callender & Osburn and further developments. *Journal of Applied Psychology* 67:835–845.
Schmidt, F. L., Hunter, J. E., Pearlman, K., & Shane, G. S. (1979). Further tests of the Schmidt-Hunter Bayesian validity generalization procedure. *Personnel Psychology* 32:257–281.
Schmidt, F. L., Hunter, J. E., & Urry, V. W. (1976). Statistical power in criterion-related validation studies. *Journal of Applied Psychology* 61:473–485.
Schwab, D. P., Olian-Gottlieb, J. D., & Heneman, H. G. (1979). Between subjects expectancy theory research: A statistical review of studies predicting effort and performance. *Psychological Bulletin* 86:139–147.
Smith, M. L., & Glass, G. V. (1977). Meta-analysis of psychotherapy outcome studies. *American Psychologist* 32:752–760.
Steele, R. P., & Ovalle, N. K. (1984). A review and meta-analysis of research on the relationship between behavioral intentions and employee turnover. *Journal of Applied Psychology* 69:673–686.
Stoffelmeyr, B. E., Dillavou, D., & Hunter, J. E. (1983). Premorbid functioning and recidivism in schizophrenia: A cumulative analysis. *Journal of Consulting and Clinical Psychology* 51:338–352.
Terborg, J. R., & Lee, T. W. (1982). Extension of the Schmidt-Hunter validity generalization procedure to the prediction of absenteeism behavior from knowledge of job satisfaction and organizational commitment. *Journal of Applied Psychology* 67:280–296.
Thorndike, E. L. (1933). The effect of the interval between test and retest on the constancy of the IQ. *Journal of Educational Psychology* 25:543–549.
U.S. Equal Employment Opportunity Commission, U.S. Civil Service Commission, U.S. Department of Labor, & U.S. Department of Justice. (1978). Uniform guidelines on employee selection procedures. *Federal Register* 43(166):38295–38309.

II DEVELOPMENTS IN APPLIED SETTINGS

7 DEVELOPMENTS IN PERSONNEL SELECTION METHODOLOGY

Robert A. Roe
Martin A. M. Greuter

Personnel selection constitutes a well-known example of the application of measurement theory and methods to practical problems. For a long time, "applied measurement" was synonymous with personnel selection. Even today there is a profitable cross-fertilization between psychometrics and personnel selection. In the past, personnel selection has benefited several times—and with encouraging results—from various psychometric concepts and procedures, such as the development of paper-and-pencil tests and everything associated, reliability and validity concepts, application of decision theory, and operations research. Another recent example is validity generalization (see chapter 6 in this book). It can be noted, too, that several subjects have drawn the attention of psychometricians after they were discovered in the application field of personnel selection. Examples such as restriction of range, stability of regression parameters, utility analysis, and the definition of criteria are just a few of these subjects. The relationship between personnel selection and measurement theory has been fruitful and will continue to be so, as we will hope to show in this chapter.

Some recent developments in personnel selection methodology will be considered here. This discussion will not focus on measurement devices as such, but rather on their significance for the design of selection procedures. This reflects our opinion that important developments in the field of personnel selection during the last decade do not lie at the level of test construction, measurement models, or validity estimation. It seems to us that here the greatest profit has already been obtained, and that the outcomes, shortcomings included, have stabilized. Schmitt and associates (1984) reported mean validity coefficients of general mental ability and special aptitudes of (approximately) .25. For personality tests, a mean coefficient of .15 was reported. Work samples and assessment centers can be considered as two of the better predictive instruments with validities of .38 and .41, respectively. For other nonpsychological predictors, analogous results are in order. The selection interview has a mean validity of .15; for reference checks .17 has been found; for academic achievement .17, and for expert recommendation .21. (These latter values are corrected for several artifacts such as differences in predictor and criterion reliability; see Hunter & Hunter, 1984, p. 83.) Most of the aforementioned tests and other predictors can be qualified as more or less well-developed instruments. Reliability and validity cannot be much improved through modifications. Concepts and methods that relate to the integration of various elements into overall selection procedures seem to be more promising. They have to do with the following issues:

1.   What predictors can be used for specific questions?
2.   Which types of predictors (tests, work samples, references, diplomas, interviews, etc.) are suitable for which type of question?
3.   How can several instruments be combined in order to maximize the utility-cost ratio?
4.   How does one arrive at a decision? What utility functions can be applied? Which decision principle, cutoffs?
5.   How can test results be communicated to executives and managers?
6.   How can acceptability of predictors be taken into account?

While concentrating on selection procedures rather than predictive tests, special attention will be given to the notion of "design." This is because we feel that systematic design of selection procedures can lead to considerable improvement over the prevailing approach in which selection procedures are little more than a clinical scenario for administering a battery of tests to a group of applicants who have applied for some type of job.

Recruitment and selection are important activities that can have far-reaching consequences for the selecting organization, the applicant, and society. From the viewpoint of the organization, these activities offer the possibility to attract and maintain an adequate work force. The presence of the proper personnel not only offers the possibility to work effectively and efficiently but also supplies the necessary creativity and energy for survival. For the individual, employment chances are at stake: selection decisions affect career perspectives, social status, the benefits of work (material as well as immaterial), and so on. At the societal level, recruitment and selection are the mechanisms by which labor is distributed. They determine largely who is going to be affected by discrimination and unemployment, and in what way. There is an important economic function of recruitment and selection as well. Selection according to appropriate procedures may lead to considerable productivity increases. The overall benefit of good selection practice may range in the order of billions of dollars each year (e.g., Schmidt et al., 1979). From these three perspectives, different requirements are being put forward for selection procedures. Employers require a quick fulfillment of vacancies by well-qualified employees at minimal costs. Applicants demand adequate procedures and fair decisions. In fact, their demands have become much stronger in recent years. A primary reason for this lies in the risk of discrimination that is implied in selection, especially from interviews and tests (Schmitt & Noe, 1986). In the United States, this has led to legislation and additional rulings (e.g., the Uniform Guidelines on Employee Selection Procedures, 1978) for nondiscriminatory selection. The discrimination issue has become more urgent because of the long-lasting condition of labor surplus. Such a condition, which implies small selection ratios, makes the opportunity for fair selection less favorable. A qualitative implication is that minority and majority groups, as well as educational groups, are competing with each other for available slots.

Other factors that influence demands regarding personnel selection result from changes in work and working conditions, caused by technological innovations and organizational restructuring. In addition, new strategies of personnel management lead to great changes in labor conditions, such as reduction of working hours, part-time work or remuneration, and so on. Finally, there is increasing pressure toward higher efficiency, effectiveness, quality, and flexibility, not only in general but also with regard to personnel management. Methods are needed to decrease labor costs, and personnel selection seems to offer attractive possibilities because it can help to create quantitative and qualitative work force changes within a relatively short period of time. The trend toward more efficiency can be found within the domain of selection itself, in the increasing orientation toward cost-benefit aspects.

It will be clear that, against this background (new technologies, changing working conditions, discrimination, displacement effects on the labor market, optimization of human resources), effective selection is not an easy objective. In the following sections, some available methods of attaining this objective will be considered.

A Technological View of Personnel Selection

Looking back over the 70-year history of personnel selection, it is striking that, while a great number of tests and other predictive instruments have been invented and many procedures for psychometric evaluation have been developed, little attention has been devoted to the actual use of tests under practical conditions, and little developmental effort has been directed at the construction of integral selection procedures that are suited for such conditions.

In fact, there seems to be only one basic recipe for developing procedures, sometimes referred to as the "classical model" (see, e.g., Cascio, 1987). This method includes such steps as: job analysis, choice of criteria, choice of predictors, validation of predictors, and revision or establishment of the predictor set on the basis of a validity study. Revisions of this model have added steps concerning the combination of predictor scores (e.g., multiple regression, multiple cutoff, multiple hurdle) and the evaluation of predictor sets in terms other than validity (decision-making accuracy and utility). All of these latter variants share the idea that a selection procedure is some optimally weighted battery of tests (or other instruments) that serves for predicting future performance. They imply that there is essentially one best solution to the selection problem, basically determined by psychometric criteria.

The approach fails to consider a number of important issues:

1. As the focus lies on prediction, issues concerning the decision-making process, the composition of the procedure, and the communication between employer, candidate, and selection consultant are given insufficient attention.

2. With regard to prediction, few options tend to be considered. The main choice is usually considered to be between a single criterion-classical regression system and a multiple criterion-clinical prediction system, while other possibilities are ignored.

3. Problems concerning the actual use of selection procedures under

practical conditions, e.g., time pressures, specific information needs of employers, withdrawals of candidates, and so on, tend to be neglected. Such aspects play a limited role in the evaluation and improvement of procedures.

We feel that personnel selection should be placed in a different perspective, one that helps to get a better view of relevant issues, facilitates the construction of procedures, and enables critical evaluation and further development. This perspective can be characterized as "technological" (Roe, 1987, 1989). It considers theoretical know-how on personnel selection to be a technology that can be drawn from when trying to find solutions for practical problems of personnel procurement within particular companies. The task for the selection specialist is to find a solution for these problems by developing suitable procedures. Thus, the central concept is "selection procedure," i.e., a series of steps to obtain relevant information from employers and applicants, and to transform this information into a valuable employment decision or advice, which has been made up in such a way that the needs of the company, the client, law, and so on, can be satisfied while all kinds of practical conditions are taken into account.

This "technological approach" defines the framework for the discussion of developments in selection testing in this chapter. The main question to be addressed is: what do we know about the development of selection procedures and what has research added to our knowledge in recent years? We will also discuss some issues for which further developmental work is needed.

Although there definitely is a tradition of designing procedures within the field of personnel selection, there are only a limited number of concepts and methods, and much of the know-how has remained implicit. We think that applied psychology and personnel selection in particular can find a proper methodology in the so-called "design methodology" from the engineering sciences. This design methodology is basically a set of rules for defining, making, and maintaining a technical product, in this case a personnel selection procedure. An important methodological concept is the "design cycle" (Eekels, 1983), which specifies a number of steps that have to be taken in the course of an iterative process. These steps are:

1. *Definition* of the functions of the selection procedure within a given context; basically, these functions are to collect relevant information, make a prediction of performance, make a decision, and report it to the employer and candidate.

2. *Analysis* of the functions in terms of specific requirements and constraints regarding the input data, the decision, and the transformation

process, and so on; here the employer's criteria, ethical standards, costs, etc., are to be specified.

3. *Synthesis*, production of a preliminary selection procedure, making use of knowledge about people and their behaviors, specific tools and procedural options, and knowledge of designing itself (choosing or constructing elements, assembling parts, etc.).

4. *Simulation*, testing the operational, predictive, and economical properties of the selection procedure; this means: establishing validity, effectiveness, utility, as well as duration, capacity, costs, and so on, either empirically or by the use of models.

5. *Evaluation*, assessing the value of the selection procedure against the requirements and constraints found in step 2; ascertaining whether the procedure as a whole is satisfactory.

6. *Decision making*, either accepting the selection procedure for operational use, or rejecting it, followed by a return to step 2 or 3.

The principle of iteration is typical for the design process: the proper solution is only found after a number of efforts. This follows from the nature of designing as a reductive rather than a deductive process. Logically speaking, several solutions are feasible; it is impossible to determine the best solution in a single round. Of course, the "design cycle" only represents the basic structure of the design process (Eekels, 1983). In real practice this process is far more complex, as there are several consecutive processes starting with a global design and proceeding in a step-by-step manner toward a completely detailed design. During specific phases of the whole process, a number of parallel design processes may take place, directed at the creation of separate components. It will be evident that the techniques and methods of personnel selection can be fitted within this framework. Most of them relate to components made in steps 3 through 5 of this cycle.

The main *functions* that selection procedures should fulfill can be described as follows (Roe, 1989):

1. Information gathering: obtaining information about job openings, job content, job requirements, and on physical, behavioral, and biographical characteristics of applicants;

2. Prediction: transforming information on (past or present) applicant characteristics into predictions about their future behavior, and the resulting contributions to organizational goals;

3. Decision: transforming predictive information on applicants into a preferred action (eventually also execution of this action);

4. Information supply: producing information on applicant characteristics, predicted behaviors, plans for actions (decisions), and communicating it to managers.

These four functions can be realized in several ways. As we will discuss below, there are some basic design options for each of them. For example, one of the options regarding the prediction function is that of sign versus sample-based prediction. Another option, which applies to each of the functions, is that of informal (clinical) versus formal information processing. It will be clear that the choices made by the designer with regard to these options largely determine what form the procedure will finally take.

Many selection procedures, especially the more advanced ones, contain prediction and/or decision models. Such models, which specify relevant variables and relationships between them, serve to operationalize the prediction and decisions functions. Developing such models, also called modeling, is a complex activity, which can be approached systematically by applying the design methodology. Such an approach implies the following steps (Roe, 1984):

1. Definition of the problem, resulting in specification of goals and conditions of use;
2. Identification of requirements that the model should satisfy, based on these goals and conditions; also specification of these requirements into design criteria;
3. Choice of the model's contents, i.e., the constituent elements;
4. Choice of the model's structure, i.e, the set of relationships between elements;
5. Choice of the model's format, i.e., type of representation of elements and relationships;
6. Choice of the model's parameters, i.e., the values that specify variables types and degrees of relationships;
7. Evaluation of the model against the design criteria;
8. Decision on the acceptability of the model or a need for revision.

What has been put forward for the design process in general pertains here as well: models can usually not be found at once. Instead, a number of iterations is necessary in order to arrive at an acceptable result.

In the following sections, we will discuss methodological developments regarding the prediction and the decision function. Consequently, we will discuss developments with regard to the overall composition of selection procedures. The information-gathering and supply functions will be left out of this review. For these latter subjects, the interested reader is referred to Roe (1989).

Prediction

Major Design Considerations

Personnel selection implies making decisions with regard to people's future behavior. Therefore, some type of prediction has to take place.

We have described the prediction function of the selection procedure as transforming information on (past or present) applicant characteristics into predictions about their future behavior, and the resulting contributions to organizational goals. With respect to this function, there seem to be two fundamental design questions:

1. Whether to predict on the basis of the deductive-nomological (or sign) approach, or the domain-sampling (or sample) approach; and
2. Whether to use formal or informal (clinical) methods for arriving at a prognostic statement on performance.

In combination, there are four basic forms of prediction, from which one or more may be chosen:

1. Prediction on the basis of a nomological model. The model contains a formalized specification of the hypothetical relationship(s) between one or more predictor variables and one or more criterion measures.
2. Prediction on the basis of work samples. "Content-oriented devices" are used to measure past or present performance; scores are generalized in a formal way (i.e., statistically) to future performance estimates, e.g., using confidence intervals.
3. Clinical prediction based on predictor comparison. The scores of applicants on predictor variables are compared in order to find the one with the best overall profile; it is assumed that this person's performance on the job will be best.
4. Clinical prediction based on criterion analogies. The work performance of applications in similar situations is analyzed in order to draw analogies; thus an idea of future performance is derived from past performance.

In this chapter, we will concentrate on prediction with the help of prediction models, as they have received most attention and are at the center of methodological developments. No further consideration will be given to clinical methods. Apart from the reconciliative reviews of the clinical-statistical controversy by Sarbin (1986), Meehl (1986), and Holt (1986), and Einhorn's (1986) proposition that clinicians and statisticians differ mainly in their conception of prediction error, there is little new to report.

Designing Prediction Models.   Prediction models can be considered as a special case of performance models. In a performance model, the performance variables (criteria) under study are explicitly related to a set of exogeneous variables. The latter variables either serve to predict outcomes on these criteria or to facilitate the understanding of performance behaviors.

Performance modeling has received considerable attention in recent years (e.g., Campbell, 1983; Naylor, 1983; Vance et al., 1989). It should be noted that several of the performance models are of a generic type; they list a large number of variables that influence performance. As an example of such a general model, the reader is referred to the well-known management performance model of Campbell and colleagues (1970). In this model, the performance of managers is depicted as a function of various individual characteristics (intelligence, aptitudes, knowledge, temperament, preferences, expectations) and environmental variables (i.e., climate and cultural conditions). Although such models are informative in the sense that the available literature and research are nicely summarized, they cannot be considered as working models for guiding interventions. In personnel selection, the model should only contain specific variables that (1) are (presumably) relevant for the problem at hand, (2) can be assessed at the moment of application, and (3) are stable enough to allow predictions over a longer time period. In addition, the number of variables should be minimized in order to get an acceptable utility-cost ratio.

In the context of personnel selection, a prediction model can be defined as a model that transforms information on applicant characteristics or behaviors into a prognostic statement about future behavior (or behavioral outcomes). Technically speaking, the model is said to transform information on predictors into information on criteria. Applying the aforementioned design methodology to prediction models leads to the following description of the design process.

1.   Defining the problem and specifying requirements: in what way is the information on applicant characteristics transformed into predictions of future work performance?
2.   Defining the model's content: what are criteria and predictors?
3.   Choosing the model's structure: how are predictor variables inter-

correlated? And how do criterion variables interrelate? How are both sets related to each other?

4. Choosing the model's format: normally, an algebraic function of the type $Y = f(X)$ is chosen.

5. Estimating model parameters: of special importance are instrumental parameters like test type and length, number of raters, etc., on the one hand, and relational parameters like regression weights and constants on the other hand.

6. Evaluating the model: part of this evaluation includes an estimation of the validity to be obtained upon actual application, but the evaluation may extend to the model's utility as well.

Sign Versus Sample-Based Prediction. In designing prediction models, two basic prediction principles can be followed. Wernimont and Campbell (1968) have called these approaches "sign" versus "sample."

The sign approach has its basis in some law (or *nomos*) on human behavior. Generally speaking, a law states that for a given set of people a relationship exists between characteristic A and a certain type of (future) behavior E. If the law is given, it suffices to know that the characteristic A is present in order to predict that behavior E will occur. This type of deductive reasoning applies not only to deterministic laws but also to probabilistic laws (see Stegmüller, 1974; Roe, 1983). The sample approach rests on the principle of generalization. The basic idea is that when it is known how a person will behave on a sample of occasions, one may generalize to behavior on other occasions belonging to the same universe. In this way the trait concept is avoided. The line of reasoning is as follows: a definition is given the domain of work, or performance, by using some type of task analysis; from this domain of work or universe of tasks, a sample is drawn which is presented to the applicant, or judged on the basis of his or her former performance. The applicant's performance in the sample is generalized to his or her future performance on the job. The assumption underlying the generalization process is that of "behavioral consistency": comparable tasks and conditions will produce similar behavior results for the same person. Because of the content similarity between predictor and criterion, this type of instrument is referred to as a "content based selection device."

In spite of the differences between the two methods of prediction, there are some common design problems. In the sign approach, performance is modeled according to the formula $Y = f(X)$ (cf., Naylor, 1983). The question is how to define Y, how to identify suitable X's, and how to choose an appropriate function f. For the sample approach, the basic formula is

$Y = f(Y')$. The identification of Y' is easier because it stems from the same domain as Y. On the other hand, the designer should answer questions on the assumed stability or consistency of work behavior, taking into account possible changes in working conditions, leadership, learning opportunity, and so on.

There is little development as far as the application of these two principles go; both are well accepted. The sign approach has remained popular as a result of validity generalization studies; the sample approach has become more popular as a result of anti-discrimination litigation, especially in the United States.

Defining Prediction Models, Contents

Choice of Criteria. The choice and definition of criteria is a traditional theme for selection psychologists (see, for example, Thorndike, 1949; Kendall, 1955; Ronan & Prien, 1971; Smith, 1976). The greatest progress in criterion theory has been accomplished in the past. Below, we would like to pinpoint three major developments.

Thorndike (1949) introduced the notion of ultimate versus substitute criteria. The ultimate criterion is the complete final goal of performance in a particular type of job. It represents the "true" order of success in the job activities; it can only be stated in very broad terms that are often not susceptible to an easy practical quantitative evaluation. Instead of trying to accomplish the almost impossible task of predicting the ultimate criterion, one proceeds in practice by predicting more concrete, "substitute" criteria of success. The distinction between ultimate and substitute criteria indicates the relative value of a diversity of performance measures and introduces the notion of criterion "relevance": the extent to which an index of success as applied is related to the true order of success in a given activity. "Relevancy" can be conceptualized as the hypothetical correlation coefficient between the criterion used and the ultimate criterion.

A shortcoming of Thorndike's way of conceptualizing is that it does not recognize the fact that criteria are mixtures of facts and values. While performance behaviors and outcomes are facts that are open to empirical study, the degree to which the performance is considered to contribute to the organization's goals is a matter of judgment or utility assignment by managers. The same performance may be judged differently by different managers, or by the same managers at different times, depending on how they define organizational goals. For this reason, Roe (1983) has suggested leaving organizational goal attainment out of the criterion notion, thus limiting it to performance and performance outcomes. Moreover, he has suggested defining criteria both at the level of theoretical notions and at the level of measures that operationalize these notions. In this chapter, we will follow his suggestion and speak of job goals, conceptual criteria, and operational criteria.

A second issue pertains to the multidimensionality of performance behaviors. An overwhelming majority of studies involving statistical analyses of sets of criterion measures (i.e., factor analysis) finds that these analyses rarely yield one single factor. Job performance tends to be complex and "multidimensional," i.e., reflects various independent aspects (Ronan & Prien, 1971). This multidimensionality gives rise to another classical problem in the history of criterion development: how many criteria should be utilized? Is it advisable to use a single overall measure or should one operationalize multiple criteria? This issue has been shown by Schmidt and Kaplan (1971) to be a pseudo-controversy. Both approaches can be of value: multiple criteria when predicting behavior and single overall criteria when making decisions about applicants.

A third development refers to the classification of criteria. Smith (1976) has developed a classification scheme for criteria. Three dimensions seem to cover most criteria:

1. The time span covered: criterion measures can be obtained either very soon after actual on-the-job behavior has occurred or many years afterwards;
2. The specificity desired: some criteria refer to specific instances of behavior, while others give rise to a global assessment;
3. Degree of closeness to organizational goals: criteria range from the description of actual behavior through the evaluation of immediate results to estimates of payoff for the organization.

Since Smith's (1976) integrative article, with few exceptions, further developments in criterion theory and criterion development have been modest, to say the least. A review article of Barrett and associates (1985), has sparked off some discussion about the concept of "dynamic criterion" (Austin et al., 1989; Barrett & Alexander, 1989).

Fleishman's work culminated in a worthwhile contribution to criterion development. In the book *Taxonomies of Human Performance*, by Fleishman and Quaintance (1984), several bases for the classification of work performance are discussed. In the "behavior description approach," categories of task activities are formulated based on observations and descriptions of what job incumbents actually do while performing a task:

emphasis is placed upon a description of overt behavior as manifested. The "behavior requirement approach" relies on the cataloguing of behaviors that should be emitted or are assumed to be required in order to achieve desired criterion levels of performance. In the "ability requirements approach," tasks are described, contrasted, and compared in terms of the abilities that are required for job performance. Finally, human performance can be classified on the basis of the "task characteristic approach." This approach is predicated on a definition of work performance that treats the task as a set of conditions that elicit and stimulate performance: tasks can be described in terms of these "triggering" conditions, placing emphasis on aspects such as task instructions, procedures, motivational contingencies, and so on.

In almost every instance, conceptual criteria are chosen on the basis of job analysis methods, especially those job analysis techniques that can be attributed to the behavior description approach mentioned above. This can be useful in stipulating conceptual criteria. In this category, a further subdivision into job-oriented (work-oriented, task-oriented) and worker-oriented methods can be made. Job-oriented methods result in a description of specific job activities, also taking into account special instruments, materials, and equipment. A recent example is the Occupation Analysis Inventory (OAI) (Cunningham et al., 1983). This instrument contains 622 individual items that fall into five generalized categories: information received, mental activities, observable behaviors, work content, and work context. The OAI attempts to achieve as much specificity in occupational descriptions as possible while maintaining its applicability to the entire occupational spectrum. Worker-oriented methods lead to a more general description of job activities. The specific job context is not considered in detail; job activities are described by means of verbs indicating relevant performance elements: for example, making decisions, reading, manipulating objects, using far-reaching tools, and so on. The traditional example is the Position Analysis Questionnaire (PAQ) (McCormick, 1972).

Which job analysis method is perferable in a specific instance depends on the nature of the prediction model (Algera & Greuter, 1989). A prerequisite for applying the sign approach is that work performance is conceptualized in an abstract manner, thereby incorporating performance dimensions that can be connected, at least in principle, to capacities, personality traits, and other stable characteristics. For this purpose, worker-oriented job analysis techniques such as the PAQ are recommended. For developing content-based selection devices following the sample approach, very detailed information on the job and the job context is necessary in order to arrive at a complete description of the job domain, and to simulate relevant parts by means of work samples. Job-oriented techniques are to be considered here.

The critical incident technique (Flanagan, 1954) might serve a dual purpose: (1) incidents of superior, average, and inferior performance do lend themselves to direct simulation in a work sample; and (2) incidents can be categorized in more abstract behavioral dimensions that form the basis for a sign-type prediction.

Studies using Schmidt and Hunter's (1977) validity generalization approach (to be discussed later) have cast some doubt on the use of job analysis. The general finding has been that more refined job analysis techniques do not lead to higher validity estimates than global techniques. It has even been suggested that the job title would give sufficient information for identifying predictors and their validity within a data base. Pearlman and associate (1980) concluded, on the basis of an extensive study on the relative merits of job analytic methods within the context of validity generalization, that refined ("molecular") analytical techniques are not needed. Or, in the words of Schmidt and colleagues (1985; p. 724), "validity generalization studies do not require fine-grained, task-based job analysis; job analysis does not have to be detailed." It should be noted that this type of research is based on validity coefficients that relate to global performance ratings in very broad job categories. It is evident that, within this context, fine-grained job analysis methods are of little use. When the prediction model has to produce information on different aspects of performance rather than on overall suitability of applicants, and/or when it should be applied within a narrow range of jobs, fine-grained methods are, of course, indispensable.

For the purpose of evaluating prediction models it is necessary to dispose of operational criteria. In contrast to the limited attention for criterion development at a conceptual and theoretical level, there is a considerable amount of research aimed at the question of how criteria can be operationalized (see, for example, Landy et al., 1983; Landy & Farr, 1983; Latham, 1986). Interest continues in the effect of the rating format, although several review articles have made clear that further refinements of rating scales do have zero effect on rating accuracy and rating error tendencies as halo. "A moratorium on rating scale development is in order" (Landy et al., 1983, p. 6). Improving performance rating by training is another traditional theme. Bernardin and Buckley (1981) suggested that training does succeed in reducing response tendencies such as halo and leniency; on the other hand, rating accuracy is not improved because training only replaces one response tendency with another. A more optimistic view results from a review by Smith (1986), who evaluated 24 studies on training effects. Several training methods (learning how to suppress rating errors, how to develop stable standards that are uniformly applied, how to come to a clearer understanding of the meaning of performance dimensions, etc.) are reported as effective in reducing leniency and halo or as contributing positively to rating accuracy. Training does seem to work after all, although the available research makes it abundantly clear that not every kind of training works for all purposes: for example, the most widely used training approach, called "rating error training," is inappropriate for improving rating accuracy, but other methods (e.g., learning to apply standardized performance standards) do have positive effects.

A final point must be made regarding the increasing interest in cognitive processes that may affect the measurement of performance criteria (see, for example, Feldman, 1981; DeNisi et al., 1984; Carroll & Schneier, 1982). This kind of study has enough potential for a better theoretical understanding of performance behaviors and their determinants but, until now, has not led to any viable suggestions for improving the rating process *in practice*. Almost all of the cognitive research has been implemented in laboratory settings, and there is not much evidence that the results of these contrived appraisal processes do generalize to performance appraisal in real work settings. On the contrary, critical aspects of real life performance appraisal, such as rater motivation, rating purposes, rater experience, outcome expectancies, rater resentment, and so on, are ignored in the laboratory (Ilgen & Favero, 1985; Banks & Murphy, 1985).

Choice of Predictors. Once the criteria are established, two steps must be taken to develop a set of suitable predictors (Roe, 1983): (1) identification of conceptual predictors, i.e., required traits or critical behaviors; and (2) operationalization into operational predictors by selecting tests that are commercially or otherwise available, or by constructing new instruments.

The first (and very obvious) requirement is that predictors should be relevant to future success criteria. Assessors should look for conceptual predictors with high validity and low intercorrelations. Several other requirements may be of importance as well, especially in finding operational predictors. Examples of such requirements are intrusion of privacy, duration of administration, costs, personnel implications, and practical aspects (paper-and-pencil).

The prediction principle that has been preferred (signs or samples) determines what type of predictors will be chosen: trait-oriented, behavior-oriented ("content-based selection devices"), or both. The strategy for identifying predictors at the conceptual level is the same, however. One can choose from four options: (1) meta-analysis of published validity

(validity generalization); (2) theoretical analysis; (3) job analysis; and (4) empirical try-out (exploratory validation).

Published validity data can be of help in identifying and selecting relevant predictor variables. Older reviews of validity data are those by Ghiselli (1966, 1973), Lent and associates (1971), [Lawshe] and Balma (1966), Guion (1965), Bemis (1968), and Asher and Sciarrino (1974, work samples). More recent reviews are given by Arvey and Campion (1982; the interview), Reilly and Chao (1982; various predictors), Campion (1983; selection for physically demanding jobs), Sackett and Harris (1984; tests for honesty), Hunter and Hunter (1984; various predictors), Schmitt and associates (1984; various predictors), Gaugler and associates (1987; Assessment Centers), Reilly and Israelski (1988), and Robertson and Downs (1989; trainability tests).

Traditionally, published validity data were analyzed in an informal, narrative manner. More recently, reviews are characterized by the use of meta-analytical techniques (see chapter 6).

Within the field of industrial and organizational psychology, the validity generalization method (Schmidt & Hunter, 1977, 1981) has become the prevailing method of analysis. The method has been applied to personnel selection as well as to several other subjects.

The validity generalization method has not remained undisputed, however (see Algera et al., 1984; Burke, 1984; James et al., 1986; Jansen et al., 1986; Kemery et al., 1987, 1989; Osburn et al., 1983; Paese & Switzer, 1988; Rasmussen & Loher, 1988; Roe, 1984; Sackett, et al., 1985, 1986; Spector & Levine, 1987; and Thomas, 1988). Some major points of criticism are: (1) the lack of classification rules that can prevent compilation and analysis of validities with widely differing referents (types of tests, criteria, and jobs), (2) the lack of power of the procedure used for tion and analysis of validities with widely differing referents (types of tests, criteria, and jobs), (2) the lack of power of the procedure used for testing situational specificity; and (3) inadequacies in the procedure for correcting for artifacts and estimating true validity.

A second method for identifying predictor constructs is by using theoretical analysis; however, this is the least developed approach. The principle is that one uses some type of job analysis for describing the tasks and the behavioral or trait requirements implied in them. In the sample approach, this idea is more or less straightforward. One needs some refined method for analyzing tasks and behavioral requirements, such as the Systems Task Vocabulary (Miller, 1973). A less elaborate method, which aims at defining a roster of task elements that can be helpful in defining critical behaviors, has been published by Guion (1978).

With the sign approach, the derivation of predictors is more cumbersome, since knowledge about the trait prerequisites for behavior patterns and behavior outcomes is far from complete. The only published systematic work in this domain is that of Fleishman on the Task Abilities Scales (TAS) (Fleishman & Quaintance, 1984). Here, the job analyst should indicate to which degree a fixed set of ability factors is supposed to play a role in the job. The scales are anchored with examples of tangible work behaviors, which were found by empirical research and expert studies. For some of the abilities, decision trees have been developed; this implies that the analyst can confine himself to a series of dichotomous (yes/no) decisions in order to determine whether a given ability factor is relevant.

The third approach is more or less related to the second in the sense that it tries to determine the traits required while performing the job analysis. The difference is that the theoretical phase is lacking; the inference of required traits is made directly by the job analyst, the job incumbent, or some other "job expert." An example of this approach can be found in the Minnesota Job Requirements Questionnaire (MJRQ) (Desmond & Weiss, 1973, 1975), which asks job incumbents and superiors for the relevance of problems that are used to define aptitudes. Another example is the Threshold Trait Analysis (TTA) (Lopez et al., 1981). Here it is the job analyst who should interpret which traits are required for adequate job performance.

In addition to judging trait relevance directly, one can also opt for an indirect procedure. The job content is described first, but it is followed by a mechanical, empirically based identification of required personal characteristics. The traditional example is that of the Position Analysis Questionnaire (PAQ) (McCormick et al., 1972). The factor structure of the PAQ has been established in two ways: (1) correlations between job elements (job data) and (2) correlations between personal characteristics (attribute data). According to subjective standards, both factor structures appear to be similar, which implies that it is possible to place an empirically based relationship between criterion and predictor variables. In addition, the relationships between job dimension scores and GATB test scores have been examined in two studies (McCormick et al., 1972, 1979). These results are promising as well, but they do not supply rules for the choice of predictors in a specific case. Also, it should be noted that considerable criticism has been leveled at the PAQ. Points of criticism are: the PAQ is hard to read (Ash & Edgell, 1975), and it would only measure common sense knowledge about jobs (Smith & Hakel, 1979; Cornelius et al., 1984). Recently, Harvey and Theodore (1986) have shown, on the basis of Monte Carlo studies, that the reliability values that have traditionally been found can be expected on the basis of mere chance. This is a result of the great number of "does not apply" answers: values of .50 are obtained when 15 percent to 20 percent of the items are answered with "does not apply" and the rest of them answered at random. A study by DeNisi and associates (1987) shows that large numbers of "does not apply" answers can also artifically inflate the agreement between expert and naive raters, thus incorrectly giving rise to the proposition that expertise is not an important factor contributing to accurate job descriptions.

A more recently developed method is the Occupational Analysis Inventory (OAI) (Cunningham et al., 1983); the developmental research is of the same nature as the PAQ. Ratings of 1,414 jobs have been made on a total of more than 600 job elements. Also, ratings for 102 human attributes were made ("attribute ratings"). Factor analyses were conducted separately for the element ratings and the attribute ratings. The resultant factors were intuitively meaningful. Furthermore, the OAI dimensions were significantly related to tested abilities of relevant job holders. Most striking is that the OAI seems to offer a certain generalizability in spite of the fact that it is "job oriented."

The fourth approach to the problem is, in fact, the classical way of working (Guion, 1965). The exploration aims at a tryout of criteria and predictors and the generation of hypotheses about possible relationships. Unfortunately, because of the rise of validity generalization, exploratory methods have lost much of their significance. But exploratory validation remains the only viable alternative when a relevant database is lacking or when jobs and situational contexts are rapidly changing.

In the preceding discussion, methods for choosing predictors that are based on expert judgments were excluded. Experienced researchers in the field of personnel selection seem to be able to make accurate estimates of the validity of predictors. According to Schmidt and associates (1983), the combined judgment of 20 experts yielded a validity estimate as accurate as a "criterion-related" validity study with N = 981. Experts with less experience, although "trained professionals in the field of personnel selection," do perform considerably less well, but still the combined judgment of 20 persons is as accurate as a local validity study with a sample size of 217 (Hirsch et al., 1985). From a logical point of view, it does not make sense to make use of expert judgment if sufficient data about comparable jobs are available. When such data are lacking, the use of expert judgments could be considered, but, since their value depends on several factors (Hamilton & Dickinson, 1987), the results would need to be interpreted carefully. Exploratory validation seems to be a more dependable strategy in this case.

With regard to the development of operational predictors, little progress has been made during recent years (Guion & Gibson, 1988; Hakel, 1986; and Zedeck & Cascio, 1984). The main trends can be summarized as follows. First, one can observe that validity generalization research has led to a certain reappreciation of the predictors that are associated with the sign approach, i.e., ability and aptitude tests. However, this is more a matter of growing confidence in existing instruments than an increased interest in the development of new instruments. In fact, publications on validity generalization seem to have hampered test development. At the same time, it is noted that predictive validities of tests tend to be somewhat lower than those of biodata and job samples (Schmitt et al., 1984).

Secondly, there is a still-growing interest in "content-based selection devices," the instruments that are based on the sample approach to prediction. Probably, this is not only a consequence of higher validity estimates but also of the good reputation that this kind of method has gained within the United States in legal cases on discrimination. Characteristics of this method are the elaborate job analysis as the first step of construction and the empirical content of the consequent construction steps. The construction method as such is not very new, as the roots of this approach lie in the critical incidents method (Flanagan, 1954), the retranslation technique (Smith & Kendall, 1963), and the sampling theory of statistical generalization. Nevertheless, several refinements have been proposed, and at present there exists a well-developed method for constructing a predictor instrument for a specific situation on the basis of the "behavioral consistency" principle. Schmitt and Ostroff (1986) distinguish between the following steps: job analysis, task generation, KSAOs generation (KSAO = knowledge, skills, aptitudes, other characteristics), importance ratings of tasks and KSAOs, selection of most important KSAOs, and construction of tests. Sackett (1987) has drawn attention to the fact that the development of instruments goes beyond the construction of stimulus materials. The presentation of stimulus materials and the scoring of responses are important aspects as well. Not only have the construction methods been formulated more precisely, but progress has also been made with regard to the development of procedures for the assessment of content validity. Lawshe (1975) developed a quantitative index, the Content Validity Ratio (CVR). Other indices, measuring some form of interrater agreement, can be found in Jones and associates (1983).

Although the behavioral consistency approach has initially been limited to job samples, several other selection methods have been developed on this basis: biographical inventories and biodata (Owens, 1976; Pannone, 1984), application forms for training and experience evaluation (Ash & Levine, 1985), accomplishment records (Hough, 1984), and interviews (Latham et al., 1980).

Third, assessment centers (see chapter 8) which combine the sign and sample approaches are still of considerable interest. But, according to the review by Schmitt and associates (1984), the validity has not been so high as initially expected. The highest validity is found against rating criteria ($r = .43$) which is not impressive because of common method variance and possible contamination of the criterion (Klimoski & Brickner, 1987). Objective criteria such as training results and salary level are predicted less well by assessment centers. In a recent meta-analysis by Gaugler and associates (1987) of 50 assessment center studies containing 107 validity coefficients, a mean validity coefficient (corrected for several statistical artifacts of .37) was reported. Higher validities were found in studies in which potential ratings were the criterion (corrected $r = .53$); promotional criteria are less well predicted (corrected $r = .30$). The validities for other types of criteria (overall performance rating, dimensional ratings, success in training, career advancement criteria) and other purposes (early potential identification, selection, research) lie somewhere in between. All in all, these findings illustrate that assessment centers are rather successful in making valid predictions.

Further Model Specification

Structure and Format.   Once the criteria and predictor variables have been identified, the *structure* of the model has to be established and parameter values have to be specified. From the various possibilities that exist here (e.g., conjunctive and disjunctive models), the linear compensatory model is the most well known and seems to be most frequently applied for both sign and sample-based prediction models. Discrete models can be mentioned as well, but their applicability seems limited: critical requirements that can be considered as "conditions sine qua non" do not occur frequently and are, at best, exemplary exceptions. The *format* of prediction models is usually algorithmic, which makes them suitable for computer processing. The tabular and graphical formats that were favored in classical textbooks seem to have lost much of their popularity.

A class of models that has been mentioned quite often during the last two decades is the moderator model. Initially, this type of model was proposed as a means for a more fair selection. The moderator variable, then, is a racial or other external characteristic. More recently, moderator models have been mentioned in the context of validity generalization. In these cases, the moderator variable is a situational or job characteristic that could serve to increase the homogeneity of a set of predictor variables.

Regarding the first application, it can be concluded that efforts to demonstrate moderator-effects for racial and group characteristics have generally failed (Schmitt & Noe, 1986). Whenever moderator-effects are observed, they are caused by differences in regression constants rather than regression weights of separate predictors. In the rare instances that differences are found, criterion scores of minority group members are, surprisingly, not underestimated, but rather overestimated. Although this has been observed several times, a satisfactory explanation is still lacking. For one part, one could think of statistical explanations: small sample sizes and little power to detect moderators. This explanation is not completely satisfactory, however, since no evidence for systematic underestimation has been found in larger samples.

Regarding the second point (situation and/or job characteristics as moderators for predictor criterion relationships within occupational classes as used for validity generalization purposes), the discussion is still going on. A study by Gutenberg and associates (1983) showed that the "information processing/decision making" job dimensions of the PAQ moderate the validity coefficients of several GATB dimensions (general ability, verbal and numerical ability). In addition to job characteristics of this type, the situational arrangement of a job, i.e., the work setting, is also a potential source of moderators (Greuter, 1988).

In applying the moderator approach, several serious statistical problems arise. A search for moderators is usually carried through by introducing a product or interaction term (predictor × moderator) in ordinary least-squares multiple regression analysis, so-called moderated regression analysis. Morris and associates (1986) pointed to the high correlation between this product-term and its constituent predictors, introducing linear dependencies in the set of regressor variables (see also Sockloff, 1976). The power of the (traditional) F-test for interaction can be quite low because of the relation among the regressor variables. As a consequence, moderator effects may have a diminished opportunity for detection, even when sample size is adequate. Morris and associates recommended principal regression analysis on the principal components of the predictor set in which the smallest principal component was deleted. However, their remedy may lead to an *over*estimation of the interaction effect as has been put forward by Cronbach (1988). Dunlap and Kemery (1988) demonstrated in a series of Monte Carlo simulations that detection of moderator effects in regression analysis is hampered by unreliability in either the predictor or the moderator variable. Although (un)reliability can always be acknowledged as a problem in prediction, it has a greater impact on the more complex moderator model: the reliability of the product-term is partly determined by the product of the reliabilities of its constituents. More precise and accurate measurement of regressor variables is called for in order to have a reasonable chance of detecting moderating effects.

Parameter Estimation. Parameters can be estimated with the help of either empirical or rational methods. The empirical methods can only be applied when a complete set of data is available. This poses a problem when validity generalization (or another type of meta-analysis) has been used as an alternative to an empirical validity study. Although the method could, in principle, be used for estimating intercorrelations as well, the required data are usually lacking, thereby forcing the designer to perform an empirical study after all, or to resort to rational methods.

The empirical methods for parameter estimation include the classical (unbiased) multiple regression analysis, and (biased) Stein and ridge regression methods. Multiple regression, according to Stein (1960), differs from classical multiple regression, because the regression weights are corrected with a factor that is similar to the shrinkage correction for multiple correlations. Since this correction factor is identical for all regression variables, the multiple correlation remains the same. The corrected weights are more reliable estimators of their population counterparts. Ridge regression is based on the same principle. Again, a correction of regression weights is carried through, but here the correction applies to the principle components, and its magnitude is variable depending on the eigenvalues. According to Darlington (1978), ridge regression leads to more reliable estimates of parameters than traditional methods, especially when there is a high degree of validity concentration, i.e., large differences in validities between principle components. Rational methods assign weights to predictors on the basis of expert judgments. The simplest method is unit weighing, but one can also ask judges to assign differential weights.

The Bayesian approach can be seen as a combination of empirical and rational approaches to parameter estimation. It offers a general method to specify a priori hypotheses on regression weights and revise these on the basis of empirical data. By applying this method iteratively, the estimates converge to their final values when more data are added. General Bayesian methods have been described by Lindley and Smith (1972) and Laughlin (1979). The method by Laughlin starts from a prior distribution of equal regression weights. These weights can be adjusted on the basis of empirical evidence. The method contains a factor by which the designer can assign a weight to the importance of the empirical data. A well-known application of the Bayesian method concerns the estimation of regression weights in comparable groups (m group regression). Molenaar and Lewis (1979) have improved the method that was originally proposed by Jackson and associates (1971). It should be noted that this m group method can be used to establish whether validities are generalizable. In a study on the prediction of grades from different curricula, Dunbar and associates (1985) showed, with the help of this technique, that validities are only generalizable within selected groups of criteria.

Evaluation of Models

Evaluation should be done against the requirements and constraints specified in advance. The main requirement is predictive validity. In the case of empirical parameter estimation, a validity estimate for the total model is usually obtained simultaneously. Rational models may require an additional analysis. There are few new developments here, apart from the biased regression methods mentioned above.

Recently there has been renewed interest in *synthetic validation* (Algera & Groenendijk, 1985; Mossholder & Arvey, 1984). A job is broken down into components for each of which a validity estimate is made. The validity of the overall procedure can be synthesized by rational/empirical methods such as the J-coefficient of Primoff (1955; see also Hamilton & Dickinson, 1987). According to Hamilton and Dickinson (1987), the job components may be specified in a job analysis as behaviors, traits, abilities, or skills, provided that the elements used can be conceived as determinants of behavior. The defining component relations of the J-coefficient can be measured with criterion-related validation designs but they can also be estimated rationally with the help of expert judgment, i.e., job incumbents and supervisors estimate indicators for job performance (relations between job elements and total job performance) and test experts give estimates of relational parameters based on test performance (validities).

The rationale for the J-coefficient offers great potential for estimating validities when an empirically based validation study is not feasible, or when a relevant database for conducting a form of meta-analysis is lacking. The concept can be applied most conveniently with inadequate sample sizes, inadequate performance ratings (or no ratings at all), new jobs without incumbents, rapidly changing jobs, or (unknown) situational variables that modify job performance or validities, and so on.

Decision Making

Major Design Considerations

While prediction models serve to yield information on future performance of candidates, the function of decision models is to transform this information into plans for action. In order to fulfill this function, some analysis has to be made, taking into account such factors as expected criterion performance, utility of these performance outcomes, and possibilities for planned action. All this can be done with the help of special analytical schemes, several of which are available in the literature. In addition, a decision strategy is needed that embodies a certain principle for dealing with utilities and uncertainty. Such strategies can be borrowed from (normative) decision theory. Some examples are:

1. Maximization of utility (in case of certain outcomes);
2. Maximization of expected utility (in case of decision making under risk);
3. Maximin, Maximax, Minimax regret (in case of decision making under full uncertainty).

Below we will discuss how features of decision models depend on the analytical scheme and the decision strategy that has been adopted. To be sure, decisions can be made, and actually quite often are made, on an informal judgmental basis, without the help of a decision model. Studies on the judgmental processes involved and on efforts to model them (so called paramorphic representation) have been discussed by Wiggins (1980) and Roe (1983).

For describing the design of decision models we can once again use the design methodology that was presented at the beginning of the chapter. By doing this, we obtain the following general description of the design of decision models:

1. Defining the problem and specifying requirements: how is the predictive information on candidates transposed in decisions such as accepting or rejecting an applicant?
2. Defining the model's content: what criterion and utility variables must be defined, and what are the possible actions to decide upon?
3. Choosing the model's structure: how are utilities related to criterion performance?

4. Choosing the model's format: again, usually an algebraic function is chosen.

5. Estimating model parameters: specifying the precise form of the relationship between each utility variable and the set of criterion variables under consideration by estimating weights of criterion variables (relational parameters) and calculating cutoff scores (instrumental parameters).

6. Evaluation of the model: analyzing the differences between expected utilities and actual utilities accomplished by applying the decision model.

Defining Decision Models' Content

Decision models can take many different forms. Some commonly used elements are:

1. Two or more possibilities for action, i.e., accepting, rejecting, assigning one or more candidates;

2. One or more criterion variables referring to job performance, on which expected scores or probabilities of scores can be expressed;

3. One or more utility dimensions, expressing the value of job performance for the organization, either subjectively or objectively.

Sometimes the models are extended by incorporating:

4. One or more predictor variables that can be associated directly with either utility dimensions or actions;

5. Costs associated with collecting and processing information on candidates.

Possible actions follow from the analysis of the organization's personnel plan and the current workforce situation. Utilities and criteria can be found in a utility analysis. This covers: (1) establishing the number and nature of utility dimensions; and (2) assessing the relationship of utility dimensions with specific criteria (e.g., by making use of published criterion studies; see, for example, Brogden & Taylor, 1950; van Naerssen, 1962). Criteria and predictors can be chosen on the basis of previously established prediction models.

It should be noted that decision modeling for personnel selection purposes is far less developed than prediction modeling. Some general schemes for analyzing decision situations that can be applied to personnel selection have been published in the context of decision theory. In addition, there are a number of methods and models that have been developed for personnel selection, but the older models tend to be poorly conceptualized, and little developmental conceptual work has been performed during the last decade.

Further Model Specification

Structure and Format. The structure of the decision model can only be established after the elements have been defined. As has been shown, the elements that take a central place are utility dimensions and criteria. Hence, a crucial question is how to relate them to each other and how to express the relationship. When the usual algebraic format is adopted, this comes down to the specification of a utility function. The general form of the utility function is $U = f(Y)$. By making certain assumptions regarding its shape or properties, one can specify this function. Well-known types of utility functions are the threshold function (e.g., Gross & Su, 1975), the linear function (Mellenbergh & van der Linden, 1977), and the normal ogive function (van Naerssen et al., 1986; Novick & Lindley, 1978).

The relationship between criteria and utility can also be established by the direct assignment of numerical values. This implies that only minimal assumptions have to be made (Hull et al., 1973).

Within this latter category, one finds objective methods based on human resources accounting (see, for example, cost-accounting approach as described by Cascio, 1982, pp. 154–156), as well as subjective methods based on ratings. A usable rating method has been proposed by Mellenbergh (see Vrijhoff et al., 1983; Gaag et al., 1986). This method has been subjected to a tryout in the context of pass-fail decisions in education. In the 1986 study, 10 teachers and 10 students were asked to give their judgment about the utility of passing and failing on examinations in the English language, French language, and biology. The utilities were scaled according to the constant sum method. It was concluded by the researchers that the method was quite reliable, that there were only limited differences between the utility functions of teachers and students, and between the utility functions for the different examinations, and, furthermore, that two of each three utility functions could be approximated by a linear function.

In order to arrive at decisions, a relationship should be laid between the utility functions and possible actions. This may be done with the help of criterion cutoff scores. The procedures for finding such cutoff scores will be discussed later.

Decision models may include predictor variables as well. Such extended models offer the possibility to define cutoff scores on the predictor variables, which simplifies the total selection process. In fact, it means that the predictor model is incorporated, either partially or completely, within the decision model. For the relevant choices regarding the structure of the model, we can therefore refer to an earlier section of this chapter.

Incorporating costs in the decision model means splitting up fixed and variable cost components of selection, and relating variable costs to the parts of the procedure. Usually a linear cost function is employed, which relates the number of candidates to be examined to the overall expenditure. To be sure, costs have also been related to the length and composition of the examination procedure, but this is of no relevance in the framework of decision making on candidates unless an adaptive procedure is followed.

Parameter Estimation. Because the utility of selection outcomes is essentially a matter of subjective judgment, procedures are called for by which such judgments can be made explicit. The rating method, as well as accounting methods, have already been referred to. When the decision has been made to use utility functions, the parameters of these functions have to be established separately. This can be done by regression methods, taking the performance criteria as "predictors" and utility ratings as "criteria." The regression function can be of any linear or nonlinear type.

The same approach can be used for finding the parameters of cost functions. When predictor variables are included, the earlier material applies.

The determination of cutoff scores on either criteria or predictors requires the application of some decision strategy. As a rule, this is "maximization of expected utility" (MEU). The usual procedure to establish criterion cutoff scores for individual decisions is to determine the criterion score at which the two utility functions intersect, i.e., the utility of rejection equals that of acceptance. A related procedure exists for collective decisions. Here, one looks for the criterion score at which the accumulated utility for the group to be accepted equals that of the group to be rejected.

De Gruijter and Hambleton (1984) and van der Linden (1984) have studied various utility functions with regard to the determination of cutoff scores. A general problem seems to be that the accuracy of utility functions for passing and failing (on examinations) is not sufficient to assess reliably the point of intersection, and hence the cutoff score. According to De Gruijter and Hambleton (1984), a solution can be found in "robustness studies" which specify the range of population cutoff values within which one single cutoff score can be used. These authors also discuss problems that can arise in relation to utility functions and cutoffs for subpopulations.

Splitting up the total population into subpopulations can lead to small sample sizes which preclude the establishment of stable cutoff scores.

The procedures for establishing predictor cutoff scores resemble those for criterion cutoff scores. In fact, the latter can be seen as a special case of the former, when predictors are assumed to have a linear relationship to criteria. A general assumption-free method for determining predictor cutoffs has been described by Roe (1983) both for the case of individual decisions and for collective decisions. The methods described by Stone and Kendall (1956) and Mellenbergh and van der Linden (1977) can be considered as special cases of the method for individual decisions. The methods described by Guttman and Raju (1965), Guilford (1965), Rorer and associates (1966), Darlington and Staufer (1966), Alf and Dorman (1967), Cronbach and Gleser (1965), Naylor and Shine (1965), and Taylor and Russell (1939) can be seen as specific instances of the method for collective decisions.

The aforementioned methods do not apply to fixed quota situations. In such situations, an important consideration is whether the number of applicants should be considered as a given premise.

If the number of applicants cannot be extended (for example, by intensifying recruitment procedures), the only possibility is to manipulate the selection ratio, i.e., the corresponding cutoff score. If predictor, criterion, and utility variables are linearly related to each other, this comes down to selecting those applicants with the highest predictor-scores until the quotum has been reached (top-down strategy). A serious drawback of this method is that cutoff scores can fluctuate considerably in time, due to quantitative and/or qualitative changes in the supply of applicants.

If the number of applicants is not to be considered as fixed, one can act as is indicated above for the quotum-free situation, i.e., placing the cutoff scores at the intersection of the utility functions for rejection and acceptance. In this situation, it is necessary to define an optimal selection ratio that can be found, for instance, following the methods of Cronbach and Gleser (1965) or van Naerssen (1962, p. 363). A recent review on cutoff scores, including legal issues, has been given by Cascio and colleagues (1988).

Evaluation of Decision Models

A basis for the evaluation of decision models can be found in the deviation of estimated utilities from actually obtained utilities. In an analogy of the concept of predictive validity, which expresses the deviation between predicted and obtained criterion performance, one can define a concept of decision validity. In the same way, one could define decision reliability as the degree to which equivalent sets of estimated utilities correspond (Roe, 1983, p. 250).

Various specific coefficients for evaluating decisions have been proposed (Hambleton & Novick, 1973; Swaminathan, Hambleton, & Algina, 1974, 1975; Huynh, 1976). A general coefficient for evaluating the "internal and external optimality" (reliability) of a decision procedure has been elaborated by Mellenbergh and van der Linden (1977).

Another approach would be to compare the overall, i.e., cumulated, utility of decisions taken with a given model. For this purpose, several methods have been developed, for example, by Taylor and Russell (1939), Naylor and Shine (1965), and Brogden, Cronbach, and Gleser (Brogden, 1949; Cronbach & Gleser, 1965).

The approach of Brogden and Cronbach and Gleser is, at this moment, by far the most popular method in the field of industrial and organizational psychology. In this model, the total utility is expressed with the following functions:

$$\Delta U = N_s \cdot SD_y \cdot r_{xy} \cdot \frac{\gamma}{\phi} - \frac{C \cdot N_s}{\phi}$$

where:

ΔU = dollar value payoff from the selection program (as contrasted with random selection);

N_s = number of selectees;

SD_y = standard deviation of performance in dollars (calculated in the group of present employees);

r_{xy} = validity of the predictor;

ϕ = selection ratio;

γ = ordinate of the normal curve associated with ϕ;

C = per applicant costs of the selection program (variable and fixed costs).

Confidence intervals for ΔU can be calculated following a procedure developed by Alexander and Barrick (1987). In deriving this model, several assumptions have been made: utility functions are assumed to be linear (as are predictor-criterion relations), utilities for rejecting employees are considered to be zero, and ΔU expresses the net gain in utility as contrasted with an a priori procedure of random selection.

The Brogden/Cronbach/Gleser model has remained almost unchanged except for some minor embellishments. Schmidt and associates (1979) multiplied the benefit component of the model by the expected tenure of the hired cohort (i.e., T), pointing out that revenues are accumulating for each year of tenure. Further improvements have been suggested by Boudreau (1983a; see also Boudreau, 1989) and Cronshaw and Alexander (1985), such as including several financial/economic concepts such as costs of capital (discount rate), taxes, service value, and so on. Also, the effects of recruitment have been made explicit (Boudreau & Rynes, 1985). The accumulation of effects due to the repeated application of selection programs can be calculated with the so-called Employee Flows Utility Model by Boudreau (1983b).

Most of the research efforts are now directed at developing accurate procedures for estimating SD_y in dollars. For a review of such methods as the 40 percent to 70 percent rule, the CREPID-procedure, and the percentile method of Schmidt and associates (1979), the reader is referred to Cascio (1982; see also Cascio, 1987). As far as the empirical evidence demonstrates (e.g., Burke & Frederick, 1986; DeSimone et al., 1986; Reilly & Smither, 1985; Weekly et al., 1985), no method seems clearly superior to others. A cautious conclusion may be that the more global estimation procedures (for example, the percentile method of Schmidt et al., 1979) give higher estimates. However, even these higher estimates can sometimes be lower than an empirically counted value (DeSimone et al., 1986). All together, it is not all clear where the research on SD_y is leading (Guion & Gibson, 1988). If the goal is to get realistic and accurate estimates, there is a long way to go considering the very large standard errors of utility estimates as reported by Alexander and Barrick (1987). If the main concern is calculating *relative* utilities of alternative selection procedures, utility research has already accomplished too much; these latter inferences can probably also be made (fairly accurately!) on the basis of comparing validities alone.

Designing Selection Procedures

In the previous paragraphs, we have focused on two functions of selection procedures, i.e., prediction and decision making, discussing some technical aspects of modeling. It should be recalled that there are other functions as well, and also that every function can be implemented in a variety of ways when designing selection procedures. The problem faced by the designer is to make a choice from the numerous technical options in such a way that the singularities of the particular selection problem are optimally met. Given the reductive nature of the design task, it is impossible to give specific recommendations with regard to the composition of selection procedures. Much depends on the "program of requirements" and the ideas and experience of the designer. For an illustration, we would like to refer to Roe (1989), who gives a short account of a project that aimed at the redesign of a set of selection procedures for a psychological selection consultancy.

Generally speaking, there are at least four types of considerations that can play a role in the design of selection procedures (Roe, 1989):

1. Effectiveness considerations, which have to do with the appropriateness of the predictive information, and the correctness of decisions yielded by the procedure. These considerations may, for example, lead to the inclusion of certain types of questions on the application form, the use of certain specific aptitude tests, or a combined use of tests, biodata, and work samples.

2. Efficiency considerations, relating to the overall costs and benefits of the use of the selection procedure, and the contribution to both by its distinctive components. Efficiency may be increased by adopting cheaper information (e.g., school grades), reducing test length, or introducing multiple selection stages (Cronbach & Gleser, 1965).

3. Ethical considerations, relating to such aspects as intrusion of privacy, right to appeal, and nondiscrimination. Leaving questions on sensitive information for the end of the procedure, including a procedure for filing and processing complaints, or setting different selection ratios for applicants of different cultural backgrounds, may be the result of these considerations.

4. Managerial considerations, concerning the commercial side of personnel selection, as well as the organization of psychologists' and staff activities. These may lead to a standardization of test duration, to a test administration program that optimizes the use of manpower, or, alternatively, to automation of particular parts of the procedure for reasons of cutting labor costs.

Many of these aspects surpass the psychometric and decision-theoretic views that have dominated personnel selection literature during the last decades. Taking into account the results from the study referred to above, it seems to us that the technological approach to selection offers an adequate framework for dealing with all of these aspects simultaneously.

References

Alexander, R. A., & Barrick, M. R. (1987). Estimating the standard error or projected dollar gains in utility. *Journal of Applied Psychology* 72:475–479.

Alf, E. F., & Dorman, D. D. (1967). The classification of individuals into two criterion groups on the basis of a discontinuous pay-off function. *Psychometrika* 32:115–123.

Algera, J. A., & Greuter, M. A. M. (1989). Job analysis for personnel selection. In M. Smith & I. T. Robertson (eds.), *Advances in selection and assessment*. New York: Wiley, pp. 7–30.

Algera, J. A., & Groenendijk, B. (1985). Synthetische validiteit: Een vergelijking van benaderingen. *Nederlands Tijdschift voor de Psychologie* 40:255–269.

Algera, J. A., Jansen, P. G. W., Roe, R. A., & Vijn, P. (1984). Validity generalization: Some critical remarks on the Schmidt-Hunter procedure. *Journal of Occupational Psychology* 57:197–210.

Arvey, R. D., & Campion, J. E. (1982). The employment interview: A summary and review of recent research. *Personnel Psychology* 35:281–322.

Ash, R. A., & Edgell, S. L. (1975). A note on the readability of the Position Analysis Questionnaire (PAQ). *Journal of Applied Psychology* 60:765–766.

Ash, R. A., & Levine, E. L. (1985). Job applicant training and work experience evaluation: An empirical comparison of four methods. *Journal of Applied Psychology* 70:572–576.

Asher, J. J., & Sciarrino, J. A. (1974). Realistic work sample tests. *Personnel Psychology* 27:519–533.

Austin, J. T., Humphreys, L. G., & Hulin, C. L. (1989). Another view of dynamic criteria: A critical reanalysis of Barrett, Caldwell, and Alexander. *Personnel Psychology* 42(3):583–596.

Banks, C. G., & Murphy, K. R. (1985). Toward narrowing the research-practice gap in performance appraisal. *Personnel Psychology* 38:335–345.

Barrett, G. V., & Alexander, R. A. (1989). Rejoinder to Austin, Humphreys, and Hulin: Critical reanalysis of Barrett, Caldwell, and Alexander. *Personnel Psychology* 42(3):597–612.

Barrett, G. V., Caldwell, M. S., & Alexander, R. A. (1985). The concept of dynamic criteria: A critical reanalysis. *Personnel Psychology* 38:41–56.

Bemis, S. E. (1968). Occupational validity of the General Aptitude Test Battery. *Personnel Psychology* 21:396–407.

Bernardin, H. J., & Buckley, M. R. (1981). Strategies in rater training. *Academy of Management Review* 6:205–212.

Boudreau, J. W. (1983a). Economic considerations in estimating the utility of human resource productivity improvement programs. *Personnel Psychology* 36:551–557.

————. (1983b). Effects of employee flows on utility analysis of human resource productivity improvement programs. *Personnel Psychology* 36:396–407.

————. (1989). Selection utility analysis: A review and agenda for future research. In M. Smith & I. T. Robertson (eds.), *Advances in selection and assessment*. New York: Wiley.

Boudreau, J. W., & Rynes, S. L. (1985). Role of recruitment in staffing utility analysis. *Journal of Applied Psychology* 70:354–366.

Brogden, H. E. (1949). When testing pays off. *Personnel Psychology* 2:171–185.

Brogden, H. E., & Taylor, E. K. (1950). The dollar criterion—Applying the cost accounting concept to criterion construction. *Personnel Psychology* 3:133–154.

Burke, M. J. (1984). Validity generalization: A review and critique of the correlation model. *Personnel Psychology* 37:93–115.

Burke, M. J., & Frederick, J. T. (1986). A comparison of economic utility estimations for alternative SDy estimation procedures. *Journal of Applied Psychology* 71:334–339.

Campbell, J. P. (1983). Some possible implications of "modeling" for the conceptualization of measurement. In F. Landy, S. Zedeck, & J. Cleveland (eds.), *Performance measurement and theory*. Hillsdale, NJ: Erlbaum, pp. 277–298.

Campbell J. P., Dunnette, M. D., Lawler, E. E., & Weick, K. E. (1970). *Managerial behavior, performance, and effectiveness*. New York: McGraw-Hill.

Campion, M. A. (1983). Personnel selection for physically demanding jobs: Review and recommendations. *Personnel Psychology* 36:527–550.

Carroll, S. J., & Schneier, C. E. (1982). *Performance appraisal and review systems*. Glenview, IL: Scott, Foresman and Company.

Cascio, W. F. (1982). *Costing human resources*. New York: Van Nostrand Reinhold Company.

————. (1987). *Applied psychology in personnel management*, 3rd ed. Englewood Cliffs, NJ: Prentice-Hall.

Cascio, W. F., Alexander, R. A., & Barrett, G. V. (1988). Setting cutoff scores: Legal, psychometric, and professional issues and guidelines. *Personnel Psychology* 41:1–24.

Cornelius, E. T., Schmidt, F. L., & Carron, T. J. (1984). Job classification approaches and the implementation of validity generalization results. *Personnel Psychology* 37:247–260.

Cronbach, L. J. (1988). Statistical tests for moderator variables: Flaws in analyses recently proposed. *Psychological Bulletin* 102:414–417.

Cronbach, L. J., & Gleser, G. C. (1965). *Psychological tests and personnel decisions*, 2nd ed. Urbana, IL: University of Illinois Press.

Cronshaw, S. F., & Alexander, R. A. (1985). One answer to the demand for accountability: Selection utility as an investment decision. *Organizational Behavior and Human Performance* 35:102–118.

Cunningham, J. W., Boese, R. R., Neeb, R. W., & Pass, J. J. (1983). Systematically derived work dimensions: Factor analysis of the occupation analysis inventory. *Journal of Applied Psychology* 68:232–252.

Darlington, R. B. (1978). Reduced variance regression. *Psychological Bulletin* 85:1238–1255.

Darlington, R. B., & Staufer, G. F. (1966). A method of choosing a cutting point on a test. *Journal of Applied Psychology* 50:229–231.

de Gruijter, D. N., & Hambleton, R. K. (1984). On problems encountered using decision theory to set cut-off scores. *Applied Psychological Measurement* 8:1–8.

DeNisi, A. S., Cafferty, T. P., & Meglino, B. M. (1984). A cognitive view of the performance appraisal process: A model and research implications. *Organization Behavior and Human Performance* 33:360–396.

DeNisi, A. S., Cornelius, E. T. III, & Blencoe, A. G. (1987). Further investigation of common knowledge effects on job analysis ratings. *Journal of Applied Psychology* 72:261–268.

DeSimone, R. L., Alexander, R. A., & Cronshaw, S. F. (1986). Accuracy and reliability of SDy estimates in utility analysis. *Journal of Occupational Psychology* 59:93–102.

Desmond, R. E., & Weiss, D. J. (1973). Supervisor estimation of abilities required in jobs. *Journal of Vocational Behavior* 3:181–194.

————. (1975). Worker estimation of abilities requirements of their jobs. *Journal of Vocational Behavior* 7:13–29.

Dunbar, S. B., Mayekawa, S., & Novick, M. R. (1985). *Simultaneous estimation of regression functions for Marine Corps technical training specialties* (ONR Technical Report 85–1). Iowa City, IA: Cada Res. Group, University of Iowa.

Dunlap, W. P., & Kemery, E. R. (1988). Failure to detect moderating effects: Is multicolinearity the problem? *Psychological Bulletin* 102:418–420.

Eekels, J. (1983). Design processes seen as decision chains: Their intuitive and discursive aspects. *Proceedings of the International Conference on Engineering Design*. Copenhagen.

Einhorn, H. J. (1986). Accepting error to make less error. *Journal of Personality Assessment* 50(3):387–395.

Feldman, J. M. (1981). Beyond attribution theory: Cognitive processes in performance appraisal. *Journal of Applied Psychology* 66(2):127–148.

Flanagan, J. C. (1954). The critical incident technique. *Psychological Bulletin* 51:327–358.

Fleishman, E. A., & Quaintance, M. K. (1984). *Taxonomies of human performance*. New York: Academic Press.

Gaugler, B. B., Rosenthal, D. B., Thornton III, G. G., & Bentson, C. (1987). Meta-analysis of assessment center validity. *Journal of Applied Psychology* 72(3):439–511.

Ghiselli, E. E. (1966). *The validity of occupational aptitude tests*. New York: Wiley.

————. (1973). The validity of aptitude tests in personnel selection. *Personnel Psychology* 26:461–477.

Greuter, M. A. M. (1988). *Personeelsselektie in perspektief*. Haarlem: Uitgeverij Thesis.

Gross, A. L., & Su, W. (1975). Defining a "fair" and "unbiased" selection model: A question of utilities. *Journal of Applied Psychology* 60:345–351.

Guilford, J. P. (1965). *Fundamental statistics in psychology and education*, 4th ed. New York: McGraw-Hill.

Guion, R. M. (1965). *Personnel testing*. New York: McGraw-Hill.

————. Scoring of content domain samples: The problem of fairness. *Journal of Applied Psychology* 63:499–506.

Guion, R. M., & Gibson, W. M. (1988). Personnel selection and placement. *Annual Review of Psychology* 39:349–374.

Gutenberg, R. L., Arvey, R. D., & Osburn, H. G. (1983). Moderating effects of decision-making/information-processing job dimensions on test validities.

Journal of Applied Psychology 68(4):602–608.

Guttman, I., & Raju, N. S. (1965). A minimum loss function as determiner of optimal cutting scores. *Personnel Psychology* 18:179–185.

Hakel, M. D. (1986). Personnel selection and placement. *Annual Review of Psychology* 37:351–382.

Hambleton, R. K., & Novick, M. R. (1973). Toward an integration of theory and method for criterion-referenced tests. *Journal of Educational Measurement* 10:159–170.

Hamilton, J. W., & Dickinson, T. L. (1987). Comparison of several procedures for generating J-coefficients. *Journal of Applied Psychology* 72(1):49–54.

Harvey, R. J., & Theodore, T. L. (1986). Monte Carlo baselines for interrater reliability correlations using the Position Analysis Questionnaire. *Personnel Psychology* 39:345–357.

Hirsch, H. R., Schmidt, F. L., & Hunter, J. F. (1985). Estimation of employment validities by less experienced judges. *Personnel Psychology* 38:337–345.

Holt, R. R. (1986). Clinical and statistical prediction: A retrospective and would-be integrative perspective. *Journal of Personality Assessment* 50(3):376–386.

Hough, L. M. (1984). Development and evaluation of the "accomplishment record" method of selecting and promoting professionals. *Journal of Applied Psychology* 69:135–146.

Hull, J. C., Moore, P. G., & Thomas, H. (1973). Utility and its measurement. *Journal of the Royal Statistical Society, Series A* 136:226–247.

Hunter, J. E., & Hunter, R. F. (1984). Validity and utility of alternative predictors of job performance. *Psychological Bulletin* 96(1):72–98.

Huynh, H. (1976). On the reliability of decisions in domain-referenced testing. *Journal of Educational Measurement* 13:253–264.

Ilgen, D. R., & Favero, J. L. (1985). Limits in generalizations from psychological research to performance appraisal processes. *Academy of Management Review* 10:311–321.

Jackson, P. H., Novick, M. R., & Thayer, D. I. (1971). Estimating regression in m-groups. *British Journal of Mathematical and Statistical Psychology* 24:129–153.

James, L. R., Demarree, R. G., & Mulaik, S. A. (1986). A note on validity generalization procedures. *Journal of Applied Psychology* 71(3):440–450.

Jansen, P. G. W., Roe, R. A., Vijn, P., & Algera, J. A. (1986). *Validity generalization revisited.* Delft: University Press.

Jones, A. P., Johnson, L. A., Butler, M. C., & Main, D. S. (1983). Apples and oranges: An empirical comparison of commonly used indices of interrater agreement. *Academy of Management Journal* 26:207–519.

Kemery, E. R., Mossholder, K. W., & Dunlap, W. P. (1989). Meta-analysis and moderator variables: Cautionary note on transportability. *Journal of Applied Psychology* 74(1):168–170.

Kemery, E. R., Mossholder, K. W., & Roth, L. (1987). The power of the Schmidt and Hunter additive model of validity generalization. *Journal of Applied Psychology* 72(1):30–37.

Kendall, W. E. (1955). Industrial psychology. *Annual Review of Psychology* 6:217–250.

Klimoski, R., & Brickner, M. (1987). Why do assessment centers work? The puzzle of assessment center validity. *Personnel Psychology* 40:243–260.

Landy, F. J., & Farr, J. L. (1983). *The measurement of work performance*. Orlando, FL: Academic Press.

Landy, F. J., Zedeck, S., & Cleveland, J. (eds.) (1983). *Performance measurement and theory*. Hillsdale, NJ: Erlbaum.

Latham, G. P. (1986). Job performance and appraisal. In C. L. Cooper & I. Robertson (eds.), *International review of industrial and organizational psychology*. New York: John Wiley and Sons, Ltd., pp. 118–155.

Latham, G. P., Saari, L. M., Pursell, E. D., & Campion, M. A. (1980). The situation interview. *Journal of Applied Psychology* 65:422–427.

Laughlin, J. E. (1979). A Bayesian alternative to least squares and equal weighting coefficient in regression. *Psychometrika* 44:271–288.

Lawshe, C. H. (1975). A quantitative approach to content validity. *Personnel Psychology* 28:563–575.

Lawshe, C. H., & Balma, M. J. (1966). *Principles of personnel testing*, 2nd ed. New York: McGraw-Hill.

Lent, R. H., Aurbach, H. A., & Levin, L. S. (1971). Predictors, criteria and significant results. *Personnel Psychology* 24:519–533.

Lindley, D. V., & Smith, A. F. M. (1972). Bayesian estimates for the linear model. *Journal of the Royal Statistical Society, Series B* 33:1–41.

Lopez, F. M., Kesselman, G. A., & Lopez, F. E. (1981). An empirical test of a trait-oriented job analysis technique. *Personnel Psychology* 34:479–502.

McCormick, E. J., DeNisi, A. S., & Shaw, J. B. (1979). Use of the Position Analysis Questionnaire for establishing the job component validity of tests. *Journal of Applied Psychology* 64(1):51–56.

McCormick, E. J., Jeanneret, R. R., & Mecham, R. C. (1972). A study of job characteristics and job dimensions as based on the Position Analysis Questionnaire. *Journal of Applied Psychology* 56:347–368.

Meehl, P. E. (1986). Causes and effects of my disturbing little book. *Journal of Personality Assessment* 50(3):370–375.

Mellenbergh, G. J., & van der Linden, W. J. (1977). *The linear utility model for optimal selection*. Amsterdam: Psychologisch Laboratorium, Universiteit van Amsterdam.

Miller, R. B. (1973). Development of a taxonomy of human performance: Design of a systems task vocabulary. *JSAS Catalog of Selected Documents in Psychology* 3:29–30 (Ms. No. 327).

Molenaar, I. W., & Lewis, C. (1979). Bayesian m-group regression: A survey and an improved model. *Methoden en Data Nieuwsbrief* 4(1):62–72.

Morris, J. H., Sherman, J. D., & Mansfield, E. R. (1986). Failures to detect moderating effects with ordinary least squares-moderated multiple regression: Some reasons and a remedy. *Psychological Bulletin* 99(2):282–288.

Mossholder, K. W., & Arvey, R. D. (1984). Synthetic validity: A conceptual and comparative review. *Journal of Applied Psychology* 69:322–333.

Naylor, J. C. (1983). Modeling performance. In F. Landy, S. Zedeck, & J. Cleveland (eds.), *Performance measurement and theory*. Hillsdale, NJ: Erlbaum, pp. 299–305.

Naylor, J. C., & Shine, L. C. (1965). A table for determining the increase in mean criterion score obtained by using a selection device. *Journal of Applied Psychology* 3:33–42.

Novick, M. R., & Lindley, D. V. (1978). The use of more realistic utility functions in educational applications. *Journal of Educational Measurement* 15:181–192.

Osburn, H. G., Callendar, J. C., Greener, J. M., & Ashworth, S. (1983). Statistical power of tests of the situational specificity hypothesis in validity generalization studies: A cautionary note. *Journal of Applied Psychology* 68(1):115–122.

Owens, W. A. (1976). Background data. In M. D. Dunnette (ed.), *Handbook of industrial and organizational psychology*. Chicago, IL: Rand McNally, pp. 609–644.

Paese, P. W., & Switzer, F. S. III. (1988). Validity generalization and hypothetical reliability distributions: A test of the Schmidt-Hunter procedure. *Journal of Applied Psychology* 73(2):267–274.

Pannone, R. D. (1984). Predicting test performance: A content valid approach to screening applicants. *Personnel Psychology* 37:507–514.

Pearlman, K., Schmidt, F. L., & Hunter, J. E. (1980). Validity generalization results for test used to predict job proficiency and training success in clerical occupations. *Journal of Applied Psychology* 65:373–406.

Primoff, E. S. (1955, May). *Test selection by job analysis: The J-coefficient*. Washington, DC: U.S. Civil Service Commission, Assembled Test Technical Edition.

Rasmussen, J. R., & Loher, B. T. (1988). Appropriate critical percentages for the Schmidt and Hunter meta-analysis procedure: Comparative evaluation of type I error rate and power. *Journal of Applied Psychology* 73(4):683–687.

Reilly, R. R., & Chao, G. T. (1982). Validity and fairness of some alternative employee selection procedures. *Personnel Psychology* 35:1–62.

Reilly, R. R., & Israelski, E. (1988). Development and validation of minicourses in the telecommunication industry. *Journal of Applied Psychology* 73(4):721–726.

Reilly, R. R., & Smither, J. W. (1985). An examination of two alternative techniques to estimate the standard deviation of job performance in dollars. *Journal of Applied Psychology* 70:651–661.

Robertson, I. T., & Downs, S. (1989). Work-sample tests of trainability: A meta-analysis. *Journal of Applied Psychology* 74(3):402–410.

Roe, R. A. (1983). *Grondslagen der personeelsselektie*. Assen: Van Gorcum.

—————. (1984, August). *Advances in performance modeling: The case of validity generalization*. Paper presented at the International Congress of Psychology, Acapulco, Mexico.

—————. (1987). Un enfoque technologico en seleccion de personal. *Revista Psicologia del Trabajo y de las Organizaciones* 3(7):95–104.

—————. (1989). Designing selection procedures. In P. Herriot (ed.), *Handbook of assessment and selection in organizations.* New York: Wiley, pp. 127–142.

Ronan, W. W. & Prien, E. P. (1971). *Perspectives on the measurement of human performance.* New York: Appleton-Century-Crofts.

Rorer, L. G., Hoffman, P. J., & Hsieh, K. C. (1966). Utilities as base-rate multipliers in the determination of optimum cutting scores for the discrimination of groups of unequal size and variance. *Journal of Applied Psychology* 50:364–368.

Sackett, P. R. (1987). Assessment centers and content validity: Some selected issues. *Personnel Psychology* 40:13–25.

Sackett, P. R., & Harris, M. M. (1984). Honesty testing for personnel selection: A review and critique. *Personnel Psychology* 37:221–245.

Sackett, P. R., Harris, M. M., & Orr, J. M. (1986). On seeking moderator variables in the meta-analysis of correlational data: A Monte Carlo investigation of statistical power and resistance to type I error. *Journal of Applied Psychology* 71(2):302–310.

Sackett, P. R., Schmidt, N., Tenopyr, M. L., & Kehoe, J. (1985). Commentary on forty questions about validity generalization and meta-analysis. *Personnel Psychology* 38(4):697–798.

Sarbin, T. (1986). Prediction and clinical inference: Forty years later. *Journal of Personality Assessment* 50(3):362–369.

Schmidt, F. L., & Hunter, J. E. (1977). Development of a general solution to the problem of validity generalization. *Journal of Applied Psychology* 62:529–540.

—————. (1981). Old theories and new research findings. *American Psychologist* 36(10):1128–1137.

Schmidt, F. L., Hunter, J. E., Croll, P. R., & McKenzie, R. C. (1983). Estimation of employment test validities by expert judgment. *Journal of Applied Psychology* 68:550–651.

Schmidt, F. L., Hunter, J. E., McKenzie, R. C., & Muldrow, T. W. (1979). Impact of valid selection procedures on work force productivity. *Journal of Applied Psychology* 64:609–626.

Schmidt, F. L., Hunter, J. E., Pearlman, K., & Shane, G. S. (1985). Forty questions about validity generalization and meta-analysis. *Personnel Psychology* 38:697–798.

Schmidt, F. L., & Kaplan, L. B. (1971). Composite vs. multiple criteria: A review and resolution of the controversy. *Personnel Psychology* 24:419–434.

Schmitt, N., Gooding, R. A., & Kirsch, M. (1984). Meta-analysis of validity studies published between 1964 and 1982 and the investigation of study characteristics. *Personnel Psychology* 37:407–422.

Schmitt, N., & Noe, R. A. (1986). Personnel selection and equal employment opportunity. In C. L. Cooper, & I. Robertson (ed.), *International review of industrial and organizational psychology.* New York: Wiley, pp. 71–115.

Schmitt, N., & Ostroff, C. (1986). Operationalizing the "behavioral consistency" approach: Selection test development based on a content-oriented strategy. *Personnel Psychology* 39:91–108.

Smith, J. E., & Hakel, M. D. (1979). Convergence among data source, response bias, and reliability and validity of a structured job analysis questionnaire. *Personnel Psychology* 32:677–692.

Smith, P. C. (1976). Behavior, results, and organizational effectiveness: The problem of criteria. In M. D. Dunnette (ed.), *Handbook of industrial and organizational psychology*. Chicago, IL: Rand McNally, pp. 745–775.

―――――. (1986). Training programs for performance appraisal: A review. *Academy and Management Review* 11(1):22–40.

Smith, P., & Kendall, L. M. (1963). Retranslation of expectations: An approach to the construction of unambiguous anchors for rating scales. *Journal of Applied Psychology* 47:149–155.

Sockloff, A. L. (1976). Spurious product correlation. *Educational and Psychological Measurement* 36:33–44(b).

Spector, P. E., & Levine, E. L. (1987). Meta-analysis for integrating study outcomes: A Monte Carlo study of its susceptibility to type I and type II errors. *Journal of Applied Psychology* 72:3–9.

Stegmüller, W. (1984). *Probleme und Resultate der Wissenschaftstheorie und Analytischen Philosophie. Band I: Wissenschaftliche Erklärung und Begründung*. Studienausgabe Teil 5. New York: Springer.

Stein, C. (1960). Multiple regression. In I. Alkin et al. (eds.), *Contributions to probability and statistics*. Stanford: Stanford University Press.

Stone, C. H., & Kendall, W. E. (1956). *Effective personnel selection procedures*. Englewood Cliffs, NJ: Prentice Hall.

Swaminathan, H., Hambleton, R. K., & Algina, J. (1974). Reliability of criterion-referenced tests: A decision theoretic formulation. *Journal of Educational Measurement* 11:263–267.

―――――. (1975). A Bayesian decision-theoretic procedure for use with criterion-referenced tests. *Journal of Educational Measurement* 12:87–98.

Taylor, H. C., & Russell, J. T. (1939). The relationship of validity coefficients to the practical effectiveness of tests in selection: Discussion and tables. *Journal of Applied Psychology* 23:565–578.

Thomas, H. (1988). What is the interpretation of the validity generalization estimate $S_p^2 = S_r^2 - S_e^2$? *Journal of Applied Psychology* 73(4):679–682.

Thorndike, R. L. (1949). *Personnel selection*. New York: Wiley.

Uniform Guidelines on Employees Selection Procedures (1978). *Federal Register* (No. 166), 38290–38309.

Vance, R. J., Coovert, M. D., MacCallum, R. C., & Hedge, J. W. (1989). Construct models of task performance. *Journal of Applied Psychology* 74(3): 447–455.

van der Gaag, N. L., Mellenbergh, G. J., & van den Brink, W. P. (1986, April). *Empirical utility functions for pass/fail situations*. Paper presented at the meeting of the American Educational Research Association, San Franciso.

van der Linden, W. J. (1984). Some thoughts on the use of decision theory to set cutoff scores: Comment on de Gruijter and Hambleton. *Applied Psychological Measurement* 8:9–17.

van Naerssen, R. F. (1962). *Selektie van chauffeurs.* Groningen: Wolters.

van Naerssen, R. F., Sandbergen, S., & Bruynis, E. (1966). Is de utiliteitskurve van examenskores een ogief? *Nederlands Tijdschrift voor de Psychologie* 21(6):358–363.

Vrijhoff, B. J., Mellenbergh, G. J., & van den Brink, W. P. (1983). Assessing and studying utility functions in psychometric decision theory. *Applied Psychological Measurement* 7:341–357.

Weekly, J. A., Frank, B., O'Connor, E. J., & Peters, L. H. (1985). A comparison of three methods of estimating the standard deviation of performance in dollars. *Journal of Applied Psychology* 70:122–126.

Wernimont, P. F., & Campbell, J. P. (1968). Signs, samples, and criteria. *Journal of Applied Psychology* 52:372–376.

Wiggins, J. S. (1980). *Personality and Prediction.* Reading, MA: Addison-Wesley.

Zedeck, S., & Cascio, W. F. (1984). Psychological issues in personnel decisions. *Annual Review of Psychology* 35:461–518.

8 ASSESSMENT CENTERS AT THE DUTCH CENTRAL GOVERNMENT

Jac N. Zaal

Interest in the new and improved is probably universal. One doesn't look for special reasons to explain, for example, the attention given to the latest models of General Motors. The popularity of assessment center methodology is no exception to this general rule. The core element of assessment centers, the situational test, was applied in educational and industrial settings long before psychological testing became a success (Guilford, 1967). The breakthrough and success of early testing might even be attributed to the adoption of work sample methods by Alphons Binet in constructing his well-known intelligence test (Cronbach, 1990). But even if we restrict ourselves to assessment centers in their modern appearance, their history goes back some 45 years.

Thornton and Byham (1982), in their excellent volume on assessment center methods, described the first applications, which took place predominantly in military settings in Germany in the thirties and in the British War Office Selection Board (WOSB) and the U.S. Office of Strategic Services (OSS) in the early forties. Although it was initially suggested to the staff of OSS to adopt a program of psychological/psychiatric assessment similar to that of the English WOSBs, the ultimate form and nature of the first assessment center program in the United States was shaped primarily by

Henry A. Murray (MacKinnon, 1974). Murray and his colleagues at Harvard had been experimenting with an approach to psychology called "personology," which was dedicated to understanding persons fully. A typical feature of their approach was the participation of several colleagues, each using a different method, and reporting their results in a final session called the "diagnostic council." The results of this work were reported in the classic volume *Explorations in Personality* (Murray, 1938) and greatly influenced the development of the first civilian assessment center undertaken in the United States at the Chicago Bell Companies (Bray, 1987).

Another characteristic of this new approach at OSS was the use of situational tests in which examiners had the opportunity to observe candidates in a "naturalistic" setting. For example, in one exercise a candidate is asked to take the part of a person who was found by a night watchman in a government building going through papers in an office. The candidate is told that he is not an employee, nor does he have any identification papers. The candidate is given 12 minutes to make up an innocent and convincing cover story that would explain his presence in the building. This exercise includes not only a simulation of an interrogation but also a post-stress interview which, in fact, is a trap to break the candidate's cover. The dimensions rated in this exercise were emotional stability, maintaining cover, and motivation for assignment, and were based, like the other dimensions, on a task analysis of the exercises (MacKinnon, 1974).

In Britain, civilian assessment center programs were adopted soon after the Second World War (Vernon & Parry, 1949; Vernon, 1950; Eysenck, 1953). In the late 1960s, assessment center methods became more widely applied in the United States (Cohen, Moses, & Byham, 1974). By then, incidental applications were also noticeable in the Netherlands (Bomers & Homan, 1978), but it took some 20 years more before these methods became used on a more general and enlarged scale. Also at that time the first applications in the Dutch Central Government took place (Zaal & Pieters, 1984, 1985). These developments and applications will be described and evaluated in this chapter.

The Need for Assessment Centers

In any organization, considerable time and effort are spent on personnel selection, appraisal, training, coaching, and developing personnel. Such activities stress the importance of the human factor in attaining the goals of the organization. Because of its central position and responsibilities, management has a special significance for the continuity and quality of the services provided by the organization. The recent, even stronger interest in the art of management is probably not attributable to advanced scientific developments in personnel and organizational psychology, but rather to the hectic situations in which many organizations find themselves as a consequence of the economic recession. Quality or lack of quality in management is more apparent than it used to be. Severe cutbacks in budget and personnel, the need to develop new markets, new products, and new production methods, and the reorganizations that are inevitably associated with them, place new and heavy demands on management. Often, the personal quality and skills of the manager are decisive for the success of these operations and even for the simple survival of the organization. The manager's success is no longer taken for granted, and failures are no longer covered up.

Governmental organizations in the Netherlands find themselves in more or less the same situation as private business. If anything is lacking, according to the governmental bodies, it must be the management tradition.

The quality of an organization's management depends on the quality of selection and promotion decisions and, in the longer run, on training and development. As is well known, it's a hard and time-consuming job to assess managerial potential effectively, and it often happens that one is far from happy with the decisions made.

One reason for this lack of satisfaction might be due to the lack of a good job analysis. Also, the efficiency of the selection methods employed might be insufficient. The frequency with which different selection methods are used (see, for example, Greuter & Roe, 1980) shows an impressive lack of correspondence with known utility data. These figures are reported in table 8–1. Since no studies are available for the Dutch population, the utility data are based on figures for the U.S. federal government published by Hunter and Hunter (1984). There is no reason to believe the Hunter and Hunter data should differ a great deal from Dutch data, especially since the instruments and procedures are so much alike.

None of the traditional methods—references, interviews with selection boards, biographical data, and so on—provides the organization with an impression of a person's managerial skills on first sight. Yet, an impression is necessary for assessing these critical skills as one could in a probe period. Performance appraisals might aid in the assessment, but they are hard to apply effectively, and the audience is, by definition, rather restrictive. The traditional psychological test might have lost its appeal to the public, the personnel manager, or even the psychologist, but it certainly did not lose

Table 8–1.   Frequency of Selection Activities and Utility

Selection Activity	Percent of Use	Utility Entry Level	Promotion
Application blank	57		
Application letter	64		
Reference check	50	2.95	—
Education	28	1.13	—
Work sample	6	—	6.13
Antecedents	19	—	—
Ability composite	25	6.24	6.24
Medical check	71	—	—
Interview	94	1.58	—
Other	8		
Biographical inventory		4.20	—
Training & experience		1.47	—
Job knowledge		—	5.45
Peer ratings		—	5.56
Assessment centers		—	4.88
Job tryout		5.00	—

Note: Utilities have been divided by utility of ability with low cut-off ($u = 2.50$).

its quality. However, it will be made clear later that the strength of a test is in the generality of its predictive power and in measuring basic traits and not in assessing specific managerial behavioral skills (Wernimont & Campbell, 1968).

Assessment centers are closely associated with the behavioral analysis of task requirements. Situational exercises and rating procedures are specifically designed to provide dependable ratings for those who are most concerned (Thornton & Byham, 1982). As such, they can make a unique contribution to the quality of selection and promotion decisions. The validity of work samples and assessment centers is well documented (Asher & Sciarrino, 1974; Robertson & Kandola, 1982; Finkle, 1976; Thornton & Byham, 1982; Gaugler, Rosenthal, Thornton, & Bentson, 1987). Although there may be theoretical and methodological arguments to support methods based on the sample approach as contrasted to the sign approach of classical tests (Wernimont & Campbell, 1968), the choice between work samples and tests will depend heavily on cost benefit considerations. From this perspective, it is important to realize not only the great losses that are at stake in making wrong decisions in hiring managers but also the unique contribution that work samples and assessment centers can make in raising the validity of selection procedures in addition to tests. The adoption of these new methods by the Dutch government illustrated its strong dedication to a policy to raise the quality of management.

Characteristics and Developments of Assessment Centers in Holland

Preliminaries

The first incidental applications of assessment center methods by the Rijks Psychologische Dienst (RPD) date from the early 1980s. A first assessment center was designed for the selection of housing managers of the Department of Agriculture. It consisted of an analysis exercise (locations), oral presentation to higher management, and drafting a policy statement to an outside organization. Soon after, procedures were designed for entrance examinations for the Dutch Police Academy (Zaal & Pieters, 1984), the academy of fire-brigade officers (Pieters, Hollenberg, Roosbroeck, & Zaal, 1985), and the graduate entrance level of the Foreign Office (Pieters & Zaal, 1984). One year after finishing the design and application of an assessment center for top level executive positions in the Dutch central government (Baker & Zaal, 1986; Zaal, 1987), methods and procedures were well enough established to open an independent office called the Center For Management Assessment to cope with the growing need for consultations.

Characteristics

Assessment centers show great variety in scope, format, and content in dimensions and exercises used, rating and reporting style, and purpose and setting in which they are applied (see, for instance, Finkle, 1976). Although two major styles—an American and a British—might be distinguished (Feltman, 1988), the assessment centers adopted by the Dutch government do not fit either of these styles. In fact, the governmental centers are characterized by a flexible structure, achieved by the use of anchored rating scales and a highly structured assessment process. As a result, both training of assessors and the assessment process itself take less time while enhancing quality standards with regard to behavior specificity and inter-rater agreement. As a rule, assessors for oral exercises are senior line managers, while, for written exercises, mostly assessment specialists are used. Assessment specialists also take responsibility for the final integration of data and preparation of reports.

Exercises and behavior dimensions are considered the "nuts and bolts" of the assessment center machinery. Both should guarantee a realistic projection of tasks and requirements of the manager in a particular position and a particular organization. Behavior dimensions reflect the critical managerial skills. They summarize descriptive statements about managerial behavior and, as such, have a more general flavor than is intended and can be warranted according to the empirical data.

Roles and activities of managers vary according to level, type of organization, type of job, the personal style of the manager, and other characteristics of the organization. Hence, governmental and other public organizations do not differ from private industries. Differences between public and business managers are often overstated and are, according to Costin (1970), mainly restricted to entrepreneurial skills, defined as taking advantage of opportunities and putting through organizational change and innovations. Even with respect to the latter activities, organizations of both types will have become more alike in past years. The dimensions used in the various programs of the Dutch government are based both on literature (Byham, 1982; Mintzberg, 1980; Thornton & Byham, 1982) and on job analysis (Pieters et al., 1985; Born, Algera, & Hoolwerf, 1986). A comprehensive list of management dimensions used in Dutch Government Assessment Centers is given below:

    I. Management
       1. Planning and Organizing
       2. Delegation
       3. Control
   II. Supervision
       4. Sensitivity
       5. Leadership
       6. Conflict Handling
  III. Decision Making
       7. Problem Analyses
       8. Knowledge/(Extra)-Organizational and Political Sensitivity
       9. Judgment
      10. Decisiveness
      11. Creativity
  IV. Personality
      12. Initiative
      13. Stress Tolerance
      14. Motivation
      15. Independence
      16. Flexibility/Innovation
      17. Perseverance
      18. Energy

V. Communication
   19. Oral
   20. Written

Nevertheless, it should be admitted that not every program is equally tailored to the data of an empirical job analysis. In some cases, short cuts are taken by rating priorities of an extended list of management dimensions and or merely choosing exercises and the dimensions that go with them.

A dimension such as Developing Staff, which does not appear in the list above, is becoming more and more important, and will be added in the future. This also holds true for Risk Taking. Some other dimensions mentioned in the literature, such as Helicopter View, are not included in our management profiles. This, however, is more a matter of semantics than of any systematic differences. Characteristics that are crucial for the manager in the public sector, like understanding and appreciation of the relationship with parliament and other political powers, are basically no different from what is meant by dimensions such as Organizational and Extra-Organizational Sensitivity, Knowledge, and Motivation. Their meaning cannot be considered separately from the specific behavioral and situational specifications, and it seems confusing to include separate entries in a dimensional taxonomy.

Each dimension is defined by specific behavioral descriptions. This is done at three levels: the general definition, the rating scales, and observ-

Table 8–2.   Matrix of Management Dimensions and Exercises

Management Dimension	IB	ANAL	Exercise LGD	INT	PRES
Leadership	X		X	X	
Sensitivity	X		X	X	X
Planning & organization	X				X
Delegation & control	X			X	
Decision making	X		X	X	X
Judgment		X	X	X	
Problem analyses	X	X	X	X	X
Oral communication			X	X	X
Written communication	X	X			

Notes: IB   = In-Basket.
        ANAL = Analysis.
        LGD   = Leaderless group discussion.
        INT   = Interview.
        PRES = Presentation.

able behaviors. The last two levels are specifically defined for each exercise.

More than anything else, the contents of an assessment center are specified and, in a way, defined by exercises. By their specific nature, exercises represent the situation in which the manager has to perform and the criteria he/she has to meet. Exercises are decisive in observing behavior.

Exercises currently used in Dutch governmental programs are: (1) group discussions either with or without assigned roles, including that of leader; (2) interviews in various settings (co-worker, client, representatives of outside organizations); (3) presentations; (4) analysis exercises such as drafting or redrafting policy statements, working out action plans according to stated policies, etc.; and (5) In-Basket, which involves working through the in-tray basket of a manager and taking appropriate actions.

Only by putting dimensions and exercises together in a matrix can one obtain a full description of the content of an assessment center program. Table 8–2 gives, for example, the matrix of the assessment center program for top executives (ac-top).

Assessor Team and the Assessment Process

Exercises, either oral or written, are situational tests in which behaviors are observed in a naturalistic way. The observers are called *assessors*. Not unlike situations in daily life, expertise is required to be a good assessor. One important requirement to qualify as an assessor is a full understanding of the criteria set for a successful completion of the exercise. Since these exercises are meant to replicate situations a manager has to face, it seems obvious that the successful manager in the real job will be the expert assessor. As a rule, this should be a manager one level above the job level for which the assessment center is designed. Other reasons for asking managers to function as assessors relate to their position in the organization since they will most likely be responsible for the development and followup of the assessees. Also, they probably influence greatly the implementation of the method in the organization. Their attendance is, therefore, also aimed at enhancing the commitment of the members of the organization, an important factor in establishing the success of the application of assessment center methods.

However, assessing people requires skills that are less familiar to the average manger but are nevertheless vital for the dependability of ratings. The manager is used to managing by objectives and setting targets, and is less accustomed to observing and rating the behavioral competencies needed to achieve these objectives. At the same time most managers are not hindered by a lack of competence in judging people. A second and no less important requirement for an assessor, therefore, is to be thoroughly trained in observing, rating, and reporting on the behavior dimensions involved in the various exercises. In the assessment process the following basic skills can be separated:

1. Observing behaviors (verbal and behavioral expressions);
2. Taking down notes of the observations;
3. Allocating behaviors to management dimensions;
4. Assigning numerical ratings on the anchored scales;
5. Evaluating the overall performance of the assessment center;
6. Reporting performance integrating three behavior levels.

These skills, taken in the above order, describe the assessment process itself and are each in turn the basic modules of the assessor training. The elements will be recognized at the same time as the remedies for the many pitfalls with which the human judge is confronted.

The length of the training strongly depends on the purpose and design of the assessment center program. Governmental assessment centers are designed in such a way that the structure and the assessment process can be adapted to different purposes. When used for selection and/or applied under time pressure, procedures are highly structured and the assessment process is kept under strict control. For developmental and descriptive purposes, assessors perform in a more independent way, taking more time working out reports and exchanging behavioral information in reporting on the overall performance.

Psychologists participate in their capacity as assessment specialists; they give methodological, scientific, and organizational support in developing the exercises and the design of the overall program and procedures, including the assessor training. In taking the assessment center in operation, the psychologists' responsibilities are to enhance working standards and procedures.

During the development and application of the assessment center program, there are many occasions when the quality of the program can be evaluated. These opportunities should be taken to improve and refine the procedures and exercises. However, assumptions about score reliability and validity should ultimately be tested, and established by research and statistical analyses of empirical data. A number of studies on the quality of various assessment centers in Holland will be reported in the next section.

DEVELOPMENTS IN APPLIED SETTINGS

An Evaluation of Assessment Centers in Holland

The criteria used to evaluate the quality of psychological measurement devices used in assessment centers are not restricted to psychometric qualities such as inter-rater reliability and various aspects of validity (see, for example, the American Educational Research Association, the National Council on Measurement in Education, and the American Psychological Association *Test Standards*). Acceptability of procedures by candidates and those who are involved in a wider sense (cf. the public) is important to evaluate whether the test is doing the job it is intended to do. It is standard practice at the RPD to ask for the opinions of candidates about the testing procedures (Vanderveer, 1990). As far as assessment center procedures are concerned, this information is important not only for accommodating procedures to the preferences of candidates but also for indicating content validity.

Opinions of Candidates and Assessors

Most candidates in Holland consider the exercises used in assessment centers relevant indicators of their managerial potential. This is fortunate because assessment centers would have limited utility if they did not at least have face validity for candidates. Face validity is probably high because of the emphasis on work samples rather than paper-and-pencil tests. Tables 8–3, 8–4, 8–5, and 8–6 include the opinion data from candidates and assessors of two assessment centers: ac-Dutch Fire Patrol Academy and ac-Top Executives.

Table 8–3. Average Opinion of Candidates (ac-Dutch Fire Patrol Academy, N = 35)

			Exercise			
Scale[1]	IB	ANAL	LGD	GDAR	INT	PRES
Realistic	4.1	4.1	2.8	3.7	4.7	4.4
Easy	2.8	2.8	3.4	2.9	2.6	3.1
Interesting	4.2	4.3	4.0	4.2	4.6	4.7
Clear	4.1	4.2	4.1	3.7	4.4	4.4
Relevancy	4.1	4.3	3.8	4.4	4.8	4.5
Showing quality	3.6	3.5	3.4	3.5	3.9	4.1

[1] Five-point rating scale, with high ratings being the most positive.

Table 8–4.   Average Judgment by Assessors (ac—Dutch Fire Patrol Academy, N = 11)

Scale[1]		Exercise			
	ANAL	GDZL	GDAR	INT	PRES
Realistic	4.0	2.8	4.1	4.5	4.3
Easy	2.5	2.6	3.0	2.3	2.6
Interesting	3.9	3.8	4.2	4.5	4.3
Clear	4.1	3.2	3.3	3.0	3.6
Relevancy	4.0	3.1	4.2	4.7	4.1
Showing quality	4.5	4.5	4.3	4.5	4.3
Easy to judge	2.6	3.0	2.7	3.1	2.9

[1] Five-point rating scale, with high ratings being the most positive.

Table 8–5.   Average Opinion of Candidates (ac-Top Executives, N = 12)

Scale[1]			Exercise		
	IB	ANAL	LGD	INT	PRES
Preparation time	3.8	4.0	4.8	4.2	3.8
Instruction	4.5	4.0	4.2	5.0	4.3
Realistic	4.4	3.0	4.2	4.2	4.0
Difficult	2.6	3.5	2.5	2.5	2.8
Interesting	3.5	3.4	4.0	4.8	4.3
Relevance	4.6	3.5	4.1	4.8	4.8
Showing quality	4.1	3.6	3.6	4.3	3.8

[1] Five-point rating scale, with high ratings being the most positive.

Table 8–6.   Average Opinion of Assessors (ac-Top Executives, N = 9)

Scale[1]		Exercise	
	LGD	INT	PRES
Realistic	3.8	4.6	4.8
Easy	3.4	2.0	2.2
Interesting	2.6	4.2	4.6
Relevance	3.6	4.8	4.8
Enough time	4.2	4.4	4.4
Instruction	4.6	4.6	4.4
Showing quality	3.8	4.6	4.6

[1] Five-point rating scale, with high ratings being the most positive.

These tables highlight data from two programs and groups, but the general picture is fairly representative of what is generally found in Holland and what is reported in the literature (Baker & Martin, 1974; Robertson & Kandola, 1982).

Besides the generally favorable attitudes and opinions, there are some interesting variations in the data that are worthy of special mention and limit the generalizability of results. On the average, none of the exercises is rated as irrelevant or impossible for candidates to show their managerial skills. Some systematic differences, however, seem to appear. Written exercises such as the In-Basket are rated more favorably than, for example, Analysis. But assessors have a higher opinion than the candidates do regarding the relevance and reality of the Analysis exercise. The point illustrates a potential lack of proper job image on the part of the candidates. The job preview that is given thereby is an example of what is called an aspect of the multiple benefits of assessment centers. The opinions of assessors and, to a lesser extent, of the candidates, taken as an expert judgment on relevance and reality of exercises, provide the empirical evidence on the content validity of assessment centers—i.e., of exercises, of course, and not of the management dimensions.

Inter-rater Agreement

In making decisions about the implementation and continuation of assessment centers, the psychometric properties of instruments such as reliability and validity should play a major role. In this section, data will be reported on the assessment centers for entrance to the Dutch Police Academy (ac-NPA) (Zaal & Pieters, 1984), the Academy for Fire-brigade Officers (ac-RBA) (Pieters et al., 1985), and the graduate entrance assessment center for the Foreign Office (ac-BUIZA) (Pieters & Zaal, 1984). RBA candidates were assessed by at least two senior officers who had been trained for one day.

All candidates entering the assessment center program were preselected on certain ability and personality tests. Selection ratios differed from about 50 percent (Foreign Office) to 15 percent (NPA). Level of education varied; the NPA could be entered after college (six grades) or high school (five grades). RBA and BUIZA required university of technology (four-year) degrees. Age varied accordingly. The reliability of the ratings in the various work samples was computed using a variance-components approach (see, e.g., Winer, 1971; Thorndike, 1982). In the case of incomplete designs, assessors did not see all candidates; and maximum likelihood

Table 8–7. Results of Inter-rater Reliability (ac-Foreign Affairs)

Area	ANAL (N = 3)	Exercise PRES (N = 3)	LGD (N = 7)
I. Planning and organization	.46	*	*
II. Sensitivity	.83	.59	.59
Interpersonal	.83	.59	.59
III. Problem analyses	.60	*	*
Knowledge & org. sensitivity	.57	*	*
Judgment	.67	*	*
Decision making	.78	*	*
IV. Initiative	*	.90	.90
Stress tolerance	*	.86	*
V. Oral communication	*	.82	*
Written communication	.67	*	*
Overall effectiveness	*	*	.88

Notes: ANAL = Analysis.
PRES = Presentation.
LGD = Group discussion without leader.

*No data were available.

procedures were used to estimate the relevant variance components using the following model:

$$X_{ij} = \mu + \pi_i + \beta_j + \varepsilon_{ij}$$

where X_{ij} is the rating of candidate i by rater j, μ is the overall mean, π_i is the candidate component of the rating, β_j is the rater effect, and ε_{ij} is the residual component. Reported reliability coefficients relate to the mean rating over the specific number of raters involved. The results of the analyses on the work samples used in the selection procedure for the Foreign Office are reported in table 8–7. The assessment center included a written exercise (Tombi Case), followed by an interview and a leaderless group discussion (LGD).

The Foreign Office program took one day, and two groups of 12 candidates participated on two successive days.

Rating procedures used in the group discussion were changed according to the wishes of the assessors who resisted the rather strict procedures of the RPD; they insisted that raters first prepare their ratings on their own and discuss them afterwards. In table 8–8, the resulting reliabilities for each separate day are presented.

As can be seen, only the reliability of Interpersonal is improved at the

Table 8–8.   Inter-rater Reliability of Group Discussion of ac-Foreign Affairs (After Each Day)

Dimension	Day 1	Day 2
Interpersonal	0.528	0.693
Initiative	0.927	0.806
Effectiveness	0.931	0.672

Table 8–9.   Results of Inter-rater Reliability (ac-Dutch Police Academy)

| | | Exercise | |
Management Dimension	IB	LGD	GDAR
I. Planning and organization	.90	*	*
II. Sensitivity/Interpersonal	.56	.82	.72
III. Problem analyses	.84	*	*
Judgment	.74	*	*
IV. Initiative	.79	*	*
Stress tolerance	.74	.74	.62
Motivation	*	.80	.67
Perseverance	.84	.83	.73
V. Oral communication	*	.84	.83
Written communication	.48	*	*

Notes: IB   = In-Basket.
       LGD   = Group discussion without leader.
       GDAR = Group discussion with assigned roles.

*No data were available.

cost of losing quite a bit of inter-rater agreement on Initiative and Effectiveness.

The ac used in the selection procedure for the Dutch Police Academy consisted of a written exercise (the In-Basket test), a leaderless group discussion (LGD), and a group discussion with rotating leadership (GDAR). The resulting reliability coefficients are reported in table 8–9, and those of ac-RBA are reported in table 8–10. The analysis exercise in ac-RBA involved relocation problems, taking into account technical, professional, social, and environmental facets. In the presentation exercise a resulting relocation plan had to be presented to local administrative and political authorities.

The reliability coefficients reported in tables 8–7, 8–9, and 8–10 range from 0.459 to 0.901 with a median reliability of 0.741. If the coefficients are

Table 8-10.   Results of Interrater Reliability (ac-Dutch Fire Patrol Academy)

		Exercise		
Management Dimension	ANAL	PRES	LGD	GDAR
I. Planning and organization	.89	*	*	*
II. Sensitivity/Interpersonal	*	.68	.79	.28
III. Judgment	.87	*	*	*
IV. Initiative/Ascendency	*	.80	.89	.82
Stress tolerance	*	.82	.62	.61
V. Oral communication	*	.80	.84	.73
Written communication	.62	*	*	*
Overall effectiveness	.89	.88	.84	.73

Notes: ANAL = Analysis.
PRES = Presentation.
LGD = Group discussion without leader.
GDAR = Group discussion with assigned roles.

*No data were available.

Table 8-11.   Reliability Coefficients of ac-Foreign Affairs (ac-BUIZA), ac-Dutch Police Academy (ac-NPA) and ac-Dutch Fire Patrol Academy (ac-RBA) According to Amount of Training of Assessors

	Amount of Training of Assessors			
Reliability Level	Low (27)	Medium (18)	High (19)	Total (64)
Poor	47%	22%	26%	35%
Reasonable	12%	39%	26%	26%
Good	41%	39%	47%	42%

classified according to the rule that $r < .70$: poor, $.70 \leq r \leq .80$: reasonable, and $.80 \leq r$: good, then table 8-11 can be prepared.

   Seventeen out of 55 reliability coefficients were poor (31 percent), 15 (27 percent) were reasonable, and 23 reliability coefficients were good (42 percent). Considering the suboptimal conditions regarding the development and implementation of these ac-procedures, the results were probably better than one would have expected, but they do not compare favorably with results reported by others (see, for example, Hall, 1979 and Thornton & Byham, 1982). A major factor was the amount of training received by assessors. Groups in table 8-11 were ordered according to the amount of training. Buiza assessors, without being trained in the management dimensions used, do worst, while senior fire-brigade officers do best after one day of training.

Besides the reliability analyses for each behavior dimension reported above, other analyses were performed on the data of the Buiza group in order to test for halo, leniency, and logical error (Guilford, 1954). It appeared that, for each exercise, halo-effect and the logical error were significant. The use of behaviorally anchored rating scales helped to overcome the tendency to apply different standards (leniency). These results again highlight the importance of proper training in the meaning of the management dimensions, and the ways in which these dimensions can be separated and inferred from observed behavior.

Dimensions requiring special attention differ from program to program. Sensitivity, for instance, was difficult to assess in the Buiza program but somewhat easier in the others, yet the overall reliability was weak as compared to other dimensions. This also seems to be the case with Stress Tolerance and Motivation. Apparently, dimensions such as these are difficult to relate to observable behaviors.

Turning to the exercises, it was noted that the dimensions were rated either poor or good, with the exception of the leaderless group discussion, where, over the three groups, eight out of 14 dimensions received good reliability ratings.

Reliability of measurements has much to do with the efficiency of getting information: in other words, how much cost should be afforded in preventing errors and how bad the losses are if one doesn't prevent them. Some measures to enhance the dependability of ratings are costly, such as increasing the amount of training and using more assessors; some are less costly, such as revising scales or giving more elaborate written examples of observable behavior for dimensions.

The major consideration, however, concerns the purpose for which assessment centers are used. Decisions about appointments, admission, and promotion are normally based on the overall rating of managerial potential. The reliability will be far better than each of the dimensions involved and will reach acceptable levels in cases such as those described in this section. However, if one has to make decisions about allocating candidates to different types of managerial jobs and/or different types of training assessment centers should have differential validity. Specifically, the dimensions of managerial skills should prove to be independent, reliable, and generalizable across exercises. These issues will be dealt with in the next section.

Validity of ac-Dutch

In discussing the validity of assessment centers, one must make a clear distinction between different type of scores like the overall performance and the performance on exercises and dimensions. Depending on the use and the decisions to be made, different types of validity are involved. The most common decisions for which assessment centers are used are single selection decisions of the reject/accept and or fast/normal/reject type. In such cases the predictive validity of the overall score (managerial potential) should be established. The most convincing proofs of the predictive power of assessment center methods have been provided by a study at the Bell Corporation (Bray, 1982, 1987). Many studies since then have demonstrated the predictive validity and generalizability of the validity of assessment centers (Hunter & Hunter, 1984; Gaugler et al., 1987). Up to now, in the relatively short period of application to the government agencies, it has been impossible to study the predictive validity. The first study undertaken will be finished within a short time (Tersmette & Zaal, in preparation).

Questions relating to management dimensions will be addressed next. As was mentioned previously, decisions to allocate candidates to different types of managerial jobs are called *placement decisions* and require differential validity (Cronbach & Gleser, 1965). For assessment centers to have differential validity they must prove that exercises or managerial dimensions are sufficiently independent. In line with Thornton and Byham's (1982) interpretations, the dimensions will be explicitly tested for generality in the following section.

First, the results of a multitrait multimethod analysis are reported, followed by some results from factor analyses. Finally, data are reported on the relation between intelligence and personality as measured by paper-and-pencil tests on the one hand, and management dimensions on the other.

The Generalizability of ac-Dimensions

There seems to have been no research effort regarding the generalizability of ac-dimensions. Yet, in the literature on the development of ac procedures, one can find at least the suggestion that the behavioral dimensions commonly used can be considered general latent traits. That is, a behavioral dimension such as "stress tolerance." rated in a leaderless group discussion and an In-Basket test, appeals to the same general latent trait.

The data gathered in the selection of police officers provided an opportunity to test this hypothesis. The rating scales used in the leaderless group discussion were also applied in the group discussion with rotated leadership. The dimensions were Motivation, Oral communication, Perseverance, Interpersonal Skills, and Stress tolerance. The hypothesis regarding common latent traits was tested in a multitrait, multimethod analysis, which

Table 8–12. Results of Multitrait Multimethod Analysis of GDAR and LGD from ac-Dutch Fire Patrol Academy

Exercise	Trait Factor				Method Factor			
	DIM	MO	OC	P	PO	ST	GDAR	LGD
GDAR MO	0.709	–	–	–	–	0.741	–(*)
OM	–(*)	0.285	–	–	–	0.875	–	
P	–	–	0.327	–	–	0.808	–	
PO	–	–	–	0.724	–	0.477	–	
ST	–	–	–	–	0.425	0.756	–	
LGD MO	0.226	–	–	–	–	–	–(*)	1.023
OC	–(*)	0.704	–	–	–	–		0.690
P	–	–	0.359	–	–	–		0.888
PO	–	–	–	0.384	–	–		0.825
ST	–	–	–	–	0.536	–		0.791

Notes: DIM = Dimension.
MO = Motivation.
OC = Oral communication.
P = Perseverance.
PO = Interpersonal.
ST = Stress tolerance.
GDAR = Group discussion with assigned roles.
LGD = Group discussion without leader.

*Fixed at O in the estimation of parameters.

allows one to separate the total variance in three components: a trait component, a method component, and an error component. The results of the analysis using the ACOVS program (Jöreskog, 1974) are reported in table 8–12.

If the behavioral dimensions common to both work samples appeal to the same latent trait, the trait components reported in table 8–13 should be substantially related to the method component. However, it is clear from table 8–13 that the method component accounts systematically for a more substantive part of the total variance than the trait component. Hence, the dimensions measured in the different work samples are method-specific.

Factor Structure of Management Dimensions and Exercises

Similar results were obtained in an analysis of ac scores in the case of the selection of candidates for the Foreign Office. Although the structure of the ac problems did not allow a multitrait, multimethod analysis of scores,

Table 8–13. Variance Components of Behavior Dimensions of GDAR and LGD

Exercise	Dimension	Trait	Method	Error
GDAR	MO	0.503	0.549	0.0
	OC	0.081	0.766	0.127
	P	0.107	0.653	0.232
	PO	0.551	0.228	0.270
	ST	0.181	0.572	0.247
LGD	MO	0.501	1.047	0.0
	OC	0.496	0.476	0.019
	P	0.129	0.789	0.183
	PO	0.147	0.681	0.248
	ST	0.287	0.626	0.080

Note: See Table 8–12 for the meaning of the pneumonics.

Table 8–14. Factor Structure Management Dimensions (ac-Foreign Affairs)

Exercise	Management Dimension	Factor I	II	III
Analysis	– Planning	.70	0.00	0.00
	– Sensitivity	.93	0.00	0.00
	– Analysis	.82	0.00	0.00
	– Judgment	.92	0.00	0.00
	– (Extra) Organizational sensitivity	.82	0.00	0.00
	– Decisiveness	.52	0.00	.39
	– Written communication	.56	0.00	0.00
Presentation	– Sensitivity	0.00	.74	0.00
	– Initiative	0.00	.95	0.00
	– Stress tolerance	0.00	.93	0.00
	– Oral communication	0.00	.86	0.00
LGD	– Interpersonal	0.00	0.00	.79
	– Initiative	0.00	0.00	.90
	– Effectiveness	0.00	0.00	.92

Note: Factor loadings ≤ 0.25 were set to zero.

it was possible to perform a factor analysis in order to check whether managerial dimensions shared sufficient common variance across exercises to appear as independent factors.

As can be seen by the results presented in table 8–14, the structure of primary factors clearly resembled the structure of the problems used in an ac procedure. Similar results were obtained in an analysis of ac scores in the case of the selection of candidates for the Foreign Office. Although the design of the assessment did not allow a multitrait, multimethod analysis of scores, a factor analysis of the data produced a factor pattern that clearly resembles the structure of the exercises used in an assessment center procedure. One may conclude that the dimensions measured in the different work samples are method-specific. The results of the analysis are reported in table 8–14.

Observations in other studies generally confirm this finding (Herriot, 1986). Thus, the dimensions measured in the different work samples are method-specific to a great extent. Caution should be used, therefore, in applying the latent-trait concept to the assessment center approach. However, more research is needed before a final conclusion can be reached.

The Relation Between Assessment Center Measures, Intelligence, and Personality Tests

One issue that is of extreme importance in introducing assessment center procedures in existing selection procedures is the relationship between a candidate's score on an intelligence test and/or a personality questionnaire and his/her performance in assessment center exercises. Contrary to the issue discussed above, there is unequivocal evidence in the literature regarding this issue (see, e.g., Thornton & Byham, 1982).

It has been established that the overlap between ac scores on the one hand and intelligence scores and/or scores on personality questionnaires on the other hand is negligible. This finding was confirmed in a number of our studies: a canonical correlation analysis was used to assess the overlap between two sets of variables. This is achieved by constructing a linear function of the variables in each set such that the correlation between these linear functions is maximized. The linear functions are called *canonical variates*, and the correlation between these variates is called the *canonical correlation*. Hence, the method can be seen as a multivariate extension of multiple regression analysis. The null hypothesis that the variates in the first set are unrelated to the variates in the second set may be tested by a chi-square test (see, e.g., Timm, 1975).

Obviously, the conclusion must be that there is no overlap between dimensions measured in intelligence tests and/or personality questionnaires (see Table 8–15). The use of these tests in assessment centers, then, depends on their predictive validity. In our view, however, intelligence tests and personality questionnaires are most effective in earlier stages of the selection process.

Table 8–15.   Results of the Canonical Correlational Analysis of Management Dimensions and Intelligence and Personality Traits (ac-Dutch Police Academy and ac-Foreign Affairs)

Group		Chi-Square	df	p
ac-Dutch Police Academy	Intelligence	247.8	252	0.563
	Personality	215.8	210	0.377
ac-Foreign Affairs	Intelligence	8.1	16	0.945
	Personality	25.9	20	0.168

Concluding Remarks

Despite differences in procedures and format such as number, position, and professional status of assessors, no systematic differences were observed in inter-rater reliabilities of the behavioral dimensions used in the work samples. Amount of training, however, evidently had a positive effect on interrater agreement. As might be expected, there were some differences with respect to the efficiency with which dimensions could be rated. Some were more difficult to observe in one exercise as compared to others. For example, Motivation was better agreed upon if rated in a leaderless group discussion as compared to a group discussion with assigned roles. Interpersonal Skills were better agreed upon in group exercises than in written exercises. The opposite held true for Planning. Hence, the efficiency of assessment center methods relies heavily upon the optimal matching of behavioral dimensions and rating scales on one hand, and specific exercises (group versus individual and written versus oral) on the other hand. Obviously, training of assessors improves the overall reliability of ratings.

A related issue is the present finding that behavioral dimensions are method-specific. The latent trait concept, which is apparently extremely useful in mental test theory, appears to be less fruitful in the area of assessment center methods. Further research is needed to ascertain whether the amount of training of assessors has an effect upon the method-specificity of ratings. That is, the method-specificity of ratings found in this study *might* be an artifact induced by the amount of training of assessors. If this hypothesis proves correct, prolonged training of assessors is not *primarily* called for to improve on the inter-rater reliability of behavioral ratings but is a necessary condition to obtain information regarding latent traits. However, the question of whether one should put more effort into training of assessors is related to the purpose of a specific assessment center. The requirements in a selection situation are quite different from the requirements in, say, a management development program.

In the latter situation, one is primarily interested in statements regarding capabilities (latent traits) of candidates which can be used to develop a specific training program to compensate for weak points. The objectives in a training program are better stated with respect to specific behavioral dimensions instead of the overall performance on a particular exercise. In a selection situation, the requirements are of a different nature. Here we are primarily concerned with the reliability of ratings and the validity of the methods in predicting the capability of the candidates to perform a particular job in order to raise the quality of decisions on hiring or promoting personnel. The overall performance on different exercises might indicate capability as well as or even better than ratings on behavioral dimensions. As a result, the need for training of assessors may vary substantially over different applications of assessment center methods.

Although a number of questions still remain and need further research, we have the strong impression that the introduction of assessment center methods in the Dutch government has been successful. There are several benefits of the new selection procedures. First, the face validity of these methods, especially for candidates, is much higher than for the traditional methods. Second, acceptance on the part of management is high. Finally, the success rate of candidates selected using ac methods is higher than it was previously. In addition, we have the impression that management, while participating in ac procedures, not only arrives at a better understanding of the major determinants of success and failure in the function but also improves its own functioning. Thus the organization as a whole benefits from the use of assessment center methods.

References

Asher, J. J., & Sciarrino, J. A. (1974). Realistic work sample tests: A review. *Personnel Psychology* 27:519–533.

Baker, D. R., & Martin, C. G. (1974). *Evaluation of the federal executive development program assessment center*. Washington, DC: Personnel Research and Development Center.

Baker, D. R., & Zaal, J. N. (1986). *Development and operation of a top management assessment center in the Dutch government*. Paper presented at the 14th International Congress on the Assessment Center Method, Dearborn, MI.

Bomers, G. B. J., & Homan, T. H. (1978). Assessment centers. *Intermediair* 14:1–9.

Born, M. Ph., Algera, J. A., & Hoolwerf, G. (1986). *Management potentieel beoordeling*. Den Haag: Rijks Psychologische Dienst.

Bray, D. W. (1982). The assessment center and the study of lives. *American Psychologist* 37(2):180–189.

—————. (1987). *The assessment centers in the United States*. Paper presented at the first European Conference on Assessment Centers, Amsterdam.

Byham, W. C. (1982). *Dimensions of managerial competence. Monograph VI*. Pittsburgh, PA: Developmental Dimensions International.

Cohen, B. M., Moses, J. L., & Byham, W. C. (1974). *The validity of assessment centers: A literature review. Monograph II*. Pittsburgh, PA: Developmental Dimensions Press.

Costin, A. A. (1970). Management profiles in business and government. Unpublished master's thesis, McGill University, Montreal.

Cronbach, L. J. (1990). *Essentials of psychological testing*, 5th ed. New York: Harper and Row.

Cronbach, L. J., & Gleser, G. C. (1965). *Psychological tests and personnel decisions*. Urbana, IL: University of Illinois Press.

Eysenck, H. J. (1953). *Uses and abuses of psychology*. Baltimore, MD: Penguin Books.

Feltman, R. (1988). Validity of a police assessment center: A 1–19–year follow up. *Journal of Occupational Psychology* 61:129–144.

Finkle, R. B. (1976). Managerial assessment centers. In M. D. Dunnette (ed.), *Handbook of industrial and organizational psychology*. Chicago, IL: Rand McNally, pp. 861–888.

Gaugler, B. B., Rosenthal, D. B., Thornton, G. C., & Bentson, C. (1987). Meta analysis of assessment center validity. *Journal of Applied Psychology* 72:493–511.

Greuter, M., & Roe, R. (1980). *Personeelsselectie in Nederland*. Amsterdam: Universiteit van Amsterdam.

Guilford, J. P. (1954). *Psychometric methods*. New York: McGraw Hill.

—————. (1967). *Nature of human intelligence*. New York: McGraw Hill.

Hall, H. L. (1979). *Analysis of an executive-level assessment center: A comparison of assessment center ratings to supervisor ratings and to biodata*. Washington, DC: Personnel Research and Development Center.

Herriot, P. (1986). *Assessment centers: Dimensions or job samples?* Paper presented at the European Conference on the Benefits of Psychology, Lausanne.

Hunter, J. E., & Hunter, R. F. (1984). Validity and utility of alternative predictors of job performance. *Psychological Bulletin* 96:72–98.

Jöreskog, K. G. (1974). Analyzing psychological data by structural analysis of covariance matrices. In D. H. Krantz, R. D. Luce, R. C. Atkinson, & P. Suppes (eds.), *Contemporary developments in mathematical psychology*, Vol. II. San Francisco, CA: Freeman.

MacKinnon, D. W. (1974). *How assessment centers were started in the United States*. Pittsburgh, PA: Developmental Dimensions International.

Mintzberg, H. (1980). *The nature of managerial work*, 2nd ed. Englewood Cliffs, NJ: Prentice Hall.

Murray, H. (1938). *Explorations in personality*. Cambridge, England: Oxford University Press.

Pieters, J. P. M., Hollenberg, W. H., Roosbroeck, H. F. M. van, & Zaal, J. N. (1985). *Selectie van Brandweerofficieren 1985: toepassing van assessment center methode*. Den Haag: Rijks Psychologische Dienst.

Pieters, J. P. M., & Zaal, J. N. (1984). *Evaluatie van Assessment Center Methoden als selectie instrument bij de R.P.D.* Den Haag: Rijks Psychologische Dienst.

Robertson, I. T., & Kandola, R. S. (1982). Work sample tests: Validity, adverse impact, and applicant reactions. *Journal of Occupational Psychology* 55:171–183.

Tersmette, M., & Zaal, J. N. (In preparation). *Follow up van aspirant brandweer officieren: de predictieve validiteit van assessment centers*. Den Haag: Rijks Psychologische Dienst.

Thorndike, R. L. (1982). *Applied psychometrics*. Boston, MA: Houghton-Mifflin.

Thornton, G. C., & Byham, W. C. (1982). *Assessment centers and managerial performance*. New York: Academic Press.

Timm, N. H. (1975). *Multivariate analysis with applications in education and psychology*. Monterey: Brooks Publishing Company.

Vanderveer, J. (1990). Het woord is aan de kandidaat. In H. Vanderflier, P. Janssen, & J. N. Zaal (eds.), *Selectieresearch in de praktijk*. Lisse: Swets & Zeitlinger.

Vernon, P. E. (1950). The validation of Civil Service Selection Board procedures. *Occupational Psychology* 24:75–95.

Vernon, P. E., & Parry, J. B. (1949). *Personnel selection in the British forces*. London: University of London Press.

Wernimont, P. F., & Campbell, J. P. (1968). Signs, samples and criteria. *Journal of Applied psychology* 52:372–376.

Winer, B. J. (1971). *Statistical principles in experimental design*. New York: McGraw-Hill.

Zaal, J. N. (1987). *Assessment centers topfuncties: Eindverslag*. Den Haag: Rijks Psychologische Dienst.

Zaal, J. N., & Pieters, J. P. M. (1984). *Evaluatie van Assessment Center Methoden bij de eindselectie van de Nederlandse Politie Academie 1984*. Den Haag: Rijks Psychologische Dienst.

————. (1985). *Assessment centers at the Rijks Psychologische Dienst*. Paper presented at the West European Conference on the Psychology of Work and Organization, Aachen.

9 CURRENT PERSPECTIVES IN THE ASSESSMENT OF THE HANDICAPPED

Stan Scarpati

Current practice for assessing the handicapped is becoming more dynamic; the concept has expanded to consider individuals and their environments as equal shareholders. At the same time the very nature of assessing the handicapped remains focused on the within-person variations that interfere with their performance in school and the community. For many, assessment of the handicapped occurs in a theoretical vacuum with little research to support why or how certain tests are given. Despite the lack of technical adequacy of norm-referenced tests, despite their bias and their limited ability to guide treatment, these tests continue to play a major role in the lives of the handicapped. Public schools, vocational rehabilitation programs, and community-based facilities consider standardized instruments a mainstay in their programs. While criterion-referenced tests (see chapter 1 of this book) and informal testing and observation techniques have made significant inroads in the evaluation process, standardized measures are not about to be abandoned. Pressure for student and program accountability and the justification for an ever-increasing need for funds will most likely keep formal norm-referenced testing as a permanent fixture.

Discussed in this chapter are current issues faced by the various professionals who work with the handicapped and advocate on their behalf.

These issues involve several overlapping topics such as measurement theory and test adequacy, and their impact on how the handicapped are identified and treated.

An understanding of the relationship between assessment and the handicapped is provided by a review of the public policy decisions rooted in case law. The discussion proceeds to ways in which assessment is used for identification and instruction of monolingual and bilingual children, its role in placing the handicapped into the community, and its method for awarding high school diplomas.

Historical and Legal Perspectives

Only since the beginning of this century have people with emotional, mental, and physical difficulties been labeled *handicapped*. Arguments have persisted since that time, and probably before, about who is *handicapped* or *disabled*, terms that are sometimes used interchangeably. Nomenclature to describe behavior and performance were constructed, primarily, to segregate a population for social and economic reasons. These labels purported to depict behavioral characteristics accurately, yet in reality they provided no information about these people's performance as individuals or identification of their positive aspects. Regardless of the terminology used, the handicapped were treated in ways that were different from, and often inferior to, the rest of society.

The decision to categorize someone as handicapped is often an imprecise judgment call. Assessment has had a considerable impact in balancing the social judgments made about people who look and behave in different ways, and about their place in society.

In many ways how we assess the handicapped today is anchored in the social and political changes the United States faced during the 1960s and 1970s. In the context of the promise for equal treatment, accessibility, and nondiscriminatory practices, questions were raised about who were handicapped and how they should be treated. Public schools in the United States were, for the most part, seen as the means through which these promises were to become a reality. It was inevitable, though, with inadequate instrumentation and untrained personnel, that sources of bias and discrimination would eventually be uncovered and confronted in courts of law.

The ways in which individuals were classified as handicapped and placed in special and segregated settings have been at the root of most litigation. Much less litigious attention has been given to the programing (instructional) function of clinical and curriculum-based assessment. It remains that the scope and sequence of curricula are local school prerogatives, and only in the most extreme cases are courts willing to overrule local autonomy.

Parents, guardians, and advocates initially used the courts to question the efficacy of intelligence tests when used with mentally or emotionally handicapped persons. When these tests unfairly led to segregated educational placements, the unacceptable "separate but equal" notion, decided in an earlier school desegregation case, was confirmed. Courts have also been the arena in which the impact of culture and of social and economic deprivation of norm-referenced tests for the handicapped have been tested. Litigation has prompted close scrutiny of tests and testing procedures, and of the purposes for which tests are used. Lawsuits have clearly been the single source through which testing the handicapped has changed in concept and practice (Fafard, Hanlon, & Bryson, 1986).

The present legal protections for the handicapped in the United States are explicit to prohibit the past discriminatory testing and evaluation procedures that led to the disproportionate representations of black and other language minority children in segregated special education classes. *Hobsen v. Hansen* (1967) was the seminal case in which a disproportionate number of poor and minority children were tracked into lower educational classes and into special education. For the first time courts questioned the technical adequacy of psychological tests and ruled that, even though tests may themselves be unbiased, their standardization samples will produce inaccurate or misleading scores for lower class and minority students. Other class action suits filed against schools charged that racially biased tests and inappropriate referral and testing procedures produced misclassification and ineffective placements that could permanently blight children (e.g., *Diana v. State Board of Education*, 1970; *Larry P. v. Riles*, 1979; *Lora v. Board of Education*, 1978; *Mattie T. v. Holladay*, 1979). Psychometric instruments used to measure intelligence and projective tests that assessed emotional disabilities were deemed flawed by the courts, resulting in too many minority children being labeled educable mentally retarded and emotionally disturbed. More importantly, making a diagnosis of mental retardation based on one test score given by one individual was permanently disallowed. Countering arguments that mental retardation appeared more often among black children due to their adverse socioeconomic status were eventually discounted. The consensus of these cases was that using a single standardized IQ test for special education placement must stop.

Some have argued that while these court decisions have yielded educational and social gains for the handicapped, the tests themselves should not bear the total burden of responsibility for discrimination. For one thing, test administrators should know if an instrument is standardized on the appropriate and relevant sample even though most test developers provide scant data about whether the handicapped have been included when the test norms and item analyses were conducted (Fuchs, Fuchs, Benowitz, & Barringer, 1987).

Current Practice

The initiative to assess the handicapped appropriately is promulgated in the United States by the Education for All Handicapped Children (EHA), PL 94–142, passed in 1975 to insure educational access to those who were previously either denied outright or provided a grossly inadequate education. Backing this legal mandate is the enforcement of civil rights guaranteed under the U.S. Constitution for equal protection and due process of law. The Vocational Rehabilitation Act of 1973 (PL 91–112), section 504, recognizes the illegality of discriminating against a handicapped person solely by reason of their handicap. Schools and work facilities have to make "reasonable accommodations" to make accessible what is naturally available to nonhandicapped people. Taking the two laws together, any agency receiving federal funds is required to provide a cascade of educational and related services to insure that appropriate individualized education is assembled for the handicapped and that it is provided in the least restrictive environment. What is a "most appropriate education" and what is "least restrictive" have been the prime sources of contention between educators, parents, and the legal system. Central to the difficulty of developing the proper educational plans and delivery systems is the evaluation procedure employed. Multifaceted assessments that screen, diagnose, place, and plan for instruction are crafted by a team into an individual education plan (IEP). These plans must be implemented in a setting that most closely represents a typical classroom.

Legislators fully intended to eradicate discriminatory testing practices when the EHA was developed. This law (EHA, 20 USC, section 1401) requires that:

1. Only children suspected of being handicapped may be evaluated;
2. Testing and evaluation materials and procedures used to evaluate and place handicapped children shall be selected and administered so as not to be racially or culturally discriminatory;

3. Tests and other evaluation materials have been validated for the specific purpose for which they are used;
4. Tests and other evaluation materials include those tailored to assess specific areas of educational need;
5. Evaluation and placement be based on a variety of sources, including aptitude and achievement tests, teacher recommendations, physical conditions, social or cultural backgrounds, adaptive behavior.
6. No single procedure is used as the sole criterion for determining an appropriate educational program;
7. The evaluation is made by a multidisciplinary team or group of persons, including at least one teacher or other specialists with knowledge in the area of suspected disability.

Interestingly, the law in no way requires the use of standardized tests. Assessment teams are fully authorized to use any appropriate informal measure to compile the data needed to development a education plan. It is rare, however, for teams not to include formal measures in their deliberations. However, unlike in the past, assessment teams must establish an assessment process that looks at the handicapped at levels of complexity and ways in which they interact with their environment. In order to do so, they must consider as part of the assessment the degree to which a person has:

1. A mental or physical irregularity—a basic criterion for the existence of a handicap is that the person has some mental or physical trait that makes him/her different from others.
2. Functional impairment—the mental or physical impairment must have a negative impact on function.
3. Impediment to activities—a functional impairment interferes with a person's ability to engage in those activities in which the function that is impaired is an essential component.
4. Career limitations—the determination is made that the impairment limits the choice of possible roles the individual can play in society.
5. Impact on life success—the determination is made that the impairment will interfere with an individual's successes and achievements during his or her life (Burgdorf, 1980, pp. 6–7).

Assessment for Identification

Testing has played a significant role in the identification (or confirmation) of handicaps and in the classification of handicapped children. Beginning with the full implementation of the EHA in 1975, schools were directed to institute a "child-find" process to search and select anyone qualified for special education and related services. Preschool screening and in-district testing programs relied primarily on standardized tests to identify those children.

Although the federal government, and most states, mandate a child-find process, they do not specify what instruments to employ, what procedures to follow, or what diagnostic criteria to use. Perlumutter and Parus (1983) verified that with children suspected of a learning disability, for instance, vast differences existed in the diagnostic and identification procedures across 14 school districts. Similar discrepancies in the identification process are also apparent at the preschool level. A survey of 508 school districts in Minnesota revealed a consistent pattern of relying on a limited number of instruments even though their technical adequacy was questionable (Ysseldyke, Thurlow, & O'Sullivan, 1986).

Preschool Assessment

Early diagnosis of existing and suspected handicaps is relatively new. Nowhere is assessment more critical than when intervening with young children to prevent or diminish the effects of an inappropriate education. Inaccurate assesssments at this stage, more than any other, run the risk of mislabeling or falsely identifying a child. The obvious characteristics present in moderately and severely handicapped children aid an early diagnosis. Others, such as the factors related to cognitive and potential learning difficulties, are harder to uncover. Developmental screening instruments, used from within a concept of school readiness, guide many preschool assessment teams. Multidimensional tests gather information about cognitive and behavioral prerequisites that are assumed to underlie skills to be learned in the future.

Very young children change rapidly, making formal assessment data unstable and imprecise when predicting future performance. In addition, cohesive norm groups with which to compare test results are often lacking, especially for tests that measure the subtle aspects of cognitive and affective development. Most importantly, at this age, assessments imple-mented in isolation from intervention and treatment are ineffective. It is suggested that assessing preschool handicapped children follows a devel-opmental and interactive process in that (1) all children develop from an interaction with their parents, siblings, peers, and teachers; (2) a develop-mental approach toward assessment and programming is more beneficial than a deficit-trait model approach; and (3) measurements of traits must be repeated in different settings and at different times for the development of effective treatment plans (Scarpati & Gillespie-Silver, 1989, p. 354).

Identification of Learning Disabilities

Along with the effort to identify handicapped children comes a disproportionate number of children (compared to all handicapped children) classified as learning disabled (LD). Children who are physically impaired, severely mentally or physically disabled, or who manifest hearing or visual impairments are identified with little difficulty. However, the lack of academic and behavioral homogeneity of children considered emotionally disturbed, educable mentally retarded, and learning disabled makes their identification more difficult.

Imprecise definitions and technically inadequate assessment instruments exacerbate the problem. For some, the identification difficulties are rooted more in the ambiguity and confusion about what a learning disability actually is than in the technical inadequacies of assessment instruments. Researchers will argue that precise measurement will only come after the definition is clarified (e.g., Berk, 1984; Adelman & Taylor, 1986). Others consider this pursuit futile since its only possible outcome is to resolve what we call these children and not how we teach them (Ysseldyke & Algozzine, 1983).

The inordinate numbers of learning disabled have resulted from diverse theory and inconclusive research as well as the change in the way mental retardation is determined. Although the mentally retarded have been a part of all societies throughout history, Binet's attempt to predict the success of school children in France initiated the use of intelligence quotients. Terman's work at the beginning of this century, followed by Weschler's subcomponents of verbal and motor ability, provide the base structure for determining intelligence. Assessment has had the greatest impact on identifying the mentally retarded by utilizing cutoff scores on IQ and adaptive behavior scales. Deficient adaptive behavior and significant subaverage intellectual ability must be present in order for someone to be considered mentally retarded. Adaptive behavior describes a person's ability to demonstrate age-appropriate independent functioning and accept social responsibility for themselves. At one time a subaverage score of one standard deviation below the mean (approximately an IQ of 85) was used. This figure, in conjunction with deficient adaptive behavior, would identify about 16 percent of the general population as retarded. Under heavy social, educational, and political pressure, Grossman's revised definition (1983) excludes children with IQ's higher than 75 (approximately two standard deviations below the mean) from categorically being considered as mentally retarded. Many persons today who are labeled "learning disabled" would, at one time, have been considered educable mentally retarded. In contrast to the struggle to refine the definition of learning disabilities and seek new and more precise instrumentation, the definition of mental retardation changed only in terms of a score.

Early theories suggested that the learning disabled's academic difficulties were correlated with sensory, motor, cognitive, and perceptual disorders. Whether neurological dysfunction truly underpinned these disorders was conjectural, and diagnoses were based more on suggestive data than on actual accounts. Assessment focused on psychoeducational variables such as the ability to process visual and auditory stimuli, to attend, store, and retrieve information selectively, and to learn through kinesthetics. Presumably all this occurred along specific learning channels. Modality assessments using, to name one, the Illinois Test of Psycholinguistic Ability (ITPA) (Kirk et al. 1968) pinpointed learning styles from which learning prescriptions were developed. At one time a survey of special education teachers revealed that nearly all of them believed modality strength and weakness could be assessed and should be taken into consideration when designing instruction (Arter & Jenkins, 1977). Matching learning strengths or preferred modalities to instruction is logical and occurs in the natural course of teaching. However, a large corpus of research has failed to produce the promised results. Kavale and Forness's (1987) meta-analysis of 39 modality testing and teaching studies yielded effect sizes of little consequence and demonstrated considerable overlap between groups exhibiting modality preference and those that didn't. This enabled the authors to call for an end to the practice of identifying the learning disabled along these lines. These results are due as much to the interdependence of cognitive processes as to the intercorrelations of the subtests used to select the research samples. While recent shifts in research posit unproductive or inactive strategic language usage and higher order cognitive processes as impediments to learning, accurate measurement remains lacking.

Intellectual capacity, and the speed and automaticity with which information is processed, are the foci of new ways to measure cognitive performance in the retarded and learning disabled. An extensive amount of research in past years has applied an information-processing framework to the analysis of mentally retarded and learning disabled children's intellectual behavior. A large portion of this research has uncovered long-term and short-term memory deficiencies that are linked to cognitive control strategies. The major advantage of this approach is that it allows for a decomposition of the components of intellectual behavior (e.g., Campione, Brown, & Ferrara, 1982). Each of the subcomponents can then theoretically be assessed. One model unique to the learning disabled subdivides intellectual performance into five multidirectional components (Swanson, 1985). Here, successful and efficient intellectual behavior would require a coherent integration of a knowledge base, meta-cognition, strategy/abstraction, executive control, and strategy plan. Each plane of the model is not presented as exclusive of the others. Other interesting componential models (Sternberg, 1988; Sternberg, see ch. 13) consider input, transfer, acquisition, and retention to translate physical movement into concepts. These models are appealing perspectives on intelligence. They do merit exhaustive research before providing the bases for new instruments.

Empirical Approaches for Identifying the Learning Disabled

Prior to the full implementation of the Education of the Handicapped Act in 1975, an identification formula, consisting of IQ, chronological age, and achievement scores, was considered to become part of the identification process for learning disabilities. Without a clear operational definition, a procedure that limited the number of children identified was considered necessary. The learning disabled are defined to have normal intelligence yet as a group fail to perform adequately on many school tasks. By definition, their poor school performance cannot be attributable to other handicapping conditions or to environmental influences. Strong arguments were raised against using formulas to select these children on the grounds that many deserving children would be denied service due to the failing of psychometrics to reflect accurately their potential and ability. Clear parameters have not yet been defined that select children on the basis of indicators that include rather than eliminate them. It is commonplace now to use the term *learning disabled* as if it described a homogeneous, well-defined group when clearly this is not the case. General school failure is the only trait shared by those served as learning disabled. The exclusionary criteria used in the definition limit the accuracy of the identification process but not the number of those selected. Schools are virtually incapable of validating the various psychometrics needed to diagnose, place, and instruct the learning disabled or differentiate them from slow learners (e.g., Ysseldyke et al., 1983). One reaction to poor assessment measures has been to disband the use of the labels and to collapse the mentally retarded, learning disabled, and emotionally disturbed into noncategorical classes where they are considered similar in the way they learn and behave. There are no current data to suggest that this approach is any more effective than past practices. Doing away with labels has more social and ethical appeal and may be totally appropriate for those reasons alone. Within this group, however, are many who are considered mildly handicapped and indistinguishable from slow learners or underachievers (Shepard, 1987).

Between 1976 and 1987 the percentage of children served as learning disabled rose from 21.6 to 43.8, respectively. At the same time the percentage served as mentally retarded declined from 26.0 to 14.7 percent (U.S. Department of Education, 1987). Critics have pointed at special education as characterized by misidentification of students who are eventually placed in inappropriate educational settings (e.g., Algozzine, Ysseldyke, & Christenson, 1983).

Fiscal, instructional, and ethical pressures have induced a series of empirical identification procedures. Advocates purport that difference scores in standard deviation units are more reliable predictors of learning problems than developmental scores from tests. Ability and achievement expectancies, ability and achievement standard score discrepancies, test cutoff scores, and other statistical techniques such as regression formulas and Bayesian estimations have been tried to determine who is learning disabled. All have significant drawbacks. Simply, the subjectivity of the identification process cannot be made unambiguous by mathematical procedures that rely on data from inadequate instruments.

Measuring the magnitude between achievement and an "expected" level of performance originated with the search for determining a child's reading ability. Ability (or potential) is assumed to be a function of intellectual capacity and thus measured by a standardized test of intelligence. The Weschler Scale for Children and the Stanford-Binet are used most often. Various formulas (e.g., Bond & Tinker, 1967; Harris, 1971) merge a variety of educationally relevant variables such as mental and chronological age, years in school, and achievement. The discrepancies are computed as differences between actual and expected standard scores or as a ratio of actual to expected performance. Although these formulas are widely used (Hoffman, 1980), they fail in two significant ways. First, all achievement measures within the same domain do not measure the same trait. For example, one standardized reading test may emphasize decoding skills while another requires good comprehension ability to score well. Yet both can be used to predict expectancy. Second, expectancy formulas are conceptualized on arbitrary mathematical relations (Wilson et al., 1983). Major shortcomings include the failure to recognize that IQ is not a ratio scale, to correlate IQ with achievement, or to accommodate for an increase in error associated with expectancy as IQ deviates from 100 (Shepard, 1980).

Flexibility in test choice can also confound the identification process in other ways. Many learning disabled persons experience reading and language deficiencies. Since it has been demonstrated that achievement is correlated with verbal but not performance intelligence scores (e.g., Prasse, Siewert, & Breen, 1983), an intelligence test that relies heavily on verbal ability to generate an IQ score may yield a biased underestimation of intelligence. When contrasted to a standardized achievement score, a conceivable conclusion would be that the student is not learning disabled per se, but of low intelligence.

Standard score ability and achievement discrepancies are psychometrically more sound than expectancy formulas and are preferred over derived scores. However, they do demand a greater "psychometric" sophistication than most school personnel have, and therefore they are less popular than expectancy score procedures. Misgivings about this procedure are that once test raw scores are converted to standard scores, their comparisons assume they have comparable distributions of equal means and standard deviations. While this occurrence is unlikely, it is necessary to use z score transformations prior to calculating the discrepancy.

The use of regression equations has gained a foothold in the procedures to identify the learning disabled (Elliot, 1981). Six states in the United States currently require the procedure to determine a severe discrepancy (Chalfant, 1984). Regression procedures rely on the benefits of knowing the correlation between achievement measures and ability (predictor variable) rather than the assumption made about the relationship in expectancy and standard score models. Shepard (1980) adds that regression techniques (1) accommodate for differences in learning opportunities by adding grade level to the formula and (2) will result in a consistent number of children identified at each grade level because discrepancy is measured in standard scores, selecting the 10 percent with the greatest deviation.

Of the several models that have been considered (see Reynolds, 1984), one that predicts the frequency of the discrepancy and includes the expected achievement of all students with the same aptitude is the most viable. This procedure, however, is contingent upon the belief that failing to identify an LD student is more perilous than falsely identifying a non-LD student. For making single comparisons, Reynolds (1984) suggests using a one-tailed test to search for a severe discrepancy. Multiple comparisons, which are most often the case, should control alpha with the Bonferroni procedure. One drawback is the computational labor involved.

Also, the lack of reliability between the ability and potential instruments and the differences in their norm samples can provide spurious results. Fortunately, using subtests within the same test or tests from a new series of achievement and cognitive instruments scaled on a common group can overcome this concern.

Others making decisions about who is learning disabled have recognized the inadequacy of the referral and evaluation process and the absence of performance data from children with similar learning difficulties. Bayesian estimations have been employed (e.g., Wissink, Kass, & Ferrell, 1975) and are appealing in that they rely on accumulated child data and consider between-subject rather than within-subject deficiencies. The procedure is limited by a need for large samples of assessment data from an appropriate reference group and by the sophisticated methodology.

Empirical techniques stimulate opinions about theory, assessment, and public policy and the learning disabled, but they do not go unopposed. Critics question their appropriateness on the grounds that, among other reasons:

1. Formulas focus on one or two academic aspects of learning disabilities to the exclusion of other aspects;

2. Technically adequate and age-appropriate instruments are lacking, particularly for preschool and adult populations; many underachieving children obtain a discrepancy between intelligence and achievement for reasons other than a learning disability;

3. The use of discrepancy formulas creates a false sense of objectivity and precision;

4. Decision making using formulas is promoted as a procedure for increasing accuracy but often represents a simplistic attempt to reduce incidence rates of learning disabilities (Board of Trustees of the Council for Learning Disabilities, 1986, p. 425).

Test Selection

Special education teachers are the primary source for gathering assessment data about children suspected to have learning or behavioral difficulties. The instruments to be used are, for the most part, decided at the local level. In a survey of 382 special education teachers in 42 states, Connelly (1985) found the most useful tests identified were: (1) Key Math (63 percent); (2) Peabody Individual Achievement Test (51 percent); (3) Woodcock Reading Mastery Test (46 percent); (4) Peabody Picture

Vocabulary Test (31 percent); (5) Brigance Diagnostic Inventory (26 percent); (6) Slosson Intelligence Test (23 percent); (7) DVMI (27 percent); (8) Detroit Test of Learning Abilities (24 percent); (9) Boehm Test of Basic Concepts (15 percent); and (10) Woodcock-Johnson Psycho-educational Battery (13 percent). With the exception of the Key Math and the Brigance Inventory, which yield criterion-referenced results, the majority of the instruments are not the most reliable available but are more attractive due to their ease in administration. The many tests used to identify the learning disabled, for example, are apparently used by specialists who tend to overrate the test's efficacy while at the same time indicating a lack of familiarity with their psychometric properties (Davis & Shepard, 1983).

Assessment for Instruction

Scant data support the position that assessment intended to diagnose a handicapped person can at the same time provide information relevant to designing a sound educational program (e.g., Glass, 1983; Jenkins & Pany, 1978). Some contend that to rely on these measures fosters a self-fulfilling prophecy and restricts low-scoring students to a future of low achievement. In addition, achievement test standard scores are considered to have un-satisfactory psychometric properties. They tend to require below-average students to gain more than average students in order to maintain the same percentile rank from grade to grade and may, therefore, create unreal expectations (Phillips & Clarizio, 1988).

The general disenchantment with formal assessment measures when applied to teaching has fostered a rapid rise in the use of criterion-referenced tests (e.g., Brigance Inventory of Basic Skills, 1979). Criterion-referenced tests are increasingly popular with special education assessment teams in that they are student centered and easily translated into instruc-tion (see, for example, Hambleton & Jurgensen, 1990). The technical aspects of these tests are provided by Hambleton and Rogers in chapter 1.

Curriculum-Based Assessment

With a renewed emphasis on keeping the handicapped in regular education classes to the greatest extent possible (referred to as the regular education initiative), the context of the local school curriculum has resurfaced as the genesis for assessing the handicapped. Popularized in the literature as "curriculum-based assessment" (CBA), informal procedures are used to assess students' performance directly within the course content through the use of frequent measures of sequentially arranged objectives. The emphasis on developmental rates of learning and the relationship between the student and the task shift the assessment focus from looking for problems within the student to inspecting the curriculum and instruction for impediments to learning. Children are paced and evaluated against themselves and the local curriculum, and are not expected to keep up with more able students or in comparison to national norms. Traditional assessment practice has children tested at the beginning and end of each academic year. CBA allows progress to be measured continually throughout the year.

Deno (1985) suggests that CBA is a promising assessment alternative for measuring achievement since it is (1) curriculum-referenced so that a student's score indicates his or her level of competence in the local school curriculum; (2) individually-referenced so that judgments can be made about whether a student's current rate of progress is an improvement over that student's past rate of progress; and (3) peer-referenced so that the "normality" of a student's performance can be reliably and regularly determined through locally developed peer sampling (p. 230).

For the special learner, assessment is only reasonable if the data collected lead to improved instruction that has known outcomes. In this way, assessment leads teachers directly to those techniques that maximize progress and at the same time assists them in selecting the academic domains that need remediation.

Assessment for Transition

More than 14 years have elapsed since the federal incentives for educating the handicapped were promulgated in the United States. Schools nationally now face a significant challenge in guaranteeing these children that their education that will allow them access to further education and full employment. The concept of "transition" (Will, 1984) has gained a foothold in school-based and residential facility curricula, with the assistance of legislation, but not without disagreement as to what constitutes appropriate assessment and instruction. Transition is an outcome-oriented process whereby a broad array of services and experiences are targeted to post-secondary education and employment. But the lack of efficient skill diagnosis, programming, and placement has impeded the transition process for the handicapped. Transition relies heavily on identifying a student's work and work-related knowledge and aptitude.

Vocational Assessment

School assessment personnel have been either reluctant and unskilled in completing career and vocational assessments. Only recently has the value been recognized of including a vocational assessment in the educational plan of a handicapped student (e.g., Levinson, 1987). Although transition services are receiving increased attention, special education workers continue to perceive the needs of handicapped students in terms not of the skills they will need as adults but of more basic academic skills (Nadolsky, 1985). Any discussion with secondary school personnel will quickly reveal an inconsistency in delivering career curricula and beliefs about who is responsible for preparing the handicapped for future schooling and employment.

A recent report has produced mixed results about the productive activity in which handicapped youths are engaged one year after graduation (Wagner, 1988). Of the handicapped who left school during the 1985–1987 school years, 36 percent dropped out while 56 percent graduated, a figure significantly less than the 71 percent graduation rate for typical students. Certain types of disabilities, such as the learning disabled, fared better and were either employed or in post-secondary education or training. But as a group the disabled were greatly underemployed compared to the general population.

In the United States the nature of the workplace is rapidly moving from being product-oriented to being information- and service-centered. Vocational assessment is hard pressed to meets the demands of matching comprehensive job analyses with an individual's ability. Jobs once available to the handicapped and other disadvantaged workers are being replaced by robotics, computer-assisted design, and international competition. Formal vocational assessment has relied heavily on commercially prepared systems that use simulated work activities and specific job skills for performance analysis. With the change in the marketplace, these instruments are quickly becoming obsolete for many entry-level jobs. In assessing the potential for the handicapped, work with computers and computer-assisted methods holds the most promise. Job-matching software programs are available that use extensive data bases of occupations to sort and align individual abilities and interest. Most exciting, however, is the emergence of authoring systems and interactive video that will dynamically measure performance in more natural ways. Artificial intelligence and natural language formats will greatly enhance the understanding of how the handicapped relate to themselves and work. Cain and Taber (1987) provide an interesting proposal of the impact that technology will have on educating disabled people in the twenty-first century.

Community Placement and Involvement

While handicapped children have moved from restrictive settings into public schools, many handicapped adults continue to be deinstitutionalized and placed in their communities to live and work. Their right to be recognized as human beings with a full opportunity to mature as citizens and contribute to the society has been socially and legally sanctioned. Indeed, community living is by itself no guarantee that the quality of life with improved social interaction and acceptance by nonhandicapped people will occur. To date most handicapped men and women in community residential facilities find little reason to go beyond the home and use a limited range of the environment when they do venture into the community (Crapps, Langone, & Swain, 1985). What role can assessment play in delivering on the expectations of normalized community participation? Traditional types of measurement are virtually useless. The assessment objectives must be conceptualized in terms of quality assurance rather than skill performance. A complete community analysis could identify the local social structure, and a functional analysis could locate health care facilities, churches, food and clothing stores, and recreation centers, to name but a few.

Post-Secondary Education

An increasing number of special education students in the United States are now leaving schools with a recognition they can continue their formal education. Two-year and four-year college education programs are designed to mediate the transition of the handicapped into campus mainstreams and are focusing their assessments on (1) admissions policies that are able to differentiate between qualified and unqualified handicapped students; (2) academic ability; (3) cognitive processing; (4) study habits and compensatory learning strategies; (5) written and oral language skills; and (6) social and emotional interpersonal skill development. The most significant barrier, of course, is pre-admission standardized tests.

Just what type of reasonable testing accommodations should postsecondary institutions make for the handicapped to give them equal access? It has been common practice to "flag" scores obtained under non-standard conditions to alert admissions officers and to protect those who took the test in the standard fashion. However, institutions run the risk of unfairly judging a handicapped applicant by reason of the flagged score alone that identifies them as handicapped. Section 504 of the Rehabilitation Act holds these institutions accountable (e.g., potential loss of federal funds) for not discriminating against these students, not only by making the physical facility accessible but also by delivering on the promise of an education. Testing under this act requires validated measures of aptitude and achievement that are not confounded by a disability or other irrelevant factors. Subsequently, what aspects of test standardization can be breached to mitigate the effects of a disability during testing, yet not compromise the results?

In one attempt, the American College Test Program administered the American College Test (ACT) to groups of specially tested and nonspecially tested examinees under standard conditions (Laing & Farmer, 1984). The special examinees had physical, visual, and auditory disabilities. When compared to the typical examinee, equal predictive validity was demonstrated under the standard conditions. Among the specially tested group, prediction was best for those with visual impairments.

In an extensive study of test modifications for learning, physically, hearing, and visually disabled students taking the Scholastic Aptitude Test (SAT), which is used in college admission, eight indicators of comparability to standard administrations were checked: (1) reliability; (2) factor structure; (3) differential item functioning (or item bias); (4) prediction of academic performance; (5) admissions decisions; (6) test content; (7) testing accommodations; and (8) test timing (Willingham, 1989; Willingham et al., 1988). The study suffered from group heterogeneity that make comparisons tenuous, but the study does provide some enlightenment to test modifications. Test accommodations included providing Braille versions for the visually impaired and audio cassettes for the hearing impaired, and extending the test time by 90 minutes for the learning disabled. When compared to the nonhandicapped taking the SAT under standard conditions, general comparability of all factors except extended test time for the learning disabled was found. Apparently the vast differences among the LD students overpredicted their college performance. As previously discussed, the lack of comon academic and cognitive traits among these students would deter any reasonable attempt to decide who should or should not take the test under extended time conditions. As intriguing as this issue may be to researchers, the safe position for college admissions officers would be to recognize the overprediction but not call for any within-group time differentiations.

Bilingual Assessment

Handicapped children from minority families add an additional tier of difficulty to the referral, assessment, and placement process. Bilingual, or limited-English-proficient (LEP), children compound the assessment process not only by the interaction of their limited or nonexistent English language but with the cultural interpretations of being handicapped made by their parents or advocates. Culture, language, test administration and interpretation, and norm representation are factors associated with the differential test performance of bilingual handicapped children. Cultural bias is disputed as influencing the performance of handicapped children when they are measured for intellectual capacity, academics, and social behavior deficiencies. The overproportion of minority children in special education classes is inevitable when norm-referenced tests are used for identification. Minority children consistently score below middle-class peers on aptitude and achievement tests, and most often have not attended school for as long or in a similarly consistent manner. These children are commonly seen as deficient in the social skills associated with "school coping behavior," leading professionals to label them as emotionally disturbed or behaviorally disordered. Poor performance on standardized tests does not uncover true deficiencies in these children but reveals the ethnocentric nature of the test and the culture on which it was developed (e.g., Lebov, 1970).

Culture-free or culture-fair tests and procedures try to compensate for these issues. From interviews of 21 local education agencies (LEA's) that had LEP handicapped children mainstreamed in bilingual classrooms, Vasquez-Nuttal (1987) found that testing most frequently employed a common culture or translated test approach. Common culture assessments overcome language barriers by relying primarily on nonverbal measures. Translated tests are standardized on an English-speaking population (with a proportional representation of the minority in the norming sample) but translated into Spanish. The districts also reported a serious problem with a shortage of bilingual assessment personnel trained to give the average of 12 educational, psychological, and language tests to each LEP child.

An increasing number of assessment instruments used to identify and instruct bilingual handicapped children are being translated into other languages. There is some question as to whether the test examiner should have the same ethnic background as the child being tested. It is more likely that the ability to administer the test proficiently in accordance with approved procedures will reduce test bias than common ethnicity, but further research is needed to resolve this question.

Translating tests (primarily into Spanish) that have been constructed on American English-speaking populations is a growing trend. With the heavy demand for assessment of the handicapped in schools, recent years have seen the production of Spanish versions of the Woodcock-Johnson Psycho-Educational Test (Woodcock & Johnson, 1979), the Peabody Picture Vocabulary Test–Revised (Dunn & Markwardt, 1988), and the Brigance Diagnostic Comprehensive Inventory (Brigance, 1984), to name a few. There is little empirical evidence, however, to support the premise that direct translation overcomes an inherent cultural and linguistic test-item bias. Gonzales (1989) has conceptualized the misgivings of others about test translation:

1. Not all words directly translate from one language to another.
2. The levels of complexity and vocabulary often change with translation.
3. Dialects complicate the task of translators, who might not understand unfamiliar idioms that are nonetheless part of the tongue.
4. When the test are translated, the original norms become immediately invalid.
5. Although the words of a test can be translated, the concepts in test items frequently cannot; many test items reflect middle-class culture which is foreign for many culturally and linguistically different children.
6. Tests written in a minority child's native tongue but normed in a foreign country would include test items reflecting that county's culture and would preclude an accurate assessment of the child's abilities (Gonzales, 1989, p. 397).

A social construction of meaning may be more representative of a child's cognitive ability than what has previously been believed to be an overall intelligence. Cognitive ability is language-based and constructed by interpreting the reciprocal influence of the event and the knowledge and beliefs of the child. Cognitive assessment should take into account how culture and language influence problem solving and adaptive behavior. Cognitive strategies should be assessed from the perspective that culture influences how children comprehend and plan to solve problems and that failure to perform efficiently on an intelligence test may not mean a trait deficiency (Miller-Jones, 1989).

Legal challenges to diagnostic procedures for identifying minorities with special needs may not result in a more accurate educational prescription but in a decline in needed service. Schools are becoming disinclined to

identify minority children as handicapped, particularly as mentally retarded, knowing the scrutiny the assessment instruments and procedures will
undergo if the identification is contested in court. This reticence may
deprive children in need of the service from getting the individualized
program they deserve. One alternative has been to serve the majority of
these students in classes for the learning disabled (Ortiz & Yates, 1983)—
a label that is more easily justified because of its "flexibility" of terms and
because it is considered less socially pejorative.

Competency Testing

Educational reform in the United States during the past decade has placed
a heavy emphasis on skill and knowledge acquisition. This is a dramatic
change from the previous two decades when schools placed a high priority
on the academic and social processes children used while they were learning. These processes were associated with the cognitive and affective
learning domains. Schools were a place where children discovered things
for themselves, and the way knowledge was communicated and how learning was facilitated were at the center of the curriculum. This general,
objective has long since been considered an "unfulfilled promise"; outside
public scrutiny challenged schools to justify their reliance on process training and account for the increase in the number of children failing basic
skills tests. A spate of reports and opinions, starting with the *Nation of
Risk* (National Commission on Excellence in Education, 1983) and Boyer's
High School: A Report on Secondary Education in America (1983) to the
recent *What Do Our 17-Year-Olds Know?* (Ravitch & Finn, 1987), spot-
light American school children as deficient in the knowledge base of fact
and information needed to compete successfully in the world's marketplace. A public outcry demanded that schools strive for excellence
and provide "proof positive" that at least basic skills were acquired
before students permanently left school. One reaction to stem the tide has
been to require high school students to take a competency test in order to
graduate from high school and receive their diplomas. Handicapped
students, although treated as special learners, are also required to pass
these tests.

Many have argued that to expect handicapped learners to pass the same
standardized test to qualify for graduation is in violation of their guaranteed right to an appropriate education. In their opinion unfair tests will
once again create a disenfranchised class that will be forever disadvantaged
by not receiving a high school diploma. If, due to their handicap, spe-

cialized individual education plans must be constructed to meet their specific learning styles, how can they be expected to pass a standard curriculum evaluated in a standard fashion without suffering discrimination? The practice of requiring the handicapped to pass minimum competency tests to qualify has not gone without legal dispute. Schools, parents, and advocates have challenged the constitutional and statutory legitimacy of requiring the test for a group of students whose class distinction affords them certain legal guarantees.

After the Illinois state superintendent of education ordered a local district to give several handicapped students a diploma even though they had not passed the competency test for graduation, the local district appealed to the United States district court challenging the order (*Brookhart v. Illinois State Board of Education*, 1982). The court held that nothing in the federal or state law stands in the way of the test. The court did recommend that minor modifications, such as a Braille version for a blind student, be made. Modifications to ensure a passing score, however, were not required since, in the court's opinion, these modifications would seriously alter the test and fail to evaluate completely the results of the educational process.

The legal guidelines regulating competency testing for the handicapped are the same as for the general school population. Sufficient prior notice to administering the test provides schools with the legal foundation to require the handicapped to pass the test. With enough advanced notice the proper assessment and instructional activities can be incorporated into a student's IEP to enable him/her to pass the test to graduate and receive a diploma (*Board of Education v. Ambach*, 1983). In general, the courts have not been persuaded to guarantee the handicapped a diploma and have restricted their interpretation to the U.S. Constitution while leaving to the schools the burden of deciding the merits of testing.

Most states have legislation addressing some type of minimal competency tests for promotion and graduation. A recent survey has shown that 39 states have outlined minimum requirements for standards concerning high school handicapped students and their quest for a diploma. These standards range from being excluded from having to take the test, to reasonable modifications to taking the test or the test situation, to no modifications at all and full participation (Grise, 1986). During the 1986–1987 school year, of the 59 percent of special education students graduating from high school, 46 percent received diplomas and 13 percent were given certificates of completion.

Competency testing adds a significant blockade to the reasonable accessibility notion of the federal mandate for the handicapped. Over 64 percent of all handicapped children in the United States are in public school settings receiving individualized instruction, for the most part in reading and mathematics. Early reports of the results of competency testing in one state (Linn, Algozzine, Schwartz, & Grise, 1984) indicated that over half of the learning disabled students taking the test were unable to master 25 of the 38 reading and math skills tested. Without the legal precedent to guard the handicapped from the potential dangers of unfair competency testing, the spirit and intent of the social mandate for an appropriate education are seriously jeopardized.

Competency testing may force special education teachers to gear their teaching curriculum toward the test, and to decrease time spent on the career, vocational, and transitional skills that these students desperately need if they are to succeed in the world. In the search for "excellence" in public schools, the "special" in special education quickly dissipates from an individually tailored education to one in which the common curriculum is held sacred. Competency testing is likely to shape public schools to the degree that the handicapped are once again denied access to the mainstream. There is clearly a conflict between excellence and equality if they are treated as separate issues. Educating handicapped students is considered a parallel enterprise in the excellence movement and has been given little recognition. Full inclusion of the handicapped would demand that they face the same standards as everyone else. At the same time, however, their unique learning patterns and aptitudes must be fully and properly evaluated and managed to meet these demands.

Conclusions

Future assessments of the handicapped will be strengthened when techniques include detailed analysis of a person's environment. Standardized measurement will and should be retained in the procedures followed during assessment. New directions need to consider ecological validity of measurement and how it is advanced when such factors as group size and expectations, type of school and home environment, and socioeconomic variables are included. In addition, tests for the handicapped must seriously consider individuals' developmental changes across time, and the beliefs and judgments they make about their learning. New assessment issues will arise, but professionals will continue to look toward formal tests to clarify who deserves specialized services and how those services can be best provided to insure the handicapped a productive and fulfilling life.

References

Adelman, H. S., & Taylor, L. (1986). Summary of the survey of the fundamental concerns confronting the LD field. *Journal of Learning Disabilities* 19:391–393.

Algozzine, B., Ysseldyke, J. E., & Christenson, S. (1983). An analysis of the incidence of special class placement: The masses are burgeoning. *Journal of Special Education* 17:141–147.

Arter, J. A., & Jenkins, J. R. (1977). Examining the benefits and prevalence of modality considerations in special education. *Journal of Special Education* 11:281–298.

Berk, R. A. (1984). An evaluation of procedures for computing an ability-achievement discrepancy score. *Journal of Learning Disabilities* 17:262–266.

Board of Education v. Ambach, 457, N. E. 2d 775 (N.Y. 1983).

Board of Trustees of the Council for Learning Disabilities. (1986). Use of discrepancy formulas in the identification of learning disabled individuals. *Learning Disabilities Quarterly* 9:245.

Bond, G. L., & Tinker, M. A. (1967). *Reading difficulties: Their diagnosis and correction*, 2nd ed. New York: Appleton-Century-Crofts.

Boyer, E. L. (1983). *High school: A report on secondary education in America*. New York: Harper and Row.

Brigance, A. (1984). *Brigance diagnostic comprehensive inventory*. Billerica, MA: Curriculum Associates, Inc.

Brookhart v. Illinois State Board of Education, 534, F.Supp. 725 (C.D. Ill. 1982).

Burgdorf, R. L. (ed.) (1980). *The legal rights of handicapped persons*. Baltimore, MD: Paul H. Brookes.

Cain, E. J., & Taber, F. M. (1987). *Educating disabled people for the 21st century*. Boston: College-Hill Press.

Campione, J. V., Brown, A. L., & Ferrara, R. A. (1982). Mental retardation and intelligence. In R. Sternberg (ed.), *Handbook of human intelligence*. New York: Cambridge.

Chalfant, J. C. (1985). Identifying learning disabled students: A summary of the national task force report. *Learning Disabilities Focus* 1:9–20.

Connelly, J. (1985). Published tests: Which ones do special education teachers perceive as useful? *Journal of Special Education* 19:129–154.

Crapps, J. M., Langone, J., & Swain, S. (1985). Quantity and quality of participation in community environments by mentally retarded adults. *Education and Training of the Mentally Retarded* 20:123–129.

Davis, W. A., & Shepard, L. A. (1983). Specialists' use of tests and clinical judgement in the diagnosis of learning disabilities. *Learning Disabilities Quarterly* 6:128–138.

Deno, S. L. (1985). Curriculum-based measurement: The emerging alternative. *Exceptional Children* 52:219–232.

Diana v. State Board of Education, 70 C. 37v (N.D.C.A. 1970).

Dunn, L. M. & Markwardt, F. C. (1988). *Peabody individual achievement test*. Circle Pines, MN: American Guidance Service.

Elliot, M. (1981). Quantitative evaluation procedures for the learning disabilities. *Journal of Learning Disabilities* 14:84–87.

Fafard, M. B., Hanlon, R. E., & Bryson, E. A. (1986). *Jose P. v. Ambach*: Progress toward compliance. *Exceptional Children* 52:313–322.

Fuchs, D., Fuchs, L. S., Benowitz, S., & Barringer, K. (1987). Norm-referenced tests: Are they valid for use with handicapped students? *Exceptional Children* 54:263–271.

Glass, G. V. (1983). Effectiveness of special education. *Policy Studies Review* 2:65–78.

Gonzales, E. (1989). Issues in the assessment of minorities. In H. L. Swanson, & B. L. Watson (eds.), *Educational and psychological assessment of exceptional children*, 2nd ed. Columbus, OH: Merrill Publishing.

Grise, P. J. (1986). Handicapped students and minimum competency testing. *Special Services in the School* 2:177–185.

Grossman, H. J. (ed.) (1983). *Manual on terminology and classification in mental retardation*. Washington, DC: American Association on Mental Deficiency.

Hambleton, R. K., & Jurgensen, C. (1990). Criterion-referenced assessment of school achievement. In C. R. Reynolds & R. W. Kamphaus (eds.), *Handbook of psychological and educational assessment of children: Vol. 1, Intelligence and achievement*. New York: The Guilford Press.

Harris, A. J. (1971). *How to increase reading ability*, 4th ed. New York: McKay.

Hobsen v. Hansen, 269 F. Supp. 401 (D.D.C. 1967).

Hoffman, J. V. (1980). The disabled reader: Forgive us for regressions and lead us not into expectations. *Journal of Learning Disabilities* 13:2–6.

Jenkins, J. R., & Pany, D. (1978). Standardized achievement tests: How useful for special education? *Exceptional Children* 44:448–453.

Kavale, K. A., & Forness, S. R. (1987). Substance over style: Assessing the efficacy of modality testing and teaching. *Exceptional Children* 54:228–239.

Kirk, S. A., McCarthy, J. J., & Kirk, N. D. (1968). *Illinois test of psycholinquistic abilities* (rev. ed.). Urbana: University of Illinois Press.

Laing, J., & Farmer, M. (1984). Use of the ACT assessment by examinees with disabilities. *ACT Research Reports*. Iowa City. IA: American College Testing Program.

Larry P. v. Riles, 495 F.Supp. 926 (N.D. Cal 1979) *aff'd*, 83–84 EHLR 555:304 (CA9 1984).

Lebov, W. (1970). The logic of non-standard English. In F. Williams (ed.), *Language and poverty: Perspectives on a theme*. Chicago: Markham, pp. 153–190.

Levinson, E. M. (1987). Incorporating a vocational component into a school psychological evaluation: A case study. *Psychology in the Schools* 24:254–264.

Linn, R. L., Algozzine, B., Schwartz, S. E., & Grise, P. (1984). Minimum competency and the learning disabled adolescent. *Diagnostique* 9:63–75.

Lora v. Board of Education, 456, F.SUPP. 1121 (E.D.N.Y. 1978) *Vac.*, 632, F2d 248 (CA2 1980).

Mattie T. v. Holladay, 3 EHLR 551:109 (N.D. Miss 1979).

Miller-Jones, D. (1989). Culture and testing. *American Psychologist* 44:360–366.

Nadolsky, J. (1985). Achieving unity in special education and rehabilitation. *Journal of Rehabilitation* 51:22–23.

National Commission on Excellence in Education. (1983). *A nation at risk.* Washington, D.C.

Ortiz, A. A., & Yates, J. R. (1983). Incidence of exceptionality among Hispanics: Implications for manpower planning. *National Association of Bilingual Education Journal* 3:41–53.

Perlumutter, B. F., & Parus, M. V. (1983). Identifying children with learning disabilities: A comparison of diagnostic procedures across school districts. *Learning Disability Quarterly* 6:321–328.

Phillips, S. E., & Clarizio, H. F. (1988). Limitations of standard scores in individual achievement testing. *Educational Measurement: Issues and Practice* 7:8–15.

Prasse, D. P., Siewert, J. C., & Breen, M. J. (1983). An analysis of performance on reading subtests from 1978 Wide Range Achievment Test and Woodcock Reading Mastery Test with the WISC-R for learning disabled and regular education students. *Journal of Learning Disabilities* 16:458–461.

Public Law 91–112, The Vocational Rehabilitation Act (1973). 29, U.S.C., 794.

Public Law 94–142, The Education for All Handicapped Children Act. (1975). 20, U.S.C., 1412.

Ravitch, D., & Finn, C. (1987). *What do our 17-year-olds know? A report of the first national assessment of history and literature.* New York: Harper & Row.

Reynolds, C. R. (1984). Critical measurement issues in learning disabilities. *Journal of Special Education* 18:451–476.

Scarpati, S., & Gillespie-Silver, P. (1989). Assessing infants and young children. In H. L. Swanson & B. L. Watson (eds.), *Educational and psychological assessment of exceptional children*, 2nd ed. Columbus, OH: Merrill Publishing.

Shepard, L. A. (1980). An evelution of the regression discrepancy method for identifying children with learning disabilities. *Journal of Special Education* 14:79–91.

Shepard, L. A. (1987). The new push for excellence: Widening the schism between regular and special education. *Exceptional Children* 53:327–329.

Sternberg, R. (1988). A unified theory of intellectual exceptionality. In J. G. Borkowski & J. Day (eds.), *Cognition and intelligence in special children: Comparative approaches to retardation, learning disabilities, and giftedness.* Norwood, NJ: Ablex.

Swanson, H. L. (1985). Assessing learning disabled children's intellectual performance. In K. D. Gadow (ed.), *Advances in learning and behavioral disorders*, Vol. 4. Greenwich, CT: JAI Press.

U.S. Department of Education, Office of Special Education and Rehabilitative Services. (1987). *Ninth annual report to Congress on the implementation of the Education of the Handicapped Act.*

Vasquez-Nuttal, E. (1987). Survey of current practices in the psychological assessment of limited-English proficiency handicapped children. *Journal of School Psychology* 25:53–61.

Wagner, M. (1988). *The transition experiences of youth with disabilities: A re-*

port from the national longitudinal transition study. Reston, VA: Council for Exceptional Children.

Will, M. (1984). *OSERS programming for the transition of youth with disabilities. Bridge from school to work*. Washington, DC: U.S. Depàrtment of Education.

Willingham, W. W. (1989). Standard testing conditions and standard score meaning for handicapped examinees. *Applied Measurement in Education* 2:97–103.

Willingham, W. W., Rogosta, M., Bennett, R. E., Braun, H., Rock, D. A., & Powers, D. E. (1988). *Testing handicapped people*. Boston: Allyn and Bacon.

Wilson, L. R., Cone, T. E., Busch, R., & Alee, T. (1983). A critique of the expectancy formula approach: Beating a dead horse. *Psychology in the Schools* 20:241–249.

Wissink, J., Kass, C., & Ferrell, W. (1975). A Bayesian approach to the identification of children with learning disabilities. *Journal of Learning Disabilities* 8:158–169.

Ysseldyke, J., Thurlow, M., Graden, J., Wesson, C., Deno, S., & Algozzine, B. (1983). Generalizations from five years of research on assessment and decision making. *Exceptional Education Quarterly* 4:75–93.

Ysseldyke, J. E., & Algozzine, B. (1983). LD or not LD: That's not the question. *Journal of Learning Disabilities* 16:29–31.

Ysseldyke, J. E., Thurlow, M. L., & O'Sullivan, P. J. (1986). Current screening and diagnostic practices in a state offering free preschool screening since 1977: Implications for the field. *Journal of Psychoeducational Assessment* 4:191–201.

10 TESTING ACROSS CULTURES

Fons J. R. van de Vijver
Ype H. Poortinga

There has been a longstanding, scientific interest in the comparison of people belonging to different cultural groups. In the course of the history of Western science, practitioners of different disciplines have been involved. During the Renaissance the equality of races was an issue for theologians. In 1550 a number of them convened at the court of Charles V in Spain to solve the question of how the American Indians could be colonized "in a Christian fashion." According to the chronicles, the debate focused on the question of whether the Indians formed an inferior race in comparison with their Spanish colonizers. The issue was never settled, even though "some of the most learned and powerful men of the age" participated (Boorstin, 1985, p. 633). During the nineteenth century, racial differences had become the domain of social philosophers, who, in turn, "passed the buck" (the use of the expression in this context coming from Mann, 1940) to psychologists.

Each scientific discipline formulated somewhat different questions: the theologians were concerned with moral equality and inequality, social philosophers studied cultural evolution, and psychologists concentrated on individual behavior. The lack of agreement already present among the sixteenth century theologians continues to exist today, in psychology notably with respect to cognitive abilities. Authors such as Jensen (1980) and Eysenck (1984) are proponents of the view that marked differences exist in cognitive abilities among individuals of various cultural groups, while others like Mercer (e.g., 1984) defend the opposite opinion. By far the most cross-cultural studies are in line with the latter position.

In these studies, ecological variables, such as climate or sociocultural variables, are postulated as the determinants of observed differences. The plasticity of human behavior is emphasized, and it is often assumed that, through formal education and technological development, intergroup differences in cognitive abilities will gradually disappear. However, it should be emphasized that most of the opinions on the nature of cultural antecedents of observed test score differences are, at least to some extent, speculative in view of the serious methodological difficulties which often arise if we want to identify the specific determinants of an observed intergroup difference. On the other hand, the occurrence of often ill-founded speculations is not restricted to "environmentalists" such as Mercer; much work which is more in line with a "geneticist" position suffers from the same problem.

An early attempt at a systematic investigation of the cognitive abilities of individuals in non-Western cultures can be found in the work of Porteus (1917), who composed the so-called Maze Test, an instrument similar to the Mazes subtest in the Wechsler Adult Intelligence Scale and Wechsler Intelligence Scale for Children batteries of today. Porteus' Maze Test has been used extensively in cross-cultural research (for a review see Porteus, 1965). David (1974) cites a number of features of this test which are meant to optimize its suitability in a cross-cultural context, namely "a high intrinsic interest for most persons, simple instructions, easy to administer and objectivity of scoring" (p. 11). Numerous studies with this test have revealed large cross-cultural differences in mean score levels. However, the interpretation of these differences is far less clear than their replicability might suggest. All kinds of factors can threaten a straight-forward interpretation of observed cross-cultural score differences. Among other things, they can be caused by differences in the familiarity of subjects with testing situations, the nature of the stimulus materials, or differences in motivation. This is true not only for Porteus' test but for all assessment instruments. The question of how to arrive at more valid explanations of observed intergroup differences is the central problem of this chapter. In the final section a procedure will be outlined which is aimed at reducing the number of rival hypotheses that can explain observed intergroup differences. In this procedure it is crucial that potential determinants of intergroup differences are recognized beforehand and that variables to assess these determinants are included in the design of a study.

A second problem of cross-cultural testing has to do with the administration of tests. In this context it is illuminating to look at the difficulties that have emerged in the application of Porteus' Maze Test. Porteus himself (1965), for instance, found it difficult to persuade Australian aboriginal subjects to solve the items by their own effort rather than in cooperation with the tester. As another example, it can be mentioned that the Maze Test, which is a paper-and-pencil test, has been applied among groups from which the members had never touched a pencil before (cf. Porteus, 1965). In the case of some cultural groups it is even debatable whether mazes are suitable as stimulus material. In a discussion on the use of the Maze Test among Bushmen, Reuning and Wortley (1973) argue that "the idea of a maze is not likely to occur to a Kalahari-dweller (like the Bushman) and must be utterly foreign to him" (p. 61). Their argument is based on the consideration that in a savannah, the natural ecology of the Bushmen, a person can invariably go along a more or less straight line from one point to another. The obvious conclusion from these examples is that the validity of the results obtained with a test will be questionable in all instances where the administration raises the kind of difficulties referred to.

The third problem of cross-cultural testing to be discussed here is that numerically identical test scores can have a psychologically different meaning. If scores are numerically comparable across cultures, they will be called *score equivalent*. However, such equivalence should be established instead of assumed. Test scores obtained in different cultural groups can have a quite distinct psychological meaning. Porteus' (1965) observation that Australian Aborigines perform significantly better than Kalahari Bushmen does not tell much about differences in planning ability between these groups. Rather, the low scores are likely to reflect the use of materials with highly unequal ecological validities across the groups and misunderstandings in the administration through the use of an interpreter, as was done among the Bushmen.

The three problems of cross-cultural testing mentioned here—the explanation of observed intergroup differences, proper test administration, and score equivalence—are interrelated. An adequate test administration procedure is a necessary, though insufficient, condition for score equivalence across groups. Score equivalence, in turn, is a necessary condition for an adequate explanation of intergroup differences.

The difficulties of cross-cultural testing have been emphasized here because their impact is greatly underrated, in our opinion. The applicability of tests in settings which are culturally widely discrepant from the usually Western context in which they are constructed is too often taken for granted. All kinds of factors may render intergroup differences invalid. Differences in formal education, unfamiliarity with tests, or even a poor nutritional state and poor general health, to mention only a few relevant factors, can form a threat to the equivalence of scores.

The underrating of testing problems in cross-cultural research is a reason for the wide gap sometimes found between psychological test data and daily observations of related phenomena. Work on (Piagetian) formal operational thinking can illustrate this point. In a review of research in this area, Neimark (1975) states that there is "clear evidence of retardation of development and even failure of attainment in most non-Western groups" (p. 578). This means that the psychological data seem to imply that many individuals in non-Western groups are incapable of abstract reasoning. It is obvious that this statement refers to the testing situation rather than to daily life, in which the same people are definitely not incapable of abstract reasoning (cf. Biesheuvel, 1949; Hutchins, 1980). It appears that for some groups the assessment procedures reviewed by Neimark have a very low generalizability to daily life.

Problems in Test Use and Administration

The proper use of tests starts with administrative procedures that are suitable to represent the psychological phenomena under study. In the introduction a few examples have been given of what can go wrong when tests are applied in a different cultural setting. In this section a broader overview is presented of the possible sources of error in test administration procedures, followed by some precautions which can be taken to reduce the effects of these errors.

Five areas are distinguished: problems related to the tester, the examinees, the interaction between tester and examinee, the response procedure, and the stimulus material.

Tester

The (obtrusive) presence of the tester during the data gathering can be a threat to the validity of the results. It is recognized that in observational studies of mother-child interactions the mere presence of the tester may provoke or inhibit particular behavior of the mother and the child (Super, 1981). The potential effect of the race of the tester on the performance of the examinee has been extensively studied in the United States, with black and white testers for both white and black subjects. The results are not very consistent, but the effects tend to be small (Jensen, 1980; Vernon,

1979). However, this conclusion cannot be generalized to other cultural settings without additional evidence.

Examinees

The second problem area involves the choice of examinees. It is a major difficulty in cross-cultural psychology to select corresponding samples of subjects across cultures (Pick, 1981; Malpass & Poortinga, 1986). Cultures differ in many ways, and hence samples recruited from these cultures will also differ in many respects. This violates the condition that samples of subjects should only differ on one variable, namely the independent variable. This condition, which is the cornerstone of experimental psychology, does not hold in cross-cultural psychology where intact groups are compared. Usually, particular cultures are selected because they are assumed to vary in terms of some background characteristic which is relevant for the construct under study. However, the researcher should be alert to the existence of other background variables—unintentionally varied through the particular choice of cultures—which can also legitimately explain intergroup differences in performance. The most clear-cut examples are studies in which the test scores of illiterates and literates are compared. Two such groups differ not only in ability to read and write but in a host of variables related to formal schooling. Comparisons between literates and illiterates are almost by definition comparisons between schoolgoing and non-schoolgoing populations. A noteworthy exception is the work of Scribner and Cole (1981) with the Vai in Liberia. Among the Vai different forms of literacy are found. Some of these people are literate in their indigeneous syllabic script which is learned in an informal setting, labeled "unschooled literacy" by the authors. By a careful choice of subjects Scribner and Cole were able to disentangle the traditionally confounded effects of schooling and literacy.

Tester-Examinee Interaction

The third problem area has to do with the interaction between tester and examinee. Establishing ways of adequate, unambiguous communication between tester and examinee is an essential condition for meaningful test use. When Reuning and Wortley (1973) planned to administer a variety of tests to the Bushmen, they were confronted with the problem of many locally different vernaculars and with the inherent difficulty of recruiting competent interpreters for each new linguistic group to be tested. Therefore, in their choice and composition of tests they tried to minimize the dependence on verbal exchange both in the instructions and in the examinees' responses. According to these authors, instructions should be understandable without any verbal explanation. Items should invite the intended action, they should have what in German is called *Aufforderungs-charakter*, i.e., incite the subject to do what is required. Also, responses should be concrete actions rather than verbal explanations (Reuning & Wortley, 1973, p. 12).

Minimal reliance on verbal communication circumvents only some of the difficulties. It is no solution for the absence in indigenous languages of particular words which are essential for a good understanding of a task. When reading Lancy's (1983) classification of indigenous counting systems among the Papuas of New Guinea,which vary considerably in their degree of complexity, it is easy to see that tests in which arithmetic reasoning plays a role may be hard to understand for certain groups, because the necessary number concepts are lacking in their language.

Sometimes it may seem possible to circumvent language problems by using the official, national language (e.g., French in Zaire) which often is also the official medium of instruction at school. However, for many subjects this national language will be their second or third language, and it is unrealistic to expect an equal proficiency in the national language as in the native tongue.

All illustration of a subtle but important communication failure in cross-cultural testing is offered in two studies among the Wolof on the Piagetian principle of conservation. Greenfield (1966, 1979) administered conservation tasks to Wolof subjects in their native language using the clinical interview method commonly found in the Piagetian tradition. In such a test, two identical short, broad beakers containing an equal amount of water are placed on a table in front of the subject. One of these beakers is poured into a tall, thin beaker. The subject is then asked which beaker contains more water. Children of preschool age—most of them "non-conservers"—typically will say that the tall glass contains more, while older children—frequently "conservers"—will give the correct answer. Greenfield's results indicated that among unschooled Wolof, nonconservation responses were found frequently, even at 12 years of age, especially with a task in which the water was distributed over more than two beakers. In an interesting replication Irvine (1978) argued that the question of which beaker held more water appeared to be ambiguous in the language of the Wolof, as "more" could refer both to the quantity and the level of the water. With this in mind, Irvine found that all subjects she tested understood the principle of conservation, although admittedly, her case is weakened by the fact that her sample included only five subjects.

Response Procedures

Response procedures are the fourth topic of discussion. We have mentioned already the use of paper-and-pencil tests among groups who have never touched a pencil before. Another example is the use of a multiple-choice format which presupposes a balanced strategy between solving a problem until one is perfectly sure and a liberal amount of guessing the correct alternative.

A further example can be found in the work of Serpell (1979). He administered a pattern design copying task to children in the United Kingdom and Zambia. Two different media were used to assess the child's skill in copying, namely pencil-drawing and iron-wire modeling, a popular pastime among boys in Zambia. The British children outperformed their Zambian counterparts in pencil-drawing, while the reverse was found for the wire-modeling task. It appears that the response medium can affect the scores to a substantial extent. It is highly unlikely that groups unfamiliar with a particular response procedure, be it iron-wire modeling, multiple-choice format, or whatever, will attain the highest level of performance with that medium.

Stimuli

The final topic to be treated, problems connected with the stimulus material, is the best documented. A factor mentioned over and over in the literature as an important determinant of intergroup differences is the differential familiarity of subjects with certain stimulus materials (e.g., Biesheuvel, 1949; Irvine & Carroll, 1980; Ord, 1970; Pick, 1981; Schwarz, 1961). An elegant demonstration of the effect of stimulus unfamiliarity is offered by Deregowski and Serpell (1971). Scottish and Zambian children were asked to sort miniature models of animals and motor vehicles in one experimental condition and photographs of these items in another condition. With the actual models no intergroup differences were found, whereas in the sorting of the photographs Scottish children obtained higher scores than Zambian children. This can be explained in terms of a lower familiarity of the Zambian children with photographs. Similarly, Price-Williams (1962) found that children in a rural Nigerian community displayed a higher ability in sorting indigenous leaves than in sorting toy models of animals.

Skill Reduction

Rather than pursuing any complete coverage of the extensive literature, we shall focus on some principles of cross-cultural test use, meant to minimize the impact of the previously mentioned problems. Van der Flier (1972, 1980) has formulated a so-called "skill reduction" approach. In this approach it is assumed that the completion of a test requires a number of "skills" from the subject. These skills can be defined as the set of abilities which are needed to perform well on the test, in addition to the construct the test is supposed to measure. The skill to recognize pictures in Deregowski and Serpell's experiment on the sorting of photographs of toys is an example. According to Van der Flier's rationale, score differences in cross-cultural research are caused not only by genuine ability differences but also by skill differences.

Van der Flier has distinguished three ways to reduce unwanted effects of skills. First, he suggests to restrict the comparison of scores to those parts of a population where the skills needed are readily available. As a check on the proper understanding of a multiple-choice response format, a researcher can administer a few extremely simple multiple-choice items, preceding the actual test items. (These simple items may even be unrelated in content to the test.) In the data analysis only those subjects with correct answers on the first simple items will be considered. Second, the researcher can try to eliminate the need for certain skills, for example, by an appropriate choice of stimulus materials. The abovementioned experiment of Price-Williams (1962), in which Nigerian subjects were asked to sort leaves found in the natural environment, is a good example of this strategy to reduce the effects of skills. Third, skill differences can be reduced by extending the test instruction and by administering training items. A classic example is the repeated administration of Raven's Matrices in Congo by Ombrédane and associates (1956), showing that the validity increased from the first to the third time. Van de Vijver (1984, 1988) included a lengthy instruction procedure with a sample item for each of the problem-solving rules which the subject needed for an inductive reasoning test. In this way the domain of responses required by the test was explicitly defined.

Similarly, Van de Vijver and colleagues (1986) gave training to Dutch, Surinam and Zambian youngsters on a test of inductive reasoning. In the test the subject had to mark the group of letters which did not fit in a group of five: for example, DDDGFH NHDTTT KLMMMB WWSXZA HHHRDS. When compared with the Dutch and Surinam groups, a remarkable score increase was found in the Zambian group at a retest after the training. Interestingly, substantial score increments were also observed in the Zambian control group. (It was not found for the control groups in the other cultures.) Since the experiences of the control groups with the tests were restricted to the first test administration, it was argued that the score increases of the Zambian subjects were caused by improved test-taking skills learned the first time.

Research such as that by Van der Flier shows that systematic approaches to cross-cultural testing can help to improve the validity of test scores. At the same time it should be clear from this section that it is impossible to offer exhaustive rules about how to design assessment instruments which are universally applicable. Rather, the use of tests requires a thorough knowledge of the local circumstances of the subjects to which the test will be administered. Serious anomalies will result unless the researcher avoids making (implicit) assumptions about testing, which can be valid in his or her own culture, but may not apply in other cultural contexts. Examples of such assumptions are that subjects can cope with multiple-choice formats, will work fast on speeded tests, will try to achieve a high score (rather than maintain good interpersonal relations with the tester), and will easily grasp the meaning of pictorial stimuli.

A Conceptual Framework for the Analysis of Cross-Cultural Score Equivalence

During the last two decades much effort has been put into developing and refining procedures to analyze score equivalence in intergroup comparisons. In the literature these are referred to as item bias studies. (The terms *unbiased* and *score equivalent* are used interchangeably here.) Although there is no agreement in the literature about the definition of item bias (Rudner et al., 1980), most differences involve the statistical analyses and the psychometric models used rather than the underlying ideas. Many definitions share the notion that an item is biased when the psychological construct represented by that item is not the same in each cultural group under study. We would like to propose a definition that is in line with this idea. Item bias is defined here as any difference in an observed score for which there is no corresponding difference in the psychological domain to which the scores are generalized (Poortinga & Malpass, 1986). Suppose that an arithmetic test contains an item, asking how many pencils will go into six dozen pencils. When "dozen" is a concept that is only known to the examinees in a subset of the cultures involved, a strange response pattern will emerge, since the item does not measure arithmetic reasoning in all groups. The psychological domain of the item in a culture in which the concept of dozen is absent is different from arithmetic reasoning, the domain of the other items of the test. Item bias analyses are implemented to detect those items in a test which do not have the same psychological meaning across cultural groups.

Bias is defined here in terms of the domain of generalization. The latter is not an intrinsic property of an instrument but depends upon the context in which the tests is used. In our opinion, the same is true for item bias. An item can be unbiased in respect to one domain but biased in respect to some (usually larger) domain. For example, suppose that an arithmetic test has been administered to a group of schooled and a group of unschooled children of the same age. If the domain of generalization would be arithmetic *achievement*, the test may well yield unbiased results. However, when the test is taken to measure arithmetic *aptitude* or, even more generally, *intelligence*, any intergroup comparison may be precluded by the presence of item bias.

An important kind of generalization domain is formed by performance criteria in organizational or educational selection. The question of bias in this context has received considerable attention in the literature on fair employment.

A Classification of Item Bias Detection Procedures

An attempted coverage of available item bias detection techniques would go well beyond the scope of the present chapter. We shall restrict ourselves here to a schematic overview of the most important approaches. For a more extensive discussion of various techniques, the reader is referred to Berk (1982) and, more recently, Cole and Moss (1989) and Mellenbergh (1989).

Our scheme is based on three criteria to distinguish bias detection techniques. First, some techniques start from the assumption that a test constitutes a common scale on which scores can be compared. Either for raw scores or for derived scores (e.g., the ability or item difficulty scale in item response theory; see below) corollaries of the assumption are tested at item level. If an item does not meet the requirements postulated, it is removed. The items remaining after item bias analysis are taken to satisfy the requirements for a common scale. In other approaches it is the objective of the analysis to establish whether such a common scale does exist. An example is exploratory factor analysis. The existence of a common scale is made plausible through the analysis rather than being assumed beforehand.

Second, techniques differ in the kind of data used in the analysis. Some methods are based on the items-by-persons matrix for each culture. In other methods the data matrix is restructured prior to the actual computations. This usually implies some aggregation of the data in the form of averages, inter-item correlations, or contingency tables. These aggregates contain all the information needed for the computation of some item bias statistic. In other words, some techniques use the information available in the full data matrix, while in other instances the relevant information on item bias is assumed to be present in the statistics.

Our third dimension reflects a distinction between so-called conditional and unconditional procedures (Mellenbergh, 1982; Van der Flier et al., 1984). In conditional methods, bias is investigated per ability level, or conditional on the ability level, hence the name. The idea behind conditional approaches is that item bias may not be invariant across the whole range of test scores; the bias effects may be larger for a particular ability level, e.g., for examinees who have a low level of ability. In unconditional procedures the data matrices are compared without any concern for possible group differences in ability levels. Mellenbergh (1982) has argued that conditional methods should be preferred over unconditional methods, because the latter yield more detailed information.

Both conditional and unconditional methods assume the existence of a common scale; hence, the first and third dimensions of our distinction of item bias techniques are not independent. Taking this into account, the three dimensions lead to a scheme as presented in table 10–1.

Table 10–1.   Schematic Overview of Item Bias Techniques

Scale	Input Data for Analysis	
	Raw Data	Aggregated Data
Common scale not assumed	None	Factor analysis, comparison of correlation matrices
Common scale assumed (unconditional)	Analysis of variance	Analysis of p-values, transformed item difficulties, linear structural models
Common scale assumed (conditional)	Item response models	χ^2-approaches

Correlational Techniques.   No common scale is assumed in a test on the equality of correlation matrices obtained in different cultures (Browne, 1978) or in exploratory factor analysis (e.g., Irvine, 1979). When using factor analytic techniques, separate analyses are carried out for each culture and the matrices of factor loadings are combined, either by rotating them to a matrix which is closest to the separate matrices (Kaiser et al., 1971) or by rotating all matrices to one target matrix—for example, the matrix obtained in one cultural group (e.g., Van der Flier, 1980). An illustration of the use of factor analysis to establish dimensional identity can be found in the work by Eysenck and colleagues (e.g., Eysenck & Eysenck, 1983). In these studies a test, usually Eysenck's Personality Questionnaire, is administered to a number of subjects in a particular culture. A factor analysis is carried out, followed by a comparison of the factors with those derived from the sample in the United Kingdom on which the original norms of the questionnaire were established. In this procedure the two matrices are rotated to one target.

In the past there has been some debate around the presumed lack of discriminatory power of these techniques (e.g., Horn, 1967; Horn & Knapp, 1973; Humphreys et al., 1969; Ten Berge, 1977). The main objection against target rotations is their "extreme kindness for the data," i.e., it is too easy to get a reasonable fit between hardly related input matrices. Only large differences will be discovered in this way. A demonstration of the extreme flexibility of target rotations as used in the Eysenck tradition has been given by Bijnen and associates (1986).

Unconditional Methods.   In most bias detection techniques the existence of a common scale is assumed rather than demonstrated. This is the case for the unconditional methods as well as the conditional methods. In the former, raw item scores or statistics derived from item scores are compared across groups. Examples of the latter approach are the comparison of p-values (Poortinga & Foden, 1975) or their normal deviates (Angoff & Ford, 1973). In these methods a scatter plot of the p-values for a set of items in two groups is prepared. The points representing unbiased items will fall in a fairly narrow region. An item that clearly falls outside that region is considered to be biased. Other examples of unconditional methods are Cleary and Hilton's (1968) use of analysis of variance and Jöreskog's linear structural models. (Applications can be found in Rock and associates, 1982, and Benson, 1987.)

At this point it should be noted that the classification of particular techniques as unconditional methods is mainly determined by their empirical use. The methods mentioned can also be applied as conditional methods, namely by including level of ability as an additional factor in the analysis. Suppose a researcher wants to compare p-values obtained in various cultural groups. An unconditional analysis entails a direct comparison of the item statistics while, in a conditional analysis, the samples of subjects will be divided according to the level of their raw score and analyzed per level. Conversely, the conditional methods that will be discussed can also be used in an unconditioned way by eliminating ability as a separate factor during the analysis.

Conditional Methods.   In the conditional methods of item bias analysis, one particular corollary of the assumption of a common scale is crucial, i.e., that subjects with equal abilities have equal probabilities of correctly answering the test items, irrespective of their group membership. Two kinds of conditional methods can be distinguished: namely, those based on item response theory and χ^2-approaches.

Within the two- and three-parameter models of item response theory, various indices of item bias have been defined (Cole & Moss, 1989; Lord, 1980; Mellenbergh, 1989; Rudner et al., 1980; Shepard et al., 1981, 1984). Some of these indices have a strong intuitive appeal, but it has to be noted that their sampling distribution is usually unknown. This means that the distinction between biased and unbiased items lacks a sound statistical basis and, hence, is arbitrary to some extent.

Within the Rasch model, the one-parameter model of item response theory, there are also various fit statistics, which can be used as bias indices. These statistics, with known sampling distributions, vary from omnibus tests in which all items are evaluated simultaneously (e.g., Andersen, 1973) to highly specific tests in which the contribution of each separate item to the overall fit can be evaluated (e.g., Van den Wollenberg, 1982).

In the second kind of conditional techniques, the χ^2-approaches, contingency tables are analyzed (Marascuilo & Slaughter, 1981; Mellenbergh, 1982). The most frequently used table has three factors, score level, culture, and response (right/wrong). The observed frequencies are entered in the cells. The table is analyzed for each test item separately. The fit of an item is evaluated by means of a χ^2-statistic, hence the name. An application can be found in Van der Flier and associates (1984).

A Procedure Based on Generalizability Theory

After this general overview of different item bias techniques, an example of a procedure and the rationale behind it will be presented in some detail;

it has previously been described by Van de Vijver and Poortinga (1982).

Our framework for the investigation of bias (or score equivalence) is based on generalizability theory (Cronbach et al., 1972). In the most simple study a test is administered to members of two culturally different groups. This design has been labeled as "Design V-B" by Cronbach and associates (1972, p. 38). It can be described as a crossing of the factors Stimulus and Persons, with the latter nested in the factor Culture, designated as Stimulus x Persons (Culture). A single item score, denoted by $X_{sp(c)}$, is assumed to consist of the following linear, additive components (Van de Vijver & Poortinga, 1982)[1]:

$$X_{sp(c)} = \mu + S_s + P_{p'}PC_{pc} + C_c + SC_{sc} + SP_{sp'}SPC_{spc'}E_{spc} \qquad (1)$$

where

μ is the overall mean;

S_s $(s = 1, \ldots, n_s)$ is the main effect for Stimulus (items);

$P_{p'}PC_{pc}(p = 1, \ldots, n_p)$ is the confounded effect for the main effect Persons (P) and the Person by Culture interaction (PC);

$C_c (c = 1, \ldots, n_c)$ is the main effect for Culture;

SC_{sc} is the interaction between Stimulus and Culture;

$SP_{sp'}SPC_{spc'}E_{spc}$ is the confounded effect of the Stimulus by Person interaction (SP), the Stimulus by Person by Culture interaction (SPC) and the error term (E).

The analysis of score equivalence starts with an analysis of variance. The sources of variance are schematically drawn in figure 10–1. On the basis of the observed mean squares, variance components can be estimated. The computational formulas are presented in table 10–2. Most current

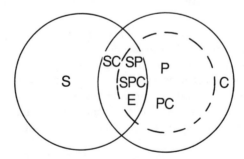

Figure 10–1. Schematic Representation of Variance Components in a Stimulus (S) by Culture (C) Design with Persons (P) Nested in Cultures

Source: From van de Vijver and Poortinga (1982). Reprinted by permission from Sage Publications.

Table 10–2. The Computation of the Estimated Variance Components

Estimated Variance Component	Computational Formula
$\sigma^2(SP, SPC, E)$	$= MS(SP, SPC, E)$
$\sigma^2(SC)$	$= (MS(SC) - MS(SP, SPC, E))/n_p$
$\sigma^2(P, PC)$	$= (MS(P, PC) - MS(SP, SPC, E))/n_s$
$\sigma^2(S)$	$= (MS(S) - MS(SC))/n_p n_c$
$\sigma^2(C)$	$= (MS(C) - MS(P, PC) - MS(SC) + MS(SP, SPC, E))/n_s n_p$

statistical computer packages contain a program for the estimation of variance components (e.g., the program P8V in BMDP; Dixon, 1981).

Generalizability Coefficients. The components of variance are used to calculate coefficients of generalizability, which reflect the impact of particular sources of variance in the dependent variable (cf. Cronbach et al., 1972). For example, when a researcher is interested in the contribution of cross-cultural score differences to the overall score variance, an estimated generalizability coefficient for the main effect culture can be computed. This coefficient indicates what proportion of the score variance is accounted for by cross-cultural differences in mean scores. Generalizability coefficients are closely related to traditional reliability coefficients; both have a lower limit of 0.00 and an upper limit of 1.00. A high value of a generalizability coefficient for a particular source indicates a high contribution of this source to the total score variance.

Generalizability coefficients also have the same disadvantage as reliability coefficients, namely that their size depends on the number of items on which they are based. In classical test theory the Spearman-Brown formula is used to estimate the reliability of a test at various lengths under the assumption of parallelism of the items (e.g., Allen & Yen, 1979, formula 4.7). The same formula applies to generalizability coefficients. Thus, given a particular number of levels for a factor in a study, the generalizability coefficient of that factor can be estimated for any other number of levels by means of the Spearman-Brown formula (Golding, 1975). This provides us with a method to overcome the disadvantage mentioned. A convenient way to get mutually comparable coefficients is to compute these at unit level, equivalent to the computation of the reliability of a one-item test in classical test theory. These unit length coefficients of generalizability are expressed on an identical scale, irrespective of the kind of factors or the number of levels in a factor.

In the present context two generalizability coefficients are of major interest. (This choice will be motivated later.) The first one, denoted by ρ_{sc}^2, evaluates the importance of the stimulus by culture interaction, the traditional item bias statistic (e.g., Cleary & Hilton, 1968; Poortinga, 1971). For the second coefficient, denoted by ρ_{c+sc}^2, both the main effect culture and the stimulus by culture interaction are of interest.

The computational formulas for these coefficients are:

$$\rho_{sc}^2 = \frac{\sigma_{sc}^2}{\sigma_{sc}^2 + \sigma_{sp,spc,e}^2/n_p'} \tag{2}$$

$$\rho_{c+sc}^2 = \frac{\sigma_c^2 + \sigma_{sc}^2}{\sigma_c^2 + \sigma_{sc}^2 + \sigma_{p,pc}^2/n_p' + \sigma_{sp,spc,e}^2/n_p'} \tag{3}$$

in which $n_p' = n_p$ for full length coefficients and $n_p' = 1$ for unit length coefficients.

In generalizability theory the statistical significance of a generalizability coefficient is considered relatively unimportant. In fact, a generalizability coefficient is an estimate of effect size rather than significance level. Although we concur with this position, it may be noted that the sampling distribution of ρ_{sc}^2 can be derived quite easily. Only the distribution of ρ_{c+sc}^2 is unknown. For a test of the hypothesis that $\rho_{sc}^2 = 0$, assuming full length estimates, the following holds (Kristof, 1963; Kraemer, 1981):

$$\frac{1}{1 - \rho_{sc}^2} = \frac{1}{1 - \sigma_{sc}^2/(\sigma_{sc}^2 + \sigma_{sp,spc,e}^2/n_p)} = \frac{\sigma_{sc}^2 + \sigma_{sp,spc,e}^2/n_p}{\sigma_{sp,spc,e}^2/n_p} \tag{4}$$

When both nominator and denominator are multiplied by n_p, the latter coefficient is the F-ratio for the SC-interaction with $(n_s - 1)(n_c - 1)$ and $n_c(n_s - 1)(n_p - 1)$ degrees of freedom; thus, it appears that ρ_{sc}^2 differs significantly from zero whenever the F-ratio for the SC-component in the analysis of variance is significant.

There are fewer conventions about effect size than about significance in the literature. What miɪ.imum value a coefficient of generalizability should attain before it can be considered to be meaningfully contributing to the score variance is a matter of debate. As a rule of thumb, a value of .05 for the unit length coefficient seems to work quite well.

ρ_{sc}^2. The size of ρ_{sc}^2 is particularly important when a researcher has good reasons to believe that bias will manifest itself primarily at the level of separate items. A value larger than .05 indicates the presence of item bias. When the value of ρ_{sc}^2 is substantial, an inspection of the residuals in each cell of the data matrix after removal of the main effects for Stimulus and Culture will indicate which items induce bias. After these have been eliminated, a new analysis of variance is carried out for the reduced data matrix. This iterative procedure can be repeated until ρ_{sc}^2 becomes acceptably low—say, less than .05.

This kind of procedure leans heavily on the particulars of a data set, thereby implicitly threatening the replicability of the results. To control for this, a researcher can split each sample randomly in two. Separate bias analyses are carried out for the two data sets. Afterwards the results are combined again. A conservative strategy to deal with bias is to discard all items that turn out to be biased in at least one of the analyses. A more lenient strategy is to exclude only those items that show evidence of bias in both data sets.

So far, the present approach does not differ from many methods of item bias analysis described in the literature. When ρ_{sc}^2 is acceptably low, the bias analysis ends and possibly remaining intergroup score differences (i.e., $\rho_c^2 > 0$ in terms of generalizability theory) are interpreted as reflections of valid cross-cultural differences.

ρ_{c+sc}^2. In our procedure, the computation of ρ_{c+sc}^2 is included in the bias analysis, as this coefficient can also reflect bias. If both ρ_{sc}^2 and ρ_{c+sc}^2 have low values, it can be concluded that the scores are equivalent across the cultural groups, but this will only be the case if there are no cross-cultural differences in the test score levels. In cross-cultural studies equal averages are the exception rather than the rule. Consequently, more often than not, ρ_{c+sc}^2 has a substantial value. The researcher is then confronted with the far from trivial problem of how to interpret the coefficient. The iterative item bias procedure just described (and most related bias detection techniques) provide adequate information only if the factors causing the bias leave a substantial proportion of the items unaffected. This presupposition, almost invariably used in item bias studies, is not self-evident and is even unlikely to be realistic when groups with a large cultural distance are compared. It is more likely that a source of bias has an effect on all items and, consequently, exerts a strong influence on the overall test score. In previous sections a number of examples have been given: The notions on which the items of a test are based may be foreign to a cultural setting (Reuning & Wortley's 1973 example of the application of Porteus' Maze Test among the Bushmen), the response medium can induce bias (Serpell's 1979 study on iron wire-modeling versus drawing), particular aspects of the test administration can cause problems (Greenfield's 1966 and Irvine's 1978 studies on conservation among the Wolof), and so on. In these cases bias leads to massive cross-cultural differences in performance, which in an analysis of variance will come out in the main effect for Culture and probably to a much lesser extent in the Stimulus by Culture interaction.

The Analysis of Item Bias Reconsidered

The shift of a bias effect from the SC-component to the C-component in an analysis of variance can easily be demonstrated in a Monte Carlo study (Poortinga & Van de Vijver, 1987). In figure 10-2 some results are presented for a low and a high level of bias. The graphs show that $\hat{\rho}_{sc}^2$ initially increases with the number of biased items, as expected. However,

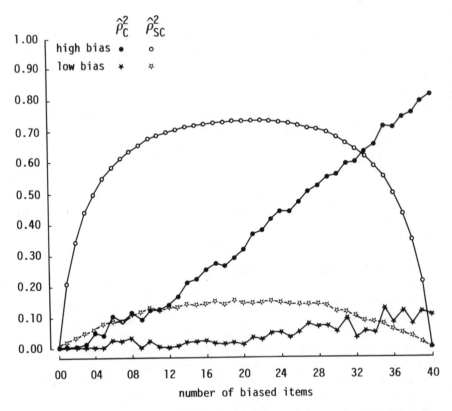

Figure 10-2. Estimated Size ($\hat{\rho}^2$) of the SC-Interaction and the Main Effect for Culture as a Function of the Number of Biased Items for Low Bias and High Bias

Source: From Poortinga and Van de Vijver (1987). Reprinted by permission from Sage Publications.

the increase is not monotonic. After reaching an upper limit, $\hat{\rho}^2_{sc}$ is going down when a still larger number of items are biased. In contrast, $\hat{\rho}^2_c$ (the generalizability coefficient for the main effect of Culture) is a monotonic function of the number of biased items. It should be noted that the simulations mentioned here were carried out under the assumption that the bias favored one group systematically. The more items are biased, the larger this shift from the interaction component to the main effect for culture will be. This situation should not be considered uncommon, since in cross-cultural psychology mostly Western tests are used to compare the performance of Western and non-Western samples. Bias effects will frequently disadvantage these latter samples (Van de Vijver & Poortinga, 1985).

A main effect can reflect either bias, valid psychological differences (that is, differences in the domain of generalization), or a combination of both. A similar argument holds for ρ^2_{sc}; this coefficient also need not be indicative of bias only, but can also reflect psychological differences (Van de Vijver & Poortinga, 1985). Therefore, the classical item bias paradigm is inadequate in its exclusive interpretation of the SC-component as bias and of the C-component as evidence for valid differences. In our opinion, a more balanced interpretation and explanation of the SC- and C-components is one of the essential tasks of the cross-cultural psychologist.

The criticisms expressed toward the item bias are not restricted to the analysis of variance model. Any other common model of bias analysis is subject to similar difficulties in interpretation. Even in item response theory, often considered as the psychometrically most advanced model to study item bias, it is impossible to arrive at unbiased intergroup comparisons when most or all items of the test are biased against a single group.

In general, it will be very difficult to distinguish bias from real differences when the only data at hand are the test data; in the last section of this chapter a model will be outlined that includes context variables as explanatory variables for the observed cross-cultural differences.

Uniform and Non-Uniform Bias

As noted before, in the item bias detection techniques a distinction has been made between conditional and unconditional methods. Within the conditional methods, Mellenbergh (1982) has introduced a further distinction, uniform and nonuniform bias. Per item, a Persons (Cultures) by Ability data matrix is composed. An item is nonuniformly biased when both the interaction between ability and culture and the main effect for culture are significant; an item is uniformly biased when only the main effect for culture is significant; if both effects are nonsignificant, the item is said to be unbiased.

In the design suggested by us, ability can be introduced as an additional factor, thereby forming a Persons (Cultures) by Stimulus by Ability design. The method of analysis is then a conditional one, with total test score being used as a separate independent variable.

An Example

Our approach to the analysis of score equivalence in intergroup comparisons will be illustrated with a set of data previously reported by Van de Vijver and Poortinga (1982). The data were collected on three samples: Indian students, Dutch students, and Dutch army conscripts. All subjects were males; each group consisted of 32 subjects.

The subjects answered 43 items of the Strength of Excitation Scale in the third experimental edition of the Temperament Inventory (Strelau, 1972). Each question of this inventory has three response alternatives: affirmative (2 points), undecided (1 point), and negative (0 points).

In the group of Indian students, a split-half reliability coefficient of .72 was observed; for the Dutch students this was .78; and for the Dutch soldiers .75.

In table 10–3 the results of the analysis of variance are given, together with the estimated components of variance. The SC-component was found to be significant, while the significance level of the main effect for culture, computed by means of a quasi-F ratio, was .09. However, as noted earlier, these F-ratios are not of primary interest here.

From the estimated variance components, the generalizability coefficients were computed. The value of $\hat{\rho}_{sc}^2$ (unit length) was .08, which exceeds the proposed criterion of .05. This means that the Temperament Inventory does not constitute a score equivalent scale for these samples from the Netherlands and India.

In subsequent analyses, potential sources of this lack of comparability were investigated; this was done by eliminating subjects or samples from the data set. The results of the analyses are presented in table 10–4. First, the two Dutch groups were taken together, thereby defining Dutch males from approximately 18 to 25 years as our population of interest. The value of $\hat{\rho}_{sc}^2$ was .02, a value which was also found for $\hat{\rho}_{c+sc}^2$. This means that within the population of young Dutch males the Temperament Inventory could be taken to yield score equivalent results. As a next step, the scores

Table 10–3.   Results of the Analysis of Variance and the Estimated Components of Variance ($\hat{\sigma}^2$)

Source	SS	df	MS	F	prob.	$\hat{\sigma}^2$
S	444.18	24	10.67	5.34	.00	.0903
C	16.52	2	8.26	2.50	.09	.0036
P,PC	172.11	93	1.85	3.37	.00	.0303
SC	168.01	84	2.00	3.64	.00	.0453
SP,SPC,E	2146.06	3906	0.55			.5494

Table 10–4.   Estimated Generalizability Coefficients

Groups[1]	$\hat{\rho}^2_{sc}$	$\hat{\rho}^2_{c+sc}$	Comments
is,ds,dc	.08	.08	All subjects
ds,dc	.02	.02	Only Dutch subjects
is,ds	.11	.11	Only students
dc	.07	.17	Only Dutch conscripts; high vs. low scorers
dc	.01	.01	Only Dutch conscripts; random split

[1] is = Indian students; ds = Dutch students; dc = Dutch conscripts.

of the Dutch and the Indian student samples were taken together, thereby defining male students of approximately 18 to 25 years as the population of interest. The value of $\hat{\rho}^2_{sc}$ was .11, clearly indicating the presence of bias.

In analyses not reported here, it was observed that many items had high endorsement rates; this led to the hypothesis that the lack of score equivalence was caused by ceiling effects. In order to test this hypothesis, one of the groups, the Dutch army conscripts, was split up into two subsamples, one with low scorers and the other group with high scorers. For these subgroups $\hat{\rho}^2_{sc}$ was .07, while for a random split of the conscripts in two subgroups a value of .01 was observed. The value of .07 seems to be high enough to conclude that ceiling effects are at least one reason for the lack of equivalence in the total data set, although there is hardly any doubt that other sources also have played a role. It may be noted that this split in high and low scorers is somewhat similar to a conditional procedure, as discussed previously. The limited number of subjects in each cultural group prohibited a finer distinction of ability in more than two score levels.

Explaining Cross-Cultural Differences

A careful analysis of bias within a given data set can provide important cues about how observed cross-cultural differences should be interpreted

(Malpass & Poortinga, 1986; Poortinga & Van der Flier, 1988). In the previous section, it was argued that the choice between bias and valid cross-cultural differences can be very complicated and definitely requires more than a simple inspection of item bias statistics. There is still another problem: in most cross-cultural studies the interpretation of the data is post hoc and, hence, tentative. In general it will be impossible to provide decisive reasons why a particular post hoc interpretation should be preferred. The existence of this problem has been recognized in cross-cultural psychology and the need for testable theories about these differences which allow less ambiguous conclusions has been emphasized (e.g., Malpass, 1977; Segall, 1986; Whiting, 1976). In this section a methodological framework will be presented which can help to structure efforts of testing such theories.

The basic idea behind our approach is that not only should the dependent variable be measured on which a researcher anticipates a difference. In the design, measurements should also include the postulated antecedent conditions, which presumably have led to an observed intergroup difference.

Since in many instances only the dependent variables are clearly identifiable and the boundary between independent variables and bias variables is fluent and somewhat arbitrary, we shall use the term *context variables* for both.

Before continuing, a brief digression on these context variables is necessary. In view of the broad range of variables related to culture, no restriction is imposed on the domain from which context variables can be recruited. On the contrary, there can be sociological variables, like mode of subsistence or socioeconomic status, measured, for instance, by family income. Other context variables will be of a more psychological nature: for example, educational background. But also physical, physiological, or economical variables can be relevant. Neither are there restrictions on the methods employed to gather data about the context variables. Self-report inventories, judgmental methods, or even external referents like the Human Research Area Files which are based on ethnographic descriptions of cultural communities (Narroll et al., 1980) are acceptable.

A Multiple Regression Model

The strategy proposed here amounts to a check on the contribution of all context variables to the observed cross-cultural differences on the

—

dependent variable. The model is presented here in the form of a multiple regression equation, although this is not the only possible choice.[2]

The statistical technique used is a hierarchical regression analysis. In the first step of the analysis, the context variables are entered as predictors. For simplicity of presentation, mutual independence of the predictors will be assumed, although it is not required by the model. The first step provides information as to whether the context variables significantly contribute to the variance in the dependent variable, which in general will be an item or test score. In the second step, culture is added to the equation as a predictor. This step gives information about the size of the remaining culture effects after elimination of the effects of the context variables.

First Step. Suppose a test is administered to people in a number of cultures and, in addition to this, data on a single context variable was also gathered. In the first step of the hierarchical regression analysis the independent variable used to predict the test score is the context variable. The regression equation for this simple linear regression model with one predictor K as context variable, is given by:

$$X_{pk} = a + b_k K_p + E_{pk} \qquad (5)$$

where
X_{pk} is the observed test score of individual p;
a is the intercept;
b_k is the regression coefficient of the context variable K;
K_p is the value of individual p for the context variable K. When more than one context variable is used, the term $b_k K_p$ will consist of the sum of these, each predictor having its own b_k;
E_{pk} is the error component.

The contribution of the context variable to the variance in the dependent variable is evaluated by means of the multiple correlation coefficient which can be tested for significance (e.g., Cohen & Cohen, 1983, formula 3.6.1). When this coefficient does not differ from zero, the context variable does not explain score differences across groups and, hence, gives no insight into the nature of the observed intergroup differences.

Second Step. A significant multiple correlation coefficient indicates that the context variable at hand is a valid predictor of cross-cultural differences. Even though this can be very important from a theoretical point of view, as it suggests that a determinant of intergroup differences has been identified, it is only one side of the coin. The question still open is how much of the total group differences on the dependent variable remains after a correction for the impact of the context variable has been carried out. This information is provided in the second step of the hierarchical analysis, in which culture is introduced as a predictor.

Culture is a nominal variable that can enter a regression equation in three ways: by dummy coding, effect coding, or contrast coding (Cohen & Cohen, 1983, ch. 5). The choice is immaterial for the present purpose as all three lead to the same multiple correlation. The regression equation for the second step of the analysis is:

$$X_{p(c)k} = a' + b_k K_p + b_{kc} C_c + E_{p(c)k} \qquad (6)$$

where
$X_{p(c)k}$ is the observed test score;
a' is the intercept;
b_{kc} is the regression coefficient for culture after removal of the effects of the context variable;
C_c is the culture effect;
$E_{p(c)k}$ is the error component.

In this model, context variables and culture are successively entered in the analysis, and the effect of culture is computed after the scores have been corrected for the effects of the context variables. The size of the multiple correlation coefficient of the second analysis gives information about how much can still be gained in prediction by including additional context variables should they be available. The difference between the multiple correlation coefficients of the first and second step in the analysis can be tested for significance (e.g., Cohen & Cohen, 1983, formula 4.4.1).

Context variables are the more valuable, as they explain a larger part of the score variance in the dependent variable. For a given value of the multiple correlation in the first analysis, the explanatory power of the context variable is highest when the introduction of culture in the second analysis does not increase the multiple correlation significantly.

An Implication

A nontrivial and at first sight paradoxical consequence of the replacement of the C-component by the K-component is that the C-component, the traditional index of cross-cultural differences, appears not to be of primary interest in cross-cultural psychology; rather, in the present approach the C-component represents the cultural differences not yet explained by context variables. *Cultural differences which have multiple interpretations are in themselves rather meaningless; they only form the starting point for further analysis. It is the task of the cross-cultural psychologist to minimize the size of the C-component by replacing it with explanatory context variables rather than to demonstrate the presence of any C-component.* In other words, cross-cultural psychologists should emphasize the interpretation and explanation of cross-cultural differences by means of context variables rather than the mere documentation of these differences in the form of a (significant) *C*-component.

A Brief Digression on Context Variables

It may seem attractive to use nominal classifications like race, nationality, cultural group, or language as context variables. For instance, McNemar (1975) states that race should be included in the regression equation as it is more often than not a significant predictor of the variables in which psychologists are interested, e.g., job success and school performance. Whatever their attractiveness, nominal classifications are methodologically invalid context variables. The major problem is their mutual interchangeability. Any score difference between groups can be ascribed to a difference in culture, or in religion, or in language, or in race, or to any combination of these. The choice is arbitrary and not logically compelling. In a regression analysis, each of these variables can be given the same coding and, hence, no distinction can be made between them. Interchangeability of the position of groups is no longer possible when context variables are measured on a scale of at least an ordinal level.

Another type of context variable that seems intuitively attractive is a psychological test that is similar to the test under study. After all, the best predictor of the score on the target test will be the subject's score on a parallel test. From a theoretical point of view, such a context variable does not yield much information beyond that provided by the original instrument. Both are likely to be affected by the same sources of intergroup variance. Therefore, the status of a test that resembles the dependent variable as context variable will often be debatable. We can carry this argument still a step further. When groups differ in test-wiseness, almost any test will show a difference. It will be test-wiseness rather than the presumed constructs underlying the tests which should be considered as the agent behind the score differences. As the dependent variable is more dissimilar to a context variable—for instance, when it is a sociological or economic measure—it becomes more unlikely that corresponding differences on the dependent and context variables are a function of a common source of error.

An Example

The data on the Strength of Excitation Scale reported earlier formed part of a larger cross-cultural project on the cultural invariance of basic personality parameters (Poortinga & Van de Vijver, 1987). In another part of the project the habituation of the orienting reflex (OR) was studied, measured by the subjects' skin conductance response (SCR). Pure tones of 500 Hz and a duration of 1 second were presented at intervals of 20 seconds. Two identical sessions were held for each subject. Four samples were involved in the study, in a 2 (groups) by 2 (cultures) design: Indian students, illiterate Indians of the Juang group, Dutch students, and Dutch military conscripts. Here we shall be concerned with the responses to the first stimulus presentation in each session.

It is instructive for our argument to consider what would be concluded on the basis of a "classical analysis," such as an analysis of variance. Two of these analyses were carried out, one per test session. The results are presented in table 10–5. In the first session, neither the independent variables (group and culture) nor their interaction turned out to be significant while, in the second session, both main effects yielded significant values. It may seem tempting to interpret the (admittedly rather weak) cross-cultural differences in terms of genuine psychological differences between the cultures at hand.

In the experiment various measurements had been collected on the "state of arousal" of the subjects in the experimental situation. One of these was used as context variable, namely the extent of spontaneous fluctuations in the skin conductance recorded during periods of rest at the beginning and at the end of each experimental session.

Prior to the analyses the question should be addressed whether spontaneous SCR meets the requirements imposed on context variables. A major objection might be that this variable constitutes a "parallel" measure of the dependent variable. However, the skin conductance recorded during rest and during the experimental task differ in one crucial aspect: the presence or absence of an external stimulus. This makes the former an adequate measure of pre-experimental individual differences in arousal.

In the first of the two regression analyses the impact of the rest SCR on the OR was evaluated. The results are presented in table 10–6. The multiple correlation coefficient was highly significant. In the second

Table 10−5. Significance Levels of the Analysis of Variance

Source	Session 1	Session 2
Culture	.19	.01
Group	.71	.01
Culture x Group	.10	.42

Table 10−6. Results of the Hierarchical Regression Analysis

Statistic	Session 1	Session 2
SMC (Rest)	.382*	.210*
Increments in SMC	G. 013	G .007
(second analysis)	GxC.014	C .021
	C .015	CxG.022

*$p < .01$.
Notes: SMC = Squared multiple correlation coefficient; G = Group; C = Culture; CxG = Culture by group internation.

analysis an additional set of independent variables was introduced, namely culture, group, and their interaction. In this analysis no remaining intercultural differences were found. The increase in squared multiple correlation from the first to the second analysis was less than 0.03 for each of the two sessions. It is important to note that the size of the factor "culture," significant in the analysis of variance, was rendered nonsignificant in the second analysis, that is, after a correction for differences in spontaneous fluctuations in skin conductance.

In conclusion, differences in spontaneous fluctuations in skin conductance accounted for cross-cultural differences in the size of the initial OR. This makes it unlikely that these differences were caused by a differential sensitivity in the two cultures for the impact of the stimulus on the neuropsychological apparatus.

It could be argued that the cultural differences in fluctuations in skin conductance should not be taken for granted as done here but require further study. We concur with this view. The fluctuations in SCR can be considered a first hypothesis to account for the cross-cultural differences observed which can be gradually shaped and refined in later studies. The major focus of the present approach—the replacement of the vague concept of culture by one or more specific variables—remains intact whatever hypothesis should prove to be the most valid explanation.

A Final Remark

The Zeitgeist of cross-cultural psychology can be described as a "difference climate," i.e., an ideological atmosphere in which the documentation of intergroup differences in psychological functioning is considered to be the major task. In this chapter we have suggested a shift in orientation. Cross-cultural psychologists should try to explain rather than explore cultural differences. Some methodological and psychometric tools that facilitate this orientation have been described in this chapter.[3]

Notes

1.   In an analysis of variance the researcher has to decide which factors in the design are random and which factors are fixed (Hays, 1973). The formulas of table 10–2 are based on an all-random model. This choice deserves some comment, in particular for the factor culture. The researcher's interest and conclusions usually go beyond the particular cultures included in a study. Treating culture as a fixed factor implies that only the cultures involved are taken to be of interest. On the other hand, the choice of particular cultures for a study is usually motivated by convenience and the presumed presence of certain characteristics and not by random selection, as would be required for a random factor. When the researcher wants to make generalizations about a dimension on which the cultures under study are assumed to vary, it seems appropriate to consider culture as a random factor.

2.   Although this will not be elaborated here, there is a close link between the analysis of variance model of the previous section and the multiple regression model (e.g., Cohen & Cohen, 1983; Pedhazur, 1982).

3.   The reader is referred to Campbell (1961) and Holland and Rubin (1983) for related approaches aimed at maximizing the interpretability of group differences.

References

Allen, M. J., & Yen, W. M. (1979). *Introduction to measurement theory*. Monterey, CA: Brooks/Cole.

Andersen, E. B. (1973). A goodness of fit test for the Rasch model. *Psychometrika* 38:123–140.

Angoff, W. H., & Ford, S. F. (1973). Item-race interaction on a test for scholastic aptitude. *Journal of Educational Measurement* 10:95–105.

Benson, J. (1987). Detecting item bias in affective scales. *Educational and Psychological Measurement* 47:55–67.

Berk, R. A. (ed.) (1982). *Handbook of methods for detecting item bias*. Baltimore: Johns Hopkins University Press.

Biesheuvel, S. (1949). Psychological tests and their application to non-European peoples. In G. B. Jeffery (ed.), *The yearbook of education*. London: Evans, pp. 87–126.

Bijnen, E. J., Van der Net, Th. Z. J., & Poortinga, Y. H. (1986). On cross-cultural comparative studies with the Eysenck Personality Questionnaire. *Journal of Cross-Cultural Psychology* 17:3–16.

Boorstin, D. J. (1985). *The discoverers.* New York: Random House.

Browne, M. W. (1978). The likelihood ratio test for the equality of correlation matrices. *British Journal of Mathematical and Statistical Psychology* 31:209–217.

Campbell, D. T. (1961). The mutual methodological relevance of anthropology and psychology. In F. L. K. Hsu (ed.), *Psychological anthropology: Approaches to culture and personality.* Homewood, IL: Dorsey Press, pp. 333–352.

Cleary, T. A., & Hilton, T. L. (1968). An investigation of item bias. *Educational and Psychological Measurement* 28:61–75.

Cohen, J., & Cohen, P. (1983). *Applied multiple regression/correlation analysis for the behavioral sciences,* 2nd ed. Hillsdale, NJ: Erlbaum.

Cole, N. S., & Moss, P. A. (1989). Bias in test use. In R. L. Linn (ed.), *Educational measurement,* 3rd ed. New York: Macmillan, pp. 201–219.

Cronbach, L. J., Gleser, G. C., Nanda, H., & Rajaratnam, N. (1972). *The dependability of behavioral instruments* New York: Wiley.

David, K. H. (1974). Cross-cultural uses of the Porteus Maze. *Journal of Social Psychology* 92:11–18.

Deregowski, J. B., & Serpell, R. (1971). Performance on a sorting task: A cross-cultural experiment. *International Journal of Psychology* 6:271–281.

Dixon, W. J. (1981). *BMDP statistical software.* Berkeley: University of California Press.

Eysenck, H. J. (1984). The effect of race on human abilities and mental test scores. In C. R. Reynolds & R. T. Brown (eds.), *Perspectives on bias in mental testing.* New York: Plenum, pp. 249–262.

Eysenck, H. J., & Eysenck, S. B. G. (1983). Recent advances in the cross-cultural study of personality. In J. N. Butcher & C. D. Spielberger (eds.), *Advances in personality assessment,* Vol. 2. Hillsdale, NJ: Erlbaum, pp. 41–70.

Golding, S. L. (1975). Flies in the ointment: Methodological problems in the analysis of the percentage of variance due to persons and situations. *Psychological Bulletin* 82:278–288.

Greenfield, P. M. (1966). On culture and conservation. In J. S. Bruner, R. R. Olver, & P. M. Greenfield (eds.), *Studies in cognitive growth.* New York: Wiley, pp. 225–256.

————. (1979). Response to Wolof "magical thinking." *Journal of Cross-Cultural Psychology* 10:251–256.

Hays, W. L. (1973). *Statistics for the social sciences.* London: Holt, Rinehart and Winston.

Holland, P. W., & Rubin, D. B. (1983). On Lord's paradox. In H. Wainer & S. Messick (eds.), *Principals of modern psychological measurement.* Hillsdale, NJ:

Horn, J. L. (1967). On subjectivity in factor analysis. *Educational and Psychological Measurement* 27:811–820.

Horn, J. L., & Knapp, J. R. (1973). On the subjective character of the empirical base of Guilford's structure-of-intellect model. *Psychological Bulletin* 80:33–43.

Erlbaum, pp. 3–26.

Humphreys, L. G., Ilgen, D., McGrath, D., & Montanelli, R. (1969). Capitalization on chance in rotation of factors. *Educational and Psychological Measurement* 29:259–271.

Hutchins, E. (1980). *Culture and inference.* Cambridge, MA: Harvard University Press.

Irvine, J. T. (1978). Wolof "magical thinking": Culture and conservation revisited. *Journal of Cross-Cultural Psychology* 9:300–310.

Irvine, S. H. (1979). The place of factor-analysis in cross-cultural methodology and its contribution to cognitive theory. In L. Eckensberger, W. Lonner, & Y. H. Poortinga (eds.), *Cross-cultural contributions to psychology.* Lisse: Swets & Zeitlinger, pp. 300–343.

Irvine, S. H., & Carroll, W. K. (1980). Testing and assessment across cultures: Issues in methodology and theory. In H. C. Triandis & J. W. Berry (eds.), *Handbook of cross-cultural psychology,* Vol. 2. Boston: Allyn & Bacon, pp. 181–244.

Jensen, A. R. (1980). *Bias in mental testing.* New York: Free Press.

Kaiser, H. F., Hunka, S., & Bianchini, J. C. (1971). Relating factors between studies based upon different individuals. *Multivariate Behavioral Research* 5:409–422.

Kraemer, H. C. (1981). Extension of Feldt's approach to testing homogeneity of coefficients of reliability. *Psychometrika* 46:41–45.

Kristof, W. (1963). The statistical theory of stepped up reliability coefficients when a test has been divided into several equivalent parts. *Psychometrika* 28:221–238.

Lancy, D. E. (1983). *Cross-cultural studies in cognition and mathematics.* London: Academic Press.

Lord, F. M. (1980). *Applications of item response theory to practical testing problems.* Hillsdale, NJ: Erlbaum.

Malpass, R. S. (1977). Theory and method in cross-cultural psychology. *American Psychologist* 32:1069–1079.

Malpass, R. S., & Poortinga, Y. H. (1986). Strategies for design and analysis. In W. J. Lonner & J. W. Berry (eds.), *Field methods in cross-cultural psychology.* Newbury Park, CA: Sage, pp. 47–83.

Mann, C. W. (1940). Mental measurement in primitive communities. *Psychological Bulletin* 37:366–395.

Marascuilo, L. A., & Slaughter, R. E. (1981). Statistical procedures for identifying possible sources of item bias based on χ^2-statistics. *Journal of Educational Measurement* 18:229–248.

McNemar, Q. (1975). On so-called test bias. *American Psychologist* 30:848–851.

Mellenbergh, G. J. (1982). Contingency table models for assessing item bias. *Journal of Educational Statistics* 7:105–118.

————. (1989). Item bias and item response theory. *International Journal of Educational Research* 13:127–143.

Mercer, J. R. (1984). What is a racially and culturally nondiscriminatory test? A sociological and pluralistic perspective. In C. R. Reynolds & R. T. Brown (eds.), *Perspectives on bias in mental testing*. New York: Plenum Press, pp. 293–356.

Narroll, R., Michick, G. L., & Narroll, F. (1980). Holocultural research methods. In H. C. Triandis & J. W. Berry (eds.), *Handbook of cross-cultural psychology*, Vol. 2. Boston: Allyn & Bacon, pp. 479–521.

Neimark, E. D. (1975). Intellectual development during adolescence. In F. D. Horowitz (ed.), *Review of child development research*, Vol. 4. Chicago: University of Chicago Press, pp. 541–594.

Ombrédane, A., Robaye, F., & Plumail, H. (1956). Résultats d'une application répétée du matrix-couleur à une population de Noirs Congolais. *Bulletin du Centre d'Etudes de Recherches Psychotechniques* 5:129–147.

Ord, I. G. (1970). *Mental tests for pre-literates*. London: Ginn.

Pedhazur, E. (1982). *Multiple regression in behavioral research*, 2nd ed. New York: Holt, Rinehart & Winston.

Pick, A. D. (1981). Cognition: Psychological perspectives. In H. C. Triandis & W. Lonner (eds.), *Handbook of cross-cultural psychology*, Vol. 3. Boston: Allyn & Bacon, pp. 117–154.

Poortinga, Y. H. (1971). Cross-cultural comparison of maximum performance tests. *Psychologia Africana Monograph* 6.

Poortinga, Y. H., & Foden, B. I. M. (1975). A comparative study of curiosity in black and white South African students. *Psychologia Africana* Monograph 8.

Poortinga, Y. H., & Malpass, R. S. (1986). Making inferences from cross-cultural data. In W. J. Lonner & J. W. Berry (eds.), *Field methods in cross-cultural psychology*. Newbury Park, CA: Sage, pp. 17–46.

Poortinga, Y. H., & Van de Vijver, F. J. R. (1987). Explaining cross-cultural differences: Bias analysis and beyond. *Journal of Cross-Cultural Psychology* 18:259–282.

Poortinga, Y. H., & Van der Flier, H. (1988). The meaning of item bias in ability tests. In S. H. Irvine & J. W. Berry (eds.), *Human abilities in cultural context*. Cambridge: Cambridge University Press, pp. 166–183.

Porteus, S. D. (1917). Mental tests with delinquents and Australian aboriginal children. *Psychological Review* 24:32–42.

Porteus, S. D. (1965). *Porteus Maze Test: Fifty years of application*. Palo Alto, CA: Pacific Books.

Price-Williams, D. R. (1962). Abstract and concrete modes of classification in a primitive society. *British Journal of Educational Psychology* 32:50–61.

Reuning, H., & Wortley, W. (1973). Psychological studies of the Bushmen. *Psychologia Africana*, Monograph Supplement, 7.

Rock, D. A., Werts, C., & Grandy, D. (1982). *Construct validity of the GTE Aptitude Test across populations* (ETS Research Report 81–57). Princeton, NJ: Educational Testing Service.

Rudner, L. M., Getson, P. R., & Knight, D. L. (1980) Biased item detection techniques. *Journal of Educational Statistics* 5:213–233.

Schwarz, P. A. (1961). *Aptitude tests for use in developing nations*. Pittsburgh: American Institute for Research.

Scribner, S., & Cole, M. (1981). *The psychology of literacy*. Cambridge, MA: Harvard University Press.

Segall, M. H. (1986). Culture and behavior: Psychology in global perspective. *Annual Review of Psychology* 37:523–564.

Serpell, R. (1979). How specific are perceptual skills? *British Journal of Psychology* 70:365–380.

Shepard, L., Camilli, G., & Averill, M. (1981). Comparisons of procedures for detecting test-item bias with both internal and external ability criteria. *Journal of Educational Statistics* 6:317–375.

Shepard, L., Camilli, G., & Williams, D. M. (1984). Accounting for statistical artifacts in item bias research. *Journal of Educational Statistics* 9:93–128.

Strelau, J. A. (1972). A diagnosis of temperament by nonexperimental techniques. *Polish Psychological Bulletin* 3:97–103.

Super, C. M. (1981). Behavior development in infancy. In R. H. Munroe, R. L. Munroe, & B. B. Whiting (eds.), *Handbook of cross-cultural human development*. New York: Garland STPM Press, pp. 181–270.

Ten Berge, J. M. F. (1977). *Optimizing factorial invariance*. Groningen: VRB Drukkerijen.

Van de Vijver, F. J. R. (1984, December). *Group differences on structured tests*. Paper presented at the Advanced Study Institute, Athens.

—————. (1988). Systematizing the item content in test design. In R. Langeheine & J. Rost (eds.), *Latent trait and latent class models*. New York: Plenum, pp. 291–307.

Van de Vijver, F. J. R., & Poortinga, Y. H. (1982). Cross-cultural generalizability and universality. *Journal of Cross-Cultural Psychology* 13:387–408.

—————. (1985). A comment on McCauley and Colberg's conception of cross-cultural transportability of tests. *Journal of Educational Measurement* 22:157–161.

Van de Vijver, F. J. R., Daal., M., & Van Zonneveld, R. (1986). The trainability of formal thinking: A cross-cultural comparison. *International Journal of Psychology* 21:589–615.

Van den Wollenberg, A. L. (1982). Two new test statistics for the Rasch model. *Psychometrika* 47:123–140.

Van der Flier, H. (1972). Evaluating environmental influences on test scores. In L. J. Cronbach & P. J. D. Drenth (eds.), *Mental tests and cultural adaptation*. The Hague: Mouton, pp. 447–452.

—————. (1980). *De vergelijkbaarheid van individuele testprestaties*. Dissertation. Lisse: Swets & Zeitlinger.

Van der Flier, H., Mellenbergh, G. J., Adèr H. J., & Wijn, M. (1984). An iterative item bias detection method. *Journal of Educational Measurement* 21:131–145.

Vernon, P. E. (1979). *Intelligence: Heredity and environment*. San Francisco: Freeman.

Whiting, B. (1976). The problem of the packaged variable. In K. F. Riegel & J. A. Meacham (eds.), *The developing individual in a changing world*. The Hague: Mouton, pp. 303–309.

11 REFLECTIONS ON LARGE-SCALE ASSESSMENTS OF STUDENT ACHIEVEMENT

Katherine MacRury
Philip Nagy
Ross E. Traub

Our purpose in this chapter is fourfold: to identify and provide brief descriptions of several large-scale assessment programs; to review the effects that such programs are alleged to cause; to consider several factors that seem likely to provoke, mediate, or otherwise influence the effects these programs may cause; and to outline an agenda for research on the effects of large-scale assessments.

First, however, we must heed Rowntree's (1977) admonition to be clear about what we mean by large-scale assessment in education. Let us start by considering the sense in which assessment is used in everyday language. *The Random House Dictionary* (Stein, 1966, 1967) gives as the first definition of assessment the "act of assessing; appraisal; evaluation." And it gives as the fourth definition of assess "to estimate or judge the value, character, etc., of; evaluate: to assess one's efforts." From these defini-

This research was partially supported by the Ontario Ministry of Education Contract No. 1206-04-804/ASN 62786 to the Ontario Institute for Studies in Education, Philip Nagy and Ross E. Traub, principal investigators. The views expressed herein reflect those of the authors and not necessarily those of the Ministry.

tions, applied to education, it is clear that there is more to assessment than the simple testing or measurement of student achievement. This was Bloom's point when he used assessment to refer to " . . . attempts to assess the characteristics of individuals in relation to a particular environment, task, or criterion situation" (1970, p. 30). Satterly, too, has offered a very broad definition:

> Educational assessment is an omnibus term which includes all the processes and products which describe the nature and extent of children's learning, its degree of correspondence with the aims and objectives of teaching and its relationship with the environments which are designed to facilitate learning (1981, pp. 3-4).

The term *large-scale assessment* incorporates all the features implied by Bloom, Satterly, and the dictionary. But the modifier *large-scale* rules out the most common kind of educational assessment, that conducted by classroom teachers as a routine part of schooling. Large-scale assessments originate outside the classroom, and are addressed to larger educational or geographical units than those represented by single classrooms or schools. Large-scale assessments occur at the level of the local educational authority (LEA), the province or state, and the nation. They also occur at the level defined by a collection of nations.

Another restriction needs to be placed on the concept of large-scale assessment. It does not include what is best described as the large-scale examination program. The latter typically consists of tests administered at the end of courses or programs of study. Satisfactory performance is required on these tests in order for examinees to gain something of extrinsic value—a diploma certifying the student's achievement or direct access to an advanced level of education. Examples of large-scale examination programs include: the Regents' Examinations of New York State (Tinkelman, 1966); the minimum competency testing (MCT) programs operated by some of the American states (Burstein, Baker, Aschbacher, & Keesling, 1985); the High School Diploma Examinations of several Canadian provinces (e.g., those for Alberta, as described by Wasserman, 1985); and the examinations in England, Wales, and Northern Ireland for the General Certificate of Education (GCE) and the Certificate of Secondary Education (CSE) (Mortimore & Mortimore, 1984).

Large-scale assessment programs differ from large-scale examination programs in several important respects. Unlike examinations, which focus on the performance of individuals, assessments focus on the performance of groups, at such levels of aggregation as the school or the LEA. They do not necessarily impose the restriction that all eligible students be tested or that examinees respond to the same questions. Thus, with subsamples of students responding to different samples of items, a large-scale assessment can cover a broad range of educational achievements. Group-level data can be obtained on many aspects of achievement, but no single student is required to write an inordinately long test. Also, in an assessment it is possible and feasible to consider a variety of nontraditional achievements, if only for small samples of students. In this way, information can be obtained on aspects of achievement that it would be impractical to assess by means of the examination. (Examples include measures of laboratory skills in science, production in oral language, and performance in music and drama.)

Another difference between examinations and assessments is the guarantee of examinee motivation. Because examinations are concerned with the performance of individuals and because relatively high performance on these tests conveys benefits not associated with relatively low performance, they carry built-in motivation for examinees to perform just as well as they can. Assessments do not provide a similar assurance of maximum performance from examinees. Indeed, because reporting is typically at a high level of aggregation, examinees often are not even apprised of their individual performances in large-scale assessments.

What may be seen as a limitation of assessment programs as compared to examination programs is that typically they do not yield information for comparing the relative achievements of students in the same class or for comparing the achievements of an individual to local or national norms. Although the different test forms administered in an assessment are often randomly equivalent, this kind of equivalence provides no guarantee of equal difficulty or equal correlation with ability. Test equating has been suggested as a way of circumventing this problem (e.g., see Wright & Stone, 1979), and is used, for example, in the California Assessment Program (Bock, Mislevy, & Woodson, 1982).

Examples of Large-Scale Assessment Programs

Descriptions can be found in the literature of programs at three levels— international, national, and intranational. Large-scale assessments have been conducted at the international level by the International Association for the Evaluation of Educational Achievement (IEA). The IEA has attempted " . . . to establish a science of empirical comparative education based on close cooperation between institutions in many countries" (Husen, 1979, p. 371). The first survey, a cross-national study of cognitive development of children, was proposed in 1958, and led to a 12-country study of mathematics achievement (Husen, 1967). It was followed by the Six Subject Survey of 21 countries (Passow, Noah, Eckstein, & Mallea, 1976). A second round of IEA studies has recently been conducted, with mathematics and science the subjects under investigation (Rosier, 1983).

Several examples can be cited of large-scale assessments at the national level. First off the mark and widely known is the National Assessment for Educational Progress of the United States. Begun in the late 1960s, this prototype of the large-scale assessment program was designed to monitor achievement at the national and regional levels. In its first incarnation, NAEP concentrated on the educational achievements of three age cohorts (9-, 13-, and 17-year-olds) in ten broad areas, including reading, writing, mathematics, and science (Greenbaum, Garet, & Solomon, 1977). Responsibility for NAEP was transferred from the Education Commission of the States to the Educational Testing Service (ETS) in 1983. In its present incarnation, NAEP is focused on the achievements of students in the grades that are modal for 9-, 13-, and 17-year-olds. Also, individual states are now being encouraged to conduct statewide assessments that will satisfy their information requirements and that are conducted so as to complement the national assessment (Sebring & Boruch, 1983).

Another prominent national program is conducted by the Assessment of Performance Unit (APU) of England, Wales, and Northern Ireland. This program was begun in 1975. Originally it involved annual testing of the achievements of 11- and 15-year-old students in mathematics and English and of 11-, 13-, and 15-year-old students in science (Gipps & Goldstein, 1983). Like NAEP, the APU assessment program has undergone recent revisions. One important change is that annual testing has been replaced with periodic testing, currently at five-year intervals (Gipps & Goldstein, 1983).

Not all national assessments have been as long-lived as NAEP and the APU. In Australia in 1975, the Australian Council for Educational Research (ACER) conducted a national survey of the literacy and numeracy skills of 10- and 14-year-old students (Bourke & Lewis, 1976; Keeves & Bourke, 1976). Subsequently, the Australian Education Council established, in 1979, the Australian Studies in Student Performance (ASSP). The ASSP commissioned the ACER to conduct a second national survey of literacy and numeracy in 1980. For several reasons, including opposition from the teachers' unions and a changed political context, the ASSP was discontinued shortly thereafter (Power, 1982; Power & Wood, 1984).

Within nations, at the level of province or state, there are many examples of large-scale assessment programs. In Canada, for instance, a recent survey identified eight provinces—British Columbia, Alberta, Manitoba, Quebec, New Brunswick (Francophone system only), Nova Scotia, Prince Edward Island, and Newfoundland—that conduct provincewide assessment programs on a more-or-less regular basis. These programs " . . . are typically administered at several grade levels and usually cover a number of subject areas," all for the purpose of providing information " . . . to assist in the evaluation of curricula, and of programs of study" (Schultz, 1985, p. 14). The two other Canadian provinces, Saskatchewan and Ontario, have conducted assessments on an ad hoc basis (Schultz, 1985, pp. 14–15).

Statewide assessment programs are found in many states of the United States. According to Burstein and associates (1985), 35 of the 50 American states were conducting assessment programs in 1985. These varied to some extent in the grade level of the students involved, in whether testing was of all students (census testing) or of a sample, in the subject areas tested (although all included reading and mathematics), and in whether the testing materials were specially constructed instruments or standardized tests.

Below the national and state (provincial) levels are the assessments conducted by local education authorities (LEAs). Many examples of large-scale assessments implemented by LEAs are either adaptations of IEA assessments or derivatives of NAEP. For example, in the province of Ontario, several school boards have used the instruments of the IEA Second International Mathematics Study to test their grade 8 and grade 13 students to obtain local data for curriculum revision and for comparing LEA results with Ontario and international results (Raphael, Wahlstrom, & Allen, 1986). Another example is provided by school districts in Connecticut. This state adapted the NAEP program in designing its statewide assessment program (CAEP) and only state-level results are reported. Individual districts have the option of using CAEP instruments to compile district results, which can then be compared with state and national results (Tirozzi et al., 1985).

Alleged Assessment Effects

The literature on the effects of large-scale assessments is sparse. What there is can be sorted into three main categories: that dealing with effects on individuals, that dealing with effects on the curriculum, including the teaching-learning process, and that dealing with effects on educational policies in the jurisdiction in which the assessment is conducted. Each of these categories is considered in turn.

Effects on Individuals

Effects on Teachers. The nature of teachers' reactions to an assessment program may depend on whether they are involved in its planning and in determining the uses to which the results will be put. In England, Wales, and Northern Ireland, the teachers' unions were invited to join a consultative committee on the development of the APU assessment program. Gipps and Goldstein (1983) reported that, although the teachers constrained the enterprise by imposing restrictions on the number of background variables measured, thus limiting the potential of the APU to study personal and social development and ethnicity in relation to educational achievement, their participation in the planning phase dissipated opposition to the assessment. The results of a subsequent survey of head teachers in England, Wales, and Northern Ireland indicated that 70 percent were in favour of the APU (Gipps, Steadman, Blackstone, & Stierer, 1983). Moreover, Wood and Gipps (1982), reporting the results of a survey of the use made of external standardized tests in England, Wales, and Northern Ireland, found less anxiety about tests among educators than was previously thought to exist.

As noted earlier, the situation was much different in Australia. There the teacher unions were not represented on the steering committee for the 1980 ASSP assessment (Power, 1982). Many teachers opposed the assessment to the point of boycotting it. As a result, 22 percent of schools chosen to participate withdrew too late in the exercise to be replaced. According to Power and Wood (1984), the failure of the ASSP to get teachers onside proved fatal to the assessment.

An obvious reason why teachers are likely to resist attempts to mount large-scale assessment programs is fear that the programs will be used to monitor their performance. According to Power and Wood,

> [a]ttempts to set up systems designed to assess the performance of public institutions have invariably met with resistance from those whose work is to be monitored. The major political problem faced in establishing a national assessment program has been to gain the cooperation of the teaching profession (1984, p. 362).

Power and Wood went on to observe that an important task for the original developers of the NAEP was to convince " . . . teachers, principals, and district superintendents that the NAEP could not and would not be used to evaluate the performance of individual teachers, schools, programs, districts, or even states" (p. 362). (The recent move in NAEP to provide state-level information on a voluntary basis leads us to wonder whether the possibility of using NAEP data to evaluate teachers, schools, and districts will again become a contentious issue.)

Madaus (1981) suggested another factor—funding—that may enter certain assessment situations and affect teacher motivation. If funding decisions hinge upon test results, teacher interest is certain to be heightened, possibly to the extent that they overemphasize the objectives tested in the assessment.

Effects on Assessment Participants. Large-scale educational assessment programs are directed more at the achievements of groups of students (aggregated to district, regional, or national levels), especially as these achievements reflect the quality of educational systems, than they are at the achievements of individuals. As such, the intended effects of assessments would not normally include effects on the examinees and their teachers. Possible adverse effects of an assessment on students and teachers would be minimized by guaranteeing individual anonymity in all reports of results and by designing the test forms so they can be completed in a moderate length of time. It is possible, of course, that decisions taken during the planning of an assessment will affect the participants' attitude and approach. For example,

- If the test items came from a large pool that is open and known to the teachers prior to testing, if the items are curriculum bound, and if the assessment results will affect resource allocation in some way or be seen to reflect on the teachers' abilities, then the teachers are likely to feel that they should teach to the test, or
- If the sampling plan is such that all students in a class, school, or LEA are administered the same test form and are told that their results will be used to compare them with other students, then the students' motivation is likely to be increased.

But these scenarios seem much more likely to characterize the effects of a large-scale examination program than those of a large-scale assessment program.

Effects on Public Groups. Regardless of their effects on students and teachers, one reason assessment programs are embraced by politicians is the expectation that the results will blunt public criticism of education. Often assessment programs are initiated in the face of public expressions of concern about standards and accountability in education. The term *educational standards* is ill-defined in both the educational literature and the popular press. In our view, educational standards are hypothetical constructs inferred from a set of educational tasks and the responses that can be given, in reality or imagination, to these tasks. Thus, the judge of a response to a task has an expectation of what an acceptable or good or high quality response is. This expectation is moderated by the judge's perception of the task—how difficult it seems—and of actual responses. The latter are likely to play a particularly important role in adjusting the judge's expectations and, therefore, his or her standards, if some of the respondents are known to the judge and these individuals respond in unexpected ways. We concur with Wood and Power (1984) that large-scale assessment programs will " . . . promote a view of 'standards' . . . " (p. 319) to the extent that the tasks that are set for students, the responses that students give, and the expectations of those who judge the responses are made public.

It follows from the foregoing considerations that educational standards cannot be raised in any way that is meaningful by the trivial act of awarding lower marks for a given set of responses to a set of tasks. The only meaningful way of raising standards is to have students learn how to give different, and in some sense better or higher quality, responses to educational tasks. Resnick and Resnick (1985) suggest that standards may be modified by developing new forms of assessment, which to us means designing new tasks and describing student responses to these tasks. Of course, whether the effect of a new form of assessment is to increase or decrease standards depends largely on how the tasks and responses are judged in relation to the tasks and responses with which members of the public are familiar. It is important to note, however, that we could find no studies that document a change in perceived educational standards by members of the public following the conduct of an assessment.

Although large-scale assessments may influence prevailing educational standards, it does not necessarily follow that a particular standard or a particular view of standards should be promoted. According to Wood and Power (1984), officials of the three national programs described earlier, the APU program, the now defunct ASSP, and NAEP, chose to remain aloof from the standards debate. This is in accord with Tyler's (1983) opinion that large-scale assessments should not be in the business of defining standards, but should only provide quality information of the sort that can be used by individuals and groups interested in defining standards. To say this, of course, is to ignore the role that is played in the establishment of standards by the tasks used in an assessment and the descriptions provided of examinee performance on these tasks. Given very different tasks or very different descriptions of examinee performance, the public perception of standards might be very different. Still, as Power and Wood

(1984) have observed, it may have been the very blandness of the reports of tasks and student performances put out by the APU and the NAEP that has enabled these assessment programs to survive as long as they have.

Effects on the Curriculum and the Teaching-Learning Process

Among the most important of the effects that an assessment can have, if it has any effect whatsoever, are those it has on the curriculum. A pervasive effect is for the tasks (items) included in the assessment to become, in effect, the curriculum. This seems rather more likely to happen if teachers believe the assessment results will be seen to reflect quality of program, in which case a tempting way to try to raise scores is to teach to the assessment tests. There is evidence, largely anecdotal in nature, that this kind of effect does occur. Wood and Power (1984, p. 316) quoted newspaper reports describing how schools in a California county registered sizeable score increases on the tests of the annual California Assessment Program by revamping the curriculum to emphasize what was tested in the assessment and by teaching students how to be test-wise. Another example of teaching to the assessment, this from England, was provided by Gipps and Goldstein (1983). The head teachers of some of the primary schools of an LEA insisted that reading be included in the timetable when it was discovered that the LEA had introduced a reading assessment program. Regrettably, the literature, as far as we know, does not contain so much as one systematic study of the phenomenon of teaching to the test or of the curriculum changing in response to a change in test content. (But, see the claims of Madaus & Macnamara, 1970, and Tinkelman, 1966.)

An assessment might also be expected to affect the breadth of the curriculum. Gipps and Goldstein (1983) suggest that if an assessment is subject specific, limited for example to mathematics, first language and science, then the curriculum might narrow as additional emphasis is placed on these subjects. If, however, the assessment is broadly based, then it might have the effect of expanding curricular coverage. Similar effects might be expected within the subjects covered in an assessment, depending on whether the assessment is focused on a narrow set of objectives or, instead, is more broadly conceived. Gipps and Goldstein reported evidence suggesting that the APU program may serve in some instances to broaden the curriculum in the areas tested (p. 159). This evidence was obtained from interviews in 30 LEAs. The interviews in 23 of the 30 yielded comments on the degree of impact of the APU; in 11 LEAs the impact of the APU was thought to be minimal, in 10 it was thought to be positive, and in two, negative. Of the LEAs in which the effect was thought to be positive, the reported impression in three was that the APU would broaden the curriculum in that students would now be exposed to material not previously covered in school but included in the APU tests. The report from another LEA was that the APU could make other areas of the curriculum seem as important as reading and mathematics. In this case, the LEA had produced guidelines for science and geography, but it was felt that complementary testing programs were needed to heighten the impact of the guidelines on teaching. Their local education committee would not accept testing programs developed within the LEA, thus the need for tests from a national agency. From interviews in two LEAs where it was felt that the APU had a negative impact, the reasons given were not curriculum-related, but rather that (1) the early APU reports were impossible to use constructively and(2) the APU program would not add in a positive sense to the existing LEA evaluation process. Gipps and Goldstein " . . . found little evidence that the APU was seen as a danger to the curriculum. On the contrary, some saw it as a tool for curriculum development and improvement" (p. 144). (In personal communication, Goldstein, 1985, reported that this effect of the APU assessments is likely to be overtaken by a new 16+ examination system for England, Wales, and Northern Ireland. Called the General Certificate of Secondary Education [GCSE], this exam replaces the two previous systems of exams for students in the final year of compulsory schooling: the General Certificate of Education, or GCE, and the Certificate of Secondary Education, CSE. The GCSE defines "a national syllabus . . . enforced via National Criteria" [Gipps, 1986]. These have been influenced by the APU, but it is likely they will crystallize the curriculum, and so hinder further APU influences.)

Another effect that an assessment can have is to motivate educators to evaluate current textbooks against the expectations established by the assessment tasks (Forbes, 1977). An example is provided by Hiebert (1981), who concluded that for elementary students to perform well on certain of the tasks in the NAEP assessment of mathematics, they needed much more experience with situational problems involving units of meas-urement than would be provided by the mathematics textbooks in common use in the United States. Lindquist, Carpenter, Silver, and Matthews (1983) considered the failure, revealed by NAEP, of students to gain a deep understanding of mathematics in the context of the content of mathematics textbooks. They questioned whether the textbooks placed sufficient stress on higher cognitive objectives, or instead gave undue emphasis to routine knowledge.

Large-scale assessments have been reported to affect what teachers do in the classroom. Sebring and Boruch (1983) surveyed the uses made by teachers of NAEP results. One use involved examining the NAEP results to identify those objectives performed poorly by students, and then considering whether the strategies for teaching those objectives are adequate. Teachers were also found to use published NAEP exercises to assess their own students, for the purposes of diagnosis and normative comparison with other students in the region and the nation.

Others have used NAEP results to suggest how instruction should be modified to reduce or eliminate apparent student misunderstandings. Hiebert (1981) analyzed elementary students' responses to questions about units of measurement in this way. After describing the basic measurement concepts that students did not seem to have grasped, he outlined several activities designed to facilitate understanding of the concepts; these activities could be used to supplement the activities suggested in a textbook. Similarly, Lindquist, et al. (1983) compared the results of the second and third NAEP assessments of mathematics for elementary and middle schools. It was discovered that the significant gains reported for these students from the second to the third assessments were due to improved performance of routine exercises, such as computation. No gains had been made on exercises intended to assess understanding of mathematical applications. From these observations, Lindquist and associates went on to argue for the enhancement of mathematics programs by making higher-level cognitive activities an instructional focus. Two types of activities were suggested: problem-solving and, in problem-solving, encouraging students to develop and evaluate a variety of solutions.

Despite the hope that large-scale assessments will affect teacher practices, there is some evidence that teachers do not make much use of external test results. Information collected in surveys of teachers (Salmon-Cox, 1981; Yeh, 1978; Stiggins & Bridgeford, 1985) suggests that standardized test scores are used by teachers primarily to confirm what they know from personal observation about a student's achievement. It seems that only if test results run contrary to the teacher's expectations are they paid any notice, and then the effect is only in one direction, to improve the teacher's impression of the student's achievement.

Herman and Dorr-Bremme (1983) surveyed principals as well as teachers, at both the elementary and secondary levels. The principals at both levels judged external test results to be valuable for curriculum evaluation and reporting to the public; these tests were judged *not* to be valuable for evaluating teachers, allocating funds or, at the high school level, deciding on student promotion. The teachers surveyed were less positively disposed to external examinations than were the principals, although the teachers did report using external test results in planning and in grouping students for instructional purposes. External test results were rated low (not used or unimportant) for deciding report card grades. Noteworthy, however, is the fact that the teachers rated their own tests and observations much more highly than external tests for all uses—planning, grouping students, and grading. If these conclusions hold for teacher use of standardized tests, which necessarily provide comparable scores on each student in the class, then they are even more likely to hold for those large-scale assessments that do not provide any scores whatsoever, let alone comparable scores, for the students in the class.

Effects on Educational Policies

An educational policy is a stated course of action used to guide the development and implementation of educational decisions within a jurisdiction. Are educational policies likely to be affected by the results of a large-scale assessment? After reviewing the evaluations by Gipps and Goldstein (1983) of the APU, Power and others (1982) of the ASSP, and Wirtz and Lapointe (1982) of NAEP, Power and Wood (1984) concluded that the educational assessment results obtained in these programs have been largely disregarded by policy makers. Evidence from other sources also leaves the impression that test results have little impact on educational policy. A hope attributed to North American educators is that test results will be used to improve the rational management of schools (Resnick, 1981). This hope is dashed, however, on the rocks of survey results. Webber (1984) was informed by members of Alberta school boards that the impact of provincial test results on board decisions was negligible. Sproull and Zubrow (1981) found that high-level educational administrators in the Pittsburgh area saw testing and test results as peripheral to the administrators' interests and activities; external testing was funded on the belief that the results would be useful to others.

There is one respect in which test results are attracting the attention of U.S. policy makers. Interest has developed recently in the use of test scores to compare states. One example of this is the recent change in policy regarding the use of NAEP data. Originally, NAEP would provide only subnational reports of results by geographic region. It had been feared that state-level comparisons would encourage the development of a national curriculum for the United States (Anderson, 1985). In 1984, however, the assessment policy committee of NAEP approved the release of results for individual states. NAEP will now report state results to states that volunteer to participate in a program of reporting at this level (Elliott & Hall, 1985).

It should be recorded that reports of state-by-state comparisons of educational achievement have not been greeted with uniform endorsement. True, the Council of Chief State School Officers of the United States voted recently in favor of comparative studies. But the motion was approved by only 54 percent of the officers (Anderson & Pipho, 1984). And although recent studies (Page & Feifs, 1985; Powell & Steelman, 1984) have attempted to draw inferences about the relative standing of states, there are methodological problems with such studies that render these inferences questionable (Wainer, 1986).

Why should it be true, if it is, that the impact of large-scale assessment programs on educational policy has been slight? One reason, advanced by Power and Wood (1984), is that assessment programs are often intended as monitoring efforts, not research studies. Gipps and Goldstein (1983) also asserted that " . . . if anything of real use is to emerge [from assessments] then it will do so as the result of a high-quality research effort rather than a narrowly conceived monitoring exercise" (p. 164).

Another reason why assessment programs have not had a substantial impact on policy is that an interpretative, judgmental, or standard-setting dimension has been lacking in reports of assessment results. Power and Wood (1984) offered this as a reason for the fact that the NAEP results have had little effect on policy. Gipps and Goldstein (1983) made the same claim about the APU. It must be acknowledged that the inclusion of a valuing component, technical issues aside, may not be acceptable politically. And in one jurisdiction where large-scale assessments have included a standard-setting component, the province of British Columbia, there is no published evidence that the assessments have had a direct and substantial impact on policy (see, e.g., Robitaille, 1981; Taylor, 1982; Jeroski, 1984).

Perhaps the most important reason of all why large-scale assessments have not had much effect on educational policy is that they are conducted in such a way that no one person or group of persons can be held accountable for the results. Individual students usually have no interest in their own performance, and in any case may not even come to know their scores. Teachers, who may see an assessment as a threat, can undermine its validity in a variety of ways, ranging from what is said to students before the assessment to outright refusal to participate. Unless an assessment program is viewed as important to the main participants, which is to say that teachers and students are accountable for the results, the results may bear no relation to the educational program and to the policies that determine the program.

A Summary of Alleged Effects

The probable effects of a large-scale assessment on individuals are almost certain to vary, depending on the purpose and design of the program. These factors will determine which individuals, if any, should be affected. It is noteworthy that no studies have been reported of the effects of assessments on the participating students. Not unexpectedly, reports exist of teacher resistance to the introduction of assessment programs, particularly in situations where teachers have not been involved in planning. Also, the effect of a large-scale assessment on teachers may be negative if they have reason to fear that the results will be used to evaluate their teaching. Members of the public may or may not be affected by an assessment. Intelligible descriptions of assessment tasks and related student performance may influence the prevailing public perception of standards.

Large-scale educational assessments have been reported to affect the curriculum and teaching-learning activities in various ways. Whether these effects occur seems to depend on how the assessment results will affect those who participate in the teaching-learning exercise. If the purpose of an assessment is to evaluate individual students, teachers, and schools, there exists a motive for preparing students by having them practice on tasks similar to those that will be used on the assessment. More important, at least when it occurs, is the use of assessment results to guide the systematic analysis of textbooks, other teaching materials, and teaching strategies. Unfortunately, what little evidence there is suggests that these effects occur all too infrequently.

The impact of large-scale assessment on educational policy is slight, to judge from the available evidence. Still, in the United States there is growing use of test results to compare states in terms of measured student achievement. This in itself is a policy, but whether the practice will affect policy governing the funding, organization and operation of schools remains to be seen.

Implications of Contextual Factors for Assessment Effects

The various contextual features of a testing program are rarely elaborated in assessment reports, yet it can be argued that these features are, in part, responsible for the particular effects that an assessment produces. In the previous section, certain alleged effects could not be discussed without also considering the context in which an assessment is conducted. In this section, we consider three contextual factors in relation to their potential impact on the scope and magnitude of assessment effects. These factors are purpose, design features, and examinee motivation.

Purposes of Assessment

The underlying reasons for conducting an assessment program should determine the effects that are intended. Moreover, the extent to which intended effects are realized is one obvious basis for evaluating program efficacy.

In a discussion of statewide testing in the United States, Anderson (1985) outlined three purposes:

1. *Monitoring performance trends:* The initial purpose stated for most statewide testing programs was that of monitoring changes in achievement over time. This was reflected in the design of the programs (i.e., coverage of widely accepted and valued basic and high-order cognitive skills in a broad range of subject areas).

2. *Ensuring accountability:* With the accountability movement of the 1970s, the purpose of state testing was extended to incorporate an evaluation function. But the nature of the tests used in these programs was not changed. In accountability testing, it must be clear who is accountable for which objectives. If the purpose of testing is to ensure that curriculum content has been covered and if the curriculum is the responsibility of the state, then it is reasonable, perhaps, to impose a state-mandated test in an effort to ensure that schools teach the curriculum. If, however, curriculum content is under local control and varies from one LEA to another, then an acceptable testing program will have to reflect this variation.

3. *Advancing the curriculum:* This purpose encourages curricular change. Tests may include tasks requiring skills and concepts not yet firmly established in the curriculum.

No systematic evidence has been collected about the implications of different purposes for either the nature of testing programs or the effects they cause. As Anderson (1985) observed: "A high priority activity for the measurement community should be to determine the implications of differing purposes for how tests are designed, administered and reported" (p. 23). We would add that high priority should also be given to the task of identifying the effects that are associated with large-scale testing programs that have been established for different purposes.

Design Features

Many facets of program design merit attention because of their potential to affect assessment outcomes. As examples, the impacts of decisions about item format, the collection of contextual data, and the dissemination of results are considered further.

Item Format. Madaus (1985) referred to the 1970s as an era of simplicity in testing, as indicated by the predominance of the multiple-choice item. Despite criticisms of this item type on the grounds that it is best suited for testing basic, low-order skills, and despite suggestions that there is need for greater commitment to the testing of high-order skills, the multiple-choice item still dominates large-scale testing programs. Exclusive use of multiple-choice assessment instruments seems almost certain to result in the emphasis of a particular subset of cognitive skills and curricular objectives, to the exclusion of other skills and objectives.

Considerations of cost enter a discussion of item types. Assessment tests composed entirely of multiple-choice items can be scored inexpensively, but, as has been noted, these items often emphasize recall and recognition memory. There are other educational objectives that can be assessed most directly, if not exclusively, by pencil-and-paper tasks that require constructed answers; responses to these items are relatively expensive to score, and the scoring is inherently subjective. Then there are educational objectives, the attainment of which cannot be assessed by written responses: performance in art and music, oral skill in language, and so forth. Assessment of these achievements is arduous and expensive. But if an assessment is to be comprehensive and if the inclusion of items testing high-order objectives encourages teachers to include them in the curriculum, as many contend, then the assessment must also address these objectives.

Contextual Data. Without measures of such ancillary variables as teacher goals and expectations, student opportunity-to-learn and teaching strategies, some would say that the research purpose of an assessment cannot be fulfilled. It is certainly true that contextual data are required for understanding the instructional process and the changes, if any, in achievement over time.

Instructional Process. There can be many reasons why students fail to achieve: the objectives may not have been taught (no "opportunity to learn"), they may be inappropriate for the age group or for students who lack enabling skills, or they may have been taught using inappropriate strategies. In the absence of ancillary information about these matters, assessment data cannot define clear implications for curriculum revision. A commitment to curriculum reform implies also a commitment to the collection of process data. Both the IEA and the national assessments have been criticized for failing to obtain adequate information about contextual variables (Theisen, Achola, & Boakari, 1983; Power & Wood, 1984).

Describing Change in Achievement over Time.   Despite interest in change and ignoring for the moment the problems inherent in measuring change, very great difficulties are encountered in attempting to interpret differences in achievement over time. One important source of these difficulties is failure to consider relevant contextual variables. For example, Stedman and Kaestle (1985) analyzed reports of test score declines in the United States throughout the 1970s and found that these reports did *not* take note of changes in minority group participation rates in the testing programs, in school dropout rates, or in the average ages of the populations of students in a grade. Recent test score increases might be interpretable in light of changed family configurations (smaller family units with more headed by single parents), increased dropout rates (the high school population has become more select), and instruction focused more on the skills measured by standardized tests (p. 209). (Madaus (1985) and Resnick and Resnick (1985) have discussed school dropout rates as an important but overlooked factor in the analysis of test results.)

In order to make direct comparisons of achievement between generations, something must be held constant—the ability level of the population of students or the curriculum they learn. Given the changes that have occurred in recent generations in the composition of the population, the most likely source of constancy is the curriculum. But it is unreasonable to hope for long-term stability in the curriculum, which evolves as do society and technology. In the final analysis, cross-generation comparisons of achievement cannot be undertaken in the belief that standards from the past are either relevant or appropriate for the present. Rather, cross-generation research should be conducted with a view to describing change—in educational tasks, in student performance of tasks, in the way students are trained—and setting standards for the future. This underlines the importance of collecting appropriate contextual data.

Goldstein (1983) has recently written about the conceptual problems that arise in the conduct of longitudinal studies. Although the APU and the NAEP gave high priority to inferences about trends over time, Goldstein could find no evidence of attempts either to define the meaning of trends over time or to discuss associated measurement problems. He outlined and criticized the most commonly used methods for attempting to measure absolute change in achievement, and proposed instead the measurement of relative change using standardized differences. Goldstein described the potential benefits of this approach as follows:

> If we discover that regional differences have narrowed and that this continues to remain the case even after a number of possible confounding variables have been allowed for, then we may have begun to uncover something interesting and useful (p. 377).

Dissemination of Results. The generation of information is a principal reason for the conduct of any large-scale assessment project, but the preparation of public reports is an activity that merits separate consideration. If the results of an assessment are not published, then the public's view of the quality of education will not be affected by the assessment. On the other hand, if the results are made public, then the nature of the reporting will determine their impact.

One view of the reporting of assessment data is that it should be neutral and factual. Another view is that it should contain judgments of the value of the results, that is, judgments of whether those involved consider the results in a particular area to be "poor," "fair," or "good." There may be a place for both types of reports. Power and Wood (1984) suggested that, although the three national assessment programs were of limited use because of the noninterpretive nature of their reports, this same low-key quality of the reporting may have accounted for the survival of at least one program, the APU, in its early days (p. 371). More recently, the dissemination of findings has become a high priority for the APU: "What is required is a means of informing teachers and others and discussing with them the implications of the APU's work within the context of the curriculum and different methods of assessment" (Gipps & Goldstein, 1983, p. 165).

The need for synthesis of results and intelligibility in reports of assessments is obvious; the problem is how best to satisfy this need. Technical considerations have been brought to bear on this problem. Bock, Mislevy, and Woodson (1982) observed that the original method for reporting the results of large-scale assessment was the fixed-item approach, typical of survey research. The idea is to report the percentage of correct responses to each item, as well as the change in this percentage from one assessment to another. An alternative approach proposed by the authors is based on the random-item concept, with the data reduced to a small number of attainment indices, each reflecting performance by students from selected populations on items from selected domains of content. Item response theory (IRT) as used in the California state assessment may provide a means to this end. Reports of achievement are couched in terms of scores on latent scales and changes from one time to another in these scores. When IRT applies, the standing of students in a population on a content sub-domain is independent of the items administered in the assessment.

McLean (1982) has stressed the importance of reporting results for meaningful curriculum domains. He also noted that while measurement professionals will, and properly should, be concerned with such issues as the factor structures of item domains and the development of within-domain sampling strategies, others will be primarily, if not exclusively, interested in the educational consequences of the results. Shepard (1980) and McLean (1982) discussed the importance of simple, clear presentations of results. Both emphasized graphical and visual displays over tabular presentations. The use of television and public forums has also been discussed (Shepard, 1980; Stevens, 1985).

The effects of an assessment report can be expected to vary depending on the information it contains. If it is possible to compare teachers or schools or LEAs on the basis of the reported results, teaching-learning may be affected. Some teachers may then be tempted to concentrate on low-order levels of achievement that can be taught (learned) effectively with relative ease. In addition, if public reports of high school results are produced, schools can be ranked on the basis of their aggregate results, and the ranks used to weight the school marks of students applying for admission. This use would affect a student's chances of entering a college or university.

Examinee Motivation

To illustrate the potential of situational factors to influence the effects of an assessment program, we consider the impact of student motivation on the validity of assessment results. Little research has been done on student attitudes to achievement testing in situations where the test results hold no extrinsic value for the students. An exception is the study of Omvig (1971), who considered the effect of student motivation on performance on standardized achievement tests. He was concerned about the impact that low student motivation might have on the results obtained in such research studies as those on the effect of class size on educational achievement. According to Omvig, "[m]ore often than not, the students [who participate

328 DEVELOPMENTS IN APPLIED SETTINGS

in the research studies] are involved only as the producers of test results," which are subsequently used to address research questions. He wondered whether " . . . the students are sufficiently motivated to put forth the effort required to insure valid test results" (p. 47).

In his experiment, Omvig designed a pre-test treatment that consisted of individual counseling to review the student's previous standardized test results and a group discussion about test-taking skills. It was hypothesized that the treatment would affect group scores on an achievement test battery. Although mean scores for the experimental group were higher on all nine subtests, the differences were statistically significant only for the subtests for English and mathematics. Omvig was unable to conclude whether the higher test scores were due to motivation, increased test-wiseness, or some other factor.

Madaus (1981) compared two studies of the uses made of standardized tests, one study American (Salmon-Cox, 1981) and the other Irish (Kellaghan, Madaus, & Airasian, 1980). In both cases, the test results were not intended for use in the formulation of educational policy. Madaus concluded that, in order for testing to affect the behavior and attitudes of students, the test results would need to be perceived as a factor in decisions affecting an individual student's life chances (e.g., grade promotion).

Recent concern about student motivation arose during the administration of the Second IEA Mathematics Study in both the United States and the Province of British Columbia. The IEA and other large-scale assessments (NAEP or the B.C. Mathematics Assessment) were being conducted concurrently, and overtesting of students on the same subject was thought to result in decreased effort (personal communications from R. G. Wolfe, July 10, 1986, and D. Bateson, July 14, 1986).

In the Province of Ontario, Talesnick and McLean (1987) conducted an assessment using items from the Chemistry item bank of the Ontario Assessment Instrument Pool (OAIP). As evidence of a motivation problem with the multiple-choice items, one might consider their comment that the p-values from the assessment were much lower than expected when compared to p-values from earlier pre-test studies. Moreover, in their analysis of each multiple-choice item, Talesnick and McLean (1987) often described student responses, particularly those for numerical calculations, as careless, which might be attributable, in part, to lack of motivation.

Talesnick and McLean's results revealed a greater motivation problem for the open-ended, problem-solving type of instrument than for the multiple-choice item. For 12 open-ended, problem-solving items, the response rate ranged from 44 percent to 71 percent. In contrast, the response rate for the multiple-choice items was generally over 99 percent. Although most students reported not having been taught the material required to answer the three open-ended items with the lowest response rates, between 50 percent and 80 percent of students indicated that the content required to answer the other nine items had been taught. Talesnick and McLean (1987) concluded that "few students were motivated to extend the effort required to solve these challenging problems when they knew the results would not count for them" (p. 133). To motivate students to try their best on open-ended items, Talesnick and McLean suggested that teachers make the problems count toward student grades or provide some other reward for good performance.

An Agenda for Research

Our review of the literature on large-scale testing programs has left us with two disturbing impressions. The first is that few systematic, empirical studies of the effects of large-scale testing programs have been conducted. This assertion applies with force to large-scale assessments. It is clear that the study of the impact of these programs is a low priority issue. Unless this situation changes, the future of large-scale assessments will, like the present, be determined not by the testing profession but instead by educational administrators interested primarily in program accountability.

The second impression we are left with is that large-scale assessment effects are unlikely to generalize widely. Large-scale testing programs are set in unique historical and political contexts, and the designs of these programs and the interpretations of the results are necessarily tailored to their contexts.

Empirical work on assessment effects is needed. We can envision two kinds of studies. One would focus on a particular assessment program. This kind of study would seek to provide before and after information about the educational system in which the assessment is being conducted, thus to describe the effects that the assessment has on the system. A second kind of study would involve the comparison of several large-scale assessment programs. This kind of study would provide detailed descriptions of the programs and the situations in which the programs were being conducted, all with a view to identifying ways in which the programs differ. Then the attempt would be made to describe each program with reference to a particular effect, to see whether there is an association between a particular kind of difference among programs and the magnitude of the effect.

Effects That Warrant Further Investigation

Earlier in this chapter we considered the literature on the effects of large-scale assessment programs on individuals, on the curriculum, and on educational policies. The most important effects, in our view, are those on the curriculum. Effects of this kind hold a great deal of interest for educators, but experts in educational measurement (Anderson, 1986; Rowley, 1986) have voiced the opinion that large-scale assessments are likely to have little impact on either curriculum or instruction. As noted earlier, there is no necessary reason for students or their teachers to value high performance on the assessment tasks, and usually no one is held directly accountable for student performance in an assessment. Systematic studies of these factors in large-scale assessments are imperative.

Effects on public opinion also warrant further study. An unanswered question of some importance to politicians and educational administrators is whether the reporting of assessment results has an effect on the public's opinion of education. It is surprising, in view of the number of assessments conducted in North America, that no systematic study of this effect has been reported.

In studies of effects, the importance of decisions taken about the design of the assessment program cannot be ignored. Traub (1985) has suggested four ways to build motivation and accountability into large-scale assessment:

1. The coverage of curriculum must be broad. The rationale for this suggestion is that participating teachers and students must recognize that student performance of at least some of the tasks in the assessment reflects on them and on what they have been trying to teach or learn. It is not reasonable to expect this if the assessment is narrowly conceived and includes none of the tasks (curricular objectives) that a teacher and class of students have been addressing.

2. Testing should be of whole populations, not samples, of students. If every student in the population is required to participate, then no student or teacher can adopt an opt-out attitude on the grounds that the students and teachers at a neighbouring school or classroom are not being required to participate.

3. The way results are reported and publicized can build increased motivation and accountability into an assessment:

- Each student should receive a report of his or her results, with whatever interpretative information can be provided. (Norms based on the performance of other students on the same set of tasks as that performed by a given student is one kind of interpretative information. Expert judgments of acceptable performance on the tasks is another.)

- Each teacher should be given a report of the results achieved by his or her class.
- Top performing individuals, classes, and schools should be identified in the media.

4. The assessment tasks should be reported so as to inform persons working outside the field of education about what is expected of students in school. If these tasks are understood by parents and others, and if at least some of the tasks are intellectually challenging, then public interest in student performance is almost certain to be greater than it will be otherwise, and student and teacher interest in performing well on the tasks will increase commensurately. Empirical research is required to test the validity of these suggestions.

A Concluding Comment

It has been almost 30 years since large-scale assessments of educational achievement first appeared on the scene. Unless educational researchers begin to pay serious attention to how large-scale assessments affect the persons and programs they purport to assess, the final chapter in the history of such assessments may have been written long before another 30 years elapses.

Epilogue

Since this chapter was initially drafted in 1986, important developments have taken place in the sphere of large-scale assessments of educational achievement. We note here developments pertaining to particular national and international assessment programs.

The IEA

The second round of IEA studies included assessment of classroom environment, and achievement in mathematics, science, and written composition. The classroom environment study and the Second International Mathematics Study (SIMS) were started in 1976, and are now essentially complete. The Second International Science Study (SISS) and the study of written composition, begun in 1980, are nearing completion (Postlethwaite, 1987a). Other studies are now in the planning stage: pre-primary education, reading literacy, and computers in education (Postlethwaite, 1987a). Approval was recently given in principle by the panjandrums of the IEA to a study of ethics and moral values (L. D. McLean, personal communication). Of course, whether these studies go ahead depends entirely on the availability of adequate funding, and funds for IEA work are apparently increasingly in short supply (Postlethwaite, 1987b). Initiatives by the NAEP on the international front—initiatives which are described in the next section of this epilogue—are also likely to affect the work of the IEA in ways that are not yet clear.

The NAEP

Two developments of importance have taken place in the activities of the U.S. National Assessment of Educational Progress. The first has been the mounting support through the 1980s for state-by-state comparisons of educational achievement, which are to be accomplished through a reformulation of NAEP. This idea was affirmed in the final report of the Study Group on National Assessment (Alexander & James, 1987, pp. 11–12). And after voting in favor of comparative studies in 1984, the Council of Chief State School Officers established a State Education Assessment Center and has been working to develop "specific recommendations for the first state-by-state assessment of student achievement in mathematics as part of the NAEP data collection in 1990" (Linn, 1988, p. 7).

Already predictions are being made as to what the likely impact of state comparisons will be on U.S. education. Ferrara and Thornton (1988) expect that " . . . schools [will] begin to teach what NAEP tests" (p. 204) and NAEP and the states will mount a concerted effort to align the curricular objectives of NAEP and the states. Although Ferrara and Thornton viewed the standardization of curriculum across the states as a means of reforming and improving the curriculum, Linn (1988) raised the issue of negative consequences of a focus on ranking the states, including narrowing of the curriculum, teaching to the test, and lack of utility to schools. Linn proposed that breadth and depth of questions be increased to prevent curricular constriction and test-focused teaching, and that multiple indicators of achievement in each subject domain be provided to identify weaknesses that teachers could then strive to address.

A second major development involving NAEP is its extension into the international arena. During 1988, the Educational Testing Service, the agency presently holding the NAEP contract, conducted the first International Assessment of Educational Progress (IAEP). NAEP items and methods were used to survey mathematics and science achievement of 13-year-old students in five countries and four (of the ten) provinces of Canada. The final report (Lapointe, Mead, & Phillips, 1989) of this project was released only one year after the data had been collected in each jurisdiction. "As the pace of change accelerates and as more countries implement educational reform, these highly efficient procedures for monitoring international progress may become increasingly useful" (Lapointe et al., 1989, p. 8). If nothing else, the presence of IAEP on the world scene places pressure on the IEA to report findings rapidly, if it wishes to be competitive. The training of indigenous educational researchers in participating countries, which has long been cited as a positive feature of IEA (see, e.g., Noah, 1987), and the increased attention paid in the second round of IEA studies to interpretation of the data in terms of circumstances local to the participating countries (see, e.g., Schwille & Burstein, 1987) may have to be sacrificed to expediency if IEA is to withstand the assault of IAEP successfully. The IAEP is now recruiting participants in a second survey, scheduled for 1990.

The APU

In 1987 the British Parliament passed a bill that mandated a national core curriculum and an associated system of student assessment in mathematics, science, and English. A report submitted in 1988 by the British Education Secretary's Task Group on Assessment and Testing recommended that assessments for every student be conducted at the end of the school years in which students reach the ages of 7, 11, 14, and 16 years, and that these assessments be based on teacher appraisals together with performance of standard tasks. It was also recommended that this assessment system be introduced gradually, over a five-year period (Surkes, 1988). Provided that the recommendations of the Task Group are implemented, the completion of the current cycle of APU assessments would coincide with the introduction of the new system, and the APU would probably be declared redundant.

References

Alexander, L., & James, H. T. (1987). *The nation's report card.* Cambridge, MA: The National Academy of Education.
Anderson, B. (1985). State testing and the educational measurement community:

Friends or foes? *Educational Measurement: Issues and Practice* 4(2):22–26.

Anderson, B., & Pipho, C. (1984). State-mandated testing and the fate of local control. *Phi Delta Kappan* 66(3):209–212.

Anderson, J. O. (1986). Discussant. In P. Nagy (chair), *Monitoring the impact of large-scale testing programs.* Symposium presented at the meeting of the National Council on Measurement in Education, San Francisco.

Bloom, B. (1970). Toward a theory of testing which includes measurement-evaluation-assessment. In M. C. Wittrock & D. E. Wiley (eds.), *The evaluation of instruction.* New York: Holt, Rinehart and Winston, pp. 25–50.

Bock, R. D., Mislevy, R., & Woodson, C. (1982). The next stage in educational assessment. *Educational Researcher* 11(3):4–11.

Bourke, S. F., & Lewis, R. (1976). *Australian studies in school performance, Vol. II: Literacy and numeracy in Australian schools: Item report.* Canberra: Australian Government Publishing Service.

Burstein, L., Baker, E. L., Aschbacher, P., & Keesling, J. W. (1985). *Using state test data for national indicators of education quality: A feasibility study.* Los Angeles: Center for the Study of Evaluation, UCLA Graduate School of Education.

Elliott, E. J., & Hall, R. (1985). Indicators of performance: Measuring the educators. *Educational Measurement: Issues and Practice* 4(2):6–9.

Ferrara, S. F., & Thornton, S. J. (1988). Using NAEP for interstate comparisons: The beginnings of a "national achievement test" and "national curriculum." *Educational Evaluation and Policy Analysis* 10(3):200–211.

Forbes, R. H. (1977). NAEP: One "tool" to improve instruction. *Educational Leadership* 34:276–281.

Gipps, C. (ed.). (1986). *The GCSE.* Bedford Way Paper No. 29. London: University of London Institute of Education.

Gipps, C., & Goldstein, H. (1983). *Monitoring children: An evaluation of the Assessment of Performance Unit.* London: Heinemann Educational Books.

Gipps, C., Steadman, S., Blackstone, T., & Stierer, B. (1983). *Testing children: Standardised testing in local education authorities and schools.* London: Heinemann Educational Books.

Goldstein, H. (1983). Measuring changes in educational attainment over time: Problems and possibilities. *Journal of Educational Measurement* 20(4):369–378.

Greenbaum, W., Garet, M. S., & Solomon, E. R. (1977). *Measuring educational progress: A study of the National Assessment.* New York: McGraw-Hill.

Herman, J. L., & Dorr-Bremme, D. W. (1983). Uses of testing in the schools: A national profile. In W. E. Hathaway (ed.), *Testing in the schools. New Directions for Testing and Measurement, No. 19.* San Francisco: Jossey-Bass, pp. 7–17.

Hiebert, J. (1981). Units of measure: Results and implications from National Assessment. *Arithmetic Teacher* 28(6):38–43.

Husen, T. (ed.). (1967). *International study of achievement in mathematics: A comparison of twelve countries.* New York: John Wiley & Sons.

Husen, T. (1979). An international research venture in retrospect: The IEA surveys. *Comparative Education Review* 23(3):371–385.

Jeroski, S. (1984). *The 1984 British Columbia reading assessment.* Victoria: British Columbia Ministry of Education.

Keeves, J. P., & Bourke, S. F. (1976). *Australian studies in school performance—Vol. I, Literacy and numeracy in Australian schools: A first report.* Canberra: Australian Government Publishing Service.

Kellaghan, T., Madaus, G. F., & Airasian, P. W. (1980). *The effects of standardized testing.* Dublin: Educational Research Centre, St. Patrick's College, and Chestnut Hill, MA: School of Education, Boston College.

Lapointe, A. E., Mead, N. A., & Phillips, G. W. (1989). *A world of differences: An international assessment of mathematics and science.* Princeton, NJ: Educational Testing Service.

Lindquist, M. M., Carpenter, T. P., Silver, E. A., & Matthews, W. (1983). The third National Mathematics Assessment: Results and implications for elementary and middle schools. *Arithmetic Teacher* 31(4):14–19.

Linn, R. L. (1988). State-by-state comparisons of achievement: Suggestions for enhancing validity. *Educational Researcher* 17(3):6–9.

Madaus, G. F. (1981). Reactions to the "Pittsburgh Papers." *Phi Delta Kappan* 62(9):634–636.

————. (1985). Public policy and the testing profession—You've never had it so good? *Educational Measurement: Issues and Practice* 4(4):5–11.

Madaus, G. F., & Macnamara, J. (1970). *Public examinations: A study of the Irish Leaving Certificate.* Dublin: Educational Research Centre, St. Patrick's College.

McLean, L. (1982). Educational assessment in the Canadian provinces. In D. L. Nuttall (ed.), Assessing educational achievement [Special issue]. *Educational Analysis,* 4(3):79–96.

Mortimore, J., & Mortimore, P. (1984). *Secondary school examinations.* London: University of London. Institute of Education.

Noah, H. J. (1987). Reflections. *Comparative Education Review* 31(1):137–149.

Omvig, C. P. (1971). Effects of guidance on the results of standardized achievement testing. *Measurement and Evaluation in Guidance* 4(1):47–51.

Page, E. B., & Feifs, H. (1985). SAT scores and American states: Seeking for useful meaning. *Journal of Educational Measurement* 22(4):305–312.

Passow, A. H., Noah, H. J., Eckstein, M. A., & Mallea, J. R. (1976). *The national case study: An empirical comparative study of twenty-one educational systems.* New York: John Wiley & Sons.

Postlethwaite, T. N. (1987a). Introduction: Special issue on the Second IEA Study. *Comparative Education Review* 31(7):7–9.

————. (1987b). Comparative educational achievement research: Can it be improved? *Comparative Education Review* 31(1):150–158.

Powell, B., & Steelman, L. C. (1984). Variations in state SAT performance: Meaningful or misleading? *Harvard Educational Review* 54:389–412.

Power, C. N. (ed.). (1982). *National assessment in Australia: An evaluation of the Australian Studies in Student Performance Project.* Canberra: Australian Government Publishing Service.

Power, C. N., & Wood, R. (1984). National assessment: A review of programs in Australia, the United Kingdom, and the United States. *Comparative Education Review* 28(3):355–377.

Raphael, D., Wahlstrom, M. W., Allen, C. (1986). *Student achievement in the North York Board of Education: Analysis of teacher coverage and student achievement on the SIMS cognitive items.* Toronto: OISE Educational Evaluation Centre.

Resnick, D. P. (1981). Testing in America: A supportive environment. *Phi Delta Kappan* 62(9):625–628.

Resnick, D. P., & Resnick, L. B. (1985). Standards, curriculum, and performance: A historical and comparative perspective. *Educational Researcher* 14(4):5–20.

Robitaille, D. F. (ed.). (1981). *British Columbia mathematics assessment: 1981.* Victoria: British Columbia Ministry of Education.

Rosier, M. J. (ed.). (1983). *IEA: Activities, institutions and people.* Oxford: Pergamon Press.

Rowley, G. L. (1986, April). Discussant. In P. Nagy (chair), *Monitoring the impact of large-scale testing programs.* Symposium presented at the meeting of the National Council on Measurement in Education, San Francisco.

Rowntree, D. (1977). *Assessing students. How shall we know them?* London: Harper & Row.

Salmon-Cox, L. (1981). Teachers and standardized achievement tests: What's really happening? *Phi Delta Kappan* 62(9):631–634.

Satterly, D. (1981). *Assessment in schools.* Oxford, England: Basil Blackwell.

Schultz, H. (1985, March). *Summary of provincial assessment practices in Canadian public education.* A report produced for the Council of Ministers of Education, Canada.

Schwille, J., & Burstein, L. (1987). The necessity of trade-offs and coalition building in cross-national reearch: A critique of Theisen, Achola, and Boakari. *Comparative Education Review* 31(4):602–611.

Sebring, P. A., & Boruch, R. F. (1983). How is National Assessment of Educational Progress used? *Educational Measurement: Issues and Practice* 2(1):16–20.

Shepard, L. A. (1980). Reporting the results of statewide assessment. *Studies in Educational Evaluation* 6:119–125.

Sproull, L., & Zubrow, D. (1981). Standardized testing from the administrative perspective. *Phi Delta Kappan* 62(9):628–631.

Stedman, L. C., & Kaestle, C. F. (1985). The test score decline is over: Now what? *Phi Delta Kappan* 67(3):204–210.

Stein, J. (ed.) (1966, 1967). *The Random House dictionary of the English language,* Unabridged edition. New York: Random House, Inc.

Stevens, F. (1985). *Challenges in implementing a testing program in a large school district.* Paper presented at the meeting of the American Educational Research Association, Chicago.

Stiggins, R. J., & Bridgeford, N. J. (1985). The ecology of classroom assessment. *Journal of Educational Measurement* 22(4):271–286.

Surkes, S. (1988, January 15). Five-year "gap" between targets and tests. *Times Educational Supplement* 3733(6):6.

Talesnick, I., & McLean, L. (1987). *Report of the 1983 field trials in chemistry — Senior division*. Toronto: Ontario Ministry of Education.

Taylor, H. (ed.). (1982). *The 1982 British Columbia science assessment*. Victoria: British Columbia Ministry of Education.

Theisen, G. L., Achola, P. P. W., & Boakari, F. M. (1983). The underachievement of cross-national studies of achievement. *Comparative Education Review* 27(1):46–68.

Tinkelman, S. N. (1966). Regents Examinations in New York State after 100 years. In *Proceedings of the 1965 Invitational Conference on Testing Problems*. Princeton, NJ: Educational Testing Service, pp. 85–94.

Tirozzi, G. N., Baron, J. B., Forgione, P. D., & Rindone, D. A. (1985). How testing is changing education in Connecticut. *Educational Measurement: Issues and Practice*, 4(2):12–16.

Traub, R. E. (1985, October). *Reflections on the inability of large-scale curriculum-based assessment to influence policy and practice*. Paper presented at the meeting of the Canadian Evaluation Society, Toronto.

Tyler, R. W. (1983). Educational assessment, standards, and quality: Can we have one without the others? *Educational Measurement: Issues and Practice* 2(2): 14–15.

Wainer, H. (1986). Five pitfalls encountered while trying to compare states on their SAT scores. *Journal of Educational Measurement* 23(1):69–81.

Wasserman, D. A. (1985, June). *Setting standards for Alberta Diploma Examinations: Intentions and practices*. Paper presented at the annual meeting of the Canadian Educational Researchers Association, Montreal.

Webber, C. F. (1984). *School board member perceptions of the utility and importance of student evaluation information in Alberta* (Planning Services Report). Edmonton: Alberta Education.

Wirtz, W., & Lapointe, A. E. (1982). *Measuring the quality of education: A report on assessing educational progress*. Washington, DC: Wirtz and Lapointe.

Wood, R., & Gipps, C. (1982). An enquiry into the use of test results for accountability purposes. In R. McCormick et al. (eds.), *Calling education to account*. London: Heinemann Educational Books, pp. 44–54.

Wood, R., & Power, C. (1984). Have national assessments made us any wiser about "standards"? *Comparative Education* 20(3):307–321.

Wright, B. D., & Stone, M. H. (1979). *Best test design*. Chicago: MESA.

Yeh, J. P. (1978). *Test use in schools* (Studies in Measurement and Methodology, Work Unit). Los Angeles: UCLA, Center for the Study of Evaluation.

III EMERGING TOPICS

12 COMPUTERIZED ADAPTIVE TESTING: THEORY, APPLICATIONS, AND STANDARDS

Ronald K. Hambleton
Jac N. Zaal
Jo P. M. Pieters

The testing industry in the United States has undergone major changes in the last 15 years. Classical test theory models and methods which have been in wide use for 60 years or more are being replaced by new test theories and methods, most notably item response theory (Hambleton & Swaminathan, 1985; and Weiss & Yoes, in Chapter 3). For example, many of the important standardized achievement and aptitude tests (e.g., Scholastic Aptitude Test, California Achievement Tests, the Stanford Achievement Tests, and the Woodcock-Johnson Psycho-Educational Battery) are developed using item response model principles and procedures.

A second major testing change in the United States has been the wide interest in and great use of criterion-referenced tests, sometimes called objectives-referenced tests, basic skills tests, competency tests, or credentialing exams (see, for example, Berk, 1984; and Hambleton & Rogers, Chapter 1). These tests provide for score interpretations in relation to well-defined bodies of content and standards of performance. These tests are being used in the United States for (1) awarding high school diplomas, (2) monitoring student progress within a grade and from one grade to the next, (3) awarding certificates or licenses to professionals in over 900 professions, and (4) determining job competence in the armed services and industry. There are many other uses for these tests as well.

Numerous changes in testing are also taking place at the present time

341

because of the availability of new computer capabilities (see, for example, Brzezinski & Hiscox, 1984; Bunderson, Inouye, & Olsen, 1989; Wainer, 1988). There is now wide recognition of the computer's immense power for storing test information (e.g., test items), and for producing, administering, and/or scoring tests. Many testing agencies in the United States already store their item pools in computer memory. These test items can be re-called on an as-needed basis. Computer software is also available now for tests to be completely constructed to fit a set of psychometric specifica-tions (see, for example, Assessment Systems Corporation, 1988; WICAT Systems, 1986). Especially attractive is the ability to prepare tests for printing without any additional typing or typesetting of test items. Errors in test production can be eliminated because of this capability.

Presently, computers are also being used in some testing programs (see, for example, experimental versions of the *Differential Aptitude Tests*) to "tailor" the particular items an examinee is administered in a test. In this way, tests can be shortened without any loss of measurement precision. After an examinee responds to a set of test items (sometimes only one item) presented at a computer terminal, an initial ability estimate for the examinee is obtained. The computer is programmed to select the next set of items from the available item bank for administration which will contri-bute the most information to the estimation of the examinee's ability. Some details for how test items are selected, and ability estimates are obtained, will be addressed later in this chapter. The administration of items to the examinee continues until some specified number of items is administered or a desired level of measurement precision is obtained.

Weiss (1985) and Reckase (1989) and others have drawn attention to the fact that the earliest application of tailored or adaptive testing goes back to the work of Binet on intelligence testing in 1908, so the idea is not a new one in testing. Still, little additional work took place on adaptive testing until Fred Lord at the Educational Testing Service began a long comprehensive research program beginning in the late 1960s (for a review of his work, see Lord, 1980). Lord's motivation for pursuing adaptive testing was that he felt fixed length tests were inefficient for many exam-inees, especially low- and high-ability examinees. With the power of the computer to select, present, and score test items, he felt that tests could be shortened without any loss of measurement precision if the test items administered to each examinee were chosen to provide maximum informa-tion about the examinee's ability. In theory, each examinee would be administered a unique set of items. Since the late 1960s, a substantial amount of research has been supported by the U.S. Armed Services, the U.S. Civil Service Commission, and other federal agencies, special conferences have been held, and the number of published papers on adaptive testing is in the hundreds (see, for example, Wainer, 1990; Weiss, 1983).

However, despite the promise of computers for facilitating test development, and opening up new possibilities for test administrations, item formats, and scoring, considerably more research is needed before we will know the full benefits, as well as shortcomings, of computer-administered achievement and aptitude tests. For comprehensive reviews of the roles and problems of computer use with testing, readers are referred to Brzezinski and Hiscox (1984) and Bunderson, Inouye, and Olsen (1989). This chapter will be focused more narrowly on the uses of computers in implementing adaptive testing strategies. Specifically, the purposes of this chapter are (1) to introduce the measurement models that underlie the applications of adaptive testing, (2) to highlight several promising adaptive testing applications, and (3) to review some developed guidelines by Green and his associates (1982, 1984) for designing and using adaptive tests.

Introduction to Item Response Theory

With few exceptions, testing is carried out in settings in which a group of individuals take the same test (or parallel forms). Typically, individuals in the group will vary in the ability being measured by the test. It can be shown easily that the test would measure maximally the ability of each individual in the group if test items were presented to each individual such that the probability of answering each item correctly was around .50, or around .60 if guessing is possible (see, for example, Hambleton & Swaminathan, 1985). Since, in general, examinees differ in their ability levels, higher-ability examinees would need to be administered relatively harder items and lower-ability examinees would need to be administered relatively easier items in order that both groups might have (approximately) 50 percent probabilities of answering correctly the test items administered. This, of course, is not possible using a single test; consequently, there is a need for "tailored tests" or "adaptive testing" (Green, 1983; Lord, 1971, 1980; Weiss, 1982, 1983) if testing time is to be reduced without loss of measurement precision.

Item response models are particularly important in adaptive testing because it is possible to derive, using item response models, ability estimates that are independent of the particular choice of test items administered. Thus, examinee abilities can be compared even though the examinees may have taken sets of test items of varying difficulty (Urry, 1977, 1983). And, in theory, each examinee will receive a different set of test items. In fact, a primary reason for Fred Lord switching his research focus from true score theory to item response theory in the late 1960s was to develop both the theoretical and practical bases for estimating ability independent of the selection of test items. Such a feature was not possible within a true score model framework.

In a few words, item response theory (IRT) postulates that (1) examinee test performance can be predicted (or explained) by a set of factors called traits, latent traits, or abilities, and (2) the relationship between examinee item performance and the set of traits assumed to be influencing item performance can be described by a monotonically increasing function called an item characteristic function. This function specifies that examinees with higher scores on the traits have higher expected probabilities for answering an item correctly than examinees with lower scores on the traits.

In applying item response theory to measurement problems, a common assumption is that there is one dominant factor or ability which can account for item performance. This assumption is made, for example, in nearly all of the current applications of adaptive testing. In the one-trait or one-dimensional model, the item characteristic function is called an item characteristic curve (ICC) and it provides the probability of examinees answering an item correctly for examinees at different points on the ability scale defined for the trait measured by the test (Hambleton & Swaminathan, 1985; Lord, 1980; and Weiss & Yoes, Chapter 3).

Corresponding to each item also is an item information function, the shape of which depends on the item statistics. The important feature of an item information function is that it is defined over the same scale on which ability is measured and indicates the contribution of the item to ability estimation at points along the ability continuum. It is this feature which is utilized in item selection. Items are preferred which provide the most information about examinee ability which can be determined once an ability estimate for the examinee is available. Items providing the most information are, generally, the same ones where the examinee has an (approximately) 50 percent chance of answering correctly though the situation is more complicated when items vary substantially in their item parameter values.

In addition to the assumption of test unidimensionality, it is common to assume that the item characteristic curves are described by one, two, or three parameters. The specification of the mathematical form of the ICCs and the corresponding number of parameters needed to describe the curves determines the particular item response model.

In any successful application of item response theory, parameter estimates corresponding to the choice of ICCs are obtained to describe the test items, and ability estimates are obtained to describe the performance of examinees. Also, successful applications require that there be evidence that the chosen item response model, at least to an adequate degree, fits the test data set (Hambleton & Swaminathan, 1985). The three-parameter logistic model is probably the model of choice by current CAT-advocates (Green & associates, 1984; Lord, 1980; Weiss, 1983). The most important reason is that a well-fitting test model is essential to the success of any CAT-applications and the three-parameter model fits test data better than either the one- or two-parameter models.

Item response theory has become a very popular topic for research in the measurement field. Numerous IRT research studies have been published in the measurement journals, many conference presentations have been made, and applications of the theory have been made to many pressing measurement problems (i.e., test score equating, study of item bias, test development, item banking, and adaptive testing) in the last several years (see, for example, Hambleton, 1983, 1989; Hambleton & Swaminathan, 1985; Lord, 1980; Weiss, 1983). Interest in item response theory stems from two desirable features which are obtained when an item response model fits a test data set: descriptors of test items (item statistics) are not dependent upon the particular sample of examinees from the population of examinees for whom the test items are intended, and the expected examinee ability scores do not depend upon the particular choice of items from the total pool of test items to which the item response model has been applied. Invariant item and examinee ability parameters, as they are called, are of immense value to measurement specialists. Neither desirable feature is obtained through the use of classical test models. The first feature removes some of the difficulties associated with obtaining statistics for a large bank of test items that is needed for adaptive testing. Sample characteristics are less important and consequently new items can be field-tested and added to the item bank on an as-needed basis. The second feature permits meaningful comparisons of examinees on the ability measured by the adaptive test, though examinees will have been administered statistically unequal tests.

Today, item response theory is being used by most of the large U.S. test publishers, state departments of education, and industrial and professional organizations, to construct norm-referenced and criterion-referenced tests, to investigate item bias, to equate tests, and to report test score information. Some issues and technical problems remain to be solved in the IRT field but it would seem that item response model technology is more than adequate at this time to serve a variety of uses, notably adaptive testing (see, for example, Lord, 1980; Wainer, 1990; Weiss, 1982, 1983, 1985). IRT is especially relevant for adaptive testing because ability estimates can be compared even though examinees take different items. Also, optimal item selection can be done because the usefulness of items for a given ability level can be determined.

Adaptive Testing

In adaptive testing, an attempt is made to match the difficulties of the test items to the ability of the examinee being measured. To match test items to ability levels requires a large pool of items whose statistical characteristics are known so that suitable items may be drawn (Millman & Arter, 1984). Since the item selection procedure does not lend itself easily to paper-and-pencil tests, the adaptive testing process is typically done by computer. (Exceptions to this rule are presented in the work of Lord, 1971.) According to Lord (1980), a computer must be programmed to accomplish the following in order to tailor a test to an examinee:

1. Predict from the examinee's previous responses how the examinee would respond to various test items not yet administered.
2. Make effective use of this knowledge to select the test item to be administered next.
3. Assign at the end of testing a numerical score that represents the ability of the examinee tested.

Advantages of computer adaptive testing (CAT), in addition to shortening tests without loss of measurement precision, include enhanced test security, testing on demand, answer sheets are not needed, test pace is keyed to the individual, quick test scoring and reporting, minimizing test frustration for some examinees, greater standardization, removal of "defective items" from the item bank when they are identified, greater flexibility in item formats and minimizing test administration supervision time (Olsen & associates, 1989).

The research on adaptive testing to date has been focused on six components:

1. The choice of IRT model,
2. The item bank,
3. Choice of starting point,
4. Selection of test items,

5. Scoring/ability estimation, and
6. Choice of stopping rule.

Each of these components will be briefly considered next.

The Choice of IRT Model

This component is important because the validity of the ability estimates depends upon the fit of the chosen model to the test data. Model selection was considered at some length in the Weiss and Yoes chapter. Most of the adaptive testing projects to date have used the three-parameter logistic model.

The Item Bank

Adaptive testing, like any fixed-length testing, requires a valid set of test items. The one main difference is that effective adaptive testing requires the presence of a large as well as valid item bank. Of special interest are highly discriminating items since these items are especially useful in producing short tests with optimal measurement characteristics. Large banks are needed to minimize problems associated with test security and to provide the basis for producing optimal tests for examinees at a wide range of abilities. A second difference is that "defective items" are apt to cause more problems in adaptive testing because these tests are relatively short. Therefore, considerable effort must be expended to insure high quality test items.

   Of course, IRT item statistics are needed, too, which are obtained through properly designed field tests involving large samples of examinees. As part of the field-testing, studies of unidimensionality are normally carried out, and items which do not meet this assumption to a reasonable degree must be deleted. In time, multi-dimensional IRT models may be operational in adaptive testing (Reckase, 1989), but, at the moment, these models are new and the amount of research on them has been low.

Choice of Starting Point

One of the factors that influences the number of items in an adaptive test is the starting place. A good starting place would probably involve administering items that are matched to the examinee's ability level. In the absence of any information about the examinee, normally an item of average difficulty is chosen. However, information about the examinee's ability level such as might be inferred from background educational data or self-reports can be helpful. Most researchers seem pretty sanguine about starting points, feeling that, as long as the test is not too short, the starting place for testing doesn't make much difference. About the only opposition on this point comes from Wainer and Kiely (1987) who feel that test anxiety and frustration are increased with inappropriate starting points.

Selection of Test Items

Research has been done on a variety of adaptive testing strategies built on the following decision rule: if an examinee answers an item correctly, the next item should be more difficult; if an examinee answers incorrectly, the next item should be easier. These strategies can be broken down into *two-stage strategies* and *multistage strategies*. The multistage strategies are either of the *fixed branching* variety or the *variable branching* variety.

In the two-stage procedure (Lord, 1980), all examinees take a routing test and, based upon this test, are directed to one of a number of tests constructed to provide maximum information at certain points along the ability continuum. Ability estimates are then derived from a combination of scores from the routing test and the optimum test. The two-stage strategy has been popular with some test developers because it is possible to implement without computers and in group test administrations. Normally, the short routing test is scored by hand, and then, based upon the examinee's score, a second and substantially longer test is assigned which is roughly matched to the examinee ability level. In practice, usually three to five tests are available for assignment following the routing test, though certainly more tests could be used. Perhaps because of the modest reliability of the routing test (due to its shortness), assignment of students to more than five tests does not seem warranted.

Whereas the two-stage strategy requires only one branching step from the routing to the optimum test, multistage strategies involve a branching decision after the examinee response to each item. If the same item structure is used for all individuals, but each individual can move through the structure in a unique way, then it is called a fixed-branching model. The question of how much item difficulty should vary from item to item leads to considerations of structures with constant, decreasing, or increasing step size. One criticism of fixed branching schemes is that they usually only consider one item statistic, item difficulty, though there are other characteristics of the item, e.g., discriminating power, that influence examinee performance, too.

For these multistage fixed-branching models, all examinees start at an item of median difficulty and, based upon a correct or an incorrect response, pass through a set of items that have been arranged in order of item difficulty. After having completed a fixed set of items, either of two scores is used to obtain an estimate of ability: the difficulty of the (hypothetical) item that would have been administered after the nth (last) item, or the average of the item difficulties, excluding the first item and including the hypothetical n + first item.

Other examples of fixed multistage strategies include the flexi-level test and the stratified-adaptive (stradaptive) test (Lord, 1971; Weiss, 1982). The flexi-level test, which can be represented in a modified pyramidal form, has only one item at each difficulty level. The decision rule for using this test is: following a correct response, the next item given is the item next higher in difficulty that has not been administered. Following an incorrect response, the item next lower in difficulty that has not been administered is given. The stradaptive test, on the other hand, has items stratified into levels according to their difficulties. Branching then occurs by difficulty level across strata and can follow any of a number of possible branching schemes.

The variable-branching structures are multistage strategies that do not operate with a fixed item structure. Rather, at each stage of the process, an item in the established item bank is selected for a certain examinee in a fashion such that the item, if administered, will maximally reduce the uncertainty of the examinee's ability estimate. After administration of the item, the ability estimate is either re-calculated using maximum likelihood procedures (Lord, 1980) or Bayesian procedures.

There are two main methods currently for item selection in variable-branching structures when conducted within an IRT framework (Kingsbury & Zara, 1989). The first, *maximum information* (Weiss, 1982), involves the selection of items which provide maximum information at the current estimate of the examinee's ability in the testing process. To avoid the same items being selected time and time again (items with the highest levels of discriminating power, in general provide the most information) and thereby (possibly) affecting test security and, subsequently, test validity, Green and associates (1982) have suggested that items be selected on a random basis from *among* those items that provide the most information at the ability level of interest.

The second method, *Bayesian item selection* (Owen, 1975), involves the selection of test items which contribute most to minimizing the "posterior belief distribution" about an examinee's ability based upon the knowledge of whether or not the examinee answered the item correctly. The method sounds complicated but it is quite straightforward to apply in practice. Like all Bayesian methods, however, the success of the method depends on the appropriateness of the initial or prior estimate of examinee ability. When the priors are not realistic, or especially when the tests are short, bias in the ability estimates can occur.

Scoring/Ability Estimation

A distinct advantage of computerized adaptive testing is that test scoring/ability estimation is being carried out while the test is being administered, thus facilitating quick feedback of results to examinees. There are two primary IRT methods of ability estimation, *maximum likelihood* (Lord, 1980) and *Bayesian* (Weiss, 1982). Both methods work fine, though maximum likelihood can be a problem with small numbers of test items (estimates are not possible with scores of 0 or n, where n is the number of items administered, for example), and Bayesian estimates tend to be biased.

Choice of Stopping Rule

One of the keys to the success of adaptive testing is knowing when to terminate the testing. Several methods and combinations of methods are currently used. In one, testing is continued until some acceptable level of measurement error is achieved. In this way, ability estimates are all at the same level of measurement when testing is terminated (this parallels measurement within a classical test theory framework) though the number of items administered to each examinee will vary. It would also be possible to specify some acceptable but unequal levels of measurement precision for different ability levels. For example, a decision could be made that more precision is needed with middle abilities than for those at the extremes.

Another method involves setting a fixed number (not too large) of test items for the set of examinees. Testing time is (approximately) constant for all examinees, but the standard error of ability estimation will vary from one examinee to the next. In some applications, a minimum number of items which must be administered is specified, and then testing is continued until the measurement error associated with the ability estimate attains some prespecified acceptable level. This method often adds credibility to the testing in the minds of the examinees. Short tests are often viewed suspiciously by examinees. By specifying a minimum number of test items, some of the criticism which might result from administering a very short test is avoided.

In practice, too, sometimes an upper-bound on the number of items that can be administered is set. In this way, examinees and computers need not be tied up for unrealistic periods of time.

One interesting variation on the above methods arises in the context of criterion-referenced testing (Weiss & Kingsbury, 1984). Here, a cut-off score is available to separate examinees into "mastery" and "nonmastery" states. Testing can continue until the probability of assigning the examinee to the correct mastery state exceeds some acceptable level (e.g., 90%). Or, alternately, testing can continue until the confidence band around the examinee's ability estimate is on one side or the other of the cut-off score.

Evaluation

There are a number of ways in which items can be tailored to ability, as well as ways of computing ability estimates. What is needed, however, is a mechanism for evaluating the results of studies obtained from these various procedures. The mechanism for evaluation should not be based on group statistics such as correlation coefficients because the crux of the problem is to determine the accuracy with which ability can be estimated for a single examinee. Almost all the comparative studies in the literature have compared tests constructed using various procedures by making use of test information functions (see, for example, Weiss, 1982). Does adaptive testing work? The evidence, simulated and live-testing, is substantial that it does. Readers are referred to Moreno and associates (1984), Ward, Kline, and Flaugher (1986), Weiss (1982, 1985), Wainer (1990), and Weiss and Kingsbury (1984) for some of this evidence. Adaptive testing procedures provide more information at the extremes of the ability distribution than do any of the standard tests used for comparative purposes and they provide adequate information at medium-difficulty and medium-ability levels (where standard tests cannot be surpassed).

Summary

In the United States in the last three or four years there have been numerous applications of computer-adaptive tests. The U.S. Armed Services, for example, is planning to administer the Armed Services Vocational Aptitude Battery using computer-adaptive testing procedures, and one testing company currently has adaptive testing projects in over 180 school districts (see Olsen & associates, 1989). In addition, most of the major testing firms in the United States are researching possible uses of computer-adaptive testing. The next few years should see many applications along with evaluative data concerning the success of these applications.

Promising Applications

In this section, two adaptive testing applications will be described: the first is in the area of criterion-referenced testing and does not require IRT methods. The second application to placement testing has not previously been described in the measurement literature. Better-known adaptive testing applications in the literature include applications (1) to grading, instructional decision-making, and ability estimation (Bunderson, Inouye, & Olsen, 1989; Weiss & Kingsbury, 1984), (2) to aptitude testing (Henly & associates, 1990), and (3) to diagnostic testing (Olsen & associates, 1989).

Hierarchically Structured Instructional Programs

To date, there have been only two investigations of adaptive testing to learning hierarchies that arise in objectives-based programs (Ferguson, 1969; Spineti & Hambleton, 1977). Ferguson (1969) was concerned with classifying students as "masters" or "nonmasters" on each objective in a learning hierarchy. His routing strategy was complex (involving the sequential ratio test) and required a computer to perform the actual routing. Ferguson found a 60 percent saving in number of items administered in the computerized administration using a variety of adaptive testing procedures. A test-retest of the adaptive testing procedure gave high reliability, with the reliabilities of the adaptive testing classifications higher than those of the paper-and-pencil conventional test approach.

An important consideration in the work of Spineti and Hambleton (1977) was that the adaptive testing strategies under investigation be implementable with or without the aid of computer terminals. Adaptive testing without the use of computers clearly sets this work apart from that of Ferguson and most of the other research on adaptive testing, with the exception of the self-scoring flexi-level testing work of Lord (1971). The primary effect of the restriction is that it eliminates the possibility of using complex decision-making rules such as the one adopted by Ferguson (1969). The concern was to study the effectiveness of a multitude of adaptive testing strategies that could easily be implemented in objectives based programs. Several additional restrictions were imposed so that the results would be of maximum usefulness. A fixed number of items was required to assess mastery of each objective tested, items were scored right or wrong, and all items measuring a particular objective were assumed to have similar statistical properties. Examinee performance on the test items was assumed to be represented by the binomial test model (Lord & Novick, 1968).

The interactive effects of several factors (test length, cut-off score, and starting point) on the accuracy of mastery classification decisions and the amount of testing time in adaptive testing schemes were investigated. Values of each factor were combined to generate a multitude of adaptive testing strategies for study with two learning hierarchies and three different distributions of true scores across the hierarchies. The study was conducted via computer simulation techniques. Therefore, there was no need to be concerned about problems of developing and validating criterion-referenced tests and learning hierarchies.

Of the many learning hierarchies reported in the educational literature, two were selected for study. These were the learning hierarchies for hydrolysis of salts (Gagné, 1970) and addition-subtraction (Ferguson, 1969). The second one was selected so some of the results of this study could be compared with Ferguson's results. The two learning hierarchies are referred to as Hierarchy A and B, respectively. With Gagné's hierarchy (Hierarchy A), the adaptive testing strategies resulted, on the average, in an overall reduction of testing time of 59.2 percent. With Ferguson's hierarchy (Hierarchy B), there was a 53.2 percent reduction in testing time. It is likely that adaptive testing strategies with Hierarchy B were not quite as effective as with Hierarchy A because Hierarchy B had two terminal objectives, whereas Hierarchy A had only one. The difference highlighted the importance of the particular form of the learning hierarchy on the effectiveness of adaptive testing strategies.

The results of this study on the saving of testing time varied from 50 to 70 percent and compared favorably with the empirical results of Ferguson (1969). Ferguson reported a saving of testing time of 60 percent over conventional testing. The similarity of the results added validity to the appropriateness of the simulation procedures.

The reduction in testing time derived from the adaptive testing strategies was impressive; however, it would have meant little if the total number of errors of classification was substantially larger than with conventional testing. In fact, with Hierarchy A, the adaptive testing strategies resulted in a slightly lower number of errors of classification than with conventional testing. The reverse was true with Hierarchy B; but, again, the differences were slight. These findings, along with the information on the comparisons of testing time for conventional and adaptive testing, provide strong support for the use of adaptive testing. That is, by using an adaptive testing strategy in the context of learning hierarchies, there is much to be gained in terms of testing efficiency without any significant loss in the accuracy of decision making.

The application of adaptive testing to learning hierarchies is substantially different from other adaptive testing applications and therefore includes some unique problems. First, there is the problem of developing and validating learning hierarchies. Because of the inter-relationship between adaptive testing schemes and a learning hierarchy, the success of any adaptive testing scheme will depend on the "validity" of the learning hierarchy under investigation. In validating learning hierarchies, there are psychological as well as statistical problems involved. For example, several researchers have reported that, while examinees may learn material in the sequence defined by a learning hierarchy, they may forget the information learned in any order. Thus, students may be able to perform a terminal objective although they have forgotten several of the prerequisite skills. The implications of this phenomenon for the validation of learning hierarchies and adaptive testing research are not clear. Second, classification problems, as opposed to measurement problems, are of interest. There has been relatively little research on using adaptive testing schemes to classify examinees into two or more categories (an exception is the work of Weiss & Kingsbury, 1984).

There are adequate technologies to develop and to validate both criterion-referenced tests and learning hierarchies (see Hambleton & Rogers, Chapter 1, and Popham, 1978). Further refinements and advancements to the technology will take place as more researchers work in the area and encounter implementation problems.

Basic Skills Testing

One new promising application of adaptive testing is to the problem of placement of adults in basic educational programs in California. Currently, placement is difficult because of the following problems:

1.   The very wide range of abilities represented among the examinees. This can result in a substantial amount of testing prior to effective placement.

2. The inconvenience of administering tests on a daily basis to accommodate applicants to the program. On some days there may be only one or
two examinees but testing must proceed anyway.

3. Difficulties in maintaining test security.

4. General dislike of conventional tests by examinees.

5. Inefficiency in test selection, test administration, and scoring by test
administrators.

All of the problems, in principle, can be overcome with computer-adaptive
testing:

1. Shorten testing time dramatically by moving examinees after a 10-
to 20-item routing test to test items pitched to their ability levels.

2. Permit examinees to begin testing as computer terminals are available. Testing can be initiated on an as-needed basis with minimal assistance
from proctors.

3. Individualize testing (i.e., in theory each examinee sees a different
test) so that test security is not a problem.

4. Provide a potentially more satisfactory test experience. At the very
least, the experience of taking a test is different and so the potential for
reducing test anxiety is present. Certainly, since the tests are "pitched" to
ability levels, examinees should encounter less frustration.

5. Improve testing efficiency by having the computer take over the test
selection, administration, scoring, and reporting functions.

The system described above is under development at the present time in
the Los Angeles County School System in the United States. Preliminary
results are very encouraging. Similar testing systems are currently being
field-tested for college admissions tests and professional credentialing
exams.

Computer Technology

Although the literature on computer-administered testing is quite extensive, one important aspect seems to have been neglected to date. The
question with which one is sooner or later confronted, when developing a
computer-adaptive testing project, is the choice of hardware, peripherals,
and, last but not least, the software. Yet, in the available literature one
searches vainly for starting points that could make the choice between
available options easier. The main purpose of this section is not to discuss
the problem in detail, but instead to point out some alternative options that
are available.

Hardware Requirements

As a result of the state of affairs in computer technology, all early attempts to develop computer-administered testing programs were centered around large mainframe computers. These projects were typically found in the U.S. Armed Forces, large testing facilities such as Educational Testing Service and the Office of Personnel Management, and universities in the United States and in Europe. However, none of these projects lasted very long. The reasons for the failure of these early projects starting in the 1960s are manifold. First, the lack of availability of adequate peripherals such as high resolution video displays hampered the implementation of various tests, especially figural tests. A second important point was the absence of suitable operating systems that would enable the interactive use of computers with fast response times. A third point concerned the shortage of techniques for setting up an adaptive testing system. However, the main reason for abandoning the early attempts was cost benefit analyses that compared the cost of computer-administered testing programs with the traditional paper-and-pencil tests. The advances made in the 1970s and 1980s in the area of chip technology leading to a dramatic decline in the cost of hardware and the availability of cheap, small computer systems with the power of early mainframes, renewed the interest in computer-administered testing programs. The problem now is not so much the cost of hardware, but rather an ever-increasing variety of available computer systems and peripherals. In addition, one is confronted with a rapidly changing technology that makes a choice even more difficult.

Due to the state of affairs in computer technology today and the availability of cost-effective high quality peripherals, any personal computer on the market can serve as a stand-alone unit to be used in computer-adaptive testing. A basic unit would typically consist of a personal computer with a powerful 16-bit processor, a numerical co-processor, a high resolution video display and a hard disk. In addition, one would have some special peripherals such as a mouse or joy-stick or a touch-screen display. A complete system would be available for $3,000 to $5,000. Such a solution would, however, only prove adequate for small testing sites such as small commercial bureaus that would test a limited number of examinees at one time. For large testing facilities, such a system would be inadequate. Procedures for the backup of test data, administrative procedures, procedures for starting the examinee program, and supervision on examinee progress would become too cumbersome. In such a situation, another solution is needed.

The most adequate solution at this time would be to choose a system with a main processor that can be used for development purposes, for data communication and data storage, and for supervision of examinee progress and analysis of results. Beside the main processor, the system would contain a number of independent co-processors that would each drive a test station or peripherals. The system would be designed in such a way that testing programs and necessary data can be down-loaded from the main processor to the co-processors that can then operate independently. Such systems are available from a number of vendors. The advantages of such an architecture are obvious. One combines the flexibility of stand-alone systems while avoiding the problems of communication between stand-alone systems. In addition, the system is easily expandable with new co-processors when needed.

One of the problems that still exists today in spite of the advances in chip technology and the quality of peripherals, especially video displays, is the presentation of figural or graphic items. Usually, video displays use what is called bit-mapped graphics. This means that a display consists of a number of points that are on or off, thus creating an image on the screen. A display with a moderate resolution would consist of a bit map of 600 by 400 points, while a high resolution display would have a resolution of 1,024 by 1,024 points. One item would therefore consist of 240,000 to 1,000,000 bits of information. If one uses a color display, these figures should be multiplied by a factor of 3 to 8, depending on the number of different colors used. A typical test consisting of 200 figural items, not uncommon in an adaptive testing program, would take between 6Mb and 30Mb of computer memory. Despite the advances in the area of chip technology, no personal computer available today on the market would have such an amount of memory on line. Therefore, the information from items would have to be loaded in memory, say, from a hard disk, and thus slow down the program, especially if several examinees were taking the same tests.

Alternatives used today are, for example, the use of video devices. A problem when using video devices such as cassettes or tapes arises, however, if one wishes to mix video images with computer-generated text. This generates a complicated synchronization problem that has yet to be solved in an elegant way. Therefore, one should be cautious to use video images if these images have to be combined with computer-generated text. An elegant solution for both problems is the use of so-called laser vision technology. Graphic images recorded on videotape can be reproduced on a laser vision disk that is computer controlled. The advantages of this system are: high quality display, large storage facilities (10,000 images per disk), fast display rates, and a high degree of flexibility. Additional features of a video disk are that, apart from displaying one frame at a time, the computer can instruct the video player to show a number of frames in sequence, thus enlarging the scope of the present tests to moving images.

A system using a multiprocessor architecture combined with laser vision technology is presently in development at the Rijks Psychologische Dienst in the Netherlands.

Software Requirements

Discussions regarding software requirements of computer-adaptive testing projects usually center around issues like exchangeability of software and the choice of a specific language. However, as ready-to-use packages are still not widely available, the problem regarding the software should, in our view, be dealt with in a pragmatic manner. The choice of a specific language such as PASCAL, BASIC, FORTRAN, FORTH, or any other language available in microcomputers today is not the main problem as long as the development tools available are adequate and the compiler used produces efficient and fast execution programs.

The main problem is to develop a flexible system that is not only adequate for present applications but is also designed in such a way that future developments in the area of ability testing can be easily implemented or at least not inhibited by the original design. In addition, a system should include all components necessary in the process between planning the test and the report regarding the results of the examinees' performance. In short, the system should include the following components: administrative procedures; item banking; test construction; test presentation; test scoring; and report formatting.

In the administrative section, data is recorded such as test date and examinees' data such as name, address, which tests are to be given and in what sequence and in what format. The item banking module should enable the user to add, update, and change items in an easy and flexible manner including item text and item parameters.

The test construction module is used to compile tests and test batteries. In addition, this module also records additional data regarding the execution of the test such as test format (adaptive testing, speeded, fixed sequence of items, recording of response times, norms, etc.). The test presentation module is the core of the program. It controls the presentation of items and tests in the specified order and records the examinees' answers, response times, and so on. In an adaptive format, it controls the sequence of items according to a specified rule or algorithm. The test scoring module transforms responses to test scores and normative scores, and prints out all results in a test profile for the examinee and/or test user. The test results may be interpreted into a more or less extensive report.

All modules should be part of an integrated program that should operate in a user friendly manner, preferably menu driven. The actual code for running a test station including the necessary data should be automatically produced by the program and be downloaded in the co-processor. The program should be constructed in such a way that one can follow the program flow in the co-processors from the main processor. Ideally, the system should be constructed in such a way that the program can be stopped and restarted from any point.

Computer-administered testing programs that are more or less closely constructed according to these guidelines are in development or operation in the U.S. Navy, the Belgian Police Selection Institute, the German Army Forces, and the Dutch Rijks Psychologische Dienst. The latter service is developing a system that resembles these guidelines and the previously described hardware most closely. At this time, it is too early to consider some sort of standardization or exchangeability. First, the systems that are developed or are already in operation should prove their merit, as more experience is gathered in operating computer-assisted programs. A definite choice between one of the available options today would be extremely imprudent merely because of the rapidly changing computer technology, especially in the area of graphic and video processors.

A number of computer packages are now available to support computerized adaptive testing (for a review, see Hsu & Yu, 1989). Probably the most comprehensive package at the present time is MicroCAT (Assessment Systems Corporation, 1988). According to Stone (1989), an integrated testing system should support item and test development, test administration, item and test analysis, and reporting test results. MicroCAT (Version 3.0) is an integrated test development, administration, and data analysis system that addresses all of Stone's concerns, as well as our earlier stated requirements for a desirable computer-assisted testing system. MicroCAT runs on microcomputers, is menu-driven, and has been in use since about 1980. Probably because of its 10-year use and up-dating, the current system contains many features that users desire and is free of errors that often plague newer systems. Features include (1) handling of multiple-item formats and items with graphics, (2) basing test development and analyses on either classical test theory or IRT principles and methods, and (3) constructing, administering, and scoring fixed length or adaptive tests.

Guidelines for Evaluating Computer-Adaptive Testing

Two main questions about computer-adaptive testing that arise concern
(1) the relationship between scores and associated decisions with conventionally administered and computer-administered tests, and (2) the viability
of IRT models for providing a technically adequate measurement system.
In the spirit of insuring that computer-adaptive tests perform as well as
paper-and-pencil tests for an important military testing program in the
United States, Green, Bock, Humphreys, Linn, and Reckase in 1982 provided a set of guidelines for evaluating computer-adaptive tests. These
guidelines, however, are generally applicable to all forms of computer-
administered tests. The authors divided the guidelines into nine main categories: content considerations, dimensionality, reliability, validity, item
parameter estimation and linking, item pool characteristics, item selection
and test scoring, and human factors. A selected list of the guidelines,
organized by category from Green and associates (1982, 1984), is contained in Figure 12–1. Also, APA (1986) prepared a set of guidelines which
apply more generally to computer-administered tests.

Recently, both Green (1988) and Wainer and Kiely (1987) have highlighted a number of difficult problems to overcome in CAT systems. Green
was especially concerned with problems in the areas of equating and item
selection. The equating problem arises because, while two tests, a paper-
and-pencil test and an adaptive test, can be equated or calibrated on the
same scale using an IRT model, in general, the two tests will not provide
the same degree of measurement precision at points along the ability
continuum (i.e., the information functions for the two tests will, in general,
differ). Therefore, the students being assessed will not (or should not) be
indifferent as to which test they prefer. Good students should prefer the
test leading to the most accurate scores; poor students should not. The
implication of this non-equivalence of the measurement properties of a
paper-and-pencil test and an adaptive test remains a problem in practice.

The problem in item selection arises because of a concern that the
context in which an item appears (e.g., item position) and its content may
influence item performance. If, for example, item performance is influenced by items that may have been administered previously, then valid
comparisons of examinees, when examinees are not administered the same
items—and, in general, they will not be in adaptive testing—are problematic. The influences of item context and content represent threats to the
validity of IRT models and, specifically, the invariance of both item and
ability parameter estimates. Wainer and Kiely (1987) also documented the
context effect of (1) item parameter estimates due to an item's location in

Figure 12–1. Guidelines for Evaluating Computer-Adaptive Testing (CAT). These guidelines were prepared by Green and associates (1982). A sample of their guidelines is offered here, with minor editing to enhance their readability without knowledge of the full text of their report.

Content Considerations

1. Specifications for item content should be the same for CAT and paper-and-pencil tests.
2. The content of items selected for the item pool should match the content specifications.
3. Test items must be designed to match the capabilities of the computer equipment.

Dimensionality

4. The fit of the IRT model should be checked.
5. Highly discriminating items should be selected.
6. A factor analysis of the inter-item tetrachoric correlations should be performed.
7. Local independence assumption should be examined.
8. Subtests should be formed when tests are not unidimensional.
9. A test should be balanced to reflect the heterogeneity of domain content and item formats.

Reliability

10. The standard error of measurement of each test score should be reported as a function of the test score, in the metric of the reported score.
11. The standard error of measurement of each test should also be reported in the ability metric.

Validity

12. The similarity of variance-covariance matrices for CAT and paper-and-pencil tests should be assessed.
13. The covariance-structures of the two versions should be compared.
14. The CAT and paper-and-pencil versions of a test should be validated against the same external criteria.
15. The extent of prediction bias should be assessed for important subpopulations.

Item Parameters — Estimation

16. The sample for item calibration should be of adequate size, currently at least 1,000 cases.
17. The calibration sample should be selected so that a sufficient number of examinees are available in the range of ability needed to estimate the lower asymptote and the point of inflection of the item characteristic curve.

Fig. 12–1. Continued

18. The procedure for estimating item parameters should be shown to be "empirically consistent" (large samples should lead to good estimates).
19. The procedure for estimating item parameters should be shown to be unbiased, or the extent and nature of the bias should be specific.
20. The item characteristic curves should fit the observed data.
21. The difficulty of items administered in the CAT and paper-and-pencil versions should be compared.

Item Parameters—Linking

22. The linking procedure for placing items on a common scale should be fully described.
23. When using an equivalent groups procedure for linking, the equivalence of groups should be demonstrated.

Item Pool Characteristics
24. The distribution of the item parameter estimates and descriptive statistics for the estimates should be presented.
25. The information for the total item pool should be presented.

Item Selection and Test Scoring

26. The procedure for item selection and ability estimation must be documented explicitly and in detail.
27. The procedure should include a method of varying the items selected, to avoid using a few items exclusively.
28. The computer algorithm must be capable of administering designated items, and recording the responses separately, without interfering with the adaptive process.
29. The computer must be able to base the choice of a first item on prior information.

Human Factors

30. The environment of the testing terminal should be quiet and comfortable, and free of distractions.
31. The display screen should be placed so that it is free of glare.
32. The legibility of the display should be assessed empirically.
33. The display must be able to include diagrams that have fine detail.

a test, and (2) ability estimates due to the sequence and emphasis (or de-emphasis) of specific test content.

Wainer and Kiely (1987) proposed that "testlets," rather than items, become the building blocks for CAT based on multistage fixed branching. Here, a testlet is

. . .a group of items related to a single content area that is developed as a unit and contains a fixed number of predetermined paths that an examinee may follow. In this way, each item is embedded in a predeveloped testlet, in effect carrying its own context with it. The paths through a testlet may follow a hierarchical branching scheme that routes examinees to successive items of greater or lesser difficulty depending on their previous responses and culminates in series of ordered score categories. Or the testlet may contain only a single linear path of a number of items that are administered to all examinees. The form chosen depends critically on the application for which it is intended.

Just as branching schemes may vary within testlets, the testlets themselves may also be combined to form a complete test by linking them hierarchically or in a linear fashion, or some combination of the two, again depending on the intended purpose of the test. This arrangement allows for the construction of a wide variety of tests for specific purposes by combining hierarchical and linear branching both between and within testlets in any desired combination (Wainer and Kiely, 1987, pp. 190–191).

Clearly, considerably more research is needed to both document the strengths and shortcomings of IRT-based CAT models as well as to pursue alternate CAT models such as testlets within an IRT framework.

Conclusions

The promise of adaptive testing has been high and now there is substantial empirical evidence to suggest that the expected advantages are being obtained in practice. In addition, Green and his associates (1982, 1984) have provided a set of guidelines for insuring that computer adaptive tests function as well as their paper-and-pencil counterparts. Finally, there exists quality computer software such as MicroCAT to support computer adaptive testing. For all of these reasons, computer adaptive testing has arrived and expanded use can be expected.

A number of topics for further research seem especially appropriate at this time. Readers are referred to Wainer (1990, Chapter 9) for a comprehensive list. Only three topics will be presented here. First, the topic of "content matching" between computer adaptive tests and their paper-and-pencil counterparts needs to be better understood. Most of the developmental work to date has not worried much about this problem, especially when the measurements from the two tests were comparable. But full acceptance of adaptive tests by examinees and test users, especially of very important tests, may require that adaptive tests adhere to the same content specifications as their full length paper-and-pencil counterparts.

A second important problem for study concerns the modelling of student item performance (Green, 1988). Successful adaptive testing based on IRT principles and methods requires an accurate match between the psychometric model used to account for examinee performance and actual examinee performance. Unidimensional models with more than three item parameters (de Ayala, 1989) or even multidimensional models (Reckase, 1989) may prove to be more valuable than one-, two-, and three-parameter logistic models which are in current use. More model-building research seems highly desirable at this time.

Finally, additional research results with respect to several of the important components of adaptive testing such as starting places, item selection, ability estimation, and stopping rules would seem to be in order. There are still many questions about the implications of these various components on the success of adaptive testing.

References

American Psychological Association. (1986). *Guidelines for computer-based tests and interpretations*. Washington, DC: Author.

Assessment Systems Corporation. (1988). *User's manual for the MicroCAT Testing System, Version 3*. St. Paul, MN: Author.

Berk, R. A. (Ed.). (1984) *A guide to criterion-referenced test construction*. Baltimore, MD: The Johns Hopkins University Press.

Brzezinski, E., & Hiscox, M. (Eds.). (1984). Microcomputers in educational measurement (Special Issue). *Educational Measurement: Issues and Practice 3*:3–50.

Bunderson, C. V., Inouye, D. K., & Olsen, J. B. (1989). The four generations of computerized educational measurement. In R. L. Linn (ed.), *Educational measurement*, 3rd ed. New York: Macmillan, pp. 367–407.

De Ayala, R. J. (1989). A comparison of the nominal response model and the three-parameter logistic model in computerized adaptive testing. *Educational and Psychological Measurement 49*:789–805.

Ferguson, R. L. (1969). The development of a computer-assisted branched test for a program of individually prescribed instruction. Unpublished doctoral dissertation, University of Pittsburgh.

Gagné, R. M. (1970). *The conditions of learning*, 2nd ed. New York: Holt, Rinehart, & Winston.

Green, B. F. (1983). The promise of tailored tests. In H. Wainer & S. Messick (eds.), *Principles of modern psychological measurement: A Festschrift for Frederic M. Lord*. Hillsdale, NJ: Lawrence Erlbaum Associates, pp. 69–80.

———— (1988). Critical problems in computer-based psychological measurement. *Applied Measurement in Education 1*:223–231.

Green, B. F., Bock, R. D., Humphreys, L. G., Linn, R. L., & Reckase, M. D.

Hambleton, R. K. (ed.). (1983). *Applications of item response theory.* Vancouver, BC: Educational Research Institute of British Columbia.

Hambleton, R. K. (1989). Principles and selected applications of item response theory. In R. L. Linn (ed.), *Educational measurement*, 3rd ed. New York: Macmillan, pp. 147–200.

Hambleton, R. K., & Swaminathan, H. (1985). *Item response theory: Principles and applications.* Hingham, MA: Kluwer Academic Publishers.

Henly, S. J., Klebe, K. J., McBride, J. R., & Cudeck, R. (1990). Adaptive and conventional versions of the DAT: The first complete test battery comparison. *Applied Psychological Measurement 13*:363–371.

Hsu, T. C., & Yu, L. (1989). Using computers to analyze item response data. *Educational Measurement: Issues and Practice 8*:21–27.

Kingsbury, G. G., & Zara, A. R. (1989). Procedures for selecting items for computerized adaptive tests. *Applied Measurement in Education 2*(4):359–375.

Lord, F. M. (1971). The self-scoring flexilevel test. *Journal of Educational Measurement 8*:147–151.

——————— (1980). *Applications of item response theory to practical testing problems.* Hillsdale, NJ: Lawrence Erlbaum Associates.

Lord, F. M., & Novick, M. R. (1968). *Statistical theories of mental test scores.* Reading, MA: Addison-Wesley.

Millman, J., & Arter, J. A. (1984). Issues in item banking. *Journal of Educational Measurement 21*:315–330.

Moreno, K. E., Wetzel, C. D., McBride, J. R., & Weiss, D. J. (1984). Relationship between corresponding Armed Services Vocational Aptitude Battery and computerized adaptive testing subtests. *Applied Psychological Measurement 8*:155–163.

Olsen, J. B., Cox, A., Price, C., & Strozeski, M. (1989, April). *Development, implementation, and validation of a predictive and prescriptive test for statewide assessment.* Paper presented at the meeting of AERA, San Francisco.

Owen, R. J. (1975). A Bayesian sequential procedure for quantal response in the context of adaptive mental testing. *Journal of the American Statistical Association 70*:351–356.

Popham, W. J. (1978). *Criterion-referenced measurement.* Englewood Cliffs, NJ: Prentice-Hall.

Reckase, M. D. (1989). Adaptive testing: The evolution of a good idea. *Educational Measurement: Issues and Practice 8*:11–15.

Spineti, J. P., & Hambleton, R. K. (1977). A computer simulation study of tailored testing strategies for objectives-based instructional programs. *Educational and Psychological Measurement 37*:139–158.

Stone, C. A. (1989). Testing software review: MicroCAT Version 3.0. *Educational Measurement: Issues and Practice 8*:33–38.

Urry, V. W. (1977). Tailored testing: A successful application of latent trait theory. *Journal of Educational Measurement 14*:181–196.

——————— (1983, August). *Tailored testing theory and practice: A basic model, normal ogive submodels, and tailored testing algorithms* (NPRDC TR 83-82).

San Diego, CA: Navy Personnel Research and Development Center.

Wainer, H. (1988). The first four millennia of mental testing: From ancient China to the computer age. In *Proceedings of 29th Annual Military Testing Association Conference*, pp. 357–362.

———— (ed.). (1990). *Computerized adaptive testing: A primer*. Hillsdale, NJ: Lawrence Erlbaum Associates.

Wainer, H., & Kiely, G. L. (1987). Item clusters and computerized adaptive testing: A case for testlets. *Journal of Educational Measurement* 24:185–201.

Ward, W. C., Kline, R .G., & Flaugher, J. (1986). *College Board Computerized Placement Tests: Validation of an adaptive test of basic skills* (Research Report 86-29). Princeton, NJ: Educational Testing Service.

Weiss, D. J. (1982). Improving measurement quality and efficiency with adaptive testing. *Applied Psychological Measurement* 6:473–492.

———— (ed.). (1983). *New horizons in testing*. New York: Academic Press.

———— (1985). Adaptive testing by computer. *Journal of Consulting and Clinical Psychology* 53:774–789.

Weiss, D. J., & Kingsbury, G. G. (1984). Application of computerized adaptive testing to educational problems. *Journal of Educational Measurement 21:* 361–375.

WICAT Systems (1986). *Educational measurement system*. Orem, UT: Author.

———— (1982, May). *Evaluation plan for the Computerized Adaptive Vocational Aptitude Battery*. Baltimore, MD: The Johns Hopkins University, Department of Psychology.

———— (1984). Technical guidelines for assessing computerized adaptive tests. *Journal of Educational Measurement* 21(4):347–360.

13 COGNITIVE THEORY AND PSYCHOMETRICS

Robert J. Sternberg

During the past decade, students of human intelligence have witnessed more development and change in our conceptions of intelligence than have any students of this topic since the early twentieth century, when such pioneers as Alfred Binet and Charles Spearman were promulgating their new ideas about the nature and assessment of intelligence. This decade of ferment and rapid progress followed several preceding decades in which relatively little had changed in our conceptions of intelligence. Why did a field that had stabilized and, in the opinion of some, become rather staid, all of a sudden take off? Different psychologists might provide different reasons, but many of them would attribute the change to the influence of a new paradigm on theory and research in the field of intelligence. The paradigm was that of cognitive psychology.

Cognitive psychology is the study of how people mentally represent and process information. As such, it includes within its domain mental abilities

Preparation of this chapter was supported by Contract N00014-85-K-0589 from the Office of Naval Research and Contract MDA903-85-K-0305 from the Army Research Institute.

such as perception, learning, memory, reasoning, problem solving, and decision making. Cognitive psychology deals with many of those abilities measured by psychometric tests of intelligence as well as those measured by more specialized aptitude tests. Thus, it would seem reasonable to believe that contemporary developments in cognitive psychology should have implications for the psychometric testing of mental abilities.

Many psychologists interested in the interface between cognitive psychology and psychometric testing believe that cognitive theories can inform testing practices. This belief dates back at least to Cronbach's (1957) seminal article on the two disciplines (correlational and experimental) of scientific psychology. The content of most mental ability tests derives from investigations of differential psychology. Because cognitive psychology studies many of the same phenomena that have been studied by differential psychology, it provides a set of converging operations for understanding mental abilities in a theoretical framework different from the one that generated most mental tests. If the two frameworks converge in their implications for how mental abilities should be tested, then the mutual support that each framework provides can potentially strengthen current testing practices. If the two frameworks diverge in their implications, then current testing practices ought to be reexamined in the light of this divergence, and changes in testing practices ought at least to be considered. In fact, there is both convergence and divergence between contemporary cognitive and psychometric theories.

This chapter is divided into two parts. First, alternative cognitive approaches to understanding and measuring human intelligence are described, then some implications of these approaches for testing are suggested.

Cognitive Approaches to Understanding and Measuring Human Intelligence

Cognitive psychologists have pursued a number of different approaches to understanding human intelligence. In just a little more than a decade, these approaches have gone through two generations of development. The first generation of development relied upon fairly standard techniques of cognitive theory and analysis for the understanding and measurement of intelligence. This generation of theory and research was, in many respects, a direct response to Cronbach's (1957) plea for the unification of the two disciplines of scientific psychology. The second generation of theory in research has been somewhat bolder than the first, expanding not only our notions about the nature of human intelligence but the boundaries of cognitive theory itself. From some points of view, the development of the first generation of theory and research can be seen as primarily methodological, whereas the contribution of the second generation can be seen as primarily substantive. Because the first generation of research extends back to 1973, whereas the second generation of research goes back only to 1983, it is much less clear where the second generation of research will lead us. Nevertheless, it is important to review this research in order to convey the exciting new developments that are at the forefront of cognitive approaches to intelligence.

In the remainder of this section, each of the two generations of theory and research will be reviewed. As noted above, the theories of the first generation are readily characterized in terms of their methodological bent. The theories of the second generation can be characterized primarily on the basis of their substantive claims. Consider each of the two kinds of theories.

The First Generation: New Methodologies for Studying and Measuring Intelligence

In the first generation of research, cognitive psychologists pursued several different approaches to understanding mental abilities. Although these approaches could be classified in a variety of ways, I have classified them into categories of cognitive correlates, cognitive components, cognitive contents, and cognitive training (Sternberg, 1981c), expanding on a more limited categorization scheme originally proposed by Pellegrino and Glaser (1979). Although I have loosely classified these different approaches into four categories, it should be understood that the categories are neither mutually exclusive nor exhaustive with respect to the first generation of research approaches in cognitive psychology. Below, I briefly describe each approach, its goals, the kinds of research it has generated, and my evaluation of that approach.

Cognitive Correlates. In the cognitive-correlates approach to understanding mental abilities, subjects are tested in their ability to perform tasks that contemporary cognitive psychologists believe measure basic human information-processing abilities. (Information processing is generally defined as the sequence of mental operations and their products involved in performing a cognitive task.) Such tasks include, among others, the Posner and Mitchell (1967) letter-matching task, in which subjects are asked to state as quickly as possible whether the letters in a pair such as "A a" constitute a physical match (which they don't) or (in another condition) a name match (which they do); and the S. Sternberg (1969) memory-scanning task, in which subjects are asked to state as quickly as possible whether a target digit or letter, such as 5, appeared in a previously memorized set of digits or letters, such as 3 6 5 2. Individuals are usually tested either via tachistoscope (a machine that provides rapid stimulus exposures) or a computer terminal, and the principal dependent measure of interest is response time.

The proximal goal in this research is to estimate parameters (characteristic quantities) representing the durations of performance for the information-processing components constituting each task, and then to investigate the extent to which these components correlate across subjects with each other and with scores on measures commonly believed to assess intelligence (e.g., Raven's Progressive Matrices test). Most commonly, correlations between parameter estimates and measured intelligence are statistically significant, but moderately low—usually around .3 (see, e.g., Hunt, Frost, & Lunneborg, 1973; Hunt, Lunneborg, & Lewis, 1975). The distal goal of cognitive-correlates research is to integrate individual-differences research and mainstream cognitive psychological research—in particular, by providing a theoretical grounding from cognitive psychology for differential research (Hunt et al., 1973). Thus, instead of trying to draw theoretical conclusions from correlating scores on one empirically derived test (e.g., vocabulary) as differential researchers have done, the cognitive-correlates researcher draws theoretical conclusions from correlating scores on an empirically derived test with parameters generated by a cognitive model of some aspect of mental functioning (e.g., memory scanning).

On the one hand, cognitive-correlates researchers like Hunt (1978), Jensen (1979), Keating and Bobbitt (1978), and Jackson and McClelland (1979) must be given credit for providing a cognitive-theoretical base for individual-differences research to supplement the psychometric (and usually factorial) theoretical base that had existed earlier. On the other hand, one might question whether these researchers are providing the optimal cognitive-theoretical base. The relatively low correlations attained between task parameters and psychometric test scores might be due to psychometric test performance's drawing on lower level perceptual and memory abilities of the kinds studied by cognitive-correlates researchers, but only in a peripheral way. It is not clear that the rather simple kinds of information processing required by many of the perceptual and memory tasks cognitive psychologists have studied in their laboratories do justice to the rather complex kinds of information processing required by many psychometric tests of intelligence—at least to the extent that the reason for studying the relationships between the two kinds of tasks is to use the first to provide a theoretical grounding for the second. Nor do the simple tasks seem to measure constructs resembling what most people mean by "intelligence" (see Neisser, 1979; Sternberg, Conway, Ketron, & Bernstein, 1981). Other explanations for the moderately low correlations between the cognitive task parameters and psychometric tests have been proposed as well. For example, Carroll (1981) has suggested that the cognitive tasks and psychometric tests may be related because they share a common speed factor; Sternberg (1981a) has proposed that the relationship may be due to a degree of shared novelty, or nonentrenchment, between the two kinds of tasks (see also Hogaboam & Pellegrino, 1978).

A final evaluation of the cognitive-correlates approach will almost certainly have to await our better understanding of the .3-level correlations between task parameters and test scores. In the meantime, cognitive-correlates researchers deserve considerable credit for reawakening interest among cognitive psychologists in individual differences and for bringing individual-differences research closer to mainstream cognitive psychological research. Although I do not believe that the cognitive-correlates approach will provide the keys to unlock the mysteries of intelligence, if only because the tasks these researchers have studied do not seem fundamental to intelligence (as opposed to, say, perception or memory), I do believe that the early contributions of Hunt and others will be remembered for having opened an area of research that for years had been all but ignored by cognitive psychologists.

Cognitive-correlates researchers would be most likely to supplement psychometric tests with information-processing tests based on standard laboratory information-processing tasks such as the memory-scanning and letter-matching tests mentioned earlier. Rose (1978) has actually constructed and tested an information-processing assessment battery based on standard laboratory tasks. Using this battery, one can isolate latency scores for a variety of different information-processing components. Rose's battery is an impressive one, although correlations across tasks are relatively low, and correlations of the information-processing tasks and parameters with psychometric tests or various types of real-world performance have yet to be reported.

Cognitive Components.   In the cognitive-components approach to understanding mental abilities, subjects are tested in their ability to perform tasks of the kinds actually found on standard psychometric tests of mental abilities—for example, analogies, series completions, mental rotations, and syllogisms. Subjects are usually tested via a tachistoscope or a computer terminal, and response time is usually the principal dependent variable, but error rate and pattern of response choices can be secondary dependent variables. These latter dependent variables are of more interest in this approach than in the cognitive-correlates approach because the tasks tend to be more difficult and thus more susceptible to erroneous responses.

The proximal goal in this research is first to formulate a model of information processing in performance on IQ-test types of tasks; second, to test the model at the same time as parameters for the model are estimated; and finally, to investigate the extent to which these components correlate across subjects with each other and with scores on standard psychometric tests. Because the tasks that are analyzed are usually taken directly from IQ tests, or else are very similar to tasks found on IQ tests, the major issue in this kind of research is not whether there is any correlation at all between cognitive task and psychometric test scores. Rather, the issue is one of isolating the locus or loci of the correlation that is obtained. One seeks to discover what components of information processing in task performance are the critical ones from the standpoint of the theory of intelligence.

The distinction between cognitive-correlates and cognitive-components research is not entirely clear-cut. There appear to be at least two major differences in emphasis in the two approaches, however. First, if one were willing to accept a continuum of levels of information processing extending from perception, to learning and memory, to reasoning and complex problem solving, cognitive-correlates researchers would tend to study tasks measuring skills at the lower end of the continuum, whereas cognitive-components researchers would tend to study tasks measuring skills at the higher end of the continuum. Thus, whereas cognitive-correlates researchers tend to study perception, learning, and memory tasks, cognitive-components researchers tend to study reasoning and problem-solving tasks. Second, cognitive-components research seems to place more emphasis on the formulation, fitting, and testing of formal information-processing models, which are usually operationalized either as sets of linear equations (e.g., Mulholland, Pellegrino, & Glaser, 1980; Sternberg, 1977, 1980a) or as computer simulations (e.g., Atwood & Polson, 1976; Simon & Kotovsky, 1963).

The differences between the two approaches are almost certainly more differences in emphasis rather than in kind. First, the theory and research of some investigators are quite difficult to classify (e.g., Carroll, 1976, 1981), as they seem to straddle the fence between the two approaches. Second, the research of some investigators who are usually seen as being in one camp or the other is sometimes on the borderline between the two approaches (e.g., MacLeod, Hunt, & Mathews, 1978).

In early cognitive-components research (e.g., Royer, 1971; Sternberg, 1977), investigators generally isolated a single kind of information-processing component. There seems to have been some evolution of cognitive-components research, however, such that investigators speak more these days of multiple kinds of information-processing components (e.g., Snow, 1979; Sternberg, 1980b), such as metacomponents (or executive processes—higher order processes that serve to organize, plan, and monitor performance) and performance components. On the one hand, the differentiation among kinds of components seems to do better justice to the variety of kinds of information processing people are required to do in their daily lives. On the other hand, it is not clear how theories regarding taxonomies of kinds of component processes can be tested, nor is it clear how one could place constraints on the kinds of components such theories could generate (and thereby avoid an endless proliferation of kinds of components). The problem is not one of proliferation per se, which may or may not be desirable, but of the absence of logical or empirical constraints on proliferation.

As in many kinds of research, there have been surprises in cognitive-components research. One of the more pleasant surprises has been the ability of formal componential models to account for large amounts of both task and person variation in response times and response choices (see, e.g., Frederiksen, 1980; Guyote & Sternberg, 1981; Mulholland et al., 1980; Pellegrino & Glaser, 1980; Schustack & Sternberg, 1981; Shepard & Metzler, 1971; Sternberg, 1977, 1980). One of the less pleasant surprises has been that the magnitudes of correlations between information-processing latencies and psychometric test scores have been only moderate (often in the .4 to .6 range). More disturbing, the identified loci of these correlations have sometimes been ones that seem theoretically questionable (e.g., when most of the identified correlation between task and test scores turns out to be isolated to the response constant—Egan, 1976; Sternberg, 1977). Recent efforts have attempted to remedy this situation by studying metacomponential or executive functioning and by studying performance in nonentrenched, or novel, tasks (e.g., Sternberg, 1981a). Studies of these kinds have yielded higher correlations (often in the .6 to .8 range) and explanations for these correlations that seem consistent with people's intuitions.

It is sometimes difficult to know where the cognitive-components approach stops and other approaches that are more than mere variants of this approach begin. The research of some investigators (e.g., Frederiksen, 1980; Embretson, 1989) although "componential" in many respects, draws on psychometric techniques such as analysis of covariance structures (in the case of Frederiksen) or item response model analysis (in the case of Embretson) that are not usually associated with the cognitive-components approach.

A final evaluation of the cognitive-components approach, like one of the cognitive-correlates approach, will have to await further developments. The approach is still being widely used and has not had sufficient time to show everything it can or cannot do. I believe that a major contribution of this approach will be its demonstration that IQ-test tasks can be understood, and understood well, in information-processing terms. Componential analyses have shown that cognitive components provide a view of mental abilities that is complementary (rather than contradictory) to that provided by the factors (Carroll, 1981; Sternberg, 1981b) characterizing differential theories of mental abilities. If the approach comes to be judged harshly, it may be because in the initial enthusiasm that accompanies new approaches to studying intelligence (or anything else), investigators following the congitive-components approach probably claimed more for their new approach than it could yield.

During the 1970s, cognitive-correlates and cognitive-components researchers were busy establishing their respective turfs, each trying to win converts to their new views on how intelligence should be studied. As investigators began to realize the fuzziness of the distinction between the two approaches and began to realize that each approach had something to contribute to the other (just as each approach had more to learn from the factor-analytic approach than had originally seemed to be the case), the competition between investigators following each of the two approaches started to wane.

Cognitive-components researchers would be most likely to supplement psychometric tests with information-processing tests based on the psychometric ones, but with test items administered in a computer-controlled setting that would enable the examiner to decompose test performance into its information-processing constituents. An information-processing analysis of a subject's inductive reasoning performance, for example, would assess skills such as the individual's ability (1) to encode stimuli, (2) to infer relations between stimulus terms, (3) to map higher order relations between relations, (4) to apply previously inferred relations to new settings, (5) to compare alternative answer options in terms of their similarities and differences, (6) to justify one answer as preferred but not necessarily ideal, (7) to respond, (8) to combine these components into a strategy that results in efficient item solution, and (9) to represent information in a way that facilitates operations on the data base stored in long-term memory (Sternberg & Gardner, 1982).

Cognitive Training. The cognitive-training approach to understanding mental abilities can be used in conjunction with either the cognitive-correlates approach or the cognitive-components approach, or in conjunction with some other approach. In this approach, one trains cognitive skills according to some theory of cognition, and views positive training results as supportive of the theory.

The cognitive-training approach has been widely used in a variety of domains. For example, Belmont and Butterfield (1971), Borkowski and Wanschura (1974), and Campione and Brown (1979) have used the approach in learning and memory; and Feuerstein (1979), Holzman, Glaser, and Pellegrino (1976), and Linn (1973) have used it in reasoning and problem solving. One conclusion has emerged with striking regularity in many studies by many different investigators: to attain both durability and generalizability of training, it seems to be necessary to train both at the level of meta-components (or executive processes) and at the level of performance components (or lower-order processes used to carry out the orders of the executive processes—see, e.g., Belmont, Butterfield, & Ferretti, 1982; Feuerstein, 1979, 1980).

At a practical level, the cognitive-training approach can be helpful in telling us what aspects of cognitive functioning are and are not trainable with reasonable amounts of effort and in actually effecting improvement in an individual's cognitive functioning. I am more impressed with the practical utility of the approach than with its theoretical utility for testing models of task performance because of interpretive problems I see in drawing theoretical conclusions about task performance from the results of training studies. I believe there are several such problems.

First, whereas successful training of a cognitive strategy for performing a particular task does imply that individuals might use the strategy in their spontaneous performance of the task, it does not imply that individuals necessarily use that strategy, or even that they are likely to use it. For example, we have found it easy to train a strategy for solving linear syllogisms that subjects only rarely use spontaneously (Sternberg & Weil, 1980). Second, training in one or more components may change the strategy subjects use. An improvement in performance as a result of training certain components may indicate improved execution of the original strategy, or instead, it may indicate the adoption of a new, more successful strategy.

The training approach, in itself, does not indicate which outcome has transpired. Third, if training fails, it is not clear what conclusions one can draw from the failure. There seem to be at least four plausible interpretations. The first is that the component is simply not a component of natural intelligence—one cannot train it because it is not a natural part of a functioning cognitive system. A second interpretation is that the component is an aspect of intelligence but that it is essentially impervious to training. Not all intelligent acts need to be accessible or even available to consciousness, and the component may be an automatic one to which the individual has no access. A third intepretation is that the component is an aspect of intelligence and is trainable, but not by the methods used by the particular investigator. A fourth interpretation is that the component is an aspect of intelligence and that it is trainable, but not in the population being investigated. Many of the cognitive training studies have been conducted on retarded populations, which scarcely provide a representative basis for drawing conclusions about trainability of cognitive processes in the population at large (Sternberg, 1981c).

On the whole, I view the cognitive-training approach as a significant and worthwhile one, but not for testing theories of intelligence. Rather, I see it as a desirable culmination of research on the nature of mental abilities that is originally undertaken following some other approach. First, one uses a set of methods such as those provided by cognitive-correlates or cognitive-components analysis to validate a particular subtheory of intelligence. If the validation is reasonably successful, then the practical utility of the theory can be tested through the cognitive-training approach, at the same time as one makes a potentially valuable contribution to people in need of intellectual improvement (which includes pretty much everyone). A given theory may be internally valid in the sense that it can account for task and subject variance, and externally valid in the sense that parameters of the theory are highly correlated with measures commonly regarded as able to provide sound measurement of mental abilities. But theoretical utility of a theory does not imply practical utility: the level of analysis may be too microscopic or too macroscopic to provide useful implications for training, or the theory may deal with processes that are too automatized to be trainable. The converse is also true: practical utility of a theory does not imply theoretical utility. Successful training outcomes can be and have been attained in the absence of any theory at all. For example, although it is quite likely that taking mathematics courses improves mathematical abilities or that taking language courses improves linguistic abilities, there is, at least at present, no satisfactory theory to account for why this should be so.

Cognitive-training researchers might follow any of a number of paths to testing depending on their choice of what to train and how to train it. One of the more interesting approaches to testing among such investigators is that of Feuerstein (1979), who has devised a "learning potential assessment device" that he believes measures cognitive modifiability, or what Vygotsky (1978) referred to as the "zone of proximal development." Modifiability is assessed by giving examinees guided instruction in solving problems that the examinees are initially unable to solve and by evaluating the examinee's ability to profit from instruction.

To conclude, I believe the cognitive-training approach provides a needed complement to other approaches for understanding mental abilities. It answers, or at least addresses, questions that other approaches do not and cannot answer or address. But the approach is not interchangeable with other approaches. It does not provide a good means for testing theories about the nature of mental abilities.

Cognitive Contents. Recently, there has emerged on the cognitive-psychological scene a new approach to research that has yet to be applied directly to the study of mental abilities but that seems to provide a good entree into such research. The approach, which might be referred to as a cognitive-contents approach, seeks to compare the performances of experts and novices in complex tasks such as the solution of physics problems (Chi, Feltovich, & Glaser, 1981; Chi, Glaser, & Rees, 1982; Larkin, McDermott, Simon, & Simon, 1980a, 1980b), the selection of moves and strategies in chess and other games (Chase & Simon, 1973; DeGroot, 1965; Reitman, 1976), and the acquisition of domain-related information by groups of people at different levels of expertise (Chiesi, Spilich, & Voss, 1979). Research on expert-novice differences in a variety of task domains suggests that the way information is stored in and retrieved from long-term memory can largely account for the substantial differences in performance between experts and novices. This view would suggest that a possible locus of differences between more and less mentally able people is in their ability to organize information in long-term memory in a way that makes it readily accessible for a variety of purposes (see, e.g., Egan & Greeno, 1973). Presumably, information stored in such a flexible way is maximally available for transfer from old to new problem situations.

Cognitive-contents researchers might supplement psychometric tests with complex learning or problem-solving tasks that elicit an examinee's knowledge base and the way in which knowledge is mentally represented. Such researchers would be particularly interested in the features of problems to which examinees pay attention. It has been found, for example, that less skilled physics problem solvers tend to pay more attention to surface features of physics problems, whereas more skilled problem solvers tend to pay more attention to deep structural features (Chi, Feltovich, & Glaser, 1981). Cognitive-contents tests might also supplement cognitive-components tests, with the former assessing knowledge deficiencies and the latter assessing processing deficiencies.

In one sense, at least, all of the information-processing approaches described have the same implication for testing—the psychometric testing procedures currently in use should be supplemented by information-processing testing procedures that have as their outcomes assessments of the information-processing components, mental representations, and strategies people use in performing tasks requiring nontrivial intelligence. The technology now exists for such supplementation to become a reality: it is possible to obtain these kinds of information for individual subject data (Sternberg, 1977, 1980a), just as it is possible to obtain factor or subtest scores for individual subject data. But although such supplementation is now technically possible, it is not clear that it is yet either practically feasible or desirable. First, administration of information-processing tests often requires expensive equipment such as computers or tachistoscopes. Second, estimation of stable parameter values for individual subjects can require quite lengthy testing sessions. Third, and perhaps most important, the incremental validity of information-processing scores over psychometric scores has yet to be demonstrated for interesting external criteria. Thus, it is not clear that we are ready to introduce information-processing tests into everyday assessment situations.

Nevertheless, I think the prognosis for eventual supplementation of psychometric testing procedures with information-processing procedures is good. Information-processing tests seem to open up diagnostic possibilities that are not available with psychometric testing. Whereas factor or subtest scores from psychometric tests are useful in pointing out broad areas in which training should take place, they do not specify just what should be trained. Component scores from information-processing tests serve this more specific purpose, pinpointing the particular information-processing skills in which improvement is needed to improve overall performance. Several training programs have already been proposed or implemented that capitalize on the usefulness of information-processing diagnosis for training purposes (Brown & Campione, 1977; Butterfield & Belmont, 1977; Feuerstein, 1980; Sternberg, 1985). For example, if one knows that an individual has difficulties in reasoning, information-processing tests enable the examiner to pinpoint the nature of these difficulties quite precisely. One can identify whether components are combined into suboptimal strategies; and whether the components and strategies operate on a suboptimal mental representation.

Thus, one might imagine a two-stage testing procedure in which cheap and efficient psychometric testing is done to pinpoint general areas of strength and weakness. Where further diagnostic testing seems to be called for, information-processing testing could be done to pinpoint specific areas of strength and weakness. Information-processing tests, because of their greater expense and time involvement, might be reserved for exceptional cases where thorough diagnosis seems to be appropriate. Eventually, if the costs in time and money of information-processing testing can be reduced, then such testing might become more widely feasible.

The Second Generation: Substantive Advances in the Understanding of Human Intelligence

In the second generation of theory and research, the major debate among cognitive theories has been not on how to study intelligence, but rather on what intelligence is. There has been a shift in emphasis from methods of groups of people to theories of individual people. Three of the main theories are those of Gardner (1983), Baron (1985), and Sternberg (1985). I will briefly describe each theory, its goals, the kinds of research it has generated, and my evaluation of it.

Gardner's Theory of Multiple Intelligences. The core claim of Gardner's theory of multiple intelligences is that there is no one intelligence, but rather multiple intelligences. A tentative list of intelligences includes linguistic intelligence, musical intelligence, logical-mathematical intelligence, spatial intelligence, bodily kinesthetic intelligence, and personal intelligence (Gardner, 1983). Each of these intelligences is asserted to be fundamentally independent from every other intelligence. So, for example, Gardner would postulate a separate memory in problem-solving facility for, say, linguistic intelligence, on the one hand, and musical intelligence, on another.

The goal of Gardner's theory is clearly to expand our conception of the nature of intelligence, and to have us reconceptualize intelligence not as a unitary construct, but as multiple constructs. The theory is an extremely bold one, and is reconceptualizing many people's thinking about intelligence. I believe that this attempt to expand the breadth of our conceptualization of intelligence is an historically important one, and that its impact has been largely positive. Traditional psychometric tests have operationally defined intelligence in a rather narrow way, despite the fact that many of the originators of these tests, such as Binet and Simon (1973) and Wechsler (1958), had quite broad conceptualizations of the nature of intelligence. Thus, Gardner's theory is monumental in its forcing of a re-examination of current thinking about the construct of human intelligence.

Despite my high regard for the role of MI (multiple-intelligences) theory in the evolutionary course of theories of intelligence, I have grave doubt about its validity. There are several reasons for this view.

1. *The notion of multiple intelligences.* Gardner's view of multiple autonomous intelligences has its roots in faculty psychology, which postulated a set of distinct human faculties that together form the human mind. Gall, the phrenologist, was a faculty theorist of sorts, although one need not postulate the existence of separate physical regions of the head to be a faculty psychologist: the regions can be mental instead. I believe there is too much of Gall in Gardner's theory.

Faculty psychology was relatively short-lived because there was just too much data to counterindicate it. I believe the same situation exists today. One of the most well-established findings in the literature on human intelligence is the existence of a "positive manifold" among the correlations of the various tests of intelligence: These tests all tend to be positively interrelated (see, e.g., Anastasi, 1958; Cronbach, 1990). Although the magnitudes of the correlations vary as a function of the particular abilities being compared—for example, the correlation between logical-mathematical scores and spatial scores is higher than the correlation between linguistic and spatial scores (see, e.g., Sternberg, 1980a)—the correlations are all positive, nevertheless. Curiously, there is not even one respectable psychometric (correlational) psychologist who denies the existence of this manifold. Such consensus is curious only because there is so little else on which psychometricians agree! Thurstone (1938), who originally argued against the existence of a general factor, eventually was forced to admit that a higher order general factor could be extracted from his "primary mental abilities." Guilford (1967) originally eschewed higher order factors (which result from correlations among factors), but more recently has started extracting such factors (Guilford, 1982). The point is that even the psychometricians most resistant to the idea of a positive manifold have eventually been forced to deal with it. Among information-processing theorists, such as Hunt (1980), Jensen (1982), Sternberg (1980b), and others, the same general view prevails; and their theories are devoted, at least in part, to trying to explain the positive manifold.

The almost universally acknowledged positive manifold is simply incon-sistent with the notion of independent multiple intelligences. In view of the overwhelming correlational and information-processing data to support this manifold, it is curious that Gardner attempts to uphold such a notion. Even Fodor (1983), the leading proponent of the "modularity" of the mind, allows for the existence of some kind of central integrative function. Gardner does not. He can argue for his independent multiple intelligences only because of his highly selective presentation of data. One could easily fill a book as long as Gardner's with counterevidence to the theory's claim of independent multiple intelligences, which, unfortunately, is the central claim of the theory as it now stands.

2.   *The scope of human intelligence.* As noted earlier, Gardner's view of human intelligence is broader than that of practically any other theorist. In my opinion, there has been a need for a broader conceptualization of intelligence than has existed in most psychometric and information-processing theories. If anything, information-processing theories, although more recent than most psychometric theories, have been even more narrowly conceived than their predecessors. Nevertheless, I am concerned that Gardner has gone too far in search of breadth.

One might wonder whether Gardner's book deals as much with mul-tiple *intelligences* as it does with multiple *talents.* Indeed, Cohn (1981), Marland (1971), and Piechowski (1979) have provided lists that are similar to Gardner's list, but these lists have been of talents rather than of intel-ligences. Although it would be hard, on the basis of existing data, to choose among these four lists one that is correct or more nearly correct, it would not be hard to characterize them as of talents rather than of intel-ligences, at least in the ordinary senses of these terms. Oddly enough, Gardner's book would have been written as a literature review organ-ized by a not-so-new taxonomy of talents rather than as a new theory of intelligence.

Although there is no unanimity on what is and is not intelligence, qualitative and quantitative analyses of experts' and laypersons' concep-tions of intelligence, as well as of existing formal theories of intelligence, reveal a reasonable degree of consensus about the range of behaviors that is and is not considered to fall within the domain of intelligence (Car-roll, 1976, 1981; Sternberg, 1981b, 1985; Sternberg, Conway, Ketron, & Bernstein, 1981). *Intelligence* appears to be a prototypically organized, family-resemblance concept (Neisser, 1979). Behaviors differ in their proto-typicality with respect to intelligence. Some of the behaviors covered by Gardner's account, such as linguistic and logical-mathematical ones, fall very close to the prototype. Other behaviors, such as those falling under "personal intelligences," are somewhat farther away from this prototype. Still other behaviors, such as those under "bodily kinesthetic intelligence," are simply outside the range of what is normally considered to be intelligence: athletic ability and dancing ability are certainly human talents; Gardner's view of them as falling under the rubric of intelligence appears to be idiosyncratic to him, at least for the time being.

One way of expressing my concern about the scope of Gardner's theory is as follows. Consider some of the attributes commonly viewed as integral parts of human intelligence, such as the ability to reason, the ability to learn, the ability to solve problems, and so on. Imagine an individual who was truly lacking in any one of these abilities—that is, had none of it at all. That individual would be utterly unable to function in the world. He or she would have to be institutionalized, and probably even institutionalization would not save the person, because even in institutions, there is at least a modest need to reason, learn, solve problems, and so on. Thus, each of these abilities seems to be a necessary but not sufficient condition for the adaptation of an individual to the world, without regard to the environment in which one lives. There exists no society or culture, for example, in which some degree of reasoning, learning, or problem solving is not required. Consider, in contrast, an attribute such as musical ability. Suppose an individual were tone-deaf, utterly unable to discriminate one musical tone from another. That person, unlike the one who could not reason or learn, would not have to be institutionalized and would not be at a stunning disadvantage in everyday life. In fact, most of the people around him or her would probably not even know that the person was tone deaf. Thus, this musical skill (as well as others) seems to be neither necessary nor sufficient for adaptation to the everyday world. Nor am I aware of any society or culture in which this ability is absolutely necessary, although such societies or cultures could, in principle, exist. The necessity test seems to be a good one in distinguishing between attributes of intelligence, on the one hand, and specialized talents, on the other, and, according to this test, what Gardner calls musical intelligence, as well as his other intelligences, would be classified as specialized talents rather than as "intelligences."

3. *The structure of a theory of intelligence.* Gardner's theory is not a psychological theory of intelligence in the usual sense. Other psychological theories of intelligence generally propose a set of interlocking constructs that together can explain, at some level, some domain of human performance. In the domain of intelligence, these constructs have included cell assemblies, factors, schemata, components, and productions, among others. One does not find in Gardner's book the requisite set of inter-

locking constructs, unless one is willing to accept the "intelligence" as an appropriate unit of analysis. The problem is that the unit that is supposed to do the explaining is identical to the phenomenon that is to be explained!

As a result of this structural oddity, Gardner's theory does not explain many of the phenomena one might expect a theory to explain. For example, although Gardner discusses information processing in intelligence, the development of intelligence, and the biology of intelligence, his theory gives no direct account of them. Consider, for example, one of Gardner's intelligences, linguistic intelligence. One might expect a theory of linguistic intelligence to specify some set of mental mechanisms or structures that accounts for, say, how children learn vocabulary, how people read, how people produce sentences, and so on. Gardner's chapter on linguistic intelligence does not explain any of these things. Instead, it consists of a set of mini-reviews of literature on topics relevant to language. The reviews, drawing on various kinds of evidence, are fascinating. But a well-organized literature review is not the same as a demonstration of support for a theory. If one were to seek to test Gardner's theory of linguistic intelligence, one would not know where to start, because there is no specifiable set of constructs to test. As a result, it is unclear what the boundaries, and even the core, of linguistic intelligence are. The same problem holds for all of the multiple intelligences.

Baron's Theory of Rationality and Intelligence. For many years, the study of decision making was separated from the study of intelligence. Baron's new theory seeks the laudable goal of integrating these two strains of theory and research. Given the obvious importance of decision making to intelligence in the real world, this contribution must be seen as a major one. Baron's basic argument is that intelligence can and should be understood in terms of rational decision making.

At the same time that I believe that Baron's goal is a laudable one, I have some reservations regarding the way in which he seeks to carry out his goal.

First, in an age in which other theorists of intelligence are seeking to expand our conception of the construct, Baron's attempt to narrow it is of some concern. For many years, psychologists and educators alike have been tied to narrow and sometimes counterproductive conceptions of intelligence as being no more than what the tests test. Recent developments have moved toward expanding our conception of intelligence. I am not certain, at this juncture, that a major contraction of this view toward only a very small aspect of what the intelligence tests measure—rational thinking—moves us forward, rather than backward.

Second, I have serious reservations regarding the view of intelligence as rationality. Consider some of the kinds of thinking that are usually considered to be intelligent:

1. Understanding ways in which two concepts are similar and different.
2. Having an insight for a scientific experiment.
3. Figuring out the meaning of an unknown word encountered in a newspaper article from the surrounding context.
4. Mentally manipulating an image of an abstract figure so as to see it from a new perspective.
5. Answering a difficult question fluently and correctly.
6. Considering a problem you have been trying to solve from a wholly different framework that finally makes the problem soluble.
7. Predicting what number should come next in a sequence of numbers.
8. Deciding how one should allocate one's priorities so as to maximize one's accomplishment for the day.
9. Realizing how one should structure a persuasive communication so as to render it maximally effective for one's audience.

Most, if not all, of the activities would seem critically to involve intelligence, but none of them seem greatly to involve rationality. Indeed, much intelligent thought, especially that within the inductive domain, simply seems to be outside the realm of rational thinking. And it is inductive thinking that has been found in study after study to be most central to general intelligence (Cronbach, 1990; Sternberg & Gardner, 1983). Thus, Baron seems to be excluding from the realm of intelligence many of those attributes that, at least traditionally, have been most central to intelligence. Even the domains of thinking that might on their face seem to be most deductive, such as mathematical reasoning, turn out to be largely intuitive. Although there are deductive elements in formulating a mathematical proof, the major difference between more and less accomplished mathematicians does not seem to be in their deductive or rational thinking at all but rather in their nonrational intuitive abilities.

Third, although incorporation of decision making into intelligence is an important step, Baron's conception of the decision-making literature in some sense seems like a throwback to earlier times, when decision making was less well understood. The thrust of recent decision-making literature (e.g., Nisbett & Ross, 1980; Tversky & Kahneman, 1974) has been toward a recognition of just how nonrational people are in their decision making. Even experts in a given field fail to solve problems within their field in the ways that rational thinking would predict. One could come to the conclusion that these experts simply aren't very intelligent, not to mention the even greater stupidity of the nonexperts. But we must be asking ourselves whether the goal of a theory of intelligence is to characterize thinking that no one does. There is certainly some value of normative models, but it should be clear that normative models sometimes characterize the thinking of nobody. Moreover, it is not at all clear that the optimal model of decision making, or of any other kind of reasoning, is always a wholly rational one. In many instances, rationality simply does not seem to be a relevant consideration. Most decisions in the everyday world are based upon incomplete information about ill-specified problems, and a rational analysis simply would not apply.

To conclude, Baron's new theory represents a novel contribution to the theory of intelligence, but it is not clear at this point that the novelty is of the kind that will most advance theory and measurement of intelligence.

Sternberg's Triarchic Theory of Intelligence. The triarchic theory of human intelligence comprises three parts (Sternberg, 1985, 1989). The first part relates intelligence to the internal world of the individual, specifying the mental mechanisms that lead to more and less intelligent behavior. This part specifies three kinds of information-processing components that are instrumental in (1) learning how to do things, (2) planning what things to do and how to do them, and (3) actually doing the things. This part of the theory thus resembles in many respects other current cognitive theories that emphasize the role of information processing in intelligence (e.g., Campione & Brown, 1979; Carroll, 1981; Hunt, 1980; Snow, 1979). The second part of the theory specifies those points along the continuum of one's experience with tasks or situations that most critically involve the use of intelligence. In particular, the account emphasizes the roles of novelty and automatization in intelligence. The third part of the theory relates intelligence to the external world of the individual, specifying three classes of acts—environmental adaptation, selection, and shaping—that characterize intelligent behavior in the everyday world. This part of the theory thus resembles contextual theories of intelligence that emphasize the role of environmental context in determining what constitutes intelligent behavior in a given milieu (see, e.g., Laboratory of Comparative Human Cognition, 1982). The three parts of the theory in combination provide a rather broad basis for characterizing the nature of intelligent behavior in the world, and for specifying the kinds of tasks that are more or less appropriate for the measurement of intelligence. A group test of intelligence based upon the triarchic theory is currently being constructed, and a training program for enhancing intellectual skills, also based on the theory, has recently been published (Sternberg, 1986).

It is always difficult to point out the limitations in one's own theory.

However, I do believe that there are some limitations to the theory as it presently stands. No doubt, others could point out further limitations.

First, the three parts or subtheories that in combination comprise this theory need to be better integrated. Although some speculations were provided as to how the three parts fit together, closer integration is necessary in order for them to constitute a wholly unified theory. Second, the theory needs to specify in much more detail forms of mental representation upon which the processes of intelligence act. Although the theory is quite specific about mental processes, it is rather vague about mental representations, and such representations play an important role in intelligent functioning.

Third, the roles of adaptation, selection, and shaping of environments need to be further articulated. These terms are rather vague, and although some progress has been made toward measuring adaptation (see, e.g., Wagner & Sternberg, 1985), absolutely nothing has been done in terms of operationalizing measures of environmental selection and shaping.

Finally, the role of automatization in intelligence needs to be further specified, and means of measuring it need to be developed. At present, cognitive psychologists just don't quite know how to measure the rate at which behavior is automatized and, without such measurements, the second part of the theory, mentioned above, will not lend itself to measurement as readily as one would like.

To conclude, the triarchic theory of human intelligence presents a new and broader theory of intelligence than has characterized many past attempts, but it, like other new theories of intelligence, needs further articulation and operationalization. The developing tests of intelligence based upon the theory will help provide some of the links that are needed to make theory-based measurement a reality.

Implications of Cognitive Theory for Psychometric Tests

The various theories of intelligence posed by cognitive psychologists have differential implications for psychometric testing of intelligence. However, it is possible to distill some general implications that cross-cut many of the theories, despite their differences. The main general implications seem to be the following:

1. *Intelligence tests should be based upon cognitive theory.* Whatever form the new generation of tests take, they will almost certainly be more theoretically based than the psychometric tests that preceded them. More-

over, these theories will be anchored in cognitive-processing conceptions of human intelligence. Without exception, all of the cognitive psychologists presently studying intelligence believe that the measurement of intelligence can be improved by tying it more closely to theory than has been the case in the past.

2. *The conception of intelligence upon which the tests are based should be broadened.* With the exception of Baron (1985), all of the cognitive theorists believe that our notion of intelligence should be expanded considerably beyond current psychometric conceptualizations. Theorists disagree as to the exact nature of this expansion. For example, Gardner (1983) includes abilities that in the past have been categorized as special talents, Hunt (1980) includes abilities that previously have been studied in investigations of basic and elementary information-processing skills, and Sternberg (1985) includes abilities that heretofore have been classified as social-competence skills. Thus, there is disagreement as to the exact form the expansion should take, but nearly unanimous agreement that some expansion is needed.

3. *Intelligence tests should be more closely linked to intellectual training.* Both Baron (1985) and Sternberg (1985, 1986) emphasize the need to link measurements of abilities not only to cognitive theory but also to training programs for enhancing abilities. On this point of view, tests are useful not because they provide an index of fixed ability, but because they indicate the starting point from which modification of abilities can take place. Cognitive theories often have clearer implications for intellectual-skills training than do psychometric theories (see Wagner & Sternberg, 1984). Intellectual-skills training in conjunction with intellectual-skills testing presents a viable option for future programs of measurement and instruction.

4. *Tests should provide diagnostic information regarding information-processing skills.* Although cognitive theorists may disagree as to the exact cognitive skills to be measured, they agree that tests should provide much more differential information than they currently provide (see, for example, Snow & Lohman, 1989). For most theorists, this differential information consists of mental-processing scores, although this is not true in every case (e.g., Gardner, 1983). The tests of the future may help us understand strengths and weaknesses in information processing that could not possibly be ascertained from the kinds of scores available for existing tests.

5. *Test scores should reflect a variety of dependent variables, not just numbers correct.* Conventional psychometric test scores are generally based upon number correct, or number correct after subtracting out some

proportion of errors. Cognitive theorists have been somewhat more catholic in the dependent variables they have considered a necessity for human performance. For example, reaction time has played an important part in some cognitive studies, and various kinds of ratings have played a role in other studies. Whatever the dependent variables of the future may be, they are likely to extend beyond mere measures of percentage of problems correctly solved. The scoring of tests in the future will probably provide a great deal more information than is currently provided by scoring just the number correct (see, for example, Embretson, 1985).

6. *Test scores should reflect qualitative as well as quantitative aspects of information processing.* In the past, test scores have yielded basically quantitative information, with this information expressed in a variety of forms. The emphasis in cognitive studies of intelligence has shifted much more to qualitative aspects of processing: strategies for problem solving, forms of mental representation, and the like. The test scores of the future should reflect this qualitative emphasis, as well as providing quantitative data of the kind used in the past.

7. *Tests should be constantly evolving as cognitive theory evolves.* Some years ago, the ex-president of the Educational Testing Service, Henry Chauncey, gave a talk at Yale, in which he noted that the content of the Scholastic Aptitude Test was roughly the same as at that time when the test was first invented. Chauncey took pride in this fact. This pride is understandable, because test constructors have indeed been able to pat themselves on the back for the great success their tests have had in predicting a variety of criterion behaviors. But I do not believe that the cognitively based tests of the future will be as static as the psychometrically based tests of the past. Cognitive theory is evolving very rapidly, and tests will have to change with it.

To conclude, cognitive theory has a great deal to offer psychometrics. Although there are differences among cognitive theorists there are certain core assumptions—such as the importance of understanding how people process and represent information—that transcend any particular theory. In basing the tests of the future on cognitive principles, we have the opportunity to measure human intelligence in a much more sophisticated and potentially instructive way than we have in the past. We have available to us a new body of theory that could be enormously fruitful in devising new kinds of intelligence tests, and I believe that the time has come to make use of this theory. Developments of the last decade or so in psychometric theory have also been impressive. But changing techniques of statistical analysis will not change the tests, and greater sophistication in both the tests and the ways in which they are analyzed are both necessary for the future progress of intelligence testing to be as auspicious as it possibly can be.

References

Anastasi, A. (1958). *Differential psychology: Individual and group differences in behavior*, 3rd ed. New York: Macmillan.

Atwood, M. E., & Polson, P. G. (1976). A process model for water jug problems. *Cognitive Psychology* 8:191–216.

Baron, J. (1985). *Rationality and intelligence.* New York: Cambridge University Press.

Belmont, J. M., & Butterfield, E. C. (1971). Learning strategies as determinants of memory deficiencies. *Cognitive Psychology* 2:411–420.

Belmont, J. M., Butterfield, E. C., & Ferretti, R. (1982). To secure transfer of training, instruct self-management skills. In D. K. Detterman & R. J. Sternberg (eds.), *How and how much can intelligence be increased?* Norwood, NJ: Ablex.

Binet, A., & Simon, T. (1973). *Classics in psychology, The development of intelligence in children.* New York: Arno Press.

Borkowski, J. G., & Wanschura, P. B. (1974). Mediational processes in the retarded. In N. R. Ellis (ed.), *International review of research in mental retardation*, Vol. 7. New York: Academic Press.

Brown, A. L. & Campione, J. (1977). Training strategy study time apportionment in educable retarded children. *Intelligence* 1:94–107.

Butterfield, E. C., & Belmont, J. M. (1977). Assessing and improving the executive cognitive functions of mentally retarded people. In I. Bialer & M. Sternlicht (eds.), *Psychological issues in mental retardation.* New York: Psychological Dimensions.

Campione, J. C., & Brown, A. L. (1979). Toward a theory of intelligence: Contributions from research with retarded children. In R. J. Sternberg & D. K. Detterman (eds.), *Human intelligence: Perspectives on its theory and measurement.* Norwood, NJ: Ablex.

Carroll, J. B. (1976). Psychometric tests as cognitive tasks: A new "structure of intellect." In L. B. Resnick (ed.), *The nature of intelligence.* Hillsdale, NJ: Erlbaum.

————. (1981). Ability and task difficulty in cognitive psychology. *Educational Researcher* 10:11–21.

Chase, W. G., & Simon, H. A. (1973). The mind's eye in chess. In W. G. Chase (ed.), *Visual information processing.* New York: Academic Press.

Chi, M. T. H., Feltovich, P., & Glaser, R. (1981). Categorization and representation of physics problems by experts and novices. *Cognitive Science* 5:121–152.

Chi, M. T. H., Glaser, R., & Rees, E. (1982). Expertise in problem solving. In R. J. Sternberg (ed.), *Advances in the psychology of human intelligence*, Vol. 1. Hillsdale, NJ: Erlbaum.

Chiesi, H. L., Spilich, G. J., & Voss, J. F. (1979). Acquisition of domain-related information in relation to high and low domain knowledge. *Journal of Verbal Learning and Verbal Behavior* 18:257–273.

Cohn, S. J. (1981). What is giftedness? A multidimensional approach. In A. H. Kramer (ed.), *Gifted children*. New York: Trillium Press.

Cronbach, L. J. (1957). The two disciplines of scientific psychology. *American Psychologist* 12:671–684.

—————. (1990). *Essentials of psychological testing*, 5th ed. New York: Harper & Row.

DeGroot, A. D. (1965). *Thought and choice in chess*. The Hague: Mouton.

Egan, D. E. (1976). *Accuracy and latency scores as measures of spatial information processing* (Research Report No. 1224). Pensacola, FL: Naval Aerospace Medical Research Laboratories.

Egan, D. E., & Greeno, J. G. (1973). Acquiring cognitive structure by discovery and rule learning. *Journal of Educational Psychology* 64:85–97.

Embretson, S. E. (ed.) (1985). *Test design: Developments in psychology and psychometrics*. New York: Academic Press.

—————. (1989). Latent trait models as an information-processing approach to testing. *International Journal of Educational Research* 13(2):189–203.

Feuerstein, R. (1979). *The dynamic assessment of retarded performers: The learning potential assessment device, theory, instruments and techniques*. Baltimore: University Park Press.

—————. (1980). *Instrumental enrichment: An intervention program for cognitive modifiability*. Baltimore: University Park Press.

Fodor, J. A. (1983). *The modularity of mind*. Cambridge, MA: MIT Press.

Frederiksen, J. R. (1980). Component skills in reading: Measurement of individual differences through chronometric analysis. In R. E. Snow, P. A. Federico, & W. E. Montagne (eds.), *Aptitude, learning, and instruction: Cognitive process analyses of aptitude*, Vol. 1. Hillsdale, NJ: Erlbaum.

Gardner, H. (1983). *Frames of mind: The theory of multiple intelligences*. New York: Basic Books.

Guilford, J. P. (1967). *The nature of human intelligence*. New York: McGraw-Hill.

—————. (1982). Cognitive psychology's ambiguities: Some suggested remedies. *Psychological Review* 89:48–59.

Guyote, M. J., & Sternberg, R. J. (1981). A transitive-chain theory of syllogistic reasoning. *Cognitive Psychology* 13:461–525.

Hogaboam, T. W., & Pellegrino, J. W. (1978). Hunting for individual differences: Verbal ability and semantic processing of pictures and words. *Memory and Cognition* 6:189–193.

Holzman, T. G., Glaser, R., & Pellegrino, J. W. (1976). Process training derived from a computer simulation theory. *Memory and Cognition* 1:349–356.

Hunt, E. B. (1978). Mechanics of verbal ability. *Psychological Review* 85:109–130.

—————. (1980). Intelligence as an information-processing concept. *British Journal of Psychology* 71:449–474.

Hunt, E. B., Frost, N., & Lunneborg, C. E. (1973). Individual differences in cognition: A new approach to intelligence. In G. Bower (ed.), *Advances in learning and motivation*, Vol. 7. New York: Academic Press.

Hunt, E. B., Lunneborg, C., & Lewis, J. (1975). What does it mean to be high verbal? *Cognitive Psychology* 7:194–227.

Jackson, M. D., & McClelland, J. L. (1979). Processing determinants of reading speed. *Journal of Experimental Psychology: General* 108:151–181.

Jensen, A. R. (1979). g: Outmoded theory or unconquered frontier? *Creative Science and Technology* 2:16–29.

———. (1982). Reaction time and psychometric g. In H. J. Eysenck (ed.), *A model for intelligence*. Berlin: Springer-Verlag.

Keating, D. P., & Bobbitt, B. L. (1978). Individual and developmental differences in cognitive processing components of mental ability. *Child Development* 49:155–167.

Laboratory of Comparative Human Cognition. (1982). Culture and intelligence. In R. J. Sternberg (ed.), *Handbook of human intelligence*. New York: Cambridge University Press.

Larkin, J., McDermott, J., Simon, D. P., & Simon, H. A. (1980a). Expert and novice performance in solving physics problems. *Science* 208:1335–1342.

———. (1980b). Models of competence in solving physics problems. *Cognitive Science* 4:317–345.

Linn, M. C. (1973). The role of intelligence in children's responses to instruction. *Psychology in the Schools* 10:67–75.

MacLeod, C. M., Hunt, E. B., & Mathews, N. N. (1978). Individual differences in the verification of sentence-picture relationships. *Journal of Verbal Learning and Verbal Behavior* 17:493–507.

Marland, S. P. (1971). *Education of the gifted and talented*, 2 vols. Washington, DC: U.S. Government Printing Office.

Matarazzo, J. D. (1972). *Wechsler's measurement and appraisal of adult intelligence*, 5th ed. Baltimore: Williams & Wilkins.

Mulholland, T., Pellegrino, J., & Glaser, R. (1980). Components of geometric analogy solution. *Cognitive Psychology* 12:252–284.

Neisser, U. (1979). The concept of intelligence. *Intelligence* 3:217–227.

Nisbett, R. E., & Ross, L. *Human inferences: Strategies and shortcomings in social judgment*. Englewood Cliffs, NJ: Prentice-Hall.

Pellegrino, J. W., & Glaser, R. (1979). Cognitive correlates and components in the analysis of individual differences. In R. J. Sternberg & D. K. Detterman (eds.), *Human intelligence: Perspectives on its theory and measurement*. Norwood, NJ: Ablex.

———. (1980). Components of inductive reasoning. In R. E. Snow, P. A. Federico, & W. Montague (eds.), *Aptitude, learning, and instruction: Cognitive process analyses of aptitude*, Vol. 1. Hillsdale, NJ: Erlbaum.

Piechowski, M. M. (1979). Developmental potential. In N. Colangelo & R. T. Zaffrann (eds.), *New voices in counseling the gifted*. Dubuque, IA: Kendall/Hunt.

Posner, M. I., & Mitchell, R. (1967). Chronometric analysis of classification. *Psychological Review* 74:392–409.

Reitman, J. S. (1976). Skilled perception in go: Deducing memory structures from inter-response times. *Cognitive Psychology* 8:336–356.

Rose, A. M. (1978). *An information processing approach to performance assessment* (NR 150–391 ONR Final Report). Washington, DC: American Institutes for Research.

Royer, F. L. (1971). Information processing of visual figures in the digit symbol substitution task. *Journal of Experimental Psychology* 87:335–342.

Schustack, M. W., & Sternberg, R. J. (1981). Evaluation of evidence in causal inference. *Journal of Experimental Psychology: General* 110:101–120.

Shepard, R. N., & Metzler, J. (1971). Mental rotation of three-dimensional objects. *Science* 171:701–703.

Simon, H. A., & Kotovsky, K. (1963). Human acquisition of concepts for sequential patterns. *Psychological Review* 70:534–546.

Snow, R. E. (1979). Theory and method for research on aptitude processes. In R. J. Sternberg & D. K. Detterman (eds.), *Human intelligence: Perspectives on its theory and measurement*. Norwood, NJ: Ablex.

Snow, R. E., & Lohman, D. F. (1989). Implications of cognitive psychology for educational measurement. In R. L. Linn (ed.), *Educational measurement*. New York: Macmillan, pp. 263–331.

Sternberg, R. J. (1977). *Intelligence, information processing, and analogical reasoning: The componential analysis of human abilities*. Hillsdale, NJ: Erlbaum.

————. (1989a). Representation and process in linear syllogistic reasoning. *Journal of Experimental Psychology: General* 109:119–159.

————. (1980b). Sketch of a componential subtheory of human intelligence. *Behavioral and Brain Sciences* 3:573–584.

————. (1981a). Intelligence and nonentrenchment. *Journal of Educational Psychology* 73:1–16.

————. (1981b). Nothing fails like success: The search for an intelligent paradigm for studying intelligence. *Journal of Educational Psychology* 73:142–155.

————. (1981c). Testing and cognitive psychology. *American Psychologist* 36:1181–1189.

————. (1985). *Beyond IQ: A triarchic theory of human intelligence*. New York: Cambridge University Press.

————. (1986). *Intelligence applied: Understanding and increasing your intellectual skills*. San Diego: Harcourt, Brace, Jovanovich.

————. (1989). *The triarchic mind: A new theory of human intelligence*. New York: Viking.

Sternberg, R. J., Conway, B. E., Ketron, J. L., & Bernstein, M. (1981). People's conceptions of intelligence. *Journal of Personality and Social Psychology* 41:37–55.

Sternberg, R. J., & Gardner, M. K. (1982). A componential interpretation of the general factor in human intelligence. In H. J. Eysenck (ed.), *A model for intelligence*. Berlin: Springer.

————. (1983). Unities in inductive reasoning. *Journal of Experimental Psychology: General* 112:80–116.

Sternberg, R. J., & Weil, E. M. (1980). An aptitude-strategy interaction in linear syllogistic reasoning. *Journal of Educational Psychology* 72:226–234.

Sternberg, S. (1969). Memory-scanning. Mental processes revealed by reaction-time experiments. *American Scientist* 4:431–457.

Thurstone, L. L. (1938). *Primary mental abilities*. Chicago: University of Chicago Press.

Tversky, A., & Kahneman, D. (1974). Judgment under uncertainty: Heuristics and biases. *Science* 185:1124–1131.

Vygotsky, L. S. (1978). *Mind in society: The development of higher psychological processes*. Cambridge, MA: Harvard University Press.

Wagner, R. K., & Sternberg, R. J. (1984). Alternative conceptions of intelligence and their implications for education. *Review of Educational Research* 54:197–224.

———. (1985). Practical intelligence in real-world pursuits: The role of tacit knowledge. *Journal of Personality and Social Psychology* 49:436–458.

Wechsler, D. (1958). *The measurement and appraisal of adult intelligence*, 4th ed. Baltimore: Williams & Wilkins.

14 THE EVOLUTION OF ETHICAL AND TECHNICAL STANDARDS FOR TESTING

Walter Haney
George Madaus

A high school newspaper carried a page one headline: "Meet the geniuses of the incoming class," and listed all pupils of IQ 120 and up with numerical scores. Then under a heading: "These are not geniuses, but good enough" were listed all the rest, with IQ scores down to the 60s.

*　　　*　　　*

A new battery of tests for reading readiness was introduced in a school. Instead of the customary two or three, 12 beginners were this year described by the test as not ready for reading. They were placed in a special group and given no reading instruction. The principal insisted that if the parents or anyone else tried to teach them to read "Their little minds would crack under the strain." In at least two cases parents did teach them to read with normal progress in the first semester, and later mental tests showed IQ's above 120 (APA, 1953).

Efforts to develop standards for tests and testing have a long history. As far back as 1895, a committee of the American Psychological Association (APA) was appointed to investigate the feasibility of standardizing the collection of mental and physical measurements. After the turn of the century, several different APA committees were set up with the goal of standardizing psychological tests and evaluating the relative merits of different kinds of assessment devices (Singleton, n.d.). Individual psychologists did prescribe specific standards for tests—for example, in 1924,

Truman Kelley wrote that a test needed a reliability of 0.94 to be useful in evaluating levels of individual accomplishment (Kelley, 1924)—but organized efforts to develop professional standards for tests bore little fruit until mid-century.

By that time, the growing popularity of psychological testing and incidents of test abuse such as those quoted above apparently prompted the APA to adopt a set of ethical principles concerning testing. Around the same time, the APA and other groups also developed technical recommendations regarding tests (APA, AERA, NCME, 1954). Sine then, the APA ethical principles have been regularly revised and the technical standards periodically updated.[1]

The purpose of this chapter is to identify the broad changes in these sorts of standards. The premise behind the chapter is that the history of past efforts to develop testing standards can inform future attempts to promote reasonable uses of tests. The chapter is organized into four sections. After this introduction, the second section traces the way tests and testing were treated in three major versions of the APA's *Ethical Standards of Psychologists*. The third section recounts the evolution of technical standards through three major versions. The fourth section summarizes the manner in which these two sets of standards—ethical and technical—evolved, and offers several suggestions about the issues which the two sets of standards do and do not treat.

Let us to consider first what is meant by the word *standard*. Apart from specialized usage, as in botany, economics, and music, the word has four general meanings that are pertinent to this chapter. Standard can mean a level of excellence or attainment regarded as a measure of adequacy. Standard can also refer to something established as a rule or basis of comparison in measuring quality or value; it may also mean a model or example commonly accepted or adhered to, that is a criterion set for usage or practice, as in moral standards. And, in an older meaning, a standard may be a figure or object used as an emblem or symbol of a person or a group of people. Which of these meanings is implied in the term *test standards* is not altogether clear. Professional standards for tests and test use seem, as we shall see, to encompass all of these different meanings, meanings with very different implications for how such standards might be viewed.

Ethical Principles of Psychologists

Arlene Kaplan Daniels (1973) has observed that psychologists "have expended considerable effort to describe and give advice about ethical problems to their members . . . " (pp. 45–46). The first formal code of ethics for psychologists was adopted by the APA in 1952. The latest version of ethical principles for psychologists was adopted by APA Council of Representatives in January 1981. In the intervening 29 years the code of ethics evolved through several versions, numerous amendments, and a title change in 1981 from *Ethical Standards of Psychologists* to *Ethical Principles of Psychologists*. Without tracing the details of this evolution, this section will compare the four major versions of the ethical code: the original 1953 standards (APA, 1953); the 1963 standards (APA, 1967); the 1977 standards (APA, 1977), and the most recent 1981 principles (APA, 1981). The analysis is limited mainly to those portions of the standards dealing directly with psychological testing.

1953 Ethical Standards

The original 1953 code of ethics of psychologists was presented in two volumes: one was a detailed statement "for use primarily by professional persons," and the other was a summary of the salient principles of the larger document. The detailed document was remarkably lengthy—around 170 pages, divided into six sections, each containing statements of general problem areas, examples of specific incidents involving ethical behavior, and specific principles relevant to each area.

One subsection of the 1953 *Standards* specifically concerned "publishing and using psychological tests and diagnostic aids." This subsection was divided into six problem areas all relating to "the sale and distribution of tests and diagnostic aids." No attempt was made "to cover the ethics or standards of test construction, or test application, although distinctions are at times difficult to make" (p. 143). The six problem areas of concern were: (1) the qualifications of test users (3 principles); (2) the role of the psychologist sponsoring test activities (4 principles); (3) the role and qualifications of test publishers' representatives (3 principles); (4) readiness of a test for release (1 principle); (5) the description of tests in manuals and publications (5 principles); and (6) safeguarding testing materials (2 principles).

Altogether, 18 out of more than 100 principles dealt specifically with testing. The first of these 18 principles, regarding the qualifications of test users, stated:

> Professional standards require that tests and diagnostic aids be released only to persons who can demonstrate that they have the knowledge and skill necessary for their effective use and interpretation.

Other principles regarding testing elaborated on the need for limiting the distribution of psychological tests. In short, the 1953 *Ethical Standards* gave considerable attention to the need for safeguarding psychological tests as "professional equipment," both to prevent misuse and to avoid their invalidation.

1963 Ethical Standards

By 1963, the ethical principles had shrunk in size. According to a later publication, "On the basis of accumulated experience, it became possible to distill from the original [1953] code, a set of more general principles" (APA, 1967, p. vii). The 1963 *Standards*, including amendments, consisted of 19 relatively general principles. Only three pertained directly to testing: specifically to test security, interpretation, and publication.

All three of these ethical principles pertaining to testing emphasized the need to control distribution of test information. The reasons for such control seemed much the same as in the previous decade. Such restrictions of test information to qualified professional users were necessary, went the apparent rationale, both to ensure proper use and to prevent invalidation of instruments due to uncontrolled dissemination.

1977 Ethical Standards

By 1977, the ethical principles had shrunk still further. Overall, the 19 principles in the 1963 *Ethical Standards* were reduced to nine principles in 1977. The three 1963 principles relating specifically to testing were merged in 1977 into a single principle concerning utilization of assessment techniques:

> In the development, publication, and utilization of psychological assessment techniques, psychologists observe relevant APA standards. Persons examined have the right to know the results, the interpretations made, and, where appropriate, the original data on which final judgements were based. Test users avoid imparting unnecessary information which would compromise test security, but they provide requested information that explains the basis for decisions that may adversely affect that person or that person's dependents.

In addition to this distillation of specific guidelines to fewer more general principles, another more qualitative change is apparent in the 1977 version of the *Ethical Standards*. Specifically, the 1977 *Standards* give much more attention to the rights of psychologists' clients, and specifically to the rights of persons tested, than did earlier versions of the *Ethical Standards*. Earlier versions gave stress mainly to the responsibilities of psychologists as scientists and professional persons. To this perspective, the 1977 *Standards* added emphasis concerning the rights of individuals served by psychologists. With respect to psychological testing, for example, consider the following statement concerning obsolete material:

> d. Psychologists accept responsibility for removing from clients' files test score information that has become obsolete, lest such information be misused or misconstrued to the disadvantage of the person tested.

> *Specific reference is made to the client, and the clause "to the disadvantage of the person tested" further focuses the concern for the client.*

This attention to consumers' rights led to an apparent contradiction. Concerning testing, the 1977 *Standards* states that "Persons examined have the right to know results, the interpretations made, and, where appropriate, the original data on which final judgments were made." In light of the very next sentence, the modifier "where appropriate" looms large and uncertain: "Test users avoid imparting unnecessary information which would comprise test security . . . ." An obvious question remains: When do the rights of test takers leave off and the need for test security begin?

1981 Ethical Principles of Psychologists

The 1981 revision of the *Ethical Standards of Psychologists* saw a name change to *Ethical Principles of Psychologists*. It contained "both substantive and grammatical changes in each of the nine ethical principles . . . plus a new tenth principle entitled Care and Use of Animals" (*Ethical Principles of Psychologists*, 1981, no page number).

Two things become apparent when the 1977 and 1981 versions are compared. First, the 1981 version re-introduces the user qualification issue: "Psychologists do not encourage or promote the use of psychological assessment techniques by inappropriately trained or otherwise unqualified persons through teaching, sponsorship, or supervision" (section f., p.8). What constitutes appropriate user qualifications is not spelled out. This lacuna has remained a serious problem for test publishers who wish to restrict sale of their products to "qualified" people.[2]

Second, the 1977 shift to the consumer seems to have been reversed. For example, the 1981 version drops reference to the clause which stipulates that, where appropriate, the test taker should be provided the original data on which final judgments were made. The section that deals with removal of obsolete materials is stated more generally in 1981 than was the case in 1977. Thus the word *client* was dropped when discussing removal of obsolete material along with the 1977 clause "lest such information be misused or misconstrued *to the disadvantage of the person tested*" (italics added). Together these changes in the ethical principles dealing with testing can be interpreted in one of two ways. First, the 1981 version is an attempt to make the principles more general and hence broader in their coverage. Alternatively, the 1981 version has been softened in favor of easier compliance by psychologists to the detriment of the rights and interests of the client.

In summary, the *Ethical Principles of Psychologists* seem to adhere most closely to the meaning of standard as a model or example commonly accepted or adhered to as a criterion for acceptable practice. Indeed, the 1967 publication of a *Casebook on Ethical Standards of Psychologists* suggests such an interpretation. The *Casebook* contains selected cases from 1959 to 1962 "illustrative of the principles involved in ethical problems" (APA, 1967, p. ix). In this respect, the materials in the *Casebook* are quite similar to the ethical incidents included in the original 1953 *Ethical Standards*. In addition, however, the 1967 *Casebook* also describes the application of ethical standards to these actual cases by the APA's Committee on Scientific and Professional Ethics and Conduct. In several instances, the conduct of individuals involved in these cases was judged to be unethical, and as a result they were dropped from membership in the APA.[3] So the *Ethical Principles* have indeed served, in at least some instances, as criteria for acceptable practice.

Nevertheless, there have been substantial changes in the ethical standards for psychologists over the last quarter-century. First, the sheer number of stated principles has dropped sharply. The original 1953 version of the standards listed more than 100 ethical principles. In the 1963 version, these were distilled to yield a set of 19 more general principles. The distillation went further in the 1977 and 1981 versions which contained just nine general principles to guide the ethical conduct of psychologists. The distillation process was evident in the number of ethical principles directly relevant to testing. The 1953 *Ethical Standards* listed 19 principles regarding testing. In the 1963 *Standards*, these were reduced to three principles, relating to test security, interpretation, and publication; the 1977 and 1981 versions contained a single general principle concerning utilization of assessment techniques. In large part the diminution in numbers of principles represented a distillation of specific principles into more general ones. For example, the 1953 document prescribed specific A, B, and C levels of tests which should be released only to people with specific sorts of training. The later versions simply stated without elaboration that tests should be released only to persons qualified to interpret them properly.

Technical Standards

In the last 30 years there have been five APA, AERA (American Educational Research Association), and NCME (National Council on Measurement in Education) committees that have formulated technical standards design to guide the development and use of tests. What follows is a description of how the technical standards evolved through each major revision.

1954 Recommendations

In the early 1950s the American Psychological Association produced the 1954 *Technical Recommendations for Psychological Tests and Diagnostic Techniques*. At the same time the American Educational Research Association and the National Council on Measurements Used in Education (the forerunner of the National Council on Measurement in Education) collaborated to produce the 1955 *Technical Recommendations for Achievment Tests*. This later document was published by the National Education Association (NEA).[4] Subsequent revisions up until the 1985 version followed the structure and format of the 1954 *Technical Recommendations for Psychological Tests and Diagnostic Techniques*. Consequently, we shall confine ourselves to a description of that document.

The 1954 *Technical Recommendations for Psychological Tests and Diagnostic Techniques* were based on the "essential principle" that "a test manual should carry information sufficient to enable any qualified user to make sound judgments regarding the usefulness and interpretations of the test" (p. 2). Altogether, the document contained more than 160 separate standards grouped into six categories:

A. dissemination of information (10 standards)
B. interpretation (18 standards)
C. validity (66 standards)
D. reliability (31 standards)
E. administration and scoring (10 standards)
F. scales and norms (29 standards).

Unlike the recent versions of the *Ethical Standards*, the technical recommendations were differentiated in two ways. First, there was a differentiation into major and subsidiary recommendations (with major ones printed in boldface type and labeled with whole numbers: for example, A3; and subsidiary standards printed in regular-face type and numbered in decimal form: for example, A3.1 and A3.11). Second, each recommendation was rated as *essential*, *very desirable*, or *desirable*. The explanation for the rating system and the description of each category went as follows:

> Manuals can never give all the information that might be desirable, because of economic limitations. At the same time, restricting this statement of recommendations to essential information might tend to discourage reporting of additional information. To avoid this, recommendations are grouped in three levels: ESSENTIAL, VERY DESIRABLE, and DESIRABLE . . . .
>
> The statements listed as ESSENTIAL are intended to be the consensus of present-day thinking as to what is normally required for operational uses of a test . . . .
>
> The category VERY DESIRABLE is used to draw attention to types of information which contribute greatly to the user's understanding of the test . . . .
>
> The category DESIRABLE includes information that would be helpful . . . (pp. 5–6).

With these distinctions, the committee seemed to be attempting to bridge two meanings of the term *standard*. Considering only *essential* recommendations, the recommendations seem to represent a statement of attainment in test development that could be regarded as a measure of adequacy. However, the recommendations taken more broadly, and including all three categories, seem to constitute a broader basis of comparison for measuring the quality of test development more generally.

Nevertheless, the authors of the 1953 recommendations seemed to have fairly flexible ideas regarding what it was they had produced. At various points it was suggested that the 1953 document was:

- a statement representing a consensus as to what information is most helpful to the test consumer (p. 1),
- a guide to test development and reporting (p. 60),
- a checklist of factors to consider in designing standardization and validation studies (p. 6),
- a reminder regarding features to be considered in choosing tests for a particular program (p. 7), and
- a statement to be used by individual members of the professions to improve their own work (p. 7).

Despite these varied purposes, the committee also pointed out some things that the document was not. The recommendations did not attempt to set out "minimal statistical specifications for tests" (p. 2). The commitee was careful to point out, too, that "the present recommendations apply to devices which are distributed for use as a basis for practical judgments rather than solely for research" (p. 4). The committee also opined:

> Almost any test can be useful for some functions and in some situations. But even the best test can have damaging consequences if used inappropriately. Therefore, ultimate responsibility for improvement of testing rests on the shoulders of test users (p. 7).

Given this sense of the locus of responsibility for testing practices, it was not surprising that the committee intended the recommendations to be used "without reference to any enforcement machinery" (p. 7).

1966 Standards

The preface to the 1966 *Standards* states that: "In view of the similarity in the nature of many (but not all) problems in educational and psychological measurement, the joint committee representing all of these organizations decided it was advantageous to issue one set of standards to cover both educational and psychological tests" (p. 1). In 1966, therefore, the APA, AERA, and NCME issued a revised version of the technical recommendations called *Standards for Educational and Psychological Tests*. In format and in length the 1966 *Standards* were very similar to the 1954 *Recommendations*. The 1966 version contained 160 separate standards, differentiated into major and subsidiary ones, with each rated as *essential*, *very desirable*, or *desirable*. Like the 1954 *Recommendations*, the 1966 standards were grouped into the same six sections as follows:

A. dissemination of information (12 standards)
B. interpretation (18 standards)
C. validity (60 standards)
D. reliability (34 standards)
E. administration and scoring (14 standards) and
F. scales and norms (22 standards).

The degree of change from 1954 to 1966 between corresponding sections varied markedly, however. The first two sections remained essentially the same, but the sections on validity and reliability were revised considerably.

The 1954 *Technical Recommendations* had defined four types of validity: content, predictive, concurrent, and construct validity corresponding to four distinct uses (p. 13). In 1966, the *Standards* listed just three aims of testing (p. 12), and correspondingly, only three types of validity: content, construct, and criterion related. Predictive validity and concurrent validity were treated in 1966 as alternative forms of the new category, criterion-related validity. The apparent reason for the change was that the two were regarded as conceptually the same; the only difference being the time at which the criterion data were gathered. If the data were collected at roughly the same time as the test was administered, the criterion data would provide an estimate of concurrent validity: if gathered at some future time, they would provide information about predictive validity.

Changes between 1954 and 1966 concerning test reliability were somewhat sharper. The 1954 document described reliability almost entirely in terms of correlation coefficients. The 1966 *Standards* continued to discuss reliability in terms of comparability of forms, internal consistency, and comparisons over time. In a sharp change, however, the 1966 document reported that the classification of "coefficients into several types (e.g., coefficient of equivalence) has been discarded. Such a terminological system breaks down as more adequate statistical analyses are applied and methods are more adequately described" (p. 26). Instead of defining reliability strictly in terms of correlation coefficients, the 1966 standards recommend that *"the estimation of clearly labeled components of error variance is the most informative outcome of a reliability study"* (p. 26; emphasis in the original). The derogation of the correlation coefficient as a measure of reliability reflected a rapprochement between the Pearsonian correlational approach to test theory and the Fisherian experimental design and analysis tradition of statistics (Stanley, 1971, pp. 371–372).

Compared to the treatment of validity and reliability issues, other sections of the 1966 *Standards* changed relatively little. The sections on *administration and scoring* and on *scales and norms* differed only slightly from the corresponding sections of the 1954 standards. Several principles were reworded and some were reorganized, but the gist of these two sections remained essentially the same.

However, the 1966 standards evidenced little effort to bridge a curious gap in the 1954 document: that is, the assertion on the one hand that the "ultimate responsibility for improvement of testing rests on the shoulders of test users" (p. 7), while on the other, the assertion that the *Technical Recommendations* were also "intended to guide test development and reporting" (p. 6). Scarcely a word of advice was offered directly to test users—on whose shoulders was placed the "ultimate responsibility" for improvement of testing. In the main, this discrepancy remained in the 1966 *Standards*. The closing lines of the introduction to the 1966 *Standards* reiterated a caveat from the 1954 document:

It is important to note that publication of superior information about tests by no means guarantees that tests will be used well. The continual improvement of courses which prepare test users and of leadership in all institutions using tests is a responsibility in which everyone must share (p. 6).

1974 Standards

By the early 1970s, "it had become apparent that problems and issues in testing, especially problems in selection for employment or for admission to educational institutions, had outdated the 1966 publication" (APA, AERA, NCME, 1974, p. 2). Consequently, a new joint committee of the three organizations was convened to revise the standards.

After three years of work, and numerous committee meetings, the revised standards were formally approved by the three organizations and were published in 1974. The new *Standards* were both a revision and an extension of the earlier version. In particular, the 1974 document attempted to bridge the gap between test manuals and test use. It was intended "to guide both test developers and test users" (p. 1).

Consequently, the 1974 technical standards had a substantially different format than earlier versions. The rating of standards as *essential, very desirable*, or *desirable* was maintained, but the domain of the 1974 standards was expanded considerably and organized into three major parts:

1. *Standards for Test Manuals and Reports*
   A. Dissemination of Information (16 standards)
   B. Aids of Interpretation (20 standards)
   C. Directions for Administration and Scoring (14 standards)
   D. Norms and Scales (28 standards)
2. *Standards for Reports of Research on Reliability and Validity*
   E. Validity (82 standards)
   F. Reliability and Measurement Error (26 standards)
3. *Standards for the use of Tests*
   G. Qualifications and Concerns of Users (9 standards)
   H. Choice or Development of Test or Method (9 standards)
   I. Administration and Scoring (16 standards)
   J. Interpretation of Scores (24 standards)

Altogether the 1974 *Standards* were expanded by more than 50 percent, from 160 in 1966 to more than 240 in 1974. Most of the new standards were found in the third section, *Standards for the Use of Tests*, but there were also substantial revisions in the topics covered in the 1966 *Standards*.

In section A could be found a new group of standards calling for inclusion in the test manual of a description of the development of the test. New standards were added to section B calling for the test manual to "describe clearly the psychological, educational, or other reasoning underlying the test and nature of the characteristic it is intended to measure" (B3, p. 15), and prescribing that "computer services for test interpretation should provide a manual reporting the rationale and evidence in support of computer based interpretations of scores" (B6, p. 7). Dropped from the standards dealing with qualifications for test administration and interpretation was any reference to level A, B, and C tests—the distinction drawn originally in the 1953 ethical standards, and referred to in both the 1954 *Recommendations* and the 1966 *Standards*.

The section on validity was revised considerably. The three categories of content-, construct-, and criterion-related validites remained. However, criterion-related validity was given far more prominence than the other two forms of validity. Indeed, in the 1974 *Standards*, more than 60 percent of the standards in the validity section dealt with criterion-related validity. This emphasis was due mainly to the concern over litigation involving the use of tests in personnel selection which motivated the 1974 revision in the first place. The predictive validity of a selection test in terms of job performance was, at that time, one of the major criteria by which the legal propriety of using a test in employment selection was judged (Lerner, 1978).

In expanding the treatment of criterion-related validity, several new standards were added, No doubt the most significant was a new essential standard concerning test bias:

> A test user should investigate the possibility of bias in tests or in test items. Wherever possible, there should be an investigation of possible differences in criterion-related validity for ethnic, sex, or other subsamples that can be identified when the test is given. The manual or research report should give the results for each subsample separately or report that no differences were found (E9, p. 43).

The addition of this standard concerning investigation of test bias was significant, but its placement in the section on criterion-related validity was peculiar. Concern over test bias would seem equally applicable to construct validity—especially in light of the long history of controversy over bias in tests of the construct of intelligence. It seems likely that the placement of the bias standard is explainable only in terms of the apparent preoccupation of the authors of the 1974 *Standards* with employment testing and litigation involving criterion-related validity.

In contrast to the treatment of validity issues, the section on reliability and measurement error was somewhat smaller in the 1974 *Standards* than the corresponding section of the 1966 *Standards*. The structure of the new section on reliability was, however, much the same as that of the earlier version. There was some shrinkage in the detailed standards and some rewording of the major standards, but it is easy to identify an exact correspondence between the six major (i.e., printed in bold-faced type) reliability standards in the 1974 standards and the 1966 reliability standards. Nevertheless, there does seem to be an important shift in the wording of the 1974 *Standards* on reliability. Specifically, this latest version of the standards gives the standard error as an index of reliability more prominence relative to reliability coefficients than did either the 1954 or the 1966 *Standards*.

One of the standards concerning users' interpretations of test scores, Standard J1, warrants a brief discussion:

> A test score should be interpreted as an estimate of performance under a given set of circumstances. It should not be interpreted as some absolute characteristic of the examinee or as something permanent and generalizable to all other circumstances. *Essential* (p. 68).

On its surface this standard seems to preclude the interpretation of test scores as indicators of innate intelligence or fixed ability. Since we have no casebook of interpretation of the 1974 *Standards* such as is available for the 1963 *Ethical Standards*, the only aid available in interpreting the meaning of the above principle is the subsidiary principle and comments appended to it:

> J1.1. A test user should consider the total context of testing in interpreting an obtained score before making any decisions (including the decision to accept the score). *Essential*.

> [Comment: The standard is that one must avoid the abdication of responsibility by relying exclusively on an obtained score. Users should, in particular, look for contaminating or irrelevant variables that may have influenced obtained scores: for example, in testing to classify school children, scores may be influenced by behavior problems, visual or hearing defects, language problems, and racial or cultural factors, as well as by ability.] (p. 68).

These elaborations seem to uphold the interpretation suggested above. Principle J1 of the 1974 *Standards* apparently proscribes the interpretation of a test score as a measure of fixed intelligence or ability unless specific consideration is given *at least* to the variables mentioned above "that may have influenced obtained test scores."

The new section of the 1974 *Standards* concerning use of tests was a clear step forward from the 1954 and 1966 *Standards*. For the first time, the *Standards* made a clear attempt to provide guidance to those upon whose shoulders had been placed the "primary responsibility for the improvement of testing" (p. 7). Nevertheless, a major problem remained concerning standards for test use. The implications of alternative uses of tests are not very clearly spelled out, and the main distinction drawn regarding differential application of standards on use seems somewhat out of touch with the realities of how tests are actually used to contribute to decision making. Although alternative uses of tests—in selection, prescription, and certification—are briefly discussed, the 1974 *Standards* do not clearly distinguish how, or even if, different standards might apply to these alternative uses.

The 1974 joint committee recognized that it had neglected standards dealing with the growing use of test results in program evaluation. However, given the pressure to publish the *Standards* to meet the employment litigation problem, the committee chose not to take the time needed to address the problem and instead recommended that this area be addressed by another committee. As a result, "the suggestion for a separate publication on guidelines for program evaluation was circulated to a number of persons having expertise in this area. It was decided that there was indeed a need for such a document and that an advisory group should be appointed to carry out the task" (Singleton, n.d., p. 11). A joint committee with members from 12 educational organizations chaired by Daniel Stufflebeam of Western Michigan University prepared and, in 1981, published through McGraw-Hill the *Standards for Evaluations of Educational Programs, Projects and Materials*.

This document evolved in such a way that testing per se became a minor concern. Instead the committee focused on all aspects of program evaluation and produced only two broad standards which dealt directly with test use in program evaluation. The first, D5 Valid Measurement, stated that:

> The information-gathering instruments and procedures should be chosen or developed and then implemented in ways that will assure that the interpretation arrived at is valid for the given use (p. 116).

The second, D6 Reliable Measurement, stated that:

> The information-gathering instruments and procedures should be chosen or developed and then implemented in ways that will assure that the information obtained is sufficiently reliable for the intended use (p. 120).

1985 Standards

By 1977 "it had become apparent that the 1974 publication was becoming outdated because of new problems and issues involving testing. Technical advances in testing and related fields, new and emerging uses of tests, and growing social concerns over the role of testing in achieving social goals indicated the need for a revision of the 1974 *Standards for Educational and Psychological Tests*" (p. v). A joint committee formed to review the 1974 *Standards* recommended that a revision be undertaken and that it adhere to the following 10 guidelines:

1. Address issues of test use in a variety of applications.
2. Be a statement of technical standards for sound professional practice and not a social action prescription.
3. Make it possible to determine the technical adequacy of a test, the appropriateness and propriety of specific applications, and the reasonableness of inferences based on the test results.
4. Require that the test developers, publishers, and users collect and make available sufficient information to enable a qualified reviewer to determine whether applicable standards were met.
5. Embody a strong ethical imperative, though it was understood that the *Standards* itself would not contain enforcement mechanisms.
6. Recognize that all standards will not be uniformly applicable across a wide range of instruments and uses.
7. Be presented at a level that would enable a wide range of people who work with tests or test results to use the *Standards*.
8. Not inhibit experimentation in the development, use, and interpretation of tests.
9. Reflect the current level of consensus of recognized experts.
10. Supersede the 1974 *Standards for Educational and Psychological Tests*.

In 1985, after four years of intensive work, the revised *Standards* were adopted by the three organizations. The number of standards dropped from more than 240 in 1974 to the 1985 level of 160. There was also a significant change in the title, to *Standards for Educational and Psychological Testing*. Anastasi, writing in *The Ninth Mental Measurements Yearbook*, observed that this simple change, from the word *Tests* to *Testing* in the title, was quite significant, reflecting "the broadened scope of the *Standards*; it calls attention to the process of test use in addition to the technical qualities of the tests themselves" (Anastasi, 1985, p. xxiv). The emphasis on test use was further highlighted by two additional modifications. First, the revised *Standards* make distinctions between test developers, test users, test takers, test reviewers, test administrators, and test sponsors. The last category, test sponsors, was included to cover state agencies that contract with a test developer for a specific instrument to implement a particular policy. The 1974 *Standards* had not included this category of user and, as a result, defendants argued in at least one trial, *Debra P. v. Turlington*[5] (a case involving the use of a competency test for high school graduation decisions), that many of the the 1974 *Standards*— particularly those dealing with reporting and manuals—did not apply to tests built by contractors for state agencies.

The second major modification of 1985 *Standards*, focusing on test use, involved its new four-part organization:

Part I: Technical Standards for Test Construction and Evaluation contains the following five chapters encompassing 82 standards:
1. Validity (25 standards);
2. Reliability (12 standards);
3. Test development and Revision (25 standards);
4. Scaling, Norming, Score Comparability, and Equating (9 standards);
5. Test Publication: Technical Manuals and Users' Guides (11 standards).

Part II: Professional Standards for Test Use, containing 62 standards, comprise the following seven chapters:
6. General Principles of Test Use (13 standards) includes a number of standards from the Test Use section of the 1974 *Standards*. The remaining six chapters of Part II focus on the following specific applications of tests:
7. Clinical Testing (6 standards);
8. Educational and Psychological Testing in the Schools (12 standards);
9. Test Use in Counseling (9 standards);
10. Employment Testing (9 standards);
11. Professional and Occupational Licensure and Certification (5 standards);
12. Program Evaluation (8 standards).[6]

Part III: Standards for Particular Applications consists of 15 standards in two chapters:
13. Testing for Linguistic Minorities (7 standards); and
14. Testing People with Handicapping Conditions (8 standards).

The final major division, Part IV: Standards for Administrative Procedures, contains two chapters with 21 standards:
15. Test Administration, Scoring, and Reporting (11 standards); and
16. Protecting the Rights of Test Takers (10 standards).

The technical standards in Parts I and II are relevant to the particular applications in Part III.

Another significant change in the 1985 *Standards* is the replacement of the classifications *essential*, *highly desirable*, and *desirable* with the categories *primary*, *secondary*, and *conditional*. The change was made in part to "avoid the troublesome distinction between *desirable* and *highly desirable* and to avoid the label *essential*" (p. 2). The principle behind the new categories was that the importance of a standard is a function of the potential impact or harm the test use has on individuals, institutions, and society. *Primary standards* "are those that should be met by all tests before their operational use, unless a sound professional reason is available to show why it is not necessary, or technically feasible, to do so in a particular case" (p. 2). Examination of common standards from 1977 to 1985 shows that the new *primary* category can be considered as equivalent to the old *essential* designation. However, the switch from the word *essential*, which conveys the sense that the standard is a requirement, to the word *primary*, which does not carry with it the sine qua non quality of *essential*, coupled with the inclusion of the escape clause, "unless a sound professional reason is available to show why it is not necessary, or technically feasible, to do so in a particular case," conspire to benefit the test publishers and contractors to the possible detriment of the test taker.

Secondary standards are "desirable as goals but are likely to be beyond reasonable expectations in many situations." The new *conditional* category is an attempt to factor in the degree of possible harm to individuals or institutions associated with particular applications. When considering whether a *conditional* standard should be considered *primary or secondary* "one should consider carefully the feasibility of meeting that standard in relation to the potential consequences to all parties involved in the testing process . . . . If the use of a test is likely to have serious consequences for test takers, especially if a large number of people may be affected, conditional standards assume increased importance" (p. 3). Thus, the *conditional* standard category was meant to cover test use in high-stakes situations such as certification or licensure, graduation or promotion decisions, or automatic assignment to remedial classes, etc., However, if the harm principle is evoked and a *conditional* standard takes on the *primary* designation, the escape clause appended to the primary designation could still be evoked by publishers, contractors, or sponsors to argue against the need to meet the standard before using the testing operationally.

In a recent analysis of the 1985 *Standards*, Della-Piana (1985) argues that the *primary-secondary* distinction lets the test developer off the hook of providing necessary validity information. Specifically, he argues that it need not be the responsibility of the developer/publisher to present evidence and argument to support test interpretation and use. Before discussing Della-Piana's analysis, and to set the stage for it, another very important revision incorporated in the 1985 *Standards* needs to be described. That is the 1985 *Standards'* treatment of validity.

In the 1974 *Standards*, validity was treated in the second section of the document, Standards for Reports of Research on Reliability and Validity. In 1985, validity stands alone—separated from reliability—as the first chapter of the document. The Validity chapter begins with the assertion that:

> Validity is the most important consideration in test evaluation. The concept refers to the appropriateness, meaningfulness, and usefulness of the specific inferences made from test scores. Test validation is the process of accumulating evidence to support such inferences (p. 9).

While the 1985 *Standards* strongly re-affirms the validity focus of the 1974 *Standards* on the appropriateness of inferences made from test scores, the 1985 joint committee went further when it argued that:

> A variety of inferences may be made from scores produced by a given test, and there are many ways of accumulating evidence to support any particular inference. *Validity, however, is a unitary concept* (p. 9; italics added).

The joint committee stopped short of asserting that the unitary concept referred to is that of construct validity; that is, that all validity questions in the final analysis involve the question of the construct validity. In the end the committee retained the traditional tri-partite categories of content-, construct-, and criterion-related validity. However, the 1985 *Standards* make clear that while these categories are convenient they

> ... [do] not imply that there are distinct types of validity or that a specific validation strategy is best for each specific inference or test use. Rigorous distinctions between the categories are not possible. Evidence identified usually with the criterion-related or content-related categories, for example, is relevant also to the construct-related category (p. 9).

Later the committee went on to discuss separately evidence related to each of the three major designations. Standards 1.1 through 1.5 are general standards related to validity; the next two standards deal with content-related validity; the next three, to construct-related validity evidence; there are 15 standards treating criterion-related validity; and one new standard deals with the use of cut-scores. Thus, the heavy emphasis on criterion-related validity found in the 1974 *Standards* is retained.

Given that validity always refers to the inferences or decisions made from test scores, let us now examine Della-Piana's argument that the present standards permit test developers or publishers to avoid providing evidence for key inferences about people or institutions made on the basis of their products. He cites as an example how test developers or publishers can avoid offering evidence to support inferences of what he feels is a contradiction between *primary* Standard 1.1 and *secondary* Standards 1.9 and 1.23. Standard 1.1 reads as follows:

> Evidence of validity should be presented for the major types of inferences for which the use of a test is recommended. A rationale should be provided to support the particular mix of evidence presented for the intended uses **Primary**.

Given its *primary* categorization, Standard 1.1 should be met by all tests before their operational use and in all tests uses, *unless a sound professional reason is available to show why it is not necessary or technically feasible to do so in a particular case.* The italized clause in the description of this *primary* standard might by itself let a test developer off the *primary* hook. However, when considered with *secondary* Standards 1.9 & 1.23—desirable but beyond reasonable expectation—Della-Piana argues that the developer is given a large, attractive loophole for not providing validity evidence for specific inferences intended to be made from test performance. For example, Standard 1.9 prescribes that:

> When a test is proposed as a measure of a construct, evidence should be presented to show that the score is more closely related to that construct when it is measured by different methods than it is to substantially different constructs. **Secondary** (p. 15).

Likewise, Standard 1.23 prescribes that:

> When a test is designed or used to classify people into specified alternative treatment groups (such as . . . educational programs) . . . evidence of the test's differential prediction for this purpose should be provided. **Secondary** (p. 18).

Thus two important types of inferences, one dealing with construct validity and the other with placement in treatment groups, fall under the secondary categorization. According to Della-Piana, this contradiction between a primary standard on the one hand and a secondary standard on the other gives test developers wide latitude to argue that certain inferences made from their instruments need not be backed up by validity evidence.

It is possible to argue that Della-Piana's analysis of the construct-related evidence is incomplete because it omits any consideration of Standard 1.8 which states:

> When a test is proposed as a measure of a construct, that construct should be distinguished from other constructs; the proposed interpretation of the test score should be explicitly stated; and construct-related evidence should be presented to support such inferences. In particular, evidence should be presented to show that a test does not depend heavily on extraneous constructs. **Primary** (p. 15).

Whether one agrees with Della-Piana's analysis or not, the important point is that the 1985 *Standards* will be interpreted and used by developers and users in ways that are most advantageous to their particular position. This is an especially troublesome problem when the *Standards* are used in litigation where lawyers and experts can, and most likely will, point to such contradictions within and between standards to argue that a client need not supply evidence for particular types of inferences either because it isn't feasible to gather such data, or because the standard is categorized as secondary. This Biblical-like, special-interest interpretability problem is further confounded by another area in which the committee left a point unclarified. That is, the harm criterion incorporated in the *conditional* category is not contained directly—though many would argue that it is inferred—in the discussion of the *primary* or *secondary* designations; this even though Standard 1.23 which is a *secondary* standard deals with placement in certain treatment groups which could have very serious consequences for test takers; in school testing situations such placement could affect relatively large numbers of students; witness the use of IQ tests for placement in special education programs.[7]

The interpretability problem associated with 1985 *Standards* is further compounded by the emphasis it places on the role of professional judgment in interpreting the individual standards, an emphasis not found in previous editions. The 1985 *Standards* state that the document "is intended to offer guidance for such judgments" (p. 2). It goes on to state that the purpose of publishing the *Standards* was to:

> . . . provide criteria for the evaluation of tests, testing practices, and the effects of test use. Although the evaluation of the appropriateness of a test or application should depend heavily on professional judgment, the *Standards* can provide a frame of reference to assure that relevant issues are addressed. The *Standards* does not attempt to assign precise responsibility for the satisfaction of individual standards. To do so would be difficult, especially since much more work in testing is done by contractual arrangement. However, all professional test developers, sponsors, publishers, and users should make reasonable efforts to observe the *Standards* and to encourage others to do so (p. 2).

Further, the *Standards* state that "evaluating acceptability involves the following: professional judgment that is based on a knowledge of behavioral science, psychometrics, and the professional field to which the tests apply . . ." (p. 2). Finally, 1985 *Standards* recognize that "in legal proceedings and elsewhere, professional judgment based on the accepted corpus of knowledge always plays an essential role in determining the relevance of particular standards in particular situations" (p. 2).

Now it is hard to argue that professional judgment should not play the predominant role in the interpretation of whether individual standards have been met. However, the recognition that "the use of the standards in litigation is inevitable" and the admission that there is no external enforcement mechanism to assure compliance, or to mediate differences in interpretation which arise between experts in the adversarial area of the courts, raises issues about the utility of the standards in resolving controversial uses of tests in high-stakes situations. The Della-Piana example certainly raises such issues. However, a recent court case, perhaps one of the first involving the use of the 1985 *Standards*, offers a more concrete example of how professional judgment becomes operationalized in the court room. *Allen et al.* v. *Alabama State Board of Education et al.* was a case heard in Federal court for the Middle District of Alabama involving the use of a series of customized tests built by a contractor for the State Department to be used for initial teacher certification.

Experts on both sides were cognizant of the introduction to chapter 1, *Validity*, in which validity was described as a unitary concept, the most important consideration in test evaluation. They were also aware of the assertion that validity "lies in the appropriateness, meaningfulness, and usefulness of specific inferences" (p. 9). Furthermore, both sides knew that the *Standards* held that the "inferences regarding specific uses of a test are validated, not the test itself" (p. 9). Standard 1.1 should have made this last point very explicit for both sides by prescribing that:

> Evidence of validity should be presented for the major types of inferences for which the use of a test is recommended. A rationale should be provided to support the particular mix of evidence presented for the intended uses. **Primary**.

With this common background in mind, plaintiffs' experts argued that the inference being made from the scores on the Alabama Initial Teacher Certification Tests (AITCT) was that if a person failed the test he/she did not have the minimal competencies, skills, or knowledge to be a minimally successful teacher; if one passed, the converse was true. Since embodied in the certification decision were explicit and implicit construct-related inferences about competence as well as criterion-related inferences about possible future success on the job, plaintiffs' experts argued that construct-related, criterion-related, and content-related evidence were needed to support the inferences.

On the other hand, defendants used the 1985 *Standards* to argue that, in their professional judgment, the only type of validity evidence necessary to support the test use was content-related. Defendants pointed to two passages from the *Standards* to support their claim. First was the statement in the introduction to chapter 11, *Professional and Occupational Licensure and Certification*, which states that:

> Investigations of criterion-related validity are more problematic in the context of licensure or certification than in many employment settings. Not all those certified or licensed are necessarily hired; those hired are likely to be in a variety of job assignments with many different employers.... These factors often make traditional studies that gather criterion-related evidence of validity infeasible (p. 63).

This was coupled with the statement from chapter 1 that, while an ideal validation includes several types of evidence spanning construct-related, criterion-related and content-related evidence:

> ...the quality of the evidence is of primary importance, and a single line of solid evidence is preferable to numerous lines of evidence of questionable quality. Professional judgment should guide the decisions regarding the forms of evidence that are most necessary and feasible in the light of intended uses of the test and any likely alternatives to testing (p. 9).

Based on these two statements, defendants' experts concluded that a solid line of content evidence was sufficient to establish validity. They argued that this was especially true given that the alternative to the test was no test at all which, they argued, would allow incompetents to teach.

One other example from the Allen case is illuminating. We saw above that the 1974 *Standards* were very explicit on the need for empirical studies of test bias. However, the 1985 *Standards* modify the treatment of bias. Two standards, 3.10 which deals with item bias and 1.20 dealing with predictive bias, are included in the 1985 *Standards*. Standard 3.10 states:

> When previous research indicates the need for studies of item or test performance differences for a particular kind of test for members of age, ethnic, cultural, and gender groups in the population of test takers, such studies should be conducted as soon as feasible. Such research should be designed to detect and eliminate aspects of test design, content, or format that might bias test scores for particular groups. **Conditional**.

Professional judgment was once again split on the interpretation of this seemingly straightforward standard. Plaintiffs argued that Standard 3.10 called for empirical bias studies. No such studies were carried out. Defendants argued that the standard had been meet when the contractor asked teachers as part of the content validation procedure to identify any objective or item which they felt was biased or offensive.

The point is not to re-argue the Allen case but to raise the more important issue of how professional judgment operates vis-a-vis the *Standards* in an adversarial hearing when there is no mechanism in place that could mediate diametrically opposed differences in interpretation. It certainly must appear confusing to lay people. But this charge is hardly unique to the 1985 *Standards*.

This raises still another issue regarding the evolution of the 1985 *Standards* through its various drafts. The process is political. Strong vested interest groups within APA demanded changes that favored their constituents at the expense of the test taker. These groups within APA were strong and unified enough to threaten that, if such modifications were not made, the *Standards* would not get through the ratification process in APA Council. There was no countervailing force from consumer groups or test takers. Thus the *Standards*, already modified in favor of the test developer and user, are further stacked in their favor by the professional judgment admonition contained in the introduction. The profession has yet to come to grips with how the *Standards* can work fairly and equitably for developer, user, and test taker without an enforcement mechanism, or a mechanism other than the courts, that could mediate differences in professional judgment.

Conclusions

This brief review of the evolution of ethical and technical standards for testing has identified several broad changes in standards over the past 35 years and has suggested specific issues that seem to need more attention.

The most apparent change in the two sets of standards over the last quarter-century is that while ethical standards directly relevant to testing have diminished in number, the technical standards have multiplied. One might interpret this discrepancy as evidence of the technocratic tendencies of professionals. After all, the very identity of professionals is probably based more on their possession of special knowledge and skills than on their possession of special ethics—although both are important in the ethos of professionalism. Also, however, the inverse relationship likely stems from a real difference between techniques and ethics. Techniques by their very nature are more precise and amenable to specific description, while ethics are more likely to be situation-bound and so best stated in more general terms. Authors of the later *Ethical Standards* may also, of course, have felt free to skip over certain specific testing issues because of the availability of technical standards.

Professional Standards and Public Practice

A major open question behind all of the foregoing discussion concerns the relationship between professional test standards and public practice. There are at least two dimensions to this relationship—the match between the standards and the test publishers/developers, and the connection between the standards and test use. On both counts, the connections seem uncertain.

What is the relationship between test standards and test publishers' practices? In a review of the 1966 *Standards for Educational and Psychological Tests*, an official of the Educational Testing Service (ETS) predicted that by the time his review appeared in print, "the major developers of tests will know the recommendations by heart and will be planning to include in future instruments those elements or standards which they have not already built into their publications" (Dobbins, 1966, pp. 752–753). Dobbins' prediction has been somewhat less than fully borne out, particularly with regard to the smaller test contracting companies that grew up in the 1970s to answer the needs of states for statewide graduation, promotion, and certification tests.

However, there is no doubt that some of the larger test publishers give serious attention to test standards. In their study of the testing industry, for example, Holmen and Doctor (1972) observed that

> [The six largest] testing organizations provide models of comprehensive and technical service which represent very high standards of professional practice within the industry . . . . With few exceptions, and most of these highly debatable, the [medium-sized testing] companies do a good job of meeting the requirements of the *Test Standards Manual* (pp. 42–43, 51).

The late Oscar Buros (1974) also observed that

> There can be no question but that the *Technical Recommendations* and *Standards* have been effective in complementing the *Mental Measurements Yearbooks* in the drive for more honest and informative test manuals. Test manuals—as inadequate as most of them still are—would certainly have been even poorer had it not been for the *Technical Recommendations*, *Standards*, and the *Mental Measurements Yearbooks* (p. 757).

Perhaps the clearest example of how seriously the major publishers regard the *Standards* is the *ETS Standards for Quality and Fairness*. These internal *Standards* adopted by the ETS Trustees "reflect and adopt the Standards for Educational and Psychological Testing" (p. vii).[8] "Adherence to the Standards is regularly assessed through a carefully structured audit process and subsequent management review" (p. iii). This compliance is monitored by a "Visiting Committee of persons outside ETS that is comprised of distinguished educational leaders, experts in testing and representatives of organizations that have been critical of ETS in the past" (p. iii).

Despite this example from the major publishers, Buros nevertheless raised the problem of nonadherence to the technical standards, and exclaimed:

> The nonobservance of the APA-AERA-NCME and MMY Standards by test authors, publishers, and users is shocking. When will test users make it unprofitable for publishers to market tests without reporting even the barest essentials of the data which were considered minimal forty-nine years ago? (Buros, 1974, p. 757).

Evidence of the weak impact of the earlier versions of the test standards comes from a 1976 survey by the APA Committee on Psychological Tests and Assessments. The survey of the content of a number of major publishers' test manuals "revealed that few manuals include all the information indicated as essential in the test standards [1974]" (Singleton, n.d., p. 12). Also in 1977, Oles and Davis (1977) reported that test publishers generally seem to violate APA standards regarding test distribution.

The apparently small impact of the *Standards* on test publishers' practices may in part be a product of ambiguity in the *Standards* themselves. To what extent do they represent levels of attainment regarded as measures of *adequacy* and to what extent do they represent standards of *excellence*? Generally the *Standards* seem to have opted for the latter with the result that test publishers have criticized them as somewhat unrealistic, overly demanding, and impossible to meet without unwarranted investment (Holmen & Doctor, 1972, p. 49).

Another explanation is the ambiguous status of test companies. On one hand, they are part of the profession, presumably with allegiance to professional standards. On the other hand, however, they are commercial institutions guided by a very different set of standards. Writing in 1960, as to why the APA principle on test publication and advertisement "is violated more flagrantly than any other in our codes of ethics," Wayne Holzman observed, "The enthusiastic author and obliging publisher cannot resist the temptation to *sell* the test as the latest word, the answer to eager personnel executives' problems" (Holtzman, 1960, p. 249; emphasis added). This ambiguous status was at the root of a 1967 case involving the Federal Trade Commission (FTC). At that time it was common practice for a number of large test companies to exchange information concerning the qualifications of individuals who might want to purchase tests. Such an exchange made it easier for publishers to adhere to standards in distribution of tests (spelled out, as noted above, in both ethical and technical standards). Such practices led to a complaint to the FTC, which subsequently charged four major test companies with restraint of trade. The case was resolved when the companies agreed to a consent decree to cease and desist from practices charged (Holmen & Doctor, 1972, pp. 129–130). In other words, publishers' cooperation to implement professional standards ran afoul of standards concerning business practices. "Persons in the testing industry feel that, as a result of this complaint and the consent decree which followed it, tests were made available to persons not necessarily qualified to use them" (Holmen & Doctor, 1972, p. 130). Presently, a working committee of the new joint APA-AERA-NCME Committee on Testing Practices is addressing this issue. The hope is that the professional organizations can offer guidelines that the commercial firms can adapt for use in deciding on test user eligibility.

This other end of the standards—practice connection, namely, the link between the test standards and test use—also seems slight. The weakness of this connection has long been noted. For example, in a review of the 1966 *Standards*, Roger Lennon (1966) wrote:

> There is little evidence to lead the reviewer to believe that many test users are now influenced in their selection of tests by the extent to which their manuals conform to the (1954) Technical Recommendation. Neither does there appear to be convincing evidence of correlation between improvement in test manuals and improvements in test use . . . . [W]hat is called for is much better dissemination of the Standards, and better training of test users in the application of the information which, thanks to the Standards, is increasingly available in test manuals (p. 755).

Only gradually is Lennon's recommendation beginning to be realized. NCME published and distributed a "translation" of the 1974 *Standards* (Brown, 1980). Furthermore, in 1985 a new joint APA-AERA-NCME Committee on Testing Practices had a subcommittee at work developing a *Code of Fair Testing in Education* that would describes what test takers and other consumers can expect from test publishers and developers. The Code was completed and published in the fall of 1988 (Fremer, Diamond, & Camara, 1989).

Nevertheless, Harold Orlans has observed the APA "has been the only major social science association which has taken effective steps to see that members observe ethical standards" (p. 80). Indeed, the 1967 casebook on the 1963 *Ethical Standards* (APA, 1967) records 11 cases in which the APA's committee on Scientific and Professional Ethics and Conduct (CSPEC) took action to adjudicate apparent violations of the three 1963 ethical standards concerning testing. The following is an account of one of those cases:

> A member of APA devised a test which was found by competent psychologists to be unreliable and invalid for the purposes for which claims were made. Responsible test publishers refused to publish or distribute the test, but the author had it printed privately and promoted its sale. He continued to do so after repeated advice and warning to desist, until finally he was dropped from membership by both the state association and APA.
>
> Opinion. In evaluating tests, writings, or other professional productions of psychologists, care must be used to distinguish between a difference in point of view and failure to meet ethical standards. When however, a number of competent peers conclude that the evidence indicates a test to be worthless, then commercial promotion of the test becomes unethical (APA, 1967, p. 58).

This example clearly indicated the limitations of this sort of professional review approach to the enforcement of testing standards. While the individual violating the standards was banished from the APA, there is no indication that the "unreliable and invalid" test was removed from the market.

In the past there have been several proposals for more stringent enforcement of testing standards. In 1950, an APA committee on test standards was charged with studying "the feasibility of and methods of implementing, A Bureau of Test Standards and a Seal of Approval to apply and enforce test standards, but took no action on these matters because of complex problems they presented" (Singleton, n.d., p. 3). In 1975, a federally sponsored project on the Classification of Exceptional Children made a proposal along similar lines:

> Because psychological tests of many kinds saturate our society and because their use can result in the irreversible deprivation of opportunity to many children, especially those already burdened by poverty and prejudice, we recommend that there be established a National Bureau of Standards for Psychological Tests and Testing [responsible to the Secretary of Health, Education, and Welfare] (Hobbs, 1975, p. 237).

This proposal for federal intervention to curtail "poor tests and testing [which] may be injurious to opportunity as impure food or drugs are injurious to health" (Hobbs, 1975, p. 238), apparently met with little enthusiasm. More recently Madaus (1985), in his presidential address to NCME, called for an independent mechanism to audit the work of test publishers and test developers, particularly with regard to the use of high-stakes tests used in educational policy. He called for:

... the establishment of an independent auditing agency that would, without vested interest, evaluate tests and testing programs that profoundly affect the lives of examinees (p. 10).

As with previous calls for some independent monitoring agency, this latest proposal also has not been implemented, although it appears that some progress will be made along these lines in the next year or two.

So we are left in a curious situation. Much effort has gone into the development of professional standards concerning testing over a period of 35 years. But there is much evidence that the test standards have limited direct impact on test publishers' practices and even less on test use. The principal exception to this statement is the reliance in the courts on the *Standards*. However, as we noted above, that adversarial setting offers judges and juries confusing interpretations of seemingly straightforward standards by opposing experts. Despite this apparent gap between standards and practice, there seems to be little professional enthusiasm for concrete proposals to enforce standards on educational and psychological testing.

This raises the question of whether professional testing standards serve functions other than improving practice. Professionals seem reluctant to set up regular enforcement mechanisms for the enforcement of their standards in part because the notion of self-governance and professional judgment is part of the self-image of professionals. As Arlene Kaplan Daniels has observed, professional "codes do not simply fulfill the function suggested by the professional ideology. Rather, they are part of the ideology, designed for public relations and justification for the status and prestige which professions assume vis-a-vis more lowly occupations" (Daniels, 1973, p. 49).

This interpretation brings us back to the older meaning of the term *standard*. Standard refers not just to criteria or measures of adequacy or excellence but also to emblems or symbols of persons or groups. In this meaning, professional standards have less to do with bettering professionals' practices than with burnishing professionals' public standing.

The public standing of professional groups increasingly seems in need of such support nowadays. Criticisms of professional groups' roles in American society are fairly widespread (Bledstein, 1977; Larson, 1977), and the public seems more and more skeptical of the idea of professional self-governance in general. The apparent gap between testing standards and actual testing practices would seem to provide fuel for that skepticism. Whatever the public image of the testing profession, those who take seriously the idea of reforming testing practice with any sort of testing standards need at the outset to take a serious look at the connection between standards and public practice.

Notes

1. There are two other sets of professional standards that also deal with testing, namely the Ethical Standards of the American Personnel and Guidance Association (APGA). One of six sections in these standards deals with testing. The Equal Employment Opportunity Commission Guidelines are another widely used set of technical standards dealing with testing. In this chapter we shall confine ourselves to the APA Ethical Standards and to the Joint APA-AERA-NCME Technical Standards.

2. A newly formed AERA-APA-NCME Joint Committee on Testing Practices is currently addressing this issue; a working group on Test User's Qualifications is attempting to formulate a model voluntary system that could be used by test publishers to develop individualized qualification systems for their potential customers.

3. At this writing, the *Casebook* is under revision.

4. Interestingly, the publication of the 1955 *Technical Recommendations for Achievement Tests* was the NEA's only formal, direct link to the joint committees that developed the test standards. Subsequent revisions were published by the APA on behalf of the three professional organizations which represented the testing community—AERA, APA, and NCME. While NEA, along with numerous other organizations, was invited to react to drafts of standards, NEA sought a membership on the Joint Committee. The joint committee refused the request. There are several probable reasons for NEA's exclusion from the various joint committees. First, the effort was seen by the three organizations as one aimed at developing technical standards, and therefore this fell into the exclusive domain of the testing community. Second, in the 1970s the NEA's call for a moratorium on testing was viewed as anti-testing by the pyschometric community. The third reason was pragmatic; if the NEA was given membership on the Joint Committee then other groups representing users or those affected by testing would also have legitimate claims to membership on the joint committee. If this were to happen, where would one draw the line and still keep the committee's size reasonable? However, this exclusion of a group partially representing perhaps the largest single group of test users in education is interesting in light of the subsequent admonishments by the 1966 and 1974 joint committees that the "ultimate responsibility for improvement of testing rests on the shoulders of the tests users" (1966, p. 7).

5. 474 F. Supp. 244 (M.D. Fla. 1979), *affd, in part, revd, in part*, 644 F.2d 397 (5th Cir. 1981), *petition for rehg, and petition for rehg, en banc denied*, 644 F.2d 397 (5th Cir. Sept. 4, 1981).

6. Chapter 12 was added because the committee did not feel that the *Standards for Evaluations of Educational Programs, Projects and Materials* adequately covered the issue of test use in program evaluation first identified as problematic by the 1974 joint committee.

7. A now famous court case, *Larry P. v. Riles*, was fought over the issue of using IQ tests for placement in special education programs. See 495 F. Supp. 926 (N.D. Cal. 1979).

8. At this writing a revision is close to finished, which brings the ETS *Standards* into line with the 1985 *Standards*.

References

AERA, APA, & NCME. (1985). *Standards for educational and psychological testing*. Washington, DC: APA.

APA (American Psychological Association). (1953). *Ethical standards of psychologists*. Washington, DC: APA.

——————. (1959). Ethical standards of psychologists. (1959). *American Psycho-*

logist 14:279–282.

—————. (1967). *Casebook on ethical standards of psychologists.* Washington, DC: APA.

—————. (1977). *Ethical standards of psychologists.* Washington, DC: APA.

—————. (1981). Ethical principles of psychologists. *American Psychologist* 36:633–638.

—————. (1981). *Ethical principles of psychologists* (1981 Revisions). Washington, DC: APA.

APA, AERA, & NCMUE (National Council on Measurements Used in Education). (1954). *Technical recommendations for psychological tests and diagnostic techniques* (Reprinted in Buros, 1972). Washington, DC: APA.

—————. (1955). *Standards for educational and psychological tests and manuals* (Reprinted in Buros, 1972). Washington, DC: National Education Association.

—————. (1974). *Standards for educational and psychological tests* (Reprinted in Buros, 1974). Washington, DC: APA.

APGA (American Personnel and Guidance Association). (1961). Ethical standards. *Personnel and Guidance Journal* 40(2):206–209.

—————. (1965). *Ethical standards casebook.* Washington, DC: APGA.

—————. (1972). *Ethical standards.* Washington, DC: APGA.

—————. (1976). *Ethical standards casebook*, 2nd ed. Washington, DC: APGA.

Bledstein, B. (1976). *The culture of professionalism.* New York: Norton.

Brown, F. G. (1980). *Guidelines for test use: A commentary on the standards for educational and psychological tests.* Washington, DC: National Council on Measurement in Education.

Buros, O. K. (1961). *Tests in print.* Highland Park, NJ: Gryphon.

—————. (1972). *Personality tests and reviews.* Highland Park, NJ: Gryphon.

—————. (1974). *Tests in print II.* Highland Park, NJ: Gryphon.

Clapp, J. (1974). *Professional ethics and insignia.* Metuchen, NJ: Scarecrow Press.

Cohen, D. K., & Garet, M. S. (1975). Reforming educational policy and applied research. *Harvard Educational Review* 45:17–43.

Cronbach, L. J., Gleser, G. C., Nanda, H., & Rajaratnam, N. (1972). *The dependability of behavioral measurements.* New York: Wiley.

Daniels, A. K. (1973). How free should professionals be? In E. Freidson (ed.), *The professions and their prospects.* Beverly Hills, CA: Sage, pp. 39–57.

Della-Piana, G. M. (1986). The 1985 test standards: Where do they leave the teacher-as-test-user? Unpublished paper, University of Utah.

Dobbins, J. E. (1966). The professional service representative of a test publisher [Review of 1966 Standards for Educational and Psychological Tests and Manuals]. *Educational and Psychological measurement* 26:751–753.

ETS (Educational Testing Service). (1971). *Handbook for STEP Series II.* Princeton, NJ: ETS.

—————. (1986). *ETS standards for quality and fairness.* Princeton, NJ: ETS.

Fremer, J., Diamond, E. E., & Camara, W. J. (1989). Developing a code of fair testing practices in education. *American Psychologist*, 44:1062–1067.

Goldstein, H., et al. (1975). Schools. In N. Hobbs (ed.), *Issues in the classification of children*, Vol. II. San Francisco: Jossey-Bass, pp. 4–61.

Hobbs, N. (ed.). (1975). *The futures of children: Report of the project on classification of exceptional children*. San Francisco: Jossey-Bass.

Holmen, M. G. (1978, September). Personal communication to Walter Haney of the Huron Institute.

Holmen, M. G., & Doctor, R. (1972). *Educational psychological testing: A study of the industry and its practices*. New York: Sage.

Holtzman, W. (1960). Some problems of defining ethical behavior. *American Psychologist* 15:247–250.

Joint Committee on Standards for Educational Evaluation. (1981). *Standards for evaluations of educational programs, projects and materials*. New York: McGraw-Hill Book Co.

Kelley, T. (1924). *Statistical method*. New York: MacMillan.

Larson, M. S. (1977). *The rise of professionalism: A sociological analysis*. Berkeley, CA: University of California Press.

Lennon, R. (1966). A measurement specialist and executive of a large test publishing firm [Review of 1966 Standards for Educational and Psychological Tests and Manuals]. *Educational and Psychological Measurement* 26:753–756.

Lerner, B. (1978, May 15). *The Supreme Court and the APA, AERA, NCME test standards: Past references and future possibilities*. Paper presented at a conference of the National Consortium, Washington, DC.

Madaus, G. (1985). Public policy and the testing profession—You've never had it so good? *Educational Measurement: Issues and Practice* 4:5–11.

Mitchell, J. V. Jr. (ed.). (1985) *The ninth mental measurements yearbook*. Lincoln, NE: University of Nebraska Press.

Oles, H. J., & Davis, G. D. (1977). Publishers violate APA standards on test distribution. *Psychological Reports* 41:713–714.

Orlans, H. (1973). *Contracting for knowledge*. San Francisco: Jossey-Bass.

Singleton, M. C. (n.d.). Historical survey of issues considered by the committee on psychological tests and assessment: 1895–1976. Unpublished paper, APA.

Stanley, J. C. (1971). Reliability. In R. L. Thorndike (ed.), *Educational measurement*, 2nd ed. Washington, DC: American Council on Education, pp. 356–442.

CHAPTER ABSTRACTS

1 Advances in Criterion-Referenced Measurement
Ronald K. Hambleton and H. Jane Rogers

Over the last 20 years, the field of criterion-referenced measurement has been developed to respond to the need in education, in industry, and in the armed services for assessments of persons in relation to objectives, skills, or tasks rather than in relation to other persons. The primary purpose of this chapter is to provide an introduction to the field of criterion-referenced measurement and to some of the technical developments that provide the measurement framework for constructing, evaluating, and using criterion-referenced tests in a wide range of settings.

In addition to a brief history of criterion-referenced measurement and a comparison of norm-referenced tests with criterion-referenced tests, several technical developments are reviewed. These include basic steps in test development, reliability and validity issues and methods, standard-setting, and guidelines for test evaluation. In a concluding section, areas for additional research and development are addressed.

427

2 Generalizability Theory
Dato N. M. de Gruijter and Leo J. Th. van der Kamp

Generalizability theory was developed by Cronbach and his co-workers in the early 1960s. The theory provides a general framework for measurements and their interpretation. In this chapter, the theory and associated analysis techniques based on ANOVA are introduced. Attention is given to variance components in one and multifaceted universes, with the corresponding definitions of error and generalizability coefficients. Regression equations can then be derived for the estimation of condition effects. Multivariate generalizability is briefly discussed. The chapter closes with a short overview of applications.

3 Item Response Theory
David J. Weiss and Michael E. Yoes

This chapter provides a nontechnical introduction to item response theory (IRT) for testing practitioners. IRT comprises a family of mathematical models which are useful in the design and analysis of a variety of psychological and educational measuring instruments. IRT has developed and become practical in the last 20 years, in part as a result of the inability of classical test theory models and methods to solve a number of applied measurement problems. The basic assumptions and concepts of the most commonly applied IRT models (i.e., those that assume a unidimensional trait and test items that can be dichotomously scored) are introduced. These concepts include the item (and test) response function, information, conditional standard errors of measurement, and the estimation of item and person parameters. Applications of IRT in the areas of test construction, equating, and adaptive testing are briefly described. An overview of other IRT models (e.g., polychotomous, multidimensional) is also presented.

4 Analysis of Covariance Structures
H. Swaminathan

In assessing the validity of a test, an important issue that must be addressed is whether the test measures the construct or constructs it is designed to measure. In order to determine this, i.e., to assess construct validity, hypotheses about the relationships between the observed variables and the underlying constructs must be formed and tested. Traditionally, the assessment of construct validity was carried out using factor analytic methods. More recently, however, factor analysis has been recognized as a special case of models for analyzing the covariance structures. Through this approach, sharper hypotheses concerning the relationships among observed variables and unobservable constructs can be formulated and tested statistically.

The purpose of this chapter is to outline the procedure for analyzing covariance structures, review the general covariance structure models that are available, and indicate how the construct validity of a test can be assessed by appropriately choosing the parametric specification of the covariance structure models.

5 Applications of Decision Theory to Test-Based Decision Making
Wim J. van der Linden

The use of Bayesian decision theory to solve problems in test-based decision making is discussed. Four basic decision problems are distinguished: selection, mastery, placement, and classification. For each type of decision, further restrictions or specifications may hold, namely multivariate test scores, sequential testing, multiple criteria, multiple populations, or quota restrictions. In some applications, combinations of the basic types of decisions may occur.

6 Meta-Analysis
John E. Hunter and Frank L. Schmidt

The meta-analysis methods for quantitatively cumulating findings across research studies advanced by Glass and his associates and by Schmidt, Hunter, and their associates are reviewed in this chapter. These meta-analytic methods are shown to be similar in many respects and complementary. The major difference is shown to be the absence from Glassian meta-analysis of procedures for correcting between-study variance in effect sizes for variance due to statistical and measurement artifacts. The most important of these artifacts is sampling error, and this article presents formulas for correcting the effect size variances in meta-analyses for sampling error. Standard significance tests are shown to give deceptive results in cumulative research, and it is recommended that confidence intervals be substituted for significance tests in most data analysis. Current reporting practices in multivariate studies are critiqued, and changes in these practices are recommended to make the data contained in individual studies more useful for cumulation across studies.

7 Developments in Personnel Selection Methodology
Robert A. Roe and Martin A. M. Greuter

Personnel selection continues to be a major field of applied testing. The developments in this field, however, do not relate to the test per se, but to the way in which tests and other instruments are used within the framework of selection procedures. This chapter discusses the developments in selection within a "technological perspective." This means that selection theory is considered as a technology from which designers draw when developing selection procedures. First, a model is presented for structuring the overall design process, and functions of selection procedures are identified. Next, the discussion focuses on prediction models and decision models as major components of procedures. Recent research on job analysis, criterion development, testing, parameter estimation, validation, decision analysis, utility theory, cost-benefit analysis, etc., are described, as well as what these areas of study have added to the general theory of selection and how they can be utilized during the successive steps of designing such models.

8 Assessment Centers at the Dutch Central Government
Jac N. Zaal

In most organizations, considerable time and effort are spent on activities such as selection, placement, transfer, coaching, training, personnel appraisal, etc. Efforts like these illustrate the importance of the human factor in meeting the objectives of the organization. The higher the responsibilities and complexities of the job, the more difficult it is to assess potential qualities, yet the more loss is involved in making the wrong judgments. This is certainly true for jobs at managerial levels.

The assessment center method is an appraisal device in which the candidate is asked to perform carefully selected exercises that can be seen as situational samples of the managerial job. As such, assessment center methods are not unlike a probe period which only consists of the most critical moments for managerial success. The manager plays the role he/she is supposed to fill, and behavioral criteria are used to assess the managerial potential of candidates.

In this chapter assessment center programs that are being used by the Dutch government are described and evaluated.

9 Current Perspectives in the Assessment of the Handicapped
Stan Scarpati

Formal tests have historically been utilized in the United States as the primary means by which people with atypical behavior are identified, classified, and treated. The tests used with the handicapped have come under close scrutiny by the legal system for evidence of unfair treatment and discrimination. As a result, specific guidelines and procedures provide a framework for assessing the handicapped. This chapter reviews the legal precedents guiding current practice and presents a perspective on the assessment issues currently confronting professionals who work with handicapped children and adults in public settings. The ways in which tests are used to identify and instruct the handicapped, and the role tests play when the handicapped are transitioned into the community are included.

10 Testing Across Cultures
Fons J. R. van de Vijver and Ype H. Poortinga

In this chapter various aspects of cross-cultural testing are discussed. First, an overview is given of the problems of test administration in a cross-cultural context. It is concluded that a thorough knowledge is required of local circumstances, which will vary from one cultural group to another. Once data have been gathered, statistical techniques can be applied to detect bias in the test items. Some important techniques are briefly mentioned, followed by the description of a more comprehensive framework for item bias analysis. A disadvantage of traditional approaches lies in their emphasis on the *documentation* rather than the *explanation* of cross-cultural differences in test scores. In the final section an approach is offered that explicitly aims at explaining cross-cultural differences by including contextual variables in the design of a study.

11 Reflections on Large-Scale Assessments of Student Achievement
Katherine MacRury, Philip Nagy, and Ross E. Traub

This chapter begins with a discussion of the meaning of large-scale assessment and of the distinction between large-scale assessment and examination programs. There follows a brief description of several large-scale assessment programs. Then, the effects alleged to be associated with large-scale assessments are considered under three headings: effects on individuals (teachers, students, members of the public), on the curriculum (including teaching-learning activities), and on educational policies. It is concluded that, although many effects are claimed, few, if any, have been documented in systematic studies. Next, three contextual factors are considered: purpose, design features (item format, collection of contextual data, dissemination of results), and examinee motivation. These factors influence the shape and possibly also the effects of an assessment program. Finally, an agenda is offered for empirical research on the effects of large-scale assessment programs.

12   Computerized Adaptive Testing: Theory, Applications, and Standards
Ronald K. Hambleton, Jac N. Zaal, and Jo P. M. Pieters

The availability of enhanced computer power for testing has opened up new options for test development, test administration, and test scoring. One particularly well-developed use of the computer is in the area of "adaptive testing." Adaptive testing involves the testing of examinees where the test items administered to examinees are dependent upon their performance on earlier items in the test. The goal is to reduce testing time by only administering test items that are "matched" to the examinees' ability levels. The primary purposes of this chapter are (1) to describe the technology, issues, and computer software that are associated with adaptive testing, (2) to highlight several of the promising adaptive testing applications, and (3) to present some newly developed guidelines for designing and using adaptive tests.

13   Cognitive Theory and Psychometrics
Robert J. Sternberg

The tremendous growth of cognitive psychology, besides having implications for training and instruction, also has implications for the psychometric testing of mental abilities. This chapter is divided into two main parts: alternative cognitive approaches to understanding and measuring human intelligence, and the implications of these approaches for testing.

In the first part, two generations of developments will be described.

One, which began around 1973, was based upon standard techniques of cognitive psychology and analysis for the understanding of intelligence. The other, which was started around 1983, is based upon broader definitions of intelligence and cognitive psychology.

In the second part of the chapter, seven general implications of the various new cognitive-based theories of intelligence for testing are described.

14 The Evolution of Ethical and Technical Standards for Testing
Walt Haney and George Madaus

Efforts to develop standards for tests and testing practices have a long history. The purpose of this chapter is to identify these various efforts to develop test standards as well as to document the nature of the changes in these standards over the years. Of special interest in this chapter are the three major revisions of the APA's *Ethical Standards of Psychologists*, and APA, AERA, and NCME's *Standards for Educational and Psychological Tests*. In a final section of the chapter, several suggestions are offered about the issues which the two sets of standards, ethical and technical, do and do not treat.

Contributing Author Biographies

Dato N. M. de Gruijter is Director of the Educational Research Center at the University of Leiden, The Netherlands. He received his Ph.D. in the social sciences from the University of Leiden. His principal research interest is educational measurement. He publishes on the topics of generalizability theory, criterion-referenced measurement, and item response theory. With Leo J. Th. van der Kamp, he published *Statistical Models in Psychological and Educational Testing*. Currently, he is serving on the editorial board of *Applied Psychological Measurement*.

Martin A. M. Greuter is a research and development consultant with Adviesbureau Psychotechniek in Utrecht, The Netherlands. He received his doctor's degree in technical sciences from Delft University of Technology in 1988, on the basis of a thesis dealing with interactive performance models (*New Perspectives in Personnel Selection*, in Dutch). His major field of interest is personnel assessment. After having finished his study of psychology in 1979, he has worked as a consultant in the field of personnel psychology, and taught at the University of Amsterdam.

Ronald K. Hambleton is Professor of Education and Psychology and Chairman of the Laboratory of Psychometric and Evaluative Research at the University of Massachusetts, Amherst. He received his Ph.D. in psychometric methods from the University of Toronto in 1969. His principal research interests are in the areas of criterion-referenced measurement and item response theory. His most recent publications are a book (co-authored with H. Swaminathan) entitled *Item Response Theory: Principles and Applications* and a book entitled *A Practical Guide to Criterion-Referenced Testing*. Both books are published by Kluwer Academic Publishers. He served as an associate editor to the *Journal of Educational Statistics* (1981–1989), and currently serves on the editorial boards of *Applied Psychological Measurement*, *Journal of Educational Measurement*, *Educational and Psychological Measurement*, and *Evaluation and the Health Professions*, and as president of the International Test Commission (1990–1994), and the president of the National Council on Measurement in Education (1989–1990).

Walt Haney is Associate Professor and Director of the Educational Technology Program in Boston College's School of Education, and a Senior Research Associate in the Center for the Study of Testing, Evaluation, and Educational Policy. He has two primary fields of professional interest: educational evaluation and testing, and educational technology. Haney has served as editor of NCME's *Educational Measurement: Issues and Practice*, staff director of the National Consortium on Testing Project at the Huron Institute, and advisor to the Joint Committee to revise the Standards for Educational and Psychological Tests.

John E. Hunter received his Ph.D. in psychology (math minor) at the University of Illinois in 1964. He is a co-author of two books: *Meta-analysis* and *Mathematical Models of Attitude Change*. He is a Fellow of the Society of Industrial and Organizational Psychology, the American Psychological Society, and the American Psychological Association. He has published over 150 articles on many topics: personnel selection, organizational interventions, attitude change, psychometric theory, personality, group dynamics, and other social processes. In personnel: job knowledge gained from training and experience, specific cognitive skills used in day-to-day performance, social skills used in management, and job analysis. In meta-analysis: corrections for artifacts not yet handled. In psychometric theory: the use of path analysis to analyze experiments and interventions, the relationship between static and dynamic causal models, and nonlinear and hierarchical measurement models. In personality: shame, the inner voice, and authoritarianism.

Katherine MacRury is a research associate in the Department of Measurement, Evaluation and Computer Applications at the Ontario Institute for Studies in Education, Toronto, Canada. She has taught in secondary schools in Canada and West Malaysia. Her current research interests include the impact of large-scale testing, the role of classroom testing in the grading practices of mathematics teachers, distance education, and comparative studies.

George Madaus is the Director of the Center for the Study of Testing, Evaluation, and Educational Policy at Boston College in the United States. Dr. Madaus has a long track record of contribution in the areas of assessment and evaluation. He has taught junior and senior high school as well as at the undergraduate and graduate levels in college. He has served on the 1974 and 1985 Joint AERA, APA, and NCME Test Standards Committees, and on the 1981 Joint Committee on Standards for Educational Evaluation which developed the *Evaluations of Educational Programs, Projects, and Materials*, was co-chair of the APA, AERA, and NCME Joint Committee on Testing Practices, and served on the subcommittee that drafted the *Code of Fair Testing Practices in Education*. He is currently the executive director of the National Commission on Testing and Public Policy.

Philip Nagy is an Associate Professor in the Department of Measurement, Evaluation and Computer Applications, and the Educational Leadership Center, of the Ontario Institute for Studies in Education. He is a former high school science teacher and supervisor of the provincial testing program for the province of Newfoundland, Canada. He received his Ph.D. from the University of Alberta in 1977. His research interests include student and program evaluation, and the assessment of understanding and problem solving. He has published in *Science Education*, the *Alberta Journal of Educational Research*, and *Review of Educational Research*. He has served on the editorial board of the Canadian Journal of Education, and is a past president of the Canadian Educational Researchers Association.

Jo P. M. Pieters studied mathematical psychology at the University of Nijmegen and entered a position as research fellow at the Institute of Mathematical Psychology at the same university. In 1983, he finished his thesis on the application of R. T. models in the measurement of individual differences in intelligence. Among his articles is a critical review of the additive factor method of Sternberg. A member of the research department at the Rijks Psychologische Dienst since 1986, he has worked on such projects as computerized testing, test fairness, and assessment centers. Pieters recently accepted the position of head of the graduate staff recruitment group at Philips in Eindhoven.

Ype H. Poortinga is an Associate Professor in cross-cultural psychology at Tilburg University, the Netherlands. He holds a Ph.D. from the Free University of Amsterdam and has worked at the National Institute for Personnel Research in Johannesburg. He is the past president of the International Association for Cross-Cultural Psychology and the Netherlands Association of Psychologists. His research interests include methodological issues in cross-cultural comparisons, intergroup relations, and the question of how much basic psychological processes are influenced by the socio-cultural or ecological environments.

Robert A. Roe is Professor of Work and Organizational Psychology at the University of Tilburg, The Netherlands. He obtained his doctor's degree in social sciences from the University of Amsterdam in 1975. He started to work in psychometrics and applied research in 1969, and lectured at the University of Amsterdam between 1973 and 1980. From 1981 until 1988, he was Professor of Work and Organizational Psychology at Delft University of Technology. His recent research has focused on personnel assessment and work behavior in technical environments. His publications include: *Foundations of Personnel Selection* and *Personnel Appraisal* (both in Dutch). He has served as editor of a number of scientific and professional journals in The Netherlands. Currently, he is associate editor of Peter Herriot's *Assessment Handbook*, published by Wiley.

H. Jane Rogers recently earned her Ph.D. from the University of Massachusetts with specializations in the areas of psychometric and statistical methods. Currently, she is an Assistant Professor at Columbia Teachers College. She is interested in goodness-of-fit applications of item response theory to criterion-referenced measurement, large-scale assessments, and the identification of biased test items. Other areas of research interest include Bayesian methods and multivariate statistics.

Stan Scarpati is an Associate Professor of Special Education at the University of Massachusetts at Amherst. He received his doctor of education degree in special education from the University of Northern Colorado in 1980. He is presently the director of the Office of Research and Development for the School of Education. His principal research interests are in the areas of applied academic and vocational testing for the handicapped and the cognitive-behavioral processes associated with social attributions of children with learning and behavioral problems.

Frank L. Schmidt is Sheets Professor of Human Resources at the University of Iowa, College of Business. He received his Ph.D. in industrial and organizational psychology from Purdue University in 1970. He previously directed a research program in personnel psychology at the U.S. Office of Personnel Management. He and John Hunter initially developed their meta-analysis methods as a means of studying the generalizability of employment test validities. Their studies in this area resulted in major revisions of earlier research conclusions in personnel psychology. Later, in their 1982 meta-analysis book with Greg Jackson, they extended these methods for use in all social areas. A revised and greatly expanded book on meta-analysis was published in 1989. Frank Schmidt is on the editorial board of *Journal of Applied Psychology* and is a Fellow of the American Psychological Association.

Robert J. Sternberg is IBM Professor of Psychology and Education at Yale University. He received his B.A. degree summa cum laude, Phi Beta Kappa, from Yale in 1972, and the Ph.D. from Stanford in 1975. He has received numerous awards, including the Early Career Award and McCandless Awards from the American Psychological Association, the Outstanding Book Award and Research Review Award from the American Educational Research Association, the Distinguished Scholar Award from the National Association on Gifted Children, and the Cattell Award from the Society for Multivariate Experimental Psychology. Professor Sternberg has written over 200 books, book chapters, and articles on the topics of intelligence and thought. Some of his most recent books include *The Triarchic Mind* (Viking-Penguin, 1988), *The Nature of Creativity* (ed., Cambridge University Press, 1988), *The Psychology of Human Thought* (ed., with Edward Smith, Cambridge University Press, 1988), and *Beyond IQ* (Cambridge University Press, 1985). His latest book, *Metaphors of Mind*, will be published by Cambridge University Press in 1990.

Hariharan Swaminathan is Professor of Education and Psychology at the University of Massachusetts at Amherst. He received his Ph.D. in psychometric methods and statistics from the University of Toronto in 1971. He has held the positions of Associate Dean of Academic Affairs and Acting Dean of the School of Education. He has served as an associate editor to the *Journal of Educational Statistics*, the president of Educational Statisticians, a special interest group of the American Educational Research Association, co-program chair of Division D of AERA, and as a member of the Graduate Records Examinations Board. His principal research interests are in the areas of item response theory, multivariate statistics, and Bayesian analysis.

Ross E. Traub is Professor and former Chairman of the Department of Measurement, Evaluation and Computer Applications, at the Ontario Institute for Studies in Education. He has served as the editor of the *Jour-*

nal of Educational Measurement and as a member of the editorial boards for the *Alberta Journal of Educational Research, Applied Psychological Measurement*, and the *Canadian Journal of Behavioural Science*. Also, he served on the board of directors of the National Council on Measurement in Education. Professor Traub has published on topics in educational measurement and test theory, and has participated in evaluations of school and government programs. A current research interest is the grading practices of high school teachers of mathematics.

Leo J. Th. van der Kamp is Professor of Research Methodology at the Department of Psychology at the University of Leiden. He holds a Ph.D. in the social sciences from the University of Leiden. His principal research interests are general research methodology, multivariate analysis, and test theory. He published, with Dato N. M. de Gruijter, the monograph *Statistical Models in Psychological and Educational Testing*.

Wim J. van der Linden is Professor of Educational Measurement and Data Analysis at the University of Twente, Enschede, The Netherlands. He holds a Ph.D. in psychometric theory from the University of Amsterdam, and studied psychology and sociology with a specialization in quantitative methods at the University of Utrecht, The Netherlands. His research interests center on item response theory and statistical decision theory as well as their applications in education. Currently, he serves on the editorial boards for the *Journal of Educational Measurement* and *Applied Psychological Measurement*.

Fons J. R. van de Vijver works at the Department of Social Sciences at Tilburg University, the Netherlands. His master's dissertation (on the robustness of Rasch estimates) has been published in *Applied Psychological Measurement*. He is now preparing a Ph.D., an empirical cross-cultural study on the universality of inductive thinking. His major research interests are cognition across cultures, and item response theory and its cross-cultural applications. He is consulting editor to the *Journal of Cross-Cultural Psychology*.

David J. Weiss is Professor of Psychology and Director of the Psychometric Methods Program at the University of Minnesota. He received his B. A. in psychology from the University of Pennsylvania in 1959 and his Ph.D. in psychology from the University of Minnesota in 1964. He began applied measurement research in 1959 as a staff member of the Work Adjustment Project at the University of Minnesota, and was the research director for that project from 1963 through 1970. In 1971, he initiated a program of research on adaptive testing that was supported by the Office of Naval

Research and other agencies in the U.S. Department of Defense from 1972 through 1985. In 1975, he founded the journal *Applied Psychological Measurement* and currently remains its editor. His current research interests include computerized adaptive testing and all aspects of item response theory.

Michael E. Yoes earned his Ph.D. in psychometric methods at the University of Minnesota Department of Psychology. He received a B. A. in psychology from San Diego State University in 1982 and has worked in a research capacity on a wide range of projects involving microcomputer-based psychological and educational assessment. His primary research interests are in the areas of computerized testing, computer-assisted instruction, and computerized adaptive testing. He is currently working as a project director for The Psychological Corporation, where he is involved with applications of IRT to achievement testing. His dissertation research is in the area of IRT item parameter estimation.

Jac N. Zaal is Manager R&D/Senior consultant with GITP in The Netherlands. Before that he was head of the Center of Management Assessment at the Department of Psychological Services of the Dutch government, studied industrial and organizational psychology at the Free University in Amsterdam, and obtained his doctor's degree at the same university in 1978. His research activities and publications focused on test construction, social behavior, and intellectual development. In 1983 he moved from the Free University to the head of the research department of the Psychological Services. He served as the president of the International Test Commission from 1986 to 1990.

Index